# MANSFIELD PARK

JANE AUSTEN

# MANSFIELD PARK

## An Annotated Edition

EDITED BY

DEIDRE SHAUNA LYNCH

The Belknap Press of Harvard University Press

Cambridge, Massachusetts

London, England

2016

Copyright © 2016 by the President and Fellows of Harvard College
All rights reserved
Printed in the United States of America
First printing

Frontispiece: Stoke Park, a mid-seventeenth-century country house in the
Palladian style. From *Ackermann's Repository,* 1826.

LIBRARY OF CONGRESS CATALOGING-IN-PUBLICATION DATA

Names: Austen, Jane, 1775–1817, author. | Lynch, Deidre, editor.
Title: Mansfield Park : an annotated edition / Jane Austen ;
edited by Deidre Shauna Lynch.
Description: Cambridge, Massachusetts : The Belknap Press of Harvard University
Press, 2016. | Includes bibliographical references.
Identifiers: LCCN 2016018027 | ISBN 9780674058101 (alk. paper)
Subjects: LCSH: Austen, Jane, 1775–1817. Mansfield Park. | Country homes—
England—Fiction. | Young women—England—Fiction. | England—Social life and
customs—19th century—Fiction.
Classification: LCC PR4034 .M3 2016 | DDC 823/.7—dc23 LC record
available at https://lccn.loc.gov/2016018027

For the students of English 323H (Jane Austen and Her
Contemporaries) and English 145a (Jane Austen's Fictions and Fans),
Toronto and Cambridge, 2008–2015

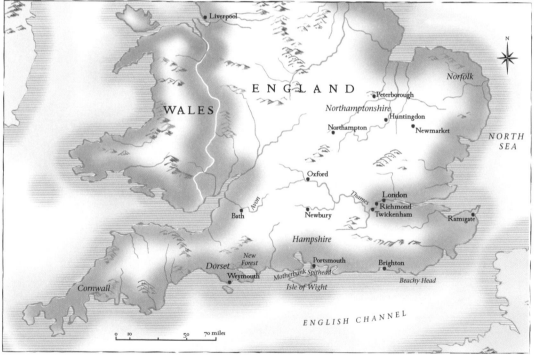

The world of *Mansfield Park*.

# Contents

# Note on the Text

Two editions of *Mansfield Park* appeared during Austen's lifetime, the second incorporating revisions she introduced. Priced at eighteen shillings, the novel was initially published in three volumes in May 1814 by the London publishing house of Thomas Egerton, earlier the publisher of *Sense and Sensibility* and *Pride and Prejudice.* That first edition of *Mansfield Park* (a print run, we think, of 1,250 copies) sold out in six months and earned Austen more money than any of her other works. In 1815 Austen began negotiations with a more prestigious London publisher, John Murray, also at this time the publisher of Lord Byron's poetry and the Waverley novels of Walter Scott. Murray brought out the second edition of *Mansfield Park* in February 1816, *Emma* having appeared under his imprint two months earlier. That 1816 edition is the basis for my text, though I have sometimes reverted to the 1814 text to correct obvious errors introduced by Murray's printers. Alterations are recorded in the list of Emendations.

In a letter to Murray on December 11, 1815, Austen states that she is returning *Mansfield Park* to him and that it is "as ready for a 2d Edit: I beleive, as I can make it" (*Jane Austen's Letters,* ed. Deirdre Le Faye, p. 318): this statement is generally construed as evidence that Austen marked up a copy of the 1814 text with marginal corrections. Beyond multiple small, interesting changes in punctuation, there are in fact few substantive changes. One exception comes in Vol. III, Chap. 7, where, perhaps as a consequence of consultations with her sailor brothers, Austen alters some of the naval slang used when William Price converses with his father.

# MANSFIELD PARK

# Introduction

IN THE SIXTEENTH CHAPTER of Vol. I of *Mansfield Park,* Fanny Price, still shaky after the bullying that her relations inflicted on her the night before, finds her way to an unfrequented upstairs room of the manor house in which she has grown up. The room, the narrator tells us, is Fanny's refuge following "any thing unpleasant below." That alliance with a specific space is one of the many things that make Fanny surprisingly different from Austen's other heroines. When Elizabeth Bennet, for example, seeks solitude behind closed doors, she asserts her right to privacy in a site that Austen's narrator leaves undescribed. In *Mansfield Park,* by contrast, the narrator takes pains both to inform us that her protagonist possesses a room of her own—a space "most dear to her"—and to show us that room itself. The more the narrator describes Fanny's room, however, the more it becomes apparent that Fanny's status as its acknowledged "mistress" is a sign of this character's privations, not her privileges. A space that was originally consigned to the governess, a storeroom for shabby hand-me-downs ("a faded footstool . . . too ill done for the drawing-room"; "a collection of family profiles thought unworthy of being anywhere else"), the East room is evidently Fanny's only because no one more important finds it desirable.

The descriptive detail that Austen's narrator uses in this chapter has been of keen interest to scholars, who see it evidencing a new departure in the novelist's career. *Mansfield Park,* planned and composed, we think, between February 1811 and July 1813, published in May 1814, was the first of the trio of novels that Austen wrote after

Castle Ashby in Northamptonshire, here pictured by the nineteenth-century landscape painter Frederick William Hulme, has been identified as a possible prototype for the fictional manor house of *Mansfield Park*.

she, her mother, sister, and friend Martha Lloyd relocated to Chawton cottage on her brother Edward's Hampshire estate.[1] What distinguishes the works she produced at that new home base from her three earlier works (which she revised at Chawton, but began in the 1790s) is, scholars propose, the way those later works emphasize setting and the influence that environment has on character.

Only two of Austen's six novels are named for a place, and *Mansfield Park* is the only one she titled herself (*Northanger Abbey* was a title devised by Austen's siblings, who saw that novel through the press following her death in August 1817). The novel fulfills the promise of that title: the manor house that belongs to Sir Thomas Bertram is name-checked both in its first sentence—where man and house are introduced in the same breath—and in its last sentence—which pictures Fanny settling into her new home at Mansfield Parsonage, and coming to find that place "as thoroughly perfect in her eyes, as everything else, within the view and patronage of Mansfield Park, had long been." The titles *Sense and Sensibility* and *Pride and Prejudice* invoke interacting characters and characteristics, but *Mansfield Park* suggests how as a mature novelist Austen tends to establish *who* an individual is by establishing *where* that individual is. She remakes the novel as an instrument for exploring how it feels to be *inside* a room, a house, a family, or a society and for exploring how those settings, more than mere backdrops, delimit opportunities and constrict thought.

The descriptive detail given when the narrative follows Fanny into her upstairs refuge is not there solely for its own sake, in other words. Instead, the narrator's engagement with the material things of the exterior world supplies Austen with a new way to get at interiority—the character's inner, mental life. The attention expended on the furnishings and ornaments of the East room—footstool, family portraits, plants, and writing desk—is a signal that in this space blessings are being counted and that, furthermore, this character is the sort of person who knows she is expected to count them. Fanny, the narrator tells us, "could scarcely see an object in that room which had not an interesting remembrance connected with it." "Every thing was a friend, or bore her thoughts to a friend."

When Fanny's attention is drawn to a table "covered with work-boxes and netting-boxes, which had been given her at different times," that "sight of present upon present" leaves the young woman "bewildered as to the amount of the debt which all these kind remembrances produced." The many claims that Fanny's aunts and cousins make on her, their calls on their poor relation's gratitude, exert an influence even in their absence: the very furnishings of the room speak them. Fanny's enumerating of their gifts connects her right back to the relations whom in this chapter she has been hoping to avoid—and it has that effect even before her cousin Edmund shows up in person a few pages later.

The privacy this room of her own affords Fanny is imperfect, then (in succeeding chapters, people will continue to show up, uninvited and unexpected, at its door). It is a problem, too, that Fanny does not use her space in the way we might wish her to—say, to express freely the feelings she has had to stifle downstairs in Mansfield Park's more public rooms. When in Vol. I, Chap. 16 Austen has us listen in on Fanny's train of thought, we come to realize instead that Fanny is making her visit to her room and her survey of its furnishings into the occasion for a self-guided tutorial on the kinds of feelings—of gratitude; indebtedness; submission—that she thinks she *ought to* feel. We realize the extent to which Fanny remains *inside* society, even after she appears to have removed herself from it. In this way, the description of the individual's physical circumstances ends up encompassing more metaphysical issues: painful questions about, for instance, socialization and the limits of mental autonomy.

The shrewdest, and sorriest, touch in this chapter's record of Fanny's thinking might be, however, the revelation that, although the remembrances that she connects with the mementoes in her room encompass incidents of "tyranny, of ridicule, and neglect," she finds "the whole . . . now so blended together, so harmonized by distance, that every former affliction had its charm." Considered one by one, her knickknacks might plausibly evidence her deprivations. (For instance, those "work boxes" that number among her cousins' gifts, boxes meant to hold sewing supplies, might register how Fanny has been introduced into the household less as family member than as maid-of-all-work. The givers might have intended with those gifts to teach Fanny a lesson in knowing her place.) When considered as an ensemble, however, a whole "blended together," those objects form the landscape in which Fanny feels at *home*. That "distance" that the narrator mentions helps as well, performing its proverbial function of lending enchantment to the view, assisting Fanny in turning the record of past sorrow and frustration into something less abrasive and more "harmonized."

The critic Nicholas Dames proposes that Fanny's room of her own may be understood as a kind of memory theater: the memory staged within its walls, he says, is that particularly modern, strangely forgetful form of memory that the later nineteenth century would call nostalgia. Dames also observes that readers' devotion to Austen's fiction has itself often involved just the kind of idealizing, selective memory that Austen's narrator analyzes, and gently derides, when she follows Fanny into this "nest of comforts."[2] Since the late Victorian period, numerous readers have greeted Austen's novels as though they were freighted with news from a bygone world, one more romantic, tasteful, cozy, or stable and settled than readers' own. The desire to experience these books has been conflated with a desire, rather more difficult to fulfill, to inhabit their time and milieu: "oh to live then, and with those characters," writes Dames, ventriloquizing this nostalgic reader response.[3] Austen scholars tend to promote a more disenchanted view, aiming to dislodge Austen's works from the placid enclave that "Jane Austen's World" represents in the popular imagination. Research on the novels' contexts is one lever they use, restoring to contemporary view the fractiousness rather than peace, and the insecurities rather than security, of Austen's historical moment. Recovering topical issues of imperial policy and class and sectarian strife, demonstrating just how incisive and wide-ranging a social commentator Austen could be, this scholarship has helped expand our understanding of her achievement. The annotations in this book draw on research in this denostalgizing mode.

But at the outset, while we are still hovering on the threshold of *Mansfield Park,* it is worth acknowledging that when Austen's twentieth- and twenty-first-century devotees have sought to satisfy their nostalgic cravings, this novel is usually *not* the first place they have looked. Even today it is much less likely than Austen's other works to be adapted by screenwriters or appropriated by writers of fan fiction. Its afterlife has been a meager thing compared with that enjoyed by *Pride and Prejudice* and *Emma,* firm favorites for nigh on a century. (The website Austenprose currently lists, for instance, 117 works inspired by *Pride and Prejudice* to a paltry 7 inspired by *Mansfield Park.*) What accounts for the difference in *Mansfield Park*'s contemporary standing? What are the difficulties it poses?[4]

The notion that her novels might offer readers a safe haven in which to feel at home has been basic to Austen's modern appeal. On Etsy one may purchase, among the many, many knickknacks that a modern Fanny Price might treasure, tea towels inscribed with the words "There's nothing like staying at home for real comfort" (a pearl of wisdom that the manufacturer ascribes to "Jane Austen" but

which belongs more properly to *Emma*'s odious Mrs. Elton). Many
screen adaptations of Austen's works open with the characters returning home, as if inviting us to follow them there.[5] But *Mansfield
Park* is seldom pressed into service as a purveyor of virtual domestic
comforts. Readers often experience with *Mansfield* the sort of unset-
tling disorientation that the narrator reports on when, in her second
chapter, she checks in on the ten-year-old Fanny not long after her
adoption into the Bertram family. Here she tells us that "it required a
longer time . . . than Mrs. Norris was inclined to allow, to reconcile
Fanny to the novelty of Mansfield Park." In *Mansfield Park,* too, it can
be hard to get your bearings.

As much as Austen's other works—even more, I would contend—
*Mansfield Park* is a great novel. But, as Bharat Tandon observes, "its
greatness [is] commensurate with its power to frustrate."[6] In this Introduction and the annotations that follow, I aim to take account of
both those dimensions—the novel's stylistic and technical prowess
and its profound capacity to disturb. It can require hard work and
generally more than one reading to get your bearings in *Mansfield
Park,* but that is part of Austen's experiment. In late 1811, when she
began writing it, there were new and daring things that she wanted
to do—and, buoyed by her first experience of seeing her words in
print, felt that she *could* do—with the novel form.

In *Mansfield Park* Austen systematically investigates just what
sorts of themes and characters her genre can accommodate. (That
investigation suggests one way to apprehend the prominence the
plot gives in its first and third volumes to plays, first *Lovers' Vows* and
then *Henry VIII:* perhaps Austen is figuring out what narrative fiction can tell us about human character by determining what theater
can't.) She takes the interpersonal dramas of the gentry drawing
room—the conventional material for the novel of manners—and
pointedly sets them against a wider social geography. Encompassing a socially diverse population without parallel in Austen's other
works, *Mansfield Park* shifts between the quiet backwater of rural
Northamptonshire and the bustle and grit of urban Portsmouth.
Through its sidelong glances at Sir Thomas's West Indian plantations, it also acknowledges the interpenetration of everyday life at

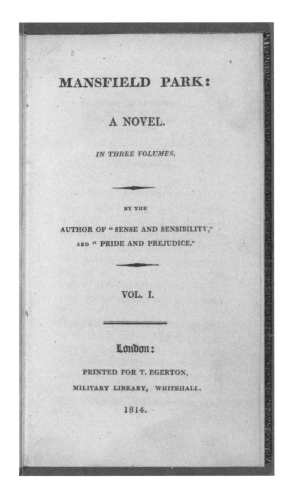

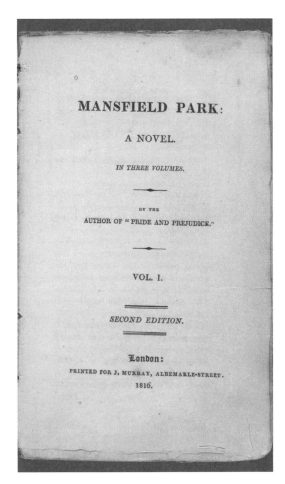

Title page for the first edition of *Mansfield Park,* published in 1814 by Thomas Egerton. As his colophon's mention of the "Military Library" indicates, Egerton tended to specialize in titles of interest to military officers (books on fortification and strategy, for example), but he also published many other titles, Austen's earlier novels, *Sense and Sensibility* and *Pride and Prejudice*, included.

Title page for the second edition of *Mansfield Park,* brought out, two years after the appearance of the first edition, by the prestigious publishing house of John Murray. This title page, like that of the first edition, refrains from identifying Austen by name. Murray nonetheless manages to create a kind of brand when he here identifies this book as a work by the author of *Pride and Prejudice*. He, like Egerton before him, was eager to trade on the success of Austen's earlier writings.

home with economic exploitation abroad—registering how the English parties that novels of manner chronicle have been subsidized by enslaved African labor. *Mansfield Park*'s renovation of its genre involves, as well, the sorts of moral knowledge the novel form can convey and the technical resources it commands to do that conveying. Through unassuming, acquiescent Fanny, a new sort of heroine in English fiction, Austen asks painful questions about the difficulties of being good. She probes the limited options for ethical life available to a character who, as Fanny says, in a statement that has more meanings than she realizes, "really cannot act."

Admittedly, its original audience might well have seen in *Mansfield Park* a book constructed along familiar, comfortable lines. A bare-bones account of its plot would have suggested a book belonging to that edifying narrative tradition in which virtue is rewarded and the meek are blessed by inheriting the earth. Fanny shares some traits with, for instance, the heroine of the 1765 children's novel *Little Goody Two-Shoes,* a book Austen owned as a girl.[7] To the approving reader, the heroine of *Mansfield Park* can look like a twin to that paragon of moral fortitude and patient endurance Margery Two-Shoes, otherwise known as Goody. (To an exasperated reader, alternately, Fanny can look like the perfect example of the priggishness for which Little Goody Two-Shoes has become a byword.) In Fanny's case, as in her predecessor's, the marriage that rescues a good girl from her straitened circumstances is presented to us as the proper reward for such virtues. Both these good girls have equally worthy sailor brothers—and by Austen's third volume William Price too is positioned (largely because Henry Crawford has mobilized his uncle's Admiralty connections on William's behalf) to make his fortune overseas, just as Little Tommy had before him.

But when, pursuing her new interest in the relationship of environment and character, Austen recounts Fanny's story of being good and making good and overcoming her marginality, she pays attention to the psychological costs that plots of this sort inflict on their pro-

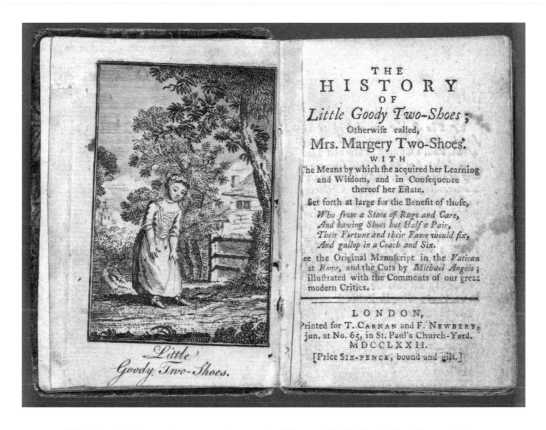

This frontispiece to the extremely popular *History of Little Goody Two-Shoes,* originally published in 1765, pictures the story's impoverished heroine at a moment when she seems particularly excited about the footwear that a charitable gentleman has just bestowed upon her.

tagonists. Over the course of the novel the Bertrams' poor relation often proves almost too adept at accommodating herself to any situation—this, even though Chap. 2's account of the homesick, tearful ten-year-old who is slow to "reconcile" herself to her new abode might seem the harbinger of a different outcome, and even though Fanny's refusal to "act" when her cousins and their friends stage *Lovers' Vows* seems, to them at least, an announcement of her inflexibilty. Fanny also proves frighteningly ready to assume that her just deserts do not encompass anything better than the little that she is generally given. Her capacity for thankfulness can appear excessive—the more so since, when one looks closely, the line between her grateful appreciation and Aunt Norris's cloying sycophancy starts to seem quite blurry.

The damage inflicted on her psyche by her early uprooting is made apparent, too, in that scene in the East room. As we saw, Fanny makes strategic use of the mementoes that have piled up in her room; with their assistance, she conjures a version of the recent past in which even the "afflictions" have become possessed of "charm." Unlike many present-day Austen scholars, who can be hard on nostalgic idealizations of the past when those shape other people's reception of Austen novels, in this episode the novel's narrator does not evidently condemn rose-colored glasses. She goes easy on Fanny's frailties. (She does, however, flag their droller aspects—as when, in this chapter, she jokily describes Fanny as hoping, when she gives some air to her potted plants, to "inhale a breeze of mental strength herself.") Assessing Fanny's proclivity for misremembering her past becomes a trickier matter, however, in the novel's third volume. Its Portsmouth chapters show us a Fanny who, after eight years of separation, is returned to her birthplace and to her parents. They show us as well a Fanny who, disappointed in her hopes for that return, is homesick once more, now for what the narrator, speaking her thoughts, calls Mansfield's "happy ways." It is a jolt to be asked to concur with Fanny in remembering Sir Thomas's household as a place where "all proceeded in a regular course of cheerful orderliness," and "every body's feelings were consulted"—since that entails forgetting all that we thought we knew about, in Deirdre Coleman's phrase, "the iron fist" in Mansfield's "velvet glove of . . . civility."[8] Austen's narrator permits us to listen in on Fanny's comparisons between Mansfield and Portsmouth, and then cryptically leaves it at that, refusing to spell out what we should think about her heroine's judgment.

Critics who present *Mansfield Park* as a conservative novel endorsing Fanny's idealization of Sir Thomas's household sometimes intimate that the faulty memory and self-deception here are also Austen's. Too enamored of both the notion that England's Sir Thomases represented its legitimate governors and the notion that the country house, patrimonial property handed down across the generations, was the proper fount of political authority, the novelist might not have grasped how hollow such praise of Mansfield would sound by this point. But there could be another reason for this seeming cognitive dissonance: Austen's wish to dramatize Fanny's susceptibility to the Bertrams' influence. Supplying further evidence of the shaping power of circumstance, she might mean to emphasize the extent to which Fanny has internalized the class prejudices by which she has been injured. By representing such "vicissitudes of the human mind" (III, 6), *Mansfield Park* makes unfamiliar—newly edgy—the familiar story of an upwardly mobile character's quest to belong to some place and to someone.

What effect does this exploration of a damaged psyche have on those notions of home that so often underwrite Austen's contemporary appeal? There are certainly characters besides Fanny who declare their love for home spaces and idealize domestic comforts. They tend to be men. Fanny's mentor, her cousin Edmund, for example—who, as she says, "taught" our heroine "to think and feel" on many subjects— also casts himself as a homebody. When in Vol. I, Chap. 16 he puts in an appearance in the East room he enthuses over what he calls Fanny's "little establishment." But Edmund blithely overlooks the East room's discomforts, which have already been enumerated for us— the room's want, for instance, even during the winter months, of a fire in the fireplace. Readers may notice, too, that the very space that Edmund calls "little" was, at the chapter's start, when the narration was threaded through Fanny's point of view, described as "spacious."

Three chapters on, Edmund's father, back at Mansfield again after his West Indian journey, makes a speech about how he appreciates anew that "domestic tranquillity" that "shuts out noisy pleasures." Fanny elaborates on that speech and allies herself with her uncle in a conversation she has with Edmund not long after, in which she says that she is sure that her uncle would now, unlike his children, resist "*any* addition" to his circle of intimates (the emphasis hints that Fanny, succumbing to the envy with which she often struggles, might

mean Mary Crawford, whom at this point Edmund evidently misses).
My uncle, Fanny says a tad primly to her cousin, values "quietness";
"the repose of his own family-circle is all he wants." The plot unfolds
in a way that ultimately ratifies Sir Thomas and Fanny's shared value
system. Its denouement, involving first the expulsion of Mary Crawford from the world of the novel and then the marriage between
cousins who have been raised almost "as brother and sister," con-
tracts the family circle almost scandalously.

Scholars who discern in the novel Austen's preemptive defense
against contemporary critiques of hereditary privilege—a demonstration of how England's landed interest might retain its authority by emulating the middle class's domestic virtues—make much of
how Sir Thomas and Fanny coincide in their views about those virtues.[9] In this account, the family values that Sir Thomas espouses
from the start foretell his moral reclamation. Much has also been
made of how the denouement, in which the Bertram household
seems to be circling its wagons, presents even conjugal love as something best kept within the family and withheld from interlopers (Sir
Thomas's wish at this point, we are told, is to bind "by the strongest
securities all that remained to him of domestic felicity," and he sees a
match between his younger son and his niece as one of those securities). But this interpretation, for all that it accounts for Fanny's passage from the peripheries of the Mansfield family to its moral center,
should not distract us from noticing how deluded, and *self*-deluded,
Sir Thomas was in ascribing repose and tranquility to the family
scene to which he had returned and in overlooking the dread and
disaffection his return had produced. Fanny's mentors at Mansfield
do share her tendency to idealize domestic life and to airbrush away
its pains. But for them that idealization is self-serving in a different
way, not a survival strategy but a prop to their complacency.

Troubled homes are the norm for this novel, and young women
seem to be the first casualties of those troubles. The orphaned Crawford siblings come to Northamptonshire from London in the first
place—setting up a face-off between urban worldliness and rural retirement and between interlopers and insiders—because their uncle
Admiral Crawford, following the death of their aunt, has chosen,

"instead of retaining his niece, to bring his mistress under his own roof." (As their half-sister, Mrs. Grant, notes, the Crawfords were in a "bad school for matrimony, in Hill-Street.") Maria Bertram goes through with her marriage to the doltish Mr. Rushworth in part because the restraint her father imposes on his daughters has come to feel unbearable and she longs to regain the liberty she enjoyed in Sir Thomas's absence. On a party of pleasure at her husband-to-be's estate, Maria doesn't, when cued by flirtatious Henry Crawford, agree as they gaze at the view that there is a "smiling scene" before her: adopting Henry's own idiom at the boundary between the literal and the figurative, Maria says that she sees an iron gate that gives her a "feeling of restraint." Comfort in this novel is often evoked in conjunction with confinement.[10]

Overall *Mansfield Park* treats with skepticism the promise, one our society inherited from eighteenth- and nineteenth-century enthusiasts for a new model of domesticity, that home is a refuge that will safeguard our personal flourishing. "Domestic happiness, thou only bliss / Of paradise that has survived the fall," Fanny's favorite poet, William Cowper, had hymned in 1785 in his poem *The Task,* but Austen is pessimistic about our postlapsarian possibilities.[11] There is little in *Mansfield Park* resembling the ringing endorsements of Pemberley in *Pride and Prejudice* and Donwell Abbey in *Emma,* country houses presented as focal points of community and models of social harmony.

Idealized understandings of home prove difficult to sustain in *Mansfield Park* because Austen repeatedly reminds us that at Mansfield domestic life is an arena of *patronage.* Austen's other works often turn on the older sense of that term, which emphasizes, in conjunction with inequalities in power, the benevolence that superiors will tender toward dependents and hangers-on. Think of all that Mr. Darcy, with the wealth of Pemberley behind him, is able to do for George and Lydia Wickham, or think of how Mr. Knightley sponsors the up-and-coming Robert Martin in his projects on Donwell Farm. In

The American painter John Singleton Copley's 1783 portrait of an elderly William
Murray, First Earl of Mansfield, shows him in the resplendent trappings—wig, gold
chain, and ermine robe—associated with the office of Lord Chief Justice.

*Mansfield Park,* however, that older sense takes on insidious meanings. It gets linked to the more modern sense of *patronage* that encompasses the *patronizing*—the officious and imperious. *Mansfield* underscores how, etched through with the power differentials that also define the public world, the private sphere of home is where some people learn lessons in domination and others lessons in obsequiousness. Her aunts' and her uncle's pursuit of a policy that makes Fanny one of the family and at the same time reinforces the status differences separating her from her cousins is the vehicle for such lessons, as Austen takes pains to demonstrate.

The household of William Murray, first Earl of Mansfield (1705–1793)—the Lord Chief Justice of Britain who is name-checked by this novel's title—may have inspired some aspects of that demonstration. Austen's knowledge of that household's history may have prompted her both to broaden the analyses of power relations that she had already built into her domestic fictions and to acknowledge the ties between English country houses and England's slave colonies. Austen knew one of the two great-nieces adopted in the 1760s by Lord Mansfield and his wife and raised together at Kenwood House, his stately home at the northern edge of London. A letter from August 1805, written from her brother Edward's Godmersham estate in Kent, records her visit to Elizabeth Finch-Hatton, née Murray. The second great-niece—whom Austen is unlikely to have met—was Dido Belle, a woman of mixed race whose father, the Royal Navy captain John Lindsay, was, like Elizabeth's father, another Mansfield nephew, and whose mother was a nameless African slave whose path crossed Lindsay's during his West Indian naval campaign. (In some versions of Dido Belle's mother's history, which is obscure, Lindsay appears to have claimed the woman as a trophy of war, following his capture of an enemy ship.) When, in 1772, Lord Mansfield issued the judgment for which he is most celebrated—the declaration, made in the case of *Somerset v. Stewart,* that was thought to make slavery illegal in England—Dido Belle had been living in his family for about nine years.[12] Yet Dido, though by all accounts as elegant and educated and accomplished as any Austen heroine, was not permitted to take her meals with the family and was kept apart from

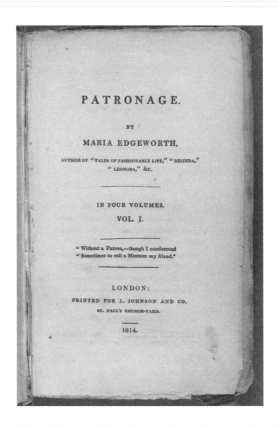

PATRONAGE.

BY

MARIA EDGEWORTH,

AUTHOR OF "TALES OF FASHIONABLE LIFE," "BELINDA,"
"LEONORA," &c.

IN FOUR VOLUMES.
VOL. I.

" Without a Patron,—though I condescend
" Sometimes to call a Minister my friend."

LONDON:
PRINTED FOR J. JOHNSON AND CO.
ST. PAUL'S CHURCH-YARD.

1814.

The title page to Maria Edgeworth's ambitious, four-volume political fiction *Patronage,* which appeared in the same year as *Mansfield Park.* Austen admired her sister novelist's writings. In the playful letter, addressed to her niece Anna Austen in September 1814, in which she pretends to wax indignant about current literary trends, she declares, "I have made up my mind to like no Novels really, but Miss Edgeworth's, Yours, & my own."

visitors to the house. (There was speculation even so, particularly on the part of apologists for slavery, that Lord Mansfield's fondness for his mixed-race niece—and not his understanding of legal justice—was the real explanation for his favoring the abolitionist cause.) When her cousin Elizabeth left Kenwood to be married, Dido Belle was left behind to be a companion and nursemaid to her great-uncle, by then an ailing, elderly widower.[13] We can only conjecture about how much of Dido Belle's history Austen might have known; but, as Austen scholar Paula Byrne has outlined, its parallels to the history of the fictional Fanny Price, who is likewise an adoptee, who is likewise betwixt and between the positions of lady and of servant, are striking. Byrne also invites us to wonder whether her acquaintance with Elizabeth Finch-Hatton contributed to Austen's decision to show the evils of slavery casting a shadow over her Northamptonshire country house.[14]

When in *Mansfield Park* Austen anatomizes the institution of the family, we witness a strange counterpoint: on the one hand, the Mansfield people promote the importance of blood ties—"Is not she a sister's child?" Aunt Norris asks rhetorically—and on the other, they insist on differences and hierarchies in ways that annul those solidarities.[15] "They cannot be equals," Sir Thomas says austerely, when the charitable plan to raise Fanny alongside his daughters is first aired. "Their rank, fortune, rights, and expectations will always be different" (I, 1). Aunt Norris, Fanny's other patron and the originator of the plan (one who wants credit for its benevolence but is agile at shirking its expense), is more brutally direct. Here she is speaking to, not of, Fanny: "I do beseech and intreat you not to be putting yourself forward, and talking and giving your opinion as if you were one of your cousins—as if you were dear Mrs. Rushworth or Julia . . . Remember, wherever you are, you must be the lowest and last" (II, 5).

By 1811, when Austen was beginning work on her Chawton novels, it was widely understood that a "special moment in the history of the novel" had arrived and that novelists, once so derided for their frivolity, had begun to pursue new intellectually serious ends.[16] Upon its first publication, however, no one recognized *Mansfield Park* as participating in this new trend in novel-writing.[17] The female-authored novel of 1814 that contemporaries did notice in this connection, some with disapproval, was Maria Edgeworth's *Patronage*—a hard-hitting, reform-minded survey of the ruinous effects that the patronage system (the valuing of family connections at the expense of merit) had on key institutions of national life such as the church, the army, and Parliament. Edgeworth threads a political polemic through the chronicle of the struggles endured by a virtuous family, the Percys, who strive to preserve their independence from the political machine. She advocates for institutional change, and she uses the Percys, who lose and then regain their landed property, almost allegorically, so as to show what an improved England's political future might hold.

Austen, as I've been suggesting, uses the lives of both Fanny and her brother William to deliver her own commentary on the topic that Edgeworth flags in her title. *Mansfield Park* too is informed by the proposition, writ large in *Patronage,* that modern fiction could be an instrument with which "to examine the very web and texture of society, as it really exists," as the essayist William Hazlitt put it in the survey of the form that he published in that banner year of 1814.[18] And yet it must be confessed that Austen's examination is a good deal more oblique than Edgeworth's. The ingredients of what, following Thomas Carlyle, commentators would later call a "Condition of England" novel are in evidence in *Mansfield Park,* but pinpointing the conclusions that Austen wishes her readers to derive is a challenge.

Certainly, as critics like Paula Byrne have emphasized, the world that *Mansfield Park*'s characters inhabit is a world that depends on overseas trade and transatlantic traverses and colonial exploitation—which Austen foregrounds. But she remains bafflingly tight-lipped about what exactly motivates Sir Thomas's journey to Antigua, even as she appears to invite her readers to notice the continuities between tyranny in the nation's overseas colonies and tyranny in the little world of the family. With similar effects, Austen seems to gesture toward the continuities between the "work" that goes on in that domestic sphere and the work done at Portsmouth, Fanny's hometown, celebrated during Austen's lifetime as both a key site of wartime defense and a center of economic modernization and rationalization. When *Mansfield Park* was published, Sir Samuel Bentham, the Inspector General of the Naval Works, had been at work for some time redesigning the industrial processes of Portsmouth's dockyard, a project that involved divesting the dockyard's traditionally rebellious labor force of their longstanding right to carry home the wood scraps created during their work.[19] With intriguing effects, wood scraps are also a matter of dispute in an episode in Vol. I, Chap. 15 in which Aunt Norris reports with pride on how she prevented the servants engaged in the carpentry for the Mansfield theater from claiming dinners as well as wages. Does Austen wish us to notice how Bentham's real-world regimen of labor discipline is being duplicated on a smaller scale at the fictional Mansfield Park? And how Bentham has a double in the ever-watchful Mrs. Norris? Then, too, there are the echoes of contemporary Evangelical writing audible in the novel's first half especially, whenever Edmund and Fanny and Mary Crawford discuss that young man's religious calling. Yet these echoes do not straightforwardly support the conclusion that Austen herself, as distinct from Edmund and Fanny, endorsed either the Evangelicals' proposals for the nation's religious revival or their criticisms of the worldliness of mainstream Anglicanism.[20]

Is the presiding genius of *Mansfield Park* the archconservative Edmund Burke, defender of hereditary honors and the political status quo, or the feminist and democrat Mary Wollstonecraft, Burke's antagonist in the 1790s debates about the Revolution in France and its possible extension to Britain? This sort of question, I've been suggesting, is hard to answer—no more easily settled now than when the critic Joseph Litvak posed it in 1992.[21] Critics have recently been sharply divided, as well, as to whether Sir Thomas represents a version of a well-meaning but blinkered Lord Mansfield or a tyrant slave-owner who imports into his genteel English home the culture of abuse that defined the West Indian plantation system.

What *is* clear is that in *Mansfield Park* Austen at least gestures toward the expanded political context that the then more celebrated early nineteenth-century practitioners of the "serious modern novel" were claiming for their home turf. Those gestures, however enigmatic, help take this book beyond the narratives of virtue rewarded set out by the novelists of the eighteenth century. One rationale for my annotations is to make Austen's engagements with the debates of the period visible to a twenty-first-century audience, so that they may draw their own conclusions about Austen's meanings.

First page of the manuscript of "Opinions of *Mansfield Park*." Austen began collecting readers' responses to her new novel sometime after May 1814.

My notes have an additional aim—to demonstrate that even after two centuries readers have been anything but unanimous about the novel's meanings and values. *Mansfield Park* has always occasioned controversy. Bemusement over its difference from Austen's other novels—and more particularly, over its heroine's difference from the heroines of those other novels—is of long standing.

We know about the disagreements it engendered among its first readers because, perhaps impelled by her disappointment over the periodical reviews' neglect of *Mansfield Park,* Austen undertook a kind of audience survey among her acquaintance. She wrote down the results in a small, hand-made booklet of eight pages that she titled "Opinions of *Mansfield Park*" (transcribed in this book's appendix). This document confirms one's suspicion that Austen's design in writing the novel in fact had been to *highlight* the conflicting feelings that her plot, and even more so her heroine, could arouse. In this novel more than any of her others, Austen seems to have wanted to stir things up.

Perhaps a simple love of mischief prompted Austen when she compiled the "Opinions" to document for the ages the rudeness of a certain Mrs. Augusta Bramstone, a Hampshire neighbor who confessed to thinking Austen's previous two novels "downright nonsense," but who "expected to like" the new book better "& having finished the 1st vol—flattered herself she had got through the worst." This lady's sister-in-law, a Mrs. Bramstone, delivered a more positive verdict on *Mansfield*. She declared herself "much pleased." But it is far from clear that Mrs. Bramstone is to be trusted, it being a bad sign that she "Thought Lady Bertram like herself." Would anyone who understood Austen's novel own up to *that* resemblance? And indeed Mrs. Bramstone herself conceded that her preference for *Mansfield Park* over the other works might be attributed to "her want of Taste—as she does not understand wit."[22] It is easy to envision Austen grinning to herself as she transcribed this response: it is funny that someone with an impaired relationship to both taste and wit should still feel entitled to hold an Opinion.

In the section of the "Opinions of *Mansfield Park*" that Austen devotes to the responses of her extended family, she seems intent, by contrast, not just on making comedy, in the manner of Mr. Bennet, from the absurdities of her neighbors, but on recording her success in creating controversy. "Edward admired Fanny—George disliked her," Austen notes in the paragraph recording the responses supplied by her nephews. Her nieces were similarly at variance, and their disagreement too is emphasized by Austen's phrasing: Fanny Knight was "delighted with Fanny"; Anna Austen "could not bear" her. "My Mother . . . Thought Fanny insipid," while sister Cassandra was "Fond of Fanny."[23]

Was Austen puzzled or gratified by the contrariety of the responses? Did it confirm her success? The answer to that last question is probably *yes:* conflicted opinions about Fanny are to be found inside the novel as well as outside it. Fanny confuses the people around her. The wonder is that so modest and quiet a young woman—whose blushes have oftentimes to speak *for* her—should center a novel that sparks so much disputatious talk. The wonder is that she creates so much debate herself. "Pray, is she out, or is she not?": thus Mary Crawford, when, shortly after her arrival at Mansfield Parsonage, she begins to feel she understands all the family in the great house, Miss Price excepted. Mary is stumped by the difficulty of placing Fanny in the social and sexual scripts of the era: at eighteen, Fanny is certainly of an age to be introduced into society, but she evidently does not attend the dinners and dances that are the normal program for a marriageable girl of the gentry class. "What is her character?—Is she solemn?—Is she queer?—Is she prudish?": these are the questions about Fanny that Henry Crawford poses to his sister at the moment, in Vol. II, when, finding himself at loose ends at Mansfield Parsonage, he announces his rakish scheme to spend his leisure making "a small hole" in the modest girl's "heart."

It has sometimes puzzled readers that Fanny is the novel's protagonist at all. In a famous essay published in 1955 Lionel Trilling observed that one way *Mansfield Park* alienated readers' affections was through Austen's "strange, . . . almost perverse, rejection of Mary Crawford's vitality in favor of Fanny's debility." Slyly framing the point as though it were a truth universally acknowledged, critic Amanda Claybaugh says something similar in the opening sentence of her recent edition of *Mansfield Park:* "Mary Crawford is the very model of a Jane Austen heroine."[24] Claybaugh means to flag the resemblance between Mary Crawford and Elizabeth Bennet, characters distinguished by what *Mansfield Park*'s narrator (in Vol. I, Chap. 8) calls "talents for the light and lively," and she means to highlight how, in making Fanny, not Mary, the heroine, Austen disrupted her readers' expectations. In the opening chapters, Mary's exchanges with Edmund—and, more so, her exchanges with her brother and half-sister—might well remind us of Elizabeth's banter with Darcy in

*Pride and Prejudice.* Mary, like Elizabeth, laughs readily—and makes others laugh, even Fanny, or nearly so. (In Vol. I, Chap. 7, when Fanny and Edmund gravely enumerate the good and bad points they have discerned in the manners of the new addition to their neighborhood, Fanny confesses to feeling entertained by Mary's conversation, which "made me almost laugh.") Mary comments cleverly on the conventionality of social games even while she is in the midst of playing them, which she generally does with more success than the others. Like Elizabeth in that scene at the Netherfield ball in which she both submits to the necessity of conversing with Darcy as they dance and succeeds in limiting the conversation to the topic of conversation, Mary Crawford has the wit simultaneously to occupy a role and to call attention to it as a role.[25] It makes sense that, like her brother, she is in her element in the theatricals.

Where Edmund and Fanny censure Mary, readers may find her wit rather enjoyable, even if she takes the irreverence that she shares with "model" Austen heroines like Elizabeth and Emma Woodhouse further than is safe or proper. (After the novel's halfway point, some readers do begin to hear notes of coarseness in Mary's dialogue, and her witty sallies misfire more often.) Still, it is a measure of Austen's readiness to overturn expectations, and of her distaste for schemes that tidily sort out a book's characters into opposing camps, that Mary, who is not the novel's heroine, cannot be categorized as the villain of the piece either, any more than her brother can be. Mary's question about whether Fanny is out or not (that is, available for courtship) suggests her perceptiveness—a sensitivity to Fanny's equivocal standing in the Bertram household that might well derive from the sympathy that one deracinated young woman is inclined to feel for another. (It is striking to consider that the passages conveying Fanny's thoughts and feelings about Mary never include one in which *she* takes note of the resemblance in their situations.) In that episode in which Tom Bertram, his aunt, his sisters, and Mr. Yates all gang up on Fanny to force her to take part in the play, Mary demonstrates her kindness when she administers comfort to the bullied girl and when, by "a look at her brother, she prevented any farther entreaty from the theatrical board."[26] Edmund, always Fanny's

preferred ally, is notably of less help at this moment of need, "too
angry to speak." Incidents like these are the reason it can be hard
work to feel as one knows one ought about Mary Crawford.

What's more, for the first two volumes of *Mansfield Park* the narrator keeps us in touch with Mary's private thoughts and feelings and
so with her nervous doubts about Edmund's intentions and about
the extent of her power over him. When Vol. II, Chap. 7, for instance, reports on the conversation between Edmund and Henry
that involves Edmund's plans for the parsonage he will inhabit after
his ordination, we are made privy to Mary's worries about the sub-
text of Edmund's statements, and we wonder what it might signify
for her romantic hopes. Austen goes out of her way to ensure that
*both* the young women who are contenders for Edmund's heart will
be able to call on our sympathies.

Shortly after the publication of *Mansfield Park,* Anna Austen, the
niece who "could not bear Fanny," appears to have been at work on
a novel of her own, which at one point bore the provisional title
"Which is the Heroine?"[27] Whatever Anna's intentions, it is a title
that pays homage to a distinctive component of her aunt's practice.
With varying effects, the heroines of *Pride and Prejudice* and *Emma*
are each invested in the idea that they are mere lookers-on, and that
the real action lies with the storylines of others. Elizabeth is so intent on watching how Bingley interacts with her sister that she is unaware of the signs that she has become an object of interest to Darcy.
Emma's schemes to make Harriet Smith into the heroine of a courtship plot of Emma's own authoring get in the way of her noticing
that Mr. Elton has his sights set on her, not Harriet. Austen often
slots Fanny into the passive role of onlooker—during Mary Crawford's riding lesson in Vol. I, Chap. 5, during the rehearsals of *Lovers'
Vows*—but overall *Mansfield* has different ways of making "which is
the heroine?" a live question. Not only balancing between Fanny's
and Mary's perspectives, the narrator, in the first third of the novel
especially, weaves in and out of the consciousnesses of multiple char-

acters. The inside view on the action that we obtain through the narrative's recording of private response is not anchored by any single character, but passes, in Austen's even-handed arrangement, from one person to another. At the start of Chap. 13 even the Honourable Mr. Yates gets a moment: through Austen's technique of free indirect style (of which, more shortly), the narrative briefly becomes a forum for his inner feelings, feelings, in this case, of exasperation over having been cheated of thespian fame, and which, alas for Mr. Yates, recur in the second volume, when he is disappointed once more.[28]

*Mansfield Park*'s opening chapters can seem, accordingly, to foretell a novel that will be a chronicle of a group rather than an individual or a pair of romantic rivals (the French translator who in 1816 equipped the novel with the subtitle *les trois cousines* evidently had this impression). Calling Fanny a "hidden heroine," critic Jo-Alyson Parker does justice to the disorienting effect of this arrangement.[29] In Vol. I, Chap. 5, having surveyed the initial impression that the Crawford siblings have created among the family at Mansfield Park, the narrator underscores how her survey has up to this point omitted her protagonist: "And Fanny, what was *she* doing and thinking all this while? and what was *her* opinion of the new-comers? Few young ladies of eighteen could be less called on to speak their opinion than Fanny." It is almost as if, her heroine having slipped from her or her readers' view, this narrator had to make an extra effort, registered by those italicized pronouns, to pull her back into the narrative field.

Ultimately, however, this emphasis on the group—unparalleled in Austen's other writings—only sets off the remarkable shift in her handling of point of view that occurs once we reach the Portsmouth chapters of Vol. III. When Sir Thomas sends Fanny back to her birthplace, the narrative follows her there and the people whose destinies have been interwoven with hers drop from view. The change occurs because Sir Thomas means, or so he thinks, to manifest his benevolence to his dependent: he is undertaking a "medicinal project" upon his niece's understanding, which "he must consider as at present diseased." (Fanny's return to her parents' house might more accurately be understood as a punitive shaming, one that, in Sir Thomas's view, Fanny deserves, because she does not think of Henry

Crawford's courtship as he would have her think.)[30] This plot turn which deposits Fanny back in Portsmouth could be understood as the set-up that enables our heroine to come into her own. And these chapters are to some extent defined by the young woman's growing consciousness that she *is* able to judge for herself—act as mentor to her younger sister, for instance, and do for Susan what Edmund once did for her.

But the emphasis falls here as much on the pain Fanny endures in her exile as it does on the achievement of independence. To John Wiltshire, Fanny in the Portsmouth chapters is "marooned," as though she were a shipwrecked sailor.[31] His metaphor captures how, when the other characters fall away from the narrative, it feels in a strange way as though the novel's plot has dropped from view too. It has begun to unfold elsewhere, at a distance from Fanny and Austen's readers. Events that affect Fanny in crucial ways now happen at a geographical remove, in London, for instance (where the newlywed Rushworths, Julia, Edmund, and Mary Crawford have all gathered), and in Newmarket (where Tom Bertram goes to attend the races and meets with a near-fatal accident). In the main, she learns of those events only belatedly, through letters that are a long time coming. Waiting anxiously for news, Fanny still cannot act.

*Mansfield Park* is throughout strangely ready to foreground non-events, Bharat Tandon has observed.[32] Tandon notes that the Portsmouth chapters—which cast action as something, happening elsewhere, that readers can access only in filtered form, through those letters and Fanny's reactions to them—conform to a pattern that has been discernible ever since that moment in which the *Lovers' Vows,* so long rehearsed, failed to be performed. Another way to describe the effect of these Portsmouth chapters, though, is to say that at this point the principal work of Austen's narrative becomes not to register action but to chart the ebb and flow of feeling. Left alone now with Fanny, we are thoroughly absorbed by the turmoil of her inner life—and maybe to a greater extent than before, since that inner life is now so disconnected from the outer life she leads among her parents and siblings. The fact that her family know nothing of the occasion for Fanny's return to Portsmouth reinforces that disconnect; so does the fact that, whereas they take minimal interest in the doings at Mansfield, Fanny herself can think of little else.

The verbal texture of these chapters is therefore distinctive: the long letters that Edmund and Mary send to Fanny and which are incorporated verbatim into the narrative are set off by passages, in a very different style, that simulate Fanny's thoughts and feelings—mental processes that in their confusion and complexity elude full articulation. The third volume never supplies Fanny's side of the epistolary exchanges with Edmund, Mary, or Lady Bertram, but we hardly mark those letters' absence. Our concern is with inner struggles that Fanny would never commit to paper.

Since that early moment when her narrator asks, "And Fanny, what was *she* doing and thinking all this while? and what was *her* opinion of the new-comers?", Austen has been teaching readers of *Mansfield Park* to conceive of its narrative discourse as a microphone of sorts, an instrument that will bring her heroine's muted mental life into audibility. This novel is, to be sure, full of instances of free indirect style: that technique, for which Austen in her later works especially is celebrated, which she uses to write "at the same time from within and without a character," and which commingles the narrator's objective vantage point on the action with that character's own thoughts and views.[33] Because of *Mansfield Park*'s extensive use of this technique, we come away feeling as though we had known very well what makes a whole range of its characters tick; we feel not just that we have been informed about the Mansfield family, both the Crawfords, and even Mr. Yates, as I have been suggesting, but also as though all these persons had *revealed* themselves to us, in all their individuality.[34]

Understandably, though, free indirect style occupies a special, complex role when it comes to making Fanny known to the reader. She is a heroine who frequently fails to make herself understood to others, who—tongue-tied, self-doubting—does not and cannot speak her mind. At the start of the third volume, Henry Crawford feels hopeful that he will succeed in winning her love, not just because of his vanity, but also because in the conversation the two have on this subject he is misled by the gentleness of her manner, which conceals "the sternness of her purpose"; Sir Thomas comes to realize that, because of that gentleness, "her emotions were beyond his discrimination." Most exasperatingly of all, Edmund knows so little about Fanny's feelings, her feelings toward him included, as to be surprised when she fails to show any signs of missing Mary Crawford after the latter's departure for London. We know Fanny more intimately than the people in the novel do because of the inside view Austen's free indirect style supplies.

And yet, when we listen in on Fanny's inner mental processes, what we hear in the main are notes of self-reproach. The book's free indirect style makes us privy not so much to Fanny's examinations of her feelings as to her struggles to control or negate them and to "check" (as the narrator puts it) "the tendency" of her "thoughts." This is especially apparent in a passage near the close of the second volume in which Edmund gratifies her by giving her the gold chain that she will wear to her first ball. At this point the narration follows Fanny's train of thought as she tiptoes painfully around the idea that she loves Edmund and that she envies Mary. Even to herself, Fanny cannot describe her state so explicitly—though she comes closer here to doing so than at any other moment, only to retreat abruptly: "Why did such an idea occur to her even enough to be reprobated and forbidden? It ought not to have touched on the confines of her imagination." In *Persuasion,* Austen's final novel, free indirect style works to ensure that a neglected, socially marginalized heroine—a nobody whose "word has no weight"—will come into her own on the page.[35] In *Mansfield Park,* resistance to this dynamic is mounted by the heroine herself. The critic John Mullan underscores how important that resistance will prove to the history of the novel, to Henry James and Virginia Woolf: "Any novelist can tell us what a character feels; Austen developed a means of declining to tell us. In doing so she bequeathed new technical possibilities to later novelists."[36]

When in the chapters devoted to the theatricals Fanny banishes herself to the sidelines of the action, and when in the Portsmouth chapters Austen herself installs Fanny in the position of bystander, this heroine ends up in a role that Austen heroines before and after her have occupied. The innovation in *Mansfield Park,* however, is that unlike Elizabeth Bennet and Emma Woodhouse, who define themselves as disinterested observers of other people's stories primarily because they do not know their own hearts, Fanny does know hers. The most audacious feature of the novel is that Fanny's erotic longing for Edmund is palpable from the opening chapters: illicit, suffused with guilt and shame, but also irrepressible.

Accounts of *Mansfield Park* that propose that the novel's conservative value system rests on its heroine's passivity and submissiveness overlook the fact that in this one respect Fanny *has* acted. She has given her heart away. She has done so without sanction, without questioning, either, that this heart *is* her own *to* give. In the novel's back story, Fanny's mother marries to "disoblige her family," but the plotline that in Vol. III the Bertrams in concert project for Fanny would see her doing the opposite—the match they wish to make for her would oblige and serve her family. As Sir Thomas insists, when he confronts his niece at the start of Vol. III, the power that Henry Crawford, with his wealth and his connections, has to procure advantage for Fanny's family should in itself be "sufficient recommendation" of this gentleman's suit. But in steadily refusing Mr. Crawford, Fanny rebels against the understanding of wedlock that guided Sir Thomas while he brought his own daughters up to "the trade of *coming out*"—an understanding that makes wedlock a business that has power-broking at the center and in which the interests of the group, and not of the individual, have to be consulted.

Dutiful and self-abnegating as she is, Fanny Price loves improperly. And she loves immodestly, even, according to the conduct-book codes of the era, in that she has loved first. (Delicate young women, according to those codes, ought to be unaware of any romantic longings they might have right up to the moment when their husbands-to-be declare themselves.)[37] That impropriety compounds the other transgressive dimension of Fanny's passion—namely, that at the novel's start Aunt Norris and Sir Thomas between them had declared any romance between Fanny and a scion of the Bertrams to be "mor-

ally impossible." After all, Fanny's adoption into the Bertram family
had initially been promoted by her aunt as the pre-emptive measure
that would ensure that Fanny would never be seen by Tom or Edmund as a marriageable cousin, but would always belong to the kinship category of unmarriageable sister. "Suppose her a pretty girl,
and seen by Tom or Edmund for the first time seven years hence, and
I dare say there would be mischief," Aunt Norris says, and then continues, "But breed her up with them from this time, and suppose her
even to have the beauty of an angel, and she will never be more to either than a sister."[38]

Her patrons cannot conceive of Fanny as someone who desires. In
the passage I just quoted, in which Aunt Norris lays out a worst-case
scenario for the family fortunes, she assumes that the troublesome
romantic urges with which the family might have to contend in the
future would naturally be those of the young men. The most compelling explanation for his niece's refusal of Henry Crawford—that her
affections are pre-engaged—is exactly the one that her uncle rules
out during their confrontation at the start of Vol. III, leaving him
with no option but to consider his niece "unaccountable."[39]

Modern readers of *Mansfield Park* sometimes come close to repli-
cating Sir Thomas's mistake. When they assume that Fanny's rejection of Henry expresses her firm sense of right and wrong, her principled objections to the vain, philandering man who so recklessly
gambled with her cousins' affections, they forget to factor in what
Austen tells us, at the very moment that Henry embarks on her conquest, both about Fanny's nature and about the nature of the new
fictional mode that *Mansfield* represents:

> although there doubtless are such unconquerable young la-
> dies of eighteen (or one should not read about them) as are
> never to be persuaded into love against their judgment by all
> that talent, manner, attention, and flattery can do, I have no
> inclination to believe Fanny one of them, or to think that
> with so much tenderness of disposition, and so much taste as
> belonged to her, she could have escaped heart-whole from
> the courtship (though the courtship only of a fortnight) of

such a man as Crawford, in spite of there being some previous ill-opinion of him to be overcome, had not her affection
been engaged elsewhere.

As John Wiltshire has said, it is desire that instigates Fanny's conduct, not rectitude.[40]

Unsurprisingly, unreciprocated and inexpressible love does not
bring out the best in Fanny. If she represents a heroine who deviates,
as Austen indicates, from those "young ladies one reads about," one
additional reason that this is so is that Fanny struggles, often in vain,
against feelings of discontent and envy. Sometimes her censures of
the Crawfords can sound peevish. In the scene in Vol. I, Chap. 5 in
which she watches Mary's riding lessons from a distance, the vexation she might reasonably feel toward Edmund, who has forgotten
that it is time for Fanny to reclaim the mare, becomes, a little ab-
surdly, a criticism of Henry Crawford for not having already provided Mary with such lessons: "She could not but think indeed that
Mr. Crawford might as well have saved [Edmund] the trouble; that
it would have been particularly proper and becoming in a brother
to have done it himself." Throughout the novel, Fanny means to be
high-minded. In her East room retreat, as we saw, she rehearses, as
though for future performances, the feelings that she knows she
ought to feel. But she finds it difficult to carry out her good intentions—as people generally do.

An astute contemporary observer of Austen's work, the bishop of
Dublin, Richard Whately, thought that she alone among contemporary novelists had sufficient strength of mind to populate her fictions with alternatives to fiction's usual paragons—to represent ugly
feelings and with them "temper the aetheriel materials of a heroine."[41] In his landmark 1821 essay, Whately singled out as evidence
of Austen's stout-heartedness Fanny's response in Vol. III, Chap. 15
to the letter that conveys the news of the adultery between Henry
and Maria Rushworth. This same letter summons her back to Mansfield from her Portsmouth exile to help out as the family prepares to
weather the scandal. To Fanny, the bad news that the letter carries is
*not* unwelcome. She receives it as a reprieve, and she has to remind

herself that she ought instead to be grieving along with the Mansfield family: "She was, she felt she was, in the greatest danger of being exquisitely happy, while so many were miserable. The evil which
brought such good to her!" It is uncomfortable for Fanny to admit to
conscious thought this realization that others who have done wrong
have inadvertently done right by her. But her sense of self-interest
asserts itself.

Not long after this passage, Austen brings *Mansfield Park* to a close by
informing us of a reversal in Sir Thomas's attitude—the man who
had expelled Fanny from the familial fold finds that she "was indeed
the daughter that he wanted." In the hasty denouement of the final
chapter, that discovery of Fanny's worth follows right after a turn-
around in Edmund's attitude—*his* discovery (narrated with surprising flippancy) that his "unconquerable passions" have been cured,
that his "unchanging attachments" have been transferred, and that
he has learned "to prefer soft light eyes to sparkling dark ones." *Mansfield Park,* as I have noted, to some readers has appeared to conform only too well to the paradigmatic storyline of how virtue is rewarded—the storyline demonstrating how a girl from the lower
middle class, "born to struggle and endure," as the narrator here puts
it, can make good by being good. This final chapter, with its brisk,
no-nonsense meting out of rewards and punishments, might well be
instanced as evidence.

But one flaw in such descriptions of this novel is that Fanny isn't
always good. Another is that the rewards distributed when Austen
brings down her curtain are meager in comparison to those proper
to the happy endings enjoyed by girls who make good. Little Goody
Two-Shoes becomes Lady Jones and rides in a coach and six. When
she makes good, Elizabeth Bennet becomes mistress of Pemberley.
Fanny gets to live in Mansfield Parsonage with Edmund.[42]

The experimentalism of *Mansfield Park* is arguably nowhere more
marked than in this disquieting conclusion, which denies us the eu-
phoric delights that, primed by the novels Austen published before

and after this one, we might suppose to be the reliable accompaniment of the wind-up of a marriage plot. Compare Elizabeth, who declares near the end of *Pride and Prejudice,* "I am happier even than Jane; she only smiles, I laugh."[43] Elizabeth's dancing spirits would be sadly out of place at sedate Mansfield Park at any time (as they would be at Mansfield Parsonage, too, as Mary Crawford might have had occasion to discover)—but the more so now, since it will take sober, strenuous work to rebuild this family, in the wake of the shame brought upon it by the home-wrecking Maria and Henry. More so, too, because at this moment we are not permitted to forget that Fanny's happiness is the accidental byproduct of other people's misconduct and mischances. There is a terribly contingent and fragile feel to this plot's resolution. This is thanks in part to the narrator's parting shot about Henry Crawford's deserts:

> Would he have deserved more, there can be no doubt that more would have been obtained; especially when that marriage had taken place, which would have given him the assistance of her conscience in subduing her first inclination and brought them very often together. Would he have persevered, and uprightly, Fanny must have been his reward—and a reward very voluntarily bestowed—within a reasonable period from Edmund's marrying Mary.

Austen doesn't go as easy on readers of *Mansfield Park*'s final chapter as she might have. She might have let us believe that Henry had been insincere in his courtship of Fanny all along, or she might have let us believe that Fanny would always have carried a torch for Edmund, even if "sparkling dark eyes" had remained his choice. But instead Austen dexterously arranges matters so that even the "tolerable comfort" to which the narrator showily restores her deserving characters becomes uncomfortable to the reader.

To a degree, the final chapter does open the novel up to an altered, renewed future. The reformed Sir Thomas is heartened by the spectacle of the members of the Price family "assisting to advance each other" and rejoices in particular in William Price's "rising fame";

looking through his eyes, we glimpse a coming history of middle-class empowerment and national and imperial progress (just the history that in *Patronage* Maria Edgeworth puts front and center). A more equivocal note has been struck, though, earlier in this same paragraph, when the future we glimpse is that unfolding within the community of Mansfield itself—at home, not abroad. The narrator mentions that Susan Price will advance from being Fanny's "auxiliary" to being Fanny's "substitute," the "stationary niece" whose permanent post is by Lady Bertram's sofa. For a vertiginous instant it seems that, instead of taking us somewhere new, the narrative has returned us to our starting point, and that the same cycle is beginning over again. Perhaps, her protests notwithstanding, our narrator has not quit the odious subjects of guilt and misery after all.

As the ball that initiates Fanny Price into the trade of coming out begins, we are told that Fanny is both pleased to have a partner for the first set of dances and displeased that the partner is Henry rather than Edmund: "Her happiness on this occasion was very much à-la-mortal, finely chequered." Working at the height of her powers, Austen created in *Mansfield Park* a book of difficult beauty that has continually sparked dissent and controversy—as well as fascination and awe. The key to these strong responses lies in part in the novel's sociological range, its shrewd analyses of the power politics of domestic life, its experiments with character and action and *in*action. But those responses are a function, above all, of this sort of clear-eyed reminder of what is involved in enduring an imperfect, unjust, fallen world: of how it is necessarily a matter of putting up with what we are given, of making do with substitutions, and thus a matter of mixed feelings, "finely chequered."

# Notes

All citations of Austen's correspondence in these notes and in the notes on the text are from *Jane Austen's Letters,* ed. Deirdre Le Faye, 4th ed. (Oxford: Oxford University Press, 2011). References to Austen's five other published novels identify passages by volume and chapter numbers.

1 That move to Chawton brought to a close the unsettled, unhappy period that followed the death of Austen's father in 1805, during which the family changed lodgings almost annually.

2 Nicholas Dames, *Amnesiac Selves: Nostalgia, Forgetting, and British Fiction, 1810–1870* (Oxford: Oxford University Press, 2001). See also his "Nostalgia" in *A Companion to Jane Austen,* ed. Claudia L. Johnson and Clara Tuite (Malden, Mass.: Wiley-Blackwell, 2009), pp. 413–421.

3 Dames, "Nostalgia," p. 415.

4 The generation of readers that followed Austen's do not, however, appear to have found *Mansfield Park* a challenge. In 1833 Arthur Hallam observed in a letter to Emily Tennyson (his fiancée and the poet Alfred Lord Tennyson's sister) that *Mansfield Park* was the work of Austen's "which many people vote the best"; two years earlier, Thomas Babington Macaulay anticipated this account of public opinion when he wrote to his sister Hannah that "everybody likes Mansfield Park." (*Emma,* Macaulay added, was liked only by the select set to which he himself belonged, "the true believers.") See Katie Halsey, *Jane Austen and Her Readers, 1786–1945* (London: Anthem, 2013), pp. 147–148.

5 As noted by Suzanne R. Pucci in "The Return Home," in *Jane Austen and Co.: Remaking the Past in Contemporary Culture,* ed. Suzanne R. Pucci and James Thompson (Albany, N.Y.: SUNY Press, 2003), pp. 133–156. As Pucci acknowledges, the 1999 Miramax film of *Mansfield Park,* directed by Patricia Rozema, broke with this pattern. Viewed through Rozema's lenses, the cavernous, starkly underfurnished rooms of Kirby Hall—the Northamptonshire location where Rozema did most of the filming—appear anything but inviting.

6 *Jane Austen and the Morality of Conversation* (London: Anthem Press, 2003), p. 195. Tandon deliberately echoes Lionel Trilling's account of the novel, which put the case more strongly: Trilling found in *Mansfield Park* a "greatness . . . commensurate with

its power to offend." See Trilling, *The Opposing Self: Nine Essays in Criticism* (New York: Viking, 1955), p. 211.

7 David Selwyn describes Austen's copy of *Little Goody Two-Shoes*—in which as a young girl she signed her name—in *Jane Austen and Children* (London: Continuum, 2010), p. 143. This work, published by John Newbery in 1765, helped launch a new tradition of children's publishing. For all its importance, however, its authorship remains uncertain.

8 Deirdre Coleman, "Imagining Sameness and Difference: Domestic and Colonial Sisters in *Mansfield Park*," in *A Companion to Jane Austen,* ed. Claudia L. Johnson and Clara Tuite (Malden, Mass.: Wiley-Blackwell, 2009), p. 301.

9 See, for instance, Alistair Duckworth, *The Improvement of the Estate: A Study of Jane Austen's Novels,* rev. ed. (Baltimore: Johns Hopkins University Press, 1994). For a compelling account of how Austen's feminism is inflected by this Tory politics of property, see Clara Tuite's *Romantic Austen: Sexual Politics and the Literary Canon* (Cambridge: Cambridge University Press, 2002).

10 On this topic, see Suvendrini Perera, *The Reaches of Empire: The English Novel from Edgeworth to Dickens* (New York: Columbia University Press, 1991), pp. 41–43; Nina Auerbach, *Romantic Imprisonment: Women and Other Glorified Outcasts* (New York: Columbia University Press, 1987).

11 William Cowper, *The Task,* in *The Task and Selected Other Poems,* ed. James Sambrook (London: Longman, 1994), book 3, p. 112, lines 41–42.

12 Mansfield's judgment, which brought about the emancipation of the African James Somerset, was widely interpreted as confirmation that English law did not recognize slavery. As William Cowper put it in the passage in *The Task* that celebrated the judgment, "Slaves cannot breathe in England; if their lungs / Receive our air, that moment they are free, / They touch our country and their shackles fall" (*The Task,* book 3, lines 40–42). Mansfield himself stated later, however, that he had never intended to be the great emancipator of English slaves, writing in the case of *King v. Inhabitants of Thames Ditton* that "the case of Somerset . . . goes no further than to determine that the master of such a servant shall not have it in his power to take him out of the kingdom against his will." Mansfield is cited in Teresa Michals's informative article "'That Sole and Despotic Dominion': Slaves, Wives, and Game in Blackstone's Commentaries," *Eighteenth-Century Studies* 27 (1993–1994): 195–216.

13 After Mansfield's death in 1793, Dido Belle, probably in her thirties by then, did marry, a French servant named John Daviniere.

14 Paula Byrne, *Belle: The Slave Daughter and the Lord Chief Justice* (New York: Harper, 2014). Byrne's book was originally marketed as the accompaniment to the 2013 Fox Searchlight film *Belle,* directed by Amma Asante and written by Misan Sagay. It corrects many of the film's historical inaccuracies.

15 On this topic see Coleman, "Imagining Sameness and Difference." That counterpoint is also discernible in the otherwise gorgeous double portrait of Dido and Elizabeth that Mansfield commissioned in 1779 and which is now on display in the Mansfields' Scottish home, Scone Palace: the black niece, who is carrying a basket full of fruit from Kenwood's hothouses, is portrayed waiting, servant-style, upon the white one.

16 Kathryn Sutherland, "Jane Austen and the Invention of the Serious Modern Novel," in *The Cambridge Companion to British Literature, 1740–1830,* ed. Thomas Keymer and Jon Mee (Cambridge: Cambridge University Press, 2004), p. 259.

17 On the contrary, it was thoroughly neglected by reviewers at the time, although *Pride and Prejudice* and *Sense and Sensibility* had been reviewed fairly extensively. Austen was especially upset that the wide-ranging review of her works that Sir Walter Scott published in the prestigious *Quarterly Review* unaccountably left *Mansfield Park* out of the picture. When she wrote to her publisher, John Murray, on April 1, 1816, she observed tartly that she could not "but be sorry that so clever a Man . . . should consider [*Mansfield Park*] unworthy of being noticed" (*Letters,* p. 327).

18 "Standard Novels and Romances," *Contributions to the "Edinburgh Review,"* in *The Collected Works of William Hazlitt* (London: J. M. Dent, 1904), vol. 10, p. 26.

19 Peter Linebaugh, *The London Hanged: Crime and Civil Society in the Eighteenth Century,* new ed. (London: Verso, 2003), pp. 397–398; see also Fraser Easton, "The Political Economy of *Mansfield Park,*" *Textual Practice* 12 (1998): 459–488.

20 It is true that Edmund approaches his ordination with a thoughtfulness that distinguishes him from Austen's other clergymen heroes, Edward Ferrars and Henry Tilney. But Edmund would serve as a more effective spokesman for Evangelical concerns if he weren't also preparing to take charge of a family living associated with his father's property: Austen has set him up to be the beneficiary of exactly the family patronage system that was often the target of the Evangelicals' critique. In a letter to her sister from September 8–9, 1816, Austen comments acerbically on how the sermons published by her Staffordshire cousin Edward Cooper "are fuller of Regeneration & Conversion than ever—with the addition of his zeal in the cause of the Bible Society" (*Letters,* p. 336). The audible impatience with the standard topics for Evangelical sermons makes it hard to agree with biographers who propose that Austen during the final years of her life came under the influence of Evangelicalism. Counterbalancing this letter, however, is the more frequently cited statement in a letter of November 18–20, 1814, in which Austen counsels her niece Fanny Knight not to be frightened off by the piety of her suitor: "I am by no means convinced that we ought not all to be Evangelicals" (*Letters,* p. 292).

21 Joseph Litvak, *Caught in the Act: Theatricality in the Nineteenth-Century English Novel* (Berkeley: University of California Press, 1992), p. 1.

22 The "Opinions" are cited from R. W. Chapman's edition of the *Minor Works,* rev. ed. (Oxford: Oxford University Press, 1969), pp. 431–435.

23  Many years later, so much later that the recollection might not be reliable, Austen's youngest niece, Louisa Knight, reported on another disagreement the book had spurred: her aunt Cassandra tried to persuade her aunt Jane "to let Mr. Crawford marry Fanny," but the novelist would not be swayed. The story is reported in Deirdre Le Faye, *Jane Austen: A Family Record*, 2nd ed. (Cambridge: Cambridge University Press, 2003), p. 275.

24  *The Opposing Self*, p. 213; Amanda Claybaugh, Introduction in Jane Austen, *Mansfield Park*, ed. Amanda Claybaugh (New York: Barnes and Noble Classics, 2004), p. xiii.

25  Darcy: "Do you talk by rule then, while you are dancing?"

Elizabeth: "Sometimes. One must speak a little, you know. It would look odd to be entirely silent for half an hour together, and yet for the advantage of *some*, conversation ought to be so arranged as that they may have the trouble of saying as little as possible" (*Pride and Prejudice*, I, 18).

26  And yet what Austen gives with one hand here, she takes away with the other, as her narrator describes the sequel to Mary's act of kindness: "the really good feelings by which she was almost purely governed," the narrator states, began "restoring her to all the little she had lost in Edmund's favour" (I, 15). The note of qualification in "almost purely governed" is disorienting enough, but the end of the sentence makes things worse, divesting Mary's kindness of its altruism, suggesting that throughout she has calculated on how she will appear in Edmund's eyes. Fanny really cannot act, as she says, but Mary, aware of her audience, can, and, though the rehearsals for *Lovers' Vows* have yet to begin, she may well be acting here.

27  See Letter to Anna Austen, August 10–18, 1814, *Letters*, p. 279.

28  Here is the passage in which the narrator ventriloquizes Mr. Yates's sensations: "To be so near happiness, so near fame, so near the long paragraph in praise of the private theatricals at Ecclesford, the seat of the Right Hon. Lord Ravenshaw, in Cornwall, which would of course have immortalised the whole party for at least a twelvemonth! and being so near, to lose it all, was an injury to be keenly felt, and Mr. Yates could talk of nothing else."

29  *The Author's Inheritance: Henry Fielding, Jane Austen, and the Establishment of the Novel* (DeKalb, IL: Northern Illinois University Press, 1998), p. 163.

30  Though the scheme opens "visions of enjoyment" to Fanny (visions that the squalid realities of the Portsmouth chapters will puncture), her enjoyment is far from being a priority for her uncle, as the narrator explains: "his prime motive in sending her away, had very little to do with the propriety of her seeing her parents again, and nothing at all with any idea of making her happy" (III, 6). That emphatic "nothing at all" makes this passage one of the book's sharpest indictments of Sir Thomas's parenting style.

31  John Wiltshire, *Jane Austen and the Body: "The Picture of Health"* (Cambridge: Cambridge University Press, 1992) p. 103.

32  Tandon, *Jane Austen and the Morality of Conversation,* p. 217.

33  Sutherland, *Jane Austen's Textual Lives,* p. 174.

34  A good example of this technique can be found in the passage in Vol. I, Chap. 5 that describes Mary Crawford's feelings on first meeting the Bertrams. It begins objectively enough with the statement, "She acknowledged, however, that the Mr. Bertrams were very fine young men. . ." By the paragraph's close, though, we feel as if we were inside Mary's mind, listening in as she begins to conduct an argument with herself about those feelings: Tom Bertram "had been much in London, and had more liveliness and gallantry than Edmund, and must, therefore, be preferred . . . She had felt an early presentiment that she *should* like the eldest best. She knew it was her way."

35  *Persuasion,* I, 1.

36  John Mullan, *What Matters in Jane Austen: Twenty Critical Puzzles Solved* (London: Bloomsbury, 2012), p. 320.

37  On Fanny's forwardness see Claudia L. Johnson, "What Became of Jane Austen?: *Mansfield Park," Persuasions: Journal of the Jane Austen Society of North America* 17 (1995): 59–70. The narrator of *Northanger Abbey* mocks this account of female virtue when in her third chapter she calls on readers to wonder whether Catherine Morland dreams of Henry Tilney on the night that follows their first introduction and then adds: "if it be true, as a celebrated writer has maintained, that no young lady can be justified in falling in love before the gentleman's love is declared, it would be very improper that a young lady should dream of a gentleman before the gentleman is first known to have dreamt of her."

38  For illuminating discussions of the status of cousin marriage during Austen's lifetime, see Mary Jean Corbett, *Family Likeness: Sex, Marriage, and Incest from Jane Austen to Virginia Woolf* (Ithaca, N.Y.: Cornell University Press, 2008); and Ruth Perry, *Novel Relations: The Transformation of Kinship in English Literature and Culture, 1748–1818* (Cambridge: Cambridge University Press, 2004). In this period Britain's aristocracy and middle classes were generally nonchalant about such unions—so that Sir Thomas's and Aunt Norris's cant about cousins in love and moral impossibility likely represents a cover for their concern with family finances. A dowerless daughter of the Prices would, after all, be no great catch for the Bertrams. See my note 13 to Vol. I, Chap. 1, for further discussion.

39  For all the anguish of this scene, one senses that Austen is also having some fun at Sir Thomas's expense. Narrating it from his point of view, she makes us feel how astonished he is at having his will thwarted by this mere slip of a girl.

40  Wiltshire, *Jane Austen and the Body,* p. 84.

41  Richard Whately, "Modern Novels," *Miscellaneous Lectures and Reviews* (London: Parker, Son, and Bourn, 1861), p. 302. This review of Austen's posthumously published *Northanger Abbey* and *Persuasion* originally appeared in the *Quarterly Review* in 1821.

42 As Thomas R. Edwards, Jr., notices, "Jane Austen resists what *must* have been the sore temptation of killing Tom to make her heroine rich: Fanny gets in effect, the life Mary could not accept, and it seems pretty minimal when we think of what Elizabeth Bennet or Emma or even Anne Elliot get. Then, too, there is Edmund!" ("The Difficult Beauty of *Mansfield Park*," *Nineteenth-Century Fiction* 20, no. 1 [1965], p. 67 n.14).

43 *Pride and Prejudice*, III, 18.

# Volume I

# I

About thirty years ago, Miss Maria Ward of Huntingdon, with only seven thousand pounds, had the good luck to captivate Sir Thomas Bertram, of Mansfield Park, in the county of Northampton,[1] and to be thereby raised to the rank of a baronet's lady,[2] with all the comforts and consequences of an handsome house and large income. All Huntingdon exclaimed on the greatness of the match, and her uncle, the lawyer, himself, allowed her to be at least three thousand pounds short of any equitable claim to it. She had two sisters to be benefited by her elevation; and such of their acquaintance as thought Miss Ward and Miss Frances quite as handsome as Miss Maria, did not scruple to predict their marrying with almost equal advantage. But there certainly are not so many men of large fortune in the world, as there are pretty women to deserve them. Miss Ward, at the end of half a dozen years, found herself obliged to be attached to the Rev. Mr. Norris, a friend of her brother-in-law, with scarcely any private fortune,[3] and Miss Frances fared yet worse. Miss Ward's match, indeed, when it came to the point, was not contemptible, Sir Thomas being happily able to give his friend an income in the living of Mansfield,[4] and Mr. and Mrs. Norris began their career of conjugal felicity with very little less than a thousand a year. But Miss Frances married, in the common phrase, to disoblige her family,[5] and by fixing on a Lieutenant of Marines, without education, fortune, or connections, did it very thoroughly.[6] She could hardly have made a more untoward choice. Sir Thomas Bertram had interest,[7] which, from principle as well as pride, from a general wish of doing right,

1 In situating Sir Thomas's country house in Northamptonshire, a county located at England's center, Austen opted to set *Mansfield Park* in a locale of which she had no first-hand experience: a choice that obliged her, in a letter written on January 29, 1813, to commission her sister to investigate whether "Northamptonshire" was "a Country of Hedgerows" (*Letters,* p. 210). The Midlands setting distinguishes this novel from the fictions Austen published before and after and has never been satisfactorily explained. Samuel Richardson's *Sir Charles Grandison* (1753–1754) identified Northamptonshire as the home ground of its heroine, Harriet Byron, and the location of Mansfield Park might be Austen's tribute to her favorite novelist (Richardson's novel also has a Mansfield House). It might be, too, that Austen uses Northamptonshire's geographical centrality to stake a claim for her country house's symbolic centrality. *Mansfield Park* has often been considered an early version of what scholars of the Victorian era call the "condition-of-England novel." Indeed, multiple details in the narration would have encouraged Austen's Regency readership to construe Sir Thomas's estate as a microcosm of the state and to discern in the story of Mansfield's government, misgovernment, and restoration parallels to the political crises of their day.

2 In becoming Lady Bertram, Maria Ward—whose middle-class origins are registered with that reference to her "uncle, the lawyer" several lines down—has vaulted up the social ladder. That she has married so advantageously, at least according to the estimate of

the community—"all Huntingdon"—whose voice we hear in this passage, is not something that would have been predicted by those who knew that her dowry was "only seven thousand pounds." Since a baronet is a commoner, the new Lady Bertram has not managed to enter the nobility, but she has ascended to the uppermost rank of the gentry. The baronetcy is a hereditary order: Sir Thomas has inherited his title and can anticipate passing it down to his son or heir in turn.

3 Austen's reference to "Miss Ward" reveals the birth order of the Ward siblings, as convention dictated that the eldest daughter in a family would be identified simply as "Miss," her first name omitted. One cannot imagine the future Mrs. Norris coping well with the psychological challenge of seeing her younger sister married before she was or of owing her own settlement in life to the patronage of that younger sister's husband.

4 The chief landowner of a parish often had the right to bestow the position of parish priest on a candidate of his choosing. This benefice came with a rent-free residence and an income derived from the tithes paid by the parishioners and the profits obtainable through the farming of the lands (the "glebe") belonging to the church. As often as not, the living in a landowner's gift went to a member of his family who had been ordained in the Church of England.

5 In choosing "to disoblige her family"—or in marrying *for love,* which under these circumstances might amount to the same thing—Miss Frances manifests her lack of regard for the very understanding of marriage that the opening of this paragraph has brought into view: the understanding that it involves the happiness of entire families ("sisters to be benefited" by their sibling's elevation, for example), not just of the husband-wife pair. There is no missing Austen's pun confirming the linkage between love and money that the saga of the three Ward sisters has asserted: Miss Frances, we see, pays a high *price* for that choice.

6 Detachments of marines, the infantry of the Royal Navy, were carried on almost all navy vessels, both to provide small-arms fire when fighting took place at close quarters and to enforce the authority of the cap-

and a desire of seeing all that were connected with him in situations of respectability, he would have been glad to exert for the advantage of Lady Bertram's sister; but her husband's profession was such as no interest could reach; and before he had time to devise any other method of assisting them, an absolute breach between the sisters had taken place. It was the natural result of the conduct of each party, and such as a very imprudent marriage almost always produces. To save herself from useless remonstrance, Mrs. Price never wrote to her family on the subject till actually married. Lady Bertram, who was a woman of very tranquil feelings, and a temper remarkably easy and indolent, would have contented herself with merely giving up her sister, and thinking no more of the matter: but Mrs. Norris had a spirit of activity, which could not be satisfied till she had written a long and angry letter to Fanny, to point out the folly of her conduct, and threaten her with all its possible ill consequences. Mrs. Price in her turn was injured and angry; and an answer which comprehended each sister in its bitterness, and bestowed such very disrespectful reflections on the pride of Sir Thomas, as Mrs. Norris could not possibly keep to herself, put an end to all intercourse between them for a considerable period.

Their homes were so distant, and the circles in which they moved so distinct, as almost to preclude the means of ever hearing of each other's existence during the eleven following years, or at least to make it very wonderful to Sir Thomas, that Mrs. Norris should ever have it in her power to tell them, as she now and then did in an angry voice, that Fanny had got another child. By the end of eleven years, however, Mrs. Price could no longer afford to cherish pride or resentment, or to lose one connection that might possibly assist her. A large and still increasing family, an husband disabled for active service, but not the less equal to company and good liquor, and a very small income to supply their wants, made her eager to regain the friends she had so carelessly sacrificed;[8] and she addressed Lady Bertram in a letter which spoke so much contrition and despondence, such a superfluity of children, and such a want of almost every thing else, as could not but dispose them all to a reconciliation. She was preparing for her ninth lying-in,[9] and after bewailing the circumstance, and imploring their countenance as sponsors to the expected child,[10] she could not conceal how important she felt they might be to the future maintenance of the eight already in being. Her eldest was a boy of ten years old, a fine spirited fellow who longed to be out in the world; but what could she do? Was there any chance of his being hereafter useful to Sir Thomas in the concerns of his West Indian property? No situation would be beneath him—or what did Sir Thomas think of Woolwich? or how could a boy be sent out to the East?[11]

The letter was not unproductive. It re-established peace and kindness. Sir Thomas sent friendly advice and professions, Lady Bertram dispatched money and baby-linen, and Mrs. Norris wrote the letters.

Such were its immediate effects, and within a twelvemonth a more important advantage to Mrs. Price resulted from it. Mrs. Norris was often observing to the others, that she could not get her poor sister and her family out of her head, and that much as they had all done for her, she seemed to be wanting to do more: and at length she could not but own it to be her wish, that poor Mrs. Price should be relieved from the charge and expense of one child entirely out of her great number. "What if they were among them to undertake the care of her eldest daughter, a girl now nine years old, of an age to require more attention than her poor mother could possibly give? The trouble and expense of it to them, would be nothing compared with the benevolence of the action." Lady Bertram agreed with her instantly. "I think we cannot do better," said she, "let us send for the child."

Sir Thomas could not give so instantaneous and unqualified a consent. He debated and hesitated;—it was a serious charge;—a girl so brought up must be adequately provided for, or there would be cruelty instead of kindness in taking her from her family. He thought of his own four children—of his two sons—of cousins in love, &c.;—but no sooner had he deliberately begun to state his objections, than Mrs. Norris interrupted him with a reply to them all whether stated or not.

"My dear Sir Thomas, I perfectly comprehend you, and do justice to the generosity and delicacy of your notions, which indeed are quite of a piece with your general conduct; and I entirely agree with

tain. The marines were generally perceived as the naval officers' inferiors—incorrigible landlubbers and idlers, who had been able to obtain their commissions without any training or experience at sea. In Mr. Price's case, mysteriously, education, fortune, and connections also appear to have been unnecessary, though their absence might help explain why, prior to the unspecified event that disabled him for active service, he failed to advance beyond his original rank. Tellingly, Captain Brilliant, the protagonist of John Davis's nautical novel of 1808, *The Post-Captain; or, The Wooden Walls Well-Manned,* uses the term "marine" as slang for an empty liquor bottle—thereby indicating that both the man and the thing are useless to him ([London: Thomas Tegg, 1808], p. 26).

7 Influence.

8 *Friends* in early nineteenth-century usage often includes family members.

9 The period of bed rest for the mother that preceded and followed the birth of a child.

10 She hopes the Bertrams will agree to be named as the baby's godparents at its christening.

11 In seeking to place William in either training or employment (a "situation"), Mrs. Price looks both near—the Royal Military Academy and Royal Ordnance Factory were alike located in Woolwich, a town on the Thames to the immediate southeast of London—and far—to the West and East Indies. To send a boy out to the East likely involves finding him work with the East India Company, which at this time administered Britain's empire in India and monopolized its trade with Asia.

12 Mrs. Norris's reference to the "mite" that she will contribute to the little girl's maintenance allies her with the scriptural figure of the "poor widow" who gives her all—"two mites, which make a farthing"—to her temple, and who, Christ says, is more praiseworthy than her richer neighbors, who have donated only a portion of their wealth (Mark, chapter 12, verse 42; Luke, chapter 21, verse 2). However, Mrs. Norris's analogy—which she evidently likes, since we will hear again of the "mite" that she gives, in Vol. II, Chap. 13—is misleading. At this point she is neither widowed nor poor: earlier we learned that the Norris household commands an income of "very little less than a thousand [pounds] a year," an income near the top of the range for men in the Rev. Norris's professional position. See Edward Copeland, "Money," in *The Cambridge Companion to Jane Austen,* ed. Edward Copeland and Juliet McMaster, 2nd ed. (Cambridge: Cambridge University Press, 2011), p. 131.

13 "Mischief" of just the sort Mrs. Norris flags launches the plot of Charlotte Smith's proto-Gothic novel *Emmeline, or, The Orphan of the Castle,* which Austen appears to have read shortly after its 1788 publication. When Delamere, the spoiled son of the haughty Lord Montreville, first encounters the young cousin whose existence had hitherto been a secret to him, he falls in love at once. Brought up in poverty and obscurity in the Welsh hinterland by Delamere's father, who hopes that by concealing her there he may likewise conceal the wrongs he did her father before her birth, the virtuous and beautiful Emmeline spends much of the novel flying from place to place attempting both to elude her unwanted cousin-suitor and to prove to her uncle just how unwilling a participant she is in Delamere's rebellion against his authority.

Cousin-marriage in itself is uncontroversial in *Emmeline.* It would have been uncontroversial for Austen too—her brother Henry had, for instance, married their cousin Eliza de Feuillide in 1797—as it was for her culture generally. In *Incest and Influence: The Private Life of Bourgeois England* (Cambridge, Mass.: Harvard University Press, 2009), the historian Adam Kuper estimates that for people born into "the great bourgeois

you in the main as to the propriety of doing every thing one could by way of providing for a child one had in a manner taken into one's own hands; and I am sure I should be the last person in the world to withhold my mite upon such an occasion.[12] Having no children of my own, who should I look to in any little matter I may ever have to bestow, but the children of my sisters?—and I am sure Mr. Norris is too just—but you know I am a woman of few words and professions. Do not let us be frightened from a good deed by a trifle. Give a girl an education, and introduce her properly into the world, and ten to one but she has the means of settling well, without farther expense to any body. A niece of our's, Sir Thomas, I may say, or, at least of *your's,* would not grow up in this neighbourhood without many advantages. I don't say she would be so handsome as her cousins. I dare say she would not; but she would be introduced into the society of this country under such very favourable circumstances as, in all human probability, would get her a creditable establishment. You are thinking of your sons—but do not you know that of all things upon earth *that* is the least likely to happen; brought up, as they would be, always together like brothers and sisters? It is morally impossible. I never knew an instance of it. It is, in fact, the only sure way of providing against the connection. Suppose her a pretty girl, and seen by Tom or Edmund for the first time seven years hence, and I dare say there would be mischief.[13] The very idea of her having been suffered to grow up at a distance from us all in poverty and neglect, would be enough to make either of the dear sweet-tempered boys in love with her. But breed her up with them from this time, and suppose her even to have the beauty of an angel, and she will never be more to either than a sister."

"There is a great deal of truth in what you say," replied Sir Thomas, "and far be it from me to throw any fanciful impediment in the way of a plan which would be so consistent with the relative situations of each. I only meant to observe, that it ought not to be lightly engaged in, and that to make it really serviceable to Mrs. Price, and creditable to ourselves, we must secure to the child, or consider ourselves engaged to secure to her hereafter, as circumstances may arise, the provision of a gentlewoman, if no such establishment should offer as you are so sanguine in expecting."[14]

"I thoroughly understand you," cried Mrs. Norris; "you are every thing that is generous and considerate, and I am sure we shall never disagree on this point. Whatever I can do, as you well know, I am always ready enough to do for the good of those I love; and, though I could never feel for this little girl the hundredth part of the regard I bear your own dear children, nor consider her, in any respect, so much my own, I should hate myself if I were capable of neglecting her. Is not she a sister's child? and could I bear to see her want, while I had a bit of bread to give her? My dear Sir Thomas, with all my faults I have a warm heart: and, poor as I am, would rather deny myself the necessaries of life, than do an ungenerous thing. So, if you are not against it, I will write to my poor sister to-morrow, and make the proposal; and, as soon as matters are settled, *I* will engage to get the child to Mansfield; *you* shall have no trouble about it. My own trouble, you know, I never regard. I will send Nanny to London on purpose, and she may have a bed at her cousin, the sadler's, and the child be appointed to meet her there. They may easily get her from Portsmouth to town by the coach, under the care of any creditable person that may chance to be going. I dare say there is always some reputable tradesman's wife or other going up."[15]

Except to the attack on Nanny's cousin, Sir Thomas no longer made any objection, and a more respectable, though less economical rendezvous being accordingly substituted, every thing was considered as settled, and the pleasures of so benevolent a scheme were already enjoyed. The division of gratifying sensations ought not, in strict justice, to have been equal; for Sir Thomas was fully resolved to be the real and consistent patron of the selected child, and Mrs. Norris had not the least intention of being at any expense whatever in her maintenance. As far as walking, talking, and contriving reached, she was thoroughly benevolent, and nobody knew better how to dictate liberality to others: but her love of money was equal to her love of directing, and she knew quite as well how to save her own as to spend that of her friends. Having married on a narrower income

clans of nineteenth-century England" more than one marriage in ten involved first or second cousins (p. 18). In *Emmeline* Delamere's passion for the heroine represents a problem for his father because and only because it may lead to a marriage across class lines that will bring no economic or social advantage to his family.

In this speech Mrs. Norris's circumlocutions and recourse to the pronoun *that* do appear to hint at unspeakable, incestuous possibilities: but this seems strategic on her part, a function of her conviction, which links her to Smith's Lord Montreville, that a marriage should advance a family's material interests. "In Mrs. Norris's framework, bringing Fanny into the immediate family functions as the only sure way of keeping her out of it" and of preventing her nephews from entering into the sort of cross-class mésalliance she disapproves (Mary Jean Corbett, *Family Likeness: Sex, Marriage, and Incest from Jane Austen to Virginia Woolf* [Ithaca, N.Y.: Cornell University Press, 2008], p. 51).

14 It is not clear what Sir Thomas commits to when he says the family will furnish the little girl with the "provision of a gentlewoman" if the advantageous marriage (the "creditable establishment") that Mrs. Norris anticipates for her in her future does not in fact come to be. The imprecision might be the point; Sir Thomas might want some wiggle room. Perhaps in future his niece will be able to count on finding a home as a poor dependent among her relations; if so, he is pledging that she will not lose caste and slip off the scale of gentility altogether, as she would if she were forced to seek employment as a governess, say, or paid companion, or even seamstress.

15 This town on England's south coast had been a significant port and naval base for centuries and was the site of a marine barracks by the start of the nineteenth century. For the first leg of her travel to Mansfield, Mrs. Norris proposes, there will be no problem with bundling her nine-year-old niece into the Portsmouth-London coach—the public transportation of the day—and consigning her to the care of a stranger for the seventy-mile, ten-hour journey.

16 Gout is a form of arthritis, occurring when crystals of uric acid are deposited in the joints, the feet particularly. The entry on "Medicine" in the first, 1771 edition of the *Encyclopedia Britannica* described "persons of acute parts, who follow their studies too closely" and "those who live high and indulge their appetites, drinking plenty of rich, generous wines" as especially prone to the ailment (vol. 3, p. 126). As that description implies, medical science in Austen's day tended to correlate gout with leisure and wealth. It was, as the historians of medicine Roy Porter and G. S. Rousseau put it, a "patrician malady" (*Gout: The Patrician Malady* [New Haven: Yale University Press, 2000]).

than she had been used to look forward to, she had, from the first, fancied a very strict line of economy necessary; and what was begun as a matter of prudence, soon grew into a matter of choice, as an object of that needful solicitude, which there were no children to supply. Had there been a family to provide for, Mrs. Norris might never have saved her money; but having no care of that kind, there was nothing to impede her frugality, or lessen the comfort of making a yearly addition to an income which they had never lived up to. Under this infatuating principle, counteracted by no real affection for her sister, it was impossible for her to aim at more than the credit of projecting and arranging so expensive a charity; though perhaps she might so little know herself, as to walk home to the Parsonage after this conversation, in the happy belief of being the most liberal-minded sister and aunt in the world.

When the subject was brought forward again, her views were more fully explained; and, in reply to Lady Bertram's calm inquiry of "Where shall the child come to first, sister, to you or to us?" Sir Thomas heard, with some surprise, that it would be totally out of Mrs. Norris's power to take any share in the personal charge of her. He had been considering her as a particularly welcome addition at the Parsonage, as a desirable companion to an aunt who had no children of her own; but he found himself wholly mistaken. Mrs. Norris was sorry to say, that the little girl's staying with them, at least as things then were, was quite out of the question. Poor Mr. Norris's indifferent state of health made it an impossibility: he could no more bear the noise of a child than he could fly; if indeed he should ever get well of his gouty complaints, it would be a different matter:[16] she should then be glad to take her turn, and think nothing of the inconvenience; but just now, poor Mr. Norris took up every moment of her time, and the very mention of such a thing she was sure would distract him.

"Then she had better come to us," said Lady Bertram with the utmost composure. After a short pause, Sir Thomas added with dignity, "Yes, let her home be in this house. We will endeavour to do our duty by her, and she will at least have the advantage of companions of her own age, and of a regular instructress."

"Very true," cried Mrs. Norris, "which are both very important considerations: and it will be just the same to Miss Lee,[17] whether she has three girls to teach, or only two—there can be no difference. I only wish I could be more useful; but you see I do all in my power. I am not one of those that spare their own trouble; and Nanny shall fetch her, however it may put me to inconvenience to have my chief counsellor away for three days. I suppose, sister, you will put the child in the little white attic, near the old nurseries. It will be much the best place for her, so near Miss Lee, and not far from the girls, and close by the housemaids, who could either of them help to dress her you know, and take care of her clothes, for I suppose you would not think it fair to expect Ellis to wait on her as well as the others. Indeed, I do not see that you could possibly place her any where else."

17  The Bertram daughters' governess.

An adoption of a very different sort from the Bertrams' adoption of Fanny shaped Austen's own family history. As a teenager, her older brother Edward was taken from his birth family to become the heir of the wealthy but childless Knights of Godmersham in Kent. This 1783 silhouette made by the London artist William Wellings commemorates the moment when this arrangement became official, depicting the boy's passage from his biological father (George Austen, pictured on the left) to his new, adoptive family.

18 Vulgarity.

Lady Bertram made no opposition.

"I hope she will prove a well-disposed girl," continued Mrs. Norris, "and be sensible of her uncommon good fortune in having such friends."

"Should her disposition be really bad," said Sir Thomas, "we must not, for our own children's sake, continue her in the family; but there is no reason to expect so great an evil. We shall probably see much to wish altered in her, and must prepare ourselves for gross ignorance, some meanness[18] of opinions, and very distressing vulgarity of manner; but these are not incurable faults—nor, I trust, can they be dangerous for her associates. Had my daughters been *younger* than herself, I should have considered the introduction of such a companion, as a matter of very serious moment; but as it is, I hope there can be nothing to fear for *them,* and every thing to hope for *her,* from the association."

"That is exactly what I think," cried Mrs. Norris, "and what I was saying to my husband this morning. It will be an education for the child said I, only being with her cousins; if Miss Lee taught her nothing, she would learn to be good and clever from *them.*"

"I hope she will not tease my poor pug," said Lady Bertram; "I have but just got Julia to leave it alone."

"There will be some difficulty in our way, Mrs. Norris," observed Sir Thomas, "as to the distinction proper to be made between the girls as they grow up; how to preserve in the minds of my *daughters* the consciousness of what they are, without making them think too lowly of their cousin; and how, without depressing her spirits too far, to make her remember that she is not a *Miss Bertram.* I should wish to see them very good friends, and would, on no account, authorize in my girls the smallest degree of arrogance towards their relation; but still they cannot be equals. Their rank, fortune, rights, and expectations, will always be different. It is a point of great delicacy, and you must assist us in our endeavours to choose exactly the right line of conduct."

Mrs. Norris was quite at his service; and though she perfectly agreed with him as to its being a most difficult thing, encouraged him to hope that between them it would be easily managed.

This portrait by William Hopkins of Lady Charlotte Finch shows the sitter with her pug on her lap, a situation in which, one imagines, Lady Bertram and her pug would often be glimpsed. Pugs were must-have pets for ladies of fashion when in 1787 Hopkins depicted Finch, then the governess to King George III's children. Lady Bertram's favoring of this dog breed two decades on might suggest that she, by contrast, has fallen out of step with the changing styles.

It will be readily believed that Mrs. Norris did not write to her sister in vain. Mrs. Price seemed rather surprised that a girl should be fixed on, when she had so many fine boys, but accepted the offer most thankfully, assuring them of her daughter's being a very well-disposed, good-humoured girl, and trusting they would never have cause to throw her off. She spoke of her farther as somewhat delicate and puny, but was sanguine in the hope of her being materially better for change of air. Poor woman! she probably thought change of air might agree with many of her children.

# 2

THE LITTLE GIRL PERFORMED her long journey in safety, and at Northampton was met by Mrs. Norris, who thus regaled[1] in the credit of being foremost to welcome her, and in the importance of leading her in to the others, and recommending her to their kindness.

Fanny Price was at this time just ten years old, and though there might not be much in her first appearance to captivate, there was, at least, nothing to disgust her relations. She was small of her age, with no glow of complexion, nor any other striking beauty; exceedingly timid and shy, and shrinking from notice; but her air, though awkward, was not vulgar, her voice was sweet, and when she spoke, her countenance was pretty. Sir Thomas and Lady Bertram received her very kindly, and Sir Thomas seeing how much she needed encouragement, tried to be all that was conciliating; but he had to work against a most untoward gravity of deportment—and Lady Bertram, without taking half so much trouble, or speaking one word where he spoke ten, by the mere aid of a good-humoured smile, became immediately the less awful[2] character of the two.

The young people were all at home, and sustained their share in the introduction very well, with much good humour, and no embarrassment, at least on the part of the sons, who at seventeen and sixteen, and tall of their age, had all the grandeur of men in the eyes of their little cousin. The two girls were more at a loss from being younger and in greater awe of their father, who addressed them on the occasion with rather an injudicious particularity.[3] But they were too much used to company and praise, to have any thing like natural shyness, and their confidence increasing from their cousin's total want of it, they were soon able to take a full survey of her face and her frock in easy indifference.

They were a remarkably fine family, the sons very well-looking, the daughters decidedly handsome, and all of them well-grown and forward of their age, which produced as striking a difference between the cousins in person, as education had given to their address;[4] and no one would have supposed the girls so nearly of an age as they really were. There were in fact but two years between the youngest and Fanny. Julia Bertram was only twelve, and Maria but a year older. The little visitor meanwhile was as unhappy as possible. Afraid of every body, ashamed of herself, and longing for the home she had left, she knew not how to look up, and could scarcely speak to be heard, or without crying. Mrs. Norris had been talking to her the whole way from Northampton of her wonderful good fortune, and the extraordinary degree of gratitude and good behaviour which it ought to produce, and her consciousness of misery was therefore increased by the idea of its being a wicked thing for her not to be happy. The fatigue too, of so long a journey, became soon no trifling evil. In vain were the well-meant condescensions of Sir Thomas, and all the officious prognostications of Mrs. Norris that she would be a good girl; in vain did Lady Bertram smile and make her sit on the sofa with herself and pug, and vain was even the sight of a gooseberry tart towards giving her comfort; she could scarcely swallow two mouthfuls before tears interrupted her, and sleep seeming to be her likeliest friend, she was taken to finish her sorrows in bed.

"This is not a very promising beginning," said Mrs. Norris when Fanny had left the room.—"After all that I said to her as we came along, I thought she would have behaved better; I told her how much might depend upon her acquitting herself well at first. I wish there may not be a little sulkiness of temper—her poor mother had a good deal; but we must make allowances for such a child—and I do not know that her being sorry to leave her home is really against her, for,

3 This reference to Sir Thomas's "injudicious particularity" suggests that he has discomfited his daughters by singling them out for attention or has spoken with excessive minuteness (another sense of *particularity*) about how he expects them to behave toward their little cousin. One imagines that Fanny has been introduced to her cousins in terms that confirm, as her uncle opined in the previous chapter, that her "'rank, fortune, rights, and expectations, will always be different'" from theirs.

4 Manner of speech, way of approaching other people.

5  Think of her with contempt.

6  A section of the grounds planted with shrubs as well
as flowers.

with all its faults, it *was* her home, and she cannot as yet understand how much she has changed for the better; but then there is moderation in all things."

It required a longer time, however, than Mrs. Norris was inclined to allow, to reconcile Fanny to the novelty of Mansfield Park, and the separation from every body she had been used to. Her feelings were very acute, and too little understood to be properly attended to. Nobody meant to be unkind, but nobody put themselves out of their way to secure her comfort.

The holiday allowed to the Miss Bertrams the next day on purpose to afford leisure for getting acquainted with, and entertaining their young cousin, produced little union. They could not but hold her cheap on finding that she had but two sashes,[5] and had never learned French; and when they perceived her to be little struck with the duet they were so good as to play, they could do no more than make her a generous present of some of their least valued toys, and leave her to herself, while they adjourned to whatever might be the favourite holiday sport of the moment, making artificial flowers or wasting gold paper.

Fanny, whether near or from her cousins, whether in the schoolroom, the drawing-room, or the shrubbery,[6] was equally forlorn, finding something to fear in every person and place. She was disheartened by Lady Bertram's silence, awed by Sir Thomas's grave looks, and quite overcome by Mrs. Norris's admonitions. Her elder cousins mortified her by reflections on her size, and abashed her by noticing her shyness; Miss Lee wondered at her ignorance, and the maid-servants sneered at her clothes; and when to these sorrows was added the idea of the brothers and sisters among whom she had always been important as play-fellow, instructress, and nurse, the despondence that sunk her little heart was severe.

The grandeur of the house astonished, but could not console her. The rooms were too large for her to move in with ease; whatever she touched she expected to injure, and she crept about in constant terror of something or other; often retreating towards her own chamber to cry; and the little girl who was spoken of in the drawing-room when she left it at night, as seeming so desirably sensible of her peculiar good fortune, ended every day's sorrows by sobbing herself to sleep. A week had passed in this way, and no suspicion of it conveyed by her quiet passive manner, when she was found one morning by her cousin Edmund, the youngest of the sons, sitting crying on the attic stairs.

"My dear little cousin," said he with all the gentleness of an excellent nature, "what can be the matter?" And sitting down by her, was at great pains to overcome her shame in being so surprised, and persuade her to speak openly. "Was she ill? or was anybody angry with her? or had she quarrelled with Maria and Julia? or was she puzzled about any thing in her lesson that he could explain? Did she, in short, want any thing he could possibly get her, or do for her?" For a long while no answer could be obtained beyond a "no, no—not at all—no, thank you;" but he still persevered, and no sooner had he begun to revert to her own home, than her increased sobs explained to him where the grievance lay. He tried to console her.

"You are sorry to leave Mamma, my dear little Fanny," said he, "which shows you to be a very good girl; but you must remember that you are with relations and friends, who all love you, and wish to make you happy. Let us walk out in the park, and you shall tell me all about your brothers and sisters."

On pursuing the subject, he found that dear as all these brothers and sisters generally were, there was one among them who ran more in her thoughts than the rest. It was William whom she talked of most and wanted most to see. William, the eldest, a year older than herself, her constant companion and friend; her advocate with her mother (of whom he was the darling) in every distress. "William did not like she should come away—he had told her he should miss her very much indeed." "But William will write to you, I dare say." "Yes, he had promised he would, but he had told *her* to write first." "And when shall you do it?" She hung her head and answered, hesitatingly, "she did not know; she had not any paper."

"If that be all your difficulty, I will furnish you with paper and every other material, and you may write your letter whenever you choose. Would it make you happy to write to William?"

"Yes, very."

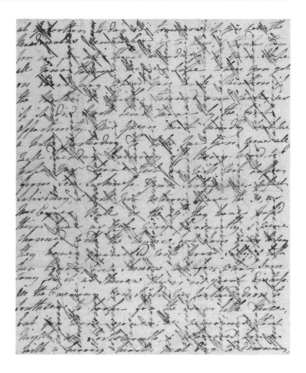

To economize at a time when sending a letter longer than a single page would be particularly costly, an early nineteenth-century letter writer would often opt for the kind of "chequer-work" that in Austen's *Emma* is associated with Jane Fairfax's letters to the Bateses. We see the technique here in a letter from 1821, addressed to George Thomas Maitland Purvis, the gentleman who would later marry into the Austen family by wedding Austen's niece Mary-Jane. Instead of continuing his letter onto a second sheet, a letter writer from this era might choose, as here, to remain on the same sheet and write the rest of his letter "crossed," that is, at a right angle across his original script.

7 To receive a letter could be a mixed blessing in the early nineteenth century: its recipient paid the postal charges, which were high. (The basic rate was four-pence for a letter of a single sheet that was to travel only fifteen miles, but costs climbed when a letter was sent on a longer journey—up to one shilling, five-pence—and letters comprising two sheets of paper were charged double. In September 1813 Austen had to pay twenty-seven pence—two shillings, threepence—for a letter she received from her sailor brother Francis, who was then aboard ship in the Baltic, though she wrote back to him that she thought it "very well worth" the money: *Letters,* p. 238.) Members of Parliament like Sir Thomas, however, were granted free carriage for their mail, a privilege they claimed by adding the word "Free" or "Frank" to a letter's address panel. Austen's own correspondence shows her exploiting her connections with acquaintance who enjoyed that privilege. A letter she wrote on October 11 and 12, 1813, to her sister, Cassandra, mentions that "Mr. Lushington MP for Canterbury . . . dines here"—a prospect that seemed to displease her, but, identifying an upside, she added, "If I can, I will get a frank from him & write to you all the sooner" (*Letters,* pp. 243–244).

8 Edmund makes himself useful by sharpening the point of the little girl's quill pen, a task even an adult could find difficult, and by assisting with the spelling *(orthography)* of her letter.

9 The guinea and half guinea owe their names to the supposed African origins of the gold from which they were manufactured. The half guinea coin was worth ten shillings, sixpence in change, making for a generous gift for William at a moment when the lowest rank of seaman in the Royal Navy would earn an amount only threepence higher for his monthly wage. Before they were posted, letters were folded up, rather than put into envelopes, and closed with a wax seal or wafer. People often placed a coin under the wax, though the practice violated post office regulations.

"Then let it be done now. Come with me into the breakfast-room, we shall find every thing there, and be sure of having the room to ourselves."

"But, cousin—will it go to the post?"

"Yes, depend upon me it shall; it shall go with the other letters; and as your uncle will frank it, it will cost William nothing."[7]

"My uncle!" repeated Fanny with a frightened look.

"Yes, when you have written the letter, I will take it to my father to frank."

Fanny thought it a bold measure, but offered no further resistance; and they went together into the breakfast-room, where Edmund prepared her paper, and ruled her lines with all the good will that her brother could himself have felt, and probably with somewhat more exactness. He continued with her the whole time of her writing, to assist her with his penknife or his orthography,[8] as either were wanted; and added to these attentions, which she felt very much, a kindness to her brother, which delighted her beyond all the rest. He wrote with his own hand his love to his cousin William, and sent him half a guinea under the seal.[9] Fanny's feelings on the occasion were such as she believed herself incapable of expressing; but her countenance and a few artless words fully conveyed all their gratitude and delight, and her cousin began to find her an interesting object. He talked to her more, and from all that she said, was convinced of her having an affectionate heart, and a strong desire of doing right; and he could perceive her to be farther entitled to attention, by great sensibility of her situation, and great timidity. He had never knowingly given her pain, but he now felt that she required more positive kindness, and with that view endeavoured, in the first place, to lessen her fears of them all, and gave her especially a great deal of good advice as to playing with Maria and Julia, and being as merry as possible.

From this day Fanny grew more comfortable. She felt that she had a friend, and the kindness of her cousin Edmund gave her better spirits with every body else. The place became less strange, and the people less formidable; and if there were some amongst them whom she could not cease to fear, she began at least to know their ways, and to catch the best manner of conforming to them. The little rusticities and awkwardnesses which had at first made grievous inroads on the tranquillity of all, and not least of herself, necessarily wore away, and she was no longer materially afraid to appear before her uncle, nor did her aunt Norris's voice make her start very much. To her cousins she became occasionally an acceptable companion. Though unworthy, from inferiority of age and strength, to be their constant associate, their pleasures and schemes were sometimes of a nature to make a third very useful, especially when that third was of an obliging, yielding temper; and they could not but own, when their aunt inquired into her faults, or their brother Edmund urged her claims to their kindness, that "Fanny was good-natured enough."

Edmund was uniformly kind himself, and she had nothing worse to endure on the part of Tom, than that sort of merriment which a young man of seventeen will always think fair with a child of ten. He was just entering into life, full of spirits, and with all the liberal dispositions of an eldest son, who feels born only for expense and enjoyment. His kindness to his little cousin was consistent with his situation and rights: he made her some very pretty presents, and laughed at her.

As her appearance and spirits improved, Sir Thomas and Mrs. Norris thought with greater satisfaction of their benevolent plan; and it was pretty soon decided between them, that though far from clever, she showed a tractable disposition, and seemed likely to give them little trouble. A mean opinion of her abilities was not confined to *them*. Fanny could read, work, and write, but she had been taught nothing more;[10] and as her cousins found her ignorant of many things with which they had been long familiar, they thought her prodigiously stupid, and for the first two or three weeks were continually bringing some fresh report of it into the drawing-room. "Dear Mamma, only think, my cousin cannot put the map of Europe together[11]—or my cousin cannot tell the principal rivers in Russia—or she never heard of Asia Minor—or she does not know the difference between water-colours and crayons!—How strange!—Did you ever hear anything so stupid?"

"My dear," their considerate aunt would reply; "it is very bad, but

10 Work here means needlework. The education Fanny has received up to this point has been restricted to subjects considered useful for female life in the lower middle class.

11 Fanny's difficulties involve the kind of educational jigsaw puzzle, known as a "dissected map," that was then a fashionable plaything in the schoolrooms of well-to-do British homes.

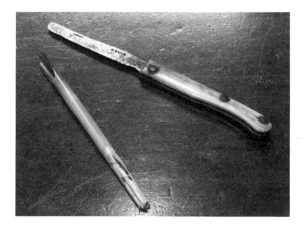

Pen-knives of the kind pictured in this photograph would be used to mend quill pens, whose points become dull quickly. Writing in this period was difficult work, involving many tools in addition to pen, ink, and paper. These pen-knives, Austen family heirlooms, are preserved at Chawton Cottage.

12 Fanny's geographical understanding and language are alike shaped by her tenacious attachment to her home ground. This would indeed be a strange route to Ireland, but for an inhabitant of Portsmouth, the Isle of Wight, just across the estuary of the Solent River, would quite naturally be "the Island," a way of referencing it that Austen used herself in her correspondence.

A puzzle map of the sort that was a staple of children's geographical education in the eighteenth and nineteenth centuries. The publisher J. Wallis manufactured this "New Dissected Map" of the United States not long after the War of Independence.

you must not expect every body to be as forward and quick at learning as yourself."

"But, aunt, she is really so very ignorant!—Do you know, we asked her last night, which way she would go to get to Ireland; and she said, she should cross to the Isle of Wight. She thinks of nothing but the Isle of Wight, and she calls it *the Island,* as if there were no other island in the world.[12] I am sure I should have been ashamed of myself, if I had not known better long before I was so old as she is. I cannot remember the time when I did not know a great deal that she has not the least notion of yet. How long ago it is, aunt, since we used to repeat the chronological order of the kings of England, with the dates of their accession, and most of the principal events of their reigns!"

"Yes," added the other; "and of the Roman emperors as low as Severus; besides a great deal of the Heathen Mythology, and all the Metals, Semi-Metals, Planets, and distinguished philosophers."

"Very true, indeed, my dears, but you are blessed with wonderful memories, and your poor cousin has probably none at all. There is a vast deal of difference in memories, as well as in everything else, and therefore you must make allowance for your cousin, and pity her deficiency. And remember that, if you are ever so forward and clever yourselves, you should always be modest; for, much as you know already, there is a great deal more for you to learn."

"Yes, I know there is, till I am seventeen. But I must tell you another thing of Fanny, so odd and so stupid. Do you know, she says she does not want to learn either music or drawing."

"To be sure, my dear, that is very stupid indeed, and shows a great want of genius and emulation.[13] But, all things considered, I do not know whether it is not as well that it should be so, for, though you know (owing to me) your papa and mamma are so good as to bring her up with you, it is not at all necessary that she should be as accomplished as you are;—on the contrary, it is much more desirable that there should be a difference."

Such were the counsels by which Mrs. Norris assisted to form her nieces' minds; and it is not very wonderful that with all their promising talents and early information,[14] they should be entirely deficient

In this 1781 portrait by George Romney, seven-year-old Margaret Casson is dwarfed by her piano and probably has to strain to read the sheet music propped on its top, but the confidence with which she meets the viewer's gaze suggests the aplomb she brings to her performances. In Austen's day, girls and young women were often expected to demonstrate their musical accomplishments during social gatherings.

13 Natural aptitude, rather than the exceptional intelligence or talent that is at issue in more modern usages of the term *genius*. In lacking "emulation," Fanny lacks a desire to excel—to equal or outshine others.

14 *Information* is a tricky word in Austen's novels, one whose meanings were in flux as she wrote. In *Why Jane Austen?*, Rachel Brownstein writes illuminatingly about the word's usage in *Emma*, focusing on Emma's query to Jane Fairfax as to whether Frank Churchill, when Jane met him at Weymouth, appeared to her a "young man of information" (II, 2). To understand Emma's question, Brownstein suggests, it helps to recall that *information* formerly encompassed more than the facts or data we associate with the term. It retained as well the meanings of the word *formation* that is at its root— and so involved notions of educational processes as distinct from the content conveyed by education. When she poses her question, Emma is not wondering whether Frank has his facts straight but—rather more consequentially—is wondering about his cultivation and personal development. Brownstein's discussion helps one grasp how, in her account of the Bertram girls' schooling, Austen seems almost to be playing information as *facts*—data about, for instance, "Metals, Semi-Metals, Planets, and distinguished philosophers"—against information as *formation*: Maria and Julia have been stuffed full of the first, at the expense of the second. See Brownstein, *Why Jane Austen?* (New York: Columbia University Press, 2011), pp. 225–234.

in the less common acquirements of self-knowledge, generosity, and humility. In every thing but disposition, they were admirably taught. Sir Thomas did not know what was wanting, because, though a truly anxious father, he was not outwardly affectionate, and the reserve of his manner repressed all the flow of their spirits before him.

To the education of her daughters, Lady Bertram paid not the smallest attention. She had not time for such cares. She was a woman who spent her days in sitting nicely dressed on a sofa, doing some long piece of needle-work, of little use and no beauty, thinking more of her pug than her children, but very indulgent to the latter, when it did not put herself to inconvenience, guided in every thing important by Sir Thomas, and in smaller concerns by her sister. Had she possessed greater leisure for the service of her girls, she would probably have supposed it unnecessary, for they were under the care of a governess, with proper masters, and could want nothing more. As for Fanny's being stupid at learning, "she could only say it was very unlucky, but some people *were* stupid, and Fanny must take more pains; she did not know what else was to be done; and except her being so dull, she must add she saw no harm in the poor little thing—and always found her very handy and quick in carrying messages, and fetching what she wanted."

Fanny, with all her faults of ignorance and timidity, was fixed at Mansfield Park, and learning to transfer in its favour much of her attachment to her former home, grew up there not unhappily among her cousins. There was no positive ill-nature in Maria or Julia; and though Fanny was often mortified by their treatment of her, she thought too lowly of her own claims to feel injured by it.

From about the time of her entering the family, Lady Bertram, in consequence of a little ill–health, and a great deal of indolence, gave up the house in town, which she had been used to occupy every spring, and remained wholly in the country, leaving Sir Thomas to attend his duty in Parliament, with whatever increase or diminution of comfort might arise from her absence. In the country, therefore, the Miss Bertrams continued to exercise their memories, practise their duets, and grow tall and womanly; and their father saw them becoming in person, manner, and accomplishments, every thing that could satisfy his anxiety. His eldest son was careless and extravagant, and had already given him much uneasiness; but his other children promised him nothing but good. His daughters he felt, while they retained the name of Bertram, must be giving it new grace, and in quitting it he trusted would extend its respectable alliances; and the character of Edmund, his strong good sense and uprightness of mind, bid most fairly for utility, honour, and happiness to himself and all his connections. He was to be a clergyman.

Amid the cares and the complacency which his own children suggested, Sir Thomas did not forget to do what he could for the children of Mrs. Price; he assisted her liberally in the education and dis-posal of her sons as they became old enough for a determinate pursuit: and Fanny, though almost totally separated from her family, was sensible of the truest satisfaction in hearing of any kindness to-wards them, or of any thing at all promising in their situation or con-duct. Once, and once only in the course of many years, had she the happiness of being with William. Of the rest she saw nothing; no-body seemed to think of her ever going amongst them again, even for a visit, nobody at home seemed to want her; but William deter-mining, soon after her removal, to be a sailor, was invited to spend a week with his sister in Northamptonshire, before he went to sea. Their eager affection in meeting, their exquisite delight in being to-gether, their hours of happy mirth, and moments of serious confer-ence, may be imagined; as well as the sanguine views and spirits of the boy even to the last, and the misery of the girl when he left her. Luckily the visit happencd in the Christmas holidays, when she could directly look for comfort to her cousin Edmund; and he told her such charming things of what William was to do, and be hereaf-ter, in consequence of his profession, as made her gradually admit that the separation might have some use. Edmund's friendship never failed her: his leaving Eton for Oxford made no change in his kind dispositions, and only afforded more frequent opportunities of proving them.[15] Without any display of doing more than the rest, or any fear of doing too much, he was always true to her interests, and considerate of her feelings, trying to make her good qualities under-stood, and to conquer the diffidence which prevented their being more apparent; giving her advice, consolation, and encouragement.

Kept back as she was by everybody else, his single support could not bring her forward, but his attentions were otherwise of the high-est importance in assisting the improvement of her mind, and ex-tending its pleasures. He knew her to be clever, to have a quick ap-prehension as well as good sense, and a fondness for reading, which, properly directed, must be an education in itself. Miss Lee taught her French, and heard her read the daily portion of History; but he recommended the books which charmed her leisure hours, he en-couraged her taste, and corrected her judgment; he made reading

15 Oxford was a day's journey from Northampton-shire. In leaving his public school, Eton, in the south of England, for his Oxford college, Edmund halves his journey from school to home. Oxford had shorter terms than Eton, another reason Edmund would be able to spend more time at home. In referencing these particular institutions of learning, Austen is not telling us about the nature of Edmund's schooling so much as she is telling us about his secure membership in the so-cial elite.

useful by talking to her of what she read, and heightened its attraction by judicious praise. In return for such services she loved him better than any body in the world except William; her heart was divided between the two.

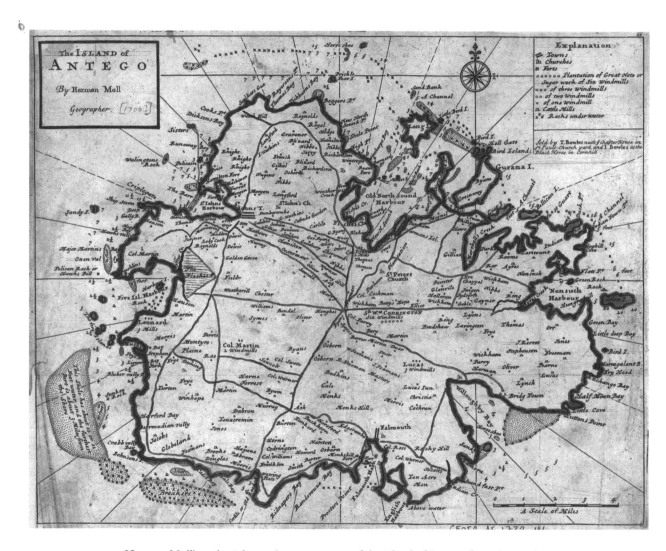

Herman Moll's early eighteenth-century map of the island of Antego (later Antigua), showing the locations of the island's forts, churches, sugarcane plantations, and mills, where raw cane was processed. The Austen family friend James Langford Nibbs inherited plantations in the northernmost peninsula of the island.

# 3

THE FIRST EVENT of any importance in the family was the death of Mr. Norris, which happened when Fanny was about fifteen, and necessarily introduced alterations and novelties. Mrs. Norris, on quitting the parsonage, removed first to the park, and afterwards to a small house of Sir Thomas's in the village, and consoled herself for the loss of her husband by considering that she could do very well without him, and for her reduction of income by the evident necessity of stricter economy.

The living was hereafter for Edmund, and had his uncle died a few years sooner, it would have been duly given to some friend to hold till he were old enough for orders. But Tom's extravagance had, previous to that event, been so great, as to render a different disposal of the next presentation necessary, and the younger brother must help to pay for the pleasures of the elder.[1] There was another family-living actually held for Edmund; but though this circumstance had made the arrangement somewhat easier to Sir Thomas's conscience, he could not but feel it to be an act of injustice, and he earnestly tried to impress his eldest son with the same conviction, in the hope of its producing a better effect than any thing he had yet been able to say or do.

"I blush for you, Tom," said he, in his most dignified manner; "I blush for the expedient which I am driven on, and I trust I may pity your feelings as a brother on the occasion. You have robbed Edmund for ten, twenty, thirty years, perhaps for life, of more than half the income which ought to be his. It may hereafter be in my power, or in

1 Sir Thomas has two family-livings in his gift, but it will no longer be possible for Edmund, after his ordination, to claim both, at least not immediately. The Mansfield living is to be sold to a new incumbent, and the income associated with that living will remain the new incumbent's for as long as he is the clergyman in charge of the parish. "Pluralism," the practice of permitting a clergyman to hold more than one living at once, was in fact controversial in this period and often identified as a cause of the declining social influence of the Church of England. Though the practice increased the income of the clergy, it was blamed for decreasing the quality of their pastoral care, since it was impossible for a pluralist to reside simultaneously in more than a single parish. The bishop of Llandaff, who in 1783 wrote publicly about the church's need to reduce pluralism and nonresidency, himself held sixteen livings. See Laura Mooneyham White, *Jane Austen's Anglicanism* (Farnham, Surrey: Ashgate, 2011), pp. 13–16.

2 Appointment to a position in the church, which Edmund would hold in conjunction with the family-livings.

3 Critics have disagreed in conjectures about the reasons for those losses, their variance a function in part of their disagreement as to whether the action of *Mansfield Park* is properly placed immediately before 1807, the date of the British Parliament's abolition of the trade in slaves, or immediately after, or, a third option, during the years in which Austen composed the novel, 1811–1812. Even before 1807, the soil in many Caribbean colonies had been depleted by the intensive farming techniques necessary for the growing of sugar cane, and what had been a sure-bet, high-profit industry for the planter class was becoming financially risky. Markets for sugar initially contracted during Britain's war with France, because of the success of the French blockade; later, when Britain recaptured sugar islands lost to the French and Dutch, the home market was flooded with the commodity and the prices it fetched plummeted. The 1807 legislation that abolished the slave trade postponed actual emancipation of the colonies' enslaved labor force until 1833, but it nevertheless exacerbated this climate of economic uncertainty.

your's (I hope it will), to procure him better preferment;[2] but it must not be forgotten, that no benefit of that sort would have been beyond his natural claims on us, and that nothing can, in fact, be an equivalent for the certain advantage which he is now obliged to forego through the urgency of your debts."

Tom listened with some shame and some sorrow; but escaping as quickly as possible, could soon with cheerful selfishness reflect, 1st, that he had not been half so much in debt as some of his friends; 2dly, that his father had made a most tiresome piece of work of it; and 3dly, that the future incumbent, whoever he might be, would, in all probability, die very soon.

On Mr. Norris's death, the presentation became the right of a Dr. Grant, who came consequently to reside at Mansfield, and on proving to be a hearty man of forty-five, seemed likely to disappoint Mr. Bertram's calculations. But "no, he was a short-neck'd, apoplectic sort of fellow, and, plied well with good things, would soon pop off."

He had a wife about fifteen years his junior, but no children, and they entered the neighbourhood with the usual fair report of being very respectable, agreeable people.

The time was now come when Sir Thomas expected his sister-in-law to claim her share in their niece, the change in Mrs. Norris's situation, and the improvement in Fanny's age, seeming not merely to do away any former objection to their living together, but even to give it the most decided eligibility; and as his own circumstances were rendered less fair than heretofore, by some recent losses on his West India Estate,[3] in addition to his eldest son's extravagance, it became not undesirable to himself to be relieved from the expense of her support, and the obligation of her future provision. In the fullness of his belief that such a thing must be, he mentioned its probability to his wife; and the first time of the subject's occurring to her again, happening to be when Fanny was present, she calmly observed to her, "So, Fanny, you are going to leave us, and live with my sister. How shall you like it?"

Fanny was too much surprised to do more than repeat her aunt's words, "Going to leave you?"

"Yes, my dear; why should you be astonished? You have been five years with us, and my sister always meant to take you when Mr. Norris died. But you must come up and tack on my patterns all the same."[4]

The news was as disagreeable to Fanny as it had been unexpected. She had never received kindness from her aunt Norris, and could not love her.

"I shall be very sorry to go away," said she, with a faltering voice.

"Yes, I dare say you will; *that's* natural enough. I suppose you have had as little to vex you, since you came into this house, as any creature in the world."

"I hope I am not ungrateful, aunt," said Fanny, modestly.

"No, my dear; I hope not. I have always found you a very good girl."

"And am I never to live here again?"

"Never, my dear; but you are sure of a comfortable home. It can make very little difference to you, whether you are in one house or the other."

Fanny left the room with a very sorrowful heart; she could not feel the difference to be so small, she could not think of living with her aunt with anything like satisfaction. As soon as she met with Edmund, she told him her distress.

"Cousin," said she, "something is going to happen which I do not like at all; and though you have often persuaded me into being reconciled to things that I disliked at first, you will not be able to do it now. I am going to live entirely with my aunt Norris."

"Indeed!"

"Yes, my aunt Bertram has just told me so. It is quite settled. I am to leave Mansfield Park, and go to the White house, I suppose, as soon as she is removed there."

"Well, Fanny, and if the plan were not unpleasant to you, I should call it an excellent one."

"Oh! Cousin!"

"It has every thing else in its favour. My aunt is acting like a sensible woman in wishing for you. She is choosing a friend and compan-

4 Baste the paper patterns used for needlework or appliqué onto the fabric.

*Andrews's New Map of the West Indies and Part of the Coast of South America,* first published in 1783. The Caribbean islands changed imperial possessors several times over the course of the wars of the eighteenth and early nineteenth centuries: the attendant changes of place names kept cartographers busy.

ion exactly where she ought, and I am glad her love of money does not interfere. You will be what you ought to be to her. I hope it does not distress you very much, Fanny."

"Indeed it does: I cannot like it. I love this house and every thing in it. I shall love nothing there. You know how uncomfortable I feel with her."

"I can say nothing for her manner to you as a child; but it was the same with us all, or nearly so. She never knew how to be pleasant to children. But you are now of an age to be treated better; I think she *is* behaving better already; and when you are her only companion, you *must* be important to her."

"I can never be important to any one."

"What is to prevent you?"

"Every thing—my situation—my foolishness and awkwardness."

"As to your foolishness and awkwardness, my dear Fanny, believe me, you never have a shadow of either, but in using the words so improperly. There is no reason in the world why you should not be important where you are known. You have good sense, and a sweet temper, and I am sure you have a grateful heart, that could never receive kindness without wishing to return it. I do not know any better qualifications for a friend and companion."

"You are too kind," said Fanny, colouring at such praise; "how shall I ever thank you as I ought, for thinking so well of me. Oh! cousin, if I am to go away, I shall remember your goodness, to the last moment of my life."

"Why, indeed, Fanny, I should hope to be remembered at such a distance as the White house. You speak as if you were going two hundred miles off instead of only across the park. But you will belong to us almost as much as ever. The two families will be meeting every day in the year. The only difference will be, that living with your aunt, you will necessarily be brought forward, as you ought to be. *Here,* there are too many, whom you can hide behind; but with *her* you will be forced to speak for yourself."

"Oh! do not say so."

"I must say it, and say it with pleasure. Mrs. Norris is much better fitted than my mother for having the charge of you now. She is of a temper to do a great deal for any body she really interests herself about, and she will force you to do justice to your natural powers."

Fanny sighed, and said, "I cannot see things as you do; but I ought to believe you to be right rather than myself, and I am very much obliged to you for trying to reconcile me to what must be. If I could suppose my aunt really to care for me, it would be delightful to feel myself of consequence to any body!—*Here,* I know I am of none, and yet I love the place so well."

"The place, Fanny, is what you will not quit, though you quit the house. You will have as free a command of the park and gardens as ever. Even *your* constant little heart need not take fright at such a nominal change. You will have the same walks to frequent, the same library to choose from, the same people to look at, the same horse to ride."

"Very true. Yes, dear old grey poney. Ah! cousin, when I remember how much I used to dread riding, what terrors it gave me to hear it talked of as likely to do me good;—(Oh! how I have trembled at my uncle's opening his lips if horses were talked of) and then think of the kind pains you took to reason and persuade me out of my fears, and convince me that I should like it after a little while, and feel how right you proved to be, I am inclined to hope you may always prophesy as well."

"And I am quite convinced that your being with Mrs. Norris, will be as good for your mind, as riding has been for your health—and as much for your ultimate happiness, too."

So ended their discourse, which, for any very appropriate service it could render Fanny, might as well have been spared, for Mrs. Norris had not the smallest intention of taking her. It had never occurred to her, on the present occasion, but as a thing to be carefully avoided. To prevent its being expected, she had fixed on the smallest habitation which could rank as genteel among the buildings of Mansfield parish; the White house being only just large enough to receive herself and her servants, and allow a spare room for a friend, of which she made a very particular point;—The spare-rooms at the parsonage had never been wanted, but the absolute necessity of a spare-room for a friend was now never forgotten. Not all her precautions, however, could save her from being suspected of something better; or, perhaps, her very display of the importance of a spare-room, might have misled Sir Thomas to suppose it really intended for Fanny. Lady Bertram soon brought the matter to a certainty, by carelessly observing to Mrs. Norris,—

"I think, sister, we need not keep Miss Lee any longer, when Fanny goes to live with you?"

Mrs. Norris almost started. "Live with me, dear Lady Bertram, what do you mean?"

"Is not she to live with you?—I thought you had settled it with Sir Thomas?"

"Me! never. I never spoke a syllable about it to Sir Thomas, nor he to me. Fanny live with me! the last thing in the world for me to think of, or for any body to wish that really knows us both. Good heaven! what could I do with Fanny?—Me! a poor helpless, forlorn widow, unfit for any thing, my spirits quite broke down, what could I do with a girl at her time of life, a girl of fifteen! the very age of all others to need most attention and care, and put the cheerfullest spirits to the test. Sure Sir Thomas could not seriously expect such a thing! Sir Thomas is too much my friend. Nobody that wishes me well, I am sure, would propose it. How came Sir Thomas to speak to you about it?"

"Indeed, I do not know. I suppose he thought it best."

"But what did he say?—He could not say he *wished* me to take Fanny. I am sure in his heart he could not wish me to do it."

"No, he only said he thought it very likely—and I thought so too. We both thought it would be a comfort to you. But if you do not like it, there is no more to be said. She is no encumbrance here."

"Dear sister! If you consider my unhappy state, how can she be any comfort to me? Here am I a poor desolate widow, deprived of the best of husbands, my health gone in attending and nursing him, my spirits still worse, all my peace in this world destroyed, with hardly enough to support me in the rank of a gentlewoman, and enable me to live so as not to disgrace the memory of the dear departed—what possible comfort could I have in taking such a charge upon me as

Fanny! If I could wish it for my own sake, I would not do so unjust a thing by the poor girl. She is in good hands, and sure of doing well. I must struggle through my sorrows and difficulties as I can."

"Then you will not mind living by yourself quite alone?"

"Dear Lady Bertram! what am I fit for but solitude? Now and then I shall hope to have a friend in my little cottage (I shall always have a bed for a friend); but the most part of my future days will be spent in utter seclusion. If I can but make both ends meet, that's all I ask for."

"I hope, sister, things are not so very bad with you neither—considering. Sir Thomas says you will have six hundred a year."[5]

"Lady Bertram, I do not complain. I know I cannot live as I have done, but I must retrench where I can, and learn to be a better manager. I *have been* a liberal housekeeper enough, but I shall not be ashamed to practise economy now. My situation is as much altered as my income. A great many things were due from poor Mr. Norris as clergyman of the parish, that cannot be expected from me. It is unknown how much was consumed in our kitchen by odd comers and goers. At the White house, matters must be better looked after. I *must* live within my income, or I shall be miserable; and I own it would give me great satisfaction to be able to do rather more—to lay by a little at the end of the year."

"I dare say you will. You always do, don't you?"

"My object, Lady Bertram, is to be of use to those that come after me. It is for your children's good that I wish to be richer. I have nobody else to care for, but I should be very glad to think I could leave a little trifle among them, worth their having."

"You are very good, but do not trouble yourself about them. They are sure of being well provided for. Sir Thomas will take care of that."

"Why, you know Sir Thomas's means will be rather straitened, if the Antigua estate is to make such poor returns."

"Oh! *that* will soon be settled. Sir Thomas has been writing about it, I know."

"Well, Lady Bertram," said Mrs. Norris, moving to go, "I can only say that my sole desire is to be of use to your family—and so, if Sir Thomas should ever speak again about my taking Fanny, you will be

5  Compare, in *Sense and Sensibility,* the 500*l* per annum that is all the income that remains to Mrs. Dashwood following her husband's death. Mrs. Dashwood has to support herself and three daughters on that sum.

6 The motives impelling Sir Thomas at this point to journey to an overseas estate that he appears previously to have left unvisited are as open to debate as the novel's references to the estate's losses. What precisely does Sir Thomas mean to do in Antigua? His aim might be to quell rebellion and reassert his property rights over his human chattel—an interpretation that seems more plausible if this section of the novel does take place before abolition. But he might alternately be prompted by reformist motives. "If the Slave-trade should really be abolished," Thomas Clarkson wrote as he explained the strategizing that had led his Committee for the Abolition to target the trade rather than slavery itself, "the bad usage of the slaves in the colonies . . . would fall. For the planters and owners being unable to procure more slaves from the coast of Africa, it would follow directly . . . that they must treat those better, whom they might then have." Sir Thomas may intend to improve working conditions on his estate, though Austen, as an avid reader of Clarkson, would certainly have been aware that such benevolence was not easily separated from the pursuit of economic self-interest. In one of the speeches to Parliament made by the abolitionist leader William Wilberforce and recorded in Clarkson's *History of the Rise, Progress, and Accomplishment of the Abolition of the African Slave-Trade,* Wilberforce even suggests that the abolition of the slave trade, in ushering in an ameliorist regime of kind treatment, might augment the value of the planters' human property. For evidence, Wilberforce pointed to conditions on the island of Antigua in particular, noting that the efforts made there by Moravian and Methodist missionaries had such happy "effects . . . that the planters themselves confessed that [the slaves'] value as property had been raised one-third by their increased habits of regularity and industry" (*The History of the Rise, Progress, and Accomplishment of the Abolition of the African Slave-Trade* [1807; rept. Philadelphia: James P. Parke, 1808], vol. 2, pp. 229; 183–184).

The Austen family's links to the Antiguan planter class are another reason Austen's reference to this particular Caribbean colony would likely have been intentional. At Oxford her father acted as tutor to the wealthy James Langford Nibbs, whose family had owned Antiguan sugar plantations for three generations, and Nibbs's marriage articles named George

able to say, that my health and spirits put it quite out of the question—besides that, I really should not have a bed to give her, for I must keep a spare room for a friend."

Lady Bertram repeated enough of this conversation to her husband, to convince him how much he had mistaken his sister-in-law's views; and she was from that moment perfectly safe from all expectation, or the slightest allusion to it from him. He could not but wonder at her refusing to do any thing for a niece, whom she had been so forward to adopt; but as she took early care to make him, as well as Lady Bertram, understand that whatever she possessed was designed for their family, he soon grew reconciled to a distinction, which at the same time that it was advantageous and complimentary to them, would enable him better to provide for Fanny himself.

Fanny soon learnt how unnecessary had been her fears of a removal; and her spontaneous, untaught felicity on the discovery, conveyed some consolation to Edmund for his disappointment in what he had expected to be so essentially serviceable to her. Mrs. Norris took possession of the White house, the Grants arrived at the parsonage, and these events over, every thing at Mansfield went on for some time as usual.

The Grants showing a disposition to be friendly and sociable, gave great satisfaction in the main among their new acquaintance. They had their faults, and Mrs. Norris soon found them out. The Dr. was very fond of eating, and would have a good dinner every day; and Mrs. Grant, instead of contriving to gratify him at little expense, gave her cook as high wages as they did at Mansfield Park, and was scarcely ever seen in her offices. Mrs. Norris could not speak with any temper of such grievances, nor of the quantity of butter and eggs that were regularly consumed in the house. "Nobody loved plenty and hospitality more than herself—nobody more hated pitiful doings—the parsonage she believed had never been wanting in comforts of any sort, had never borne a bad character in *her time,* but this was a way of going on that she could not understand. A fine lady in a country parsonage was quite out of place. *Her* store-room she thought might have been good enough for Mrs. Grant to go into. Enquire where she would, she could not find out that Mrs. Grant had ever had more than five thousand pounds."

Lady Bertram listened without much interest to this sort of invective. She could not enter into the wrongs of an economist, but she felt all the injuries of beauty in Mrs. Grant's being so well settled in life without being handsome, and expressed her astonishment on that point almost as often, though not so diffusely, as Mrs. Norris discussed the other.

These opinions had been hardly canvassed a year, before another event arose of such importance in the family, as might fairly claim some place in the thoughts and conversation of the ladies. Sir Thomas found it expedient to go to Antigua himself, for the better arrangement of his affairs, and he took his eldest son with him, in the hope of detaching him from some bad connections at home.[6] They left England with the probability of being nearly a twelvemonth absent.

The necessity of the measure in a pecuniary light, and the hope of its utility to his son, reconciled Sir Thomas to the effort of quitting the rest of his family, and of leaving his daughters to the direction of others at their present most interesting time of life. He could not think Lady Bertram quite equal to supply his place with them, or rather to perform what should have been her own; but in Mrs. Norris's watchful attention, and in Edmund's judgment, he had sufficient confidence to make him go without fears for their conduct.

Lady Bertram did not at all like to have her husband leave her; but she was not disturbed by any alarm for his safety, or solicitude for his comfort, being one of those persons who think nothing can be dangerous or difficult, or fatiguing to any body but themselves.

The Miss Bertrams were much to be pitied on the occasion; not for their sorrow, but for their want of it. Their father was no object of love to them, he had never seemed the friend of their pleasures, and his absence was unhappily most welcome. They were relieved by it from all restraint; and without aiming at one gratification that would probably have been forbidden by Sir Thomas, they felt themselves immediately at their own disposal, and to have every indulgence within their reach. Fanny's relief, and her consciousness of it, were quite equal to her cousins', but a more tender nature suggested that her feelings were ungrateful, and she really grieved because she could not grieve. "Sir Thomas, who had done so much for her and

Austen as a trustee of his Antiguan property. Nibbs's son appears to have been as disappointing to his father as Tom Bertram was to his and was likewise taken to Antigua to detach him from "unwholesome connections." He died there, disinherited.

On this Austen family connection, see especially Brian Southam, "The Silence of the Bertrams," *Times Literary Supplement,* Feb. 17, 1995, 13–14, one of many responses to Edward W. Said's *Culture and Imperialism* (New York: Alfred A. Knopf, 1993). Said's book proposed that *Mansfield Park,* like the nineteenth-century British novel more generally, demands a "contrapuntal reading," a mode of criticism that would take account both of imperialism and of the resistance to it: "Just because Austen referred to Antigua . . . without any thought of possible responses by the Caribbean . . . natives resident there is no reason for us to do the same. We now know that these non-European people did not accept with indifference the authority projected over them, or the general silence on which their presence in variously attenuated forms is predicated. We must therefore read the great canonical texts . . . with an effort to draw out, extend, give emphasis and voice to what is silent or marginally present . . . in such works" (*Culture and Imperialism,* p. 66). Said's statement later in this discussion that Austen *assumes,* by a "very odd combination of casualness and stress," that even insulated English places require the sustenance of the colonies (*Culture and Imperialism,* p. 89) has in itself sparked much debate since the 1990s, Southam's *TLS* essay being one of the earliest and most notable salvos. While Said appeared to suggest that Austen was somehow inattentive or irresponsible, that she marginalized exactly the issues of geopolitical justice she should have put front and center, these critics draw different conclusions as they examine *Mansfield Park* in its contemporary context—in conjunction with abolitionist literature, for instance, or with the novels in which Austen's contemporaries also treated the transits of English husbands and fathers between their Caribbean properties and their families at home. For a fine example of this line of argument, see Katie Trumpener's discussion of *Mansfield Park* in *Bardic Nationalism: The Romantic Novel and the British Empire* (Princeton: Princeton University Press, 1997), pp. 162–182.

7 Indifference, lack of sympathetic feeling.

her brothers, and who was gone perhaps never to return! that she should see him go without a tear!—it was a shameful insensibility."[7] He had said to her moreover, on the very last morning, that he hoped she might see William again in the course of the ensuing winter, and had charged her to write and invite him to Mansfield as soon as the squadron to which he belonged should be known to be in England. "This was so thoughtful and kind!"—and would he only have smiled upon her and called her "my dear Fanny," while he said it, every former frown or cold address might have been forgotten. But he had ended his speech in a way to sink her in sad mortification, by adding, "If William does come to Mansfield, I hope you may be able to convince him that the many years which have passed since you parted, have not been spent on your side entirely without improvement—though I fear he must find his sister at sixteen in some respects too much like his sister at ten." She cried bitterly over this reflection when her uncle was gone; and her cousins, on seeing her with red eyes, set her down as a hypocrite.

Kirby Hall in Northamptonshire doubled as Sir Thomas Bertram's country house in Patricia Rozema's 1999 film adaptation of *Mansfield Park*.

# 4

Tom Bertram had of late spent so little of his time at home, that he could be only nominally missed; and Lady Bertram was soon astonished to find how very well they did even without his father, how well Edmund could supply his place in carving, talking to the steward, writing to the attorney, settling with the servants, and equally saving her from all possible fatigue or exertion in every particular, but that of directing her letters.

The earliest intelligence of the travellers' safe arrival in Antigua after a favourable voyage, was received; though not before Mrs. Norris had been indulging in very dreadful fears, and trying to make Edmund participate them whenever she could get him alone; and as she depended on being the first person made acquainted with any fatal catastrophe, she had already arranged the manner of breaking it to all the others, when Sir Thomas's assurances of their both being alive and well, made it necessary to lay by her agitation and affectionate preparatory speeches for a while.

The winter came and passed without their being called for; the accounts continued perfectly good;—and Mrs. Norris in promoting gaieties for her nieces, assisting their toilets, displaying their accomplishments,[1] and looking about for their future husbands, had so much to do as, in addition to all her own household cares, some interference in those of her sister, and Mrs. Grant's wasteful doings to overlook, left her very little occasion to be occupied in fears for the absent.

1 In *Pride and Prejudice* Miss Bingley outlines (a tad self-servingly) what it takes to qualify as an accomplished woman: one "must have a thorough knowledge of music, singing, drawing, dancing, and the modern languages, to deserve the word" (I, 8). Those who identified such knowledge as a proper goal of the education of young ladies often did so with one eye to their pupils' advantage in a competitive marriage market. The talents and conversational powers of the young wife who had been so educated would help her to keep her husband entertained and at home. As Hester Chapone proposed in her much reprinted *Letters on the Improvement of the Mind* (first published 1773), accomplishments would also give their possessor the wherewithal to entertain herself—to fill "agreeably those intervals of time which too often hang heavily on the hands of a woman" ([London: John Hearne, 1829], p. 133).

The Miss Bertrams were now fully established among the belles of the neighbourhood; and as they joined to beauty and brilliant acquirements, a manner naturally easy, and carefully formed to general civility and obligingness, they possessed its favour as well as its admiration. Their vanity was in such good order, that they seemed to be quite free from it, and gave themselves no airs; while the praises attending such behaviour, secured, and brought round by their aunt, served to strengthen them in believing they had no faults.

Lady Bertram did not go into public with her daughters. She was too indolent even to accept a mother's gratification in witnessing their success and enjoyment at the expense of any personal trouble, and the charge was made over to her sister, who desired nothing better than a post of such honourable representation, and very thoroughly relished the means it afforded her of mixing in society without having horses to hire.

Fanny had no share in the festivities of the season; but she enjoyed being avowedly useful as her aunt's companion, when they called away the rest of the family; and as Miss Lee had left Mansfield, she naturally became everything to Lady Bertram during the night of a ball or a party. She talked to her, listened to her, read to her; and the tranquillity of such evenings, her perfect security in such a *tête-à-tête* from any sound of unkindness, was unspeakably welcome to a mind which had seldom known a pause in its alarms or embarrassments. As to her cousins' gaieties, she loved to hear an account of them, especially of the balls, and whom Edmund had danced with; but thought too lowly of her own situation to imagine she should ever be admitted to the same, and listened therefore without an idea of any nearer concern in them. Upon the whole, it was a comfortable winter to her; for though it brought no William to England, the never failing hope of his arrival was worth much.

The ensuing spring deprived her of her valued friend the old grey poney, and for some time she was in danger of feeling the loss in her health as well as in her affections, for in spite of the acknowledged importance of her riding on horseback, no measures were taken for mounting her again, "because," as it was observed by her aunts, "she might ride one of her cousins' horses at any time when they did not want them;" and as the Miss Bertrams regularly wanted their horses every fine day, and had no idea of carrying their obliging manners to the sacrifice of any real pleasure, that time of course never came. They took their cheerful rides in the fine mornings of April and May; and Fanny either sat at home the whole day with one aunt, or walked beyond her strength at the instigation of the other; Lady Bertram holding exercise to be as unnecessary for every body as it was unpleasant to herself; and Mrs. Norris, who was walking all day, thinking every body ought to walk as much. Edmund was absent at this time, or the evil would have been earlier remedied. When he returned to understand how Fanny was situated, and perceived its ill effects, there seemed with him but one thing to be done, and that "Fanny must have a horse," was the resolute declaration with which he opposed whatever could be urged by the supineness of his mother, or the economy of his aunt, to make it appear unimportant. Mrs. Norris could not help thinking that some steady old thing might be found among the numbers belonging to the Park, that would do vastly well, or that one might be borrowed of the steward, or that perhaps Dr. Grant might now and then lend them the pony he sent to the post. She could not but consider it as absolutely unnecessary, and even improper, that Fanny should have a regular lady's horse of her own in the style of her cousins. She was sure Sir Thomas had never intended it; and she must say, that to be making such a purchase in his absence, and adding to the great expenses of his stable, at a time when a large part of his income was unsettled, seemed to her very unjustifiable. "Fanny must have a horse," was Edmund's only reply. Mrs. Norris could not see it in the same light. Lady Bertram did; she entirely agreed with her son as to the necessity of it, and as to its being considered necessary by his father;—she only pleaded against there being any hurry, she only wanted him to wait till Sir Thomas's return, and then Sir Thomas might settle it all himself. He would be at home in September, and where would be the harm of only waiting till September?

Though Edmund was much more displeased with his aunt than with his mother, as evincing least regard for her niece, he could not help paying more attention to what she said, and at length determined on a method of proceeding which would obviate the risk of his father's thinking he had done too much, and at the same time procure for Fanny the immediate means of exercise, which he could not bear she should be without. He had three horses of his own, but not one that would carry a woman. Two of them were hunters;[2] the third, a useful road-horse: this third he resolved to exchange for one that his cousin might ride; he knew where such a one was to be met with, and having once made up his mind, the whole business was soon completed. The new mare proved a treasure; with a very little trouble, she became exactly calculated for the purpose, and Fanny was then put in almost full possession of her. She had not supposed before, that any thing could ever suit her like the old grey pony; but her delight in Edmund's mare was far beyond any former pleasure of the sort; and the addition it was ever receiving in the consideration of that kindness from which her pleasure sprung, was beyond all her words to express. She regarded her cousin as an example of everything good and great, as possessing worth, which no one but herself could ever appreciate, and as entitled to such gratitude from her, as no feelings could be strong enough to pay. Her sentiments towards him were compounded of all that was respectful, grateful, confiding, and tender.

As the horse continued in name as well as fact, the property of Edmund, Mrs. Norris could tolerate its being for Fanny's use; and had Lady Bertram ever thought about her own objection again, he might have been excused in her eyes, for not waiting till Sir Thomas's return in September, for when September came, Sir Thomas was still abroad, and without any near prospect of finishing his business. Unfavourable circumstances had suddenly arisen at a moment when he was beginning to turn all his thoughts towards England, and the very great uncertainty in which every thing was then involved, determined him on sending home his son, and waiting the final arrangement by himself. Tom arrived safely, bringing an excellent account of his father's health; but to very little purpose, as far as Mrs. Norris was concerned. Sir Thomas's sending away his son, seemed to her so like a parent's care, under the influence of a foreboding of evil to himself, that she could not help feeling dreadful presentiments; and as the long evenings of autumn came on, was so terribly haunted by these ideas, in the sad solitariness of her cottage, as to be obliged to take daily refuge in the dining room of the park. The return of winter engagements, however, was not without its effect; and in the course of their progress, her mind became so pleasantly occupied in superintending the fortunes of her eldest niece, as tolerably to quiet her nerves. "If poor Sir Thomas were fated never to return, it would be peculiarly consoling to see their dear Maria well married," she very often thought; always when they were in the company of men of fortune, and particularly on the introduction of a young man who had recently succeeded to one of the largest estates and finest places in the country.

Mr. Rushworth was from the first struck with the beauty of Miss Bertram, and being inclined to marry, soon fancied himself in love. He was a heavy young man,[3] with not more than common sense; but as there was nothing disagreeable in his figure or address, the young lady was well pleased with her conquest. Being now in her twenty-first year, Maria Bertram was beginning to think matrimony a duty; and as a marriage with Mr. Rushworth would give her the enjoyment of a larger income than her father's, as well as ensure her the house in town, which was now a prime object, it became, by the same rule of moral obligation, her evident duty to marry Mr. Rushworth if she could. Mrs. Norris was most zealous in promoting the match, by every suggestion and contrivance, likely to enhance its desirableness to either party; and, among other means, by seeking an intimacy with the gentleman's mother, who at present lived with him, and to whom she even forced Lady Bertram to go through ten miles of indifferent road to pay a morning visit.[4] It was not long before a good understanding took place between this lady and herself. Mrs. Rushworth acknowledged herself very desirous that her son should marry, and declared that of all the young ladies she had ever seen, Miss Bertram seemed, by her amiable qualities and accomplishments, the best adapted to make him happy. Mrs. Norris accepted the compliment, and admired the nice discernment of character which could so well distinguish merit. Maria was indeed the pride and delight of them all—perfectly faultless—an angel; and of course, so surrounded by

3 A comment not on Mr. Rushworth's physical size but on his intellect: he is slow-witted and ponderous.

4 Since "morning" in Austen's time denoted the whole of the period between breakfast and dinner, it is tricky to identify the exact time of day when Lady Bertram and her sister called on Mrs. Rushworth or how long they might have stayed.

5 One who is *difficult in her choice* is, we would say, choosey. In the previous sentence, which references Mrs. Rushworth's "nice discernment of character," the same claim is being made about her, with "nice" carrying there its older sense of "careful" or "fastidious."

6 A fellow landholder, Mr. Rushworth is part of the same political grouping ("interest") as his future father-in-law.

admirers, must be difficult in her choice;[5] but yet as far as Mrs. Norris could allow herself to decide on so short an acquaintance, Mr. Rushworth appeared precisely the young man to deserve and attach her.

After dancing with each other at a proper number of balls, the young people justified these opinions, and an engagement, with a due reference to the absent Sir Thomas, was entered into, much to the satisfaction of their respective families, and of the general lookers-on of the neighbourhood, who had, for many weeks past, felt the expediency of Mr. Rushworth's marrying Miss Bertram.

It was some months before Sir Thomas's consent could be received; but in the mean while, as no one felt a doubt of his most cordial pleasure in the connection, the intercourse of the two families was carried on without restraint, and no other attempt made at secrecy, than Mrs. Norris's talking of it every where as a matter not to be talked of at present.

Edmund was the only one of the family who could see a fault in the business; but no representation of his aunt's could induce him to find Mr. Rushworth a desirable companion. He could allow his sister to be the best judge of her own happiness, but he was not pleased that her happiness should centre in a large income; nor could he refrain from often saying to himself, in Mr. Rushworth's company, "If this man had not twelve thousand a year, he would be a very stupid fellow."

Sir Thomas, however, was truly happy in the prospect of an alliance so unquestionably advantageous, and of which he heard nothing but the perfectly good and agreeable. It was a connection exactly of the right sort; in the same county, and the same interest;[6] and his most hearty concurrence was conveyed as soon as possible. He only conditioned that the marriage should not take place before his return, which he was again looking eagerly forward to. He wrote in April, and had strong hopes of settling everything to his entire satisfaction, and leaving Antigua before the end of the summer.

Such was the state of affairs in the month of July, and Fanny had just reached her eighteenth year, when the society of the village received an addition in the brother and sister of Mrs. Grant, a Mr. and

Miss Crawford, the children of her mother by a second marriage. They were young people of fortune. The son had a good estate in Norfolk, the daughter twenty thousand pounds.[7] As children, their sister had been always very fond of them; but, as her own marriage had been soon followed by the death of their common parent, which left them to the care of a brother of their father, of whom Mrs. Grant knew nothing, she had scarcely seen them since. In their uncle's house they had found a kind home. Admiral and Mrs. Crawford, though agreeing in nothing else, were united in affection for these children, or at least were no farther adverse in their feelings than that each had their favourite, to whom they showed the greatest fondness of the two. The Admiral delighted in the boy, Mrs. Crawford doted on the girl; and it was the lady's death which now obliged her *protegée,* after some months further trial at her uncle's house, to find another home. Admiral Crawford was a man of vicious conduct, who chose, instead of retaining his niece, to bring his mistress under his own roof; and to this Mrs. Grant was indebted for her sister's proposal of coming to her, a measure quite as welcome on one side, as it could be expedient on the other; for Mrs. Grant having by this time run through the usual resources of ladies residing in the country without a family of children; having more than filled her favourite sitting room with pretty furniture, and made a choice collection of plants and poultry, was very much in want of some variety at home. The arrival, therefore, of a sister whom she had always loved, and now hoped to retain with her as long as she remained single, was highly agreeable; and her chief anxiety was lest Mansfield should not satisfy the habits of a young woman who had been mostly used to London.

Miss Crawford was not entirely free from similar apprehensions, though they arose principally from doubts of her sister's style of living and tone of society; and it was not till after she had tried in vain to persuade her brother to settle with her at his own country-house, that she could resolve to hazard herself among her other relations. To any thing like a permanence of abode, or limitation of society, Henry Crawford had, unluckily, a great dislike; he could not accommodate his sister in an article of such importance, but he escorted

7 Miss Crawford's fortune of twenty thousand pounds is likely invested in government funds at an annual interest rate of 5 percent. It yields her a yearly income of a thousand pounds, underwriting some of the self-confidence that is audible at the close of this chapter when she explains what it means to marry "properly."

8 Mrs. Grant is both more polished in her manners and less of a stickler for the proprieties (less devoted to "preciseness") than her half-sister expected.

9 A look of self-assurance.

her, with the utmost kindness, into Northamptonshire, and as readily engaged to fetch her away again at half an hour's notice, whenever she were weary of the place.

The meeting was very satisfactory on each side. Miss Crawford found a sister without preciseness or rusticity[8]—a sister's husband who looked the gentleman, and a house commodious and well fitted up; and Mrs. Grant received in those whom she hoped to love better than ever, a young man and woman of very prepossessing appearance. Mary Crawford was remarkably pretty; Henry, though not handsome, had air and countenance;[9] the manners of both were lively and pleasant, and Mrs. Grant immediately gave them credit for every thing else. She was delighted with each, but Mary was her dearest object; and having never been able to glory in beauty of her own, she thoroughly enjoyed the power of being proud of her sister's. She had not waited her arrival to look out for a suitable match for her; she had fixed on Tom Bertram; the eldest son of a Baronet was not too good for a girl of twenty thousand pounds, with all the elegance and accomplishments which Mrs. Grant foresaw in her; and being a warm-hearted, unreserved woman, Mary had not been three hours in the house before she told her what she had planned.

Miss Crawford was glad to find a family of such consequence so very near them, and not at all displeased either at her sister's early care, or the choice it had fallen on. Matrimony was her object, provided she could marry well, and having seen Mr. Bertram in town, she knew that objection could no more be made to his person than to his situation in life. While she treated it as a joke, therefore, she did not forget to think of it seriously. The scheme was soon repeated to Henry.

"And now," added Mrs. Grant, "I have thought of something to make it quite complete. I should dearly love to settle you both in this country, and therefore, Henry, you shall marry the youngest Miss Bertram, a nice, handsome, good-humoured, accomplished girl, who will make you very happy."

Henry bowed and thanked her.

"My dear sister," said Mary, "if you can persuade him into any thing of the sort, it will be a fresh matter of delight to me, to find myself allied to any body so clever, and I shall only regret that you have not half-a-dozen daughters to dispose of. If you can persuade Henry to marry, you must have the address of a Frenchwoman.[10] All that English abilities can do, has been tried already. I have three very particular friends who have been all dying for him in their turn; and the pains which they, their mothers, (very clever women,) as well as my dear aunt and myself, have taken to reason, coax, or trick him into marrying, is inconceivable! He is the most horrible flirt that can be imagined. If your Miss Bertrams do not like to have their hearts broke, let them avoid Henry."

"My dear brother, I will not believe this of you."

"No, I am sure you are too good. You will be kinder than Mary. You will allow for the doubts of youth and inexperience. I am of a cautious temper, and unwilling to risk my happiness in a hurry. Nobody can think more highly of the matrimonial state than myself. I consider the blessing of a wife as most justly described in those discreet lines of the poet, "Heaven's *last* best gift."[11]

"There, Mrs. Grant, you see how he dwells on one word, and only look at his smile. I assure you he is very detestable—the admiral's lessons have quite spoiled him."

"I pay very little regard," said Mrs. Grant, "to what any young person says on the subject of marriage. If they profess a disinclination for it, I only set it down that they have not yet seen the right person."

Dr. Grant laughingly congratulated Miss Crawford on feeling no disinclination to the state herself.

"Oh! yes, I am not at all ashamed of it. I would have every body marry if they can do it properly; I do not like to have people throw themselves away; but every body should marry as soon as they can do it to advantage."

10 The British novel during Austen's lifetime often featured Frenchwomen with dangerous powers of persuasion and manipulation, thus trading in an account of the deviousness of the French national character that had been standard for a century or more and recently reinvigorated by the Revolutionary and Napoleonic wars. In *Leonora,* for instance, the "tale of fashionable life" she published in 1805, Maria Edgeworth portrays her heroine's false friend as a Frenchified Englishwoman who simultaneously deplores and exploits Leonora's very English reluctance to wield her erotic power to her advantage. As Olivia attests in a letter to a Parisian correspondent, Leonora "enters a room without producing, or thinking of producing, any sensation; she moves often without seeming to have any intention than to change her place; and her fine eyes generally look as if they were made only to see with" (*Works of Maria Edgeworth* [Boston: Samuel H. Parker, 1824], vol. 2, p. 160). A Parisienne would conduct herself very differently.

11 The marriage-averse Henry puts a mischievous spin on Adam's loving description of Eve in Milton's *Paradise Lost:* "My fairest, my espoused, my latest found, / Heav'n's last best gift, my ever new delight" (Book V, lines 18–19).

# 5

1 Martin Price comments admiringly on how this passage captures "the rapid, almost mechanical process of rationalization by which a marriageable gentleman is found to have extraordinary charms"; Austen, he states, uses free indirect discourse here to catch her characters' idiom and at the same time to compress their reasoning, much "as a speeded-up film mechanizes motion" (*Forms of Life: Character and Moral Imagination in the Novel* [New Haven: Yale University Press, 1983], p. 26).

THE YOUNG PEOPLE were pleased with each other from the first. On each side there was much to attract, and their acquaintance soon promised as early an intimacy as good manners would warrant. Miss Crawford's beauty did her no disservice with the Miss Bertrams. They were too handsome themselves to dislike any woman for being so too, and were almost as much charmed as their brothers, with her lively dark eye, clear brown complexion, and general prettiness. Had she been tall, full formed, and fair, it might have been more of a trial; but as it was, there could be no comparison, and she was most allowably a sweet pretty girl, while they were the finest young women in the country.

Her brother was not handsome; no, when they first saw him, he was absolutely plain, black and plain; but still he was the gentleman, with a pleasing address. The second meeting proved him not so very plain; he was plain, to be sure, but then he had so much countenance, and his teeth were so good, and he was so well made, that one soon forgot he was plain; and after a third interview, after dining in company with him at the parsonage, he was no longer allowed to be called so by any body.[1] He was, in fact, the most agreeable young man the sisters had ever known, and they were equally delighted with him. Miss Bertram's engagement made him in equity the property of Julia, of which Julia was fully aware, and before he had been at Mansfield a week, she was quite ready to be fallen in love with.

Maria's notions on the subject were more confused and indistinct. She did not want to see or understand. "There could be no harm in her liking an agreeable man—every body knew her situation—Mr. Crawford must take care of himself." Mr. Crawford did not mean to be in any danger; the Miss Bertrams were worth pleasing, and were ready to be pleased; and he began with no object but of making them like him. He did not want them to die of love; but with sense and temper which ought to have made him judge and feel better, he allowed himself great latitude on such points.

"I like your Miss Bertrams exceedingly, sister," said he, as he returned from attending them to their carriage after the said dinner visit; "they are very elegant, agreeable girls."

"So they are, indeed, and I am delighted to hear you say it. But you like Julia best."

"Oh! yes, I like Julia best."

"But do you really? for Miss Bertram is in general thought the handsomest."

"So I should suppose. She has the advantage in every feature, and I prefer her countenance—but I like Julia best. Miss Bertram is certainly the handsomest, and I have found her the most agreeable, but I shall always like Julia best, because you order me."

This is how the 1999 film *Mansfield Park* imagines the Bertram family at the moment when Mary and Henry Crawford, off screen, make their first entrance into the Mansfield Park drawing room. It is clear from the expressions and body language that the newcomers make a good first impression.

3 When *Mansfield Park* appeared in 1814, the word *manoeuvring*—as a designation for subterfuge and scheming—had only recently entered English from French and tended to be used in ways that acknowledged that cross-Channel origin. In *Jane Austen and Her Predecessors* (Cambridge: Cambridge University Press, 1966), Frank W. Bradbrook observed that the number of French words and phrases included in *Mansfield Park* outstrips that in any of Austen's other fictions (seventeen examples, according to Bradbrook's tally [p. 122], compared with five in *Sense and Sensibility,* four in *Pride and Prejudice,* seven in *Emma,* and three in *Northanger Abbey*). The bulk of the French terms in Austen's novel are to be found, tellingly, in passages spoken by the Crawford siblings. See, for instance, Mary's reference below to the *esprit du corps* (team spirit) she honors in her sister. In the opening to the "Tale of Fashionable Life" entitled *Manoeuvring* that Maria Edgeworth published in 1809, the heroine's father harrumphs that their match-making neighbor Mrs. Beaumont "is a *manoeuvrer.* We can't well make an English word of it. The species, thank Heaven! is not so numerous yet in England as to require a generic name" (*Tales of Fashionable Life in Five Volumes* [London: Baldwin and Cradock, 1832], vol. 2, p. 3).

"I shall not talk to you, Henry, but I know you *will* like her best at last."

"Do not I tell you, that I like her best *at first?*"

"And besides, Miss Bertram is engaged. Remember that, my dear brother. Her choice is made."

"Yes, and I like her the better for it. An engaged woman is always more agreeable than a disengaged. She is satisfied with herself. Her cares are over, and she feels that she may exert all her powers of pleasing without suspicion. All is safe with a lady engaged; no harm can be done."

"Why as to that—Mr. Rushworth is a very good sort of young man, and it is a great match for her."

"But Miss Bertram does not care three straws for him; *that* is your opinion of your intimate friend. *I* do not subscribe to it. I am sure Miss Bertram is very much attached to Mr. Rushworth. I could see it in her eyes, when he was mentioned. I think too well of Miss Bertram to suppose she would ever give her hand without her heart."

"Mary, how shall we manage him?"

"We must leave him to himself, I believe. Talking does no good. He will be taken in at last."

"But I would not have him *taken in,* I would not have him duped; I would have it all fair and honourable."

"Oh! dear—Let him stand his chance and be taken in. It will do just as well. Every body is taken in at some period or other."

"Not always in marriage, dear Mary."

"In marriage especially. With all due respect to such of the present company as chance to be married, my dear Mrs. Grant, there is not one in a hundred of either sex, who is not taken in when they marry. Look where I will, I see that it *is* so; and I feel that it *must* be so, when I consider that it is, of all transactions, the one in which people expect most from others, and are least honest themselves."

"Ah! You have been in a bad school for matrimony, in Hill Street."[2]

"My poor aunt had certainly little cause to love the state; but, however, speaking from my own observation, it is a manoeuvring business.[3] I know so many who have married in the full expectation and confidence of some one particular advantage in the connection, or accomplishment or good quality in the person, who have found themselves entirely deceived, and been obliged to put up with exactly the reverse! What is this, but a take in?"

"My dear child, there must be a little imagination here. I beg your pardon, but I cannot quite believe you. Depend upon it, you see but half. You see the evil, but you do not see the consolation. There will be little rubs and disappointments every where, and we are all apt to expect too much; but then, if one scheme of happiness fails, human nature turns to another; if the first calculation is wrong, we make a second better; we find comfort somewhere—and those evil–minded observers, dearest Mary, who make much of a little, are more taken in and deceived than the parties themselves."

"Well done, sister! I honour your *esprit du corps*. When I am a wife, I mean to be just as staunch myself; and I wish my friends in general would be so too. It would save me many a heart-ache."

"You are as bad as your brother, Mary; but we will cure you both. Mansfield shall cure you both—and without any taking in. Stay with us and we will cure you."

The Crawfords, without wanting to be cured, were very willing to stay. Mary was satisfied with the parsonage as a present home, and Henry equally ready to lengthen his visit. He had come, intending to spend only a few days with them, but Mansfield promised well, and there was nothing to call him elsewhere. It delighted Mrs. Grant to keep them both with her, and Dr. Grant was exceedingly well contented to have it so; a talking pretty young woman like Miss Crawford, is always pleasant society to an indolent, stay-at-home man; and Mr. Crawford's being his guest was an excuse for drinking claret every day.

The Miss Bertrams' admiration of Mr. Crawford was more rapturous than any thing which Miss Crawford's habits made her likely to feel. She acknowledged, however, that the Mr. Bertrams were very fine young men, that two such young men were not often seen together even in London, and that their manners, particularly those of the eldest, were very good. *He* had been much in London, and had more liveliness and gallantry than Edmund, and must, therefore, be preferred; and, indeed, his being the eldest was another strong claim.

4  The right to succeed to the property.

5  "Modern-built" is generally construed as a reference to the Palladian style of architecture that was the fashion for the houses of the rich in the first part of the eighteenth century. The adjective differentiates Mansfield Park from Sotherton, the Elizabethan mansion, centuries old, that the Bertrams and Crawfords will visit in Chaps. 9 and 10. That Sir Thomas's house is modern-built may be a subtle indication that the family has not been long settled in Northamptonshire and that the Bertram title and wealth are of recent date. Through the eighteenth century, slave labor in the Caribbean colonies bankrolled many sudden ascents in family fortunes, enabling the grandsons of colonists of humble means to be accepted (as James Langford Nibbs was) as well-bred English gentlemen.

6  Books assembling engraved views of the great houses and parks of the British nobility and gentry were steady sellers for eighteenth- and nineteenth-century publishers. These picture books offered opportunities for armchair tourism. They were also patriotic productions, exhibiting the taste and affluence of the nation's social elite.

A country house that was rebuilt in the Palladian style in the mid-seventeenth century, Stoke Park, now almost entirely destroyed, has been identified as a possible prototype for Austen's Mansfield Park, alongside other Northamptonshire landmarks like Castle Ashby, Harleston House, and Cottesbrooke Hall. The periodical *Ackermann's Repository* included this view of Stoke Park in its pages in 1826.

She had felt an early presentiment that she *should* like the eldest best. She knew it was her way.

Tom Bertram must have been thought pleasant, indeed, at any rate; he was the sort of young man to be generally liked, his agreeableness was of the kind to be oftener found agreeable than some endowments of a higher stamp, for he had easy manners, excellent spirits, a large acquaintance, and a great deal to say; and the reversion of Mansfield Park,[4] and a baronetcy, did no harm to all this. Miss Crawford soon felt, that he and his situation might do. She looked about her with due consideration, and found almost every thing in his favour, a park, a real park five miles round, a spacious modern-built house,[5] so well placed and well screened as to deserve to be in any collection of engravings of gentlemen's seats in the kingdom,[6] and wanting only to be completely new furnished—pleasant sisters, a quiet mother, and an agreeable man himself—with the advantage of being tied up from much gaming at present, by a promise to his father, and of being Sir Thomas hereafter. It might do very well; she believed she should accept him; and she began accordingly to interest herself a little about the horse which he had to run at the B——races.[7]

These races were to call him away not long after their acquaintance began; and as it appeared that the family did not, from his usual goings on, expect him back again for many weeks, it would bring his passion to an early proof. Much was said on his side to induce her to attend the races, and schemes were made for a large party to them, with all the eagerness of inclination, but it would only do to be talked of.

And Fanny, what was *she* doing and thinking all this while? and what was *her* opinion of the new-comers? Few young ladies of eighteen could be less called on to speak their opinion than Fanny. In a quiet way, very little attended to, she paid her tribute of admiration to Miss Crawford's beauty; but as she still continued to think Mr. Crawford very plain, in spite of her two cousins having repeatedly proved the contrary, she never mentioned *him*. The notice which she excited herself, was to this effect. "I begin now to understand you all, except Miss Price," said Miss Crawford, as she was walking with the Mr. Bertrams. "Pray, is she out, or is she not?—I am puzzled.—She dined at the Parsonage, with the rest of you, which seemed like being *out;* and yet she says so little, that I can hardly suppose she *is*."[8]

Edmund, to whom this was chiefly addressed, replied, "I believe I know what you mean—but I will not undertake to answer the question. My cousin is grown up. She has the age and sense of a woman, but the outs and not outs are beyond me."

"And yet in general, nothing can be more easily ascertained. The distinction is so broad. Manners as well as appearance are, generally speaking, so totally different. Till now, I could not have supposed it possible to be mistaken as to a girl's being out or not. A girl not out, has always the same sort of dress; a close bonnet for instance,[9] looks very demure, and never says a word. You may smile—but it is so I assure you—and except that it is sometimes carried a little too far, it is all very proper. Girls should be quiet and modest. The most objec-

7 Tom Bertram evidently is the owner of a race horse and can afford to hire a jockey to ride it. The sport of horse racing had an ardent and fashionable patron at the turn of the nineteenth century in the person of the Prince Regent (later King George IV), whose colossal debts were increased by his unlucky bets at the race track.

8 A girl who was "out" had been formally introduced to society, an event that marked her accession to maturity and, more important, marriageability.

9 A hat with a stiff brim in the front that shaded the face.

10  A slang expression that originated in the 1790s, *to quiz* is "to regard with amusement or scorn; to appraise mockingly" *(Oxford English Dictionary)*.

11  Another fashionable address in London's West End.

tionable part is, that the alteration of manners on being introduced into company is frequently too sudden. They sometimes pass in such very little time from reserve to quite the opposite—to confidence! *That* is the faulty part of the present system. One does not like to see a girl of eighteen or nineteen so immediately up to every thing—and perhaps when one has seen her hardly able to speak the year before. Mr. Bertram, I dare say *you* have sometimes met with such changes."

"I believe I have; but this is hardly fair; I see what you are at. You are quizzing me and Miss Anderson."[10]

"No indeed. Miss Anderson! I do not know who or what you mean. I am quite in the dark. But I *will* quiz you with a great deal of pleasure, if you will tell me what about."

"Ah! you carry it off very well, but I cannot be quite so far imposed on. You must have had Miss Anderson in your eye, in describing an altered young lady. You paint too accurately for mistake. It was exactly so. The Andersons of Baker Street.[11] We were speaking of them the other day, you know. Edmund, you have heard me mention Charles Anderson. The circumstance was precisely as this lady has represented it. When Anderson first introduced me to his family, about two years ago, his sister was not *out,* and I could not get her to speak to me. I sat there an hour one morning waiting for Anderson, with only her and a little girl or two in the room—the governess being sick or run away, and the mother in and out every moment with letters of business; and I could hardly get a word or a look from the young lady—nothing like a civil answer—she screwed up her mouth, and turned from me with such an air! I did not see her again for a twelvemonth. She was then *out.* I met her at Mrs. Holford's—and did not recollect her. She came up to me, claimed me as an acquaintance, stared me out of countenance, and talked and laughed till I did not know which way to look. I felt that I must be the jest of the room at the time—and Miss Crawford, it is plain, has heard the story."

"And a very pretty story it is, and with more truth in it, I dare say, than does credit to Miss Anderson. It is too common a fault. Mothers certainly have not yet got quite the right way of managing their daughters. I do not know where the error lies. I do not pretend to set people right, but I do see that they are often wrong."

"Those who are showing the world what female manners *should be*," said Mr. Bertram, gallantly, "are doing a great deal to set them right."

"The error is plain enough," said the less courteous Edmund; "such girls are ill brought up. They are given wrong notions from the beginning. They are always acting upon motives of vanity—and there is no more real modesty in their behaviour *before* they appear in public than afterwards."[12]

"I do not know," replied Miss Crawford hesitatingly. "Yes, I cannot agree with you there. It is certainly the modestest part of the business. It is much worse to have girls *not out,* give themselves the same airs and take the same liberties as if they were, which I *have* seen done. *That* is worse than any thing—quite disgusting!"[13]

"Yes, *that* is very inconvenient indeed," said Mr. Bertram. "It leads one astray; one does not know what to do. The close bonnet and demure air you describe so well, (and nothing was ever juster,) tell one what is expected; but I got into a dreadful scrape last year from the want of them. I went down to Ramsgate for a week with a friend last September[14]—just after my return from the West Indies—my friend Sneyd—you have heard me speak of Sneyd, Edmund—; his father and mother and sisters were there, all new to me. When we reached Albion place they were out; we went after them, and found them on the pier. Mrs. and the two Miss Sneyds, with others of their acquaintance. I made my bow in form, and as Mrs. Sneyd was surrounded by men, attached myself to one of her daughters, walked by her side all the way home, and made myself as agreeable as I could; the young lady perfectly easy in her manners, and as ready to talk as to listen. I had not a suspicion that I could be doing anything wrong. They looked just the same; both well dressed, with veils and parasols like other girls; but I afterwards found that I had been giving all my attention to the youngest, who was not *out,* and had most excessively offended the eldest. Miss Augusta ought not to have been noticed for the next six months, and Miss Sneyd, I believe, has never forgiven me."

"That was bad indeed. Poor Miss Sneyd! Though I have no younger sister, I feel for her. To be neglected before one's time, must be very vexatious. But it was entirely the mother's fault. Miss Augusta

12 Mary Wollstonecraft in 1792 found the system of "outs and not outs" fundamentally flawed: "what can be more indelicate than a girl's *coming out* in the fashionable world? Which, in other words, is to bring to market a marriageable miss, whose person is taken from one public place to another, richly caparisoned" (*A Vindication of the Rights of Woman,* ed. Deidre Shauna Lynch, 3rd ed. [New York: W. W. Norton, 2006], p. 179). The problem highlighted in this passage of Wollstonecraft's *Vindication* is the immodest forwardness of the girl who is out. But Edmund is arguing that the reserve of the girl who has not yet made her coming out is sometimes not so different from that forwardness. If put on simply for show, to be discarded on demand, reserve can be its own kind of brazenness.

13 "By presuming that the only alternative to the girl who abruptly alters her behavior when she comes out is the girl who acts immodestly from the start, Mary unwittingly reveals that she finds a modest consciousness unimaginable": Ruth Bernard Yeazell, *Fictions of Modesty: Women and Courtship in the English Novel* (Chicago: University of Chicago Press, 1991), p. 157.

14 Ramsgate is a seaside resort on England's southeast coast, a small fishing village that almost overnight had mushroomed into a chic vacation destination. It figures in *Pride and Prejudice* as the place where Georgiana Darcy and her fortune nearly fall victim to Mr. Wickham's wiles.

should have been with her governess. Such half and half doings never prosper. But now I must be satisfied about Miss Price. Does she go to balls? Does she dine out every where, as well as at my sister's?"

"No," replied Edmund, "I do not think she has ever been to a ball. My mother seldom goes into company herself, and dines no where but with Mrs. Grant, and Fanny stays at home with *her.*"

"Oh! then the point is clear. Miss Price is *not* out."

The moorpark apricot, as pictured in William Hooker's *Pomona Londinensis,* a catalog of "the most esteemed fruits cultivated in British gardens."

# 6

MR. BERTRAM SET OFF FOR————,[1] and Miss Crawford was prepared to find a great chasm in their society, and to miss him decidedly in the meetings which were now becoming almost daily between the families; and on their all dining together at the park soon after his going, she retook her chosen place near the bottom of the table, fully expecting to feel a most melancholy difference in the change of masters. It would be a very flat business, she was sure. In comparison with his brother, Edmund would have nothing to say. The soup would be sent round in a most spiritless manner, wine drank without any smiles, or agreeable trifling, and the venison cut up without supplying one pleasant anecdote of any former haunch, or a single entertaining story about "my friend such a one." She must try to find amusement in what was passing at the upper end of the table, and in observing Mr. Rushworth, who was now making his appearance at Mansfield, for the first time since the Crawfords' arrival. He had been visiting a friend in the neighbouring county, and that friend having recently had his grounds laid out by an improver, Mr. Rushworth was returned with his head full of the subject, and very eager to be improving his own place in the same way; and though not saying much to the purpose, could talk of nothing else.[2] The subject had been already handled in the drawing-room; it was revived in the dining-parlour. Miss Bertram's attention and opinion was evidently his chief aim; and though her deportment showed rather conscious superiority than any solicitude to oblige him, the mention of Sotherton Court, and the ideas attached to it, gave her a feeling of complacency, which prevented her from being very ungracious.

1 In *Mansfield Park* the narrator and characters generally mention real places by their real names, which makes Austen's use of long dashes in these early references to Tom Bertram's sporting travels disconcerting: it almost suggests that particular discretion is required on the part of the author who wishes to send a character to the races. Dashes like these were frequent in the fiction of the eighteenth century, part of the apparatus that the early novelists used to present themselves as telling histories firmly grounded in the readers' reality rather than romances that evaded that reality.

2 A keyword for Austen and her contemporaries, the term *improvement* was applied variously to both people and things. Education was described as an "improvement of the mind"—a phrase that appears in Hester Chapone's conduct book, in the definition that Mr. Darcy gives, early in *Pride and Prejudice,* of a truly accomplished woman (I, 8), and in Vol. I, Chap. 2 of *Mansfield Park,* when the narrator describes the effects of Edmund's informal supervision of his young cousin's education. Sometimes the word *improvement* was used in ways that make it correspond to the terms we use, like *development* or *modernization:* in Mr. Rushworth's second speech in this chapter, for instance, his claim that "Sotherton wants improvement beyond any thing" is simply his way of saying that the property needs to be brought up-to-date. The term *improver* could also designate, as here, a specific vocation: a professional designer hired by a landowner to bring the layout of his house and grounds into conformity with the taste of the day.

As country pursuits became fashionable in the last part of the eighteenth century, Britain's landed gentry and aristocracy enrolled themselves in multiple dimensions of the project of improvement. They augmented the agricultural productivity of the nation, as well as their incomes, as they adopted new farming techniques, drained fields, reclaimed waste lands for cultivation, enclosed common lands, and began concerning themselves more directly in the farming practices of their tenants. They also took on the renovations of their country estates that increased the contact between their living spaces and the countryside around them. They built conservatories, for instance, introduced windows cut down to the ground to frame the view, and moved their main rooms onto ground floors so that the rooms might open up onto greenery and gardens. The intended net effect of such renovations was supposed to be a "'natural' house in a 'natural' landscape" (Mark Girouard, *Life in the English Country House: A Social and Architectural History* [New Haven: Yale University Press, 1978], p. 226)—though of course the nature that those wealthy Britons hoped to commune with was generally preferred in an edited version. This was where the improver came into the picture.

3 In their pitches to their clients, improvers placed particular emphasis on the importance of managing a visitor's first impressions of the property. An improver would introduce new windings or sudden turns into the drive that led through the park and up to the house, aiming to lead visitors through a variety of scenes before suddenly granting them their first view of the house. *Pride and Prejudice* captures the effect of such arrangements at the start of its third volume, which narrates in detail the approach Elizabeth and the Gardiners make to Pemberley. They first turn in at the lodge, entering the estate at one of its lowest points, and then begin to drive through a wood: "Elizabeth's mind was too full for conversation, but she saw and admired every remarkable spot and point of view. They gradually ascended for half a mile, and then found themselves at the top of a considerable eminence, where the wood ceased, and the eye was instantly caught by Pemberley House, situated on the opposite side of a valley, into which the road with some abruptness wound" (III, 1).

A specimen of the watercolor self-portraits that the landscape architect Humphry Repton regularly included in the "red books" he prepared for his clients; these handmade volumes documented his alterations of these landowners' grounds. Here Repton is the figure standing behind a surveyor's theodolite, an instrument for measuring angles.

"I wish you could see Compton," said he, "it is the most complete thing! I never saw a place so altered in my life. I told Smith I did not know where I was. The approach *now* is one of the finest things in the country. You see the house in the most surprising manner.[3] I declare when I got back to Sotherton yesterday, it looked like a prison—quite a dismal old prison."

"Oh! for shame!" cried Mrs. Norris. "A prison, indeed! Sotherton Court is the noblest old place in the world."

"It wants improvement, ma'am, beyond any thing. I never saw a place that wanted so much improvement in my life; and it is so forlorn, that I do not know what can be done with it."

"No wonder that Mr. Rushworth should think so at present," said Mrs. Grant to Mrs. Norris, with a smile; "but depend upon it, Sotherton will have *every* improvement in time which his heart can desire."

"I must try to do something with it," said Mr. Rushworth, "but I do not know what. I hope I shall have some good friend to help me."

"Your best friend upon such an occasion," said Miss Bertram, calmly, "would be Mr. Repton, I imagine."[4]

"That is what I was thinking of. As he has done so well by Smith, I think I had better have him at once. His terms are five guineas a day."

"Well, and if they were *ten*," cried Mrs. Norris, "I am sure *you* need not regard it. The expense need not be any impediment. If I were you, I should not think of the expense.[5] I would have every thing done in the best style, and made as nice as possible. Such a place as Sotherton Court deserves every thing that taste and money can do. You have space to work upon there, and grounds that will well reward you. For my own part, if I had anything within the fiftieth part of the size of Sotherton, I should be always planting and improving, for naturally I am excessively fond of it. It would be too ridiculous for me to attempt any thing where I am now, with my little half acre. It would be quite a burlesque. But if I had more room, I should take a prodigious delight in improving and planting. We did a vast deal in that way at the parsonage; we made it quite a different place from what it was when we first had it. You young ones do not remember much about it, perhaps. But if dear Sir Thomas were here, he could tell you what improvements we made; and a great deal more would have been done, but for poor Mr. Norris's sad state of health. He could hardly ever get out, poor man, to enjoy any thing, and *that* disheartened me from doing several things that Sir Thomas and I used to talk of. If it had not been for *that*, we should have carried on the garden wall, and made the plantation to shut out the churchyard, just as Dr. Grant has done. We were always doing something, as it was. It was only the spring twelvemonth before Mr. Norris's death, that we put in the apricot against the stable wall, which is now grown such a noble tree, and getting to such perfection, sir," addressing herself then to Dr. Grant.

"The tree thrives well beyond a doubt, madam," replied Dr. Grant. "The soil is good; and I never pass it without regretting, that the fruit should be so little worth the trouble of gathering."

"Sir, it is a moor park, we bought it as a moor park, and it cost us— that is, it was a present from Sir Thomas, but I saw the bill, and I know it cost seven shillings, and was charged as a moor park."[6]

4 Austen would have been closely acquainted with the landscaping projects of Humphry Repton (1752–1818), the celebrity designer of her day, since her mother's cousin Thomas Leigh hired Repton twice. The first time was to renovate the grounds of the rectory and great house at Adlestrop in Gloucestershire, a project that Repton undertook some time around 1802, and which Austen, her sister, and mother were able to see for themselves on a visit they paid their cousin in 1806. That same year Rev. Leigh inherited Stoneleigh Abbey, a grand Elizabethan mansion in Warwickshire built on the foundations of a Cistercian abbey that had come into the Leigh family at the time of the Reformation. He then turned to Repton for a second time.

5 We have already seen enough of Mrs. Norris to know that she generally does think of the expense.

6 William Hooker in his *Pomona Londinensis* (London: by the author, 1818) states that the Moor Park is the variety of apricot "held in esteem over any other at present cultivated" and that it owes its name to "Lord Anson, by whom it was introduced into this country, and cultivated in his garden at Moor Park, near Rickmansworth, in Hertfordshire" (Vol. I, p. 18).

7 The sums covering deterioration of the property that would be charged to the former occupant of a parsonage at the moment the new minister took up his living.

8 Clashing with the naturalistic effects prized by the landscapers of Austen's day, the rows of trees ranged in long parallel lines that were standard features of early-eighteenth-century garden design were frequent casualties of improvers' projects. The avenue that blocked the view risked being thinned, if not uprooted altogether. In 1794 Repton stated that "the greatest objection to an avenue is, that . . . it will often act as a curtain

From the 1803 book *Cowper Illustrated in a Series of Views,* which retraces for literary tourists the poet's daily walks in the countryside. The engraving pictures the sole portion of the avenue of limes (called basswood trees in North America) that remained following the grounds' "improvement" by the local landowner.

"You were imposed on, ma'am," replied Dr. Grant; "these potatoes have as much the flavour of a moor park apricot, as the fruit from that tree. It is an insipid fruit at the best; but a good apricot is eatable, which none from my garden are."

"The truth is, ma'am," said Mrs. Grant, pretending to whisper across the table to Mrs. Norris, "that Dr. Grant hardly knows what the natural taste of our apricot is; he is scarcely ever indulged with one, for it is so valuable a fruit, with a little assistance, and ours is such a remarkably large, fair sort, that what with early tarts and preserves, my cook contrives to get them all."

Mrs. Norris, who had begun to redden, was appeased, and, for a little while, other subjects took place of the improvements of Sotherton. Dr. Grant and Mrs. Norris were seldom good friends; their acquaintance had begun in dilapidations,[7] and their habits were totally dissimilar.

After a short interruption, Mr. Rushworth began again. "Smith's place is the admiration of all the country; and it was a mere nothing before Repton took it in hand. I think I shall have Repton."

"Mr. Rushworth," said Lady Bertram, "if I were you, I would have a very pretty shrubbery. One likes to get out into a shrubbery in fine weather."

Mr. Rushworth was eager to assure her ladyship of his acquiescence, and tried to make out something complimentary; but between his submission to *her* taste, and his having always intended the same himself, with the super-added objects of professing attention to the comfort of ladies in general, and of insinuating, that there was one only whom he was anxious to please, he grew puzzled; and Edmund was glad to put an end to his speech by a proposal of wine. Mr. Rushworth, however, though not usually a great talker, had still more to say on the subject next his heart. "Smith has not much above a hundred acres altogether in his grounds, which is little enough, and makes it more surprising that the place can have been so improved. Now, at Sotherton, we have a good seven hundred, without reckoning the water meadows; so that I think, if so much could be done at Compton, we need not despair. There have been two or three fine old trees cut down that grew too near the house, and it opens the prospect amazingly, which makes me think that Repton, or any body of that sort, would certainly have the avenue at Sotherton down;[8] the avenue that leads from the west front to the top of the hill you know," turning to Miss Bertram particularly as he spoke. But Miss Bertram thought it most becoming to reply:

"The avenue! Oh! I do not recollect it. I really know very little of Sotherton."

Fanny, who was sitting on the other side of Edmund, exactly opposite Miss Crawford, and who had been attentively listening, now looked at him, and said in a low voice,

"Cut down an avenue! What a pity! Does not it make you think of Cowper?" 'Ye fallen avenues, once more I mourn your fate unmerited.'"[9]

He smiled as he answered, "I am afraid the avenue stands a bad chance, Fanny."

"I should like to see Sotherton before it is cut down, to see the place as it is now, in its old state; but I do not suppose I shall."

"Have you never been there? No, you never can; and unluckily it is out of distance for a ride. I wish we could contrive it."

"Oh! it does not signify. Whenever I do see it, you will tell me how it has been altered."

"I collect," said Miss Crawford, "that Sotherton is an old place, and a place of some grandeur. In any particular style of building?"

"The house was built in Elizabeth's time, and is a large, regular, brick building—heavy, but respectable looking, and has many good rooms. It is ill placed. It stands in one of the lowest spots of the park; in that respect, unfavourable for improvement. But the woods are fine, and there is a stream, which, I dare say, might be made a good deal of.[10] Mr. Rushworth is quite right, I think, in meaning to give it a modern dress, and I have no doubt that it will be all done extremely well."

Miss Crawford listened with submission, and said to herself, "He is a well bred man; he makes the best of it."

"I do not wish to influence Mr. Rushworth," he continued, "but had I a place to new fashion, I should not put myself into the hands of an improver. I would rather have an inferior degree of beauty, of my own choice, and acquired progressively. I would rather abide by my own blunders than by his."

drawn across to exclude what is infinitely more interesting than any row of trees, however venerable or beautiful in themselves"; he went on to commend drawing this curtain to reveal the prospect (*Sketches and Hints on Landscape Gardening* [London: J. and J. Boydell, 1794], p. 23). In later writing, however, perhaps aware that his contemporaries were all too ready to equate the leveling of trees with dangerously democratic political leveling, Repton advised caution on just this point: "Where the long and formal line of a majestic avenue shall be submitted to his decision, the man of taste will pause, and not always break their venerable ranks, for his hand is not guided by the levelling principles or sudden innovations of modern fashion; he will reverence the glory of former ages" (*Observations on the Theory and Practice of Landscape Gardening* [London: J. Taylor, 1805], p. 76). Austen in *Sense and Sensibility* establishes the bad taste of John and Fanny Dashwood when she has these new proprietors of Norland Park cut down some old walnut trees to make room for Fanny's greenhouse (II, 11).

9 Fanny remembers lines from William Cowper's long poem *The Task* (1785), in which, describing his walk in the Buckinghamshire countryside, in an area bordering Northamptonshire, the poet mourns the trees that were felled as a consequence of his neighbors' improvements (*The Task and Selected Other Poems,* ed. James Sambrook [London: Longman, 1994], Book 1, p. 68, lines 338–339). Later in the poem Cowper deplores improvement as the "idol of the age" (3: 764), targeting in particular Repton's predecessor Launcelot "Capability" Brown. He depicts Brown's landscaping as a kind of black magic:

> He speaks. The lake in front becomes a lawn,
> Woods vanish, hills subside, and vallies rise,
> And streams as if created for his use,
> Pursue the track of his directing wand
> Sinuous or strait, now rapid and now slow,
> Now murm'ring soft, nor roaring in cascades
> Ev'n as he bids. (3: 774–780)

10 Edmund knows his theory of landscape design. The improvements that Repton undertook for Thomas Leigh at Adlestrop Park had for their centerpiece, as Repton reported in *Observations on the Theory and Prac-*

*tice of Landscape Gardening,* a newly created "lively stream of water," which was "led through the flower garden" and then over some ledges of rock—imported into the landscape for this purpose—until it fell into a lake at some distance (p. 36). To make way for this effect, a small pool close to the house had to be removed. The improvements at Stoneleigh Abbey proved even more ambitious: Repton not only converted a mill race into an ornamental cascade but also widened the river Avon and altered its course so as to bring it nearer the south face of the abbey.

11 Ten miles from London, on the river Thames, Twickenham was a fashionable rural retreat from the city.

An engraving of William Cowper, Fanny's (and Austen's) favorite poet, showing him tending his garden while one of his pet hares sits beside him.

"*You* would know what you were about of course—but that would not suit *me*. I have no eye or ingenuity for such matters, but as they are before me; and had I a place of my own in the country, I should be most thankful to any Mr. Repton who would undertake it, and give me as much beauty as he could for my money; and I should never look at it, till it was complete."

"It would be delightful to *me* to see the progress of it all," said Fanny.

"Ay—you have been brought up to it. It was no part of my education; and the only dose I ever had, being administered by not the first favourite in the world, has made me consider improvements *in hand* as the greatest of nuisances. Three years ago, the admiral, my honoured uncle, bought a cottage at Twickenham for us all to spend our summers in;[11] and my aunt and I went down to it quite in raptures; but it being excessively pretty, it was soon found necessary to be improved; and for three months we were all dirt and confusion, without a gravel walk to step on, or a bench fit for use. I would have everything as complete as possible in the country, shrubberies and flower gardens, and rustic seats innumerable; but it must be all done without my care. Henry is different; he loves to be doing."

Edmund was sorry to hear Miss Crawford, whom he was much disposed to admire, speak so freely of her uncle. It did not suit his sense of propriety, and he was silenced, till induced by further smiles and liveliness, to put the matter by for the present.

"Mr. Bertram," said she, "I have tidings of my harp at last. I am assured that it is safe at Northampton; and there it has probably been these ten days, in spite of the solemn assurances we have so often received to the contrary." Edmund expressed his pleasure and surprise. "The truth is, that our inquiries were too direct; we sent a servant, we went ourselves: this will not do seventy miles from London—but this morning we heard of it in the right way. It was seen by some farmer, and he told the miller, and the miller told the butcher, and the butcher's son-in-law left word at the shop."

"I am very glad that you have heard of it, by whatever means; and hope there will be no further delay."

"I am to have it to-morrow; but how do you think it is to be conveyed? Not by a wagon or cart;—Oh! no, nothing of that kind could be hired in the village. I might as well have asked for porters and a hand-barrow."

"You would find it difficult, I dare say, just now, in the middle of a very late hay harvest, to hire a horse and cart?"

"I was astonished to find what a piece of work was made of it! To want a horse and cart in the country seemed impossible, so I told my maid to speak for one directly; and as I cannot look out of my dressing-closet without seeing one farm yard, nor walk in the shrubbery without passing another, I thought it would be only ask and have, and was rather grieved that I could not give the advantage to all. Guess my surprise, when I found that I had been asking the most unreasonable, most impossible thing in the world, had offended all the farmers, all the labourers, all the hay in the parish. As for Dr. Grant's bailiff, I believe I had better keep out of *his* way;[12] and my brother-in-law himself, who is all kindness in general, looked rather black upon me, when he found what I had been at."

"You could not be expected to have thought on the subject before, but when you *do* think of it, you must see the importance of getting in the grass. The hire of a cart at any time might not be so easy as you suppose; our farmers are not in the habit of letting them out; but in harvest, it must be quite out of their power to spare a horse."

"I shall understand all your ways in time; but, coming down with the true London maxim, that everything is to be got with money, I was a little embarrassed at first by the sturdy independence of your country customs. However, I am to have my harp fetched to-morrow. Henry, who is good-nature itself, has offered to fetch it in his barouche.[13] Will it not be honourably conveyed?"

Edmund spoke of the harp as his favourite instrument, and hoped to be soon allowed to hear her.[14] Fanny had never heard the harp at all, and wished for it very much.

"I shall be most happy to play to you both," said Miss Crawford; "at least, as long as you can like to listen; probably much longer, for I dearly love music myself, and where the natural taste is equal, the player must always be best off, for she is gratified in more ways than one. Now, Mr. Bertram, if you write to your brother, I entreat you to tell him that my harp *is* come, he heard so much of my misery about it. And you may say, if you please, that I shall prepare my most plain-

12 A portion of Dr. Grant's income at Mansfield is derived from the farm land that is a part of the living, and he evidently employs a bailiff to oversee the farm work.

13 A four-wheeled carriage, with a collapsible roof and seating inside for four. Henry has the latest thing in carriages. In *Sense and Sensibility*, Austen's narrator, after describing how Edward Ferrars has proved a disappointment to his family, tells us that although his sister hopes to see Edward get into Parliament or connected with "some of the great men of the day," "it would have quieted her ambition to see him driving a barouche" (I, 3). As Susan J. Wolfson notes in her edition of *Northanger Abbey*, "carriages, fittings, and horses are important social displays; Austen frequently represents character in such material elements" (*Northanger Abbey: An Annotated Edition* [Cambridge, Mass.: Belknap Press of Harvard University Press, 2014], p. 116).

14 Harp-playing heroines are frequent in early nineteenth-century fictions, especially novels set in Britain's Celtic margins, which represent them as keepers of memory and votaries of vanishing musical traditions. At the same time these heroines can also, as in Sydney Owenson's *The Wild Irish Girl* (1806) and Walter Scott's *Waverley* (1814), be portrayed as figures of a dangerous charm—sirens whose songs lure the heroes into imprudence. Commentators noticed that this instrument was one that showed off to advantage the body of its female performer and sometimes intimated that for many young women this had been reason enough to take up the harp. In the contrasting sets of drawings of female accomplishments that the artist Maria Cosway executed in 1800 to depict the "Progress of Female Dissipation" and the "Progress of Female Virtue," Cosway seems to make this argument. She depicts her dissipated young lady at once playing on her harp and admiring her reflection in a mirror. Cosway's virtuous young lady opts, by contrast, for sketching as her pastime.

15 Henry's letters to her are so short, Mary says, that he has never needed to turn his paper over and continue his missive on the back. Given the high cost of postage at this time, Mary would be well within her rights to expect more effort from her brother; recipients of letters felt entitled to their money's worth. On September 25, 1815, Austen assures *her* brother Francis that she feels very much obliged to him for "filling . . . so long a sheet a [sic] paper, you are a good one to traffic with in that way, You pay most liberally" (*Letters*, p. 238).

16 *Letters to William* was to be the title of the opera adapting *Mansfield Park* that Benjamin Britten began writing in 1946 and which he abandoned only a few months into the project, when he turned to *Albert Herring*. The librettist Ronald Duncan saw in the title an index of Britten's wish to write something like Tatyana's letter scene in Tchaikovsky's *Eugene Onegin*. The title suggests in addition, though, something of Britten's astuteness as a reader of Fanny's story: he evidently recognized how consequential for Fanny's emotional well-being those "letters to William" would have been. For what is known of the plans for this opera, see *Letters from a Life: The Selected Letters of Benjamin Britten, 1913–1967*, 6 vols., ed. Donald Mitchell, Philip Reed, and Mervyn Cooke (Berkeley: University of California Press, 2004), vol. 3, pp. 232–234.

17 Mary means to ascertain whether William is employed aboard a commercial ship or instead serving in the Royal Navy.

18 The Fleet was divided into three grades—in ascending order of status, the Blue, the White, and the Red—and ships would fly different colored flags according to the grade of the division to which they were assigned. There were three ranks of admiral in each division, full admirals being the most senior, followed by vice admirals and then rear admirals.

tive airs against his return, in compassion to his feelings, as I know his horse will lose."

"If I write, I will say whatever you wish me; but I do not at present foresee any occasion for writing."

"No, I dare say, nor if he were to be gone a twelvemonth, would you ever write to him, nor he to you, if it could be helped. The occasion would never be foreseen. What strange creatures brothers are! You would not write to each other but upon the most urgent necessity in the world; and when obliged to take up the pen to say that such a horse is ill, or such a relation dead, it is done in the fewest possible words. You have but one style among you. I know it perfectly. Henry, who is in every other respect exactly what a brother should be, who loves me, consults me, confides in me, and will talk to me by the hour together, has never yet turned the page in a letter;[15] and very often it is nothing more than, 'Dear Mary, I am just arrived. Bath seems full, and every thing as usual. Your's sincerely.' That is the true manly style; that is a complete brother's letter."

"When they are at a distance from all their family," said Fanny, colouring for William's sake, "they can write long letters."[16]

"Miss Price has a brother at sea," said Edmund, "whose excellence as a correspondent, makes her think you too severe upon us."

"At sea, has she?—In the King's service of course."[17]

Fanny would rather have had Edmund tell the story, but his determined silence obliged her to relate her brother's situation; her voice was animated in speaking of his profession, and the foreign stations he had been on, but she could not mention the number of years that he had been absent without tears in her eyes. Miss Crawford civilly wished him an early promotion.

"Do you know any thing of my cousin's captain?" said Edmund; "Captain Marshall? You have a large acquaintance in the navy, I conclude?"

"Among Admirals, large enough; but," with an air of grandeur, "we know very little of the inferior ranks. Post captains may be very good sort of men, but they do not belong to *us*. Of various admirals I could tell you a great deal; of them and their flags, and the gradation of their pay, and their bickerings and jealousies.[18] But in general, I can

A Barouche with Ackermann's Patent Moveable Axles.

Image from an 1818 advertisement touting the latest thing in coach-building. Readers of *Ackermann's Repository* are assured that the new "patented moveable axle" will afford the riders in this barouche "complete security against upsetting."

19 Of course, despite her demurral, Mary's auditors *must* suspect her of punning—but whether Austen intends for readers to hear one pun or two has been a subject of much dispute. There is certainly a pun on vices, serving to conjoin vice as wickedness with the rank of vice admiral. Whether readers are right to hear in Mary's witticism a second pun on "rears" is less sure. Edmund would surely do more than look grave if he were forced to ponder the possibility that Mary, moving between rear admirals and admirals' rears, might be alluding knowingly to the frequency of the floggings suffered by the ships' crews or even to those sailors' notorious association with sodomitical practices. On the other hand, that Edmund doesn't pick up on the steamier meanings that lurk in Mary's playful speech need not prevent *our* doing so. For contrasting views on this passage, see Brian Southam, *Jane Austen and the Navy* (London: Hambledon and London, 2000), pp. 184–185, and Jillian Heydt-Stevenson, *Austen's Unbecoming Conjunctions* (Basingstoke: Palgrave, 2005), pp. 137–141.

assure you that they are all passed over, and all very ill used. Certainly, my home at my uncle's brought me acquainted with a circle of admirals. Of *Rears,* and *Vices,* I saw enough. Now, do not be suspecting me of a pun, I entreat."[19]

Edmund again felt grave, and only replied, "It is a noble profession."

"Yes, the profession is well enough under two circumstances; if it make the fortune, and there be discretion in spending it. But, in short, it is not a favourite profession of mine. It has never worn an amiable form to *me.*"

Edmund reverted to the harp, and was again very happy in the prospect of hearing her play.

The subject of improving grounds meanwhile was still under consideration among the others; and Mrs. Grant could not help addressing her brother, though it was calling his attention from Miss Julia Bertram. "My dear Henry, have *you* nothing to say? You have been an improver yourself, and from what I hear of Everingham, it may vie with any place in England. Its natural beauties, I am sure, are great.

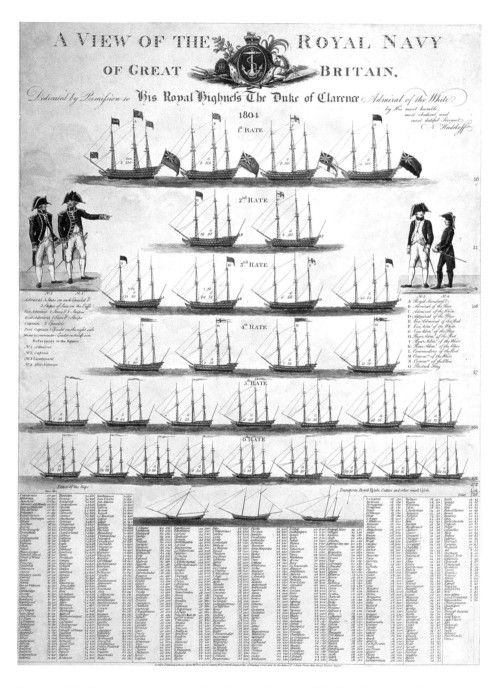

Buyers of this 1804 engraving visualizing the organization of the Royal Navy would also have been demonstrating their patriotism through their purchase.

Everingham as it *used* to be was perfect in my estimation; such a happy fall of ground, and such timber! What would not I give to see it again!"

"Nothing could be so gratifying to me as to hear your opinion of it," was his answer. "But I fear there would be some disappointment. You would not find it equal to your present ideas. In extent it is a mere nothing—you would be surprised at its insignificance; and as for improvement, there was very little for me to do; too little—I should like to have been busy much longer."

"You are fond of the sort of thing?" said Julia.

"Excessively: but what with the natural advantages of the ground, which pointed out even to a very young eye what little remained to be done, and my own consequent resolutions, I had not been of age three months before Everingham was all that it is now. My plan was laid at Westminster[20]—a little altered perhaps at Cambridge, and at one and twenty executed. I am inclined to envy Mr. Rushworth for having so much happiness yet before him. I have been a devourer of my own."

"Those who see quickly, will resolve quickly and act quickly," said Julia. "*You* can never want employment. Instead of envying Mr. Rushworth, you should assist him with your opinion."

Mrs. Grant hearing the latter part of this speech, enforced it warmly, persuaded that no judgment could be equal to her brother's; and as Miss Bertram caught at the idea likewise, and gave it her full support, declaring that in her opinion it was infinitely better to consult with friends and disinterested advisers, than immediately to throw the business into the hands of a professional man, Mr. Rushworth was very ready to request the favour of Mr. Crawford's assistance; and Mr. Crawford after properly depreciating his own abilities, was quite at his service in any way that could be useful. Mr. Rushworth then began to propose Mr. Crawford's doing him the honour of coming over to Sotherton, and taking a bed there; when Mrs. Norris, as if reading in her two nieces' minds their little approbation of a plan which was to take Mr. Crawford away, interposed with an amendment. "There can be no doubt of Mr. Crawford's willingness; but why should not more of us go?—Why should not we make a little party? Here are many that would be interested in your

20  An elite public school, counterpart to Eton.

Pair of contrasting images included in Humphry Repton's *Observations on the Theory and Practice of Landscape Gardening* (1805). Found in a section that instructs the reader on how and where to plant trees, this page is also a manifesto declaring Repton's aesthetic principles.

improvements, my dear Mr. Rushworth, and that would like to hear Mr. Crawford's opinion on the spot, and that might be of some small use to you with *their* opinions; and for my own part I have been long wishing to wait upon your good mother again; nothing but having no horses of my own, could have made me so remiss; but now I could go and sit a few hours with Mrs. Rushworth while the rest of you walked about and settled things, and then we could all return to a late dinner here, or dine at Sotherton just as might be most agreeable to your mother, and have a pleasant drive home by moonlight. I dare say Mr. Crawford would take my two nieces and me in his barouche, and Edmund can go on horseback, you know, sister, and Fanny will stay at home with you."

Lady Bertram made no objection, and every one concerned in the going, was forward in expressing their ready concurrence, excepting Edmund, who heard it all and said nothing.

# 7

"WELL FANNY, AND HOW DO YOU like Miss Crawford *now?*" said Edmund the next day, after thinking some time on the subject himself. "How did you like her yesterday?"

"Very well—very much. I like to hear her talk. She entertains me; and she is so extremely pretty, that I have great pleasure in looking at her."

"It is her countenance that is so attractive. She has a wonderful play of feature! But was there nothing in her conversation that struck you Fanny, as not quite right?"

"Oh! yes, she ought not to have spoken of her uncle as she did. I was quite astonished. An uncle with whom she has been living so many years, and who, whatever his faults may be, is so very fond of her brother, treating him, they say, quite like a son. I could not have believed it!"

"I thought you would be struck. It was very wrong—very indecorous."

"And very ungrateful, I think."

"Ungrateful is a strong word. I do not know that her uncle has any claim to her *gratitude;* his wife certainly had; and it is the warmth of her respect for her aunt's memory which misleads her here. She is awkwardly circumstanced. With such warm feelings and lively spirits it must be difficult to do justice to her affection for Mrs. Crawford, without throwing a shade on the admiral. I do not pretend to know which was most to blame in their disagreements, though the admiral's present conduct might incline one to the side of his wife: but it is natural and amiable that Miss Crawford should acquit her aunt entirely. I do not censure her *opinions;* but there certainly *is* impropriety in making them public."

"Do not you think," said Fanny, after a little consideration, "that this impropriety is a reflection itself upon Mrs. Crawford, as her niece has been entirely brought up by her? She cannot have given her right notions of what was due to the admiral."

"That is a fair remark. Yes, we must suppose the faults of the niece to have been those of the aunt; and it makes one more sensible of the disadvantages she has been under. But I think her present home must do her good. Mrs. Grant's manners are just what they ought to be. She speaks of her brother with a very pleasing affection."

"Yes, except as to his writing her such short letters. She made me almost laugh; but I cannot rate so very highly the love or good nature of a brother, who will not give himself the trouble of writing anything worth reading, to his sisters, when they are separated. I am sure William would never have used *me* so, under any circumstances. And what right had she to suppose, that *you* would not write long letters when you were absent?"

"The right of a lively mind, Fanny, seizing whatever may contribute to its own amusement or that of others; perfectly allowable, when untinctured by ill humour or roughness; and there is not a shadow of either in the countenance or manner of Miss Crawford, nothing sharp, or loud, or coarse. She is perfectly feminine, except in the instances we have been speaking of. *There* she cannot be justified. I am glad you saw it all as I did."

Having formed her mind and gained her affections, he had a good chance of her thinking like him; though at this period, and on this subject, there began now to be some danger of dissimilarity, for he was in a line of admiration of Miss Crawford, which might lead him where Fanny could not follow. Miss Crawford's attractions did not lessen. The harp arrived, and rather added to her beauty, wit, and good humour, for she played with the greatest obligingness, with an expression and taste which were peculiarly becoming, and there was something clever to be said at the close of every air. Edmund was at the parsonage every day to be indulged with his favourite instrument; one morning secured an invitation for the next, for the lady could not be unwilling to have a listener, and every thing was soon in a fair train.

A young woman, pretty, lively, with a harp as elegant as herself; and both placed near a window, cut down to the ground, and opening on a little lawn, surrounded by shrubs in the rich foliage of summer, was enough to catch any man's heart. The season, the scene, the air, were all favourable to tenderness and sentiment. Mrs. Grant and her tambour frame[1] were not without their use; it was all in harmony; and as every thing will turn to account when love is once set going, even the sandwich tray, and Dr. Grant doing the honours of it, were worth looking at. Without studying the business, however, or knowing what he was about, Edmund was beginning, at the end of a week of such intercourse, to be a good deal in love; and to the credit of the lady it may be added, that without his being a man of the world or an elder brother, without any of the arts of flattery or the gaieties of small talk, he began to be agreeable to her. She felt it to be so, though she had not foreseen and could hardly understand it; for he was not pleasant by any common rule, he talked no nonsense, he paid no compliments, his opinions were unbending, his attentions tranquil and simple. There was a charm, perhaps, in his sincerity, his steadiness, his integrity, which Miss Crawford might be equal to feel, though not equal to discuss with herself. She did not think very much about it, however; he pleased her for the present; she liked to have him near her; it was enough.

Fanny could not wonder that Edmund was at the parsonage every morning; she would gladly have been there too, might she have gone in uninvited and unnoticed to hear the harp; neither could she wonder, that when the evening stroll was over, and the two families parted again, he should think it right to attend Mrs. Grant and her sister to their home, while Mr. Crawford was devoted to the ladies of the park; but she thought it a very bad exchange, and if Edmund were not there to mix the wine and water for her, would rather go without it than not. She was a little surprised that he could spend so many hours with Miss Crawford, and not see more of the sort of fault which he had already observed, and of which *she* was almost

1 Circular frame for embroidery.

Mary's newfound love of horsemanship might supply her with a reason to add to her wardrobe. This 1806 fashion plate picturing a stylish riding costume suggests the possibilities now open to her.

always reminded by a something of the same nature whenever she was in her company; but so it was. Edmund was fond of speaking to her of Miss Crawford, but he seemed to think it enough that the admiral had since been spared; and she scrupled to point out her own remarks to him, lest it should appear like ill-nature. The first actual pain which Miss Crawford occasioned her, was the consequence of an inclination to learn to ride, which the former caught soon after her being settled at Mansfield from the example of the young ladies at the park, and which, when Edmund's acquaintance with her increased, led to his encouraging the wish, and the offer of his own quiet mare for the purpose of her first attempts, as the best fitted for a beginner that either stable could furnish. No pain, no injury, however, was designed by him to his cousin in this offer: *she* was not to lose a day's exercise by it. The mare was only to be taken down to the parsonage half an hour before her ride were to begin; and Fanny, on its being first proposed, so far from feeling slighted, was almost overpowered with gratitude that he should be asking her leave for it.

Miss Crawford made her first essay with great credit to herself, and no inconvenience to Fanny. Edmund, who had taken down the mare and presided at the whole, returned with it in excellent time, before either Fanny or the steady old coachman, who always attended her when she rode without her cousins, were ready to set forward. The second day's trial was not so guiltless. Miss Crawford's enjoyment of riding was such that she did not know how to leave off. Active and fearless, and, though rather small, strongly made, she seemed formed for a horsewoman; and to the pure genuine pleasure of the exercise, something was probably added in Edmund's attendance and instructions, and something more in the conviction of very much surpassing her sex in general by her early progress, to make her unwilling to dismount. Fanny was ready and waiting, and Mrs. Norris was beginning to scold her for not being gone, and still no horse was announced, no Edmund appeared. To avoid her aunt, and look for him, she went out.

The houses, though scarcely half a mile apart, were not within sight of each other; but by walking fifty yards from the hall door, she could look down the park, and command a view of the parsonage and all its demesnes,[2] gently rising beyond the village road; and in Dr. Grant's meadow she immediately saw the group—Edmund and Miss Crawford both on horseback, riding side by side, Dr. and Mrs. Grant, and Mr. Crawford, with two or three grooms, standing about and looking on. A happy party it appeared to her—all interested in one object—cheerful beyond a doubt, for the sound of merriment ascended even to her. It was a sound which did not make *her* cheerful; she wondered that Edmund should forget her, and felt a pang. She could not turn her eyes from the meadow, she could not help watching all that passed. At first Miss Crawford and her companion made the circuit of the field, which was not small, at a foot's pace; then, at *her* apparent suggestion, they rose into a canter; and to Fanny's timid nature it was most astonishing to see how well she sat. After a few minutes they stopped entirely, Edmund was close to her, he was speaking to her, he was evidently directing her management of the bridle, he had hold of her hand; she saw it, or the imagination supplied what the eye could not reach. She must not wonder at all this; what could be more natural than that Edmund should be making himself useful, and proving his good-nature by any one? She could not but think indeed that Mr. Crawford might as well have saved him the trouble; that it would have been particularly proper and becoming in a brother to have done it himself; but Mr. Crawford, with all his boasted good-nature, and all his coachmanship, probably knew nothing of the matter, and had no active kindness in comparison of Edmund. She began to think it rather hard upon the mare to have such double duty; if she were forgotten the poor mare should be remembered.

Her feelings for one and the other were soon a little tranquillized, by seeing the party in the meadow disperse, and Miss Crawford still on horseback, but attended by Edmund on foot, pass through a gate into the lane, and so into the park, and make towards the spot where she stood. She began then to be afraid of appearing rude and impatient; and walked to meet them with a great anxiety to avoid the suspicion.

"My dear Miss Price," said Miss Crawford, as soon as she was at all within hearing, "I am come to make my own apologies for keeping

2 Lands belonging to the parsonage.

you waiting—but I have nothing in the world to say for myself—I knew it was very late, and that I was behaving extremely ill; and, therefore, if you please, you must forgive me. Selfishness must always be forgiven you know, because there is no hope of a cure."

Fanny's answer was extremely civil, and Edmund added his conviction that she could be in no hurry. "For there is more than time enough for my cousin to ride twice as far as she ever goes," said he, "and you have been promoting her comfort by preventing her from setting off half an hour sooner; clouds are now coming up, and she will not suffer from the heat as she would have done then. I wish *you* may not be fatigued by so much exercise. I wish you had saved yourself this walk home."

"No part of it fatigues me but getting off this horse, I assure you," said she, as she sprang down with his help; "I am very strong. Nothing ever fatigues me, but doing what I do not like. Miss Price, I give way to you with a very bad grace; but I sincerely hope you will have a pleasant ride, and that I may have nothing but good to hear of this dear, delightful, beautiful animal."

The old coachman, who had been waiting about with his own horse, now joining them, Fanny was lifted on her's, and they set off across another part of the park; her feelings of discomfort not lightened by seeing, as she looked back, that the others were walking down the hill together to the village; nor did her attendant do her much good by his comments on Miss Crawford's great cleverness as a horsewoman, which he had been watching with an interest almost equal to her own.

"It is a pleasure to see a lady with such a good heart for riding!" said he. "I never see one sit a horse better. She did not seem to have a thought of fear. Very different from you, miss, when you first began, six years ago come next Easter. Lord bless me! how you did tremble when Sir Thomas first had you put on!"

In the drawing-room Miss Crawford was also celebrated. Her merit in being gifted by nature with strength and courage was fully appreciated by the Miss Bertrams; her delight in riding was like their own; her early excellence in it was like their own, and they had great pleasure in praising it.

"I was sure she would ride well," said Julia; "she has the make for it. Her figure is as neat as her brother's."

"Yes," added Maria, "and her spirits are as good, and she has the same energy of character. I cannot but think that good horsemanship has a great deal to do with the mind."

When they parted at night, Edmund asked Fanny whether she meant to ride the next day.

"No, I do not know, not if you want the mare," was her answer.

"I do not want her at all for myself," said he; "but whenever you are next inclined to stay at home, I think Miss Crawford would be glad to have her for a longer time—for a whole morning in short. She has a great desire to get as far as Mansfield common,[3] Mrs. Grant has been telling her of its fine views, and I have no doubt of her being perfectly equal to it. But any morning will do for this. She would be extremely sorry to interfere with you. It would be very wrong if she did.—*She* rides only for pleasure, *you* for health."

"I shall not ride to-morrow, certainly," said Fanny; "I have been out very often lately, and would rather stay at home. You know I am strong enough now to walk very well."

Edmund looked pleased, which must be Fanny's comfort, and the ride to Mansfield common took place the next morning;—the party included all the young people but herself, and was much enjoyed at the time, and doubly enjoyed again in the evening discussion. A successful scheme of this sort generally brings on another; and the having been to Mansfield-common, disposed them all for going somewhere else the day after. There were many other views to be shewn, and though the weather was hot, there were shady lanes wherever they wanted to go. A young party is always provided with a shady lane. Four fine mornings successively were spent in this manner, in shewing the Crawfords the country, and doing the honours of its finest spots. Every thing answered;[4] it was all gaiety and good-humour, the heat only supplying inconvenience enough to be talked of with pleasure—till the fourth day, when the happiness of one of the party was exceedingly clouded. Miss Bertram was the one. Edmund and Julia were invited to dine at the parsonage, and *she* was excluded. It was meant and done by Mrs. Grant, with perfect good humour, on

3 The village of Mansfield appears to retain its unenclosed common: land held jointly by the community on which even the poorest inhabitants would have the right to pasture their cattle or sheep or gather firewood. In the long term, however, Northamptonshire was one of the counties most drastically affected by the enclosures movement that was gathering momentum in Austen's day; there landowners intent on schemes of improvement bit by bit eliminated the older open field system of agriculture.

4 Everything fulfilled their expectations.

5 This basket contained the cheap fabrics that were kept on hand for making clothes for the poor. Such charitable works were considered a lady's duty.

Mr. Rushworth's account, who was partly expected at the park that day; but it was felt as a very grievous injury, and her good manners were severely taxed to conceal her vexation and anger, till she reached home. As Mr. Rushworth did *not* come, the injury was increased, and she had not even the relief of shewing her power over him; she could only be sullen to her mother, aunt, and cousin, and throw as great a gloom as possible over their dinner and dessert.

Between ten and eleven, Edmund and Julia walked into the drawing-room, fresh with the evening air, glowing and cheerful, the very reverse of what they found in the three ladies sitting there, for Maria would scarcely raise her eyes from her book, and Lady Bertram was half asleep; and even Mrs. Norris, discomposed by her niece's ill-humour, and having asked one or two questions about the dinner, which were not immediately attended to, seemed almost determined to say no more. For a few minutes, the brother and sister were too eager in their praise of the night and their remarks on the stars, to think beyond themselves; but when the first pause came, Edmund, looking around, said, "But where is Fanny?—Is she gone to bed?"

"No, not that I know of," replied Mrs. Norris; "she was here a moment ago."

Her own gentle voice speaking from the other end of the room, which was a very long one, told them that she was on the sofa. Mrs. Norris began scolding.

"That is a very foolish trick, Fanny, to be idling away all the evening upon a sofa. Why cannot you come and sit here, and employ yourself as *we* do?—If you have no work of your own, I can supply you from the poor-basket.⁵ There is all the new calico that was bought last week, not touched yet. I am sure I almost broke my back by cutting it out. You should learn to think of other people; and take my word for it, it is a shocking trick for a young person to be always lolling upon a sofa."

Before half this was said, Fanny was returned to her seat at the table, and had taken up her work again; and Julia, who was in high good-humour, from the pleasures of the day, did her the justice of exclaiming, "I must say, ma'am, that Fanny is as little upon the sofa as anybody in the house."

"Fanny," said Edmund, after looking at her attentively; "I am sure you have the headach?"

She could not deny it, but said it was not very bad.

"I can hardly believe you," he replied; "I know your looks too well. How long have you had it?"

"Since a little before dinner. It is nothing but the heat."

"Did you go out in the heat?"

"Go out! to be sure she did," said Mrs. Norris; "would you have her stay within such a fine day as this? Were not we *all* out? Even your mother was out to-day for above an hour."

"Yes, indeed, Edmund," added her ladyship, who had been thoroughly awakened by Mrs. Norris's sharp reprimand to Fanny; "I was out above an hour. I sat three-quarters of an hour in the flower

The amateur artist John Harden (1772–1847) captures beautifully the look of concentration on his sitters' faces, but his sketch also evokes these women's capacity to be together in their separateness. In so doing it evokes the way women's work—the sewing, for instance, that Aunt Norris urges on Fanny—could double as an occasion for female sociability. It seems unlikely that the Mansfield Park drawing room would ever witness the solidarities that Harden's sketch honors.

6 A concoction used as smelling salts would be.

7 Mrs. Norris appears to have claimed the Mansfield roses and Fanny's labor in order to prepare potpourri for her house.

garden, while Fanny cut the roses, and very pleasant it was I assure you, but very hot. It was shady enough in the alcove, but I declare I quite dreaded the coming home again."

"Fanny has been cutting roses, has she?"

"Yes, and I am afraid they will be the last this year. Poor thing! *She* found it hot enough, but they were so full blown, that one could not wait."

"There was no help for it, certainly," rejoined Mrs. Norris, in a rather softened voice; "but I question whether her headach might not be caught *then,* sister. There is nothing so likely to give it as standing and stooping in a hot sun. But I dare say it will be well to-morrow. Suppose you let her have your aromatic vinegar;[6] I always forget to have mine filled."

"She has got it," said Lady Bertram; "she has had it ever since she came back from your house the second time."

"What!" cried Edmund; "has she been walking as well as cutting roses; walking across the hot park to your house, and doing it twice, ma'am?—No wonder her head aches."

Mrs. Norris was talking to Julia, and did not hear.

"I was afraid it would be too much for her," said Lady Bertram; "but when the roses were gathered, your aunt wished to have them, and then you know they must be taken home."

"But were there roses enough to oblige her to go twice?"

"No; but they were to be put into the spare room to dry;[7] and, unluckily, Fanny forgot to lock the door of the room and bring away the key, so she was obliged to go again."

Edmund got up and walked about the room, saying, "And could nobody be employed on such an errand but Fanny?—Upon my word, ma'am, it has been a very ill-managed business."

"I am sure I do not know how it was to have been done better," cried Mrs. Norris, unable to be longer deaf; "unless I had gone myself indeed; but I cannot be in two places at once; and I was talking to Mr. Green at that very time about your mother's dairymaid, by *her* desire, and had promised John Groom to write to Mrs. Jefferies about his son, and the poor fellow was waiting for me half an hour. I think nobody can justly accuse me of sparing myself upon any occasion, but really I cannot do every thing at once. And as for Fanny's just stepping down to my house for me, it is not much above a quarter of a mile, I cannot think I was unreasonable to ask it. How often do I pace it three times a-day, early and late, ay and in all weathers too, and say nothing about it."

"I wish Fanny had half your strength, ma'am."

"If Fanny would be more regular in her exercise, she would not be knocked up so soon. She has not been out on horseback now this long while, and I am persuaded, that when she does not ride, she ought to walk. If she had been riding before, I should not have asked it of her. But I thought it would rather do her good after being stooping among the roses; for there is nothing so refreshing as a walk after a fatigue of that kind; and though the sun was strong, it was not so very hot. Between ourselves, Edmund," nodding significantly at his mother, "it was cutting the roses, and dawdling about in the flower-garden, that did the mischief."

"I am afraid it was, indeed," said the more candid Lady Bertram, who had overheard her, "I am very much afraid she caught the headach there, for the heat was enough to kill any body. It was as much as I could bear myself. Sitting and calling to Pug, and trying to keep him from the flower-beds, was almost too much for me."

Edmund said no more to either lady; but going quietly to another table, on which the supper tray yet remained, brought a glass of Madeira to Fanny, and obliged her to drink the greater part. She wished to be able to decline it; but the tears which a variety of feelings created, made it easier to swallow than to speak.

Vexed as Edmund was with his mother and aunt, he was still more angry with himself. His own forgetfulness of her was worse than any thing which they had done. Nothing of this would have happened had she been properly considered; but she had been left four days together without any choice of companions or exercise, and without any excuse for avoiding whatever her unreasonable aunts might require. He was ashamed to think that for four days together she had not had the power of riding, and very seriously resolved, however unwilling he must be to check a pleasure of Miss Crawford's, that it should never happen again.

Fanny went to bed with her heart as full as on the first evening of her arrival at the Park. The state of her spirits had probably had its share in her indisposition; for she had been feeling neglected, and been struggling against discontent and envy for some days past. As she leant on the sofa, to which she had retreated that she might not be seen, the pain of her mind had been much beyond that in her head; and the sudden change which Edmund's kindness had then occasioned, made her hardly know how to support herself.

James Andrews's portrait of Jane Austen, done in 1869, was based on Cassandra Austen's sketch of her sister, which it prettifies and softens. An engraving of this watercolor served as the frontispiece in 1870 for J. E. Austen-Leigh's *A Memoir of Jane Austen* and after 2017 will be seen on the Bank of England's new ten-pound note.

# 8

FANNY'S RIDES RECOMMENCED the very next day, and as it was a pleasant fresh-feeling morning, less hot than the weather had lately been, Edmund trusted that her losses both of health and pleasure would be soon made good. While she was gone, Mr. Rushworth arrived, escorting his mother, who came to be civil, and to shew her civility especially, in urging the execution of the plan for visiting Sotherton, which had been started a fortnight before, and which, in consequence of her subsequent absence from home, had since lain dormant. Mrs. Norris and her nieces were all well pleased with its revival, and an early day was named, and agreed to, provided Mr. Crawford should be disengaged; the young ladies did not forget that stipulation, and though Mrs. Norris would willingly have answered for his being so, they would neither authorize the liberty, nor run the risk; and at last on a hint from Miss Bertram, Mr. Rushworth discovered that the properest thing to be done, was for him to walk down to the Parsonage directly, and call on Mr. Crawford, and inquire whether Wednesday would suit him or not.

Before his return Mrs. Grant and Miss Crawford came in. Having been out some time, and taken a different route to the house, they had not met him. Comfortable hopes, however, were given that he would find Mr. Crawford at home. The Sotherton scheme was mentioned of course. It was hardly possible indeed that any thing else should be talked of, for Mrs. Norris was in high spirits about it, and Mrs. Rushworth, a well-meaning, civil, prosing, pompous woman,

1 Lady Bertram's health does not seem so very bad: could it really be compromised by a road trip of ten miles in a carriage drawn by four horses? Even taking into account the poor road conditions between Mansfield and Sotherton, one cannot imagine the journey requiring much more than two hours. By way of contrast with Lady Bertram's evident preference for immobility, consider Frank Churchill in *Emma,* who travels thirty-two miles in a hired chaise, from Highbury to London and back again in a single day, merely (as he tells people) to get his hair cut (II, 7).

who thought nothing of consequence, but as it related to her own and her son's concerns, had not yet given over pressing Lady Bertram to be of the party. Lady Bertram constantly declined it; but her placid manner of refusal made Mrs. Rushworth still think she wished to come, till Mrs. Norris's more numerous words and louder tone convinced her of the truth.

"The fatigue would be too much for my sister, a great deal too much I assure you, my dear Mrs. Rushworth. Ten miles there, and ten back, you know.[1] You must excuse my sister on this occasion, and accept of our two dear girls and myself without her. Sotherton is the only place that could give her a *wish* to go so far, but it cannot be indeed. She will have a companion in Fanny Price you know, so it will all do very well; and as for Edmund, as he is not here to speak for himself, I will answer for his being most happy to join the party. He can go on horseback, you know."

Mrs. Rushworth being obliged to yield to Lady Bertram's staying at home, could only be sorry. "The loss of her Ladyship's company would be a great drawback, and she should have been extremely happy to have seen the young lady too, Miss Price, who had never been at Sotherton yet, and it was a pity she should not see the place."

"You are very kind, you are all kindness, my dear madam," cried Mrs. Norris; "but as to Fanny, she will have opportunities in plenty of seeing Sotherton. She has time enough before her; and her going now is quite out of the question. Lady Bertram could not possibly spare her."

"Oh! no — I cannot do without Fanny."

Mrs. Rushworth proceeded next, under the conviction that every body must be wanting to see Sotherton, to include Miss Crawford in the invitation; and though Mrs. Grant, who had not been at the trouble of visiting Mrs. Rushworth on her coming into the neighbourhood, civilly declined it on her own account, she was glad to secure any pleasure for her sister; and Mary, properly pressed and persuaded, was not long in accepting her share of the civility. Mr. Rushworth came back from the parsonage successful; and Edmund made his appearance just in time to learn what had been settled for Wednesday, to attend Mrs. Rushworth to her carriage, and walk half way down the park with the two other ladies.

On his return to the breakfast-room, he found Mrs. Norris trying to make up her mind as to whether Miss Crawford's being of the party were desirable or not, or whether her brother's barouche would not be full without her. The Miss Bertrams laughed at the idea, assuring her that the barouche would hold four perfectly well, independent of the box, on which *one* might go with him.

"But why is it necessary," said Edmund, "that Crawford's carriage, or his *only* should be employed? Why is no use to be made of my mother's chaise? I could not, when the scheme was first mentioned the other day, understand why a visit from the family were not to be made in the carriage of the family."

"What!" cried Julia: "go box'd up three in a post-chaise in this weather, when we may have seats in a barouche! No, my dear Edmund, that will not quite do."[2]

"Besides," said Maria, "I know that Mr. Crawford depends upon taking us. After what passed at first, he would claim it as a promise."

"And my dear Edmund," added Mrs. Norris, "taking out *two* carriages when *one* will do, would be trouble for nothing; and, between ourselves, coachman is not very fond of the roads between this and Sotherton; he always complains bitterly of the narrow lanes scratching his carriage, and you know one should not like to have dear Sir Thomas when he comes home find all the varnish scratched off."

"That would not be a very handsome reason for using Mr. Crawford's," said Maria; "but the truth is, that Wilcox is a stupid old fellow, and does not know how to drive. I will answer for it that we shall find no inconvenience from narrow roads on Wednesday."

"There is no hardship, I suppose, nothing unpleasant," said Edmund, "in going on the barouche box."

"Unpleasant!" cried Maria: "Oh! dear, I believe it would be generally thought the favourite seat. There can be no comparison as to one's view of the country.[3] Probably, Miss Crawford will choose the barouche box herself."

"There can be no objection then to Fanny's going with you; there can be no doubt of your having room for her."

"Fanny!" repeated Mrs. Norris; "my dear Edmund, there is no idea of her going with us. She stays with her aunt. I told Mrs. Rushworth so. She is not expected."

2 A post-chaise was a closed carriage, built for long-distance travel. Generally such chaises were drawn by one or two pairs of horses, which would be changed for new horses at each post on the traveler's route. Julia's preference for Henry Crawford's stylish barouche over her mother's more staid and cumbersome carriage is understandable. In a barouche four passengers could be seated in two facing rows; the driver would be perched on a high seat at the front of the carriage (the "box" that Edmund references later in this dialogue), sometimes sitting alongside a companion. In Lady Bertram's chaise a group of three passengers would sit in a single row together, on a warm summer's day likely with some discomfort.

3 Countryside.

"You can have no reason I imagine madam," said he, addressing his mother, "for wishing Fanny *not* to be of the party, but as it relates to yourself, to your own comfort. If you could do without her, you would not wish to keep her at home?"

"To be sure not, but I *cannot* do without her."

"You can, if I stay at home with you, as I mean to do."

There was a general cry out at this. "Yes," he continued, "there is no necessity for my going, and I mean to stay at home. Fanny has a great desire to see Sotherton. I know she wishes it very much. She has not often a gratification of the kind, and I am sure ma'am you would be glad to give her the pleasure now?"

"Oh! yes, very glad, if your aunt sees no objection."

Mrs. Norris was very ready with the only objection which could remain, their having positively assured Mrs. Rushworth, that Fanny could not go, and the very strange appearance there would consequently be in taking her, which seemed to her a difficulty quite impossible to be got over. It must have the strangest appearance! It would be something so very unceremonious, so bordering on disrespect for Mrs. Rushworth, whose own manners were such a pattern of good-breeding and attention, that she really did not feel equal to it. Mrs. Norris had no affection for Fanny, and no wish of procuring her pleasure at any time, but her opposition to Edmund *now* arose more from partiality for her own scheme because it *was* her own, than from any thing else. She felt that she had arranged everything extremely well, and that any alteration must be for the worse. When Edmund, therefore, told her in reply, as he did when she would give him the hearing, that she need not distress herself on Mrs. Rushworth's account, because he had taken the opportunity as he walked with her through the hall, of mentioning Miss Price as one who would probably be of the party, and had directly received a very sufficient invitation for his cousin, Mrs. Norris was too much vexed to submit with a very good grace, and would only say, "Very well, very well, just as you chuse, settle it your own way, I am sure I do not care about it."

"It seems very odd," said Maria, "that you should be staying at home instead of Fanny."

"I am sure she ought to be very much obliged to you," added Julia, hastily leaving the room as she spoke, from a consciousness that she ought to offer to stay at home herself.

"Fanny will feel quite as grateful as the occasion requires," was Edmund's only reply, and the subject dropt.

Fanny's gratitude when she heard the plan, was in fact much greater than her pleasure. She felt Edmund's kindness with all, and more than all, the sensibility which he, unsuspicious of her fond attachment, could be aware of;[4] but that he should forego any enjoyment on her account gave her pain, and her own satisfaction in seeing Sotherton would be nothing without him.

The next meeting of the two Mansfield families produced another alteration in the plan, and one that was admitted with general approbation. Mrs. Grant offered herself as companion for the day to Lady Bertram in lieu of her son, and Dr. Grant was to join them at dinner. Lady Bertram was very well pleased to have it so, and the young ladies were in spirits again. Even Edmund was very thankful for an arrangement which restored him to his share of the party; and Mrs. Norris thought it an excellent plan, and had it at her tongue's end, and was on the point of proposing it, when Mrs. Grant spoke.

Wednesday was fine, and soon after breakfast the barouche arrived, Mr. Crawford driving his sisters; and as every body was ready, there was nothing to be done but for Mrs. Grant to alight and the others to take their places. The place of all places, the envied seat, the post of honour, was unappropriated. To whose happy lot was it to fall? While each of the Miss Bertrams were meditating how best, and with the most appearance of obliging the others, to secure it, the matter was settled by Mrs. Grant's saying, as she stepped from the carriage, "As there are five of you, it will be better that one should sit with Henry, and as you were saying lately, that you wished you could drive, Julia, I think this will be a good opportunity for you to take a lesson."

Happy Julia! Unhappy Maria! The former was on the barouche-box in a moment, the latter took her seat within, in gloom and mortification; and the carriage drove off amid the good wishes of the two remaining ladies, and the barking of pug in his mistress's arms.

4 Referring to this "fond attachment" the narrator may be indicating not simply that Fanny loves but also that she is foolish in doing so. *Fond* was often used in the latter, reproachful sense in the early nineteenth century.

Their road was through a pleasant country; and Fanny, whose rides had never been extensive, was soon beyond her knowledge, and was very happy in observing all that was new, and admiring all that was pretty. She was not often invited to join in the conversation of the others, nor did she desire it. Her own thoughts and reflections were habitually her best companions; and in observing the appearance of the country, the bearings of the roads, the difference of soil, the state of the harvest, the cottages, the cattle, the children, she found entertainment that could only have been heightened by having Edmund to speak to of what she felt. That was the only point of resemblance between her and the lady who sat by her; in every thing but a value for Edmund, Miss Crawford was very unlike her. She had none of Fanny's delicacy of taste, of mind, of feeling; she saw nature, inanimate nature, with little observation; her attention was all for men and women, her talents for the light and lively. In looking back after Edmund, however, when there was any stretch of road behind them, or when he gained on them in ascending a considerable hill, they were united, and a "there he is" broke at the same moment from them both, more than once.

For the first seven miles Miss Bertram had very little real comfort; her prospect always ended in Mr. Crawford and her sister sitting side by side full of conversation and merriment; and to see only his expressive profile as he turned with a smile to Julia, or to catch the laugh of the other was a perpetual source of irritation, which her own sense of propriety could but just smooth over. When Julia looked back, it was with a countenance of delight, and whenever she spoke to them, it was in the highest spirits; "her view of the country was charming, she wished they could all see it, &c." but her only offer of exchange was addressed to Miss Crawford, as they gained the summit of a long hill, and was not more inviting than this, "Here is a fine burst of country. I wish you had my seat, but I dare say you will not take it, let me press you ever so much," and Miss Crawford could hardly answer, before they were moving again at a good pace.

When they came within the influence of Sotherton associations, it was better for Miss Bertram, who might be said to have two strings to her bow. She had Rushworth-feelings, and Crawford-feelings, and in the vicinity of Sotherton, the former had considerable effect. Mr. Rushworth's consequence was hers. She could not tell Miss Crawford that "those woods belonged to Sotherton," she could not carelessly observe that "she believed that it was now all Mr. Rushworth's property on each side of the road," without elation of heart; and it was a pleasure to increase with their approach to the capital freehold mansion,[5] and ancient manorial residence of the family, with all its rights of Court-Leet and Court-Baron.[6]

"Now we shall have no more rough road, Miss Crawford, our difficulties are over. The rest of the way is such as it ought to be. Mr. Rushworth has made it since he succeeded to the estate. Here begins the village. Those cottages are really a disgrace.[7] The church spire is reckoned remarkably handsome. I am glad the church is not so close to the Great House as often happens in old places. The annoyance of the bells must be terrible. There is the parsonage; a tidy-looking house, and I understand the clergyman and his wife are very decent people. Those are alms-houses, built by some of the family. To the right is the steward's house; he is a very respectable man. Now we are coming to the lodge gates; but we have nearly a mile through the park still. It is not ugly, you see, at this end; there is some fine timber, but the situation of the house is dreadful. We go down hill to it for half-a-mile, and it is a pity, for it would not be an ill-looking place if it had a better approach."

Miss Crawford was not slow to admire; she pretty well guessed Miss Bertram's feelings, and made it a point of honour to promote her enjoyment to the utmost. Mrs. Norris was all delight and volubility; and even Fanny had something to say in admiration, and might be heard with complacency. Her eye was eagerly taking in every thing within her reach; and after being at some pains to get a view of the house, and observing that "it was a sort of building which she could not look at but with respect," she added, "Now, where is the avenue? The house fronts the east, I perceive. The avenue, therefore, must be at the back of it. Mr. Rushworth talked of the west front."

"Yes, it is exactly behind the house; begins at a little distance, and

5 *Freehold* in that the mansion is the property for life of Mr. Rushworth and his to transmit to his heirs.

6 These archaic legal terms advertise Sotherton's antiquity. They denote the legal powers—the "liberties of the manor"—that in feudal times the lord of the manor or his agent would have exercised, in for instance acting as the judge who heard the civil and criminal cases involving the tenants on his estate.

7 That these cottages are deemed disgraceful by Mr. Rushworth's bride-to-be does not bode well for their continued existence. When in *Northanger Abbey* General Tilney, another enthusiastic improver, takes Catherine Morland on a tour of the grounds surrounding his son's parsonage at Woodston, he seems alarmingly ready to tear down any buildings—including people's homes—that do not meet with Catherine's approval. One particular cottage is declared safe from demolition explicitly because she has happened to declare it "pretty" (II, 11).

For some contemporary commentators, the landed classes' enthusiasm for improving their estates seemed to go hand in hand with their growing disengagement from their social responsibilities. Maria's reference to the disgraceful look of the village near Sotherton suggests such disengagement. The implication is that for her rural poverty is a problem primarily because it spoils the view. As a great landscape designer, Humphry Repton was more reluctant to sweep away entire settlements than his predecessor Capability Brown had been before him, worrying, as he put it, that "a mistaken idea has prevailed, that the house should stand detached from every surrounding object" and finding it injudicious that "in many parts of the kingdom" whole villages had been destroyed "to give solitary importance to the insulated mansion" (*Observations on the Theory and Practice of Landscape Gardening*, p. 192). Even so, the designs for plantings that he proposed to his clients frequently served to screen from view all signs of the work and workers that sustained their estates.

8 The late seventeenth century had seen the beginnings of a national romance with oak woods that in Austen's day showed no signs of abating. Furnishing the hardwood timber needed for the warships of the Royal Navy, they were celebrated as a source of the nation's maritime power. Portrait painters like Thomas Gainsborough posed their sitters in front of oak trees to testify to their patriotism.

ascends for half-a-mile to the extremity of the grounds. You may see something of it here—something of the more distant trees. It is oak entirely."[8]

Miss Bertram could now speak with decided information of what she had known nothing about when Mr. Rushworth had asked her opinion; and her spirits were in as happy a flutter as vanity and pride could furnish, when they drove up to the spacious stone steps before the principal entrance.

Stoneleigh Abbey, a grand Elizabethan manor house in Warwickshire, is often said to be Austen's model for Sotherton. This early twentieth-century photograph shows the effects at Stoneleigh of the improvements Repton carried out a century earlier. It was Repton who diverted the river Avon so that it ran directly by the house.

## 9

MR. RUSHWORTH WAS AT THE DOOR to receive his fair lady, and the whole party were welcomed by him with due attention. In the drawing-room they were met with equal cordiality by the mother, and Miss Bertram had all the distinction with each that she could wish. After the business of arriving was over, it was first necessary to eat, and the doors were thrown open to admit them through one or two intermediate rooms into the appointed dining-parlour, where a collation was prepared with abundance and elegance. Much was said, and much was ate, and all went well. The particular object of the day was then considered. How would Mr. Crawford like, in what manner would he choose, to take a survey of the grounds?—Mr. Rushworth mentioned his curricle.[1] Mr. Crawford suggested the greater desirableness of some carriage which might convey more than two. "To be depriving themselves of the advantage of other eyes and other judgments, might be an evil even beyond the loss of present pleasure."

Mrs. Rushworth proposed that the chaise should be taken also; but this was scarcely received as an amendment; the young ladies neither smiled nor spoke. Her next proposition, of shewing the house to such of them as had not been there before, was more acceptable, for Miss Bertram was pleased to have its size displayed, and all were glad to be doing something.

The whole party rose accordingly, and under Mrs. Rushworth's guidance were shewn through a number of rooms, all lofty, and many large, and amply furnished in the taste of fifty years back, with shining floors, solid mahogany, rich damask, marble, gilding and carving,

1 A light, two-wheeled carriage seating a driver and a single passenger—often quite expensive, and a rather sporty vehicle for a character who has been introduced as a heavy young man. Henry Tilney in *Northanger Abbey* drives a curricle.

John Cordrey, the artist who in 1806 painted this gentleman with his curricle and matched pair of horses to pull it, appears to have specialized in oil paintings of horses and carriages.

2 Mrs. Rushworth's housekeeper would be an experienced guide because country house visiting was an increasingly popular pastime for genteel travelers—one in which the jaded Mary Crawford has apparently participated more often than she might like. In *Pride and Prejudice* Mrs. Reynolds, Darcy's housekeeper at Pemberley, has a well-defined sense of the itinerary that tourists like Elizabeth and her aunt and uncle should follow on their visit and of which rooms in the house will be open "to general inspection" (III, 1). At a time when few public art galleries or museums were in existence, houses like Sotherton were attractions for visitors in part because they offered experiences of history and art not available elsewhere.

3 The fictional Sotherton resembles in many respects the real Stoneleigh Abbey in Warwickshire, which the Austens visited with its new owner, their cousin Rev. Leigh, in 1806. Sotherton's past likewise looks to have been shaped by its owners' loyalty to the Stuart monarchy during the seventeenth-century Civil War. Stoneleigh had sheltered Charles I in 1642. The Leighs' loyalty to the Stuart line was so pronounced that in 1745 the family had been ready as well, at tremendous risk to their own safety, to harbor Charles Edward Stuart, the Young Pretender and leader of the third Jacobite rebellion.

4 Mr. Rushworth mentioned in Chap. 6 that Sotherton "stands in one of the lowest spots of the park," which precludes there being much of a view, or *prospect,* from the manor house's windows.

5 A form of property tax, based on the number of windows in a house, the window tax had been increased substantially in recent memory as a result of the Crown's need to fund its wars with France.

6 Through her reading of Walter Scott's poetry Fanny has already warmed her imagination with scenes of the past, even before this visit to Sotherton. She quotes Scott's wildly popular *The Lay of the Last Minstrel* (1805), a "romance of Border Chivalry" in six cantos, set in the Scottish borders in the sixteenth century and so at a time of violent feuding between English and Scottish clans. The lines Fanny remembers, misquoting slightly, are from the opening of the second canto. The Lady of

each handsome in its way. Of pictures there were abundance, and some few good, but the larger part were family portraits, no longer anything to any body but Mrs. Rushworth, who had been at great pains to learn all that the housekeeper could teach, and was now almost equally well qualified to shew the house.[2] On the present occasion, she addressed herself chiefly to Miss Crawford and Fanny, but there was no comparison in the willingness of their attention, for Miss Crawford, who had seen scores of great houses, and cared for none of them, had only the appearance of civilly listening, while Fanny, to whom every thing was almost as interesting as it was new, attended with unaffected earnestness to all that Mrs. Rushworth could relate of the family in former times, its rise and grandeur, regal visits and loyal efforts,[3] delighted to connect any thing with history already known, or warm her imagination with scenes of the past.

The situation of the house excluded the possibility of much prospect from any of the rooms;[4] and while Fanny and some of the others were attending Mrs. Rushworth, Henry Crawford was looking grave and shaking his head at the windows. Every room on the west front looked across a lawn to the beginning of the avenue immediately beyond tall iron palisades and gates.

Having visited many more rooms than could be supposed to be of any other use than to contribute to the window tax,[5] and find employment for housemaids, "Now," said Mrs. Rushworth, "we are coming to the chapel, which properly we ought to enter from above, and look down upon; but as we are quite among friends, I will take you in this way, if you will excuse me."

They entered. Fanny's imagination had prepared her for something grander than a mere, spacious, oblong room, fitted up for the purpose of devotion—with nothing more striking or more solemn than the profusion of mahogany, and the crimson velvet cushions appearing over the ledge of the family gallery above. "I am disappointed," said she, in a low voice, to Edmund. "This is not my idea of a chapel. There is nothing awful here, nothing melancholy, nothing grand. Here are no aisles, no arches, no inscriptions, no banners. No banners, cousin, to be 'blown by the night wind of Heaven.' No signs that a 'Scottish monarch sleeps below.'"[6]

"You forget, Fanny, how lately all this has been built, and for how confined a purpose, compared with the old chapels of castles and monasteries. It was only for the private use of the family. They have been buried, I suppose, in the parish church. *There* you must look for the banners and the atchievements."[7]

"It was foolish of me not to think of all that, but I am disappointed."

Mrs. Rushworth began her relation. "This chapel was fitted up as you see it, in James the Second's time.[8] Before that period, as I understand, the pews were only wainscot; and there is some reason to think that the linings and cushions of the pulpit and family-seat were only purple cloth; but this is not quite certain. It is a handsome chapel, and was formerly in constant use both morning and evening. Prayers were always read in it by the domestic chaplain, within the memory of many. But the late Mr. Rushworth left it off."

"Every generation has its improvements," said Miss Crawford, with a smile, to Edmund.

Mrs. Rushworth was gone to repeat her lesson to Mr. Crawford; and Edmund, Fanny, and Miss Crawford remained in a cluster together.

"It is a pity," cried Fanny, "that the custom should have been discontinued. It was a valuable part of former times. There is something in a chapel and chaplain so much in character with a great house, with one's ideas of what such a household should be! A whole family assembling regularly for the purpose of prayer, is fine!"

"Very fine indeed!" said Miss Crawford, laughing. "It must do the heads of the family a great deal of good to force all the poor housemaids and footmen to leave business and pleasure, and say their prayers here twice a day, while they are inventing excuses themselves for staying away."

"*That* is hardly Fanny's idea of a family assembling," said Edmund. "If the master and mistress do *not* attend themselves, there must be more harm than good in the custom."

"At any rate, it is safer to leave people to their own devices on such subjects. Every body likes to go their own way—to choose their own time and manner of devotion. The obligation of attendance, the for-

Branksome Hall has sent her retainer William Deloraine on a mysterious mission in the dead of night to Melrose Abbey, where he is to recover a magic book that she means to use for evil purposes. The abbey, a traditional burial place for the kings of Scotland, is described in canto 2, stanza 10, as a place where "Full many a scutcheon and banner, riven,/Shook to the cold night-wind of heaven" (*The Poetical Works of Sir Walter Scott* [Glasgow: Grand Colosseum Warehouse, n.d.], p. 13). Melrose's ruins may still be visited.

7 Square- or diamond-shaped panels which are placed in a church and display the coats of arms of the dead.

8 Mrs. Rushworth's spiel would reveal to attentive listeners that the refurbishing of the Sotherton chapel occurred at a crucial moment of turmoil in the history of the Anglican Church. The three-year reign of King James II came to an end in 1688. In that year of "Glorious Revolution," his son-in-law, Prince William of Orange, deposed him with the support of the English Parliament, which feared that the king aimed to restore Catholicism in England. If, by means of this detail, the chapel is being presented to us, as Colin Jager has proposed, as "a repository of the religious history of the eighteenth century," it is that much more troubling that the most recent generation of Rushworths has retreated from this space and left it, as the narrator tells us later, to "silence and stillness" (Colin Jager, "*Mansfield Park* and the End of Natural Theology," *Modern Language Quarterly* 63, 1 [2002]: 36). Mrs. Rushworth (or Austen) seems to be getting her dates wrong in implying here that the chapel furnishings were redone in mahogany during King James's reign. This wood was not commonly used for furniture in England until the 1710s or 1720s, when it first began to be imported in large quantities from the Caribbean, where it was harvested by the colonies' slave population. The narrator's earlier reference to the "solid mahogany" found in the other rooms of the house and her explanation that those rooms were "furnished in the taste of fifty years back" are more easily accommodated by the chronology that historians of English furniture propose when they speak of an "age of mahogany" extending from the 1710s or 1720s into the 1760s or 1770s.

9 In her vision of the tedium of Sotherton life in the last century, Mary both refers to the household's servant-girls using the old-fashioned honorific "Mrs." (then applied to both unmarried and married women) and bestows on them two markedly old-fashioned names, the better to make her point about the distance separating Sotherton's past from her up-to-date present.

10 In the older sense of the term denoting a space for private devotion.

An engraved portrait of Sir Walter Scott, author of *The Lay of the Last Minstrel,* based on an 1808 painting by Sir Henry Raeburn. Scott, like Fanny, loved to warm his "imagination with scenes of the past." Raeburn acknowledges that aspect of his character by picturing Scott sitting among the ruins of a medieval tower.

mality, the restraint, the length of time—altogether it is a formidable thing, and what nobody likes: and if the good people who used to kneel and gape in that gallery could have foreseen that the time would ever come when men and women might lie another ten minutes in bed, when they woke with a headach, without danger of reprobation, because chapel was missed, they would have jumped with joy and envy. Cannot you imagine with what unwilling feelings the former belles of the house of Rushworth did many a time repair to this chapel? The young Mrs. Eleanors and Mrs. Bridgets[9]—starched up into seeming piety, but with heads full of something very different—especially if the poor chaplain were not worth looking at—and, in those days, I fancy parsons were very inferior even to what they are now."

For a few moments she was unanswered. Fanny coloured and looked at Edmund, but felt too angry for speech; and he needed a little recollection before he could say, "Your lively mind can hardly be serious even on serious subjects. You have given us an amusing sketch, and human nature cannot say it was not so. We must all feel *at times* the difficulty of fixing our thoughts as we could wish; but if you are supposing it a frequent thing, that is to say, a weakness grown into a habit from neglect, what could be expected from the *private* devotions of such persons? Do you think the minds which are suffered, which are indulged in wanderings in a chapel, would be more collected in a closet?"[10]

"Yes, very likely. They would have two chances at least in their favour. There would be less to distract the attention from without, and it would not be tried so long."

"The mind which does not struggle against itself under *one* circumstance, would find objects to distract it in the *other,* I believe; and the influence of the place and of example may often rouse better feelings than are begun with. The greater length of the service, however, I admit to be sometimes too hard a stretch upon the mind. One wishes it were not so—but I have not yet left Oxford long enough to forget what chapel prayers are."

While this was passing, the rest of the party being scattered about the chapel, Julia called Mr. Crawford's attention to her sister, by saying, "Do look at Mr. Rushworth and Maria, standing side by side, exactly as if the ceremony were going to be performed. Have not they completely the air of it?"

Mr. Crawford smiled his acquiescence, and stepping forward to Maria, said, in a voice which she only could hear, "I do not like to see Miss Bertram so near the altar."

Starting, the lady instinctively moved a step or two, but recovering herself in a moment, affected to laugh, and asked him, in a tone not much louder, "if he would give her away?"

"I am afraid I should do it very awkwardly," was his reply, with a look of meaning.

Julia joining them at the moment, carried on the joke.

"Upon my word, it is really a pity that it should not take place directly, if we had but a proper license,[11] for here we are altogether, and nothing in the world could be more snug and pleasant." And she talked and laughed about it with so little caution, as to catch the comprehension of Mr. Rushworth and his mother, and expose her sister to the whispered gallantries of her lover, while Mrs. Rushworth spoke with proper smiles and dignity of its being a most happy event to her whenever it took place.

"If Edmund were but in orders!" cried Julia, and running to where he stood with Miss Crawford and Fanny; "My dear Edmund, if you were but in orders now, you might perform the ceremony directly. How unlucky that you are not ordained, Mr. Rushworth and Maria are quite ready."

Miss Crawford's countenance, as Julia spoke, might have amused a disinterested observer. She looked almost aghast under the new idea she was receiving. Fanny pitied her. "How distressed she will be at what she said just now," passed across her mind.

"Ordained!" said Miss Crawford; "what, are you to be a clergyman?"

"Yes, I shall take orders soon after my father's return—probably at Christmas."

Miss Crawford rallying her spirits, and recovering her complexion, replied only, "If I had known this before, I would have spoken of the cloth with more respect," and turned the subject.[12]

The chapel was soon afterwards left to the silence and stillness which reigned in it with few interruptions throughout the year. Miss

11 In the wake of England's 1753 reform of its marriage laws, for a marriage to be valid it had to have been performed in a church either after the banns had been read from the pulpit on three consecutive Sundays or after a license had been obtained from the bishop of the diocese or his surrogate. Couples hoping to avoid publicity and opting for the latter method had to pay a fee for their license.

12 The cloth are the clergy.

J. M. W. Turner's *Melrose Abbey by Midnight,* picturing the site that Scott's *The Lay of the Last Minstrel* had made famous, might represent Fanny's "idea of a chapel" better than the Sotherton chapel does.

13 The ornamental part of the grounds, as distinct from the kitchen gardens or orchards.

14 Those walls are a gift to the improver, Henry appears to suggest, likely because they so evidently invite demolition. In the ancient style of gardening that Repton hoped to see superseded, the views on an estate were, he said, too often made "confined, formal, and dull by lofty walls and clipped hedges" (*Observations on the Theory and Practice of Landscape Gardening*, p. 187).

15 The part of the grounds that was planted with fast-growing trees and laid out in shady, winding walks. The letter to her daughter-in-law Mary that Mrs. Austen wrote in 1806 while visiting Stoneleigh Abbey described how she and her daughters walked a good deal in the abbey's beautiful woods during their visit, the more happily because the woods were "impenetrable to the sun, even in the middle of an August day" (quoted in Constance Hill, *Jane Austen: Her Homes and Her Friends* [London: Bodley Head, 1923], p. 164). In the mornings the visitors joined in family prayers in the house's handsome chapel.

Bertram, displeased with her sister, led the way, and all seemed to feel that they had been there long enough.

The lower part of the house had been now entirely shown, and Mrs. Rushworth, never weary in the cause, would have proceeded towards the principal stair-case, and taken them through all the rooms above, if her son had not interposed with a doubt of there being time enough. "For if," said he, with the sort of self-evident proposition which many a clearer head does not always avoid—"we are *too* long going over the house, we shall not have time for what is to be done out of doors. It is past two, and we are to dine at five."

Mrs. Rushworth submitted, and the question of surveying the grounds, with the who and the how, was likely to be more fully agitated, and Mrs. Norris was beginning to arrange by what junction of carriages and horses most could be done, when the young people, meeting with an outward door, temptingly open on a flight of steps which led immediately to turf and shrubs, and all the sweets of pleasure-grounds,[13] as by one impulse, one wish for air and liberty, all walked out.

"Suppose we turn down here for the present," said Mrs. Rushworth, civilly taking the hint and following them. "Here are the greatest number of our plants, and here are the curious pheasants."

"Query," said Mr. Crawford, looking round him, "whether we may not find something to employ us here, before we go farther? I see walls of great promise.[14] Mr. Rushworth, shall we summon a council on this lawn?"

"James," said Mrs. Rushworth to her son, "I believe the wilderness will be new to all the party.[15] The Miss Bertrams have never seen the wilderness yet."

No objection was made, but for some time there seemed no inclination to move in any plan, or to any distance. All were attracted at first by the plants or the pheasants, and all dispersed about in happy independence. Mr. Crawford was the first to move forward, to examine the capabilities of that end of the house. The lawn, bounded on each side by a high wall, contained beyond the first planted area a bowling-green, and beyond the bowling-green a long terrace walk, backed by iron palissades, and commanding a view over them into the tops of the trees of the wilderness immediately adjoining. It was a good spot for fault-finding. Mr. Crawford was soon followed by Miss Bertram and Mr. Rushworth, and when after a little time the others began to form into parties, these three were found in busy consultation on the terrace by Edmund, Miss Crawford and Fanny, who seemed as naturally to unite, and who after a short participation of their regrets and difficulties, left them and walked on. The remaining three, Mrs. Rushworth, Mrs. Norris, and Julia, were still far behind; for Julia, whose happy star no longer prevailed, was obliged to keep by the side of Mrs. Rushworth, and restrain her impatient feet to that lady's slow pace, while her aunt, having fallen in with the housekeeper, who was come out to feed the pheasants, was lingering behind in gossip with her. Poor Julia, the only one out of the nine not tolerably satisfied with their lot, was now in a state of complete penance, and as different from the Julia of the barouche-box as could well be imagined. The politeness which she had been brought up to practise as a duty, made it impossible for her to escape; while the want of that higher species of self-command, that just consideration of others, that knowledge of her own heart, that principle of right which had not formed any essential part of her education, made her miserable under it.

"This is insufferably hot," said Miss Crawford when they had taken one turn on the terrace, and were drawing a second time to the door in the middle which opened to the wilderness. "Shall any of us object to being comfortable? Here is a nice little wood, if one can but get into it. What happiness if the door should not be locked!—but of course it is, for in these great places, the gardeners are the only people who can go where they like."

The door, however, proved not to be locked, and they were all agreed in turning joyfully through it, and leaving the unmitigated glare of day behind. A considerable flight of steps landed them in the wilderness, which was a planted wood of about two acres, and though chiefly of larch and laurel, and beech cut down, and though laid out with too much regularity,[16] was darkness and shade, and natural beauty, compared with the bowling-green and the terrace. They all felt the refreshment of it, and for some time could only walk and

16 The grounds at Sotherton are laid out in an early eighteenth-century style that is no longer fashionable, as this description of the Sotherton wilderness, and in particular its walks lined with trimmed beech hedges ("beech cut down"), confirms.

17 To set the *ton* is to be a trendsetter.

18 The Reverend Hugh Blair was widely admired both for the five volumes of sermons he published between 1777 and 1801 and for the *Lectures on Rhetoric and Belles-Lettres* (1783), which set out the fundamentals of tasteful composition and literary appreciation. Mary is being a bit facetious when she ascribes good sense to clergymen who borrow their sermons from others' books, but the practice had in fact been encouraged by the eighteenth-century Church of England, which favored highly crafted formal sermons and deplored the way Methodist preachers seemed by contrast to make a point of extemporizing in the pulpit. A handbook from 1753 thus advised young clergymen in the Church of England "not to trust at first to their own compositions, but to furnish themselves with a provision of the best sermons" (quoted in Christina Lupton, "Creating the Writer of the Cleric's Words," *Journal for Eighteenth-Century Studies*, vol. 34, no. 2 [2011]: 171). Attitudes were changing, however. In his critique of the fashionable clergy of his day, William Cowper pointed out in *The Task* that as their office should have made them "messengers of truth," it was objectionable to see them "reading what they never wrote" (*The Task and Selected Other Poems*, book 2, p. 98, line 411).

admire. At length, after a short pause, Miss Crawford began with, "So you are to be a clergyman, Mr. Bertram. This is rather a surprise to me."

"Why should it surprise you? You must suppose me designed for some profession, and might perceive that I am neither a lawyer, nor a soldier, nor a sailor."

"Very true; but, in short, it had not occurred to me. And you know there is generally an uncle or a grandfather to leave a fortune to the second son."

"A very praiseworthy practice," said Edmund, "but not quite universal. I am one of the exceptions, and *being* one, must do something for myself."

"But why are you to be a clergyman? I thought *that* was always the lot of the youngest, where there were many to choose before him."

"Do you think the church itself never chosen then?"

"*Never* is a black word. But yes, in the *never* of conversation which means *not very often,* I do think it. For what is to be done in the church? Men love to distinguish themselves, and in either of the other lines, distinction may be gained, but not in the church. A clergyman is nothing."

"The *nothing* of conversation has its gradations, I hope, as well as the *never.* A clergyman cannot be high in state or fashion. He must not head mobs, or set the ton in dress.[17] But I cannot call that situation nothing, which has the charge of all that is of the first importance to mankind, individually or collectively considered, temporally and eternally—which has the guardianship of religion and morals, and consequently of the manners which result from their influence. No one here can call the *office* nothing. If the man who holds it is so, it is by the neglect of his duty, by foregoing its just importance, and stepping out of his place to appear what he ought not to appear."

"*You* assign greater consequence to the clergyman than one has been used to hear given, or than I can quite comprehend. One does not see much of this influence and importance in society, and how can it be acquired where they are so seldom seen themselves? How can two sermons a week, even supposing them worth hearing, supposing the preacher to have the sense to prefer Blair's to his own, do all that you speak of?[18] govern the conduct and fashion the manners of a large congregation for the rest of the week? One scarcely sees a clergyman out of his pulpit."

"*You* are speaking of London, *I* am speaking of the nation at large."

"The metropolis, I imagine, is a pretty fair sample of the rest."

"Not, I should hope, of the proportion of virtue to vice throughout the kingdom. We do not look in great cities for our best morality. It is not there, that respectable people of any denomination can do most good; and it certainly is not there, that the influence of the clergy can be most felt. A fine preacher is followed and admired; but it is not in fine preaching only that a good clergyman will be useful in his parish and his neighbourhood, where the parish and neighbourhood are of a size capable of knowing his private character, and observing his general conduct, which in London can rarely be the case. The clergy are lost there in the crowds of their parishioners. They are known to the largest part only as preachers. And with regard to their influencing public manners, Miss Crawford must not misunderstand me, or suppose I mean to call them the arbiters of good breeding, the regulators of refinement and courtesy, the masters of the ceremonies of life. The *manners* I speak of, might rather be called *conduct,* perhaps, the result of good principles; the effect, in short, of those doctrines which it is their duty to teach and recommend; and it will, I believe, be everywhere found, that as the clergy are, or are not what they ought to be, so are the rest of the nation."

"Certainly," said Fanny with gentle earnestness.

"There," cried Miss Crawford, "you have quite convinced Miss Price already."

"I wish I could convince Miss Crawford too."

"I do not think you ever will," said she with an arch smile; "I am just as much surprised now as I was at first that you should intend to take orders. You really are fit for something better. Come, do change your mind. It is not too late. Go into the law."

"Go into the law! With as much ease as I was told to go into this wilderness."

"Now you are going to say something about law being the worst wilderness of the two, but I forestall you; remember I have forestalled you."

"You need not hurry when the object is only to prevent my saying

19 Witticism.

20 A furlong is an eighth of a mile.

a bon-mot,[19] for there is not the least wit in my nature. I am a very matter of fact, plain spoken being, and may blunder on the borders of a repartee for half an hour together without striking it out."

A general silence succeeded. Each was thoughtful. Fanny made the first interruption by saying, "I wonder that I should be tired with only walking in this sweet wood; but the next time we come to a seat, if it is not disagreeable to you, I should be glad to sit down for a little while."

"My dear Fanny," cried Edmund, immediately drawing her arm within his, "how thoughtless I have been! I hope you are not very tired. Perhaps," turning to Miss Crawford, "my other companion may do me the honour of taking an arm."

"Thank you, but I am not at all tired." She took it, however, as she spoke, and the gratification of having her do so, of feeling such a connection for the first time, made him a little forgetful of Fanny. "You scarcely touch me," said he. "You do not make me of any use. What a difference in the weight of a woman's arm from that of a man! At Oxford I have been a good deal used to have a man lean on me for the length of a street, and you are only a fly in the comparison."

"I am really not tired, which I almost wonder at; for we must have walked at least a mile in this wood. Do not you think we have?"

"Not half a mile," was his sturdy answer; for he was not yet so much in love as to measure distance, or reckon time, with feminine lawlessness.

"Oh! you do not consider how much we have wound about. We have taken such a very serpentine course; and the wood itself must be half a mile long in a straight line, for we have never seen the end of it yet, since we left the first great path."

"But if you remember, before we left that first great path, we saw directly to the end of it. We looked down the whole vista, and saw it closed by iron gates, and it could not have been more than a furlong in length."[20]

"Oh! I know nothing of your furlongs, but I am sure it is a very long wood; and that we have been winding in and out ever since we came into it; and therefore when I say that we have walked a mile in it, I must speak within compass."

"We have been exactly a quarter of an hour here," said Edmund, taking out his watch. "Do you think we are walking four miles an hour?"

"Oh! do not attack me with your watch. A watch is always too fast or too slow. I cannot be dictated to by a watch."

A few steps farther brought them out at the bottom of the very walk they had been talking of; and standing back, well shaded and sheltered, and looking over a ha-ha into the park, was a comfortable-sized bench, on which they all sat down.[21]

"I am afraid you are very tired, Fanny," said Edmund, observing her; "why would not you speak sooner? This will be a bad day's amusement for you, if you are to be knocked up. Every sort of exercise fatigues her so soon, Miss Crawford, except riding."

"How abominable in you, then, to let me engross her horse as I did all last week! I am ashamed of you and of myself, but it shall never happen again."

"*Your* attentiveness and consideration makes me more sensible of my own neglect. Fanny's interest seems in safer hands with you than with me."

21 For Horace Walpole in his "History of the Modern Taste in Gardening," a watershed moment in the development of the modern English garden occurred in the early eighteenth century when the royal gardener at Kew, Charles Bridgeman, ceased to use walls for boundaries and invented the ha-ha to take their place—"an attempt then deemed so astonishing, that the common people called them Ha! Ha's! to express their surprize at finding a sudden and unperceived check to their walk" (*Anecdotes of Painting in England . . . To which is added The History of the Modern Taste in Gardening,* 2nd ed. [London: J. Dodsley, 1782], vol. 4, p. 288). A ha-ha was a turfed ditch constructed in such a way as to be invisible from the country house, so ensuring the landowners an uninterrupted view across their estate while nonetheless preventing deer and cattle from straying into the pleasure grounds. Through this device, the park lying beyond the ha-ha was, as Walpole put it, "harmonized" with the "lawn within," and "the garden in its turn was set free from its prim regularity" and permitted to "assort with the wilder country without" (p. 288).

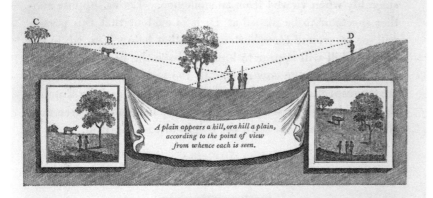

to advantage.   The difference betwixt viewing ground from the bottom of a valley, or the side of a hill, will be best explained by the following diagram, where the rules of perspective again assist the scientific improver.

*A plain appears a hill, or a hill a plain, according to the point of view from whence each is seen.*

The spectator at A. in looking up the hill towards C. will lose all the ground that is fore-shortened ; and every object

With this diagram in his *Observations on the Theory and Practice of Landscape Gardening,* Humphry Repton demonstrates the principle that, as he says, the "apparent shape of the ground will be altered by the situation of the spectator." The effect of the ha-ha in a landscape is equally a function of the laws of perspective exemplified here.

22 It is well past noon when Mary says this, but, as noted earlier, "morning" in the early nineteenth century named the whole of the period between dawn and dinner.

"That she should be tired now, however, gives me no surprise; for there is nothing in the course of one's duties so fatiguing as what we have been doing this morning[22]—seeing a great house, dawdling from one room to another—straining one's eyes and one's attention—hearing what one does not understand—admiring what one does not care for.—It is generally allowed to be the greatest bore in the world, and Miss Price has found it so, though she did not know it."

"I shall soon be rested," said Fanny; "to sit in the shade on a fine day, and look upon verdure, is the most perfect refreshment."

After sitting a little while, Miss Crawford was up again. "I must move," said she, "resting fatigues me.—I have looked across the ha-ha till I am weary. I must go and look through that iron gate at the same view, without being able to see it so well."

Edmund left the seat likewise. "Now, Miss Crawford, if you will look up the walk, you will convince yourself that it cannot be half a mile long, or half half a mile."

"It is an immense distance," said she; "I see *that* with a glance."

He still reasoned with her, but in vain. She would not calculate, she would not compare. She would only smile and assert. The greatest degree of rational consistency could not have been more engaging, and they talked with mutual satisfaction. At last it was agreed that they should endeavour to determine the dimensions of the wood by walking a little more about it. They would go to one end of it, in the line they were then in (for there was a straight green walk along the bottom by the side of the ha-ha,) and perhaps turn a little way in some other direction, if it seemed likely to assist them, and be back in a few minutes. Fanny said she was rested, and would have moved too, but this was not suffered. Edmund urged her remaining where she was with an earnestness which she could not resist, and she was left on the bench to think with pleasure of her cousin's care, but with great regret that she was not stronger. She watched them till they had turned the corner, and listened till all sound of them had ceased.

# IO

A QUARTER OF AN HOUR, twenty minutes, passed away, and Fanny was still thinking of Edmund, Miss Crawford, and herself, without interruption from any one. She began to be surprised at being left so long, and to listen with an anxious desire of hearing their steps and their voices again. She listened, and at length she heard; she heard voices and feet approaching; but she had just satisfied herself that it was not those she wanted, when Miss Bertram, Mr. Rushworth, and Mr. Crawford issued from the same path which she had trod herself, and were before her.

"Miss Price all alone!" and "My dear Fanny, how comes this?" were the first salutations. She told her story. "Poor dear Fanny," cried her cousin, "how ill you have been used by them! You had better have staid with us."

Then seating herself with a gentleman on each side, she resumed the conversation which had engaged them before, and discussed the possibility of improvements with much animation. Nothing was fixed on—but Henry Crawford was full of ideas and projects, and, generally speaking, whatever he proposed was immediately approved, first by her, and then by Mr. Rushworth, whose principal business seemed to be to hear the others, and who scarcely risked an original thought of his own beyond a wish that they had seen his friend Smith's place.

After some minutes spent in this way, Miss Bertram observing the iron gate, expressed a wish of passing through it into the park, that

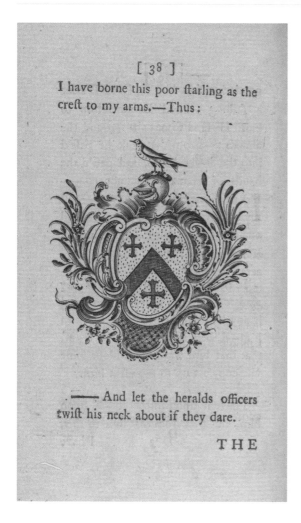

[ 38 ]

I have borne this poor ſtarling as the creſt to my arms.——Thus:

——— And let the heralds officers twiſt his neck about if they dare.

THE

Page in the first edition of Sterne's *A Sentimental Journey through France and Italy*. Here, to memorialize the caged starling who "cannot get out," Parson Yorick adds it in effigy to his coat of arms.

their views and their plans might be more comprehensive. It was the very thing of all others to be wished, it was the best, it was the only way of proceeding with any advantage, in Henry Crawford's opinion; and he directly saw a knoll not half a mile off, which would give them exactly the requisite command of the house. Go therefore they must to that knoll, and through that gate; but the gate was locked. Mr. Rushworth wished he had brought the key; he had been very near thinking whether he should not bring the key; he was determined he would never come without the key again; but still this did not remove the present evil. They could not get through; and as Miss Bertram's inclination for so doing did by no means lessen, it ended in Mr. Rushworth's declaring outright that he would go and fetch the key. He set off accordingly.

"It is undoubtedly the best thing we can do now, as we are so far from the house already," said Mr. Crawford, when he was gone.

"Yes, there is nothing else to be done. But now, sincerely, do not you find the place altogether worse than you expected?"

"No, indeed, far otherwise. I find it better, grander, more complete in its style, though that style may not be the best. And to tell you the truth," speaking rather lower, "I do not think that *I* shall ever see Sotherton again with so much pleasure as I do now. Another summer will hardly improve it to me."

After a moment's embarrassment the lady replied, "You are too much a man of the world not to see with the eyes of the world. If other people think Sotherton improved, I have no doubt that you will."

"I am afraid I am not quite so much the man of the world as might be good for me in some points. My feelings are not quite so evanescent, nor my memory of the past under such easy dominion as one finds to be the case with men of the world."

This was followed by a short silence. Miss Bertram began again. "You seemed to enjoy your drive here very much this morning. I was glad to see you so well entertained. You and Julia were laughing the whole way."

"Were we? Yes, I believe we were; but I have not the least recollection at what. Oh! I believe I was relating to her some ridiculous stories of an old Irish groom of my uncle's. Your sister loves to laugh."

"You think her more light-hearted than I am."

"More easily amused," he replied, "consequently you know," smiling, "better company. I could not have hoped to entertain *you* with Irish anecdotes during a ten miles' drive."

"Naturally, I believe, I am as lively as Julia, but I have more to think of now."

"You have undoubtedly—and there are situations in which very high spirits would denote insensibility. Your prospects, however, are too fair to justify want of spirits. You have a very smiling scene before you."

"Do you mean literally or figuratively? Literally, I conclude. Yes, certainly, the sun shines and the park looks very cheerful. But unluckily that iron gate, that ha-ha, give me a feeling of restraint and hardship. I cannot get out, as the starling said."[1] As she spoke, and it was with expression, she walked to the gate; he followed her. "Mr. Rushworth is so long fetching this key!"

"And for the world you would not get out without the key and without Mr. Rushworth's authority and protection, or I think you might with little difficulty pass round the edge of the gate, here, with my assistance; I think it might be done, if you really wished to be more at large, and could allow yourself to think it not prohibited."

"Prohibited! nonsense! I certainly can get out that way, and I will. Mr. Rushworth will be here in a moment, you know—we shall not be out of sight."

"Or if we are, Miss Price will be so good as to tell him, that he will find us near that knoll, the grove of oak on the knoll."

Fanny, feeling all this to be wrong, could not help making an effort to prevent it. "You will hurt yourself, Miss Bertram," she cried, "you will certainly hurt yourself against those spikes—you will tear your gown—you will be in danger of slipping into the ha-ha. You had better not go."

Her cousin was safe on the other side, while these words were spoken, and smiling with all the good-humour of success, she said, "Thank you, my dear Fanny, but I and my gown are alive and well, and so good bye."

1 Maria alludes to an episode in Laurence Sterne's 1769 novel, *A Sentimental Journey through France and Italy*. Yorick, Sterne's first-person narrator, has forgotten to bring his passport with him on a visit to Paris. When he hears that a police lieutenant has been inquiring after him at his hotel, he begins to fear for his liberty and think gloomily about Paris's notorious prison, the Bastille. At this point Yorick overhears a starling kept in a cage at his hotel which has been taught to speak the words "I can't get out." Knowing that the words are uttered mechanically and that the starling must speak without understanding, Yorick nonetheless is haunted by the bird's cry, but he fails in his attempt to liberate the bird from its cage. The encounter sets him musing on slavery, the bitter draught that "thousands in all ages have been made to drink" (*A Sentimental Journey*, ed. Ian Jack [Oxford: Oxford University Press, 1984], pp. 71–72).

Sterne reiterates here a contrast between British liberty and French despotism that would have been very familiar to his late eighteenth-century readership. It structured discussions of the nations' respective styles of gardening as well. Austen's allusion to Sterne's episode transforms it, by eliminating the comparison between the nations and intimating instead to her British readers that confinement may equally define the landscape of home. Sotherton, we've already heard Mr. Rushworth say, feels like a prison. Still, as John Wiltshire points out in his edition of *Mansfield Park* (Cambridge: Cambridge University Press, 2005), Austen may wish readers to infer that, like Sterne's starling, "Maria is speaking what she does not understand" (p. 670, n. 3).

Fanny was again left to her solitude, and with no increase of pleasant feelings, for she was sorry for almost all that she had seen and heard, astonished at Miss Bertram, and angry with Mr. Crawford. By taking a circuitous, and as it appeared to her, very unreasonable direction to the knoll, they were soon beyond her eye; and for some minutes longer she remained without sight or sound of any companion. She seemed to have the little wood all to herself. She could almost have thought, that Edmund and Miss Crawford had left it, but that it was impossible for Edmund to forget her so entirely.

She was again roused from disagreeable musings by sudden footsteps, somebody was coming at a quick pace down the principal walk. She expected Mr. Rushworth, but it was Julia, who hot and out of breath, and with a look of disappointment, cried out on seeing her, "Heyday! Where are the others? I thought Maria and Mr. Crawford were with you."

Fanny explained.

"A pretty trick, upon my word! I cannot see them any where," looking eagerly into the park. "But they cannot be very far off, and I think I am equal to as much as Maria, even without help."

"But, Julia, Mr. Rushworth will be here in a moment with the key. Do wait for Mr. Rushworth."

"Not I, indeed. I have had enough of the family for one morning. Why, child, I have but this moment escaped from his horrible mother. Such a penance as I have been enduring, while you were sitting here so composed and so happy! It might have been as well, perhaps, if you had been in my place, but you always contrive to keep out of these scrapes."

This was a most unjust reflection, but Fanny could allow for it, and let it pass; Julia was vexed, and her temper was hasty, but she felt that it would not last, and therefore taking no notice, only asked her if she had not seen Mr. Rushworth.

"Yes, yes, we saw him. He was posting away as if upon life and death, and could but just spare time to tell us his errand, and where you all were."

"It is a pity he should have so much trouble for nothing."

"*That* is Miss Maria's concern. I am not obliged to punish myself for *her* sins. The mother I could not avoid, as long as my tiresome aunt was dancing about with the housekeeper, but the son I *can* get away from."

And she immediately scrambled across the fence, and walked away, not attending to Fanny's last question of whether she had seen anything of Miss Crawford and Edmund. The sort of dread in which Fanny now sat of seeing Mr. Rushworth prevented her thinking so much of their continued absence, however, as she might have done. She felt that he had been very ill-used, and was quite unhappy in having to communicate what had passed. He joined her within five minutes after Julia's exit; and though she made the best of the story, he was evidently mortified and displeased in no common degree. At first he scarcely said any thing; his looks only expressed his extreme surprise and vexation, and he walked to the gate and stood there, without seeming to know what to do.

"They desired me to stay—my cousin Maria charged me to say that you would find them at that knoll, or thereabouts."

"I do not believe I shall go any farther," said he sullenly; "I see nothing of them. By the time I get to the knoll, they may be gone some where else. I have had walking enough."

And he sat down with a most gloomy countenance by Fanny.

"I am very sorry," said she; "it is very unlucky." And she longed to be able to say something more to the purpose.

After an interval of silence, "I think they might as well have staid for me," said he.

"Miss Bertram thought you would follow her."

"I should not have had to follow her if she had staid."

This could not be denied, and Fanny was silenced. After another pause, he went on: "Pray, Miss Price, are you such a great admirer of this Mr. Crawford as some people are? For my part, I can see nothing in him."

"I do not think him at all handsome."

"Handsome! Nobody can call such an under-sized man handsome. He is not five foot nine. I should not wonder if he is not more than

Sir Joshua Reynolds's 1760 portrait, here in a copy engraved by Edward Fisher, pictures Laurence Sterne with the manuscript for his famous work, *The Life and Opinions of Tristram Shandy,* at his elbow and with his wig askew. The pose gives the clergyman turned novelist a fittingly raffish look.

*He walked to the gate and stood there without seeming to know what to do.*

Charles Edmund Brock, who at the end of the nineteenth century first supplied the illustrations for the often-reprinted J. M. Dent reissue of Austen's novels, evokes nicely just how puzzled Mr. Rushworth is when he finds that his bride-to-be has slipped away during his absence.

five foot eight. I think he is an ill-looking fellow. In my opinion, these Crawfords are no addition at all. We did very well without them."

A small sigh escaped Fanny here, and she did not know how to contradict him.

"If I had made any difficulty about fetching the key, there might have been some excuse, but I went the very moment she said she wanted it."

"Nothing could be more obliging than your manner, I am sure, and I dare say you walked as fast as you could; but still it is some distance, you know, from this spot to the house, quite into the house; and when people are waiting, they are bad judges of time, and every half minute seems like five."

He got up and walked to the gate again, and "wished he had had the key about him at the time." Fanny thought she discerned in his standing there, an indication of relenting, which encouraged her to another attempt, and she said, therefore, "It is a pity you should not join them. They expected to have a better view of the house from that part of the park, and will be thinking how it may be improved; and nothing of that sort, you know, can be settled without you."

She found herself more successful in sending away, than in retaining a companion. Mr. Rushworth was worked on. "Well," said he, "if you really think I had better go; it would be foolish to bring the key for nothing." And letting himself out, he walked off without farther ceremony.

Fanny's thoughts were now all engrossed by the two who had left her so long ago, and getting quite impatient, she resolved to go in search of them. She followed their steps along the bottom walk, and had just turned up into another, when the voice and the laugh of Miss Crawford once more caught her ear; the sound approached, and a few more windings brought them before her. They were just returned into the wilderness from the park, to which a side gate, not fastened, had tempted them very soon after their leaving her, and they had been across a portion of the park into the very avenue which Fanny had been hoping the whole morning to reach at last; and had been sitting down under one of the trees. This was their history. It was evident that they had been spending their time pleasantly, and were not aware of the length of their absence. Fanny's best consolation was in being assured that Edmund had wished for her very much, and that he should certainly have come back for her, had she not been tired already; but this was not quite sufficient to do away with the pain of having been left a whole hour, when he had talked of only a few minutes, nor to banish the sort of curiosity she felt, to know what they had been conversing about all that time; and the result of the whole was to her disappointment and depression, as they prepared, by general agreement, to return to the house.

On reaching the bottom of the steps to the terrace, Mrs. Rushworth and Mrs. Norris presented themselves at the top, just ready for the wilderness, at the end of an hour and a half from their leaving the house. Mrs. Norris had been too well employed to move faster. Whatever cross accidents had occurred to intercept the pleasures of her nieces, she had found a morning of complete enjoyment—for the housekeeper, after a great many courtesies on the subject of pheasants, had taken her to the dairy, told her all about their cows, and given her the receipt[2] for a famous cream cheese; and since Julia's leaving them, they had been met by the gardener, with whom she had made a most satisfactory acquaintance, for she had set him right as to his grandson's illness, convinced him that it was an ague, and promised him a charm for it;[3] and he, in return, had shewn her all his choicest nursery of plants, and actually presented her with a very curious specimen of heath.

On this rencontre they all returned to the house together, there to lounge away the time as they could with sofas, and chit-chat, and Quarterly Reviews,[4] till the return of the others, and the arrival of dinner. It was late before the Miss Bertrams and the two gentlemen came in, and their ramble did not appear to have been more than partially agreeable, or at all productive of anything useful with regard to the object of the day. By their own accounts they had been all walking after each other, and the junction which had taken place at last seemed, to Fanny's observation, to have been as much too late for re-establishing harmony, as it confessedly had been for determining on any alteration. She felt, as she looked at Julia and Mr. Rush-

2 Recipe.

3 The charm that Mrs. Norris recommends is probably an amulet that the grandson is to wear around his neck. She practices a medicine that is more superstition than science. An ague is a chronic fever, with shivering its primary symptom.

4 The *Quarterly Review* was one of the two major periodicals of the period, devoted to reviews of the most important recent publications in literature, politics, and science. It was owned by John Murray, the publisher with whom Austen would, as it happens, begin working in 1815 and who would publish the second edition of *Mansfield Park* the year after. Austen demonstrates her sociological precision in having Rushworth subscribe to the *Quarterly*. It had been founded in 1808 to provide a conservative alternative to the liberal politics of its rival the *Edinburgh Review,* which had been founded six years earlier. The detail also furnishes evidence in support of the theory that *Mansfield Park* is set after the 1807 abolition of the slave trade.

worth, that her's was not the only dissatisfied bosom amongst them; there was gloom on the face of each. Mr. Crawford and Miss Bertram were much more gay, and she thought that he was taking particular pains, during dinner, to do away any little resentment of the other two, and restore general good humour.

Dinner was soon followed by tea and coffee, a ten miles' drive home allowed no waste of hours, and from the time of their sitting down to table, it was a quick succession of busy nothings till the carriage came to the door, and Mrs. Norris, having fidgeted about, and obtained a few pheasants' eggs and a cream cheese from the housekeeper, and made abundance of civil speeches to Mrs. Rushworth, was ready to lead the way. At the same moment Mr. Crawford, approaching Julia, said, "I hope I am not to lose my companion, unless she is afraid of the evening air in so exposed a seat." The request had not been foreseen, but was very graciously received, and Julia's day was likely to end almost as well as it began. Miss Bertram had made up her mind to something different, and was a little disappointed—but her conviction of being really the one preferred, comforted her under it, and enabled her to receive Mr. Rushworth's parting attentions as she ought. He was certainly better pleased to hand her into the barouche than to assist her in ascending the box—and his complacency seemed confirmed by the arrangement.

"Well, Fanny, this has been a fine day for you, upon my word!" said Mrs. Norris, as they drove through the park. "Nothing but pleasure from beginning to end! I am sure you ought to be very much obliged to your aunt Bertram and me, for contriving to let you go. A pretty good day's amusement you have had!"

Maria was just discontented enough to say directly, "I think *you* have done pretty well yourself, ma'am. Your lap seems full of good things, and here is a basket of something between us, which has been knocking my elbow unmercifully."

"My dear, it is only a beautiful little heath, which that nice old gardener would make me take; but if it is in your way, I will have it in my lap directly. There Fanny, you shall carry that parcel for me—take great care of it—do not let it fall; it is a cream cheese, just like the excellent one we had at dinner. Nothing would satisfy that good old

Portrait of John Murray II (1778–1843), a founder of the *Quarterly Review* and, after 1815, Austen's publisher.

Mrs. Whitaker, but my taking one of the cheeses. I stood out as long as I could, till the tears almost came into her eyes, and I knew it was just the sort that my sister would be delighted with. That Mrs. Whitaker is a treasure! She was quite shocked when I asked her whether wine was allowed at the second table, and she has turned away two housemaids for wearing white gowns.[5] Take care of the cheese, Fanny. Now I can manage the other parcel and the basket very well."

"What else have you been spunging?" said Maria, half pleased that Sotherton should be so complimented.

"Spunging, my dear! It is nothing but four of those beautiful pheasants' eggs, which Mrs. Whitaker would quite force upon me; she would not take a denial. She said it must be such an amusement to me, as she understood I lived quite alone, to have a few living creatures of that sort; and so to be sure it will. I shall get the dairy maid to set them under the first spare hen, and if they come to good I can have them moved to my own house and borrow a coop; and it will be a great delight to me in my lonely hours to attend to them. And if I have good luck, your mother shall have some."

It was a beautiful evening, mild and still, and the drive was as pleasant as the serenity of nature could make it; but when Mrs. Norris ceased speaking it was altogether a silent drive to those within. Their spirits were in general exhausted – and to determine whether the day had afforded most pleasure or pain, might occupy the meditations of almost all.

5 In Mrs. Whitaker, Mrs. Norris finds an ally in her favorite project of ensuring that people know their place. The Sotherton housekeeper regulates what is served even to the upper domestics who take their dinner in her room or the steward's ("second table") rather than the servants' hall, and she fires any maidservant bold enough to wear the light-colored fabrics that were the genteel fashion at this moment instead of restricting herself to the dark colors that would mark off her class position properly.

# II

THE DAY AT SOTHERTON, with all its imperfections, afforded the Miss Bertrams much more agreeable feelings than were derived from the letters from Antigua, which soon afterwards reached Mansfield. It was much pleasanter to think of Henry Crawford than of their father; and to think of their father in England again within a certain period, which these letters obliged them to do, was a most unwelcome exercise.

November was the black month fixed for his return. Sir Thomas wrote of it with as much decision as experience and anxiety could authorize. His business was so nearly concluded as to justify him in proposing to take his passage in the September packet,[1] and he consequently looked forward with the hope of being with his beloved family again early in November.

Maria was more to be pitied than Julia, for to her the father brought a husband, and the return of the friend most solicitous for her happiness,[2] would unite her to the lover, on whom she had chosen that happiness should depend. It was a gloomy prospect, and all she could do was to throw a mist over it, and hope when the mist cleared away, she should see something else. It would hardly be *early* in November, there were generally delays, a bad passage or *something;* that favouring *something* which every body who shuts their eyes while they look, or their understandings while they reason, feels the comfort of. It would probably be the middle of November at least; the middle of November was three months off. Three months comprised thirteen weeks. Much might happen in thirteen weeks.

Sir Thomas would have been deeply mortified by a suspicion of

1 Packet-boat, a ship carrying the overseas mail and traveling at scheduled intervals between two ports.

2 Meaning Sir Thomas. *Friend,* as noted earlier, could be used to designate a closely related kinsman or—since friendship still was thought of as organizing the relations of public life as well as private—a patron or benefactor.

half that his daughters felt on the subject of his return, and would hardly have found consolation in a knowledge of the interest it excited in the breast of another young lady. Miss Crawford, on walking up with her brother to spend the evening at Mansfield Park, heard the good news; and though seeming to have no concern in the affair beyond politeness, and to have vented all her feelings in a quiet congratulation, heard it with an attention not so easily satisfied. Mrs. Norris gave the particulars of the letters, and the subject was dropt; but after tea, as Miss Crawford was standing at an open window with Edmund and Fanny looking out on a twilight scene, while the Miss Bertrams, Mr. Rushworth, and Henry Crawford, were all busy with candles at the piano-forte, she suddenly revived it by turning round towards the group, and saying, "How happy Mr. Rushworth looks! He is thinking of November."

Edmund looked round at Mr. Rushworth too, but had nothing to say. "Your father's return will be a very interesting event."

"It will, indeed, after such an absence; an absence not only long, but including so many dangers."

"It will be the fore-runner also of other interesting events; your sister's marriage, and your taking orders."

"Yes."

"Don't be affronted," said she laughing; "but it does put me in mind of some of the old heathen heroes, who after performing great exploits in a foreign land, offered sacrifices to the gods on their safe return."

"There is no sacrifice in the case," replied Edmund with a serious smile, and glancing at the piano-forte again, "it is entirely her own doing."

"Oh! yes, I know it is. I was merely joking. She has done no more than what every young woman would do; and I have no doubt of her being extremely happy. My other sacrifice of course you do not understand."

"My taking orders I assure you is quite as voluntary as Maria's marrying."

"It is fortunate that your inclination and your father's convenience should accord so well. There is a very good living kept for you, I understand, hereabouts."

3 Means for a comfortable life. Samuel Johnson in his *Dictionary* defines *competence* as "such a fortune as, without exuberance, is equal to the conveniences of life." In *Sense and Sensibility* Elinor and Marianne Dashwood have a conversation in which it becomes clear that the younger sister's "competence"—an income that would, Marianne calculates, ensure a family a "proper establishment of servants, a carriage, perhaps two," and horses with which to hunt—would in fact be the older sister's "wealth" (I,18). (As Patricia Meyer Spacks says in her annotations on this scene, "Marianne refuses to accept the idea of restriction for herself; Elinor assumes it": *Sense and Sensibility: An Annotated Edition* [Cambridge, Mass.: Belknap Press of Harvard University Press, 2013], p. 135.) Edward's and Mary's ideas of a competence are at variance in similar ways.

"Which you suppose has biassed me."

"But *that* I am sure it has not," cried Fanny.

"Thank you for your good word, Fanny, but it is more than I would affirm myself. On the contrary, the knowing that there was such a provision for me, probably did bias me. Nor can I think it wrong that it should. There was no natural disinclination to be overcome, and I see no reason why a man should make a worse clergyman for knowing that he will have a competence early in life.[3] I was in safe hands. I hope I should not have been influenced myself in a wrong way, and I am sure my father was too conscientious to have allowed it. I have no doubt that I was biased, but I think it was blamelessly."

"It is the same sort of thing," said Fanny, after a short pause, "as for the son of an admiral to go into the navy, or the son of a general to be in the army, and nobody sees anything wrong in that. Nobody wonders that they should prefer the line where their friends can serve them best, or suspects them to be less in earnest in it than they appear."

"No, my dear Miss Price, and for reasons good. The profession, either navy or army, is its own justification. It has every thing in its favour; heroism, danger, bustle, fashion. Soldiers and sailors are always acceptable in society. Nobody can wonder that men are soldiers and sailors."

"But the motives of a man who takes orders with the certainty of preferment, may be fairly suspected, you think?" said Edmund. "To be justified in your eyes, he must do it in the most complete uncertainty of any provision."

"What! take orders without a living! No, that is madness indeed, absolute madness!"

"Shall I ask you how the church is to be filled, if a man is neither to take orders with a living, nor without? No, for you certainly would not know what to say. But I must beg some advantage to the clergyman from your own argument. As he cannot be influenced by those feelings which you rank highly as temptation and reward to the soldier and sailor in their choice of a profession, as heroism, and noise, and fashion are all against him, he ought to be less liable to the suspicion of wanting sincerity or good intentions in the choice of his."

"Oh! no doubt he is very sincere in preferring an income ready made, to the trouble of working for one; and has the best intentions of doing nothing all the rest of his days but eat, drink, and grow fat. It is indolence Mr. Bertram, indeed. Indolence and love of ease—a want of all laudable ambition, of taste for good company, or of inclination to take the trouble of being agreeable, which make men clergymen. A clergyman has nothing to do but be slovenly and selfish—read the newspaper, watch the weather, and quarrel with his wife. His curate does all the work,[4] and the business of his own life is to dine."

"There are such clergymen, no doubt, but I think they are not so common as to justify Miss Crawford in esteeming it their general character. I suspect that in this comprehensive and (may I say) common-place censure, you are not judging from yourself, but from prejudiced persons, whose opinions you have been in the habit of hearing. It is impossible that your own observation can have given you much knowledge of the clergy. You can have been personally acquainted with very few of a set of men you condemn so conclusively. You are speaking what you have been told at your uncle's table."

"I speak what appears to me the general opinion; and where an opinion is general, it is usually correct. Though *I* have not seen much of the domestic lives of clergymen, it is seen by too many to leave any deficiency of information."

"Where any one body of educated men, of whatever denomination, are condemned indiscriminately, there must be a deficiency of information, or (smiling) of something else. Your uncle, and his brother admirals, perhaps, knew little of clergymen beyond the chaplains whom, good or bad, they were always wishing away."[5]

"Poor William! He has met with great kindness from the chaplain of the Antwerp," was a tender apostrophe of Fanny's, very much to the purpose of her own feelings, if not of the conversation.[6]

"I have been so little addicted to take my opinions from my uncle," said Miss Crawford, "that I can hardly suppose;—and since you push me so hard, I must observe, that I am not entirely without the means of seeing what clergymen are, being at this present time the guest of my own brother, Dr. Grant.[7] And though Dr. Grant is most

4 A curate is an ordained clergyman who has not been appointed to a living of his own, and who earns a salary (generally meager) by assisting the parish priest in his performance of his duties. Austen's father, the Rev. George Austen, never could afford to hire a curate.

5 As Brian Southam explains, Royal Navy officers of Admiral Crawford's generation looked with disdain or outright hostility on the chaplains who were assigned to their ships. However, as politicians with Evangelical leanings gained more influence in the Admiralty near the end of the Napoleonic wars, such opinions began to be challenged (*Jane Austen and the Navy*, pp. 187–188).

6 This is not the only occasion in the novel on which Austen's narrator—here underlining Fanny's limitations as a conversationalist as she points out that her comment about William's chaplain really is something of a non sequitur—invites readers to notice the droll side to the devotion that defines this heroine's character. Fanny's thoughts turn to William very, very readily. Her comment would have been more informative to Austen's first readers than to us, though, since that audience would have been able to infer from her mention of his chaplain that William was currently serving aboard a man-of-war. In short supply, chaplains were stationed aboard larger ships, of seventy-four guns or more, almost exclusively (see Southam, *Jane Austen and the Navy*, p. 187).

7 *Brother* and *brother-in-law* were often used interchangeably in Austen's day.

8 A young (green) goose, not yet fattened up. Geese
were traditionally served later in the year, at the end of
September, after they had grazed on the stubble left in
the fields after the harvest. Perhaps Dr. Grant's dinner
plans have gone awry because the lean meat has not
been cooked properly.

kind and obliging to me, and though he is really a gentleman, and I
dare say a good scholar and clever, and often preaches good sermons,
and is very respectable, *I* see him to be an indolent selfish bon vivant,
who must have his palate consulted in every thing, who will not stir a
finger for the convenience of any one, and who, moreover, if the
cook makes a blunder, is out of humour with his excellent wife. To
own the truth, Henry and I were partly driven out this very evening,
by a disappointment about a green goose,[8] which he could not get
the better of. My poor sister was forced to stay and bear it."

"I do not wonder at your disapprobation, upon my word. It is a
great defect of temper, made worse by a very faulty habit of self-
indulgence; and to see your sister suffering from it, must be exceedingly painful to such feelings as your's. Fanny, it goes against us. We
cannot attempt to defend Dr. Grant."

"No," replied Fanny, "but we need not give up his profession for all
that; because, whatever profession Dr. Grant had chosen, he would
have taken a—not a good temper into it; and as he must either in the
navy or army have had a great many more people under his command
than he has now, I think more would have been made unhappy by
him as a sailor or soldier than as a clergyman. Besides, I cannot but
suppose that whatever there may be to wish otherwise in Dr. Grant,
would have been in a greater danger of becoming worse in a more active and worldly profession, where he would have had less time and
obligation—where he might have escaped that knowledge of himself, the *frequency,* at least, of that knowledge which it is impossible
he should escape as he is now. A man—a sensible man like Dr. Grant,
cannot be in the habit of teaching others their duty every week, cannot go to church twice every Sunday and preach such very good sermons in so good a manner as he does, without being the better for it
himself. It must make him think, and I have no doubt that he oftener
endeavours to restrain himself than he would if he had been any
thing but a clergyman."

"We cannot prove to the contrary, to be sure—but I wish you a
better fate Miss Price, than to be the wife of a man whose amiable-
ness depends upon his own sermons; for though he may preach him-

self into a good humour every Sunday, it will be bad enough to have him quarrelling about green geese from Monday morning till Saturday night."

"I think the man who could often quarrel with Fanny," said Edmund affectionately, "must be beyond the reach of any sermons."

Fanny turned farther into the window; and Miss Crawford had only time to say in a pleasant manner, "I fancy Miss Price has been more used to deserve praise than to hear it;" when being earnestly invited by the Miss Bertrams to join in a glee,[9] she tripped off to the instrument, leaving Edmund looking after her in an ecstasy of admiration of all her many virtues, from her obliging manners down to her light and graceful tread.

"There goes good humour I am sure," said he presently. "There goes a temper which would never give pain! How well she walks! and how readily she falls in with the inclination of others! joining them the moment she is asked. What a pity," he added, after an instant's reflection, "that she should have been in such hands!"

Fanny agreed to it, and had the pleasure of seeing him continue at the window with her, in spite of the expected glee; and of having his eyes soon turned like her's, towards the scene without, where all that was solemn and soothing, and lovely, appeared in the brilliancy of an unclouded night, and the contrast of the deep shade of the woods. Fanny spoke her feelings. "Here's harmony!" said she, "Here's repose! Here's what may leave all painting and all music behind, and what poetry only can attempt to describe. Here's what may tranquillize every care, and lift the heart to rapture! When I look out on such a night as this, I feel as if there could be neither wickedness nor sorrow in the world; and there certainly would be less of both if the sublimity of Nature were more attended to, and people were carried more out of themselves by contemplating such a scene."

"I like to hear your enthusiasm, Fanny. It is a lovely night, and they are much to be pitied who have not been taught to feel in some degree as you do—who have not at least been given a taste for nature in early life. They lose a great deal."

"*You* taught me to think and feel on the subject, cousin."

9 A song written for three or more voices, with each voice taking a different part.

10 Arcturus (Greek for "guardian of the bear") is a bright star in the northern sky, in the constellation next to Ursa Major, the Great Bear, also known as the Big Dipper. Cassiopeia is another constellation in the northern sky. In the chapter of *Letters on the Improvement of the Mind* devoted to female accomplishments, Hester Chapone recommends that young women's education include an acquaintance with astronomy because, as she explains in a long, rhapsodic passage, lessons of this kind will cultivate their religious feelings and lead them from the works of Creation to the Creator. When "the philosophic eye is raised towards the heavens, what a stupendous scene there opens to its view!—those brilliant lights that sparkle to the eye of ignorance as gems adorning the sky, or as lamps to guide the traveller by night, assume an importance that amazes the understanding! . . . Who can contemplate such a scene unmoved?" (p. 142).

11 Fanny's melancholy sigh belies her earlier claim about the transporting effect of nature's sublimity. In the Gothic romances she published in the 1790s, Ann Radcliffe likewise endowed her heroines with minds "highly elevated, or sweetly smoothed by scenes of nature." Ellena di Rosalba in Radcliffe's *The Italian* (1796), for example, even at moments when she fears for her life, is able to find peace when she looks out a window at the grandeur of the mountain scenery around her prison and construes the prospect as evidence of the Creator's benevolence: "dwelling as with a present God in the midst of his sublime works . . . how insignificant would appear to her the transactions, and the sufferings of this world," states Radcliffe's narrator (*The Italian, or, the Confessional of the Black Penitents* [London: Penguin, 2004], p. 106). Despite her portrayal as a figure of firm religious conviction, Fanny is not the paragon that a Radcliffe heroine is: Fanny's faith can be derailed by her desire.

"I had a very apt scholar. There's Arcturus looking very bright."

"Yes, and the bear. I wish I could see Cassiopeia."[10]

"We must go out on the lawn for that. Should you be afraid?"

"Not in the least. It is a great while since we have had any stargazing."

"Yes, I do not know how it has happened." The glee began. "We will stay till this is finished, Fanny," said he, turning his back on the window; and as it advanced, she had the mortification of seeing him advance too, moving forward by gentle degrees towards the instrument, and when it ceased, he was close by the singers, among the most urgent in requesting to hear the glee again.

Fanny sighed alone at the window till scolded away by Mrs. Norris's threats of catching cold.[11]

This frontispiece to an 1829 edition of Hester Chapone's often-reprinted *Letters on the Improvement of the Mind* pictures the tutelage in astronomy that Chapone promotes as part of her educational program for young women.

1 The "duties," so called, that take Tom Bertram back to Mansfield and (as we learn two paragraphs down) that take Henry Crawford to his estate in Norfolk involve partridges. The start of September is the traditional beginning of that particular phase of the shooting season.

2 Like Ramsgate, mentioned by Tom in Chap. 5, Weymouth is a seaside resort on England's south coast (and the setting for the off-stage romance between Jane Fairfax and Frank Churchill in *Emma*). Tom seems to gravitate toward such towns.

3 *Conscious* in this context means self-conscious or self-aware.

SIR THOMAS WAS TO RETURN in November, and his eldest son had duties to call him earlier home. The approach of September brought tidings of Mr. Bertram first in a letter to the gamekeeper, and then in a letter to Edmund;[1] and by the end of August he arrived himself, to be gay, agreeable, and gallant again as occasion served, or Miss Crawford demanded, to tell of races and Weymouth,[2] and parties and friends, to which she might have listened six weeks before with some interest, and altogether to give her the fullest conviction, by the power of actual comparison, of her preferring his younger brother.

It was very vexatious, and she was heartily sorry for it; but so it was; and so far from now meaning to marry the elder, she did not even want to attract him beyond what the simplest claims of conscious beauty required;[3] his lengthened absence from Mansfield, without any thing but pleasure in view, and his own will to consult, made it perfectly clear that he did not care about her; and his indifference was so much more than equalled by her own, that were he now to step forth the owner of Mansfield Park, the Sir Thomas complete, which he was to be in time, she did not believe she could accept him.

The season and duties which brought Mr. Bertram back to Mansfield, took Mr. Crawford into Norfolk. Everingham could not do without him in the beginning of September. He went for a fortnight; a fortnight of such dullness to the Miss Bertrams, as ought to have put them both on their guard, and made even Julia admit in her jealousy of her sister, the absolute necessity of distrusting his attentions, and wishing him not to return; and a fortnight of sufficient leisure in the intervals of shooting and sleeping, to have convinced the gentleman that he ought to keep longer away, had he been more in the habit of examining his own motives, and of reflecting to what the indulgence of his idle vanity was tending; but, thoughtless and selfish from prosperity and bad example, he would not look beyond the present moment. The sisters, handsome, clever, and encouraging, were an amusement to his sated mind; and finding nothing in Norfolk to equal the social pleasures of Mansfield, he gladly returned to it at the time appointed, and was welcomed thither quite as gladly by those whom he came to trifle with further.

Maria, with only Mr. Rushworth to attend to her, and doomed to the repeated details of his day's sport, good or bad, his boast of his dogs, his jealousy of his neighbours, his doubts of their qualifications,[4] and his zeal after poachers,—subjects which will not find their way to female feelings without some talent on one side, or some attachment on the other, had missed Mr. Crawford grievously; and Julia, unengaged and unemployed, felt all the right of missing him much more. Each sister believed herself the favourite. Julia might be justified in so doing by the hints of Mrs. Grant, inclined to credit what she wished, and Maria by the hints of Mr. Crawford himself. Every thing returned into the same channel as before his absence; his manners being to each so animated and agreeable, as to lose no ground with either, and just stopping short of the consistence, the steadiness, the solicitude, and the warmth which might excite general notice.

Fanny was the only one of the party who found any thing to dislike; but since the day at Sotherton, she could never see Mr. Crawford with either sister without observation, and seldom without wonder or censure; and had her confidence in her own judgment been equal to her exercise of it in every other respect, had she been sure that she was seeing clearly, and judging candidly, she would probably have made some important communications to her usual confidant. As it was, however, she only hazarded a hint, and the hint was lost. "I am rather surprised," said she, "that Mr. Crawford should come back again so soon, after being here so long before, full seven

4 The right to shoot game was legally restricted to men who met certain property qualifications.

weeks; for I had understood he was so very fond of change and moving about, that I thought something would certainly occur when he was once gone, to take him elsewhere. He is used to much gayer places than Mansfield."

"It is to his credit," was Edmund's answer, "and I dare say it gives his sister pleasure. She does not like his unsettled habits."

"What a favourite he is with my cousins!"

"Yes, his manners to women are such as must please. Mrs. Grant, I believe, suspects him of a preference for Julia; I have never seen much symptom of it, but I wish it may be so. He has no faults but what a serious attachment would remove."

"If Miss Bertram were not engaged," said Fanny, cautiously, "I could sometimes almost think that he admired her more than Julia."

"Which is, perhaps, more in favour of his liking Julia best, than you, Fanny, may be aware; for I believe it often happens, that a man, before he has quite made up his own mind, will distinguish the sister or intimate friend of the woman he is really thinking of, more than the woman herself. Crawford has too much sense to stay here if he found himself in any danger from Maria; and I am not at all afraid for her, after such a proof as she has given, that her feelings are not strong."

Fanny supposed she must have been mistaken, and meant to think differently in future; but with all that submission to Edmund could do, and all the help of the coinciding looks and hints which she occasionally noticed in some of the others, and which seemed to say that Julia was Mr. Crawford's choice, she knew not always what to think. She was privy, one evening, to the hopes of her aunt Norris on the subject, as well as to her feelings, and the feelings of Mrs. Rushworth, on a point of some similarity, and could not help wondering as she listened; and glad would she have been not to be obliged to listen, for it was while all the other young people were dancing, and she sitting, most unwillingly, among the chaperons at the fire, longing for the re-entrance of her elder cousin, on whom all her own hopes of a partner then depended. It was Fanny's first ball, though without the preparation or splendour of many a young lady's first ball, being the thought only of the afternoon, built on the late acquisition of a violin player in the servants' hall, and the possibility of raising five couple with the help of Mrs. Grant and a new intimate friend of Mr. Bertram's just arrived on a visit. It had, however, been a very happy one to Fanny through four dances, and she was quite grieved to be losing even a quarter of an hour.—While waiting and wishing, looking now at the dancers and now at the door, this dialogue between the two above-mentioned ladies was forced on her.

"I think, ma'am," said Mrs. Norris—her eyes directed towards Mr. Rushworth and Maria, who were partners for the second time—"we shall see some happy faces again now."

"Yes, ma'am, indeed"—replied the other, with a stately simper—"there will be some satisfaction in looking on *now,* and I think it was rather a pity they should have been obliged to part. Young folks in their situation should be excused complying with the common forms.[5]—I wonder my son did not propose it."

"I dare say he did, ma'am.—Mr. Rushworth is never remiss. But dear Maria has such a strict sense of propriety, so much of that true delicacy which one seldom meets with now-a-days, Mrs. Rushworth, that wish of avoiding particularity!—Dear ma'am, only look at her face at this moment;—how different from what it was the two last dances!"

Miss Bertram did indeed look happy, her eyes were sparkling with pleasure, and she was speaking with great animation, for Julia and her partner, Mr. Crawford, were close to her; they were all in a cluster together. How she had looked before, Fanny could not recollect, for she had been dancing with Edmund herself, and had not thought about her.

Mrs. Norris continued, "It is quite delightful, ma'am, to see young people so properly happy, so well suited, and so much the thing! I cannot but think of dear Sir Thomas's delight. And what do you say, ma'am, to the chance of another match? Mr. Rushworth has set a good example, and such things are very catching."

Mrs. Rushworth, who saw nothing but her son, was quite at a loss. "The couple above, ma'am. Do you see no symptoms there?"

"Oh! dear—Miss Julia and Mr. Crawford. Yes, indeed, a very pretty match. What is his property?"

5 The lists of rules that were posted in the assembly rooms in which public balls were held generally stated that partners were to be changed after every second dance. However, Mrs. Rushworth thinks that because her son and Maria are practically engaged—only awaiting the return of Sir Thomas to make things official—this bit of dance-floor etiquette should be waived in their case; they should get to comport themselves as engaged couples would and dance exclusively with each other. It is clear, though, that Maria would be happy to comply with the stricter etiquette if that compliance would give her the chance to dance with some one other than Mr. Rushworth—with Henry Crawford in particular.

6 Tom could be referring either to the skirmishes between the British and American navies that led up to
America's declaration of war on Britain in 1812 or (if
Austen indeed set *Mansfield Park* in the years in which
she wrote it) to the war itself. In the decade preceding
the formal outbreak of hostilities, the Royal Navy repeatedly violated America's neutrality and disrupted
American shipping; in response, President Thomas
Jefferson's government passed the Embargo Act in
1807 that closed U.S. ports to foreign vessels.

7 To make up a table for whist for Mrs. Rushworth,
Mrs. Norris needs four players, as the card game was
played by two couples. A rubber is a set of three games.
Lady Bertram's dedication to the fringe—ornamental
trimming—that she is sewing is such that by the beginning of Vol. II of *Mansfield Park* she will have produced
"many yards" of it. It is never made clear just what this
fringe will ornament.

"Four thousand a year."

"Very well.—Those who have not more, must be satisfied with
what they have.—Four thousand a year is a pretty estate, and he
seems a very genteel, steady young man, so I hope Miss Julia will be
very happy."

"It is not a settled thing, ma'am, yet.—We only speak of it among
friends. But I have very little doubt it *will* be.—He is growing extremely particular in his attentions."

Fanny could listen no farther. Listening and wondering were all
suspended for a time, for Mr. Bertram was in the room again, and
though feeling it would be a great honour to be asked by him, she
thought it must happen. He came towards their little circle; but instead of asking her to dance, drew a chair near her, and gave her an
account of the present state of a sick horse, and the opinion of the
groom, from whom he had just parted. Fanny found that it was not
to be, and in the modesty of her nature immediately felt that she had
been unreasonable in expecting it. When he had told of his horse, he
took a newspaper from the table, and looking over it said in a languid
way, "If you want to dance, Fanny, I will stand up with you."—With
more than equal civility the offer was declined;—she did not wish to
dance.—"I am glad of it," said he in a much brisker tone, and throwing down the newspaper again—"for I am tired to death. I only wonder how the good people can keep it up so long.—They had need be
*all* in love, to find any amusement in such folly—and so they are, I
fancy.—If you look at them, you may see they are so many couple of
lovers—all but Yates and Mrs. Grant—and, between ourselves, she,
poor woman! must want a lover as much as any one of them. A desperate dull life her's must be with the doctor," making a sly face as he
spoke towards the chair of the latter, who proving, however, to be
close at his elbow, made so instantaneous a change of expression and
subject necessary, as Fanny, in spite of every thing, could hardly help
laughing at.—"A strange business this in America, Dr. Grant!—What
is your opinion?—I always come to you to know what I am to think
of public matters."6

"My dear Tom," cried his aunt soon afterwards, "as you are not
dancing, I dare say you will have no objection to join us in a rubber;7

The dramatic activities of the group of aristocratic amateurs who called themselves the Pic-Nic Society are the satiric target of this ebullient cartoon by James Gillray. Gillray's original audience in 1803 would easily have identified the figures from the political elite being skewered here. At the cartoon's center one sees, for instance, the corpulent Lady Buckinghamshire readying herself for performance in Nathaniel Lee's tragedy *Alexander the Great, or, The Rival Queens.* The oversized cupid to the left is Lord Cholmondeley, chamberlain to the prince of Wales.

8 Mrs. Norris hopes to sway Tom by suggesting that he and Dr. Grant might play for higher stakes than the ladies will. However, even a half-crown was a sizeable bet, since it was a coin worth one-eighth of a pound (two shillings, sixpence).

shall you?"—then, leaving her seat, and coming to him to enforce the proposal, added in a whisper—"We want to make a table for Mrs. Rushworth, you know.—Your mother is quite anxious about it, but cannot very well spare time to sit down herself, because of her fringe. Now, you and I and Dr. Grant will just do; and though *we* play but half-crowns, you know, you may bet half-guineas with *him*."[8]

"I should be most happy," replied he aloud, and jumping up with alacrity, "it would give me the greatest pleasure—but that I am this moment going to dance. Come, Fanny,"—taking her hand—"do not be dawdling any longer, or the dance will be over."

Fanny was led off very willingly, though it was impossible for her to feel much gratitude towards her cousin, or distinguish, as he certainly did, between the selfishness of another person and his own.

"A pretty modest request upon my word!" he indignantly exclaimed as they walked away. "To want to nail me to card table for the next two hours with herself and Dr. Grant, who are always quarrelling, and that poking old woman, who knows no more of whist than of algebra. I wish my good aunt would be a little less busy! And to ask me in such a way too! without ceremony, before them all, so as to leave me no possibility of refusing! *That* is what I dislike most particularly. It raises my spleen more than any thing, to have the pretence of being asked, of being given a choice, and at the same time addressed in such a way as to oblige one to do the very thing—whatever it be! If I had not luckily thought of standing up with you, I could not have got out of it. It is a great deal too bad. But when my aunt has got a fancy in her head, nothing can stop her."

# 13

THE HONOURABLE JOHN YATES, this new friend, had not much to recommend him beyond habits of fashion and expense, and being the younger son of a lord with a tolerable independence;[1] and Sir Thomas would probably have thought his introduction at Mansfield by no means desirable. Mr. Bertram's acquaintance with him had begun at Weymouth, where they had spent ten days together in the same society, and the friendship, if friendship it might be called, had been proved and perfected by Mr. Yates's being invited to take Mansfield in his way, whenever he could, and by his promising to come; and he did come rather earlier than had been expected, in consequence of the sudden breaking-up of a large party assembled for gaiety at the house of another friend, which he had left Weymouth to join. He came on the wings of disappointment, and with his head full of acting, for it had been a theatrical party; and the play, in which he had borne a part, was within two days of representation, when the sudden death of one of the nearest connections of the family had destroyed the scheme and dispersed the performers. To be so near happiness, so near fame, so near the long paragraph in praise of the private theatricals at Ecclesford, the seat of the Right Hon. Lord Ravenshaw, in Cornwall, which would of course have immortalised the whole party for at least a twelvemonth![2] and being so near, to lose it all, was an injury to be keenly felt, and Mr. Yates could talk of nothing else. Ecclesford and its theatre, with its arrangements and dresses, rehearsals and jokes, was his never-failing subject, and to boast of the past his only consolation.

1 Mr. Yates's aristocratic birth endows him with an "Honourable" before his name, but his income is merely sufficient, "a tolerable independence."

2 Amateur acting was a tremendously popular pastime in Austen's day. Plays were staged in schools, in army barracks, and aboard navy ships. At the high-tide moment of the "Theatrico Mania," as the Reverend Richard Graves declared hyperbolically in 1801, there was "hardly a family in high or low life that ha[d] not its theatre of some kind or other, and its occasional performers" (*Senilities; or Solitary Amusements: in Prose and Verse* [London: Longman and Rees, 1801], p. 58). At the end of the eighteenth century the Austens were one of those families. Between 1782 and 1789, Austen's eldest brother, James, produced several plays from the theatrical repertory of the earlier eighteenth century, using family members and neighbors as his cast. His stagings would have been less elaborate than those put on within aristocratic households, which had money to spend on decor and costumes that the commercial theaters of the day might have envied. In those households, "private" theatricals were hardly private at all, since the performances attracted large audiences and were the occasions for much gossip, some of which made its way into newspapers—a fate that Mr. Yates had been anticipating with pleasure. Compounding this assault on their own domestic privacy, these amateur players sometimes brought in professionals as consultants or participants.

3 *Lovers' Vows* was the title that Elizabeth Inchbald gave to her adaptation of the German playwright August von Kotzebue's *Das Kind der Liebe* ("The Love Child"), first published in 1790. Inchbald wrote her script for Covent Garden, one of the patent theaters in London, which premiered it in 1798. While Austen was living in Bath between 1801 and 1806, the play was staged fifteen times, and it seems likely that she attended a performance.

4 In law the term *dowager* identifies a woman whose husband is dead but who continues in possession of a title or some income—a *dower* or, as below, a *jointure*—that derives from him.

The chatty barber Dicky Gossip, as portrayed by the actor Richard Suett in the short-lived theatrical hit of 1793 Prince Hoare's *My Grandmother.* Throughout this episode of *Mansfield Park* Tom Bertram is tellingly ready to imagine himself performing in the roles that made the careers of the era's so-called low comedians.

Happily for him, a love of the theatre is so general, an itch for acting so strong among young people, that he could hardly out-talk the interest of his hearers. From the first casting of the parts, to the epilogue, it was all bewitching, and there were few who did not wish to have been a party concerned, or would have hesitated to try their skill. The play had been Lovers' Vows,[3] and Mr. Yates was to have been Count Cassel. "A trifling part," said he, "and not at all to my taste, and such a one as I certainly would not accept again; but I was determined to make no difficulties. Lord Ravenshaw and the duke had appropriated the only two characters worth playing before I reached Ecclesford; and though Lord Ravenshaw offered to resign his to me, it was impossible to take it, you know. I was sorry for *him* that he should have so mistaken his powers, for he was no more equal to the Baron! A little man, with a weak voice, always hoarse after the first ten minutes! It must have injured the piece materially; but *I* was resolved to make no difficulties. Sir Henry thought the duke not equal to Frederick, but that was because Sir Henry wanted the part himself; whereas it was certainly in the best hands of the two. I was surprised to see Sir Henry such a stick. Luckily the strength of the piece did not depend upon him. Our Agatha was inimitable, and the duke was thought very great by many. And upon the whole it would certainly have gone off wonderfully."

"It was a hard case, upon my word;" and, "I do think you were very much to be pitied;" were the kind responses of listening sympathy.

"It is not worth complaining about, but to be sure the poor old dowager could not have died at a worse time;[4] and it is impossible to help wishing, that the news could have been suppressed for just the three days we wanted. It was but three days; and being only a grandmother, and all happening two hundred miles off, I think there would have been no great harm, and it *was* suggested, I know; but Lord Ravenshaw, who I suppose is one of the most correct men in England, would not hear of it."

"An after-piece instead of a comedy," said Mr. Bertram. "Lovers' Vows were at an end, and Lord and Lady Ravenshaw left to act my Grandmother by themselves.[5] Well, the jointure may comfort *him;*[6] and perhaps, between friends, he began to tremble for his credit and

Sir Joshua Reynolds's celebration from 1761 of the versatile talents of the actor and theatrical impresario David Garrick burlesques the classical story of Hercules's choice between virtue and pleasure. Reynolds depicts his friend as a latter-day Hercules divided between the muses of Tragedy and Comedy, smiling at Tragedy apologetically while letting himself be tugged away by Comedy. In his 1870 memoir of his aunt, Austen's nephew J. E. Austen-Leigh discusses Reynolds's allegory at length as he examines Austen's ways of creating fictional characters.

5 Tom Bertram shows off his thorough acquaintance with contemporary theatrical culture with this punning reference to Prince Hoare's *My Grandmother,* a "musical farce in two acts" first staged in 1793. *My Grandmother* was an afterpiece—an example of the kind of brief comic piece that theaters of this period customarily mounted immediately after a five-act play in order to round out a night's entertainment.

6 A jointure is property jointly owned by a husband and wife, designed to provide the latter with an income should her husband predecease her. With her death the property would revert to their descendants. Tom is calculating on Lord Ravenshaw, despite the loss of his grandmother and of his chance to shine on stage, receiving some comfort from this addition to his income.

7 In the professional theaters of Austen's day the manager combined in one person roles that are at present distributed among several individuals: artistic director for the company, producer, chief financial officer, and director of the play.

his lungs in the Baron, and was not sorry to withdraw; and to make *you* amends, Yates, I think we must raise a little theatre at Mansfield, and ask you to be our manager."[7]

This, though the thought of the moment, did not end with the moment; for the inclination to act was awakened, and in no one more strongly than in him who was now master of the house; and who having so much leisure as to make almost any novelty a certain good, had likewise such a degree of lively talents and comic taste, as were exactly adapted to the novelty of acting. The thought returned again and again. "Oh, for the Ecclesford theatre and scenery to try something with." Each sister could echo the wish; and Henry Crawford,

8 Henry Crawford names Shakespearean roles closely associated in the early nineteenth century with the actor and theater manager Edmund Kean (1787–1833). The brio with which Henry declares himself for any and all theatrical genres, a declaration that signals his own changeableness, would also have reminded Austen's first readers of an earlier actor-manager, David Garrick (1717–1779), since the versatility that made Garrick a star in both comic and tragic roles was a key ingredient in his fame. The painter Joshua Reynolds memorialized that versatility in a 1761 portrait that Austen would have seen in 1813 when visiting a retrospective exhibition of his art. Reynolds portrayed Garrick wavering between the claims of the Muse of Comedy and those of the Muse of Tragedy: each female figure has taken hold of his arm, so that, looking a bit foolish, he is tugged in opposing directions. That Henry Crawford is not a tall man, as the jealous Mr. Rushworth has already pointed out (Chap. 10), is another sign that Austen has both Garrick (5 foot, 6 inches) and Kean (5 foot, 7 inches) in her sights.

9 Yates wants more than a curtain. So as to enhance the dramatic illusion, he aims to procure wings for placement on either side of their stage, flats that will conjure up the appearance of buildings, and painted backdrops ("scenes to be let down").

10 Early nineteenth-century commentators in Britain were often scandalized by German plays, and the more popular that the works of Kotzebue and of Friedrich Schiller became in Britain in the 1790s, the more vehement the opposition they elicited. In his Preface to *Lyrical Ballads* (1800) William Wordsworth blamed the "savage torpor" of urban audiences on their diet of "sickly and stupid German Tragedies" (*The Oxford Authors: William Wordsworth,* ed. Stephen Gill [Oxford: Oxford University Press, 1984], p. 599). In *Strictures on the Modern System of Female Education* (1799), Hannah More warned that proponents of a dangerous revolution in Britain's political and domestic institutions had begun to deploy German writings for their cause, with their primary "weapon" being the "German drama" (*The Works of Hannah More* [New York: Harper, 1840], vol. 1, p. 320).

to whom, in all the riot of his gratifications, it was yet an untasted pleasure, was quite alive at the idea. "I really believe," said he, "I could be fool enough at this moment to undertake any character that ever was written, from Shylock or Richard III down to the singing hero of a farce in his scarlet coat and cocked hat. I feel as if I could be any thing or every thing, as if I could rant and storm, or sigh, or cut capers in any tragedy or comedy in the English language.[8] Let us be doing something. Be it only half a play—an act—a scene; what should prevent us? Not these countenances I am sure," looking towards the Miss Bertrams, "and for a theatre, what signifies a theatre? We shall be only amusing ourselves. Any room in this house might suffice."

"We must have a curtain," said Tom Bertram, "a few yards of green baize for a curtain, and perhaps that may be enough."

"Oh, quite enough," cried Mr. Yates, "with only just a side wing or two run up, doors in flat, and three or four scenes to be let down;[9] nothing more would be necessary on such a plan as this. For mere amusement among ourselves, we should want nothing more."

"I believe we must be satisfied with *less,*" said Maria. "There would not be time, and other difficulties would arise. We must rather adopt Mr. Crawford's views, and make the *performance,* not the *theatre,* our object. Many parts of our best plays are independent of scenery."

"Nay," said Edmund, who began to listen with alarm. "Let us do nothing by halves. If we are to act, let it be in a theatre completely fitted up with pit, box, and gallery, and let us have a play entire from beginning to end; so as it be a German play,[10] no matter what, with a good tricking, shifting after-piece, and a figure-dance, and a hornpipe, and a song between the acts.[11] If we do not out do Ecclesford, we do nothing."

"Now, Edmund, do not be disagreeable," said Julia. "Nobody loves a play better than you do, or can have gone much farther to see one."

"True, to see real acting, good hardened real acting; but I would hardly walk from this room to the next, to look at the raw efforts of those who have not been bred to the trade—a set of gentlemen and ladies, who have all the disadvantages of education and decorum to struggle through."

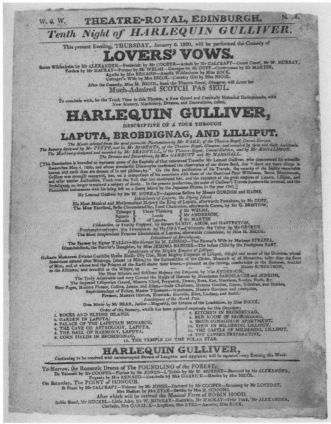

11 Edmund's list captures the miscellaneous nature of the theatrical entertainments of the period and the limited role allotted to the spoken word within this medley. The German Friedrich August Wendeborn, author of a 1791 travelogue, was struck on his visit to England by how the theater managers seemed determined to keep up good humor between the acts "by means of songs, dances, processions and things of that kind," and added, "I have observed that this was necessary even in many of Shakespeare's plays, to prevent drowsiness among the audience" (*A View of England Towards the Close of the Eighteenth Century* [Dublin: P. Wogan et al., 1791], vol. 2, p. 183).

Edmund's scornful comment about the miscellaneity of contemporary theatrical culture is borne out by the hodgepodge contents of this playbill from 1820. During a single evening's entertainment, patrons of Edinburgh's Theatre-Royal can count on seeing not only the tragi-comedy *Lovers' Vows* but also some ballet ("Miss M. Nicol . . . will dance her Much-Admired Scotch Pas Seul") and a pantomime, *Harlequin Gulliver,* "with New Scenery, Machinery, Dresses, and Decorations."

After a short pause, however, the subject still continued, and was discussed with unabated eagerness, every one's inclination increasing by the discussion, and a knowledge of the inclination of the rest; and though nothing was settled but that Tom Bertram would prefer a comedy, and his sisters and Henry Crawford a tragedy, and that nothing in the world could be easier than to find a piece which would please them all, the resolution to act something or other, seemed so decided, as to make Edmund quite uncomfortable. He was

12 The green room is where the players wait before their entrance onto the stage. "My father's room" refers not to Sir Thomas's bedchamber but to his study.

Thomas Rowlandson suggests the role the billiard room played in the social life of the early nineteenth-century English country house in this illustration to *The Tour of Dr. Syntax in Search of a Wife,* William Combe's comic poem of 1821. In this episode, Syntax loses badly to the billiard-playing daughters of the family, one of many mishaps that befall him at Tulip Hall.

determined to prevent it, if possible, though his mother, who equally heard the conversation which passed at table, did not evince the least disapprobation.

The same evening afforded him an opportunity of trying his strength. Maria, Julia, Henry Crawford, and Mr. Yates, were in the billiard-room. Tom returning from them into the drawing-room, where Edmund was standing thoughtfully by the fire, while Lady Bertram was on the sofa at a little distance, and Fanny close beside her arranging her work, thus began as he entered. "Such a horribly vile billiard-table as ours, is not to be met with, I believe, above ground! I can stand it no longer, and I think, I may say, that nothing shall ever tempt me to it again. But one good thing I have just ascertained. It is the very room for a theatre, precisely the shape and length for it, and the doors at the farther end, communicating with each other as they may be made to do in five minutes, by merely moving the book-case in my father's room, is the very thing we could have desired, if we had sat down to wish for it. And my father's room will be an excellent green-room.[12] It seems to join the billiard-room on purpose."

"You are not serious, Tom, in meaning to act?" said Edmund in a low voice, as his brother approached the fire.

"Not serious! never more so, I assure you. What is there to surprise you in it?"

"I think it would be very wrong. In a *general* light, private theatricals are open to some objections, but as *we* are circumstanced, I must think it would be highly injudicious, and more than injudicious, to attempt any thing of the kind. It would show great want of feeling on my father's account, absent as he is, and in some degree of constant danger; and it would be imprudent, I think, with regard to Maria, whose situation is a very delicate one, considering every thing, extremely delicate."

"You take up a thing so seriously! as if we were going to act three times a week till my father's return, and invite all the country. But it is not to be a display of that sort. We mean nothing but a little amusement among ourselves, just to vary the scene, and exercise our powers in something new. We want no audience, no publicity. We may be trusted, I think, in choosing some play most perfectly unexceptionable, and I can conceive no greater harm or danger to any of us in conversing in the elegant written language of some respectable author than in chattering in words of our own. I have no fears, and no scruples. And as to my father's being absent, it is so far from an objection, that I consider it rather as a motive; for the expectation of his return must be a very anxious period to my mother, and if we can be the means of amusing that anxiety, and keeping up her spirits for the next few weeks, I shall think our time very well spent, and so I am sure will he. — It is a *very* anxious period for her."

As he said this, each looked towards their mother. Lady Bertram, sunk back in one corner of the sofa, the picture of health, wealth, ease, and tranquillity, was just falling into a gentle doze, while Fanny was getting through the few difficulties of her work for her.

Edmund smiled and shook his head.

"By Jove! this won't do"—cried Tom, throwing himself into a chair with a hearty laugh. "To be sure, my dear mother, your anxiety—I was unlucky there."

"What is the matter?" asked her ladyship in the heavy tone of one half roused,—"I was not asleep."

13 Tom mentions three set-pieces used to train school-boys in elocution: Mark Antony's funeral oration from Shakespeare's *Julius Caesar,* the famous soliloquy by Hamlet, and a speech the hero delivers in John Home's *Douglas: A Tragedy* (1756). In "Theatro mania" Richard Graves acknowledges that declaiming speeches forms a part of boys' education and helps prepare them for public speaking in Parliament, the law courts, or the church, but, in contrast to Tom Bertram, Graves denies that this could be an argument in support of staging plays in the home. There is, Graves warns, no need to make a boy "a mimic or buffoon" (*Senilities,* p. 61).

14 Edmund echoes commentators who were certain that play-acting, even play-going, were harmful to female morals in particular. Thomas Gisborne, for instance, in his much reprinted *An Enquiry into the Duties of the Female Sex* (1797), which Austen appears to have read in 1805, warned that to act would excite in a young woman "a thirst of applause and admiration," would destroy her "diffidence, by the unrestrained familiarity with persons of the other sex which inevitably results from being joined with them in the drama," and would create in her "a general fondness for the perusal of plays, of which so many are improper to be read; and for attending dramatic representations, of which so many are unfit to be witnessed" ([London: T. Cadell and W. Davies, 1797], p. 175).

"Oh! dear, no ma'am—nobody suspected you—Well, Edmund," he continued, returning to the former subject, posture, and voice, as soon as Lady Bertram began to nod again—"But *this* I *will* maintain—that we shall be doing no harm."

"I cannot agree with you—I am convinced that my father would totally disapprove it."

"And I am convinced to the contrary.—Nobody is fonder of the exercise of talent in young people, or promotes it more, than my father; and for any thing of the acting, spouting, reciting kind, I think he has always a decided taste. I am sure he encouraged it in us as boys. How many a time have we mourned over the dead body of Julius Caesar, and *to be'd* and not *to be'd,* in this very room, for his amusement! And I am sure, *my name was Norval,* every evening of my life through one Christmas holidays."[13]

"It was a very different thing.—You must see the difference yourself. My father wished us, as school-boys, to speak well, but he would never wish his grown up daughters to be acting plays. His sense of decorum is strict."[14]

"I know all that," said Tom, displeased. "I know my father as well as you do, and I'll take care that his daughters do nothing to distress him. Manage your own concerns, Edmund, and I'll take care of the rest of the family."

"If you are resolved on acting," replied the persevering Edmund, "I must hope it will be in a very small and quiet way; and I think a theatre ought not to be attempted.—It would be taking liberties with my father's house in his absence which could not be justified."

"For every thing of that nature, I will be answerable,"—said Tom, in a decided tone.—"His house shall not be hurt. I have quite as great an interest in being careful of his house as you can have; and as to such alterations as I was suggesting just now, such as moving a book-case, or unlocking a door, or even as using the billiard-room for the space of a week without playing at billiards in it, you might just as well suppose he would object to our sitting more in this room, and less in the breakfast-room, than we did before he went away, or to my sister's piano forte being moved from one side of the room to the other.[15]—Absolute nonsense!"

"The innovation, if not wrong as an innovation, will be wrong as an expense."

"Yes, the expense of such an undertaking would be prodigious! Perhaps it might cost a whole twenty pounds.—Something of a Theatre we must have undoubtedly, but it will be on the simplest plan;—a green curtain and a little carpenter's work—and that's all; and as the carpenter's work may be all done at home by Christopher Jackson himself, it will be too absurd to talk of expense;—and as long as Jackson is employed, every thing will be right with Sir Thomas.—Don't imagine that nobody in this house can see or judge but yourself.—Don't act yourself, if you do not like it, but don't expect to govern every body else."

"No, as to acting myself," said Edmund, "*that* I absolutely protest against."

Tom walked out of the room as he said it, and Edmund was left to sit down and stir the fire in thoughtful vexation.

Fanny, who had heard it all, and borne Edmund company in every feeling throughout the whole, now ventured to say, in her anxiety to suggest some comfort, "Perhaps they may not be able to find any play to suit them. Your brother's taste, and your sisters', seem very different."

"I have no hope there, Fanny. If they persist in the scheme they will find something—I shall speak to my sisters, and try to dissuade *them,* and that is all I can do."

"I should think my aunt Norris would be on your side."

"I dare say she would; but she has no influence with either Tom or my sisters that could be of any use; and if I cannot convince them myself, I shall let things take their course, without attempting it through her. Family squabbling is the greatest evil of all, and we had better do any thing than be altogether by the ears."[16]

His sisters, to whom he had an opportunity of speaking the next morning, were quite as impatient of his advice, quite as unyielding to his representation, quite as determined in the cause of pleasure, as Tom.—Their mother had no objection to the plan, and they were not in the least afraid of their father's disapprobation.—There could be no harm in what had been done in so many respectable families, and

15  Though he is its heir, Tom's eagerness to rearrange the house seems cheeky at best. Austen's first readers might have been reminded of the behavior of the Prince of Wales (later George IV), who early in 1811 had become Regent in the place of his ailing father, George III. As Prince Regent he appeared to his many critics less intent on governing than in using his position to party and to embark on ostentatious redecoration projects in his houses. In *Jane Austen and Representations of Regency England,* Roger Sales points out the parallel between the two men's styles of rule, noting that when Tom, in his father's absence, "becomes regent, he is only interested in the ceremonial and theatrical aspects of government. He too moves the furniture about in order to create an elaborate theatrical set" ([London: Routledge, 1994], p. 72).

Austen's editors have tended to shift the apostrophe in this closing bit of Tom's dialogue, assuming that the singular form, "my sister's piano forte," was a printer's error and that Austen's original punctuation would have signaled that the piano belonged to both sisters. However, it is not implausible, given what we know of Bertram family life, that the piano is Maria's property exclusively.

16  Do anything rather than quarrel.

17 Mary politely offers to play a minor female character, an elderly chaperone or the companion in whom a
heroine confides. Under strappers are underlings or as-
sistants.

by so many women of the first consideration; and it must be scru-
pulousness run mad, that could see any thing to censure in a plan
like their's, comprehending only brothers and sisters, and intimate
friends, and which would never be heard of beyond themselves. Julia
*did* seem inclined to admit that Maria's situation might require particular caution and delicacy—but that could not extend to *her*—*she*
was at liberty; and Maria evidently considered her engagement as
only raising her so much more above restraint, and leaving her less
occasion than Julia, to consult either father or mother. Edmund had
little to hope, but he was still urging the subject, when Henry Crawford entered the room, fresh from the Parsonage, calling out, "No
want of hands in our Theatre, Miss Bertram. No want of under strappers—My sister desires her love, and hopes to be admitted into the
company, and will be happy to take the part of any old Duenna or
tame Confidante, that you may not like to do yourselves."[17]

Maria gave Edmund a glance, which meant, "What say you now?
Can we be wrong if Mary Crawford feels the same?" And Edmund
silenced, was obliged to acknowledge that the charm of acting might
well carry fascination to the mind of genius; and with the ingenuity
of love, to dwell more on the obliging, accommodating purport of
the message than on any thing else.

The scheme advanced. Opposition was vain; and as to Mrs. Norris, he was mistaken in supposing she would wish to make any. She
started no difficulties that were not talked down in five minutes by
her eldest nephew and niece, who were all-powerful with her; and, as
the whole arrangement was to bring very little expense to any body,
and none at all to herself, as she foresaw in it all the comforts of
hurry, bustle and importance, and derived the immediate advantage
of fancying herself obliged to leave her own house, where she had
been living a month at her own cost, and take up her abode in their's,
that every hour might be spent in their service; she was, in fact, exceedingly delighted with the project.

# 14

Fanny seemed nearer being right than Edmund had supposed. The business of finding a play that would suit every body, proved to be no trifle; and the carpenter had received his orders and taken his measurements, had suggested and removed at least two sets of difficulties, and having made the necessity of an enlargement of plan and expense fully evident, was already at work, while a play was still to seek. Other preparations were also in hand. An enormous roll of green baize had arrived from Northampton, and been cut out by Mrs. Norris (with a saving, by her good management, of full three-quarters of a yard), and was actually forming into a curtain by the housemaids, and still the play was wanting; and as two or three days passed away in this manner, Edmund began almost to hope that none might ever be found.

There were, in fact, so many things to be attended to, so many people to be pleased, so many best characters required, and above all, such a need that the play should be at once both tragedy and comedy, that there did seem as little chance of a decision, as any thing pursued by youth and zeal could hold out.

On the tragic side were the Miss Bertrams, Henry Crawford, and Mr. Yates;[1] on the comic, Tom Bertram, not *quite* alone, because it was evident that Mary Crawford's wishes, though politely kept back, inclined the same way; but his determinateness and his power, seemed to make allies unnecessary; and independent of this great irreconcilable difference, they wanted a piece containing very few characters in the whole, but every character first-rate, and three

1 Mr. Yates's preference for tragedy is overdetermined by his surname, which he shares with Mary Ann Yates (1728–1787), one of the leading ladies of the eighteenth-century theater. She was portrayed as the Tragic Muse in a 1771 painting by George Romney and a 1783 engraving by Thomas Stothard.

Mary Ann Yates is depicted in this mezzotint from 1771 in her signature role as Medea.

2 The rejected plays are standard works from the theatrical repertory of Austen's era: in addition to the three works of Shakespeare's that head up the list, they are John Home's *Douglas* (1756); Edward Moore's *The Gamester* (1753); Richard Brinsley Sheridan's comedies *The Rivals* (1775) and *The School for Scandal* (1777); Richard Cumberland's comedy *The Wheel of Fortune* (1791); and *The Heir at Law,* a comedy by George Colman the Younger (1808). Austen family members staged an amateur production of Sheridan's *The Rivals* in 1784.

3 Tom uses "nice" as a synonym for "fastidious" or "discriminating" rather than "kind" or "amiable." His usage would meet with the approval of Henry Tilney in *Northanger Abbey* (I, 14).

4 Tom Bertram's advice is that each member of the group be ready to play two roles in whichever play they choose. In Letter the Fifteenth of *Love and Freindship* (1790), a teenaged Austen had to comic effect imagined a troupe of strolling players rising to exactly the challenge that Tom is trying to cope with in this episode of *Mansfield Park*. As the heroine's distant relative Gustavus explains to her, whenever this company performed *Macbeth,* their Manager would play Banquo, his wife would play Lady Macbeth, he himself would do "the *Three Witches,*" and his brother Philander would act *"all the rest."* "Our Company was indeed rather small," Gustavus admits, in that it numbered only those four members, "but there were fewer to pay"; he then adds, with a philosophic spirit that Tom might applaud, "We did not mind trifles" (Jane Austen, *Juvenilia,* ed. Peter Sabor [Cambridge: Cambridge University Press, 2006], p. 139).

5 The characters in *The Heir at Law* whom Tom can imagine playing are Lord Duberly, a former tradesman who has come unexpectedly into his aristocratic title, and Dr. Pangloss, the pedantic tutor hired by this new peer of the realm. Pangloss's task is to help Duberly cope with his sudden social elevation and correct his grammar. Colman adapted the character of Pangloss from Voltaire's *Candide.*

6 *Lovers' Vows* offers two tragic leads for male actors: the parts of the Baron Wildenhaim, a nobleman

principal women. All the best plays were run over in vain. Neither Hamlet, nor Macbeth, nor Othello, nor Douglas, nor The Gamester, presented any thing that could satisfy even the tragedians; and The Rivals, The School for Scandal, Wheel of Fortune, Heir at Law, and a long etcetera, were successively dismissed with yet warmer objections.[2] No piece could be proposed that did not supply somebody with a difficulty, and on one side or the other it was a continual repetition of, "Oh! no, *that* will never do. Let us have no ranting tragedies. Too many characters—Not a tolerable woman's part in the play—Any thing but *that,* my dear Tom. It would be impossible to fill it up—One could not expect any body to take such a part—Nothing but buffoonery from beginning to end. *That* might do, perhaps, but for the low parts—If I *must* give my opinion, I have always thought it the most insipid play in the English language—*I* do not wish to make objections, I shall be happy to be of any use, but I think we could not choose worse."

Fanny looked on and listened, not unamused to observe the selfishness which, more or less disguised, seemed to govern them all, and wondering how it would end. For her own gratification she could have wished that something might be acted, for she had never seen even half a play, but everything of higher consequence was against it.

"This will never do," said Tom Bertram at last. "We are wasting time most abominably. Something must be fixed on. No matter what, so that something is chosen. We must not be so nice.[3] A few characters too many must not frighten us. We must *double* them.[4] We must descend a little. If a part is insignificant, the greater our credit in making any thing of it. From this moment *I* make no difficulties. I take any part you choose to give me, so as it be comic. Let it but be comic, I condition for nothing more."

For about the fifth time he then proposed the Heir at Law, doubting only whether to prefer Lord Duberley or Dr. Pangloss for himself, and very earnestly, but very unsuccessfully, trying to persuade the others that there were some fine tragic parts in the rest of the Dramatis Personae.[5]

The pause which followed this fruitless effort was ended by the same speaker, who taking up one of the many volumes of plays that lay on the table, and turning it over, suddenly exclaimed, "Lovers' Vows! And why should not Lovers' Vows do for *us* as well as for the Ravenshaws? How came it never to be thought of before? It strikes me as if it would do exactly. What say you all?—Here are two capital tragic parts for Yates and Crawford,[6] and here is the rhyming butler for me[7]—if nobody else wants it—a trifling part, but the sort of thing I should not dislike, and as I said before, I am determined to take any thing and do my best. And as for the rest, they may be filled up by any body. It is only Count Cassel and Anhalt."

The suggestion was generally welcome. Every body was growing weary of indecision, and the first idea with every body was, that nothing had been proposed before so likely to suit them all. Mr. Yates was particularly pleased; he had been sighing and longing to do the Baron at Ecclesford, had grudged every rant of Lord Ravenshaw's, and been forced to re-rant it all in his own room. To storm through Baron Wildenhaim was the height of his theatrical ambition, and with the advantage of knowing half the scenes by heart already, he did now with the greatest alacrity offer his services for the part. To do him justice, however, he did not resolve to appropriate it—for remembering that there was some very good ranting ground in Frederick, he professed an equal willingness for that. Henry Crawford was ready to take either. Whichever Mr. Yates did not choose, would perfectly satisfy him, and a short parley of compliment ensued. Miss Bertram feeling all the interest of an Agatha in the question,[8] took on her to decide it, by observing to Mr. Yates, that this was a point in which height and figure ought to be considered, and that *his* being the tallest, seemed to fit him peculiarly for the Baron. She was acknowledged to be quite right, and the two parts being accepted accordingly, she was certain of the proper Frederick. Three of the characters were now cast, besides Mr. Rushworth, who was always answered for by Maria as willing to do any thing; when Julia, meaning like her sister to be Agatha, began to be scrupulous on Miss Crawford's account.

"This is not behaving well by the absent," said she. "Here are not women enough. Amelia and Agatha may do for Maria and me, but here is nothing for your sister, Mr. Crawford."

haunted by guilt over the libertinism of his youth, and Frederick, a poor soldier on leave from the army. Over the course of the play's first act, Frederick not only discovers his illegitimacy but also learns the story of his mother's seduction and the name of the father whom he has never known—Baron Wildenhaim. Act III looks back to Sophocles' *Oedipus Rex* as it brings these two men together: Frederick turns highwayman to assist his starving mother, and the man he tries to rob turns out to be none other than the baron himself, recently returned to his birthplace.

7 The rhyming Butler whom Tom mentions is a comic role that Inchbald added to Kotzebue's original play to offset its overall mood of "amazement, guilt, shame, and horror"—as she put it herself in a stage direction (*The British Theatre, or, A Collection of Plays,* 25 vols. [London: Longman, 1808], vol. 23, p. 60). As Tom remembers, the Butler insists whenever possible on delivering the bad news that accumulates through the play's first three acts in poetry of his own composing rather than everyday prose. Tom evidently does not share the reluctance to perform "low parts"—plebeian characters—that his companions voiced earlier in this chapter.

8 The curtain rises in Act I to reveal Agatha, mother to Frederick and, as we learn, the lover of the baron many years before: sick, starving, she is being turned out of doors by an innkeeper for her inability to pay for her lodging. This is the part the prosperous, patrician Maria Bertram hopes to claim for herself. Agatha and the baron do not occupy the stage at the same time until Act V, but, as Maria evidently knows, from their reunion in Act I on, Agatha and Frederick do play several sentimental scenes together involving considerable physical contact. If Maria is to play Agatha, rather than Amelia, the heroine of the comic subplot of *Lovers' Vows,* it only makes sense that it should matter to her which man is cast as Frederick.

9 Inchbald's stage directions for Act I specify that Frederick will make his entrance "dressed in a soldier's uniform" and with "a knapsack on his shoulders" (*British Theatre,* vol. 23, p. 13). This soldier on leave from his regiment is seeking to obtain lodgings at the inn when he notices the beggar woman who will turn out to be Agatha, his own mother. The more Henry insists that Julia Bertram is constitutionally better suited to a comic role than she is to that of the tragic Agatha, the more he makes his preference for Maria Bertram apparent. Austen once again seems to invite readers to consider how Henry's situation resembles David Garrick's as portrayed in the Reynolds painting: like the eighteenth-century actor, Henry appears to be pulled in two directions, by a comic woman and a tragic one.

10 This is a bit part, as both Mr. Yates and Mr. Crawford will confirm. At the end of Act I of *Lovers' Vows,* the poor but virtuous couple who live in a nearby cottage will offer Agatha refuge.

Mr. Crawford desired *that* might not be thought of; he was very sure his sister had no wish of acting, but as she might be useful, and that she would not allow herself to be considered in the present case. But this was immediately opposed by Tom Bertram, who asserted the part of Amelia to be in every respect the property of Miss Crawford if she would accept it. "It falls as naturally, as necessarily to her," said he, "as Agatha does to one or other of my sisters. It can be no sacrifice on their side, for it is highly comic."

A short silence followed. Each sister looked anxious; for each felt the best claim to Agatha, and was hoping to have it pressed on her by the rest. Henry Crawford, who meanwhile had taken up the play, and with seeming carelessness was turning over the first act, soon settled the business. "I must entreat Miss *Julia* Bertram," said he, "not to engage in the part of Agatha, or it will be the ruin of all my solemnity. You must not, indeed you must not—(turning to her). I could not stand your countenance dressed up in woe and paleness. The many laughs we have had together would infallibly come across me, and Frederick and his knapsack would be obliged to run away."[9]

Pleasantly, courteously it was spoken; but the manner was lost in the matter to Julia's feelings. She saw a glance at Maria, which confirmed the injury to herself; it was a scheme—a trick; she was slighted, Maria was preferred; the smile of triumph which Maria was trying to suppress shewed how well it was understood, and before Julia could command herself enough to speak, her brother gave his weight against her too, by saying, "Oh! yes! Maria must be Agatha. Maria will be the best Agatha. Though Julia fancies she prefers tragedy, I would not trust her in it. There is nothing of tragedy about her. She has not the look of it. Her features are not tragic features, and she walks too quick, and speaks too quick, and would not keep her countenance. She had better do the old countrywoman; the Cottager's wife; you had, indeed, Julia. Cottager's wife is a very pretty part I assure you. The old lady relieves the high-flown benevolence of her husband with a good deal of spirit. You shall be Cottager's wife."[10]

"Cottager's wife!" cried Mr. Yates. "What are you talking of? The most trivial, paltry, insignificant part; the merest common-place— not a tolerable speech in the whole. Your sister do that! It is an insult to propose it. At Ecclesford the governess was to have done it. We all agreed that it could not be offered to any body else. A little more justice, Mr. Manager, if you please. You do not deserve the office, if you cannot appreciate the talents of your company a little better."

"Why as to *that,* my good friend, till I and my company have really acted there must be some guess-work; but I mean no disparagement to Julia. We cannot have two Agathas, and we must have one Cottager's wife; and I am sure I set her the example of moderation myself in being satisfied with the old Butler. If the part is trifling she will have more credit in making something of it; and if she is so desperately bent against every thing humorous, let her take Cottager's speeches instead of Cottager's wife's, and so change the parts all through; *he* is solemn and pathetic enough I am sure. It could make no difference in the play; and as for Cottager himself, when he has got his wife's speeches, *I* would undertake him with all my heart."

"With all your partiality for Cottager's wife," said Henry Crawford, "it will be impossible to make any thing of it fit for your sister, and we must not suffer her good nature to be imposed on. We must not *allow* her to accept the part. She must not be left to her own complaisance.[11] Her talents will be wanted in Amelia. Amelia is a character more difficult to be well represented than even Agatha. I consider Amelia is the most difficult character in the whole piece. It requires great powers, great nicety, to give her playfulness and simplicity without extravagance. I have seen good actresses fail in the part. Simplicity, indeed, is beyond the reach of almost every actress by profession. It requires a delicacy of feeling which they have not.[12] It requires a gentlewoman—a Julia Bertram. You *will* undertake it I hope?" turning to her with a look of anxious entreaty, which softened her a little; but while she hesitated what to say, her brother again interposed with Miss Crawford's better claim.

"No, no, Julia must not be Amelia. It is not at all the part for her. She would not like it. She would not do well. She is too tall and robust. Amelia should be a small, light, girlish, skipping figure. It is fit for Miss Crawford and Miss Crawford only. She looks the part, and I am persuaded will do it admirably."

Without attending to this, Henry Crawford continued his supplication. "You must oblige us," said he, "indeed you must. When you have studied the character, I am sure you will feel it suit you. Tragedy

11 Her desire to do what is agreeable.

12 Amelia is Baron Wildenhaim's young daughter. When she is introduced in Act II she is on the point of marriage to the foppish Count Cassel, a husband chosen for her by her father, but his plans are derailed as the innocent but enthusiastic girl sets out determinedly to educate herself about the true nature of love. She proves a quick study, which is key to the comedy of this subplot. Henry's comments on Amelia echo reviews of *Lovers' Vows:* the reviewer for the *Star,* for example, spoke of the "fascinating . . . coquetry" that the actress H. Johnston brought to the role and proposed that "the character of Amelia is that of arch simplicity; the most elegant, but perhaps the most difficult character in nature faithfully to pourtray" (quoted in Colin Pedley, "'Terrific and Unprincipled Compositions': The Reception of *Lovers' Vows* and *Mansfield Park,*" *Philological Quarterly* 74 [1995], p. 307).

13 In Act IV, Amelia pays a charitable visit to Frederick in his prison cell in the baron's castle.

may be your choice, but it will certainly appear that comedy chooses *you*. You will be to visit me in prison with a basket of provisions; you will not refuse to visit me in prison? I think I see you coming in with your basket."[13]

The influence of his voice was felt. Julia wavered: but was he only trying to soothe and pacify her, and make her overlook the previous affront? She distrusted him. The slight had been most determined. He was, perhaps, but at treacherous play with her. She looked suspiciously at her sister; Maria's countenance was to decide it; if she were vexed and alarmed—but Maria looked all serenity and satisfaction, and Julia well knew that on this ground Maria could not be happy but at her expense. With hasty indignation therefore, and a tremulous voice, she said to him, "You do not seem afraid of not keeping your countenance when I come in with a basket of provisions—though one might have supposed—but it is only as Agatha that I was to be so overpowering!"—She stopped—Henry Crawford looked rather foolish, and as if he did not know what to say. Tom Bertram began again,

"Miss Crawford must be Amelia.—She will be an excellent Amelia."

"Do not be afraid of *my* wanting the character," cried Julia with angry quickness;—"I am *not* to be Agatha, and I am sure I will do nothing else; and as to Amelia, it is of all parts in the world the most disgusting to me. I quite detest her. An odious, little, pert, unnatural, impudent girl. I have always protested against comedy, and this is comedy in its worst form." And so saying, she walked hastily out of the room, leaving awkward feelings to more than one, but exciting small compassion in any except Fanny, who had been a quiet auditor of the whole, and who could not think of her as under the agitations of *jealousy,* without great pity.

A short silence succeeded her leaving them; but her brother soon returned to business and Lovers' Vows, and was eagerly looking over the play, with Mr. Yates's help, to ascertain what scenery would be necessary—while Maria and Henry Crawford conversed together in an under voice, and the declaration with which she began of, "I am sure I would give up the part to Julia most willingly, but that though I shall probably do it very ill, I feel persuaded *she* would do it worse," was doubtless receiving all the compliments it called for.

When this had lasted some time, the division of the party was completed by Tom Bertram and Mr. Yates walking off together to consult farther in the room now beginning to be called *the Theatre,* and Miss Bertram's resolving to go down to the Parsonage herself with the offer of Amelia to Miss Crawford; and Fanny remained alone.

The first use she made of her solitude was to take up the volume which had been left on the table, and begin to acquaint herself with the play of which she had heard so much. Her curiosity was all awake, and she ran through it with an eagerness which was suspended only by intervals of astonishment, that it could be chosen in the present instance—that it could be proposed and accepted in a private Theatre! Agatha and Amelia appeared to her in their different ways so totally improper for home representation—the situation of one, and the language of the other, so unfit to be expressed by any woman of modesty,[14] that she could hardly suppose her cousins could be aware of what they were engaging in;[15] and longed to have them roused as soon as possible by the remonstrance which Edmund would certainly make.

[14] As Fanny has just learned from her reading, the play is full of sexually suggestive material. Agatha is an unwed mother who speaks rather explicitly about her sexual initiation as a matter of "fervent caresses" and "delirium" (I, i, p. 13), and Amelia is indelicately blunt in her pursuit of love, exhibiting, as the *Times* reviewer of *Lovers' Vows* complained, "the boldness and pert manners of a country hoyden" (quoted in Pedley, "'Terrific and Unprincipled Compositions,'" p. 307).

[15] The Bertram sisters' rivalry over the role of Agatha indicates that Fanny is wrong. They know exactly what the play will demand.

## 15

1 One of the first things we learn about Count Cassel is that he is "a tedious time dressing" (II, ii, p. 28). The count is ultimately discovered to be a philanderer as well as a vain dandy.

MISS CRAWFORD ACCEPTED THE PART very readily, and soon after Miss Bertram's return from the Parsonage, Mr. Rushworth arrived, and another character was consequently cast. He had the offer of Count Cassel and Anhalt, and at first did not know which to choose, and wanted Miss Bertram to direct him, but upon being made to understand the different style of the characters, and which was which, and recollecting that he had once seen the play in London, and had thought Anhalt a very stupid fellow, he soon decided for the Count. Miss Bertram approved the decision, for the less he had to learn the better; and though she could not sympathize in his wish that the Count and Agatha might be to act together, nor wait very patiently while he was slowly turning over the leaves with the hope of still discovering such a scene, she very kindly took his part in hand, and curtailed every speech that admitted being shortened;—besides pointing out the necessity of his being very much dressed, and choosing his colours.[1] Mr. Rushworth liked the idea of his finery very well, though affecting to despise it, and was too much engaged with what his own appearance would be, to think of the others, or draw any of those conclusions, or feel any of that displeasure, which Maria had been half prepared for.

Thus much was settled before Edmund, who had been out all the morning, knew anything of the matter; but when he entered the drawing-room before dinner, the buz of discussion was high between Tom, Maria, and Mr. Yates; and Mr. Rushworth stepped forward with great alacrity to tell him the agreeable news.

"We have got a play," said he.—"It is to be Lovers' Vows; and I am to be Count Cassel, and am to come in first with a blue dress, and a pink satin cloak, and afterwards am to have another fine fancy suit by way of a shooting dress.[2]—I do not know how I shall like it."

Fanny's eyes followed Edmund, and her heart beat for him as she heard this speech, and saw his look, and felt what his sensations must be.

"Lovers' Vows!"—in a tone of the greatest amazement, was his only reply to Mr. Rushworth; and he turned towards his brother and sisters as if hardly doubting a contradiction.

"Yes," cried Mr. Yates.—"After all our debatings and difficulties, we find there is nothing that will suit us altogether so well, nothing so unexceptionable, as Lovers' Vows. The wonder is that it should not have been thought of before. My stupidity was abominable, for here we have all the advantage of what I saw at Ecclesford; and it is so useful to have anything of a model!—We have cast almost every part."

"But what do you do for women?" said Edmund gravely, and looking at Maria.

Maria blushed in spite of herself as she answered, "I take the part which Lady Ravenshaw was to have done, and (with a bolder eye) Miss Crawford is to be Amelia."

"I should not have thought it the sort of play to be so easily filled up, with *us*," replied Edmund, turning away to the fire where sat his mother, aunt, and Fanny, and seating himself with a look of great vexation.

Mr. Rushworth followed him to say, "I come in three times, and have two-and-forty speeches. That's something, is not it?—But I do not much like the idea of being so fine.—I shall hardly know myself in a blue dress, and a pink satin cloak."

Edmund could not answer him.—In a few minutes Mr. Bertram was called out of the room to satisfy some doubts of the carpenter, and being accompanied by Mr. Yates, and followed soon afterwards by Mr. Rushworth, Edmund almost immediately took the opportunity of saying, "I cannot before Mr. Yates speak what I feel as to this play, without reflecting on his friends at Ecclesford—but I must

2 The baron and count go hunting in Act III, giving the count, as he notes with boastful anticipation, the opportunity to use his "elegant gun" with its "mother-of-pearl" butt (II, ii, p. 29).

now, my dear Maria, tell *you,* that I think it exceedingly unfit for private representation, and that I hope you will give it up.—I cannot but suppose you *will* when you have read it carefully over.—Read only the first Act aloud, to either your mother or aunt, and see how you can approve it.—It will not be necessary to send you to your *father's* judgment, I am convinced."

"We see things very differently," cried Maria—"I am perfectly acquainted with the play, I assure you—and with a very few omissions, and so forth, which will be made, of course, I can see nothing objectionable in it; and *I* am not the *only* young woman you find, who thinks it very fit for private representation."

"I am sorry for it," was his answer—"But in this matter it is *you* who are to lead. *You* must set the example.—If others have blundered, it is your place to put them right, and show them what true delicacy is.—In all points of decorum, *your* conduct must be law to the rest of the party."

This picture of her consequence had some effect, for no one loved better to lead than Maria;—and with far more good humour she answered, "I am much obliged to you, Edmund;—you mean very well, I am sure—but I still think you see things too strongly; and I really cannot undertake to harangue all the rest upon a subject of this kind.—*There* would be the greatest indecorum I think."

"Do you imagine that I could have such an idea in my head? No—let your conduct be the only harangue.—Say that, on examining the part, you feel yourself unequal to it, that you find it requiring more exertion and confidence than you can be supposed to have.—Say this with firmness, and it will be quite enough.—All who can distinguish, will understand your motive.—The play will be given up, and your delicacy honoured as it ought."

"Do not act anything improper, my dear," said Lady Bertram. "Sir Thomas would not like it.—Fanny, ring the bell; I must have my dinner.—To be sure Julia is dressed by this time."

"I am convinced, madam," said Edmund, preventing Fanny, "that Sir Thomas would not like it."

"There, my dear, do you hear what Edmund says?"

"If I were to decline the part," said Maria with renewed zeal, "Julia would certainly take it."

"What!"—cried Edmund, "if she knew your reasons!"

"Oh! she might think the difference between us—the difference in our situations—that *she* need not be so scrupulous as *I* might feel necessary. I am sure she would argue so. No, you must excuse me, I cannot retract my consent. It is too far settled; every body would be so disappointed. Tom would be quite angry: and if we are so very nice,[3] we shall never act any thing."

"I was just going to say the very same thing," said Mrs. Norris. "If every play is to be objected to, you will act nothing—and the preparations will be all so much money thrown away—and I am sure *that* would be a discredit to us all. I do not know the play; but, as Maria says, if there is any thing a little too warm (and it is so with most of them) it can be easily left out.—We must not be over precise Edmund.[4] As Mr. Rushworth is to act too, there can be no harm.—I only wish Tom had known his own mind when the carpenters began, for there was the loss of half a day's work about those side-doors.—The curtain will be a good job, however. The maids do their work very well, and I think we shall be able to send back some dozens of the rings.—There is no occasion to put them so very close together. I *am* of some use I hope in preventing waste and making the most of things. There should always be one steady head to superintend so many young ones. I forgot to tell Tom of something that happened to me this very day.—I had been looking about me in the poultry yard, and was just coming out, when who should I see but Dick Jackson making up to the servants' hall door with two bits of deal board in his hand, bringing them to father, you may be sure; mother had chanced to send him of a message to father, and then father had bid him bring up them two bits of board, for he could not no how do without them. I knew what all this meant, for the servants' dinner bell was ringing at the very moment over our heads, and as I hate such encroaching people, (the Jacksons are very encroaching, I have always said so,—just the sort of people to get all they can), I said to the boy directly—(a great lubberly fellow of ten years old you know,

3 Fastidious, choosey.

4 Overly scrupulous.

5 A "lubberly fellow" is a clumsy oaf. The Jackson family might well understand themselves as claiming the usual perquisites of their employment on the estate in claiming leftover bits of lumber ("deal board") or meals in the servant's hall, but Mrs. Norris, with her talk of their "encroaching" and "marauding," takes a hard line on such traditional entitlements and reinterprets them as greedy theft. The critic Fraser Easton has outlined the attack on the "customary reciprocity" of domestic service that is lodged within Mrs. Norris's complaint about the Jacksons. He demonstrates how her wish to enforce discipline among the Mansfield servants can be connected to a host of contemporary initiatives, rural landowners' enclosures of the commons included, that aimed, in the name of economic modernization, to eliminate the customary rights of the poor. See "The Political Economy of *Mansfield Park:* Fanny Price and the Atlantic Working Class," *Textual Practice* 12 (1998): 451–488.

6 Dirty weather is wet, squally weather.

who ought to be ashamed of himself,) *I'll* take the boards to your father, Dick; so get you home again as fast as you can.—The boy looked very silly and turned away without offering a word, for I believe I might speak pretty sharp; and I dare say it will cure him of coming marauding about the house for one while,—I hate such greediness—so good as your father is to the family, employing the man all the year round!"[5]

Nobody was at the trouble of an answer; the others soon returned, and Edmund found that to have endeavoured to set them right must be his only satisfaction.

Dinner passed heavily. Mrs. Norris related again her triumph over Dick Jackson, but neither play nor preparation were otherwise much talked of, for Edmund's disapprobation was felt even by his brother, though he would not have owned it. Maria, wanting Henry Crawford's animating support, thought the subject better avoided. Mr. Yates, who was trying to make himself agreeable to Julia, found her gloom less impenetrable on any topic than that of his regret at her secession from their company, and Mr. Rushworth having only his own part, and his own dress in his head, had soon talked away all that could be said of either.

But the concerns of the theatre were suspended only for an hour or two; there was still a great deal to be settled; and the spirits of evening giving fresh courage, Tom, Maria, and Mr. Yates, soon after their being re-assembled in the drawing-room, seated themselves in committee at a separate table, with the play open before them, and were just getting deep in the subject when a most welcome interruption was given by the entrance of Mr. and Miss Crawford, who, late and dark and dirty as it was,[6] could not help coming, and were received with the most grateful joy.

"Well, how do you go on?" and "What have you settled?" and "Oh! we can do nothing without you," followed the first salutations; and Henry Crawford was soon seated with the other three at the table, while his sister made her way to Lady Bertram, and with pleasant attention was complimenting *her.* "I must really congratulate your ladyship," said she, "on the play being chosen; for though you have borne it with exemplary patience, I am sure you must be sick of all our noise and difficulties. The actors may be glad, but the by-standers must be infinitely more thankful for a decision; and I do sincerely give you joy, madam, as well as Mrs. Norris, and every body else who is in the same predicament," glancing half fearfully, half slyly, beyond Fanny to Edmund.

She was very civilly answered by Lady Bertram, but Edmund said nothing. His being only a by-stander was not disclaimed. After continuing in chat with the party round the fire a few minutes, Miss Crawford returned to the party round the table; and standing by them, seemed to interest herself in their arrangements till, as if struck by a sudden recollection, she exclaimed, "My good friends, you are most composedly at work upon these cottages and ale-houses, inside and out—but pray let me know my fate in the mean-while. Who is to be Anhalt? What gentleman among you am I to have the pleasure of making love to?"[7]

For a moment no one spoke; and then many spoke together to tell the same melancholy truth—that they had not yet got any Anhalt. "Mr. Rushworth was to be Count Cassel, but no one had yet under-taken Anhalt."

"I had my choice of the parts," said Mr. Rushworth; "but I thought I should like the Count best—though I do not much relish the finery I am to have."

"You chose very wisely, I am sure," replied Miss Crawford, with a brightened look. "Anhalt is a heavy part."

"*The Count* has two and forty speeches," returned Mr. Rushworth, "which is no trifle."

"I am not at all surprised," said Miss Crawford, after a short pause, "at this want of an Anhalt. Amelia deserves no better. Such a forward young lady may well frighten the men."

"I should be but too happy in taking the part if it were possible," cried Tom, "but unluckily the Butler and Anhalt are in together. I will not entirely give it up, however—I will try what can be done—I will look it over again."

"Your *brother* should take the part," said Mr. Yates, in a low voice. "Do not you think he would?"

"*I* shall not ask him," replied Tom, in a cold, determined manner.

7 Anhalt is the chaplain in the baron's household and serves as tutor and mentor to the baron's motherless daughter, Amelia. He is also the man whom Amelia, after she learns to examine her heart, discovers she loves. Mary's question about the identity of the gentleman to whom she as Amelia will be "making love" is not as im-modest as it seems, for she uses the term in the nine-teenth-century sense that makes it synonymous with *wooing* or *sweet-talking*. Yet as Mary tacitly acknowl-edges, that Inchbald has a female character take the lead in making love is itself something of a shocker. "As you have for a long time instructed me, why should not I now begin to teach you?" Amelia asks Anhalt in Act III, scene ii: she proceeds to "make love" to him as she teaches him the "science of herself" (p. 38).

Miss Crawford talked of something else, and soon afterwards rejoined the party at the fire. "They do not want me at all," said she, seating herself. "I only puzzle them, and oblige them to make civil speeches. Mr. Edmund Bertram, as you do not act yourself, you will be a disinterested adviser; and, therefore, I apply to *you*. What shall we do for an Anhalt? Is it practicable for any of the others to double it? What is your advice?"

"My advice," said he, calmly, "is that you change the play."

"*I* should have no objection," she replied; "for though I should not particularly dislike the part of Amelia if well supported—that is, if every thing went well—I shall be sorry to be an inconvenience—but as they do not choose to hear your advice at *that table*—(looking round)—it certainly will not be taken."

Edmund said no more.

"If *any* part could tempt *you* to act, I suppose it would be Anhalt," observed the lady, archly, after a short pause—"for he is a clergyman you know."

"*That* circumstance would by no means tempt me," he replied, "for I should be sorry to make the character ridiculous by bad acting. It must be very difficult to keep Anhalt from appearing a formal, solemn lecturer; and the man who chooses the profession itself, is, perhaps, one of the last who would wish to represent it on the stage."

Miss Crawford was silenced; and with some feelings of resentment and mortification, moved her chair considerably nearer the tea-table, and gave all her attention to Mrs. Norris, who was presiding there.

"Fanny," cried Tom Bertram, from the other table, where the conference was eagerly carrying on, and the conversation incessant, "we want your services."

Fanny was up in a moment, expecting some errand, for the habit of employing her in that way was not yet overcome, in spite of all that Edmund could do.

"Oh! we do not want to disturb you from your seat. We do not want your *present* services. We shall only want you in our play. You must be Cottager's wife."

"Me!" cried Fanny, sitting down again with a most frightened look. "Indeed you must excuse me. I could not act any thing if you were to give me the world. No, indeed, I cannot act."

"Indeed but you must, for we cannot excuse you. It need not frighten you; it is a nothing of a part, a mere nothing, not above half a dozen speeches altogether, and it will not much signify if nobody hears a word you say, so you may be as creepmouse as you like, but we must have you to look at."

"If you are afraid of half a dozen speeches," cried Mr. Rushworth, "what would you do with such a part as mine? I have forty-two to learn."

"It is not that I am afraid of learning by heart," said Fanny, shocked to find herself at that moment the only speaker in the room, and to feel that almost every eye was upon her; "but I really cannot act."

"Yes, yes, you can act well enough for *us*. Learn your part, and we will teach you all the rest. You have only two scenes, and as I shall be Cottager, I'll put you in and push you about, and you will do it very well I'll answer for it."

"No, indeed, Mr. Bertram, you must excuse me. You cannot have an idea. It would be absolutely impossible for me. If I were to undertake it, I should only disappoint you."

"Phoo! Phoo! Do not be so shamefaced. You'll do it very well. Every allowance will be made for you. We do not expect perfection. You must get a brown gown, and a white apron, and a mob cap, and we must make you a few wrinkles, and a little of the crowsfoot at the corner of your eyes, and you will be a very proper, little old woman."

"You must excuse me, indeed you must excuse me," cried Fanny, growing more and more red from excessive agitation, and looking distressfully at Edmund, who was kindly observing her, but unwilling to exasperate his brother by interference, gave her only an encouraging smile. Her entreaty had no effect on Tom; he only said again what he had said before; and it was not merely Tom, for the requisition was now backed by Maria and Mr. Crawford, and Mr. Yates, with an urgency which differed from his, but in being more gentle or more ceremonious, and which altogether was quite overpowering to

Fanny; and before she could breathe after it, Mrs. Norris completed the whole, by thus addressing her in a whisper at once angry and audible: "What a piece of work here is about nothing,—I am quite ashamed of you, Fanny, to make such a difficulty of obliging your cousins in a trifle of this sort,—So kind as they are to you!—Take the part with a good grace, and let us hear no more of the matter, I entreat."

"Do not urge her, madam," said Edmund. "It is not fair to urge her in this manner.—You see she does not like to act.—Let her choose for herself as well as the rest of us.—Her judgment may be quite as safely trusted.—Do not urge her any more."

"I am not going to urge her,"—replied Mrs. Norris sharply, "but I shall think her a very obstinate, ungrateful girl, if she does not do what her aunt and cousins wish her—very ungrateful indeed, considering who and what she is."

Edmund was too angry to speak; but Miss Crawford looking for a moment with astonished eyes at Mrs. Norris, and then at Fanny, whose tears were beginning to show themselves, immediately said with some keenness, "I do not like my situation; this *place* is too hot for me"—and moved away her chair to the opposite side of the table close to Fanny, saying to her, in a kind low whisper as she placed herself, "Never mind, my dear Miss Price—this is a cross evening,—everybody is cross and teasing—but do not let us mind them"; and with pointed attention continued to talk to her and endeavour to raise her spirits, in spite of being out of spirits herself.—By a look at her brother, she prevented any farther entreaty from the theatrical board, and the really good feelings by which she was almost purely governed, were rapidly restoring her to all the little she had lost in Edmund's favour.

Fanny did not love Miss Crawford; but she felt very much obliged to her for her present kindness; and when from taking notice of her work and wishing *she* could work as well, and begging for the pattern, and supposing Fanny was now preparing for her *appearance* as of course she would come out when her cousin was married, Miss Crawford proceeded to inquire if she had heard lately from her brother at sea, and said that she had quite a curiosity to see him, and imagined him a very fine young man, and advised Fanny to get his picture drawn before he went to sea again.—She could not help admitting it to be very agreeable flattery, or help listening, and answering with more animation than she had intended.

The consultation upon the play still went on, and Miss Crawford's attention was first called from Fanny by Tom Bertram's telling her, with infinite regret, that he found it absolutely impossible for him to undertake the part of Anhalt in addition to the Butler;—he had been most anxiously trying to make it out to be feasible,—but it would not do,—he must give it up. "But there will not be the smallest difficulty in filling it," he added.—"We have but to speak the word; we may pick and choose.—I could name at this moment at least six young men within six miles of us, who are wild to be admitted into our company, and there are one or two that would not disgrace us.— I should not be afraid to trust either of the Olivers or Charles Maddox.—Tom Oliver is a very clever fellow, and Charles Maddox is as gentlemanlike a man as you will see any where, so I will take my horse early to-morrow morning, and ride over to Stoke, and settle with one of them."[8]

While he spoke, Maria was looking apprehensively round at Edmund in full expectation that he must oppose such an enlargement of the plan as this—so contrary to all their first protestations; but Edmund said nothing.—After a moment's thought, Miss Crawford calmly replied, "As far as I am concerned, I can have no objection to any thing that you all think eligible. Have I ever seen either of the gentlemen?—Yes, Mr. Charles Maddox dined at my sister's one day, did not he Henry?—A quiet-looking young man. I remember him. Let *him* be applied to, if you please, for it will be less unpleasant to me than to have a perfect stranger."

Charles Maddox was to be the man.—Tom repeated his resolution of going to him early on the morrow; and though Julia, who had scarcely opened her lips before, observed in a sarcastic manner, and with a glance, first at Maria, and then at Edmund, that "the Mansfield Theatricals would enliven the whole neighbourhood exceedingly"—Edmund still held his peace, and shewed his feelings only by a determined gravity.

8 There are several real towns named Stoke in Northamptonshire.

"I am not very sanguine as to our play"—said Miss Crawford in an under voice, to Fanny, after some consideration; "and I can tell Mr. Maddox, that I shall shorten some of *his* speeches, and a great many of *my own,* before we rehearse together.—It will be very disagreeable, and by no means what I expected."

An unflattering satiric depiction by Henry Wigstead of the author of *Lovers' Vows,* Elizabeth Inchbald, complete with a cat who appears to be passing judgment on her talents by relieving itself atop one of her manuscripts. Wigstead uses the manuscript that is placed on the author's writing table to propose that "puffing"—self-promotion—is the prime ingredient of her writing. The poster on the back wall is inscribed with the titles of three of Inchbald's most celebrated plays.

# 16

IT WAS NOT in Miss Crawford's power to talk Fanny into any real forgetfulness of what had passed.—When the evening was over, she went to bed full of it, her nerves still agitated by the shock of such an attack from her cousin Tom, so public and so persevered in, and her spirits sinking under her aunt's unkind reflection and reproach. To be called into notice in such a manner, to hear that it was but the prelude to something so infinitely worse, to be told that she must do what was so impossible as to act; and then to have the charge of obstinacy and ingratitude follow it, enforced with such a hint at the dependence of her situation, had been too distressing at the time, to make the remembrance when she was alone much less so,—especially with the supcradded dread of what the morrow might produce in continuation of the subject. Miss Crawford had protected her only for the time; and if she were applied to again among themselves with all the authoritative urgency that Tom and Maria were capable of; and Edmund perhaps away—what should she do? She fell asleep before she could answer the question, and found it quite as puzzling when she awoke the next morning. The little white attic, which had continued her sleeping room ever since her first entering the family, proving incompetent to suggest any reply, she had recourse, as soon as she was dressed, to another apartment, more spacious and more meet for walking about in, and thinking, and of which she had now for some time been almost equally mistress. It had been their school-room; so called till the Miss Bertrams would not allow it to be called so any longer, and inhabited as such to a later

1 That Fanny is "mistress" of this room suggests the sort of alignment of privacy and property with personality that also conditions Austen's characterization of Sir Thomas. In the novel's first sentence Fanny's uncle is introduced in close conjunction with his house, and the novel's mentions of his study ensure that he stands as the only character besides Fanny who is explicitly granted a room of his own. There is a tenuousness to Fanny's relationship to her possessions, however, which means that finally the East room is not much of a sanctuary; throughout the novel Fanny's room is also a place other people enter at will. See Anne B. McGrail, "Fanny Price's 'Customary' Subjectivity: Rereading the Individual in *Mansfield Park*," in *A Companion to Jane Austen Studies,* ed. Laura Lambdin and Robert Lambdin (Westport, Conn.: Greenwood Press, 2000), pp. 57–70.

2 Facing east, the room is warmed by the morning sun.

3 Transparent prints were drawings or watercolors that one covered with a varnish so that they would be translucent when positioned in front of a light source. Instructions for this "extremely fashionable and popular" handicraft are given in a manual by James Roberts, "portrait-painter to His Royal Highness the Duke of Clarence," who also states that the proper subjects for such images should be "Abbeys in ruin, Gothic painted windows [i.e. stained glass], illuminated temples and gardens, moonlight, fires, and groupes of gypsies sitting round a fire in a thick wood, with the moon glimmering behind the trees" (*Introductory Lessons . . . for the Use of Those who are Desirous of Gaining Some Knowledge of the Pleasing Art of Painting in Water Colours* [London: for the author, 1800], p. 30). Fanny's selection of images adheres closely to this advice. Tintern Abbey, the ruined abbey on the banks of the River Wye, was a standard destination in Austen's day for tourists in quest of the picturesque (William Wordsworth most famously), as was the Lake District (much of which lies within the county of Cumberland). Fanny's taste runs to new, Romantic notions of scenic beauty.

period. There Miss Lee had lived, and there they had read and written, and talked and laughed, till within the last three years, when she had quitted them.—The room had then become useless, and for some time was quite deserted, except by Fanny, when she visited her plants, or wanted one of the books, which she was still glad to keep there, from the deficiency of space and accommodation in her little chamber above;—but gradually, as her value for the comforts of it increased, she had added to her possessions, and spent more of her time there; and having nothing to oppose her, had so naturally and so artlessly worked herself into it, that it was now generally admitted to be her's.[1] The East room as it had been called, ever since Maria Bertram was sixteen, was now considered Fanny's, almost as decidedly as the white attic;—the smallness of the one making the use of the other so evidently reasonable, that the Miss Bertrams, with every superiority in their own apartments, which their own sense of superiority could demand, were entirely approving it;—and Mrs. Norris having stipulated for there never being a fire in it on Fanny's account, was tolerably resigned to her having the use of what nobody else wanted, though the terms in which she sometimes spoke of the indulgence, seemed to imply that it was the best room in the house.

The aspect was so favourable,[2] that even without a fire it was habitable in many an early spring, and late autumn morning, to such a willing mind as Fanny's, and while there was a gleam of sunshine, she hoped not to be driven from it entirely, even when winter came. The comfort of it in her hours of leisure was extreme. She could go there after any thing unpleasant below, and find immediate consolation in some pursuit, or some train of thought at hand.—Her plants, her books—of which she had been a collector, from the first hour of her commanding a shilling—her writing desk, and her works of charity and ingenuity, were all within her reach;—or if indisposed for employment, if nothing but musing would do, she could scarcely see an object in that room which had not an interesting remembrance connected with it.—Every thing was a friend, or bore her thoughts to a friend; and though there had been sometimes much of suffering to her—though her motives had often been misunderstood, her feelings disregarded, and her comprehension undervalued; though she had known the pains of tyranny, of ridicule, and neglect, yet almost every recurrence of either had led to something consolatory; her aunt Bertram had spoken for her, or Miss Lee had been encouraging, or what was yet more frequent or more dear—Edmund had been her champion and her friend;—he had supported her cause, or explained her meaning, he had told her not to cry, or had given her some proof of affection which made her tears delightful—and the whole was now so blended together, so harmonized by distance, that every former affliction had its charm. The room was most dear to her, and she would not have changed its furniture for the handsomest in the house, though what had been originally plain, had suffered all the ill-usage of children—and its greatest elegancies and ornaments were a faded footstool of Julia's work, too ill done for the drawing room, three transparencies, made in a rage for transparencies, for the three lower panes of one window, where Tintern Abbey held its station between a cave in Italy, and a moonlight lake in Cumberland;[3] a collection of family profiles thought unworthy of being anywhere else, over the mantelpiece, and by their side and pinned against the wall, a small sketch of a ship sent four years ago from the Mediterranean by William, with H. M. S. Antwerp at the bottom, in letters as tall as the mainmast.

   To this nest of comforts Fanny now walked down to try its influence on an agitated, doubting spirit—to see if by looking at Edmund's profile she could catch any of his counsel, or by giving air to her geraniums she might inhale a breeze of mental strength herself. But she had more than fears of her own perseverance to remove; she had begun to feel undecided as to what she *ought to do;* and as she walked round the room her doubts were increasing. Was she *right* in refusing what was so warmly asked, so strongly wished for? What might be so essential to a scheme on which some of those to whom she owed the greatest complaisance, had set their hearts? Was it not ill-nature—selfishness—and a fear of exposing herself? And would Edmund's judgment, would his persuasion of Sir Thomas's disapprobation of the whole, be enough to justify her in a determined denial in spite of all the rest? It would be so horrible to her to act, that she was inclined to suspect the truth and purity of her own scruples, and

Two views of a transparent print marketed in 1798, the second showing the effect created after a light source is placed behind the translucent paper. These might resemble the sort of images the young women of Mansfield Park created during their "rage for transparencies."

4 Netting-boxes would contain hooks and yarn for a form of crochet, and work-boxes would contain materials for sewing and needlework. Barbara M. Benedict notes that Fanny uses her possessions "as moral prompts to instruct her in self-denial and gratitude" ("The Trouble with Things," in *A Companion to Jane Austen,* ed. Claudia L. Johnson and Clara Tuite [Malden, Mass.: Wiley-Blackwell, 2009], p. 347).

as she looked around her, the claims of her cousins to being obliged, were strengthened by the sight of present upon present that she had received from them. The table between the windows was covered with work-boxes and netting-boxes, which had been given her at different times, principally by Tom; and she grew bewildered as to the amount of the debt which all these kind remembrances produced.[4] A tap at the door roused her in the midst of this attempt to find her way to her duty, and her gentle "come in," was answered by the appearance of one, before whom all her doubts were wont to be laid. Her eyes brightened at the sight of Edmund.

"Can I speak with you, Fanny, for a few minutes?" said he.

"Yes, certainly."

"I want to consult. I want your opinion."

"My opinion!" she cried, shrinking from such a compliment, highly as it gratified her.

"Yes, your advice and opinion. I do not know what to do. This acting scheme gets worse and worse, you see. They have chosen almost as bad a play as they could; and now, to complete the business, are going to ask the help of a young man very slightly known to any of us. This is the end of all the privacy and propriety which was talked about at first. I know no harm of Charles Maddox; but the excessive intimacy which must spring from his being admitted among us in this manner, is highly objectionable, the *more* than intimacy—the familiarity. I cannot think of it with any patience—and it does appear to me an evil of such magnitude as must, *if possible,* be prevented. Do not you see it in the same light?"

"Yes, but what can be done? Your brother is so determined?"

"There is but *one* thing to be done, Fanny. I must take Anhalt myself. I am well aware that nothing else will quiet Tom."

Fanny could not answer him.

"It is not at all what I like," he continued. "No man can like being driven into the *appearance* of such inconsistency. After being known to oppose the scheme from the beginning, there is absurdity in the face of my joining them *now,* when they are exceeding their first plan in every respect; but I can think of no other alternative. Can you, Fanny?"

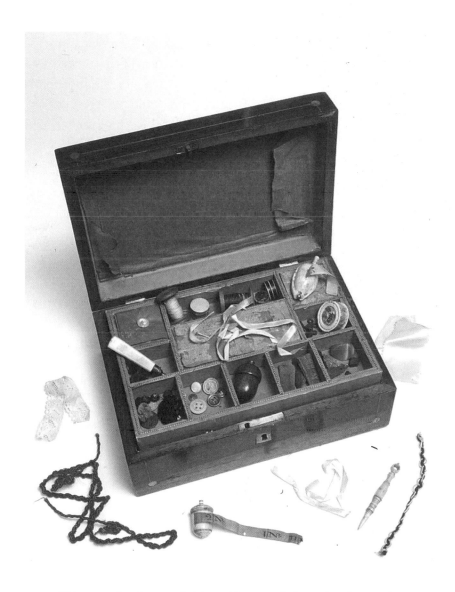

This example of a young lady's workbox once belonged to the novelist
Charlotte Brontë.

The poet George Crabbe, as portrayed in 1819 by Henry William Pickersgill, author of one of the books that Edmund singles out from his cousin's library.

"No," said Fanny, slowly, "not immediately—but—"

"But what? I see your judgment is not with me. Think it a little over. Perhaps you are not so much aware as I am, of the mischief that *may,* of the unpleasantness that *must,* arise from a young man's being received in this manner—domesticated among us—authorized to come at all hours—and placed suddenly on a footing which must do away all restraints. To think only of the license which every rehearsal must tend to create. It is all very bad! Put yourself in Miss Crawford's place, Fanny. Consider what it would be to act Amelia with a stranger. She has a right to be felt for, because she evidently feels for herself. I heard enough of what she said to you last night to understand her unwillingness to be acting with a stranger; and as she probably engaged in the part with different expectations—perhaps, without considering the subject enough to know what was likely to be, it would be ungenerous, it would be really wrong to expose her to it. Her feelings ought to be respected. Does it not strike you so, Fanny? You hesitate."

"I am sorry for Miss Crawford; but I am more sorry to see you drawn in to do what you had resolved against, and what you are known to think will be disagreeable to my uncle. It will be such a triumph to the others!"

"They will not have much cause of triumph, when they see how infamously I act. But, however, triumph there certainly will be, and I must brave it. But if I can be the means of restraining the publicity of the business, of limiting the exhibition, of concentrating our folly, I shall be well repaid. As I am now, I have no influence, I can do nothing; I have offended them, and they will not hear me; but when I have put them in good humour by this concession, I am not without hopes of persuading them to confine the representation within a much smaller circle than they are now in the high road for. This will be a material gain. My object is to confine it to Mrs. Rushworth and the Grants. Will not this be worth gaining?"

"Yes, it will be a great point."

"But still it has not your approbation. Can you mention any other measure by which I have a chance of doing equal good?"

"No, I cannot think of anything else."

"Give me your approbation, then, Fanny. I am not comfortable without it."

"Oh! cousin."

"If you are against me, I ought to distrust myself—and yet—But it is absolutely impossible to let Tom go on in this way, riding about the country in quest of any body who can be persuaded to act—no matter whom; the look of a gentleman is to be enough. I thought *you* would have entered more into Miss Crawford's feelings."

"No doubt she will be very glad. It must be a great relief to her," said Fanny, trying for greater warmth of manner.

"She never appeared more amiable than in her behaviour to you last night. It gave her a very strong claim on my good will."

"She *was* very kind indeed, and I am glad to have her spared.". . . .

She could not finish the generous effusion. Her conscience stopt her in the middle, but Edmund was satisfied.

"I shall walk down immediately after breakfast," said he, "and am sure of giving pleasure there. And now, dear Fanny, I will not interrupt you any longer. You want to be reading. But I could not be easy till I had spoken to you, and come to a decision. Sleeping or waking, my head has been full of this matter all night. It is an evil—but I am certainly making it less than it might be. If Tom is up, I shall go to him directly and get it over; and when we meet at breakfast we shall be all in high good humour at the prospect of acting the fool together with such unanimity. *You* in the meanwhile will be taking a trip into China, I suppose. How does Lord Macartney go on?"—(opening a volume on the table and then taking up some others).[5] And here are Crabbe's Tales, and the Idler, at hand to relieve you, if you tire of your great book.[6] I admire your little establishment exceedingly; and as soon as I am gone, you will empty your head of all this nonsense of acting, and sit comfortably down to your table. But do not stay here to be cold."

He went; but there was no reading, no China, no composure for Fanny. He had told her the most extraordinary, the most inconceivable, the most unwelcome news; and she could think of nothing else. To be acting! After all his objections—objections so just and so public! After all that she had heard him say, and seen him look, and

5 The book on the table is usually identified as John Barrow's 1807 *Some Account of the Public Life and a Selection from the Unpublished Writings of the Earl of Macartney,* which incorporated the journal in which Lord Macartney had chronicled the fortunes of the unsuccessful trade embassy that he led to Beijing in 1792. In 1804 Barrow became the second secretary to the First Lord of the Admiralty, an administrative position that would have made him a consequential figure for Austen's sailor brothers. Earlier in the 1790s his language skills had won him a place in Lord Macartney's entourage. Fanny, who has been coping with her relations at their overbearing worst, might well find much to interest her as she reads about Macartney's experience of absolutist power at the court of the Chinese emperor.

6 The poet George Crabbe published *Tales in Verse* in 1812, but "Tale" can be a generic term applicable to any narrative poem, and some critics suggest that the reference is to Crabbe's earlier poem *The Parish Register* (1807). They note, too, that Fanny Price shares her name with a character in that poem, a virtuous maiden who says no to the sexual advances of a wealthy aristocrat. The *Idler* is the title of the much-reprinted periodical essay series that Samuel Johnson published between 1758 and 1760.

Fanny's favorite authors are also her creator's. In his 1870 *Memoir* of his aunt, Austen's nephew J. E. Austen-Leigh reported that her favorite writers were "Johnson in prose, Crabbe in verse, and Cowper in both" (ed. Kathryn Sutherland [Oxford: Oxford University Press, 2009], p. 71).

known him to be feeling. Could it be possible? Edmund so inconsistent. Was he not deceiving himself? Was he not wrong? Alas! it was all Miss Crawford's doing. She had seen her influence in every speech, and was miserable. The doubts and alarms as to her own conduct, which had previously distressed her, and which had all slept while she listened to him, were become of little consequence now. This deeper anxiety swallowed them up. Things should take their course; she cared not how it ended. Her cousins might attack, but could hardly tease her. She was beyond their reach; and if at last obliged to yield—no matter—it was all misery *now*.

James Gillray's c. 1793 satiric print represents a climactic moment of Lord Macartney's embassy to China, an enterprise memorialized in more upbeat terms in Fanny's "great book." The embassy was an abject failure: almost the only concession wrested from the Chinese court was that Macartney would be permitted to kneel to the emperor, as here, rather than bow to him. By contrast, the faceless men in Western dress immediately behind Macartney have no compunction when it comes to self-abasement.

# 17

It was, indeed, a triumphant day to Mr. Bertram and Maria. Such a victory over Edmund's discretion had been beyond their hopes, and was most delightful. There was no longer any thing to disturb them in their darling project, and they congratulated each other in private on the jealous weakness to which they attributed the change, with all the glee of feelings gratified in every way. Edmund might still look grave, and say he did not like the scheme in general, and must disapprove the play in particular; their point was gained; he was to act, and he was driven to it by the force of selfish inclinations only. Edmund had descended from that moral elevation which he had maintained before, and they were both as much the better as the happier for the descent.

They behaved very well, however, *to him* on the occasion, betraying no exultation beyond the lines about the corners of the mouth, and seemed to think it as great an escape to be quit of the intrusion of Charles Maddox, as if they had been forced into admitting him against their inclination. "To have it quite in their own family circle was what they had particularly wished. A stranger among them would have been the destruction of all their comfort," and when Edmund, pursuing that idea, gave a hint of his hope as to the limitation of the audience, they were ready, in the complaisance of the moment, to promise any thing. It was all good humour and encouragement. Mrs. Norris offered to contrive his dress, Mr. Yates assured him, that Anhalt's last scene with the Baron admitted a good deal of action and emphasis,[1] and Mr. Rushworth undertook to count his speeches.

[1] In Act V, Anhalt persuades the baron to heed his conscience and marry Agatha, making amends to her for robbing her of her honor years before.

"Perhaps," said Tom, *Fanny* may be more disposed to oblige us now. Perhaps you may persuade *her*."

"No, she is quite determined. She certainly will not act."

"Oh! very well." And not another word was said: but Fanny felt herself again in danger, and her indifference to the danger was beginning to fail her already.

There were not fewer smiles at the parsonage than at the park on this change in Edmund; Miss Crawford looked very lovely in her's, and entered with such an instantaneous renewal of cheerfulness into the whole affair, as could have but one effect on him. "He was certainly right in respecting such feelings; he was glad he had determined on it." And the morning wore away in satisfactions very sweet, if not very sound. One advantage resulted from it to Fanny; at the earnest request of Miss Crawford, Mrs. Grant had with her usual good humour agreed to undertake the part for which Fanny had been wanted—and this was all that occurred to gladden *her* heart during the day; and even this, when imparted by Edmund, brought a pang with it, for it was Miss Crawford to whom she was obliged, it was Miss Crawford whose kind exertions were to excite her gratitude, and whose merit in making them was spoken of with a glow of admiration. She was safe; but peace and safety were unconnected here. Her mind had been never farther from peace. She could not feel that she had done wrong herself, but she was disquieted in every other way. Her heart and her judgment were equally against Edmund's decision; she could not acquit his unsteadiness and his happiness under it made her wretched. She was full of jealousy and agitation. Miss Crawford came with looks of gaiety which seemed an insult, with friendly expressions towards herself which she could hardly answer calmly. Every body around her was gay and busy, prosperous and important, each had their object of interest, their part, their dress, their favourite scene, their friends and confederates, all were finding employment in consultations and comparisons, or diversion in the playful conceits they suggested. She alone was sad and insignificant; she had no share in any thing; she might go or stay, she might be in the midst of their noise, or retreat from it to the solitude of the East room, without being seen or missed. She could almost think any

thing would have been preferable to this. Mrs. Grant was of consequence; *her* good nature had honourable mention—her taste and her
time were considered—her presence was wanted—she was sought
for and attended, and praised; and Fanny was at first in some danger of envying her the character she had accepted. But reflection
brought better feelings, and shewed her that Mrs. Grant was entitled to respect, which could never have belonged to *her,* and that had
she received even the greatest, she could never have been easy in
joining a scheme which, considering only her uncle, she must condemn altogether.

Fanny's heart was not absolutely the only saddened one amongst
them, as she soon began to acknowledge to herself,—Julia was a suf
ferer too, though not quite so blamelessly.

Henry Crawford had trifled with her feelings; but she had very
long allowed and even sought his attentions, with a jealousy of her
sister so reasonable as ought to have been their cure; and now that
the conviction of his preference for Maria had been forced on her,
she submitted to it without any alarm for Maria's situation, or any
endeavour at rational tranquillity for herself.—She either sat in
gloomy silence, wrapt in such gravity as nothing could subdue, no curiosity touch, no wit amuse; or allowing the attentions of Mr. Yates,
was talking with forced gaiety to him alone, and ridiculing the acting
of the others.

For a day or two after the affront was given, Henry Crawford had
endeavoured to do it away by the usual attack of gallantry and compliment, but he had not cared enough about it to persevere against
a few repulses; and becoming soon too busy with his play to have
time for more than one flirtation, he grew indifferent to the quarrel,
or rather thought it a lucky occurrence, as quietly putting an end
to what might ere long have raised expectations in more than Mrs.
Grant.—She was not pleased to see Julia excluded from the play, and
sitting by disregarded; but as it was not a matter which really involved her happiness, as Henry must be the best judge of his own,
and as he did assure her, with a most persuasive smile, that neither
he nor Julia had ever had a serious thought of each other, she could
only renew her former caution as to the elder sister, entreat him not

2 Before the political reforms of the later nineteenth century and the implementation of secret ballots, it was easy for great landowners to influence local electors in ways that would guarantee them the results they wanted in parliamentary elections. There may well be some nearby pocket borough—so called because there the choice of an M. P. was for all intents and purposes in the pocket of a single person or family—where Mr. Rushworth, unqualified as he is, can count on being elected. In *Melincourt,* Thomas Love Peacock's satirical novel of 1817, an orangutan caught young in the jungles of Angola, christened Oran Haut-Ton, and endowed with a purchased baronetcy, is elected to Parliament as one of two representatives of the ancient borough of Onevote. Sir Oran Haut-Ton is an even worse speaker than Mr. Rushworth.

3 Mary's lines rewrite a poem that was already a rewriting. Isaac Hawkins Browne's couplet praising the "Blest leaf" of tobacco opens one of the poems composing his *A Pipe of Tobacco: In Imitation of Six Several Authors.* The six poems of Hawkins Browne's stylistic medley—each of them about tobacco—were published together in 1736 and then reprinted in one of the eighteenth century's most famous anthologies, Robert Dodsley's 1748 *Collection of Poems;* Browne's skillful impersonations of other writers' poetic styles make *A Pipe of Tobacco* a miniaturized anthology in and of itself.

4 She seems even more of a nonentity.

to risk his tranquillity by too much admiration there, and then gladly take her share in anything that brought cheerfulness to the young people in general, and that did so particularly promote the pleasure of the two so dear to her.

"I rather wonder Julia is not in love with Henry," was her observation to Mary.

"I dare say she is," replied Mary, coldly. "I imagine both sisters are."

"Both! no, no, that must not be. Do not give him a hint of it. Think of Mr. Rushworth."

"You had better tell Miss Bertram to think of Mr. Rushworth. It may do *her* some good. I often think of Mr. Rushworth's property and independence, and wish them in other hands—but I never think of *him.* A man might represent the county with such an estate; a man might escape a profession and represent the county."

"I dare say he *will* be in parliament soon. When Sir Thomas comes, I dare say he will be in for some borough, but there has been nobody to put him in the way of doing any thing yet."[2]

"Sir Thomas is to achieve many mighty things when he comes home," said Mary, after a pause. "Do you remember Hawkins Browne's 'Address to Tobacco,' in imitation of Pope?—

"Blest leaf! whose aromatic gales dispense
"To Templars modesty, to Parsons sense."

I will parody them:

Blest Knight! whose dictatorial looks dispense
To Children affluence, to Rushworth sense.[3]

Will not that do, Mrs. Grant? Every thing seems to depend upon Sir Thomas's return."

"You will find his consequence very just and reasonable when you see him in his family, I assure you. I do not think we do so well without him. He has a fine dignified manner, which suits the head of such a house, and keeps every body in their place. Lady Bertram seems more of a cipher now than when he is at home;[4] and nobody else can keep Mrs. Norris in order. But, Mary, do not fancy that Maria Bertram cares for Henry. I am sure *Julia* does not, or she would not have flirted as she did last night with Mr. Yates; and though he and Maria are very good friends, I think she likes Sotherton too well to be inconstant."

"I would not give much for Mr. Rushworth's chance, if Henry stept in before the articles were signed."[5]

"If you have such a suspicion, something must be done, and as soon as the play is all over, we will talk to him seriously, and make him know his own mind; and if he means nothing, we will send him off, though he is Henry, for a time."

Julia *did* suffer, however, though Mrs. Grant discerned it not, and though it escaped the notice of many of her own family likewise. She had loved, she did love still, and she had all the suffering which a warm temper and a high spirit were likely to endure under the disappointment of a dear, though irrational hope, with a strong sense of ill-usage. Her heart was sore and angry, and she was capable only of angry consolations. The sister with whom she was used to be on easy terms, was now become her greatest enemy; they were alienated from each other, and Julia was not superior to the hope of some distressing end to the attentions which were still carrying on there, some punishment to Maria for conduct so shameful towards herself, as well as towards Mr. Rushworth. With no material fault of temper, or difference of opinion, to prevent their being very good friends while their interests were the same, the sisters, under such a trial as this, had not affection or principle enough to make them merciful or just, to give them honour or compassion. Maria felt her triumph, and pursued her purpose careless of Julia; and Julia could never see Maria distinguished by Henry Crawford, without trusting that it would create jealousy, and bring a public disturbance at last.

Fanny saw and pitied much of this in Julia; but there was no outward fellowship between them. Julia made no communication, and Fanny took no liberties. They were two solitary sufferers, or connected only by Fanny's consciousness.

The inattention of the two brothers and the aunt to Julia's discomposure, and their blindness to its true cause, must be imputed to

5 Before the parties involved agree on the details of the private legal contract that is to be ratified prior to their union. The articles will establish the kind of financial transaction this marriage will be. They might set up, for instance, the individual allowance or "pin money" that Mr. Rushworth will be obliged to pay out to the future Mrs. Rushworth, or they might specify the amount of money that will be settled on her should she become a widow.

the fullness of their own minds. They were totally preoccupied. Tom was engrossed by the concerns of his theatre, and saw nothing that did not immediately relate to it. Edmund, between his theatrical and his real part, between Miss Crawford's claims and his own conduct, between love and consistency, was equally unobservant; and Mrs. Norris was too busy in contriving and directing the general little matters of the company, superintending their various dresses with economical expedient, for which nobody thanked her, and saving, with delighted integrity, half-a-crown here and there to the absent Sir Thomas, to have leisure for watching the behaviour, or guarding the happiness of his daughters.

# 18

Every thing was now in a regular train; theatre, actors, actresses, and dresses, were all getting forward: but though no other great impediments arose, Fanny found, before many days were past, that it was not all uninterrupted enjoyment to the party themselves, and that she had not to witness the continuance of such unanimity and delight, as had been almost too much for her at first. Every body began to have their vexation. Edmund had many. Entirely against *his* judgment, a scene painter arrived from town,[1] and was at work, much to the increase of the expenses, and what was worse, of the eclat of their proceedings;[2] and his brother, instead of being really guided by him as to the privacy of the representation, was giving an invitation to every family who came in his way. Tom himself began to fret over the scene painter's slow progress, and to feel the miseries of waiting. He had learned his part—all his parts—for he took every trifling one that could be united with the Butler, and began to be impatient to be acting; and every day thus unemployed, was tending to increase his sense of the insignificance of all his parts together, and make him more ready to regret that some other play had not been chosen.

Fanny, being always a very courteous listener, and often the only listener at hand, came in for the complaints and the distresses of most of them. *She* knew that Mr. Yates was in general thought to rant dreadfully,[3] that Mr. Yates was disappointed in Henry Crawford, that Tom Bertram spoke so quick he would be unintelligible, that Mrs. Grant spoilt every thing by laughing, that Edmund was behind-hand with his part, and that it was misery to have any thing to do with Mr.

1 This likely means from London.

2 From the French *faire éclat*—to create a stir or make a sensation. Richard Graves had deplored in his essay on private theatricals how deficiently private they actually were. He noted how the "nobility and gentry" stricken by the "theatrico mania" seemed determined to give "their *rural retreat* some semblance of a public place" (*Senilities,* p. 59). To Edmund's vexation, Tom's invitations threaten to have just that effect.

3 Yates appears to be importing into the billiard room a declamatory acting style better suited to the stadium-like public theaters of the early nineteenth century (recently rebuilt and enlarged, Covent Garden and Drury Lane each seated more than 3,000 spectators). In these venues booming voices and grand gestures were crucial components in the actor's bag of tricks.

4 Fanny is clearly thinking of how little feigning Maria is required to do in the part of Agatha, especially in the opening scene, being rehearsed "with needless frequency," in which she is called on to demonstrate her affection for the character of Frederick / Henry Crawford. Acting *well* might require no acting at all. As Marilyn Butler points out in a famous discussion of *Mansfield Park*, Maria is not alone in playing a version of herself, as this is the case for almost all the members of this cast of *Lovers' Vows* (*Jane Austen and the War of Ideas*, 2nd ed. [Oxford: Oxford University Press, 1987], p. 232). In Chap. 13 Tom Bertram had defended their theatrical project with the statement, "I can conceive no greater harm or danger to any of us in conversing in the elegant language of some respectable author than in chattering in words of our own." But the contrast this statement draws between an author's words and their own words has been eroded: Maria Bertram has found in Inchbald's script the means by which she may be liberated into self-expression.

Rushworth, who was wanting a prompter through every speech. She knew, also, that poor Mr. Rushworth could seldom get any body to rehearse with him; *his* complaint came before her as well as the rest; and so decided to her eye was her cousin Maria's avoidance of him, and so needlessly often the rehearsal of the first scene between her and Mr. Crawford, that she had soon all the terror of other complaints from *him*.—So far from being all satisfied and all enjoying, she found every body requiring something they had not, and giving occasion of discontent to the others.—Every body had a part either too long or too short;—nobody would attend as they ought, nobody would remember on which side they were to come in—nobody but the complainer would observe any directions.

Fanny believed herself to derive as much innocent enjoyment from the play as any of them;—Henry Crawford acted well, and it was a pleasure to *her* to creep into the theatre, and attend the rehearsal of the first act—in spite of the feelings it excited in some speeches for Maria.—Maria she also thought acted well—too well;[4]—and after the first rehearsal or two, Fanny began to be their only audience—and sometimes as prompter, sometimes as spectator—was often very useful.—As far as she could judge, Mr. Crawford was considerably the best actor of all; he had more confidence than Edmund, more judgment than Tom, more talent and taste than Mr. Yates.—She did not like him as a man, but she must admit him to be the best actor, and on this point there were not many who differed from her. Mr. Yates, indeed, exclaimed against his tameness and insipidity—and the day came at last, when Mr. Rushworth turned to her with a black look, and said—"Do you think there is anything so very fine in all this? For the life and soul of me, I cannot admire him;—and between ourselves, to see such an undersized, little, mean-looking man, set up for a fine actor, is very ridiculous in my opinion."

From this moment there was a return of his former jealousy, which Maria, from increasing hopes of Crawford, was at little pains to remove; and the chances of Mr. Rushworth's ever attaining to the knowledge of his two and forty speeches became much less. As to his ever making anything *tolerable* of them, nobody had the smallest idea of that except his mother—*She*, indeed, regretted that his part

This view of Covent Garden Theatre, from Thomas Rowlandson and William Combe's *The Tour of Doctor Syntax in Search of the Picturesque* (1812), suggests the theater's gargantuan dimensions: Doctor Syntax finds that in this "vast profound" the spectator can neither hear nor see. Such architecture explains why some critics of the early nineteenth-century English stage felt that dreadful ranting had become business as usual.

5 They hope that Mr. Rushworth will remember his cue.

6 Mrs. Norris implies that Fanny is fortunate that her role is only to work (fulfill the "executive part") so as to carry out the commands of others; she herself, or so she appears to believe, fills the more burdensome role of supervisor.

was not more considerable, and deferred coming over to Mansfield till they were forward enough in their rehearsal to comprehend all his scenes, but the others aspired at nothing beyond his remembering the catchword,[5] and the first line of his speech, and being able to follow the prompter through the rest. Fanny, in her pity and kindheartedness, was at great pains to teach him how to learn, giving him all the helps and directions in her power, trying to make an artificial memory for him, and learning every word of his part herself, but without his being much the forwarder.

Many uncomfortable, anxious, apprehensive feelings she certainly had; but with all these, and other claims on her time and attention, she was as far from finding herself without employment or utility amongst them, as without a companion in uneasiness; quite as far from having no demand on her leisure as on her compassion. The gloom of her first anticipations was proved to have been unfounded. She was occasionally useful to all; she was perhaps as much at peace as any.

There was a great deal of needle-work to be done moreover, in which her help was wanted; and that Mrs. Norris thought her quite as well off as the rest, was evident by the manner in which she claimed it: "Come Fanny," she cried, "these are fine times for you, but you must not be always walking from one room to the other and doing the lookings on, at your ease, in this way,—I want you here.—I have been slaving myself till I can hardly stand, to contrive Mr. Rushworth's cloak without sending for any more satin; and now I think you may give me your help in putting it together.—There are but three seams, you may do them in a trice.—It would be lucky for me if I had nothing but the executive part to do.[6]—*You* are best off, I can tell you; but if nobody did more than *you*, we should not get on very fast."

Fanny took the work very quietly, without attempting any defence; but her kinder aunt Bertram observed on her behalf,

"One cannot wonder, sister, that Fanny *should* be delighted; it is all new to her, you know,—you and I used to be very fond of a play ourselves—and so am I still;—and as soon as I am a little more at leisure,

*I* mean to look in at their rehearsals too. What is the play about, Fanny, you have never told me?"

"Oh! sister, pray do not ask her now; for Fanny is not one of those who can talk and work at the same time.—It is about Lovers' Vows."

"I believe," said Fanny to her aunt Bertram, "there will be three acts rehearsed to-morrow evening, and that will give you an opportunity of seeing all the actors at once."

"You had better stay till the curtain is hung," interposed Mrs. Norris—"the curtain will be hung in a day or two,—there is very little sense in a play without a curtain—and I am much mistaken if you do not find it draw up into very handsome festoons."

Lady Bertram seemed quite resigned to waiting.—Fanny did not share her aunt's composure; she thought of the morrow a great deal,—for if the three acts were rehearsed, Edmund and Miss Crawford would then be acting together for the first time;—the third act would bring a scene between them which interested her most particularly, and which she was longing and dreading to see how they would perform. The whole subject of it was love—a marriage of love was to be described by the gentleman, and very little short of a declaration of love be made by the lady.[7]

She had read, and read the scene again with many painful, many wondering emotions, and looked forward to their representation of it as a circumstance almost too interesting. She did not *believe* they had yet rehearsed it, even in private.

The morrow came, the plan for the evening continued, and Fanny's consideration of it did not become less agitated. She worked very diligently under her aunt's directions, but her diligence and her silence concealed a very absent, anxious mind; and about noon she made her escape with her work to the East room, that she might have no concern in another, and, as she deemed it, most unnecessary rehearsal of the first act, which Henry Crawford was just proposing, desirous at once of having her time to herself, and of avoiding the sight of Mr. Rushworth. A glimpse, as she passed through the hall, of the two ladies walking up from the parsonage, made no change in her wish of retreat, and she worked and meditated in the East room,

7 This scene comes about because, clinging to the faint hope that Cassel might prove an acceptable son-in-law, the baron has asked Anhalt to meet with Amelia in his capacity as family chaplain and explain to her the duties of a wife. In Act III, scene ii, Anhalt tries to carry out this office, but Amelia turns the tables on him and intentionally misconstrues a sermon on marriage as his own proposal of marriage:

> Anhalt: You misconstrue—you misconceive every thing I say or do. The subject I came to you upon was marriage.
> Amelia: A very proper subject for the man, who has taught me love, and I accept the proposal. (p. 39)

8 Mary's plan initially involved some private practic-ing with Edmund—insurance against the mistakes they might otherwise make that evening—but Edmund is not around ("in the way").

9 The critic David Marshall suspects a "finely tuned sadism" in Mary's conscription of Fanny for this rehearsal. "Fanny is asked to play a love scene with Mary in which she must not only witness her rival speak the lines that she herself would like to say to Edmund but also take Edmund's place and imagine him receiving and reciprocating Mary's lover's vows" (*The Frame of Art: Fictions of Aesthetic Experience, 1750–1815* [Baltimore: Johns Hopkins University Press, 2005], p. 77).

10 Mary is complying with Inchbald's stage direction for Act III, scene ii, which requires Anhalt to set out two chairs in preparation for his conversation with Amelia. The East room's history as a former schoolroom makes it an apt space for rehearsing a scene between Anhalt and his former pupil.

undisturbed, for a quarter of an hour, when a gentle tap at the door was followed by the entrance of Miss Crawford.

"Am I right?—Yes; this is the East room. My dear Miss Price, I beg your pardon, but I have made my way to you on purpose to entreat your help."

Fanny, quite surprised, endeavoured to show herself mistress of the room by her civilities, and looked at the bright bars of her empty grate with concern.

"Thank you—I am quite warm, very warm. Allow me to stay here a little while, and do have the goodness to hear me my third act. I have brought my book, and if you would but rehearse it with me, I should be *so* obliged! I came here to-day intending to rehearse it with Edmund—by ourselves—against the evening, but he is not in the way;[8] and if he *were,* I do not think I could go through it with *him,* till I have hardened myself a little, for really there *is* a speech or two— You will be so good, won't you?"

Fanny was most civil in her assurances, though she could not give them in a very steady voice.

"Have you ever happened to look at the part I mean?" continued Miss Crawford, opening her book. "Here it is. I did not think much of it at first—but, upon my word—. There, look at *that* speech, and *that,* and *that.* How am I ever to look him in the face and say such things? Could you do it? But then he is your cousin, which makes all the difference. You must rehearse it with me, that I may fancy *you* him, and get on by degrees. You *have* a look of *his* sometimes."[9]

"Have I?—I will do my best with the greatest readiness—but I must *read* the part, for I can *say* very little of it."

"*None* of it, I suppose. You are to have the book, of course. Now for it. We must have two chairs at hand for you to bring forward to the front of the stage.[10] There—very good school-room chairs, not made for a theatre, I dare say; much more fitted for little girls to sit and kick their feet against when they are learning a lesson. What would your governess and your uncle say to see them used for such a purpose? Could Sir Thomas look in upon us just now, he would bless himself, for we are rehearsing all over the house. Yates is storming away in the dining room. I heard him as I came up stairs, and the theatre is engaged of course by those indefatigable rehearsers, Agatha and Frederick. If *they* are not perfect, I *shall* be surprised. By the bye, I looked in upon them five minutes ago, and it happened to be exactly at one of the times when they were trying *not* to embrace, and Mr. Rushworth was with me. I thought he began to look a little queer, so I turned it off as well as I could, by whispering to him, 'We shall have an excellent Agatha, there is something so *maternal* in her manner, so completely *maternal* in her voice and countenance.' Was not that well done of me? He brightened up directly. Now for my soliloquy."

She began, and Fanny joined in with all the modest feeling which the idea of representing Edmund was so strongly calculated to inspire; but with looks and voice so truly feminine, as to be no very good picture of a man. With such an Anhalt, however, Miss Crawford had courage enough, and they had got through half the scene, when a tap at the door brought a pause, and the entrance of Edmund the next moment, suspended it all.

Surprise, consciousness,[11] and pleasure, appeared in each of the three on this unexpected meeting; and as Edmund was come on the very same business that had brought Miss Crawford, consciousness and pleasure were likely to be more than momentary in *them.* He too had his book, and was seeking Fanny, to ask her to rehearse with him, and help him to prepare for the evening, without knowing Miss Crawford to be in the house; and great was the joy and animation of being thus thrown together—of comparing schemes—and sympathizing in praise of Fanny's kind offices.

*She* could not equal them in their warmth. *Her* spirits sank under the glow of theirs, and she felt herself becoming too nearly nothing to both, to have any comfort in having been sought by either. They must now rehearse together. Edmund proposed, urged, entreated it—till the lady, not very unwilling at first, could refuse no longer— and Fanny was wanted only to prompt and observe them. She was invested, indeed, with the office of judge and critic, and earnestly desired to exercise it and tell them all their faults; but from doing so every feeling within her shrank, she could not, would not, dared not attempt it; had she been otherwise qualified for criticism, her con-

11 Self-consciousness.

science must have restrained her from venturing at disapprobation. She believed herself to feel too much of it in the aggregate for honesty or safety in particulars. To prompt them must be enough for her; and it was sometimes *more* than enough; for she could not always pay attention to the book. In watching them she forgot herself; and, agitated by the increasing spirit of Edmund's manner, had once closed the page and turned away exactly as he wanted help. It was imputed to very reasonable weariness, and she was thanked and pitied; but she deserved their pity, more than she hoped they would ever surmise. At last the scene was over, and Fanny forced herself to add her praise to the compliments each was giving the other; and when again alone and able to recall the whole, she was inclined to believe their performance would, indeed, have such nature and feeling in it, as must ensure their credit, and make it a very suffering exhibition to herself. Whatever might be its effect, however, she must stand the brunt of it again that very day.

The first regular rehearsal of the three first acts was certainly to take place in the evening; Mrs. Grant and the Crawfords were engaged to return for that purpose as soon as they could after dinner; and every one concerned was looking forward with eagerness. There seemed a general diffusion of cheerfulness on the occasion; Tom was enjoying such an advance towards the end, Edmund was in spirits from the morning's rehearsal, and little vexations seemed every where smoothed away. All were alert and impatient; the ladies moved soon, the gentlemen soon followed them, and with the exception of Lady Bertram, Mrs. Norris, and Julia, every body was in the theatre at an early hour, and having lighted it up as well as its unfinished state admitted, were waiting only the arrival of Mrs. Grant and the Crawfords to begin.

They did not wait long for the Crawfords, but there was no Mrs. Grant. She could not come. Dr. Grant, professing an indisposition, for which he had little credit with his fair sister-in-law, could not spare his wife.

"Dr. Grant is ill," said she, with mock solemnity. "He has been ill ever since; he did not eat any of the pheasant to day. He fancied it tough—sent away his plate—and has been suffering ever since."

'My father is come!'

Hugh Thomson's 1897 illustration of the episode that brings down the curtain on the first volume of *Mansfield Park*.

12 Austen likely intended for the break between the separate volumes of the novel to coincide with this abrupt interruption of the play. With this arrangement, she manages to conclude Vol. I theatrically in her turn, ensuring that her readers' sense of suspense and their curiosity about the consequences of Sir Thomas's return would be compounded by their anxiety about the current availability of Vol. II.

Here was disappointment! Mrs. Grant's non-attendance was sad indeed. Her pleasant manners and cheerful conformity made her always valuable amongst them—but *now* she was absolutely necessary. They could not act, they could not rehearse with any satisfaction without her. The comfort of the whole evening was destroyed. What was to be done? Tom, as Cottager, was in despair. After a pause of perplexity, some eyes began to be turned towards Fanny, and a voice or two, to say, "If Miss Price would be so good as to *read* the part." She was immediately surrounded by supplications, every body asked it, even Edmund said, "Do Fanny, if it is not *very* disagreeable to you."

But Fanny still hung back. She could not endure the idea of it. Why was not Miss Crawford to be applied to as well? Or why had not she rather gone to her own room, as she had felt to be safest, instead of attending the rehearsal at all? She had known it would irritate and distress her—she had known it her duty to keep away. She was properly punished.

"You have only to *read* the part," said Henry Crawford, with renewed entreaty.

"And I do believe she can say every word of it," added Maria, "for she could put Mrs. Grant right the other day in twenty places. Fanny, I am sure you know the part."

Fanny could not say she did *not*—and as they all persevered—as Edmund repeated his wish, and with a look of even fond dependence on her good nature, she must yield. She would do her best. Every body was satisfied—and she was left to the tremors of a most palpitating heart, while the others prepared to begin.

They *did* begin—and being too much engaged in their own noise, to be struck by unusual noise in the other part of the house, had proceeded some way, when the door of the room was thrown open, and Julia appearing at it, with a face all aghast, exclaimed, "My father is come! He is in the hall at this moment."[12]

# Volume II

# I

How is the consternation of the party to be described? To the greater number it was a moment of absolute horror. Sir Thomas in the house! All felt the instantaneous conviction. Not a hope of imposition or mistake was harboured any where. Julia's looks were an evidence of the fact that made it indisputable; and after the first starts and exclamations, not a word was spoken for half a minute; each with an altered countenance was looking at some other, and almost each was feeling it a stroke the most unwelcome, most ill-timed, most appalling! Mr. Yates might consider it only as a vexatious interruption for the evening, and Mr. Rushworth might imagine it a blessing, but every other heart was sinking under some degree of self-condemnation or undefined alarm, every other heart was suggesting "What will become of us? what is to be done now?" It was a terrible pause; and terrible to every ear were the corroborating sounds of opening doors and passing footsteps.

Julia was the first to move and speak again. Jealousy and bitterness had been suspended: selfishness was lost in the common cause; but at the moment of her appearance, Frederick was listening with looks of devotion to Agatha's narrative, and pressing her hand to his heart,[1] and as soon as she could notice this, and see that, in spite of the shock of her words, he still kept his station and retained her sister's hand, her wounded heart swelled again with injury, and looking as red as she had been white before, she turned out of the room, saying "*I* need not be afraid of appearing before him."

1 Here is more evidence of how conscientiously these two actors comply with Inchbald's stage directions: in Act I, scene i, Frederick takes Agatha's hand "and puts it to his heart" (*British Theatre*, vol. 23, p. 13).

2 *Stoutest* meaning the bravest and most resolute.

3 Revelation awaiting him.

Her going roused the rest; and at the same moment, the two brothers stepped forward, feeling the necessity of doing something. A very few words between them were sufficient. The case admitted no difference of opinion; they must go to the drawing-room directly. Maria joined them with the same intent, just then the stoutest of the three;[2] for the very circumstance which had driven Julia away, was to her the sweetest support. Henry Crawford's retaining her hand at such a moment, a moment of such peculiar proof and importance, was worth ages of doubt and anxiety. She hailed it as an earnest of the most serious determination, and was equal even to encounter her father. They walked off, utterly heedless of Mr. Rushworth's repeated question of, "Shall I go too?—Had not I better go too?—Will not it be right for me to go too?" but they were no sooner through the door than Henry Crawford undertook to answer the anxious inquiry, and, encouraging him by all means to pay his respects to Sir Thomas without delay, sent him after the others with delighted haste.

Fanny was left with only the Crawfords and Mr. Yates. She had been quite overlooked by her cousins; and as her own opinion of her claims on Sir Thomas's affection was much too humble to give her any idea of classing herself with his children, she was glad to remain behind and gain a little breathing time. Her agitation and alarm exceeded all that was endured by the rest, by the right of a disposition which not even innocence could keep from suffering. She was nearly fainting: all her former habitual dread of her uncle was returning, and with it compassion for him and for almost every one of the party on the development before him[3]—with solicitude on Edmund's account indescribable. She had found a seat, where in excessive trembling she was enduring all these fearful thoughts, while the other three, no longer under any restraint, were giving vent to their feelings of vexation, lamenting over such an unlooked-for premature arrival as a most untoward event, and without mercy wishing poor Sir Thomas had been twice as long on his passage, or were still in Antigua.

The Crawfords were more warm on the subject than Mr. Yates, from better understanding the family and judging more clearly of the mischief that must ensue. The ruin of the play was to them a certainty, they felt the total destruction of the scheme to be inevitably at hand; while Mr. Yates considered it only as a temporary interruption, a disaster for the evening, and could even suggest the possibility of the rehearsal being renewed after tea, when the bustle of receiving Sir Thomas were over and he might be at leisure to be amused by it. The Crawfords laughed at the idea; and having soon agreed on the propriety of their walking quietly home and leaving the family to themselves, proposed Mr. Yates's accompanying them and spending the evening at the Parsonage. But Mr. Yates, having never been with those who thought much of parental claims, or family confidence,[4] could not perceive that any thing of the kind was necessary, and therefore, thanking them, said, "he preferred remaining where he was that he might pay his respects to the old gentleman handsomely since he *was* come; and besides, he did not think it would be fair by the others to have every body run away."

Fanny was just beginning to collect herself, and to feel that if she staid longer behind it might seem disrespectful, when this point was settled, and being commissioned with the brother and sister's apology, saw them preparing to go as she quitted the room herself to perform the dreadful duty of appearing before her uncle.

Too soon did she find herself at the drawing-room door, and after pausing a moment for what she knew would not come, for a courage which the outside of no door had ever supplied to her, she turned the lock in desperation, and the lights of the drawing-room, and all the collected family were before her. As she entered, her own name caught her ear. Sir Thomas was at that moment looking round him, and saying "But where is Fanny?—Why do not I see my little Fanny?", and on perceiving her, came forward with a kindness which astonished and penetrated her, calling her his dear Fanny, kissing her affectionately, and observing with decided pleasure how much she was grown! Fanny knew not how to feel, nor where to look. She was quite oppressed. He had never been so kind, so *very* kind to her in his life. His manner seemed changed; his voice was quick from the agitation of joy, and all that had been awful in his dignity seemed lost in tenderness. He led her nearer the light and looked at her again—

4  Relations of intimacy or trust.

inquired particularly after her health, and then correcting himself, observed, that he need *not* inquire, for her appearance spoke sufficiently on that point. A fine blush having succeeded the previous paleness of her face, he was justified in his belief of her equal improvement in health and beauty. He inquired next after her family, especially William; and his kindness altogether was such as made her reproach herself for loving him so little, and thinking his return a misfortune; and when, on having courage to lift her eyes to his face, she saw that he was grown thinner and had the burnt, fagged, worn look of fatigue and a hot climate, every tender feeling was increased, and she was miserable in considering how much unsuspected vexation was probably ready to burst on him.

Sir Thomas was indeed the life of the party, who at his suggestion now seated themselves round the fire. He had the best right to be the talker; and the delight of his sensations in being again in his own house, in the centre of his family, after such a separation, made him communicative and chatty in a very unusual degree; and he was ready to give every information as to his voyage, and answer every question of his two sons almost before it was put. His business in Antigua had latterly been prosperously rapid, and he came directly from Liverpool, having had an opportunity of making his passage thither in a private vessel, instead of waiting for the packet; and all the little particulars of his proceedings and events, his arrivals and departures, were most promptly delivered, as he sat by Lady Bertram and looked with heartfelt satisfaction on the faces around him—interrupting himself more than once, however, to remark on his good fortune in finding them all at home—coming unexpectedly as he did—all collected together exactly as he could have wished, but dared not depend on. Mr. Rushworth was not forgotten; a most friendly reception and warmth of hand-shaking had already met him, and with pointed attention he was now included in the objects most intimately connected with Mansfield. There was nothing disagreeable in Mr. Rushworth's appearance, and Sir Thomas was liking him already.

By not one of the circle was he listened to with such unbroken unalloyed enjoyment as by his wife, who was really extremely happy to see him, and whose feelings were so warmed by his sudden arrival, as to place her nearer agitation than she had been for the last twenty years. She had been *almost* fluttered for a few minutes, and still remained so sensibly animated as to put away her work,[5] move Pug from her side, and give all her attention and all the rest of her sofa to her husband. She had no anxieties for any body to cloud *her* pleasure; her own time had been irreproachably spent during his absence; she had done a great deal of carpet work and made many yards of fringe; and she would have answered as freely for the good conduct and useful pursuits of all the young people as for her own. It was so agreeable to her to see him again, and hear him talk, to have her ear amused and her whole comprehension filled by his narratives, that she began particularly to feel how dreadfully she must have missed him, and how impossible it would have been for her to bear a lengthened absence.

Mrs. Norris was by no means to be compared in happiness to her sister. Not that *she* was incommoded by many fears of Sir Thomas's disapprobation when the present state of his house should be known, for her judgment had been so blinded, that except by the instinctive caution with which she had whisked away Mr. Rushworth's pink satin cloak as her brother-in-law entered, she could hardly be said to shew any sign of alarm; but she was vexed by the *manner* of his return. It had left her nothing to do. Instead of being sent for out of the room, and seeing him first, and having to spread the happy news through the house, Sir Thomas, with a very reasonable dependance perhaps on the nerves of his wife and children, had sought no confidant but the butler, and had been following him almost instantaneously into the drawing-room. Mrs. Norris felt herself defrauded of an office on which she had always depended, whether his arrival or his death were to be the thing unfolded; and was now trying to be in a bustle without having any thing to bustle about, and labouring to be important where nothing was wanted but tranquillity and silence. Would Sir Thomas have consented to eat, she might have gone to the house-keeper with troublesome directions, and insulted the footmen with injunctions of dispatch; but Sir Thomas resolutely declined all dinner; he would take nothing, nothing till tea came—he would rather wait for tea. Still Mrs. Norris was at intervals urging

5  Meaning that her animation is visible; one may *sense* it.

6 A privateer was a merchant vessel licensed by its government to capture and plunder the ships of the nation's enemies. Attacks on Britain's commercial shipping were an important element in Napoleon's strategy. This mention of the privateer compounds the effect of the earlier reference to Sir Thomas's "burnt, fagged, worn look," a suggestion that his health has suffered in a tropical climate that was in the early nineteenth century thought to be perilous for Europeans. These details underscore the dangers his Antiguan journey has involved and to which his children have been oblivious.

7 Tom stresses his responsible stewardship of the game on the estate. Six brace of pheasants are six pair.

something different, and in the most interesting moment of his passage to England, when the alarm of a French privateer was at the height,[6] she burst through his recital with the proposal of soup. "Sure, my dear Sir Thomas, a basin of soup would be a much better thing for you than tea. Do have a basin of soup."

Sir Thomas could not be provoked. "Still the same anxiety for every body's comfort, my dear Mrs. Norris," was his answer. "But indeed I would rather have nothing but tea."

"Well then, Lady Bertram, suppose you speak for tea directly, suppose you hurry Baddeley a little, he seems behind hand to-night." She carried this point, and Sir Thomas's narrative proceeded.

At length there was a pause. His immediate communications were exhausted, and it seemed enough to be looking joyfully around him, now at one, now at another of the beloved circle; but the pause was not long: in the elation of her spirits Lady Bertram became talkative, and what were the sensations of her children upon hearing her say, "How do you think the young people have been amusing themselves lately, Sir Thomas? They have been acting. We have been all alive with acting."

"Indeed! and what have you been acting?"

"Oh! They'll tell you all about it."

"The *all* will be soon told," cried Tom hastily, and with affected unconcern; "but it is not worth while to bore my father with it now. You will hear enough of it to-morrow, sir. We have just been trying, by way of doing something, and amusing my mother, just within the last week, to get up a few scenes, a mere trifle. We have had such incessant rains almost since October began, that we have been nearly confined to the house for days together. I have hardly taken out a gun since the 3d. Tolerable sport the first three days, but there has been no attempting any thing since. The first day I went over Mansfield Wood, and Edmund took the copses beyond Easton, and we brought home six brace between us, and might each have killed six times as many; but we respect your pheasants, sir, I assure you, as much as you could desire. I do not think you will find your woods by any means worse stocked than they were.[7] *I* never saw Mansfield

Wood so full of pheasants in my life as this year. I hope you will take a day's sport there yourself, sir, soon."

For the present the danger was over, and Fanny's sick feelings subsided; but when tea was soon afterwards brought in, and Sir Thomas, getting up, said that he found that he could not be any longer in the house without just looking into his own dear room, every agitation was returning. He was gone before any thing had been said to prepare him for the change he must find there; and a pause of alarm followed his disappearance. Edmund was the first to speak:

"Something must be done," said he.

"It is time to think of our visitors," said Maria, still feeling her hand pressed to Henry Crawford's heart, and caring little for any thing else.—"Where did you leave Miss Crawford, Fanny?"

Fanny told of their departure, and delivered their message.

"Then poor Yates is all alone," cried Tom. "I will go and fetch him. He will be no bad assistant when it all comes out."

To the Theatre he went, and reached it just in time to witness the first meeting of his father and his friend. Sir Thomas had been a good deal surprized to find candles burning in his room; and on casting his eye round it, to see other symptoms of recent habitation, and a general air of confusion in the furniture. The removal of the book-case from before the billiard room door struck him especially, but he had scarcely more than time to feel astonished at all this, before there were sounds from the billiard room to astonish him still further. Some one was talking there in a very loud accent—he did not know the voice—*more* than talking—almost hallooing. He stept to the door, rejoicing at that moment in having the means of immediate communication, and opening it, found himself on the stage of a theatre, and opposed to a ranting young man, who appeared likely to knock him down backwards. At the very moment of Yates perceiving Sir Thomas, and giving perhaps the very best start he had ever given in the whole course of his rehearsals,[8] Tom Bertram entered at the other end of the room; and never had he found greater difficulty in keeping his countenance. His father's looks of solemnity and amazement on this his first appearance on any stage, and the gradual meta-

8 In this sly report on a moment when real life and theatricality collide, Austen might again be thinking of the acting of David Garrick. The highpoint of Garrick's performance of the role of Hamlet was said to be his execution of Hamlet's start of horror upon beholding the ghost of his father. Garrick was even reported to have commissioned a mechanical wig to wear for the part, one contrived so that in the ghost scene he could arrange for his hair suddenly to stand on end: through such artificial means he secured the naturalistic effects that made his acting famous. Mr. Yates's role as the baron in *Lovers' Vows* ought to have supplied him with plenty of opportunities for expressive starts and shudders. Notably, those sensational moments in Inchbald's play often involve unanticipated family reunions—for instance, the baron's reunion with the son he never knew he had in Act IV, scene ii, which has him ranting "Who am I? What am I? Mad—raving—no—I have a son!—A son!" (*British Theatre*, vol. 23, p. 60). By reintroducing Sir Thomas into her book when he is least expected, Austen pays her own wry homage to the dramatic potential of such moments.

9  The cunning joke Austen imbeds in that phrase "true acting" is that Mr. Yates's best performance comes at the moment he ceases to play his part and plays himself, but Austen might also be calling on us to wonder whether his acting ever does cease. A well-bred and easy gentleman making a bow may also be playing a role in the real-world theater of everyday life.

10  *House* is used here as a designation for a theater, as in *playhouse*.

11  Ornamental plaster.

morphosis of the impassioned Baron Wildenheim into the well-bred and easy Mr. Yates, making his bow and apology to Sir Thomas Bertram, was such an exhibition, such a piece of true acting as he would not have lost upon any account.[9] It would be the last—in all probability the last scene on that stage; but he was sure there could not be a finer. The house would close with the greatest eclat.[10]

There was little time, however, for the indulgence of any images of merriment. It was necessary for him to step forward too and assist the introduction, and with many awkward sensations he did his best. Sir Thomas received Mr. Yates with all the appearance of cordiality which was due to his own character, but was really as far from pleased with the necessity of the acquaintance as with the manner of its commencement. Mr. Yates's family and connections were sufficiently known to him, to render his introduction as the "particular friend," another of the hundred particular friends of his son, exceedingly unwelcome; and it needed all the felicity of being again at home, and all the forbearance it could supply, to save Sir Thomas from anger on finding himself thus bewildered in his own house, making part of a ridiculous exhibition in the midst of theatrical nonsense, and forced in so untoward a moment to admit the acquaintance of a young man whom he felt sure of disapproving, and whose easy indifference and volubility in the course of the first five minutes seemed to mark him the most at home of the two.

Tom understood his father's thoughts, and heartily wishing he might be always as well disposed to give them but partial expression, began to see more clearly than he had ever done before that there might be some ground of offence—that there might be some reason for the glance his father gave towards the ceiling and stucco[11] of the room; and that when he inquired with mild gravity after the fate of the billiard table, he was not proceeding beyond a very allowable curiosity. A few minutes were enough for such unsatisfactory sensations on each side; and Sir Thomas, having exerted himself so far as to speak a few words of calm approbation in reply to an eager appeal of Mr. Yates, as to the happiness of the arrangement, the three gentlemen returned to the drawing-room together, Sir Thomas with an increase of gravity which was not lost on all.

"I come from your theatre," said he composedly, as he sat down; "I found myself in it rather unexpectedly. Its vicinity to my own room—but in every respect indeed it took me by surprise, as I had not the smallest suspicion of your acting having assumed so serious a character. It appears a neat job, however, as far as I could judge by candle-light, and does my friend Christopher Jackson credit." And then he would have changed the subject, and sipped his coffee in peace over domestic matters of a calmer hue; but Mr. Yates, without discernment to catch Sir Thomas's meaning, or diffidence, or delicacy, or discretion enough to allow him to lead the discourse while he mingled among the others with the least obtrusiveness himself, would keep him on the topic of the theatre, would torment him with questions and remarks relative to it, and finally would make him hear the whole history of his disappointment at Ecclesford. Sir Thomas listened most politely, but found much to offend his ideas of decorum and confirm his ill-opinion of Mr. Yates's habits of thinking from the beginning to the end of the story; and when it was over, could give him no other assurance of sympathy than what a slight bow conveyed.

"This was in fact the origin of *our* acting," said Tom after a moment's thought. "My friend Yates brought the infection from Ecclesford, and it spread as those things always spread you know, sir—the faster probably from *your* having so often encouraged the sort of thing in us formerly. It was like treading old ground again."

Mr. Yates took the subject from his friend as soon as possible, and immediately gave Sir Thomas an account of what they had done and were doing, told him of the gradual increase of their views, the happy conclusion of their first difficulties, and present promising state of affairs; relating every thing with so blind an interest as made him not only totally unconscious of the uneasy movements of many of his friends as they sat, the change of countenance, the fidget, the hem! of unquietness, but prevented him even from seeing the expression of the face on which his own eyes were fixed—from seeing Sir Thomas's dark brow contract as he looked with inquiring earnestness at his daughters and Edmund, dwelling particularly on the latter, and speaking a language, a remonstrance, a reproof, which *he* felt at his

Charles Heath's frontispiece to *Lovers' Vows*, which appeared in Elizabeth Inchbald's multivolume anthology *The British Theatre*, pictures the tender family reunion that closes the play: part of Austen's wit is to remind us of that reunion at the very moment in which *she* stages Sir Thomas's homecoming to his family. In this image, Agatha is flanked by her former lover, the Baron Wildenhaim, and by their illegitimate son, Frederick, while behind her the newly engaged Amelia and Anhalt look on.

12 Unwisely, given the circumstances, Mr. Yates adheres to the idiom of the playhouse: "we bespeak your indulgence" was a frequent request to the audience made by the players who spoke the dramatic prologues and epilogues of the eighteenth century.

heart. Not less acutely was it felt by Fanny, who had edged back her chair behind her aunt's end of the sofa, and, screened from notice herself, saw all that was passing before her. Such a look of reproach at Edmund from his father she could never have expected to witness; and to feel that it was in any degree deserved, was an aggravation indeed. Sir Thomas's look implied, "On your judgment, Edmund, I depended; what have you been about?"—She knelt in spirit to her uncle, and her bosom swelled to utter, "Oh! not to *him*. Look so to all the others, but not to *him!*"

Mr. Yates was still talking. "To own the truth, Sir Thomas, we were in the middle of a rehearsal when you arrived this evening. We were going through the three first acts, and not unsuccessfully upon the whole. Our company is now so dispersed from the Crawfords being gone home, that nothing more can be done to-night; but if you will give us the honour of your company to-morrow evening, I should not be afraid of the result. We bespeak your indulgence, you understand, as young performers; we bespeak your indulgence."[12]

"My indulgence shall be given, sir," replied Sir Thomas gravely, "but without any other rehearsal."—And with a relenting smile he added, "I come home to be happy and indulgent." Then turning away towards any or all of the rest, he tranquilly said, "Mr. and Miss Crawford were mentioned in my last letters from Mansfield. Do you find them agreeable acquaintance?"

Tom was the only one at all ready with an answer, but he being entirely without particular regard for either, without jealousy either in love or acting, could speak very handsomely of both. "Mr. Crawford was a most pleasant, gentleman-like man;—his sister a sweet, pretty, elegant, lively girl."

Mr. Rushworth could be silent no longer. "I do not say he is not gentleman-like, considering; but you should tell your father he is not above five feet eight, or he will be expecting a well-looking man."

Sir Thomas did not quite understand this, and looked with some surprize at the speaker.

"If I must say what I think," continued Mr. Rushworth, "in my opinion it is very disagreeable to be always rehearsing. It is having too much of a good thing. I am not so fond of acting as I was at first.

I think we are a great deal better employed, sitting comfortably here among ourselves, and doing nothing."

Sir Thomas looked again, and then replied with an approving smile, "I am happy to find our sentiments on this subject so much the same. It gives me sincere satisfaction. That I should be cautious and quick-sighted, and feel many scruples which my children do *not* feel, is perfectly natural; and equally so that *my* value for domestic tranquillity, for a home which shuts out noisy pleasures, should much exceed theirs. But at your time of life to feel all this, is a most favourable circumstance for yourself and for every body connected with you; and I am sensible of the importance of having an ally of such weight."

Sir Thomas meant to be giving Mr. Rushworth's opinion in better words than he could find himself. He was aware that he must not expect a genius in Mr. Rushworth; but as a well-judging steady young man, with better notions than his elocution would do justice to, he intended to value him very highly. It was impossible for many of the others not to smile. Mr. Rushworth hardly knew what to do with so much meaning; but by looking, as he really felt, most exceedingly pleased with Sir Thomas's good opinion, and saying scarcely any thing, he did his best towards preserving that good opinion a little longer.

## 2

EDMUND'S FIRST OBJECT the next morning was to see his father alone, and give him a fair statement of the whole acting scheme, defending his own share in it as far only as he could then, in a soberer moment, feel his motives to deserve, and acknowledging with perfect ingenuousness that his concession had been attended with such partial good as to make his judgment in it very doubtful. He was anxious, while vindicating himself, to say nothing unkind of the others; but there was only one amongst them whose conduct he could mention without some necessity of defence or palliation. "We have all been more or less to blame," said he, "every one of us, excepting Fanny. Fanny is the only one who has judged rightly throughout, who has been consistent. *Her* feelings have been steadily against it from first to last. She never ceased to think of what was due to you. You will find Fanny every thing you could wish."

Sir Thomas saw all the impropriety of such a scheme among such a party, and at such a time, as strongly as his son had ever supposed he must; he felt it too much indeed for many words; and having shaken hands with Edmund, meant to try to lose the disagreeable impression, and forget how much he had been forgotten himself as soon as he could, after the house had been cleared of every object enforcing the remembrance, and restored to its proper state. He did not enter into any remonstrance with his other children: he was more willing to believe they felt their error, than to run the risk of investigation. The reproof of an immediate conclusion of every thing, the sweep of every preparation would be sufficient.

There was one person, however, in the house whom he could not leave to learn his sentiments merely through his conduct. He could not help giving Mrs. Norris a hint of his having hoped, that her advice might have been interposed to prevent what her judgment must certainly have disapproved. The young people had been very inconsiderate in forming the plan; they ought to have been capable of a better decision themselves; but they were young, and, excepting Edmund, he believed of unsteady characters; and with greater surprize therefore he must regard her acquiescence in their wrong measures, her countenance of their unsafe amusements, than that such measures and such amusements should have been suggested. Mrs. Norris was a little confounded, and as nearly being silenced as ever she had been in her life; for she was ashamed to confess having never seen any of the impropriety which was so glaring to Sir Thomas, and would not have admitted that her influence was insufficient, that she might have talked in vain. Her only resource was to get out of the subject as fast as possible, and turn the current of Sir Thomas's ideas into a happier channel. She had a great deal to insinuate in her own praise as to *general* attention to the interest and comfort of his family, much exertion and many sacrifices to glance at in the form of hurried walks and sudden removals from her own fire-side, and many excellent hints of distrust and economy to Lady Bertram and Edmund to detail, whereby a most considerable saving had always arisen, and more than one bad servant been detected. But her chief strength lay in Sotherton. Her greatest support and glory was in having formed the connection with the Rushworths. *There* she was impregnable. She took to herself all the credit of bringing Mr. Rushworth's admiration of Maria to any effect. "If I had not been active," said she, "and made a point of being introduced to his mother, and then prevailed on my sister to pay the first visit, I am as certain as I sit here, that nothing would have come of it—for Mr. Rushworth is the sort of amiable modest young man who wants a great deal of encouragement, and there were girls enough on the catch for him if we had been idle. But I left no stone unturned. I was ready to move heaven

1 September 29, the feast day of St. Michael, mentioned as the start of autumn.

2 Managed the reins of the front pair of horses in the team of four drawing a carriage.

and earth to persuade my sister, and at last I did persuade her. You know the distance to Sotherton; it was in the middle of winter, and the roads almost impassable, but I did persuade her."

"I know how great, how justly great your influence is with Lady Bertram and her children, and am the more concerned that it should not have been— —"

"My dear Sir Thomas, if you had seen the state of the roads *that* day! I thought we should never have got through them, though we had the four horses of course; and poor old coachman would attend us, out of his great love and kindness, though he was hardly able to sit the box on account of the rheumatism which I had been doctoring him for, ever since Michaelmas.[1] I cured him at last; but he was very bad all the winter—and this was such a day, I could not help going to him up in his room before we set off to advise him not to venture: he was putting on his wig—so I said, 'Coachman, you had much better not go, your Lady and I shall be very safe; you know how steady Stephen is, and Charles has been upon the leaders so often now,[2] that I am sure there is no fear.' But, however, I soon found it would not do; he was bent upon going, and as I hate to be worrying and officious, I said no more; but my heart quite ached for him at every jolt, and when we got into the rough lanes about Stoke, where what with frost and snow upon beds of stones, it was worse than any thing you can imagine, I was quite in an agony about him. And then the poor horses too!—To see them straining away! You know how I always feel for the horses. And when we got to the bottom of Sandcroft Hill, what do you think I did? You will laugh at me—but I got out and walked up. I did indeed. It might not be saving them much, but it was something, and I could not bear to sit at my ease, and be dragged up at the expense of those noble animals. I caught a dreadful cold, but *that* I did not regard. My object was accomplished in the visit."

"I hope we shall always think the acquaintance worth any trouble that might be taken to establish it. There is nothing very striking in Mr. Rushworth's manners, but I was pleased last night with what appeared to be his opinion on *one* subject—his decided preference of a quiet family-party to the bustle and confusion of acting. He seemed to feel exactly as one could wish."

"Yes, indeed,—and the more you know of him, the better you will like him. He is not a shining character, but he has a thousand good qualities! and is so disposed to look up to you, that I am quite laughed at about it, for every body considers it as my doing. 'Upon my word, Mrs. Norris,' said Mrs. Grant, the other day, 'if Mr. Rushworth were a son of your own he could not hold Sir Thomas in greater respect.'"

Sir Thomas gave up the point, foiled by her evasions, disarmed by her flattery; and was obliged to rest satisfied with the conviction that where the present pleasure of those she loved was at stake, her kindness did sometimes overpower her judgment.

It was a busy morning with him. Conversation with any of them occupied but a small part of it. He had to reinstate himself in all the wonted concerns of his Mansfield life, to see his steward and his bailiff—to examine and compute—and, in the intervals of business, to walk into his stables and his gardens, and nearest plantations; but active and methodical, he had not only done all this before he resumed his seat as master of the house at dinner, he had also set the carpenter to work in pulling down what had been so lately put up in the billiard room, and given the scene painter his dismissal, long enough to justify the pleasing belief of his being then at least as far off as Northampton. The scene painter was gone, having spoilt only the floor of one room, ruined all the coachman's sponges, and made five of the under-servants idle and dissatisfied; and Sir Thomas was in hopes that another day or two would suffice to wipe away every outward memento of what had been, even to the destruction of every unbound copy of Lovers' Vows in the house, for he was burning all that met his eye.

Mr. Yates was beginning now to understand Sir Thomas's intentions, though as far as ever from understanding their source. He and his friend had been out with their guns the chief of the morning, and Tom had taken the opportunity of explaining, with proper apologies for his father's particularity,[3] what was to be expected. Mr. Yates felt it as acutely as might be supposed. To be a second time disappointed

3 *Particularity* as Tom uses it here means oddity or singularity.

Mr. Yates felt it acutely.

Charles Edmund Brock's illustration captures the moment when Mr. Yates realizes that his theatrical ambitions have been stymied yet again.

4 Enlightenment, explanation.

in the same way was an instance of very severe ill-luck; and his indignation was such, that had it not been for delicacy towards his friend and his friend's youngest sister, he believed he should certainly attack the Baronet on the absurdity of his proceedings, and argue him into a little more rationality. He believed this very stoutly while he was in Mansfield Wood, and all the way home; but there was a something in Sir Thomas, when they sat round the same table, which made Mr. Yates think it wiser to let him pursue his own way, and feel the folly of it without opposition. He had known many disagreeable fathers before, and often been struck with the inconveniences they occasioned, but never in the whole course of his life, had he seen one of that class, so unintelligibly moral, so infamously tyrannical as Sir Thomas. He was not a man to be endured but for his children's sake, and he might be thankful to his fair daughter Julia that Mr. Yates did yet mean to stay a few days longer under his roof.

The evening passed with external smoothness, though almost every mind was ruffled; and the music which Sir Thomas called for from his daughters helped to conceal the want of real harmony. Maria was in a good deal of agitation. It was of the utmost consequence to her that Crawford should now lose no time in declaring himself, and she was disturbed that even a day should be gone by without seeming to advance that point. She had been expecting to see him the whole morning—and all the evening too was still expecting him. Mr. Rushworth had set off early with the great news for Sotherton; and she had fondly hoped for such an immediate eclaircissement[4] as might save him the trouble of ever coming back again. But they had seen no one from the Parsonage—not a creature, and had heard no tidings beyond a friendly note of congratulation and inquiry from Mrs. Grant to Lady Bertram. It was the first day for many, many weeks, in which the families had been wholly divided. Four-and-twenty hours had never passed before, since August began, without bringing them together in some way or other. It was a sad anxious day; and the morrow, though differing in the sort of evil, did by no means bring less. A few moments of feverish enjoyment were followed by hours of acute suffering. Henry Crawford was again in the house; he walked up with Dr. Grant, who was anxious to pay his respects to Sir Thomas, and at rather an early hour they were ushered into the breakfast-room, where were most of the family. Sir Thomas soon appeared, and Maria saw with delight and agitation the introduction of the man she loved to her father. Her sensations were indefinable, and so were they a few minutes afterwards upon hearing Henry Crawford, who had a chair between herself and Tom, ask the latter in an under voice whether there were any plans for resuming the play after the present happy interruption, (with a courteous glance at Sir Thomas,) because in that case, he should make a point of returning to Mansfield, at any time required by the party; he was going away immediately, being to meet his uncle at Bath without delay,[5] but if there were any prospect of a renewal of Lovers' Vows, he should hold himself positively engaged, he should break through every other claim, he should absolutely condition with his uncle for attending them whenever he might be wanted. The play should not be lost by *his* absence.

"From Bath, Norfolk, London, York—wherever I may be," said he, "I will attend you from any place in England, at an hour's notice."

It was well at that moment that Tom had to speak and not his sister. He could immediately say with easy fluency, "I am sorry you are going—but as to our play, *that* is all over—entirely at an end (looking significantly at his father). The painter was sent off yesterday, and very little will remain of the theatre to-morrow.—I knew how *that* would be from the first.—It is early for Bath.—You will find nobody there."

"It is about my uncle's usual time."

"When do you think of going?"

"I may perhaps get as far as Banbury to-day."[6]

"Whose stables do you use at Bath?" was the next question; and while this branch of the subject was under discussion, Maria, who wanted neither pride nor resolution, was preparing to encounter her share of it with tolerable calmness.

To her he soon turned, repeating much of what he had already said, with only a softened air and stronger expressions of regret. But what availed his expressions or his air?—He was going—and if not voluntarily going, voluntarily intending to stay away; for, excepting

5  By 1814 the most fashionable time to visit Bath, the spa town in southwest England, was the winter, so the season is now only beginning. Austen's *Persuasion* shows us some of Admiral Crawford's brother admirals wintering there to benefit from the medicinal hot springs and to take part in the town's fashionable social life.

6  Banbury is a town in Oxfordshire.

what might be due to his uncle, his engagements were all self-imposed.—He might talk of necessity, but she knew his independence.—The hand which had so pressed her's to his heart!—The hand and the heart were alike motionless and passive now! Her spirit supported her, but the agony of her mind was severe.—She had not long to endure what arose from listening to language, which his actions contradicted, or to bury the tumult of her feelings under the restraint of society; for general civilities soon called his notice from her, and the farewell visit, as it then became openly acknowledged, was a very short one.—He was gone—he had touched her hand for the last time, he had made his parting bow, and she might seek directly all that solitude could do for her. Henry Crawford was gone—gone from the house, and within two hours afterwards from the parish; and so ended all the hopes his selfish vanity had raised in Maria and Julia Bertram.

Julia could rejoice that he was gone.—His presence was beginning to be odious to her; and if Maria gained him not, she was now cool enough to dispense with any other revenge.—She did not want exposure to be added to desertion.—Henry Crawford gone, she could even pity her sister.

With a purer spirit did Fanny rejoice in the intelligence.—She heard it at dinner and felt it a blessing. By all the others it was mentioned with regret, and his merits honoured with due gradation of feeling, from the sincerity of Edmund's too partial regard, to the unconcern of his mother speaking entirely by rote. Mrs. Norris began to look about her and wonder that his falling in love with Julia had come to nothing; and could almost fear that she had been remiss herself in forwarding it; but with so many to care for, how was it possible for even *her* activity to keep pace with her wishes?

Another day or two, and Mr. Yates was gone likewise. In *his* departure Sir Thomas felt the chief interest; wanting to be alone with his family, the presence of a stranger superior to Mr. Yates must have been irksome; but of him, trifling and confident, idle and expensive, it was every way vexatious. In himself he was wearisome, but as the friend of Tom and the admirer of Julia he became offensive. Sir Thomas had been quite indifferent to Mr. Crawford's going or staying—but his good wishes for Mr. Yates's having a pleasant journey, as he walked with him to the hall door, were given with genuine satisfaction. Mr. Yates had staid to see the destruction of every theatrical preparation at Mansfield, the removal of every thing appertaining to the play; he left the house in all the soberness of its general character; and Sir Thomas hoped, in seeing him out of it, to be rid of the worst object connected with the scheme, and the last that must be inevitably reminding him of its existence.

Mrs. Norris contrived to remove one article from his sight that might have distressed him. The curtain over which she had presided with such talent and such success, went off with her to her cottage, where she happened to be particularly in want of green baize.

# 3

SIR THOMAS'S RETURN made a striking change in the ways of the family, independent of Lovers' Vows. Under his government, Mansfield was an altered place. Some members of their society sent away and the spirits of many others saddened, it was all sameness and gloom, compared with the past; a sombre family-party rarely enlivened. There was little intercourse with the Parsonage. Sir Thomas drawing back from intimacies in general, was particularly disinclined, at this time, for any engagements but in one quarter. The Rushworths were the only addition to his own domestic circle which he could solicit.

Edmund did not wonder that such should be his father's feelings, nor could he regret any thing but the exclusion of the Grants. "But they," he observed to Fanny, "have a claim. They seem to belong to us—they seem to be part of ourselves. I could wish my father were more sensible of their very great attention to my mother and sisters while he was away. I am afraid they may feel themselves neglected. But the truth is that my father hardly knows them. They had not been here a twelvemonth when he left England. If he knew them better, he would value their society as it deserves, for they are in fact exactly the sort of people he would like. We are sometimes a little in want of animation among ourselves; my sisters seem out of spirits, and Tom is certainly not at his ease. Dr. and Mrs. Grant would enliven us, and make our evenings pass away with more enjoyment even to my father."

Emanuel Bowen's *New and Accurate Map of the Island of Antigua or Antego:* a 1747 updating of Herman Moll's earlier map. Notice Willoughby Bay on the island's south coast, an evocative place name for a reader of Austen's fiction.

Portrait of Thomas Clarkson, anti–slave trade campaigner and author in 1807 of *The History of the Rise, Progress, and Accomplishment of the Abolition of the Slave Trade,* a book that Austen's correspondence suggests she read with admiration. Clarkson's influential writings represent one reason the slave trade and slave labor were debated not only in the British Parliament but also in British drawing rooms.

"Do you think so?" said Fanny "In my opinion, my uncle would not like *any* addition. I think he values the very quietness you speak of, and that the repose of his own family-circle is all he wants. And it does not appear to me that we are more serious than we used to be; I mean before my uncle went abroad. As well as I can recollect, it was always much the same. There was never much laughing in his presence; or, if there is any difference, it is not more I think than such an absence has a tendency to produce at first. There must be a sort of shyness. But I cannot recollect that our evenings formerly were ever merry, except when my uncle was in town. No young people's are, I suppose, when those they look up to are at home."

"I believe you are right, Fanny," was his reply, after a short consideration. "I believe our evenings are rather returned to what they were, than assuming a new character. The novelty was in their being lively.—Yet, how strong the impression that only a few weeks will give! I have been feeling as if we had never lived so before."

"I suppose I am graver than other people," said Fanny. "The evenings do not appear long to me. I love to hear my uncle talk of the West Indies. I could listen to him for an hour together. It entertains *me* more than many other things have done—but then I am unlike other people I dare say."

"Why should you dare say *that?* (smiling)—Do you want to be told that you are only unlike other people in being more wise and discreet? But when did you or any body ever get a compliment from me, Fanny? Go to my father if you want to be complimented. He will satisfy you. Ask your uncle what he thinks, and you will hear compliments enough; and though they may be chiefly on your person, you must put up with it, and trust to his seeing as much beauty of mind in time."

Such language was so new to Fanny that it quite embarrassed her.

"Your uncle thinks you very pretty, dear Fanny—and that is the long and the short of the matter. Any body but myself would have made something more of it, and any body but you would resent that you had not been thought very pretty before; but the truth is, that your uncle never did admire you till now—and now he does. Your complexion is so improved!—and you have gained so much counte-

"Slaves Planting Cane Cuttings" from William Clark's *Ten Views in the Island of Antigua* (1823), a portfolio of lithographs depicting the several stages in the production of sugar, the island's primary commodity. Clark lived on a sugar estate in Antigua for three years while making his drawings.

nance!—and your figure—Nay, Fanny, do not turn away about it—it is but an uncle. If you cannot bear an uncle's admiration what is to become of you? You must really begin to harden yourself to the idea of being worth looking at.—You must try not to mind growing up into a pretty woman."

"Oh! don't talk so, don't talk so," cried Fanny, distressed by more feelings than he was aware of; but seeing that she was distressed, he had done with the subject, and only added more seriously, "Your uncle is disposed to be pleased with you in every respect; and I only wish you would talk to him more.—You are one of those who are too silent in the evening circle."

"But I do talk to him more than I used. I am sure I do. Did not you hear me ask him about the slave-trade last night?"

"I did—and was in hopes the question would be followed up by others. It would have pleased your uncle to be inquired of farther."

"And I longed to do it—but there was such a dead silence![1] And

1 What exactly Fanny might have asked about the slave trade and whether the lack of a response suggests the Bertrams' sense of guilt or instead their imperturbable self-preoccupation are questions much discussed in criticism of *Mansfield Park*. Most critics agree in interpreting Fanny's question as motivated by her own support for the abolition of the trade and perhaps by her interest (assuming that the novel postdates Parliament's passage of the abolition bill in 1807) in how the new law's provisions were being enforced. This stance would fit with Fanny's piety and even her love of William Cowper's poetry—Cowper's *Task* had explicitly celebrated the legal decision of 1772 in which the Lord Chief Justice, Lord Mansfield, had abolished slavery on English soil. (In the colonies, by contrast, slavery would remain legal until 1833.) The views of the other characters in this scene are more difficult to gauge. Edmund will shortly indicate that his father was eager to expatiate on this topic, which suggests to some commentators that Sir Thomas is what Mrs. Elton in *Emma* would call "a friend to the abolition" (II, xvii). Most critics have felt, however, that Fanny's question must have hit a nerve, given how the talkativeness that was so noticeable in the Sir Thomas we saw two chapters ago apparently failed him at this moment.

The scene's importance lies as well in how it testifies to Fanny's intellectual and moral development. The girl whose inability to put the map of Europe together occasioned her cousins' mockery at the start of the novel now appears, as an adult, much more knowledgeable than they do about Britain's place in its empire.

2 *Repulsive* did not carry then the strongly negative charge that it does now; Edmund means simply that his father's reserve will feel uninviting to Mary.

3 Tunbridge Wells and Cheltenham are spa towns in Kent and Gloucestershire respectively. A moralizing mentor to the hero of Frances Burney's *Camilla* (1796), a novel that figures in *Northanger Abbey,* laments the time that fashionable young women in search of amusement spend in towns of this kind: "those who, after meeting them all the winter at the opera, and all the spring at Ranelagh, hear of them all the summer at Cheltenham, Tunbridge, &c. and all the autumn at Bath, are apt to inquire, when is the season for home" (*Camilla,* ed. Edward A. Bloom and Lillian D. Bloom [Oxford: Oxford University Press, 1983], p. 472).

while my cousins were sitting by without speaking a word, or seeming at all interested in the subject, I did not like—I thought it would appear as if I wanted to set myself off at their expense, by shewing a curiosity and pleasure in his information which he must wish his own daughters to feel."

"Miss Crawford was very right in what she said of you the other day—that you seemed almost as fearful of notice and praise as other women were of neglect. We were talking of you at the Parsonage, and those were her words. She has great discernment. I know nobody who distinguishes characters better.—For so young a woman it is remarkable! She certainly understands *you* better than you are understood by the greater part of those who have known you so long; and with regard to some others, I can perceive, from occasional lively hints, the unguarded expressions of the moment, that she could define *many* as accurately, did not delicacy forbid it. I wonder what she thinks of my father! She must admire him as a fine looking man, with most gentleman-like, dignified, consistent manners; but perhaps having seen him so seldom, his reserve may be a little repulsive.[2] Could they be much together I feel sure of their liking each other. He would enjoy her liveliness—and she has talents to value his powers. I wish they met more frequently!—I hope she does not suppose there is any dislike on his side."

"She must know herself too secure of the regard of all the rest of you," said Fanny with half a sigh, "to have any such apprehension. And Sir Thomas's wishing just at first to be only with his family is so very natural, that she can argue nothing from that. After a little while I dare say we shall be meeting again in the same sort of way, allowing for the difference of the time of year."

"This is the first October that she has passed in the country since her infancy. I do not call Tunbridge or Cheltenham the country;[3] and November is a still more serious month, and I can see that Mrs. Grant is very anxious for her not finding Mansfield dull as winter comes on."

Fanny could have said a great deal, but it was safer to say nothing, and leave untouched all Miss Crawford's resources, her accomplishments, her spirits, her importance, her friends, lest it should betray her into any observations seemingly unhandsome. Miss Crawford's kind opinion of herself deserved at least a grateful forbearance, and she began to talk of something else.

"To-morrow, I think, my uncle dines at Sotherton, and you and Mr. Bertram too. We shall be quite a small party at home. I hope my uncle may continue to like Mr. Rushworth."

"That is impossible, Fanny. He must like him less after to-morrow's visit, for we shall be five hours in his company. I should dread the stupidity of the day, if there were not a much greater evil to follow—the impression it must leave on Sir Thomas. He cannot much longer deceive himself. I am sorry for them all, and would give something that Rushworth and Maria had never met."

In this quarter, indeed, disappointment was impending over Sir Thomas. Not all his good-will for Mr. Rushworth, not all Mr. Rushworth's deference for him, could prevent him from soon discerning some part of the truth—that Mr. Rushworth was an inferior young man, as ignorant in business as in books, with opinions in general unfixed, and without seeming much aware of it himself.

He had expected a very different son-in-law; and beginning to feel grave on Maria's account, tried to understand *her* feelings. Little observation there was necessary to tell him that indifference was the most favourable state they could be in. Her behaviour to Mr. Rushworth was careless and cold. She could not, did not like him. Sir Thomas resolved to speak seriously to her. Advantageous as would be the alliance, and long standing and public as was the engagement, her happiness must not be sacrificed to it. Mr. Rushworth had perhaps been accepted on too short an acquaintance, and on knowing him better she was repenting.

With solemn kindness Sir Thomas addressed her; told her his fears, inquired into her wishes, entreated her to be open and sincere, and assured her that every inconvenience should be braved, and the connection entirely given up, if she felt herself unhappy in the prospect of it. He would act for her and release her. Maria had a moment's struggle as she listened, and only a moment's: when her father ceased, she was able to give her answer immediately, decidedly, and with no apparent agitation. She thanked him for his great attention,

An early nineteenth-century seal with the motto "Am I not a Woman and a Sister." The design adapts that of a 1787 Wedgwood medallion that pictured an enslaved African man asking, "Am I not a Man and a Brother": with this redesign, campaigners for the abolition of the slave trade acknowledged the value that Englishwomen's opinions might have for their cause.

4 *Lovers' Vows* continues to be relevant here, despite Sir Thomas's bonfire of the books. Readers of *Mansfield Park* who knew Inchbald's play would notice the contrast between Sir Thomas and the Baron Wildenhaim, who takes considerable trouble to ascertain his daughter Amelia's feelings when she is on the point of marriage to Count Cassel.

his paternal kindness, but he was quite mistaken in supposing she had the smallest desire of breaking through her engagement, or was sensible of any change of opinion or inclination since her forming it. She had the highest esteem for Mr. Rushworth's character and disposition, and could not have a doubt of her happiness with him.

Sir Thomas was satisfied; too glad to be satisfied perhaps to urge the matter quite so far as his judgment might have dictated to others.[4] It was an alliance which he could not have relinquished without pain; and thus he reasoned. Mr. Rushworth was young enough to improve;—Mr. Rushworth must and would improve in good society; and if Maria could now speak so securely of her happiness with him, speaking certainly without the prejudice, the blindness of love, she ought to be believed. Her feelings probably were not acute; he had never supposed them to be so; but her comforts might not be less on that account, and if she could dispense with seeing her husband a leading, shining character, there would certainly be every thing else in her favour. A well-disposed young woman, who did not marry for love, was in general but the more attached to her own family, and the nearness of Sotherton to Mansfield must naturally hold out the greatest temptation, and would, in all probability, be a continual supply of the most amiable and innocent enjoyments. Such and such-like were the reasonings of Sir Thomas—happy to escape the embarrassing evils of a rupture, the wonder, the reflections, the reproach that must attend it, happy to secure a marriage which would bring him such an addition of respectability and influence, and very happy to think any thing of his daughter's disposition that was most favourable for the purpose.

To her the conference closed as satisfactorily as to him. She was in a state of mind to be glad that she had secured her fate beyond recall—that she had pledged herself anew to Sotherton—that she was safe from the possibility of giving Crawford the triumph of governing her actions, and destroying her prospects; and retired in proud resolve, determined only to behave more cautiously to Mr. Rushworth in future, that her father might not be again suspecting her.

Had Sir Thomas applied to his daughter within the first three or four days after Henry Crawford's leaving Mansfield, before her feelings were at all tranquillized, before she had given up every hope of him, or absolutely resolved on enduring his rival, her answer might have been different; but after another three or four days, when there was no return, no letter, no message—no symptom of a softened heart—no hope of advantage from separation—her mind became cool enough to seek all the comfort that pride and self-revenge could give.

Henry Crawford had destroyed her happiness, but he should not know that he had done it; he should not destroy her credit, her appearance, her prosperity too. He should not have to think of her as pining in the retirement of Mansfield for *him,* rejecting Sotherton and London, independence and splendour for *his* sake. Independence was more needful than ever; the want of it at Mansfield more sensibly felt. She was less and less able to endure the restraint which her father imposed. The liberty which his absence had given was now become absolutely necessary. She must escape from him and Mansfield as soon as possible, and find consolation in fortune and consequence, bustle and the world,[5] for a wounded spirit. Her mind was quite determined and varied not.

To such feelings, delay, even the delay of much preparation, would have been an evil, and Mr. Rushworth could hardly be more impatient for the marriage than herself. In all the important preparations of the mind she was complete; being prepared for matrimony by an hatred of home, restraint, and tranquillity; by the misery of disappointed affection, and contempt of the man she was to marry. The rest might wait. The preparations of new carriages and furniture might wait for London and spring, when her own taste could have fairer play.

The principals being all agreed in this respect, it soon appeared that a very few weeks would be sufficient for such arrangements as must precede the wedding.

Mrs. Rushworth was quite ready to retire, and make way for the fortunate young woman whom her dear son had selected;—and very early in November removed herself, her maid, her footman, and her chariot, with true dowager propriety, to Bath—there to parade over the wonders of Sotherton in her evening-parties—enjoying them as

5 Her entrance into fashionable society—"the world"—will console her, Maria believes.

6 Smelling salts, to be inhaled should she feel faint.

7 The seaside resort on the south coast also favored by the Prince Regent, who had his palace of pleasure, the Marine Pavilion, built there.

thoroughly perhaps in the animation of a card-table as she had ever done on the spot—and before the middle of the same month the ceremony had taken place, which gave Sotherton another mistress.

It was a very proper wedding. The bride was elegantly dressed—the two bridesmaids were duly inferior—her father gave her away—her mother stood with salts in her hand,[6] expecting to be agitated—her aunt tried to cry—and the service was impressively read by Dr. Grant. Nothing could be objected to when it came under the discussion of the neighbourhood, except that the carriage which conveyed the bride and bridegroom and Julia from the church door to Sotherton, was the same chaise which Mr. Rushworth had used for a twelve-month before. In every thing else the etiquette of the day might stand the strictest investigation.

It was done, and they were gone. Sir Thomas felt as an anxious father must feel, and was indeed experiencing much of the agitation which his wife had been apprehensive of for herself, but had fortunately escaped. Mrs. Norris, most happy to assist in the duties of the day, by spending it at the Park to support her sister's spirits, and drinking the health of Mr. and Mrs. Rushworth in a supernumerary glass or two, was all joyous delight—for she had made the match—she had done every thing—and no one would have supposed, from her confident triumph, that she had ever heard of conjugal infelicity in her life, or could have the smallest insight into the disposition of the niece who had been brought up under her eye.

The plan of the young couple was to proceed after a few days to Brighton,[7] and take a house there for some weeks. Every public place was new to Maria, and Brighton is almost as gay in winter as in summer. When the novelty of amusement there were over, it would be time for the wider range of London.

Julia was to go with them to Brighton. Since rivalry between the sisters had ceased, they had been gradually recovering much of their former good understanding; and were at least sufficiently friends to make each of them exceedingly glad to be with the other at such a time. Some other companion than Mr. Rushworth was of the first consequence to his lady, and Julia was quite as eager for novelty and pleasure as Maria, though she might not have struggled through so much to obtain them, and could better bear a subordinate situation.

Their departure made another material change at Mansfield, a chasm which required some time to fill up. The family circle became greatly contracted, and though the Miss Bertrams had latterly added little to its gaiety, they could not but be missed. Even their mother missed them—and how much more their tender-hearted cousin, who wandered about the house, and thought of them, and felt for them, with a degree of affectionate regret which they had never done much to deserve!

# 4

Fanny's consequence increased on the departure of her cousins. Becoming, as she then did, the only young woman in the drawing-room, the only occupier of that interesting division of a family in which she had hitherto held so humble a third, it was impossible for her not to be more looked at, more thought of and attended to, than she had ever been before; and "where is Fanny?" became no uncommon question, even without her being wanted for any one's convenience.

Not only at home did her value increase, but at the Parsonage too. In that house which she had hardly entered twice a year since Mr. Norris's death, she became a welcome, an invited guest; and in the gloom and dirt of a November day, most acceptable to Mary Crawford. Her visits there, beginning by chance, were continued by solicitation. Mrs. Grant, really eager to get any change for her sister, could by the easiest self-deceit persuade herself that she was doing the kindest thing by Fanny, and giving her the most important opportunities of improvement in pressing her frequent calls.

Fanny, having been sent into the village on some errand by her aunt Norris, was overtaken by a heavy shower close to the Parsonage, and being descried from one of the windows endeavouring to find shelter under the branches and lingering leaves of an oak just beyond their premises, was forced, though not without some modest reluctance on her part, to come in. A civil servant she had withstood; but when Dr. Grant himself went out with an umbrella, there was nothing to be done but to be very much ashamed and to get into the house as fast as possible; and to poor Miss Crawford, who had just been contemplating the dismal rain in a very desponding state of mind, sighing over the ruin of all her plan of exercise for that morning, and of every chance of seeing a single creature beyond themselves for the next twenty-four hours; the sound of a little bustle at the front door, and the sight of Miss Price dripping with wet in the vestibule, was delightful. The value of an event on a wet day in the country, was most forcibly brought before her. She was all alive again directly, and among the most active in being useful to Fanny, in detecting her to be wetter than she would at first allow, and providing her with dry clothes; and Fanny, after being obliged to submit to all this attention, and to being assisted and waited on by mistresses and maids, being also obliged on returning down stairs, to be fixed in their drawing-room for an hour while the rain continued, the blessing of something fresh to see and think of was thus extended to Miss Crawford, and might carry on her spirits to the period of dressing and dinner.

The two sisters were so kind to her and so pleasant, that Fanny might have enjoyed her visit could she have believed herself not in the way, and could she have foreseen that the weather would certainly clear at the end of the hour, and save her from the shame of having Dr. Grant's carriage and horses out to take her home, with which she was threatened. As to anxiety for any alarm that her absence in such weather might occasion at home, she had nothing to suffer on that score; for as her being out was known only to her two aunts, she was perfectly aware that none would be felt, and that in whatever cottage aunt Norris might chuse to establish her during the rain, her being in such cottage would be indubitable to aunt Bertram.

It was beginning to look brighter, when Fanny, observing a harp in the room, asked some questions about it, which soon led to an acknowledgment of her wishing very much to hear it, and a confession, which could hardly be believed, of her having never yet heard it since its being in Mansfield. To Fanny herself it appeared a very simple and natural circumstance. She had scarcely ever been at the Parsonage since the instrument's arrival, there had been no reason that she

Plate 5 from *The Progress of Female Dissipation* (1800), a series of etchings based on drawings by Maria Cosway. Mary Crawford's proficiency as a harpist sets her apart from Fanny, who, it seems, has never even heard harp music before. Borrowing for its caption a couplet from Alexander Pope's *The Rape of the Lock* that details its anti-heroine's vanity, Cosway's *Progress* equates such musicianship with moral deficiency.

should; but Miss Crawford, calling to mind an early-expressed wish on the subject, was concerned at her own neglect;—and "shall I play to you now?"—and "what will you have?" were questions immediately following with the readiest good humour.

She played accordingly; happy to have a new listener, and a listener who seemed so much obliged, so full of wonder at the performance, and who shewed herself not wanting in taste. She played till Fanny's eyes, straying to the window on the weather's being evidently fair, spoke what she felt must be done.

"Another quarter of an hour," said Miss Crawford, "and we shall see how it will be. Do not run away the first moment of its holding up. Those clouds look alarming."

"But they are passed over," said Fanny.—"I have been watching them.—This weather is all from the south."

"South or north, I know a black cloud when I see it; and you must not set forward while it is so threatening. And besides, I want to play something more to you—a very pretty piece—and your cousin Edmund's prime favourite. You must stay and hear your cousin's favourite."

Fanny felt that she must; and though she had not waited for that sentence to be thinking of Edmund, such a memento made her particularly awake to his idea, and she fancied him sitting in that room again and again, perhaps in the very spot where she sat now, listening with constant delight to the favourite air, played, as it appeared to her, with superior tone and expression; and though pleased with it herself, and glad to like whatever was liked by him, she was more sincerely impatient to go away at the conclusion of it than she had been before; and on this being evident, she was so kindly asked to call again, to take them in her walk whenever she could, to come and hear more of the harp, that she felt it necessary to be done, if no objection arose at home.

Such was the origin of the sort of intimacy which took place between them within the first fortnight after the Miss Bertrams' going away, an intimacy resulting principally from Miss Crawford's desire of something new, and which had little reality in Fanny's feelings. Fanny went to her every two or three days; it seemed a kind of fascination;[1] she could not be easy without going, and yet it was without loving her, without ever thinking like her, without any sense of obligation for being sought after now when nobody else was to be had; and deriving no higher pleasure from her conversation than occasional amusement, and *that* often at the expense of her judgment, when it was raised by pleasantry on people or subjects which she wished to be respected. She went however, and they sauntered about together many an half hour in Mrs. Grant's shrubbery, the weather being unusually mild for the time of year; and venturing sometimes even to sit down on one of the benches now comparatively unsheltered, remaining there perhaps till in the midst of some tender ejaculation of Fanny's, on the sweets of so protracted an autumn, they

1 Since Austen's day, some of the darker meanings of the word *fascination* have faded from view, but Austen may wish her readers to be mindful of the term's association with "bewitching" or "enchantment" (Johnson's *Dictionary*) or even with "the action and the faculty of fascinating their prey attributed to serpents" (*Oxford English Dictionary*).

2 The Grants' newly planted shrubbery, the critic Robert Clark observes, typifies a Romantic period "vogue for using loose arrangements of shrubs to conceal or soften the bounds of relatively modest grounds." See "Wilderness and Shrubbery in Austen's Works," *Persuasions On-Line,* vol. 36, no. 1 (Winter 2015).

3 Strikingly.

4 Fanny's reading of Samuel Johnson's essays, part of her library in the East room, might inspire her reflections on memory. The *Idler* essay dated September 15, 1759, for instance, considers the inequality with which powers of memory seem to be distributed, points out how often, even among those with the best memories, memory "deceives our trust," and assesses some of the contrivances people develop "to secure its fidelity" (*The Yale Edition of the Works of Samuel Johnson,* vol. 2, *"The Idler" and "The Adventurer,"* ed. W. J. Bate, John M. Bullitt, and L. F. Powell [New Haven: Yale University Press, 1963], p. 231). Fanny, who as a child was belittled for her poor memory (I, 2), would have reason to remember this essay of Johnson's, which concludes by outlining the difficulties of mindful reading: "If the mind is employed on the past and future, the book will be held before the eyes in vain" (p. 232).

were forced by the sudden swell of a cold gust shaking down the last few yellow leaves about them, to jump up and walk for warmth.

"This is pretty—very pretty," said Fanny, looking around her as they were thus sitting together one day: "Every time I come into this shrubbery I am more struck with its growth and beauty. Three years ago, this was nothing but a rough hedgerow along the upper side of the field, never thought of as any thing, or capable of becoming any thing; and now it is converted into a walk, and it would be difficult to say whether most valuable as a convenience or an ornament; and perhaps in another three years we may be forgetting—almost forgetting what it was before.[2] How wonderful, how very wonderful the operations of time, and the changes of the human mind!" And following the latter train of thought, she soon afterwards added: "If any one faculty of our nature may be called *more* wonderful than the rest, I do think it is memory. There seems something more speakingly[3] incomprehensible in the powers, the failures, the inequalities of memory, than in any other of our intelligences. The memory is sometimes so retentive, so serviceable, so obedient—at others, so bewildered and so weak—and at others again, so tyrannic, so beyond controul!—We are to be sure a miracle every way—but our powers of recollecting and of forgetting, do seem peculiarly past finding out."[4]

Miss Crawford, untouched and inattentive, had nothing to say; and Fanny, perceiving it, brought back her own mind to what she thought must interest.

"It may seem impertinent in *me* to praise, but I must admire the taste Mrs. Grant has shewn in all this. There is such a quiet simplicity in the plan of the walk!—not too much attempted!"

"Yes," replied Miss Crawford carelessly, "it does very well for a place of this sort. One does not think of extent *here*—and between ourselves, till I came to Mansfield, I had not imagined a country parson ever aspired to a shrubbery or any thing of the kind."

"I am so glad to see the evergreens thrive!" said Fanny in reply. "My uncle's gardener always says the soil here is better than his own, and so it appears from the growth of the laurels and evergreens in general.—The evergreen!—How beautiful, how welcome, how wonderful the evergreen!—When one thinks of it, how astonishing a variety of nature!—In some countries we know the tree that sheds its leaf is the variety,[5] but that does not make it less amazing, that the same soil and the same sun should nurture plants differing in the first rule and law of their existence.[6] You will think me rhapsodizing; but when I am out of doors, especially when I am sitting out of doors, I am very apt to get into this sort of wondering strain. One cannot fix one's eyes on the commonest natural production without finding food for a rambling fancy."

"To say the truth," replied Miss Crawford, "I am something like the famous Doge at the court of Lewis XIV; and may declare that I see no wonder in this shrubbery equal to seeing myself in it.[7] If any body had told me a year ago that this place would be my home, that I should be spending month after month here, as I have done, I certainly should not have believed them!—I have now been here nearly five months! and moreover the quietest five months I ever passed."

"*Too* quiet for you I believe."

"I should have thought so *theoretically* myself, but"—and her eyes brightened as she spoke—"take it all and all, I never spent so happy a summer.—But then"—with a more thoughtful air and lowered voice—"there is no saying what it may lead to."

Fanny's heart beat quick, and she felt quite unequal to surmizing or soliciting any thing more. Miss Crawford however, with renewed animation, soon went on:

"I am conscious of being far better reconciled to a country residence than I had ever expected to be. I can even suppose it pleasant to spend *half* the year in the country, under certain circumstances —very pleasant. An elegant, moderate-sized house in the centre of family connections—continual engagements among them—commanding the first society in the neighbourhood—looked-up to perhaps as leading it even more than those of larger fortune, and turning from the cheerful round of such amusements to nothing worse than a tête-à-tête with the person one feels most agreeable in the world. There is nothing frightful in such a picture, is there, Miss Price? One need not envy the new Mrs. Rushworth with such a home as *that*."

"Envy Mrs. Rushworth!" was all that Fanny attempted to say. "Come, come, it would be very unhandsome in us to be severe on Mrs. Rush-

5 The exception.

6 If, as seems probable, they include the magnolias, pines, and laurels that at this period were still quite recent introductions from America and Asia, the evergreens composing this shrubbery might be considered horticultural counterparts to Fanny herself, and there might be an element of projection in Fanny's somewhat bookish rhapsodizing. In Chap. 10 of this volume, Fanny's "transplantation" from Portsmouth will be identified as the cause of her improvement in beauty. By contrast, English gardeners of this period often questioned whether the exotic evergreen species were as transplants hardy enough for the English climate.

7 The story of the witty Doge (the title given a chief magistrate in Italy) had been relayed in Voltaire's history *Le Siècle du Louis XIV* (1751). As John Wiltshire points out in his edition of *Mansfield Park* (p. 696 n. 10), Austen certainly knew Samuel Johnson's repurposing of that anecdote, in a 1773 letter that Johnson sent from Scotland to his friend Hester Thrale: "You remember the Doge of Genoa, who being asked what struck him most at the French court? answered, 'Myself.' I cannot think many things here more likely to affect the fancy than to see Johnson ending his sixty-fourth year in the wilderness of the Hebrides" (*Letters to and from the Late Samuel Johnson* [London: A. Strahan, 1788], vol. 1, p. 114).

8 Fanny's reading has likely introduced her to several Edmunds: the poet Edmund Spenser, for instance, whose *Faerie Queene* (1590/1596) commemorates the glories of knighthood, or, from a later era, Sir Edmund Verney, whose fatal loyalty to King Charles I figured in histories of the English Civil War. Austen's first readers might have been reminded, too, of the conservative politician Edmund Burke. His *Reflections on the Revolution in France* (1790) bitterly denounced the democratic politics of the Revolutionary era with the declaration that "the age of chivalry is gone.—That of sophisters, oeconomists, and calculators, has succeeded; and the glory of Europe is extinguished forever" (*Reflections on the Revolution in France,* ed. Conor Cruise O'Brien [Harmondsworth: Penguin, 1982], p. 170).

worth, for I look forward to our owing her a great many gay, brilliant, happy hours. I expect we shall be all very much at Sotherton another year. Such a match as Miss Bertram has made is a public blessing, for the first pleasures of Mr. Rushworth's wife must be to fill her house, and give the best balls in the country."

Fanny was silent—and Miss Crawford relapsed into thoughtfulness, till suddenly looking up at the end of a few minutes, she exclaimed, "Ah! here he is." It was not Mr. Rushworth, however, but Edmund, who then appeared walking towards them with Mrs. Grant. "My sister and Mr. Bertram—I am so glad your eldest cousin is gone that he *may* be Mr. Bertram again. There is something in the sound of Mr. *Edmund* Bertram so formal, so pitiful, so younger-brother-like, that I detest it."

"How differently we feel!" cried Fanny. "To me, the sound of *Mr.* Bertram is so cold and nothing-meaning—so entirely without warmth or character!—It just stands for a gentleman, and that's all. But there is nobleness in the name of Edmund. It is a name of heroism and renown—of kings, princes, and knights; and seems to breathe the spirit of chivalry and warm affections."[8]

"I grant you the name is good in itself, and *Lord* Edmund or *Sir* Edmund sound delightfully; but sink it under the chill, the annihilation of a Mr.—and Mr. Edmund is no more than Mr. John or Mr. Thomas. Well, shall we join and disappoint them of half their lecture upon sitting down out of doors at this time of year, by being up before they can begin?"

Edmund met them with particular pleasure. It was the first time of his seeing them together since the beginning of that better acquaintance which he had been hearing of with great satisfaction. A friendship between two so very dear to him was exactly what he could have wished; and to the credit of the lover's understanding be it stated, that he did not by any means consider Fanny as the only, or even as the greater gainer by such a friendship.

"Well," said Miss Crawford, "and do you not scold us for our imprudence? What do you think we have been sitting down for but to be talked to about it, and entreated and supplicated never to do so again?"

"Perhaps I might have scolded," said Edmund, "if either of you had been sitting down alone; but while you do wrong together I can overlook a great deal."

"They cannot have been sitting long," cried Mrs. Grant, "for when I went up for my shawl I saw them from the staircase window, and then they were walking."

"And really," added Edmund, "the day is so mild, that your sitting down for a few minutes can be hardly thought imprudent. Our weather must not always be judged by the Calendar. We may sometimes take greater liberties in November than in May."

"Upon my word," cried Miss Crawford, "you are two of the most disappointing and unfeeling kind friends I ever met with! There is no giving you a moment's uneasiness. You do not know how much we have been suffering, nor what chills we have felt! But I have long thought Mr. Bertram one of the worst subjects to work on, in any little manœuvre against common sense that a woman could be plagued with. I had very little hope of *him* from the first; but you, Mrs. Grant, my sister, my own sister, I think I had a right to alarm you a little."

"Do not flatter yourself, my dearest Mary. You have not the smallest chance of moving me. I have my alarms, but they are quite in a different quarter: and if I could have altered the weather, you would have had a good sharp east wind blowing on you the whole time—for here are some of my plants which Robert *will* leave out because the nights are so mild, and I know the end of it will be that we shall have a sudden change of weather, a hard frost setting in all at once, taking every body (at least Robert) by surprize, and I shall lose every one; and what is worse, cook has just been telling me that the turkey, which I particularly wished not to be dressed till Sunday, because I know how much more Dr. Grant would enjoy it on Sunday after the fatigues of the day, will not keep beyond to-morrow. These are something like grievances, and make me think the weather most unseasonably close."

"The sweets of housekeeping in a country village!" said Miss Crawford archly. "Commend me to the nurseryman and the poulterer."

9 Promotion to the position of dean at St. Paul's Cathedral or Westminster Abbey would take the Grants to London, where amenities such as poulterers' shops or nursery gardens would be easier to access than in rural Northamptonshire.

10 A myrtle is an evergreen shrub. Mary's point may be that with enough money worries about one's garden or dinner vanish. That the myrtle is a plant sacred to the goddess of love gives her quip an aggressive edge.

"My dear child, commend Dr. Grant to the deanery of Westminster or St. Paul's, and I should be as glad of your nurseryman and poulterer as you could be.[9] But we have no such people in Mansfield. What would you have me do?"

"Oh! you can do nothing but what you do already; be plagued very often and never lose your temper."

"Thank you—but there is no escaping these little vexations, Mary, live where we may; and when you are settled in town and I come to see you, I dare say I shall find you with yours, in spite of the nurseryman and the poulterer—perhaps on their very account. Their remoteness and unpunctuality, or their exorbitant charges and frauds will be drawing forth bitter lamentations."

"I mean to be too rich to lament or to feel any thing of the sort. A large income is the best recipé for happiness I ever heard of. It certainly may secure all the myrtle and turkey part of it."[10]

"You intend to be very rich," said Edmund, with a look which, to Fanny's eye, had a great deal of serious meaning.

"To be sure. Do not you?—Do not we all?"

"I cannot intend any thing which it must be so completely beyond my power to command. Miss Crawford may chuse her degree of wealth. She has only to fix on her number of thousands a year, and there can be no doubt of their coming. My intentions are only not to be poor."

"By moderation and economy, and bringing down your wants to your income, and all that. I understand you—and a very proper plan it is for a person at your time of life, with such limited means and indifferent connections.—What can *you* want but a decent maintenance? You have not much time before you; and your relations are in no situation to do any thing for you, or to mortify you by the contrast of their own wealth and consequence. Be honest and poor, by all means—but I shall not envy you; I do not much think I shall even respect you. I have a much greater respect for those that are honest and rich."

"Your degree of respect for honesty, rich or poor, is precisely what I have no manner of concern with. I do not mean to be poor. Poverty is exactly what I have determined against. Honesty, in the something between, in the middle state of worldly circumstances, is all that I am anxious for your not looking down on."

"But I do look down upon it, if it might have been higher. I must look down upon any thing contented with obscurity when it might rise to distinction."

"But how may it rise?—How may my honesty at least rise to any distinction?"

This was not so very easy a question to answer, and occasioned an "Oh!" of some length from the fair lady before she could add "You ought to be in parliament, or you should have gone into the army ten years ago."

"*That* is not much to the purpose now; and as to my being in parliament, I believe I must wait till there is an especial assembly for the representation of younger sons who have little to live on. No, Miss Crawford," he added, in a more serious tone, "there *are* distinctions which I should be miserable if I thought myself without any chance—absolutely without chance or possibility of obtaining—but they are of a different character."

A look of consciousness as he spoke,[11] and what seemed a consciousness of manner on Miss Crawford's side as she made some laughing answer, was sorrowful food for Fanny's observation; and finding herself quite unable to attend as she ought to Mrs. Grant, by whose side she was now following the others, she had nearly resolved on going home immediately, and only waited for courage to say so, when the sound of the great clock at Mansfield Park, striking three, made her feel that she had really been much longer absent than usual, and brought the previous self-inquiry of whether she should take leave or not just then, and how, to a very speedy issue. With undoubting decision she directly began her adieus; and Edmund began at the same time to recollect, that his mother had been inquiring for her, and that he had walked down to the Parsonage on purpose to bring her back.

Fanny's hurry increased; and without in the least expecting Edmund's attendance, she would have hastened away alone; but the general pace was quickened, and they all accompanied her into the house through which it was necessary to pass. Dr. Grant was in the vestibule, and as they stopt to speak to him, she found from Edmund's manner that he *did* mean to go with her.—He too was taking

11 Here as elsewhere Austen uses *consciousness* where we would use *self-consciousness*.

12 A man who asks another to take his mutton with him is inviting him to dine. Fanny's father will use the same expression in Vol. III, Chap. 10.

leave.—She could not but be thankful.—In the moment of parting, Edmund was invited by Dr. Grant to eat his mutton with him the next day;[12] and Fanny had barely time for an unpleasant feeling on the occasion, when Mrs. Grant, with sudden recollection, turned to her and asked for the pleasure of her company too. This was so new an attention, so perfectly new a circumstance in the events of Fanny's life, that she was all surprize and embarrassment; and while stammering out her great obligation, and her—"but she did not suppose it would be in her power," was looking at Edmund for his opinion and help.—But Edmund, delighted with her having such an happiness offered, and ascertaining with half a look, and half a sentence, that she had no objection but on her aunt's account, could not imagine that his mother would make any difficulty of sparing her, and therefore gave his decided open advice that the invitation should be accepted; and though Fanny would not venture, even on his encouragement, to such a flight of audacious independence, it was soon settled that if nothing were heard to the contrary, Mrs. Grant might expect her.

"And you know what your dinner will be," said Mrs. Grant, smiling—"the turkey—and I assure you a very fine one; for, my dear"—turning to her husband—"cook insists upon the turkey's being dressed to-morrow."

"Very well, very well," cried Dr. Grant, "all the better. I am glad to hear you have any thing so good in the house. But Miss Price and Mr. Edmund Bertram, I dare say, would take their chance. We none of us want to hear the bill of fare. A friendly meeting, and not a fine dinner, is all we have in view. A turkey or a goose, or a leg of mutton, or whatever you and your cook chuse to give us."

The two cousins walked home together; and except in the immediate discussion of this engagement, which Edmund spoke of with the warmest satisfaction, as so particularly desirable for her in the intimacy which he saw with so much pleasure established, it was a silent walk—for having finished that subject, he grew thoughtful and indisposed for any other.

# 5

"But why should Mrs. Grant ask Fanny?" said Lady Bertram. "How came she to think of asking Fanny?—Fanny never dines there, you know, in this sort of way. I cannot spare her, and I am sure she does not want to go.—Fanny, you do not want to go, do you?"

"If you put such a question to her," cried Edmund, preventing his cousin's speaking, "Fanny will immediately say, no; but I am sure, my dear mother, she would like to go; and I can see no reason why she should not."

"I cannot imagine why Mrs. Grant should think of asking her—She never did before.—She used to ask your sisters now and then, but she never asked Fanny."

"If you cannot do without me, ma'am," said Fanny, in a self-denying tone—

"But my mother will have my father with her all the evening."

"To be sure, so I shall."

"Suppose you take my father's opinion, ma'am."

"That's well thought of. So I will, Edmund. I will ask Sir Thomas, as soon as he comes in, whether I can do without her."

"As you please, ma'am, on that head; but I meant my father's opinion as to the *propriety* of the invitation's being accepted or not; and I think he will consider it a right thing by Mrs. Grant, as well as by Fanny, that being the *first* invitation it should be accepted."

"I do not know. We will ask him. But he will be very much surprized that Mrs. Grant should ask Fanny at all."

There was nothing more to be said, or that could be said to any purpose, till Sir Thomas were present; but the subject involving, as it did, her own evening's comfort for the morrow, was so much uppermost in Lady Bertram's mind, that half an hour afterwards, on his looking in for a minute in his way from his plantation to his dressing-room, she called him back again, when he had almost closed the door, with "Sir Thomas, stop a moment—I have something to say to you."

Her tone of calm languor, for she never took the trouble of raising her voice, was always heard and attended to; and Sir Thomas came back. Her story began; and Fanny immediately slipped out of the room; for to hear herself the subject of any discussion with her uncle, was more than her nerves could bear. She was anxious, she knew—more anxious perhaps than she ought to be—for what was it after all whether she went or staid?—but if her uncle were to be a great while considering and deciding, and with very grave looks, and those grave looks directed to her, and at last decide against her, she might not be able to appear properly submissive and indifferent. Her cause meanwhile went on well. It began, on Lady Bertram's part, with, "I have something to tell you that will surprize you. Mrs. Grant has asked Fanny to dinner!"

"Well," said Sir Thomas, as if waiting more to accomplish the surprize.

"Edmund wants her to go. But how can I spare her?"

"She will be late," said Sir Thomas, taking out his watch, "but what is your difficulty?"

Edmund found himself obliged to speak and fill up the blanks in his mother's story. He told the whole, and she had only to add, "So strange! for Mrs. Grant never used to ask her."

"But is it not very natural," observed Edmund, "that Mrs. Grant should wish to procure so agreeable a visitor for her sister?"

"Nothing can be more natural," said Sir Thomas, after a short deliberation; "nor, were there no sister in the case, could any thing in my opinion be more natural. Mrs. Grant's shewing civility to Miss Price, to Lady Bertram's niece, could never want explanation. The only surprize I can feel is that this should be the *first* time of its being paid. Fanny was perfectly right in giving only a conditional answer. She appears to feel as she ought. But as I conclude that she must wish to go, since all young people like to be together, I can see no reason why she should be denied the indulgence."

"But can I do without her, Sir Thomas?"

"Indeed I think you may."

"She always makes tea, you know, when my sister is not here."

"Your sister perhaps may be prevailed on to spend the day with us, and I shall certainly be at home."

"Very well, then, Fanny may go, Edmund."

The good news soon followed her. Edmund knocked at her door in his way to his own.

"Well, Fanny, it is all happily settled, and without the smallest hesitation on your uncle's side. He had but one opinion. You are to go."

"Thank you, I am *so* glad," was Fanny's instinctive reply; though when she had turned from him and shut the door, she could not help feeling, "And yet, why should I be glad? for am I not certain of seeing or hearing something there to pain me?"

In spite of this conviction, however, she was glad. Simple as such an engagement might appear in other eyes, it had novelty and importance in her's, for excepting the day at Sotherton, she had scarcely ever dined out before; and though now going only half a mile and only to three people, still it was dining out, and all the little interests of preparation were enjoyments in themselves. She had neither sympathy nor assistance from those who ought to have entered into her feelings and directed her taste; for Lady Bertram never thought of being useful to any body, and Mrs. Norris, when she came on the morrow, in consequence of an early call and invitation from Sir Thomas, was in a very ill humour, and seemed intent only on lessening her niece's pleasure, both present and future, as much as possible.

"Upon my word, Fanny, you are in high luck to meet with such attention and indulgence! You ought to be very much obliged to Mrs. Grant for thinking of you, and to your aunt for letting you go, and you ought to look upon it as something extraordinary: for I hope you are aware that there is no real occasion for your going into company in this sort of way, or ever dining out at all; and it is what you must not depend upon ever being repeated. Nor must you be fancying, that the invitation is meant as any particular compliment to *you;* the compliment is intended to your uncle and aunt, and me. Mrs. Grant thinks it a civility due to *us* to take a little notice of you, or else it would never have come into her head, and you may be very certain, that if your cousin Julia had been at home, you would not have been asked at all."

Mrs. Norris had now so ingeniously done away all Mrs. Grant's part of the favour, that Fanny, who found herself expected to speak, could only say that she was very much obliged to her aunt Bertram for sparing her, and that she was endeavouring to put her aunt's evening work in such a state as to prevent her being missed.

"Oh! depend upon it, your aunt can do very well without you, or you would not be allowed to go. *I* shall be here, so you may be quite easy about your aunt. And I hope you will have a very *agreeable* day and find it all mighty *delightful.* But I must observe, that five is the very awkwardest of all possible numbers to sit down to table; and I cannot but be surprized that such an *elegant* lady as Mrs. Grant should not contrive better! And round their enormous great wide table too, which fills up the room so dreadfully! Had the Doctor been contented to take my dining table when I came away, as any body in their senses would have done, instead of having that absurd new one of his own, which is wider, literally wider than the dinner table here—how infinitely better it would have been! and how much more he would have been respected! for people are never respected when they step out of their proper sphere. Remember *that,* Fanny. Five, only five to be sitting round that table! However, you will have dinner enough on it for ten I dare say."

Mrs. Norris fetched breath and went on again.

"The nonsense and folly of people's stepping out of their rank and trying to appear above themselves, makes me think it right to give *you* a hint, Fanny, now that you are going into company without any of us; and I do beseech and intreat you not to be putting yourself forward, and talking and giving your opinion as if you were one of your cousins—as if you were dear Mrs. Rushworth or Julia. *That* will never do, believe me. Remember, wherever you are, you must be the lowest and last; and though Miss Crawford is in a manner at home, at the Parsonage, you are not to be taking place of her.[1] And as to coming away at night, you are to stay just as long as Edmund chuses. Leave him to settle *that*."

"Yes, ma'am, I should not think of any thing else."

"And if it should rain, which I think exceedingly likely, for I never saw it more threatening for a wet evening in my life—you must manage as well as you can, and not be expecting the carriage to be sent for you. I certainly do not go home to night, and, therefore, the carriage will not be out on my account; so you must make up your mind to what may happen, and take your things accordingly."

Her niece thought it perfectly reasonable. She rated her own claims to comfort as low even as Mrs. Norris could; and when Sir Thomas, soon afterwards, just opening the door, said, "Fanny, at what time would you have the carriage come round?" she felt a degree of astonishment which made it impossible for her to speak.

"My dear Sir Thomas!" cried Mrs. Norris, red with anger, "Fanny can walk."

"Walk!" repeated Sir Thomas, in a tone of most unanswerable dignity, and coming farther into the room.—"My niece walk to a dinner engagement at this time of the year! Will twenty minutes after four suit you?"

"Yes, sir," was Fanny's humble answer, given with the feelings almost of a criminal towards Mrs. Norris; and not bearing to remain with her in what might seem a state of triumph, she followed her uncle out of the room, having staid behind him only long enough to hear these words spoken in angry agitation:

"Quite unnecessary!—a great deal too kind! But Edmund goes;—true—it is upon Edmund's account. I observed he was hoarse on Thursday night."

But this could not impose on Fanny. She felt that the carriage was for herself and herself alone; and her uncle's consideration of her, coming immediately after such representations from her aunt, cost her some tears of gratitude when she was alone.

The coachman drove round to a minute; another minute brought down the gentleman, and as the lady had, with a most scrupulous fear of being late, been many minutes seated in the drawing room,

[1] Mrs. Norris ensures that the rules of etiquette are interpreted in a way that reinforces Fanny's low station. If Mary Crawford were really thought of as being at home at the Parsonage, then convention would dictate that, as the sole female guest at the Parsonage dinner, Fanny would enter the dining room first and Mary would follow.

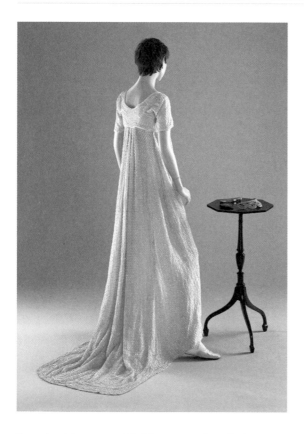

Fanny's white gown with "glossy spots" might have resembled this muslin dress with glass beads from about 1800.

Sir Thomas saw them off in as good time as his own correctly punctual habits required.

"Now I must look at you, Fanny," said Edmund, with the kind smile of an affectionate brother, "and tell you how I like you; and as well as I can judge by this light, you look very nicely indeed. What have you got on?"

"The new dress that my uncle was so good as to give me on my cousin's marriage. I hope it is not too fine; but I thought I ought to wear it as soon as I could, and that I might not have such another opportunity all the winter. I hope you do not think me too fine."

"A woman can never be too fine while she is all in white. No, I see no finery about you; nothing but what is perfectly proper. Your gown seems very pretty. I like these glossy spots. Has not Miss Crawford a gown something the same?"

In approaching the Parsonage they passed close by the stable-yard and coach-house. —

"Hey day!" said Edmund, "here's company, here's a carriage! who have they got to meet us?" And letting down the side-glass to distinguish, "'Tis Crawford's, Crawford's barouche, I protest! There are his own two men pushing it back into its old quarters. He is here of course. This is quite a surprize, Fanny. I shall be very glad to see him."

There was no occasion, there was no time for Fanny to say how very differently she felt; but the idea of having such another to observe her, was a great increase of the trepidation with which she performed the very aweful ceremony of walking into the drawing-room.

In the drawing-room Mr. Crawford certainly was; having been just long enough arrived to be ready for dinner; and the smiles and pleased looks of the three others standing round him, shewed how welcome was his sudden resolution of coming to them for a few days on leaving Bath. A very cordial meeting passed between him and Edmund; and with the exception of Fanny, the pleasure was general; and even to *her,* there might be some advantage in his presence, since every addition to the party must rather forward her favourite indulgence of being suffered to sit silent and unattended to. She was soon aware of this herself; for though she must submit, as her own propriety of mind directed, in spite of her aunt Norris's opinion, to being

the principal lady in company, and to all the little distinctions consequent thereon, she found, while they were at table, such a happy flow
of conversation prevailing in which she was not required to take any
part—there was so much to be said between the brother and sister
about Bath, so much between the two young men about hunting, so
much of politics between Mr. Crawford and Dr. Grant, and of every
thing, and all together between Mr. Crawford and Mrs. Grant, as
to leave her the fairest prospect of having only to listen in quiet,
and of passing a very agreeable day. She could not compliment the
newly-arrived gentleman however with any appearance of interest in
a scheme for extending his stay at Mansfield, and sending for his
hunters from Norfolk, which, suggested by Dr. Grant, advised by
Edmund, and warmly urged by the two sisters, was soon in possession of his mind, and which he seemed to want to be encouraged
even by her to resolve on. Her opinion was sought as to the probable
continuance of the open weather, but her answers were as short and
indifferent as civility allowed. She could not wish him to stay, and
would much rather not have him speak to her.

Her two absent cousins, especially Maria, were much in her
thoughts on seeing him; but no embarrassing remembrance affected
*his* spirits. Here he was again on the same ground where all had
passed before, and apparently as willing to stay and be happy without the Miss Bertrams, as if he had never known Mansfield in any
other state. She heard them spoken of by him only in a general way,
till they were all re-assembled in the drawing-room,[2] when Edmund,
being engaged apart in some matter of business with Dr. Grant,
which seemed entirely to engross them, and Mrs. Grant occupied at
the tea-table, he began talking of them with more particularity to his
other sister. With a significant smile, which made Fanny quite hate
him, he said, "So! Rushworth and his fair bride are at Brighton, I understand—Happy man!"

"Yes, they have been there—about a fortnight, Miss Price, have
they not?—And Julia is with them."

"And Mr. Yates, I presume, is not far off."

"Mr. Yates!—Oh! we hear nothing of Mr. Yates. I do not imagine he figures much in the letters to Mansfield Park; do you, Miss

2 The group of six at this dinner party reassemble after the interval, following the meal, in which the sexes
have been separated. It was the convention in genteel
society for the men to remain at the dining table, while
the ladies withdrew to the drawing room.

Price?—I think my friend Julia knows better than to entertain her father with Mr. Yates."

"Poor Rushworth and his two-and-forty speeches!" continued Crawford. "Nobody can ever forget them. Poor fellow!—I see him now;—his toil and his despair. Well, I am much mistaken if his lovely Maria will ever want him to make two-and-forty speeches to her"—adding, with a momentary seriousness, "She is too good for him—much too good." And then changing his tone again to one of gentle gallantry, and addressing Fanny, he said, "You were Mr. Rushworth's best friend. Your kindness and patience can never be forgotten, your indefatigable patience in trying to make it possible for him to learn his part—in trying to give him a brain which nature had denied—to mix up an understanding for him out of the superfluity of your own! *He* might not have sense enough himself to estimate your kindness, but I may venture to say that it had honour from all the rest of the party."

Fanny coloured, and said nothing.

"It is as a dream, a pleasant dream!" he exclaimed, breaking forth again after a few minutes musing. "I shall always look back on our theatricals with exquisite pleasure. There was such an interest, such an animation, such a spirit diffused! Every body felt it. We were all alive. There was employment, hope, solicitude, bustle, for every hour of the day. Always some little objection, some little doubt, some little anxiety to be got over. I never was happier."

With silent indignation, Fanny repeated to herself, "Never happier!—never happier than when doing what you must know was not justifiable!—never happier than when behaving so dishonourably and unfeelingly!—Oh! what a corrupted mind!"

"We were unlucky, Miss Price," he continued in a lower tone, to avoid the possibility of being heard by Edmund, and not at all aware of her feelings, "we certainly were very unlucky. Another week, only one other week, would have been enough for us. I think if we had had the disposal of events—if Mansfield Park had had the government of the winds just for a week or two about the equinox, there would have been a difference. Not that we would have endangered his safety by any tremendous weather—but only by a steady contrary wind, or a calm. I think, Miss Price, we would have indulged our selves with a week's calm in the Atlantic at that season."

He seemed determined to be answered; and Fanny, averting her face, said with a firmer tone than usual, "As far as *I* am concerned, sir, I would not have delayed his return for a day. My uncle disapproved it all so entirely when he did arrive, that in my opinion, every thing had gone quite far enough."

She had never spoken so much at once to him in her life before, and never so angrily to any one; and when her speech was over, she trembled and blushed at her own daring. He was surprized; but after a few moments silent consideration of her, replied in a calmer, graver tone, and as if the candid result of conviction, "I believe you are right. It was more pleasant than prudent. We were getting too noisy." And then turning the conversation, he would have engaged her on some other subject, but her answers were so shy and reluctant that he could not advance in any.

Miss Crawford, who had been repeatedly eyeing Dr. Grant and Edmund, now observed, "Those gentlemen must have some very interesting point to discuss."

"The most interesting in the world," replied her brother—"how to make money—how to turn a good income into a better. Dr. Grant is giving Bertram instructions about the living he is to step into so soon. I find he takes orders in a few weeks. They were at it in the dining-parlour. I am glad to hear Bertram will be so well off. He will have a very pretty income to make ducks and drakes with,[3] and earned without much trouble. I apprehend he will not have less than seven hundred a year. Seven hundred a year is a fine thing for a younger brother; and as of course he will still live at home, it will be all for his *menus plaisirs*;[4] and a sermon at Christmas and Easter, I suppose, will be the sum total of sacrifice."

His sister tried to laugh off her feelings by saying, "Nothing amuses me more than the easy manner with which every body settles the abundance of those who have a great deal less than themselves. You would look rather blank, Henry, if your menus plaisirs were to be limited to seven hundred a year."

"Perhaps I might; but all *that* you know is entirely comparative. Birthright and habit must settle the business. Bertram is certainly well off for a cadet[5] of even a Baronet's family. By the time he is four

3  Money to squander. To play at ducks and drakes is to throw flat stones so that they skim and skip along the surface of a flat body of water.

4  A term for pocket money, from the French for "small pleasures."

5  Younger son.

or five-and-twenty he will have seven hundred a year, and nothing to do for it."

Miss Crawford *could* have said that there would be a something to do and to suffer for it, which she could not think lightly of; but she checked herself and let it pass; and tried to look calm and unconcerned when the two gentlemen shortly afterwards joined them.

"Bertram," said Henry Crawford, "I shall make a point of coming to Mansfield to hear you preach your first sermon. I shall come on purpose to encourage a young beginner. When is it to be? Miss Price, will not you join me in encouraging your cousin? Will not you engage to attend with your eyes steadily fixed on him the whole time—as I shall do—not to lose a word; or only looking off just to note down any sentence pre-eminently beautiful? We will provide ourselves with tablets[6] and a pencil. When will it be? You must preach at Mansfield, you know, that Sir Thomas and Lady Bertram may hear you."

"I shall keep clear of you, Crawford, as long as I can," said Edmund, "for you would be more likely to disconcert me, and I should be more sorry to see you trying at it, than almost any other man."

"Will he not feel this?" thought Fanny. "No, he can feel nothing as he ought."

The party being now all united, and the chief talkers attracting each other, she remained in tranquillity; and as a whist table was formed after tea—formed really for the amusement of Dr. Grant, by his attentive wife, though it was not to be supposed so—and Miss Crawford took her harp, she had nothing to do but to listen, and her tranquillity remained undisturbed the rest of the evening, except when Mr. Crawford now and then addressed to her a question or observation, which she could not avoid answering. Miss Crawford was too much vexed by what had passed to be in a humour for any thing but music. With that, she soothed herself and amused her friend.

The assurance of Edmund's being so soon to take orders, coming upon her like a blow that had been suspended, and still hoped uncertain and at a distance, was felt with resentment and mortification. She was very angry with him. She had thought her influence more. She *had* begun to think of him—she felt that she had—with great regard, with almost decided intentions; but she would now meet him with his own cool feelings. It was plain that he could have no serious views, no true attachment, by fixing himself in a situation which he must know she would never stoop to. She would learn to match him in his indifference. She would henceforth admit his attentions without any idea beyond immediate amusement. If *he* could so command his affections, *her's* should do her no harm.

# 6

1 A biblical phrase: in *Proverbs* chapter 31 the good woman "looketh well to the ways of her household, and eateth not the bread of idleness."

HENRY CRAWFORD HAD quite made up his mind by the next morning to give another fortnight to Mansfield, and having sent for his hunters and written a few lines of explanation to the Admiral, he looked round at his sister as he sealed and threw the letter from him, and seeing the coast clear of the rest of the family, said, with a smile, "And how do you think I mean to amuse myself, Mary, on the days that I do not hunt? I am grown too old to go out more than three times a week; but I have a plan for the intermediate days, and what do you think it is?"

"To walk and ride with me, to be sure."

"Not exactly, though I shall be happy to do both, but *that* would be exercise only to my body, and I must take care of my mind. Besides *that* would be all recreation and indulgence, without the wholesome alloy of labour, and I do not like to eat the bread of idleness.[1] No, my plan is to make Fanny Price in love with me."

"Fanny Price! Nonsense! No, no. You ought to be satisfied with her two cousins."

"But I cannot be satisfied without Fanny Price, without making a small hole in Fanny Price's heart. You do not seem properly aware of her claims to notice. When we talked of her last night, you none of you seemed sensible of the wonderful improvement that has taken place in her looks within the last six weeks. You see her every day, and therefore do not notice it, but I assure you, she is quite a different creature from what she was in the autumn. She was then merely a quiet, modest, not plain looking girl, but she is now absolutely pretty. I used to think she had neither complexion nor countenance; but in that soft skin of her's, so frequently tinged with a blush as it was yesterday, there is decided beauty; and from what I observed of her eyes and mouth, I do not despair of their being capable of expression enough when she has any thing to express. And then—her air, her manner, her tout ensemble[2] is so indescribably improved! She must be grown two inches, at least, since October."

"Phoo! phoo! This is only because there were no tall women to compare her with, and because she has got a new gown, and you never saw her so well dressed before. She is just what she was in October, believe me. The truth is, that she was the only girl in company for you to notice, and you must have a somebody. I have always thought her pretty—not strikingly pretty—but 'pretty enough' as people say; a sort of beauty that grows on one. Her eyes should be darker, but she has a sweet smile; but as for this wonderful degree of improvement, I am sure it may all be resolved into a better style of dress and your having nobody else to look at; and therefore, if you do set about a flirtation with her, you never will persuade me that it is in compliment to her beauty, or that it proceeds from any thing but your own idleness and folly."

Her brother gave only a smile to this accusation, and soon afterwards said, "I do not quite know what to make of Miss Fanny. I do not understand her. I could not tell what she would be at yesterday. What is her character?—Is she solemn?—Is she queer?—Is she prudish? Why did she draw back and look so grave at me? I could hardly get her to speak. I never was so long in company with a girl in my life—trying to entertain her—and succeed so ill! Never met with a girl who looked so grave on me! I must try to get the better of this. Her looks say, 'I will not like you, I am determined not to like you,' and I say, she shall."

"Foolish fellow! And so this is her attraction after all! This it is— her not caring about you—which gives her such a soft skin and makes her so much taller, and produces all these charms and graces! I do desire that you will not be making her really unhappy; a *little* love

2 Her appearance in its entirety (French).

3 In his edition of *Mansfield Park* (p. 699 n. 5), Wiltshire discerns in Mary's warning an echo of a song that the poet Robert Burns had published in *The Scots Musical Museum* (1788): "Talk not of love, it gives me pain, / For Love has been my foe; / He bound me with an iron chain / And plunged me deep in woe."

4 Readers perturbed by the cold-blooded way in which the Crawford siblings discuss Fanny's fate have often heard in their discussion echoes of the epistolary novel *Les Liaisons dangereuses (Dangerous Liaisons)* by the Frenchman Choderlos de Laclos (1782). Henry's plot to put a small hole in Fanny's heart may represent an anglicized version of the schemes of Laclos's libertine hero, the Vicomte de Valmont, who as *Liaisons* commences sets out to conquer the virtuous (and married) Madame de Tourvel. The cynical Marquise de Merteuil, his former lover, partner in sexual crime, and equal in malice, is kept abreast of his progress through the letters that Valmont sends off to her at every stage in Madame de Tourvel's seduction. In this account of the shaping influences of Austen's novel, Mary Crawford would, as the confidante of Henry's plot, be *Mansfield Park*'s stand-in for the Marquise. The latter has more often, however, been identified as an inspiration for Austen's Lady Susan Vernon, the master manipulator who propels the action of the novella named after her, an epistolary fiction Austen drafted some time before 1805, or so most critics think, and which remained unpublished until 1871.

perhaps may animate and do her good, but I will not have you plunge her deep,[3] for she is as good a little creature as ever lived, and has a great deal of feeling."

"It can be but for a fortnight," said Henry, "and if a fortnight can kill her, she must have a constitution which nothing could save. No, I will not do her any harm, dear little soul! I only want her to look kindly on me, to give me smiles as well as blushes, to keep a chair for me by herself wherever we are, and be all animation when I take it and talk to her; to think as I think, be interested in all my possessions and pleasures, try to keep me longer at Mansfield, and feel when I go away that she shall be never happy again. I want nothing more."

"Moderation itself!" said Mary. "I can have no scruples now.[4] Well, you will have opportunities enough of endeavouring to recommend yourself, for we are a great deal together."

And without attempting any further remonstrance, she left Fanny to her fate—a fate which, had not Fanny's heart been guarded in a way unsuspected by Miss Crawford, might have been a little harder than she deserved; for although there doubtless are such unconquerable young ladies of eighteen (or one should not read about them) as are never to be persuaded into love against their judgment by all that talent, manner, attention, and flattery can do, I have no inclination to believe Fanny one of them, or to think that with so much tenderness of disposition, and so much taste as belonged to her, she could have escaped heart-whole from the courtship (though the courtship only of a fortnight) of such a man as Crawford, in spite of there being some previous ill-opinion of him to be overcome, had not her affection been engaged elsewhere. With all the security which love of another and disesteem of him could give to the peace of mind he was attacking, his continued attentions—continued, but not obtrusive, and adapting themselves more and more to the gentleness and delicacy of her character,—obliged her very soon to dislike him less than formerly. She had by no means forgotten the past, and she thought as ill of him as ever; but she felt his powers; he was entertaining, and his manners were so improved, so polite, so seriously and blamelessly polite, that it was impossible not to be civil to him in return.

A very few days were enough to effect this; and at the end of those few days, circumstances arose which had a tendency rather to forward his views of pleasing her, inasmuch as they gave her a degree of happiness which must dispose her to be pleased with every body. William, her brother, the so long absent and dearly loved brother, was in England again. She had a letter from him herself, a few hurried happy lines, written as the ship came up Channel, and sent into Portsmouth, with the first boat that left the Antwerp, at anchor, in Spithead;[5] and when Crawford walked up with the newspaper in his hand, which he had hoped would bring the first tidings, he found her trembling with joy over this letter, and listening with a glowing, grateful countenance to the kind invitation which her uncle was most collectedly dictating in reply.

5 At Portsmouth, writes the town's historian Lake Allen in 1817, "the most distinguished part of the harbour" was Spithead, which "takes its name from a sandbank, which extends from the right side of the harbour" (*The History of Portsmouth* [London: Mills, Whitehead, and Johnson, 1817], p. 150). The crews of ships anchored there would transfer to shore in small boats.

In Patricia Rozema's 1999 film adaptation of *Mansfield Park,* both casting choices and costume design play up the libertinism that Austen only hints at in her characterization of the Crawford siblings. In this still we see the duo in the Mansfield Park billiard room, readying themselves to entangle Fanny in their erotic game-playing.

6 Henry's intelligence gathering exploits the latest in communications technologies. Forty years before the introduction of the electric telegraph, the British Admiralty relied on a network of signaling stations that transmitted messages using semaphore: "The stations customarily consisted of a squat tower on the top of which was mounted a metal pole equipped with two wooden beams, which could be manipulated like semaphore flags to convey the letters of the alphabet. Each station was staffed by two or more operators, one to watch for incoming signals through a telescope, the others to relay the message to the next station" (Jay Clayton, *Charles Dickens in Cyberspace* [New York: Oxford University Press, 2003], p. 58). Thanks to this telegraph line, the Admiralty Office could be apprised of a ship's arrival in Portsmouth harbor within five minutes of its dropping anchor, "naval intelligence" that the Admiralty would then disseminate among London newspapers like the *Morning Post* or *London Gazette.*

7 Leave was not a right but granted at the discretion of the individual captain. However, each naval vessel generally included many midshipmen among its crew (as many as twenty on the largest ships), and so an individual midshipman might well be deemed dispensable.

It was but the day before, that Crawford had made himself thoroughly master of the subject, or had in fact become at all aware of her having such a brother, or his being in such a ship, but the interest then excited had been very properly lively, determining him on his return to town to apply for information as to the probable period of the Antwerp's return from the Mediterranean, &c.; and the good luck which attended his early examination of ship news, the next morning, seemed the reward of his ingenuity in finding out such a method of pleasing her, as well as of his dutiful attention to the Admiral, in having for many years taken in the paper esteemed to have the earliest naval intelligence.[6] He proved, however, to be too late. All those fine first feelings, of which he had hoped to be the excitor, were already given. But his intention, the kindness of his intention, was thankfully acknowledged—quite thankfully and warmly, for she was elevated beyond the common timidity of her mind by the flow of her love for William.

This dear William would soon be amongst them. There could be no doubt of his obtaining leave of absence immediately, for he was still only a midshipman;[7] and as his parents, from living on the spot, must already have seen him and be seeing him perhaps daily, his direct holidays might with justice be instantly given to the sister, who had been his best correspondent through a period of seven years, and the uncle who had done most for his support and advancement; and accordingly the reply to her reply, fixing a very early day for his arrival, came as soon as possible; and scarcely ten days had passed since Fanny had been in the agitation of her first dinner visit, when she found herself in an agitation of a higher nature—watching in the hall, in the lobby, on the stairs, for the first sound of the carriage which was to bring her a brother.

It came happily while she was thus waiting; and there being neither ceremony nor fearfulness to delay the moment of meeting, she was with him as he entered the house, and the first minutes of exquisite feeling had no interruption and no witnesses, unless the servants chiefly intent upon opening the proper doors could be called such. This was exactly what Sir Thomas and Edmund had been separately conniving at, as each proved to the other by the sympathetic alacrity with which they both advised Mrs. Norris's continuing where she was, instead of rushing out into the hall as soon as the noises of the arrival reached them.

William and Fanny soon shewed themselves; and Sir Thomas had the pleasure of receiving, in his protégé, certainly a very different person from the one he had equipped seven years ago, but a young man of an open, pleasant countenance, and frank, unstudied, but feeling and respectful manners, and such as confirmed him his friend.

It was long before Fanny could recover from the agitating happiness of such an hour as was formed by the last thirty minutes of expectation and the first of fruition; it was some time even before her happiness could be said to make her happy, before the disappointment inseparable from the alteration of person had vanished, and she could see in him the same William as before, and talk to him, as her heart had been yearning to do, through many a past year. That time, however, did gradually come, forwarded by an affection on his side as warm as her own, and much less incumbered by refinement or self-distrust. She was the first object of his love, but it was a love which his stronger spirits, and bolder temper, made it as natural for him to express as to feel. On the morrow they were walking about together with true enjoyment, and every succeeding morrow renewed a tête-à-tête, which Sir Thomas could not but observe with complacency, even before Edmund had pointed it out to him.

Excepting the moments of peculiar delight, which any marked or unlooked-for instance of Edmund's consideration of her in the last few months had excited, Fanny had never known so much felicity in her life, as in this unchecked, equal, fearless intercourse with the brother and friend, who was opening all his heart to her, telling her all his hopes and fears, plans, and solicitudes respecting that long thought of, dearly earned, and justly valued blessing of promotion—who could give her direct and minute information of the father and mother, brothers and sisters, of whom she very seldom heard—who was interested in all the comforts and all the little hardships of her home, at Mansfield—ready to think of every member of that home as she directed, or differing only by a less scrupulous opinion, and

8 The second half of this paragraph on the nature of familial attachments is transcribed, in beautiful handwriting, onto two pages in an anonymous nineteenth-century commonplace book that is now housed at the Houghton Library, Harvard University. The book is said to have been the property of the master of the *Europa,* the ship on which Lord Byron was supposed to have taken passage when he traveled to Greece in 1823.

9 Teasing his sister, William uses *trim,* sailors' jargon identifying a ship that is fully rigged and ready to sail, to name the accessories or *trimmings*—bandeaux, silk flowers, or ornamental combs—that fashionable Regency ladies used to style their hair. Since William first went to sea, women's fashion has taken a neoclassical turn. In the second decade of the nineteenth century shorter hair styles imitating the loose curls and upswept hair seen on Greek and Roman statues became the height of style. A letter to Cassandra dated January 24, 1813, reveals that Austen originally had William encountering these stylish women at Government House in Gibraltar, but, through reading Sir John Carr's *Descriptive Travels in the Southern and Eastern Parts of Spain* (1811), she had learned "there is no Government House at Gibraltar.—I must alter it to the Commissioner's" (*Letters,* p. 207).

more noisy abuse of their aunt Norris—and with whom (perhaps the dearest indulgence of the whole) all the evil and good of their earliest years could be gone over again, and every former united pain and pleasure retraced with the fondest recollection. An advantage this, a strengthener of love, in which even the conjugal tie is beneath the fraternal. Children of the same family, the same blood, with the same first associations and habits, have some means of enjoyment in their power, which no subsequent connections can supply; and it must be by a long and unnatural estrangement, by a divorce which no subsequent connection can justify, if such precious remains of the earliest attachments are ever entirely outlived. Too often, alas! it is so.—Fraternal love, sometimes almost every thing, is at others worse than nothing. But with William and Fanny Price, it was still a sentiment in all its prime and freshness, wounded by no opposition of interest, cooled by no separate attachment, and feeling the influence of time and absence only in its increase.[8]

An affection so amiable was advancing each in the opinion of all who had hearts to value any thing good. Henry Crawford was as much struck with it as any. He honoured the warm hearted, blunt fondness of the young sailor, which led him to say, with his hand stretched towards Fanny's head, "Do you know, I begin to like that queer fashion already, though when I first heard of such things being done in England I could not believe it, and when Mrs. Brown, and the other women, at the Commissioner's, at Gibraltar, appeared in the same trim, I thought they were mad; but Fanny can reconcile me to any thing"[9]—and saw, with lively admiration, the glow of Fanny's cheek, the brightness of her eye, the deep interest, the absorbed attention, while her brother was describing any of the imminent hazards, or terrific scenes, which such a period, at sea, must supply.

It was a picture which Henry Crawford had moral taste enough to value. Fanny's attractions increased—increased two-fold—for the sensibility which beautified her complexion and illumined her countenance, was an attraction in itself. He was no longer in doubt of the capabilities of her heart. She had feeling, genuine feeling. It would be something to be loved by such a girl, to excite the first ardours of her young, unsophisticated mind! She interested him more than he

Portrait of Jane, Lady Orde, by Thomas Lawrence, ca. 1810–1812. Female hairstyles took a neoclassical turn in the early nineteenth century, exemplified by Lady Orde's hairband and the curls that escape it to frame her face. This might be the "queer fashion" that has caught William Price's eye.

10 The service William reports on in his stirring tales has taken him to two of the major theaters of naval warfare in the era. In the Mediterranean the Royal Navy enforced a long-running blockade against Napoleon's France. In the West Indies, its duties involved in large part the protection of the mercantile shipping passing between Britain and its colonial possessions. But in addition to ensuring that the wealth of those colonies would continue to flow to the imperial metropole, the navy was also repeatedly charged with assisting the planter class in the policing of the slave populations who produced that wealth. As Margaret Anne Doody notes, there is accordingly "a real economic relation between the seafaring William Price . . . and the aloof and spiritually landlocked Sir Thomas" (*Jane Austen's Names: Riddles, Persons, Places* [Chicago: University of Chicago Press, 2015], p. 316); William has been helping protect his uncle's investments.

11 The critic Gillian Russell detects in Henry Crawford—who in assuming the role of Frederick in *Lovers' Vows* has already played at being a soldier—symptoms of what she calls "war envy," "a sign of how the ideological security of the gentleman was beginning to be threatened by changes in the reputation of the military profession" ("The Army, the Navy, and the Napoleonic Wars," in *A Companion to Jane Austen,* ed. Claudia L. Johnson and Clara Tuite [Malden, Mass.: Wiley-Blackwell, 2011], p. 266).

had foreseen. A fortnight was not enough. His stay became indefinite.

William was often called on by his uncle to be the talker. His recitals were amusing in themselves to Sir Thomas, but the chief object in seeking them, was to understand the recitor, to know the young man by his histories; and he listened to his clear, simple, spirited details with full satisfaction—seeing in them, the proof of good principles, professional knowledge, energy, courage, and cheerfulness—every thing that could deserve or promise well. Young as he was, William had already seen a great deal. He had been in the Mediterranean—in the West Indies—in the Mediterranean again[10]—had been often taken on shore by the favour of his Captain, and in the course of seven years had known every variety of danger, which sea and war together could offer. With such means in his power he had a right to be listened to; and though Mrs. Norris could fidget about the room, and disturb every body in quest of two needlefulls of thread or a second hand shirt button in the midst of her nephew's account of a shipwreck or an engagement, every body else was attentive; and even Lady Bertram could not hear of such horrors unmoved, or without sometimes lifting her eyes from her work to say, "Dear me! how disagreeable!—I wonder any body can ever go to sea."

To Henry Crawford they gave a different feeling. He longed to have been at sea, and seen and done and suffered as much. His heart was warmed, his fancy fired, and he felt the highest respect for a lad who, before he was twenty, had gone through such bodily hardships, and given such proofs of mind. The glory of heroism, of usefulness, of exertion, of endurance, made his own habits of selfish indulgence appear in shameful contrast; and he wished he had been a William Price, distinguishing himself and working his way to fortune and consequence with so much self-respect and happy ardour, instead of what he was![11]

The wish was rather eager than lasting. He was roused from the reverie of retrospection and regret produced by it, by some inquiry from Edmund as to his plans for the next day's hunting; and he found it was as well to be a man of fortune at once with horses and grooms at his command. In one respect it was better, as it gave him the means of conferring a kindness where he wished to oblige. With spirits, courage, and curiosity up to any thing, William expressed an inclination to hunt; and Crawford could mount him without the slightest inconvenience to himself, and with only some scruples to obviate in Sir Thomas, who knew better than his nephew the value of such a loan, and some alarms to reason away in Fanny. She feared for William; by no means convinced by all that he could relate of his own horsemanship in various countries, of the scrambling parties in which he had been engaged, the rough horses and mules he had ridden, or his many narrow escapes from dreadful falls, that he was at all equal to the management of a high-fed hunter in an English fox-chase; nor till he returned safe and well, without accident or discredit, could she be reconciled to the risk, or feel any of that obligation to Mr. Crawford for lending the horse which he had fully intended it should produce. When it was proved however to have done William no harm, she could allow it to be a kindness, and even reward the owner with a smile when the animal was one minute tendered to his use again; and the next, with the greatest cordiality, and in a manner not to be resisted, made over to his use entirely so long as he remained in Northamptonshire.

The capture of *La Tribune* by *H. M. S. Unicorn*, June 8, 1796. Nicholas Pocock's painting of this important sea battle in the campaign against Napoleon evokes the sort of "terrific scene" William Price might be recalling for his listeners. Austen's brother Charles was serving aboard the *Unicorn* as a midshipman at this time.

# 7

THE INTERCOURSE OF THE TWO FAMILIES was at this period more nearly restored to what it had been in the autumn, than any member of the old intimacy had thought ever likely to be again. The return of Henry Crawford, and the arrival of William Price, had much to do with it, but much was still owing to Sir Thomas's more than toleration of the neighbourly attempts at the Parsonage. His mind, now disengaged from the cares which had pressed on him at first, was at leisure to find the Grants and their young inmates really worth visiting; and though infinitely above scheming or contriving for any the most advantageous matrimonial establishment that could be among the apparent possibilities of any one most dear to him, and disdaining even as a littleness the being quick-sighted on such points, he could not avoid perceiving in a grand and careless way that Mr. Crawford was somewhat distinguishing his niece—nor perhaps refrain (though unconsciously) from giving a more willing assent to invitations on that account.

His readiness, however, in agreeing to dine at the Parsonage, when the general invitation was at last hazarded, after many debates and many doubts as to whether it were worth while, "because Sir Thomas seemed so ill inclined! and Lady Bertram was so indolent!"—proceeded from good breeding and good-will alone, and had nothing to do with Mr. Crawford, but as being one in an agreeable group; for it was in the course of that very visit, that he first began to think, that any one in the habit of such idle observations *would have thought* that Mr. Crawford was the admirer of Fanny Price.

A certain friction between the players is detectable in this print's comic depiction of a game of whist.

The meeting was generally felt to be a pleasant one, being composed in a good proportion of those who would talk and those who would listen; and the dinner itself was elegant and plentiful, according to the usual style of the Grants, and too much according to the usual habits of all to raise any emotion except in Mrs. Norris, who could never behold either the wide table or the number of dishes on it with patience, and who did always contrive to experience some evil from the passing of the servants behind her chair, and to bring away some fresh conviction of its being impossible among so many dishes but that some must be cold.

In the evening it was found, according to the predetermination of Mrs. Grant and her sister, that after making up the Whist table there would remain sufficient for a round game, and every body being as perfectly complying and without a choice as on such occasions they always are, Speculation was decided on almost as soon as Whist; and Lady Bertram soon found herself in the critical situation of being applied to for her own choice between the games, and being required either to draw a card for Whist or not. She hesitated. Luckily Sir Thomas was at hand.

1 Any large number of people can play speculation, since players compete individually, whereas whist, a forerunner to modern bridge, accommodates two pairs of players only. The 1812 edition of *Hoyle's Games Improved* (London: W. Lowndes et al., 1812) describes speculation as a "noisy" game, presumably because of the bargaining that occurred as players bid upon one another's cards. "In order to play this game well," *Hoyle's Games Improved* explains, "little more is required, than to recollect what superior cards of that particular suit have appeared in the preceding deals, and calculating the probability of the trump offered proving the highest trump out." Because it was an easy game to learn, as Lady Bertram's companions insist, speculation was often played by children. In 1808 Jane Austen introduced it to her brother Edward's sons Edward and George, then aged twelve and eleven, "and it was so much approved that we hardly knew how to leave off" (Letter to Cassandra, October 24–25, 1808; *Letters*, p. 158). Whist, however, is a game of strategy requiring "great attention and silence" according to *Hoyle's Games Improved,* which bestows seventy-five pages of explanation on it while according speculation only one.

"What shall I do, Sir Thomas?—Whist and Speculation; which will amuse me most?"

Sir Thomas, after a moment's thought, recommended Speculation. He was a Whist player himself, and perhaps might feel that it would not much amuse him to have her for a partner.

"Very well," was her ladyship's contented answer—"then Speculation if you please, Mrs. Grant. I know nothing about it, but Fanny must teach me."

Here Fanny interposed however with anxious protestations of her own equal ignorance; she had never played the game nor seen it played in her life; and Lady Bertram felt a moment's indecision again—but upon every body's assuring her that nothing could be so easy, that it was the easiest game on the cards, and Henry Crawford's stepping forward with a most earnest request to be allowed to sit between her ladyship and Miss Price, and teach them both, it was so settled; and Sir Thomas, Mrs. Norris, and Dr. and Mrs. Grant, being seated at the table of prime intellectual state and dignity, the remaining six, under Miss Crawford's direction, were arranged round the other.[1] It was a fine arrangement for Henry Crawford, who was close to Fanny, and with his hands full of business, having two persons' cards to manage as well as his own—for though it was impossible for Fanny not to feel herself mistress of the rules of the game in three minutes, he had yet to inspirit her play, sharpen her avarice, and harden her heart, which, especially in any competition with William, was a work of some difficulty; and as for Lady Bertram, he must continue in charge of all her fame and fortune through the whole evening; and if quick enough to keep her from looking at her cards when the deal began, must direct her in whatever was to be done with them to the end of it.

He was in high spirits, doing everything with happy ease, and pre-eminent in all the lively turns, quick resources, and playful impudence that could do honour to the game; and the round table was altogether a very comfortable contrast to the steady sobriety and orderly silence of the other.

Twice had Sir Thomas inquired into the enjoyment and success of his lady, but in vain; no pause was long enough for the time his measured manner needed; and very little of her state could be known till Mrs. Grant was able, at the end of the first rubber,[2] to go to her and pay her compliments.

"I hope your ladyship is pleased with the game."

"Oh! dear, yes.—Very entertaining indeed. A very odd game. I do not know what it is all about. I am never to see my cards; and Mr. Crawford does all the rest."

"Bertram," said Crawford some time afterwards, taking the opportunity of a little languor in the game, "I have never told you what happened to me yesterday in my ride home." They had been hunting together, and were in the midst of a good run, and at some distance from Mansfield, when his horse being found to have flung a shoe, Henry Crawford had been obliged to give up, and make the best of his way back. "I told you I lost my way after passing that old farmhouse with the yew trees, because I can never bear to ask; but I have not told you that, with my usual luck—for I never do wrong without gaining by it—I found myself in due time in the very place which I had a curiosity to see. I was suddenly, upon turning the corner of a steepish downy field, in the midst of a retired little village between gently rising hills; a small stream before me to be forded, a church standing on a sort of knoll to my right—which church was strikingly large and handsome for the place, and not a gentleman or half a gentleman's house to be seen excepting one—to be presumed the Parsonage, within a stone's throw of the said knoll and church. I found myself in short in Thornton Lacey."

"It sounds like it," said Edmund; "but which way did you turn after passing Sewell's farm?"

"I answer no such irrelevant and insidious questions; though were I to answer all that you could put in the course of an hour, you would never be able to prove that it was *not* Thornton Lacey—for such it certainly was."

"You inquired then?"

"No, I never inquire. But I *told* a man mending a hedge that it was Thornton Lacey, and he agreed to it."

"You have a good memory. I had forgotten having ever told you half so much of the place."

2  At the end of the first round, when three games have been played.

3 In the conversation in Vol. I, Chap. 6, in which
Mr. Rushworth reports on the transformations an improver has wrought at his friend Smith's place, Austen
has already acknowledged how often those improvements involved resituating the approach to the country house. In *Observations on the Theory and Practice of
Landscape Gardening,* Repton advises as a general principle that an approach should pass "through the most
interesting part of the grounds, and . . . display the
scenery of the place to the greatest advantage, without
making any violent or unnecessary circuit, to include
objects that do not naturally come within its reach"
(p. 34).

Thornton Lacey was the name of his impending living, as Miss Crawford well knew; and her interest in a negotiation for William Price's knave increased.

"Well," continued Edmund, "and how did you like what you saw?"

"Very much indeed. You are a lucky fellow. There will be work for five summers at least before the place is live-able."

"No, no, not so bad as that. The farm-yard must be moved, I grant you; but I am not aware of anything else. The house is by no means bad, and when the yard is removed, there may be a very tolerable approach to it."

"The farm-yard must be cleared away entirely, and planted up to shut out the blacksmith's shop. The house must be turned to front the east instead of the north—the entrance and principal rooms, I mean, must be on that side, where the view is really very pretty; I am sure it may be done. And *there* must be your approach—through what is at present the garden.[3] You must make a new garden at what is now the back of the house; which will be giving it the best aspect in the world—sloping to the south-east. The ground seems precisely formed for it. I rode fifty yards up the lane between the church and the house in order to look about me; and saw how it might all be. Nothing can be easier. The meadows beyond what *will be* the garden, as well as what now *is,* sweeping round from the lane I stood in to the north-east, that is, to the principal road through the village, must be all laid together of course; very pretty meadows they are, finely sprinkled with timber. They belong to the living, I suppose. If not, you must purchase them. Then the stream—something must be done with the stream; but I could not quite determine what. I had two or three ideas."

"And I have two or three ideas also," said Edmund, "and one of them is that very little of your plan for Thornton Lacey will ever be put in practice. I must be satisfied with rather less ornament and beauty. I think the house and premises may be made comfortable, and given the air of a gentleman's residence without any very heavy expense, and that must suffice me; and I hope may suffice all who care about me."

Miss Crawford, a little suspicious and resentful of a certain tone of voice and a certain half-look attending the last expression of his hope, made a hasty finish of her dealings with William Price, and securing his knave at an exorbitant rate, exclaimed, "There, I will stake my last like a woman of spirit. No cold prudence for me. I am not born to sit still and do nothing. If I lose the game, it shall not be from not striving for it."

The game was her's, and only did not pay her for what she had given to secure it. Another deal proceeded, and Crawford began again about Thornton Lacey.

"My plan may not be the best possible; I had not many minutes to form it in: but you must do a good deal. The place deserves it, and you will find yourself not satisfied with much less than it is capable of.—(Excuse me, your ladyship must not see your cards. There, let them lie just before you.) The place deserves it, Bertram. You talk of giving it the air of a gentleman's residence. *That* will be done, by the removal of the farm-yard, for, independent of that terrible nuisance, I never saw a house of the kind which had in itself so much the air of a gentleman's residence, so much the look of a something above a mere Parsonage House, above the expenditure of a few hundreds a year. It is not a scrambling collection of low single rooms, with as many roofs as windows—it is not cramped into the vulgar compactness of a square farm-house—it is a solid, roomy, mansion-like looking house,[4] such as one might suppose a respectable old country family had lived in from generation to generation, through two centuries at least, and were now spending from two to three thousand a year in." Miss Crawford listened, and Edmund agreed to this. "The air of a gentleman's residence, therefore, you cannot but give it, if you do any thing. But it is capable of much more. (Let me see, Mary; Lady Bertram bids a dozen for that queen; no, no, a dozen is more than it is worth.[5] Lady Bertram does *not* bid a dozen. She will have nothing to say to it. Go on, go on.) By some such improvements as I have suggested, (I do not really require you to proceed upon my plan, though by the bye I doubt anybody's striking out a better)—you may give it a higher character. You may raise it into a *place*. From being the mere

4 The 1814 edition of *Mansfield Park* reads "solid walled, roomy, mansion-like looking house."

5 The buying and selling in speculation involve counters rather than money. These were often shaped like fish, which is why in *Pride and Prejudice*, after a visit to her Aunt Philips's, "Lydia talked incessantly . . . of the fish she had lost and the fish she had won" (I, 16).

gentleman's residence, it becomes, by judicious improvement, the residence of a man of education, taste, modern manners, good connections. All this may be stamped on it; and that house receive such an air as to make its owner be set down as the great land-holder of the parish, by every creature travelling the road; especially as there is no real squire's house to dispute the point; a circumstance between ourselves to enhance the value of such a situation in point of privilege and independence beyond all calculation. *You* think with me, I hope—(turning with a softened voice to Fanny).—Have you ever seen the place?"

Fanny gave a quick negative, and tried to hide her interest in the subject by an eager attention to her brother, who was driving as hard a bargain and imposing on her as much as he could; but Crawford pursued with "No, no, you must not part with the queen. You have bought her too dearly, and your brother does not offer half her value. No, no, sir, hands off—hands off. Your sister does not part with the queen. She is quite determined. The game will be yours (turning to her again)—it will certainly be yours."

"And Fanny had much rather it were William's," said Edmund, smiling at her. "Poor Fanny! not allowed to cheat herself as she wishes!"

"Mr. Bertram," said Miss Crawford, a few minutes afterwards, "you know Henry to be such a capital improver, that you cannot possibly engage in anything of the sort at Thornton Lacey, without accepting his help. Only think how useful he was at Sotherton! Only think what grand things were produced there by our all going with him one hot day in August to drive about the grounds, and see his genius take fire. There we went, and there we came home again; and what was done there is not to be told!"

Fanny's eyes were turned on Crawford for a moment with an expression more than grave, even reproachful; but on catching his were instantly withdrawn. With something of consciousness he shook his head at his sister, and laughingly replied, "I cannot say there was much done at Sotherton; but it was a hot day, and we were all walking after each other and bewildered." As soon as a general buz gave him

The Regency equivalent of poker chips: mother-of-pearl "fish" counters.

shelter, he added, in a low voice directed solely at Fanny, "I should be sorry to have my powers of *planning* judged of by the day at Sotherton. I see things very differently now. Do not think of me as I appeared then."

Sotherton was a word to catch Mrs. Norris, and being just then in the happy leisure which followed securing the odd trick by Sir Thomas's capital play and her own,[6] against Dr. and Mrs. Grant's great hands, she called out in high good-humour, "Sotherton! Yes, that is a place indeed, and we had a charming day there. William, you are quite out of luck; but the next time you come I hope dear Mr. and Mrs. Rushworth will be at home, and I am sure I can answer for your being kindly received by both. Your cousins are not of a sort to forget their relations, and Mr. Rushworth is a most amiable man. They are at Brighton now, you know—in one of the best houses there, as Mr. Rushworth's fine fortune gives them a right to be. I do not exactly know the distance, but when you get back to Portsmouth, if it is not very far off, you ought to go over and pay your respects to them; and I could send a little parcel by you that I want to get conveyed to your cousins."

"I should be very happy, aunt—but Brighton is almost by Beachey Head;[7] and if I could get so far, I could not expect to be welcome in such a smart place as that—poor scrubby midshipman as I am."

Mrs. Norris was beginning an eager assurance of the affability he might depend on, when she was stopped by Sir Thomas's saying with authority, "I do not advise your going to Brighton, William, as I trust you may soon have more convenient opportunities of meeting, but my daughters would be happy to see their cousins any where; and you will find Mr. Rushworth most sincerely disposed to regard all the connections of our family as his own."

"I would rather find him private secretary to the first Lord than any thing else," was William's only answer; in an under voice, not meant to reach far, and the subject dropped.[8]

As yet Sir Thomas had seen nothing to remark in Mr. Crawford's behaviour; but when the Whist table broke up at the end of the second rubber, and leaving Dr. Grant and Mrs. Norris to dispute over

6  In whist, the odd trick is the tie-breaking thirteenth round of a game.

7  A headland on the south coast of England, fifteen miles east of Brighton. The prominence of Beachy Head's high chalk cliffs made it a landmark for sailors.

8  Brian Southam notes Austen's "sure grasp of Admiralty procedures" in this passage (*Jane Austen and the Navy*, p. 197). The private secretary to the First Lord of the Admiralty would be more than a mere functionary; senior captains often occupied that role. William, a midshipman who has long been waiting promotion to the rank of lieutenant, could use a friend in high places.

E. Fane's watercolor from the 1770s, said to picture Horatio Nelson when he was a rather cherubic-looking midshipman. Nelson (1758–1805), who eventually became Vice-Admiral of the White and commander in chief of the Mediterranean Fleet, is likely the individual Fanny has in mind when she reminds William that "the greatest admirals" when young would also have experienced the slights that he has had to endure.

their last play, he became a looker-on at the other, he found his niece the object of attentions, or rather of professions of a somewhat pointed character.

Henry Crawford was in the first glow of another scheme about Thornton Lacey, and not being able to catch Edmund's ear, was detailing it to his fair neighbour with a look of considerable earnestness. His scheme was to rent the house himself the following winter, that he might have a home of his own in that neighbourhood; and it was not merely for the use of it in the hunting season, (as he was then telling her), though *that* consideration had certainly some weight, feeling as he did, that in spite of all Dr. Grant's very great kindness, it was impossible for him and his horses to be accommodated where they now were without material inconvenience; but his attachment to that neighbourhood did not depend upon one amusement or one season of the year: he had set his heart upon having a something there that he could come to at any time, a little homestall at his command where all the holidays of his year might be spent, and he might find himself continuing, improving, and *perfecting* that friendship and intimacy with the Mansfield Park family which was increasing in value to him every day. Sir Thomas heard and was not offended. There was no want of respect in the young man's address; and Fanny's reception of it was so proper and modest, so calm and uninviting, that he had nothing to censure in her. She said little, assented only here and there, and betrayed no inclination either of appropriating any part of the compliment to herself or of strengthening his views in favour of Northamptonshire. Finding by whom he was observed, Henry Crawford addressed himself on the same subject to Sir Thomas, in a more every day tone, but still with feeling.

"I want to be your neighbour, Sir Thomas, as you have perhaps heard me telling Miss Price. May I hope for your acquiescence and for your not influencing your son against such a tenant?"

Sir Thomas, politely bowing, replied—"It is the only way, sir, in which I could *not* wish you established as a permanent neighbour; but I hope, and believe, that Edmund will occupy his own house at Thornton Lacey. Edmund, am I saying too much?"

Edmund, on this appeal, had first to hear what was going on, but on understanding the question, was at no loss for an answer.

"Certainly, sir, I have no idea but of residence. But, Crawford, though I refuse you as a tenant, come to me as a friend. Consider the house as half your own every winter, and we will add to the stables on your own improved plan, and with all the improvements of your improved plan that may occur to you this spring."

"We shall be the losers," continued Sir Thomas. "His going, though only eight miles, will be an unwelcome contraction of our family circle; but I should have been deeply mortified, if any son of mine could reconcile himself to doing less. It is perfectly natural that you should not have thought much on the subject, Mr. Crawford. But a parish has wants and claims which can be known only by a clergyman constantly resident, and which no proxy can be capable of satisfying to the same extent. Edmund might, in the common phrase, do the duty of Thornton, that is, he might read prayers and preach, without giving up Mansfield Park; he might ride over, every Sunday, to a house nominally inhabited, and go through divine service; he might be the clergyman of Thornton Lacey every seventh day, for three or four hours, if that would content him. But it will not. He knows that human nature needs more lessons than a weekly sermon can convey, and that if he does not live among his parishioners and prove himself by constant attention their well-wisher and friend, he does very little either for their good or his own."[9]

Mr. Crawford bowed his acquiescence.

"I repeat again," added Sir Thomas, "that Thornton Lacey is the only house in the neighbourhood in which I should *not* be happy to wait on Mr. Crawford as occupier."

Mr. Crawford bowed his thanks.

"Sir Thomas," said Edmund, "undoubtedly understands the duty of a parish priest.—We must hope his son may prove that *he* knows it too."

Whatever effect Sir Thomas's little harangue might really produce on Mr. Crawford, it raised some awkward sensations in two of the others, two of his most attentive listeners, Miss Crawford and

9 Praising clergymen who reside among their parishioners, Sir Thomas engages a topical issue dear to Evangelical reformers of the Anglican church. There is some ethical inconsistency in his position, given that he is himself an absentee landlord where his Antigua property is concerned. As Austen knew from Thomas Clarkson's *History of the Abolition of the Slave Trade* (1807), abolitionists like William Wilberforce argued that the nonresidence of the West Indian planters left the slaves on their plantations more vulnerable to oppression at the hands of brutal overseers; the slaves' owners would surely have resented that brutality, it was said, had they been present to witness it.

10 Assemblies were public balls, which in the Portsmouth of Austen's day were held in the Crown Inn on High Street every two weeks during the winter. Subscribers paid fifteen shillings for six assemblies, three shillings for one, and tea was included (B. C. Thomas, "Portsmouth in Jane Austen's Time," *Persuasions* 12 [1990], p. 36).

11 William does not have a "commission." Because he has served as a midshipman for more than six years, he more than qualifies for the rank of lieutenant and appears already to have passed the examination that was required for promotion to that rank. However, William continues to await the decision by the Board of Admiralty that would appoint him to the position of lieutenant on board a particular vessel. Those commissions, as such appointments were called, generally depended less on the candidate's service record than on his personal connections, the more so because, as Brian Southam notes, there were far more eligible midshipmen than there were vacancies at the rank of lieutenant: "In 1813 the actual queue of passed Midshipmen awaiting commissions was almost two thousand long" (*Jane Austen and the Navy,* p. 41).

Fanny.—One of whom, having never before understood that Thornton was so soon and so completely to be his home, was pondering with downcast eyes on what it would be, *not* to see Edmund every day; and the other, startled from the agreeable fancies she had been previously indulging on the strength of her brother's description, no longer able, in the picture she had been forming of a future Thornton, to shut out the church, sink the clergyman, and see only the respectable, elegant, modernized, and occasional residence of a man of independent fortune—was considering Sir Thomas, with decided ill-will, as the destroyer of all this, and suffering the more from that involuntary forbearance which his character and manner commanded, and from not daring to relieve herself by a single attempt at throwing ridicule on his cause.

All the agreeable of *her* speculation was over for that hour. It was time to have done with cards if sermons prevailed, and she was glad to find it necessary to come to a conclusion and be able to refresh her spirits by a change of place and neighbour.

The chief of the party were now collected irregularly round the fire, and waiting the final break up. William and Fanny were the most detached. They remained together at the otherwise deserted card-table, talking very comfortably and not thinking of the rest, till some of the rest began to think of them. Henry Crawford's chair was the first to be given a direction towards them, and he sat silently observing them for a few minutes; himself in the meanwhile observed by Sir Thomas, who was standing in chat with Dr. Grant.

"This is the Assembly night," said William. "If I were at Portsmouth, I should be at it perhaps."[10]

"But you do not wish yourself at Portsmouth, William?"

"No, Fanny, that I do not. I shall have enough of Portsmouth, and of dancing too, when I cannot have you. And I do not know that there would be any good in going to the Assembly, for I might not get a partner. The Portsmouth girls turn up their noses at any body who has not a commission.[11] One might as well be nothing as a midshipman. One *is* nothing, indeed. You remember the Gregorys; they are grown up amazing fine girls, but they will hardly speak to *me,* because Lucy is courted by a lieutenant."

"Oh! shame, shame!—But never mind it, William. (Her own cheeks in a glow of indignation as she spoke.) It is not worth minding. It is no reflection on *you*; it is no more than what the greatest admirals have all experienced, more or less, in their time. You must think of that; you must try to make up your mind to it as one of the hardships which fall to every sailor's share—like bad weather and hard living—only with this advantage, that there will be an end to it, that there will come a time when you will have nothing of that sort to endure. When you are a lieutenant!—only think, William, when you are a lieutenant, how little you will care for any nonsense of this kind."

"I begin to think I shall never be a lieutenant, Fanny. Every body gets made but me."[12]

"Oh! my dear William, do not talk so, do not be so desponding. My uncle says nothing, but I am sure he will do everything in his power to get you made. He knows, as well as you do, of what consequence it is."

She was checked by the sight of her uncle much nearer to them than she had any suspicion of, and each found it necessary to talk of something else.

"Are you fond of dancing, Fanny?"

"Yes, very;—only I am soon tired."

"I should like to go to a ball with you and see you dance. Have you never any balls at Northampton?—I should like to see you dance, and I'd dance with you if you *would,* for nobody would know who I was here, and I should like to be your partner once more. We used to jump about together many a time, did not we? when the hand-organ was in the street?[13] I am a pretty good dancer in my way, but I dare say you are a better."—And turning to his uncle, who was now close to them—"Is not Fanny a very good dancer, sir?"

Fanny, in dismay at such an unprecedented question, did not know which way to look, or how to be prepared for the answer. Some very grave reproof, or at least the coldest expression of indifference must be coming to distress her brother, and sink her to the ground. But, on the contrary, it was no worse than, "I am sorry to say that I am unable to answer your question. I have never seen Fanny dance since

12 Gets promoted.

13 Street musicians performing on hand organs, also called barrel organs, were among the principal providers of entertainment for the urban poor. By this point Austen's readers are used to thinking of Fanny as someone who lacks the stamina for walking or for dancing, so William's recollection of his sister's liveliness as a little girl comes as a surprise. It makes one wonder whether the move from Portsmouth to Mansfield has in fact benefited Fanny's health, as her benefactors appear to assume.

"The School for Love, or Beauty and Music," an anonymous mezzotint from the 1780s, celebrates street music of the sort that William remembers as he looks back nostalgically at his and Fanny's childhood pleasures.

Hugh Thomson's 1897 illustration captures the moment when Fanny, to her dismay, ends up "indebted" to Mr. Crawford for his gallantry; as the Mansfield family leaves the parsonage, he, rather than Edmund, puts her shawl around her shoulders.

she was a little girl; but I trust we shall both think she acquits herself like a gentlewoman when we do see her, which perhaps we may have an opportunity of doing ere long."

"I have had the pleasure of seeing your sister dance, Mr. Price," said Henry Crawford, leaning forward, "and will engage to answer every inquiry which you can make on the subject, to your entire satisfaction. But I believe (seeing Fanny looked distressed) it must be at some other time. There is *one* person in company who does not like to have Miss Price spoken of."

True enough, he had once seen Fanny dance; and it was equally true that he would now have answered for her gliding about with quiet, light elegance, and in admirable time, but in fact he could not for the life of him recall what her dancing had been, and rather took it for granted that she had been present than remembered any thing about her.

He passed, however, for an admirer of her dancing; and Sir Thomas, by no means displeased, prolonged the conversation on dancing in general, and was so well engaged in describing the balls of Antigua, and listening to what his nephew could relate of the different modes of dancing which had fallen within his observation, that he had not heard his carriage announced, and was first called to the knowledge of it by the bustle of Mrs. Norris.

"Come, Fanny, Fanny, what are you about? We are going. Do not you see your aunt is going? Quick, quick. I cannot bear to keep good old Wilcox waiting. You should always remember the coachman and horses. My dear Sir Thomas, we have settled it that the carriage should come back for you, and Edmund, and William."

Sir Thomas could not dissent, as it had been his own arrangement, previously communicated to his wife and sister; but *that* seemed forgotten by Mrs. Norris, who must fancy that she settled it all herself.

Fanny's last feeling in the visit was disappointment—for the shawl which Edmund was quietly taking from the servant to bring and put round her shoulders, was seized by Mr. Crawford's quicker hand, and she was obliged to be indebted to his more prominent attention.

# 8

WILLIAM'S DESIRE OF SEEING Fanny dance, made more than a momentary impression on his uncle. The hope of an opportunity, which Sir Thomas had then given, was not given to be thought of no more. He remained steadily inclined to gratify so amiable a feeling—to gratify any body else who might wish to see Fanny dance, and to give pleasure to the young people in general; and having thought the matter over and taken his resolution in quiet independence, the result of it appeared the next morning at breakfast, when, after recalling and commending what his nephew had said, he added, "I do not like, William, that you should leave Northamptonshire without this indulgence. It would give me pleasure to see you both dance. You spoke of the balls at Northampton. Your cousins have occasionally attended them; but they would not altogether suit us now. The fatigue would be too much for your aunt. I believe, we must not think of a Northampton ball. A dance at home would be more eligible, and if"—

"Ah! my dear Sir Thomas," interrupted Mrs. Norris, "I knew what was coming. I knew what you were going to say. If dear Julia were at home, or dearest Mrs. Rushworth at Sotherton, to afford a reason, an occasion for such a thing, you would be tempted to give the young people a dance at Mansfield. I know you would. If *they* were at home to grace the ball, a ball you would have this very Christmas. Thank your uncle, William, thank your uncle."

"My daughters," replied Sir Thomas, gravely interposing, "have their pleasures at Brighton, and I hope are very happy; but the dance

The topaz crosses that Lieutenant Charles Austen purchased for his sisters around 1801.

Miniature portrait of Jane Austen's sailor brother Charles, painted in the 1840s when he had attained the rank of Rear Admiral of the Fleet.

which I think of giving at Mansfield, will be for their cousins. Could we be all assembled, our satisfaction would undoubtedly be more complete, but the absence of some is not to debar the others of amusement."

Mrs. Norris had not another word to say. She saw decision in his looks, and her surprize and vexation required some minutes silence to be settled into composure. A ball at such a time! His daughters absent and herself not consulted! There was comfort, however, soon at hand. *She* must be the doer of every thing; Lady Bertram would of course be spared all thought and exertion, and it would all fall upon *her*. She should have to do the honours of the evening, and this reflection quickly restored so much of her good humour as enabled her to join in with the others, before their happiness and thanks were all expressed.

Edmund, William, and Fanny, did, in their different ways, look and speak as much grateful pleasure in the promised ball, as Sir Thomas could desire. Edmund's feelings were for the other two. His father had never conferred a favour or shewn a kindness more to his satisfaction.

Lady Bertram was perfectly quiescent and contented, and had no objections to make. Sir Thomas engaged for its giving her very little trouble, and she assured him, "that she was not at all afraid of the trouble, indeed she could not imagine there would be any."

Mrs. Norris was ready with her suggestions as to the rooms he would think fittest to be used, but found it all prearranged; and when she would have conjectured and hinted about the day, it appeared that the day was settled too. Sir Thomas had been amusing himself with shaping a very complete outline of the business; and as soon as she would listen quietly, could read his list of the families to be invited, from whom he calculated, with all necessary allowance for the shortness of the notice, to collect young people enough to form twelve or fourteen couple; and could detail the considerations which had induced him to fix on the 22d, as the most eligible day. William was required to be at Portsmouth on the 24th; the 22d would therefore be the last day of his visit; but where the days were so few it would be unwise to fix on any earlier. Mrs. Norris was obliged to be satisfied with thinking just the same, and with having been on the point of proposing the 22d herself, as by far the best day for the purpose.

The ball was now a settled thing, and before the evening a proclaimed thing to all whom it concerned. Invitations were sent with dispatch, and many a young lady went to bed that night with her head full of happy cares as well as Fanny.—To her, the cares were sometimes almost beyond the happiness; for young and inexperienced, with small means of choice and no confidence in her own taste—the "how she should be dressed" was a point of painful solicitude; and the almost solitary ornament in her possession, a very pretty amber cross which William had brought her from Sicily,[1] was the greatest distress of all, for she had nothing but a bit of ribbon to fasten it to; and though she had worn it in that manner once, would it be allowable at such a time, in the midst of all the rich ornaments which she supposed all the other young ladies would appear in? And yet not to wear it! William had wanted to buy her a gold chain too, but the purchase had been beyond his means, and therefore not to wear the cross might be mortifying him. These were anxious considerations; enough to sober her spirits even under the prospect of a ball given principally for her gratification.

The preparations meanwhile went on, and Lady Bertram continued to sit on her sofa without any inconvenience from them. She had some extra visits from the housekeeper, and her maid was rather hurried in making up a new dress for her; Sir Thomas gave orders and Mrs. Norris ran about, but all this gave *her* no trouble, and as she had foreseen, "there was in fact no trouble in the business."

Edmund was at this time particularly full of cares; his mind being deeply occupied in the consideration of two important events now at hand, which were to fix his fate in life—ordination and matrimony—events of such a serious character as to make the ball, which would be very quickly followed by one of them, appear of less moment in his eyes than in those of any other person in the house. On the 23d he was going to a friend near Peterborough in the same situation as himself,[2] and they were to receive ordination in the course of the Christmas week. Half his destiny would then be determined—

1 With William's gift to Fanny, Austen recalls the topaz crosses and gold chains that her brother Charles presented to her and her sister in 1801. To purchase them Charles drew on the prize money he had received when the *Endymion*, on which he was serving as lieutenant, captured a French privateer in the Mediterranean. Austen's letter to Cassandra from May 27, 1801, reports on their youngest brother's good fortune: "Charles . . . has received 30*l* for his share of the privateer, and expects 10*l* more; but of what avail is it to take prizes if he lays out the produce in presents to his sisters . . . He must be well scolded" (*Letters*, p. 95).

2 A cathedral town in Cambridgeshire. Edmund is to be ordained by the bishop of Peterborough.

but the other half might not be so very smoothly wooed. His duties would be established, but the wife who was to share, and animate, and reward those duties might yet be unattainable. He knew his own mind, but he was not always perfectly assured of knowing Miss Crawford's. There were points on which they did not quite agree, there were moments in which she did not seem propitious, and though trusting altogether to her affection, so far as to be resolved (almost resolved) on bringing it to a decision within a very short time, as soon as the variety of business before him were arranged, and he knew what he had to offer her—he had many anxious feelings, many doubting hours as to the result. His conviction of her regard for him was sometimes very strong; he could look back on a long course of encouragement, and she was as perfect in disinterested attachment as in everything else. But at other times doubt and alarm intermingled with his hopes, and when he thought of her acknowledged disinclination for privacy and retirement, her decided preference of a London life—what could he expect but a determined rejection? unless it were an acceptance even more to be deprecated, demanding such sacrifices of situation and employment on his side as conscience must forbid.

The issue of all depended on one question. Did she love him well enough to forego what had used to be essential points—Did she love him well enough to make them no longer essential? And this question, which he was continually repeating to himself, though oftenest answered with a "Yes," had sometimes its "No."

Miss Crawford was soon to leave Mansfield, and on this circumstance the "no" and the "yes" had been very recently in alternation. He had seen her eyes sparkle as she spoke of the dear friend's letter, which claimed a long visit from her in London, and of the kindness of Henry, in engaging to remain where he was till January, that he might convey her thither; he had heard her speak of the pleasure of such a journey with an animation which had "no" in every tone. But this had occurred on the first day of its being settled, within the first hour of the burst of such enjoyment, when nothing but the friends she was to visit, was before her. He had since heard her express herself differently—with other feelings—more chequered feelings; he had heard her tell Mrs. Grant that she should leave her with regret; that she began to believe neither the friends nor the pleasures she was going to were worth those she left behind; and that though she felt she must go, and knew she should enjoy herself when once away, she was already looking forward to being at Mansfield again. Was there not a "yes" in all this?

With such matters to ponder over, and arrange, and re-arrange, Edmund could not, on his own account, think very much of the evening, which the rest of the family were looking forward to with a more equal degree of strong interest. Independent of his two cousins' enjoyment in it, the evening was to him of no higher value than any other appointed meeting of the two families might be. In every meeting there was a hope of receiving further confirmation of Miss Crawford's attachment; but the whirl of a ball-room perhaps was not particularly favourable to the excitement or expression of serious feelings. To engage her early for the two first dances, was all the command of individual happiness which he felt in his power, and the only preparation for the ball which he could enter into, in spite of all that was passing around him on the subject, from morning till night.

Thursday was the day of the ball: and on Wednesday morning, Fanny, still unable to satisfy herself, as to what she ought to wear, determined to seek the counsel of the more enlightened, and apply to Mrs. Grant and her sister, whose acknowledged taste would certainly bear her blameless; and as Edmund and William were gone to Northampton, and she had reason to think Mr. Crawford likewise out, she walked down to the Parsonage without much fear of wanting an opportunity for private discussion; and the privacy of such a discussion was a most important part of it to Fanny, being more than half ashamed of her own solicitude.

She met Miss Crawford within a few yards of the Parsonage, just setting out to call on her, and as it seemed to her, that her friend, though obliged to insist on turning back, was unwilling to lose her walk, she explained her business at once and observed that if she would be so kind as to give her opinion, it might be all talked over as well without doors as within. Miss Crawford appeared gratified by the application, and after a moment's thought, urged Fanny's re-

MANSFIELD PARK.

*Miss Crawford smiled her approbation, and hastened to complete her gift by putting the necklace round her, and making her see how well it looked.*

*London, Published by Richard Bentley 1833.*

The frontispiece for the publisher Richard Bentley's 1833 edition of *Mansfield Park* pictures the moment when Fanny settles on one particular necklace among the many contained in Mary Crawford's trinket box. To disconcerting effect, this illustrator clothes the characters in the fashionable dress of 1833 rather than of 1814.

turning with her in a much more cordial manner than before, and proposed their going up into her room, where they might have a comfortable coze,[3] without disturbing Dr. and Mrs. Grant, who were together in the drawing-room. It was just the plan to suit Fanny; and with a great deal of gratitude on her side for such ready and kind attention, they proceeded in doors and upstairs, and were soon deep in the interesting subject. Miss Crawford, pleased with the appeal, gave her all her best judgment and taste, made everything easy by her suggestions, and tried to make every thing agreeable by her encouragement. The dress being settled in all its grander parts,—"But what shall you have by way of necklace?" said Miss Crawford. "Shall not you wear your brother's cross?" And as she spoke she was undoing a small parcel, which Fanny had observed in her hand when they met. Fanny acknowledged her wishes and doubts on this point; she did not know how either to wear the cross, or to refrain from wearing it. She was answered by having a small trinket-box placed before her, and being requested to chuse from among several gold chains and necklaces. Such had been the parcel with which Miss Crawford was provided, and such the object of her intended visit; and in the kindest manner she now urged Fanny's taking one for the cross and to keep for her sake, saying every thing she could think of to obviate the scruples which were making Fanny start back at first with a look of horror at the proposal.

"You see what a collection I have," said she, "more by half than I ever use or think of. I do not offer them as new. I offer nothing but an old necklace. You must forgive the liberty and oblige me."

Fanny still resisted, and from her heart. The gift was too valuable. But, Miss Crawford persevered, and argued the case with so much affectionate earnestness through all the heads of William and the cross, and the ball, and herself, as to be finally successful.[4] Fanny found herself obliged to yield, that she might not be accused of pride or indifference, or some other littleness; and having with modest reluctance given her consent, proceeded to make the selection. She looked and looked, longing to know which might be least valuable; and was determined in her choice at last, by fancying there was one necklace more frequently placed before her eyes than the rest. It was of gold, prettily worked; and though Fanny would have preferred a longer and a plainer chain as more adapted for her purpose, she hoped in fixing on this, to be chusing what Miss Crawford least wished to keep. Miss Crawford smiled her perfect approbation; and hastened to complete the gift by putting the necklace round her and making her see how well it looked.

Fanny had not a word to say against its becomingness, and excepting what remained of her scruples, was exceedingly pleased with an acquisition so very apropos. She would rather perhaps have been obliged to some other person. But this was an unworthy feeling. Miss Crawford had anticipated her wants with a kindness which proved her a real friend. "When I wear this necklace I shall always think of you," said she, "and feel how very kind you were."

"You must think of somebody else too, when you wear that necklace," replied Miss Crawford. "You must think of Henry, for it was his choice in the first place. He gave it to me, and with the necklace I make over to you all the duty of remembering the original giver. It is to be a family remembrancer. The sister is not to be in your mind without bringing the brother too."

Fanny, in great astonishment and confusion, would have returned the present instantly. To take what had been the gift of another person—of a brother too—impossible!—it must not be!—and with an eagerness and embarrassment quite diverting to her companion, she laid down the necklace again on its cotton, and seemed resolved either to take another or none at all. Miss Crawford thought she had never seen a prettier consciousness. "My dear child," said she laughing, "what are you afraid of? Do you think Henry will claim the necklace as mine, and fancy you did not come honestly by it?—or are you imagining he would be too much flattered by seeing round your lovely throat an ornament which his money purchased three years ago, before he knew there was such a throat in the world?—or perhaps—looking archly—you suspect a confederacy between us, and that what I am now doing is with his knowledge and at his desire?"

With the deepest blushes Fanny protested against such a thought.

"Well then," replied Miss Crawford more seriously but without at all believing her, "to convince me that you suspect no trick, and are

5 The choice of the word *complaisant*, a synonym for *accommodating* or *yielding*, registers Fanny's insight into Mary's motives in this episode. Fanny's "friend" Mary acts to please her brother and do his bidding, and, even while allowing herself to be manipulated by Mary, Fanny knows it.

as unsuspicious of compliment as I have always found you, take the necklace, and say no more about it. Its being a gift of my brother's need not make the smallest difference in your accepting it, as I assure you it makes none in my willingness to part with it. He is always giving me something or other. I have such innumerable presents from him that it is quite impossible for me to value, or for him to remember half. And as for this necklace, I do not suppose I have worn it six times; it is very pretty—but I never think of it; and though you would be most heartily welcome to any other in my trinket-box, you have happened to fix on the very one which, if I have a choice, I would rather part with and see in your possession than any other. Say no more against it, I entreat you. Such a trifle is not worth half so many words."

Fanny dared not make any further opposition; and with renewed but less happy thanks accepted the necklace again, for there was an expression in Miss Crawford's eyes which she could not be satisfied with.

It was impossible for her to be insensible of Mr. Crawford's change of manners. She had long seen it. He evidently tried to please her—he was gallant—he was attentive—he was something like what he had been to her cousins: he wanted, she supposed, to cheat her of her tranquillity as he had cheated them; and whether he might not have some concern in this necklace!—She could not be convinced that he had not, for Miss Crawford, complaisant as a sister, was careless as a woman and a friend.[5]

Reflecting and doubting, and feeling that the possession of what she had so much wished for, did not bring much satisfaction, she now walked home again—with a change rather than a diminution of cares since her treading that path before.

# 9

On reaching home, Fanny went immediatcly up stairs to deposit this unexpected acquisition, this doubtful good of a necklace, in some favourite box in the east room which held all her smaller treasures; but on opening the door, what was her surprize to find her cousin Edmund there writing at the table! Such a sight having never occurred before, was almost as wonderful as it was welcome.

"Fanny," said he directly, leaving his seat and his pen, and meeting her with something in his hand, "I beg your pardon for being here. I came to look for you, and after waiting a little while in hope of your coming in, was making use of your inkstand to explain my errand. You will find the beginning of a note to yourself; but I can now speak my business, which is merely to beg your acceptance of this little trifle—a chain for William's cross. You ought to have had it a week ago, but there has been a delay from my brother's not being in town by several days so soon as I expected; and I have only just now received it at Northampton. I hope you will like the chain itself, Fanny. I endeavoured to consult the simplicity of your taste, but at any rate I know you will be kind to my intentions, and consider it, as it really is, a token of the love of one of your oldest friends."

And so saying, he was hurrying away, before Fanny, overpowered by a thousand feelings of pain and pleasure, could attempt to speak; but quickened by one sovereign wish she then called out, "Oh! cousin, stop a moment, pray stop."

He turned back.

"I cannot attempt to thank you," she continued in a very agitated manner, "thanks are out of the question. I feel much more than I can possibly express. Your goodness in thinking of me in such a way is beyond"—

"If that is all you have to say, Fanny" smiling and turning away again—

"No, no, it is not. I want to consult you."

Almost unconsciously she had now undone the parcel he had just put into her hand, and seeing before her, in all the niceness of jewellers' packing, a plain gold chain perfectly simple and neat, she could not help bursting forth again. "Oh! this is beautiful indeed! this is the very thing, precisely what I wished for! this is the only ornament I have ever had a desire to possess. It will exactly suit my cross. They must and shall be worn together. It comes too in such an acceptable moment. Oh! cousin, you do not know how acceptable it is."

"My dear Fanny, you feel these things a great deal too much. I am most happy that you like the chain, and that it should be here in time for to-morrow: but your thanks are far beyond the occasion. Believe me, I have no pleasure in the world superior to that of contributing to yours. No, I can safely say, I have no pleasure so complete, so unalloyed. It is without a drawback."

Upon such expressions of affection, Fanny could have lived an hour without saying another word; but Edmund, after waiting a moment, obliged her to bring down her mind from its heavenly flight by saying, "But what is it that you want to consult me about?"

It was about the necklace, which she was now most earnestly longing to return, and hoped to obtain his approbation of her doing. She gave the history of her recent visit, and now her raptures might well be over, for Edmund was so struck with the circumstance, so delighted with what Miss Crawford had done, so gratified by such a coincidence of conduct between them, that Fanny could not but admit the superior power of *one* pleasure over his own mind, though it might have its drawback. It was some time before she could get his attention to her plan, or any answer to her demand of his opinion; he was in a reverie of fond reflection, uttering only now and then a few half-sentences of praise; but when he did awake and understand, he was very decided in opposing what she wished.

"Return the necklace! No, my dear Fanny, upon no account. It would be mortifying her severely. There can hardly be a more unpleasant sensation than the having any thing returned on our hands, which we have given with a reasonable hope of its contributing to the comfort of a friend. Why should she lose a pleasure which she has shewn herself so deserving of?"

"If it had been given to me in the first instance," said Fanny, "I should not have thought of returning it; but being her brother's present, is not it fair to suppose that she would rather not part with it, when it is not wanted?"

"She must not suppose it not wanted, not acceptable at least; and its having been originally her brother's gift makes no difference, for as she was not prevented from offering, nor you from taking it on that account, it ought not to affect your keeping it. No doubt it is handsomer than mine, and fitter for a ball-room."

"No, it is not handsomer, not at all handsomer in its way, and for my purpose not half so fit. The chain will agree with William's cross beyond all comparison better than the necklace."

"For one night, Fanny, for only one night, if it *be* a sacrifice—I am sure you will, upon consideration, make that sacrifice rather than give pain to one who has been so studious of your comfort. Miss Crawford's attentions to you have been—not more than you were justly entitled to—I am the last person to think that *could be*—but they have been invariable; and to be returning them with what must have something the *air* of ingratitude, though I know it could never have the *meaning*, is not in your nature I am sure. Wear the necklace, as you are engaged to do to-morrow evening, and let the chain, which was not ordered with any reference to the ball, be kept for commoner occasions. This is my advice. I would not have the shadow of a coolness between the two whose intimacy I have been observing with the greatest pleasure, and in whose characters there is so much general resemblance in true generosity and natural delicacy as to make the few slight differences, resulting principally from situation,

Watercolor and pencil portrait of Jane Austen by her sister, Cassandra, circa 1810. Austen's "fondest biographers" have often lamented their inability to know just what the novelist looked like. Though this portrait, the only fully authenticated image of Austen, became the basis for the much prettified and softened engraving that the sisters' Victorian nephew J. E. Austen-Leigh included in *A Memoir of Jane Austen*, his sister, half-sister, and cousins declared it an imperfect likeness that at best gave "some idea of the truth."

no reasonable hindrance to a perfect friendship. I would not have the shadow of a coolness arise," he repeated, his voice sinking a little, "between the two dearest objects I have on earth."

He was gone as he spoke; and Fanny remained to tranquillise herself as she could. She was one of his two dearest—that must support her. But the other!—the first! She had never heard him speak so openly before, and though it told her no more than what she had long perceived, it was a stab;—for it told of his own convictions and views. They were decided. He would marry Miss Crawford. It was a stab, in spite of every long-standing expectation; and she was obliged to repeat again and again that she was one of his two dearest, before the words gave her any sensation. Could she believe Miss Crawford to deserve him, it would be—Oh! how different would it be—how far more tolerable! But he was deceived in her; he gave her merits which she had not; her faults were what they had ever been, but he saw them no longer. Till she had shed many tears over this deception, Fanny could not subdue her agitation; and the dejection which followed could only be relieved by the influence of fervent prayers for his happiness.

It was her intention, as she felt it to be her duty, to try to overcome all that was excessive, all that bordered on selfishness in her affection for Edmund. To call or to fancy it a loss, a disappointment, would be a presumption; for which she had not words strong enough to satisfy her own humility. To think of him as Miss Crawford might be justified in thinking, would in her be insanity. To her, he could be nothing under any circumstances—nothing dearer than a friend. Why did such an idea occur to her even enough to be reprobated and forbidden? It ought not to have touched on the confines of her imagination. She would endeavour to be rational, and to deserve the right of judging of Miss Crawford's character and the privilege of true solicitude for him by a sound intellect and an honest heart.

She had all the heroism of principle, and was determined to do her duty; but having also many of the feelings of youth and nature, let her not be much wondered at if, after making all these good resolutions on the side of self-government, she seized the scrap of paper on which Edmund had begun writing to her, as a treasure beyond all her hopes, and reading with the tenderest emotion these words, "My very dear Fanny, you must do me the favour to accept"—locked it up with the chain, as the dearest part of the gift. It was the only thing approaching to a letter which she had ever received from him; she might never receive another; it was impossible that she ever should receive another so perfectly gratifying in the occasion and the style. Two lines more prized had never fallen from the pen of the most distinguished author—never more completely blessed the researches of the fondest biographer. The enthusiasm of a woman's love is even beyond the biographer's.[1] To her, the hand-writing itself, independent of any thing it may convey, is a blessedness. Never were such characters cut by any other human being, as Edmund's commonest hand-writing gave! This specimen, written in haste as it was, had not a fault; and there was a felicity in the flow of the first four words, in the arrangement of "My very dear Fanny," which she could have looked at for ever.

Having regulated her thoughts and comforted her feelings by this happy mixture of reason and weakness, she was able, in due time, to go down and resume her usual employments near her aunt Bertram, and pay her the usual observances without any apparent want of spirits.

Thursday, predestined to hope and enjoyment, came; and opened with more kindness to Fanny than such self-willed, unmanageable days often volunteer, for soon after breakfast a very friendly note was brought from Mr. Crawford to William stating, that as he found himself obliged to go to London on the morrow for a few days, he could not help trying to procure a companion; and therefore hoped that if William could make up his mind to leave Mansfield half a day earlier than had been proposed, he would accept a place in his carriage. Mr. Crawford meant to be in town by his uncle's accustomary late dinner-hour,[2] and William was invited to dine with him at the Admiral's. The proposal was a very pleasant one to William himself, who enjoyed the idea of travelling post with four horses and such a good-humoured agreeable friend; and in likening it to going up with dispatches, was saying at once every thing in favour of its happiness and dignity which his imagination could suggest;[3] and Fanny, from a

1 Samuel Johnson's biographer James Boswell is likely the zealous and indiscriminate collector of textual scraps Austen's narrator has in view. Boswell opens the *Life of Johnson* (1791) by touting his efforts to obtain "materials concerning him, from every quarter where I could discover that they were to be found" and declares himself justified "in preserving rather too many of Johnson's sayings, than too few; especially as . . . it cannot be known with certainty beforehand, whether what may seem trifling to some . . . may not be most agreeable to many" (*Life of Johnson,* ed. R. W. Chapman [Oxford: Oxford University Press, 1980], pp. 19, 26).

That some mockery has crept into the narrator's description of Fanny's devotion to a "scrap of paper" is borne out by a more straightforwardly comic episode that Austen included in her next novel. As we discover in Vol. III, Chap. 4 of *Emma,* Harriet Smith, following in Fanny's footsteps, also preserves the treasured relics of the man she loves. When Emma learns about the existence of a box marked "Most Precious Treasures" and its contents—"the end of an old pencil" which Reverend Elton once used to write down a recipe for spruce beer and a bit of "court plaister" left over after he bandaged his cut finger—she will have to struggle to conceal her amusement from her friend. The narrator of *Mansfield Park* seems likewise to find amusement an appropriate reaction to such a collection.

2 Admiral Crawford keeps fashionable London hours.

3 William anticipates with pleasure the chance to participate in Crawford's expensive and swift mode of travel. Traveling post involved the use both of a private carriage and of relays of fresh horses obtained at each of a series of stops (*posts*) en route. The comparison of this journey with those taken by the messengers who go up to London with dispatches—official communications—registers William's excitement. To be selected to carry the news of a victory to the Admiralty was an honor and an opportunity, since it put the lucky officer who served as messenger in the way of reward and promotion.

4 The reference is to the cheaper public transportation of the era. The mail coaches which ran at scheduled times between Northampton and London and between London and Portsmouth carried passengers along with letters and packages.

PARTRIDGE SHOOTING

SNIPE SHOOTING

different motive, was exceedingly pleased: for the original plan was that William should go up by the mail from Northampton the following night which would not have allowed him an hour's rest before he must have got into a Portsmouth coach;[4] and though this offer of Mr. Crawford's would rob her of many hours of his company, she was too happy in having William spared from the fatigue of such a journey, to think of any thing else. Sir Thomas approved of it for another reason. His nephew's introduction to Admiral Crawford might be of service. The Admiral he believed had interest. Upon the whole, it was a very joyous note. Fanny's spirits lived on it half the morning, deriving some accession of pleasure from its writer being himself to go away.

As for the ball so near at hand, she had too many agitations and fears to have half the enjoyment in anticipation which she ought to have had, or must have been supposed to have, by the many young ladies looking forward to the same event in situations more at ease, but under circumstances of less novelty, less interest, less peculiar gratification than would be attributed to her. Miss Price, known only by name to half the people invited, was now to make her first appearance, and must be regarded as the Queen of the evening. Who could be happier than Miss Price? But Miss Price had not been brought up to the trade of *coming out;* and had she known in what light this ball was, in general, considered respecting her, it would very much have lessened her comfort by increasing the fears she already had, of doing wrong and being looked at. To dance without much observation or any extraordinary fatigue, to have strength and partners for about half the evening, to dance a little with Edmund, and not a great deal with Mr. Crawford, to see William enjoy himself, and be able to keep away from her aunt Norris, was the height of her ambition, and seemed to comprehend her greatest possibility of happiness. As these were the best of her hopes, they could not always prevail; and in the course of a long morning, spent principally with her two aunts, she was often under the influence of much less sanguine views. William, determined to make this last day a day of thorough enjoyment, was out snipe shooting; Edmund, she had too much reason to suppose, was at the Parsonage; and left alone to bear the worrying of

Mrs. Norris, who was cross because the house-keeper would have her own way with the supper, and whom *she* could not avoid though the house-keeper might, Fanny was worn down at last to think every thing an evil belonging to the ball, and when sent off with a parting worry to dress, moved as languidly towards her own room, and felt as incapable of happiness as if she had been allowed no share in it.

As she walked slowly up stairs she thought of yesterday; it had been about the same hour that she had returned from the Parsonage, and found Edmund in the east room.—"Suppose I were to find him there again to-day!" said she to herself in a fond indulgence of fancy.

"Fanny," said a voice at that moment near her. Starting and looking up, she saw, across the lobby she had just reached Edmund himself, standing at the head of a different staircase. He came towards her. "You look tired and fagged, Fanny. You have been walking too far."

"No, I have not been out at all."

"Then you have had fatigues within doors, which are worse. You had better have gone out."

Fanny, not liking to complain, found it easiest to make no answer; and though he looked at her with his usual kindness, she believed he had soon ceased to think of her countenance. He did not appear in spirits: something unconnected with her was probably amiss. They proceeded up stairs together, their rooms being on the same floor above.

"I come from Dr. Grant's," said Edmund presently. "You may guess my errand there, Fanny." And he looked so conscious, that Fanny could think but of one errand, which turned her too sick for speech.—"I wished to engage Miss Crawford for the two first dances," was the explanation that followed, and brought Fanny to life again, enabling her, as she found she was expected to speak, to utter something like an inquiry as to the result.

"Yes," he answered, "she is engaged to me; but (with a smile that did not sit easy) she says it is to be the last time that she ever will dance with me. She is not serious. I think, I hope, I am sure she is not serious—but I would rather not hear it. She never has danced with a clergyman she says, and she never *will*. For my own sake, I

These Victorian lithograph prints based on a series of "Shooting Pieces" by the late eighteenth-century artist George Morland, depict some of the characteristic sporting activities of the English country gentleman. William Price's stay at Mansfield introduces him belatedly to these rural sports.

DUCK SHOOTING

DUCK SHOOTING

5 As Edmund strains to understand Mary's character, biblical echoes begin to be audible in his language. In 1 *Corinthians* chapter 13, verse 5, for instance, one reads that love "thinketh no evil," and in 2 *Peter* chapter 2, verse 12, that the unrighteous "speak evil of the things that they understand not."

6 This discussion that identifies Mary Crawford as the victim of an improper education links *Mansfield Park* to the novels of Austen's predecessors, densely populated with neglectful or over-indulgent parents and obsequious governesses. Elizabeth Inchbald, for example, rounds off her first novel, *A Simple Story* (1791), by contrasting the ill-fated Miss Milner, the wealthy coquette whose tragic story unfolded in the book's first volume, with this character's more fortunate and more self-disciplined daughter, Matilda:

> Mr Milner, Matilda's grandfather, had better have given his fortune to a distant branch of his family . . . so he had bestowed upon his daughter A PROPER EDUCATION.

At the beginning of the novel readers learn that Miss Milner's boarding school education made her an accomplished woman but "left her mind without one ornament, except those which nature gave" (*A Simple Story,* ed. J. M. S. Tompkins [Oxford: Oxford University Press, 1988], pp. 338, 5).

could wish there had been no ball just at—I mean not this very week, this very day—to-morrow I leave home."

Fanny struggled for speech, and said, "I am very sorry that any thing has occurred to distress you. This ought to be a day of pleasure. My uncle meant it so."

"Oh! yes, yes, and it will be a day of pleasure. It will all end right. I am only vexed for a moment. In fact, it is not that I consider the ball as ill-timed;—what does it signify? But, Fanny,"—stopping her by taking her hand, and speaking low and seriously, "you know what all this means. You see how it is; and could tell me, perhaps better than I could tell you, how and why I am vexed. Let me talk to you a little. You are a kind, kind listener. I have been pained by her manner this morning, and cannot get the better of it. I know her disposition to be as sweet and faultless as your own, but the influence of her former companions makes her seem, gives to her conversation, to her professed opinions, sometimes a tinge of wrong. She does not *think* evil, but she speaks it—speaks it in playfulness—and though I know it to be playfulness, it grieves me to the soul."[5]

"The effect of education," said Fanny gently.[6]

Edmund could not but agree to it. "Yes, that uncle and aunt! They have injured the finest mind!—for sometimes, Fanny, I own to you, it does appear more than manner; it appears as if the mind itself was tainted."

Fanny imagined this to be an appeal to her judgment, and therefore, after a moment's consideration, said, "If you only want me as a listener, cousin, I will be as useful as I can; but I am not qualified for an adviser. Do not ask advice of *me.* I am not competent."

"You are right, Fanny, to protest against such an office, but you need not be afraid. It is a subject on which I should never ask advice. It is the sort of subject on which it had better never be asked; and few I imagine do ask it, but when they want to be influenced against their conscience. I only want to talk to you."

"One thing more. Excuse the liberty—but take care *how* you talk to me. Do not tell me any thing now, which hereafter you may be sorry for. The time may come—"

The colour rushed into her cheeks as she spoke.

"Dearest Fanny!" cried Edmund, pressing her hand to his lips, with almost as much warmth as if it had been Miss Crawford's, "you are all considerate thought!—But it is unnecessary here. The time will never come. No such time as you allude to will ever come. I begin to think it most improbable: the chances grow less and less. And even if it should—there will be nothing to be remembered by either you or me, that we need be afraid of, for I can never be ashamed of my own scruples; and if they are removed, it must be by changes that will only raise her character the more by the recollection of the faults she once had. You are the only being upon earth to whom I should say what I have said; but you have always known my opinion of her; you can bear me witness, Fanny, that I have never been blinded. How many a time have we talked over her little errors! You need not fear me. I have almost given up every serious idea of her; but I must be a blockhead indeed if, whatever befell me, I could think of your kindness and sympathy without the sincerest gratitude."

He had said enough to shake the experience of eighteen. He had said enough to give Fanny some happier feelings than she had lately known, and with a brighter look, she answered, "Yes, cousin, I am convinced that *you* would be incapable of any thing else, though perhaps some might not. I cannot be afraid of hearing any thing you wish to say. Do not check yourself. Tell me whatever you like."

They were now on the second floor, and the appearance of a housemaid prevented any further conversation.[7] For Fanny's present comfort it was concluded perhaps at the happiest moment; had he been able to talk another five minutes, there is no saying that he might not have talked away all Miss Crawford's faults and his own despondence. But as it was, they parted with looks on his side of grateful affection, and with some very precious sensations on her's. She had felt nothing like it for hours. Since the first joy from Mr. Crawford's note to William had worn away, she had been in a state absolutely the reverse; there had been no comfort around, no hope within her. Now, every thing was smiling. William's good fortune returned again upon her mind, and seemed of greater value than at first. The ball too—such an evening of pleasure before her! It was now a real animation! and she began to dress for it with much of the

7 Virginia Woolf comments beautifully on the quiet art of this scene: "Here is nothing out of the way; it is midday in Northamptonshire; a dull young man is talking to rather a weakly young woman on the stairs as they go up to dress for dinner, with housemaids passing. But from triviality, from commonplace, their words become suddenly full of meaning, and the moment for both one of the most memorable in their lives. It fills itself; it shines; it glows; it hangs before us, deep, trembling, serene for a second; next, the housemaid passes, and this drop, in which all the happiness of life has collected, gently subsides again to become part of the ebb and flow of ordinary existence" (*The Common Reader* [London: Hogarth Press, 1925], p. 178).

happy flutter which belongs to a ball. All went well—she did not dislike her own looks; and when she came to the necklaces again, her good fortune seemed complete, for upon trial the one given her by Miss Crawford would by no means go through the ring of the cross. She had, to oblige Edmund, resolved to wear it—but it was too large for the purpose. His therefore must be worn; and having, with delightful feelings, joined the chain and the cross, those memorials of the two most beloved of her heart, those dearest tokens so formed for each other by every thing real and imaginary—and put them round her neck, and seen and felt how full of William and Edmund they were, she was able, without an effort, to resolve on wearing Miss Crawford's necklace too. She acknowledged it to be right. Miss Crawford had a claim; and when it was no longer to encroach on, to interfere with the stronger claims, the truer kindness of another, she could do her justice even with pleasure to herself. The necklace really looked very well; and Fanny left her room at last, comfortably satisfied with herself and all about her.

Her aunt Bertram had recollected her on this occasion, with an unusual degree of wakefulness. It had really occurred to her, unprompted, that Fanny, preparing for a ball, might be glad of better help than the upper housemaid's, and when dressed herself, she actually sent her own maid to assist her; too late of course to be of any use. Mrs. Chapman had just reached the attic floor, when Miss Price came out of her room completely dressed, and only civilities were necessary—but Fanny felt her aunt's attention almost as much as Lady Bertram or Mrs. Chapman could do themselves.

# 10

HER UNCLE AND BOTH HER AUNTS were in the drawing-room when Fanny went down. To the former she was an interesting object, and he saw with pleasure the general elegance of her appearance and her being in remarkably good looks. The neatness and propriety of her dress was all that he would allow himself to commend in her presence, but upon her leaving the room again soon afterwards, he spoke of her beauty with very decided praise.

"Yes," said Lady Bertram, "she looks very well. I sent Chapman to her."

"Look well! Oh yes," cried Mrs. Norris, "she has good reason to look well with all her advantages: brought up in this family as she has been, with all the benefit of her cousins' manners before her. Only think, my dear Sir Thomas, what extraordinary advantages you and I have been the means of giving her. The very gown you have been taking notice of, is your own generous present to her when dear Mrs. Rushworth married. What would she have been if we had not taken her by the hand?"

Sir Thomas said no more; but when they sat down to table the eyes of the two young men assured him, that the subject might be gently touched again when the ladies withdrew, with more success. Fanny saw that she was approved; and the consciousness of looking well, made her look still better. From a variety of causes she was happy, and she was soon made still happier; for in following her aunts out of the room, Edmund, who was holding open the door, said as she passed him, "You must dance with me, Fanny; you must keep two dances for me; any two that you like, except the first." She had nothing more to wish for. She had hardly ever been in a state so nearly approaching high spirits in her life. Her cousins' former gaiety on the day of a ball was no longer surprizing to her; she felt it to be indeed very charming, and was actually practising her steps about the drawing-room as long as she could be safe from the notice of her aunt Norris, who was entirely taken up at first in fresh arranging and injuring the noble fire which the butler had prepared.

Half an hour followed, that would have been at least languid under any other circumstances, but Fanny's happiness still prevailed. It was but to think of her conversation with Edmund; and what was the restlessness of Mrs. Norris? What were the yawns of Lady Bertram?

The gentlemen joined them; and soon after began the sweet expectation of a carriage, when a general spirit of ease and enjoyment seemed diffused, and they all stood about and talked and laughed, and every moment had its pleasure and its hope. Fanny felt that

George Cruikshank's 1817 cartoon *La Belle Assemblée, or Sketches of Characteristic Dancing.* Cruikshank's dancing couples form a motley crew, especially in combination with the various dancing animals pictured on the wall behind them.

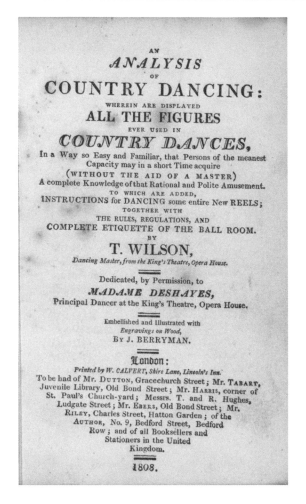

Title page of T. Wilson's how-to book, *An Analysis of Country Dancing*, from 1808.

there must be a struggle in Edmund's cheerfulness, but it was delightful to see the effort so successfully made.

When the carriages were really heard, when the guests began really to assemble, her own gaiety of heart was much subdued; the sight of so many strangers threw her back into herself; and besides the gravity and formality of the first great circle, which the manners of neither Sir Thomas nor Lady Bertram were of a kind to do away, she found herself occasionally called on to endure something worse. She was introduced here and there by her uncle, and forced to be spoken to, and to curtsey, and speak again. This was a hard duty, and she was never summoned to it, without looking at William, as he walked about at his ease in the back ground of the scene, and longing to be with him.

The entrance of the Grants and Crawfords was a favourable epoch. The stiffness of the meeting soon gave way before their popular manners and more diffused intimacies:—little groups were formed and every body grew comfortable. Fanny felt the advantage; and, drawing back from the toils of civility, would have been again most happy, could she have kept her eyes from wandering between Edmund and Mary Crawford. *She* looked all loveliness—and what might not be the end of it? Her own musings were brought to an end on perceiving Mr. Crawford before her, and her thoughts were put into another channel by his engaging her almost instantly for the first two dances. Her happiness on this occasion was very much à-la-mortal, finely chequered. To be secure of a partner at first, was a most essential good—for the moment of beginning was now growing seriously near, and she so little understood her own claims as to think, that if Mr. Crawford had not asked her, she must have been the last to be sought after, and should have received a partner only through a series of inquiry, and bustle, and interference which would have been terrible; but at the same time there was a pointedness in his manner of asking her, which she did not like, and she saw his eye glancing for a moment at her necklace—with a smile—she thought there was a smile—which made her blush and feel wretched. And though there was no second glance to disturb her, though his object seemed then to be only quietly agreeable, she could not get the better of her embarrassment, heightened as it was by the idea of his perceiving it, and had no composure till he turned away to some one else. Then she could gradually rise up to the genuine satisfaction of having a partner, a voluntary partner secured against the dancing began.

When the company were moving into the ball-room she found herself for the first time near Miss Crawford, whose eyes and smiles were immediately and more unequivocally directed as her brother's had been, and who was beginning to speak on the subject, when Fanny, anxious to get the story over, hastened to give the explanation of the second necklace—the real chain. Miss Crawford listened; and all her intended compliments and insinuations to Fanny were forgotten; she felt only one thing; and her eyes, bright as they had been before, shewing they could yet be brighter, she exclaimed with eager pleasure, "Did he? Did Edmund? That was like himself. No other man would have thought of it. I honour him beyond expression." And she looked around as if longing to tell him so. He was not near, he was attending a party of ladies out of the room; and Mrs. Grant coming up to the two girls and taking an arm of each, they followed with the rest.

Fanny's heart sunk, but there was no leisure for thinking long even of Miss Crawford's feelings. They were in the ball-room, the violins were playing, and her mind was in a flutter that forbad its fixing on any thing serious. She must watch the general arrangements and see how every thing was done.

In a few minutes Sir Thomas came to her, and asked if she were engaged; and the "Yes, sir, to Mr. Crawford," was exactly what he had intended to hear. Mr. Crawford was not far off; Sir Thomas brought him to her, saying something which discovered to Fanny, that *she* was to lead the way and open the ball; an idea that had never occurred to her before. Whenever she had thought of the minutiæ of the evening, it had been as a matter of course that Edmund would begin with Miss Crawford, and the impression was so strong, that though *her uncle* spoke the contrary, she could not help an exclamation of surprize, a hint of her unfitness, an entreaty even to be excused. To be urging her opinion against Sir Thomas's, was a proof of the ex-

1 Since the ball is in her honor, Sir Thomas expects Fanny and her partner to lead the set and start off the opening country dance of the evening. Fanny herself, however, has been assuming that the order of couples will be determined by rank and that Mary Crawford and Edmund will be the lead couple who stand at the top of the room. In a country dance, the dancers stand opposite each other in a row, and each couple by turns makes its progress down the line of dancers. The "higher" one stood in the set the more conspicuous one's dancing and one's partner's dancing would be, as Fanny well knows.

tremity of the case, but such was her horror at the first suggestion, that she could actually look him in the face and say that she hoped it might be settled otherwise; in vain, however;—Sir Thomas smiled, tried to encourage her, and then looked too serious and said too decidedly—"It must be so, my dear," for her to hazard another word; and she found herself the next moment conducted by Mr. Crawford to the top of the room, and standing there to be joined by the rest of the dancers, couple after couple as they were formed.[1]

She could hardly believe it. To be placed above so many elegant young women! The distinction was too great. It was treating her like her cousins! And her thoughts flew to those absent cousins with most unfeigned and truly tender regret, that they were not at home to take their own place in the room, and have their share of a pleasure which would have been so very delightful to them. So often as she had heard them wish for a ball at home as the greatest of all felicities! And to have them away when it was given—and for *her* to be opening the ball—and with Mr. Crawford too! She hoped they would not envy her that distinction *now;* but when she looked back to the state of things in the autumn, to what they had all been to each other when once dancing in that house before, the present arrangement was almost more than she could understand herself.

The ball began. It was rather honour than happiness to Fanny, for the first dance at least; her partner was in excellent spirits and tried to impart them to her, but she was a great deal too much frightened to have any enjoyment, till she could suppose herself no longer looked at. Young, pretty, and gentle, however, she had no awkwardnesses that were not as good as graces, and there were few persons present that were not disposed to praise her. She was attractive, she was modest, she was Sir Thomas's niece, and she was soon said to be admired by Mr. Crawford. It was enough to give her general favour. Sir Thomas himself was watching her progress down the dance with much complacency; he was proud of his niece, and without attributing all her personal beauty, as Mrs. Norris seemed to do, to her transplantation to Mansfield, he was pleased with himself for having supplied everything else;—education and manners she owed to him.

Miss Crawford saw much of Sir Thomas's thoughts as he stood, and having, in spite of all his wrongs towards her, a generally prevail-

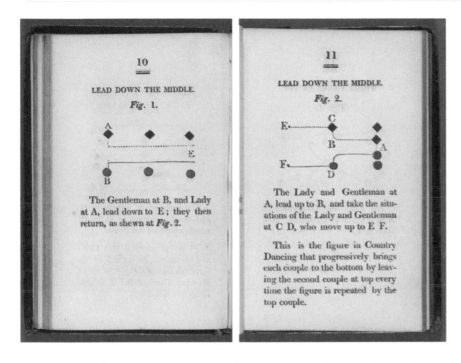

This two-part diagram from *An Analysis of Country Dancing* illustrates how each couple in succession progresses down the line of dancers involved in the set.

ing desire of recommending herself to him, took an opportunity of stepping aside to say something agreeable of Fanny. Her praise was warm, and he received it as she could wish, joining in it as far as discretion, and politeness, and slowness of speech would allow, and certainly appearing to greater advantage on the subject, than his lady did, soon afterwards, when Mary, perceiving her on a sofa very near, turned round before she began to dance, to compliment her on Miss Price's looks.

"Yes, she does look very well," was Lady Bertram's placid reply. "Chapman helped her to dress. I sent Chapman to her." Not but that she was really pleased to have Fanny admired; but she was so much more struck with her own kindness in sending Chapman to her, that she could not get it out of her head.

Miss Crawford knew Mrs. Norris too well to think of gratifying *her* by commendation of Fanny; to her, it was as the occasion offered.—"Ah! ma'am, how much we want dear Mrs. Rushworth and

Julia to night!" and Mrs. Norris paid her with as many smiles and
courteous words as she had time for, amid so much occupation as
she found for herself, in making up card-tables, giving hints to Sir
Thomas, and trying to move all the chaperons to a better part of the
room.

Miss Crawford blundered most towards Fanny herself, in her intentions to please. She meant to be giving her little heart a happy
flutter, and filling her with sensations of delightful self-consequence;
and misinterpreting Fanny's blushes, still thought she must be doing
so—when she went to her after the two first dances and said, with a
significant look, "perhaps *you* can tell me why my brother goes to
town to-morrow? He says, he has business there, but will not tell me
what. The first time he ever denied me his confidence![2] But this is
what we all come to. All are supplanted sooner or later. Now, I must
apply to you for information. Pray what is Henry going for?"

Fanny protested her ignorance as steadily as her embarrassment
allowed.

"Well, then," replied Miss Crawford laughing, "I must suppose it
to be purely for the pleasure of conveying your brother and talking
of you by the way."

Fanny was confused, but it was the confusion of discontent; while
Miss Crawford wondered she did not smile, and thought her over-
anxious, or thought her odd, or thought her any thing rather than
insensible of pleasure in Henry's attentions. Fanny had a good deal of
enjoyment in the course of the evening—but Henry's attentions had
very little to do with it. She would much rather *not* have been asked
by him again so very soon, and she wished she had not been obliged
to suspect that his previous inquiries of Mrs. Norris, about the
supper-hour, were all for the sake of securing her at that part of the
evening. But it was not to be avoided; he made her feel that she was
the object of all; though she could not say that it was unpleasantly done, that there was indelicacy or ostentation in his manner—
and sometimes, when he talked of William, he was really not un-
agreeable, and shewed even a warmth of heart which did him credit.
But still his attentions made no part of her satisfaction. She was
happy whenever she looked at William, and saw how perfectly he

was enjoying himself, in every five minutes that she could walk about with him and hear his account of his partners; she was happy in knowing herself admired, and she was happy in having the two dances with Edmund still to look forward to, during the greatest part of the evening, her hand being so eagerly sought after, that her indefinite engagement with *him* was in continual perspective. She was happy even when they did take place; but not from any flow of spirits on his side, or any such expressions of tender gallantry as had blessed the morning. His mind was fagged, and her happiness sprung from being the friend with whom it could find repose. "I am worn out with civility," said he. "I have been talking incessantly all night, and with nothing to say. But with *you,* Fanny, there may be peace. You will not want to be talked to. Let us have the luxury of silence." Fanny would hardly even speak her agreement. A weariness arising probably, in great measure, from the same feelings which he had acknowledged in the morning, was peculiarly to be respected, and they went down their two dances together with such sober tranquillity as might satisfy any looker-on, that Sir Thomas had been bringing up no wife for his younger son.

The evening had afforded Edmund little pleasure. Miss Crawford had been in gay spirits when they first danced together, but it was not her gaiety that could do him good; it rather sank than raised his comfort; and afterwards—for he found himself still impelled to seek her again, she had absolutely pained him by her manner of speaking of the profession to which he was now on the point of belonging. They had talked—and they had been silent—he had reasoned—she had ridiculed—and they had parted at last with mutual vexation. Fanny, not able to refrain entirely from observing them, had seen enough to be tolerably satisfied. It was barbarous to be happy when Edmund was suffering. Yet some happiness must and would arise, from the very conviction, that he did suffer.

When her two dances with him were over, her inclination and strength for more were pretty well at an end; and Sir Thomas having seen her walk rather than dance down the shortening set, breathless and with her hand at her side, gave his orders for her sitting down entirely. From that time Mr. Crawford sat down likewise.

3 Overcome with tiredness.

LAY OF THE LAST MINSTREL.

SHE THOUGHT SOME SPIRIT OF THE SKY

HAD DONE THE BOLD MOSS-TROOPER WRONG;
Canto III. Stan.XXII.

LONDON, PUBLISHED JUNE 1.1809, BY JOHN SHARPE PICCADILLY.

Richard Westall's 1809 illustration for *The Lay of the Last Minstrel* follows Scott's poem in emphasizing the imperious spirit of his Lady of Branksome Hall. The narrator's quotation from the *Lay* incongruously aligns submissive Fanny with this domineering Lady.

"Poor Fanny!" cried William, coming for a moment to visit her and working away his partner's fan as if for life:—"how soon she is knocked up![3] Why, the sport is but just begun. I hope we shall keep it up these two hours. How can you be tired so soon?"

"So soon! my good friend," said Sir Thomas, producing his watch with all necessary caution—"it is three o'clock, and your sister is not used to these sort of hours."

"Well then, Fanny, you shall not get up to-morrow before I go. Sleep as long as you can and never mind me."

"Oh! William."

"What! Did she think of being up before you set off?"

"Oh! yes, sir," cried Fanny, rising eagerly from her seat to be nearer her uncle, "I must get up and breakfast with him. It will be the last time you know, the last morning."

"You had better not.—He is to have breakfasted and be gone by half past nine.—Mr. Crawford, I think you call for him at half past nine?"

Fanny was too urgent, however, and had too many tears in her eyes for denial; and it ended in a gracious, "Well, well," which was permission.

"Yes, half past nine," said Crawford to William, as the latter was leaving them, "and I shall be punctual, for there will be no kind sister to get up for *me*." And in a lower tone to Fanny, "I shall have only a desolate house to hurry from. Your brother will find my ideas of time and his own very different to-morrow."

After a short consideration, Sir Thomas asked Crawford to join the early breakfast party in that house instead of eating alone; he should himself be of it; and the readiness with which his invitation was accepted, convinced him that the suspicions whence, he must confess to himself, this very ball had in great measure sprung, were well founded. Mr. Crawford was in love with Fanny. He had a pleasing anticipation of what would be. His niece, meanwhile, did not thank him for what he had just done. She had hoped to have William all to herself, the last morning. It would have been an unspeakable indulgence. But though her wishes were overthrown there was no spirit of murmuring within her. On the contrary, she was so totally unused to have her pleasure consulted, or to have any thing take place at all in the way she could desire, that she was more disposed to wonder and rejoice in having carried her point so far, than to repine at the counteraction which followed.

Shortly afterwards, Sir Thomas was again interfering a little with her inclination, by advising her to go immediately to bed. "Advise" was his word, but it was the advice of absolute power, and she had only to rise and, with Mr. Crawford's very cordial adieus, pass quietly away; stopping at the entrance door, like the Lady of Branxholm Hall, "one moment and no more,"[4] to view the happy scene, and take a last look at the five or six determined couple, who were still hard at work—and then, creeping slowly up the principal staircase, pursued by the ceaseless country-dance, feverish with hopes and fears, soup and negus,[5] sore-footed and fatigued, restless and agitated, yet feeling, in spite of every thing, that a ball was indeed delightful.

In thus sending her away, Sir Thomas perhaps might not be thinking merely of her health. It might occur to him, that Mr. Crawford had been sitting by her long enough, or he might mean to recommend her as a wife by shewing her persuadableness.

4 The quotation is from *The Lay of the Last Minstrel* (canto I, stanza 20), the narrative poem by Sir Walter Scott that Fanny herself cited earlier, during the visit to the disued chapel at Sotherton (see Vol. I, Chap. 9). The quoted passage describes the widowed Lady of Branksome Hall, a woman, as Scott put it in his endnotes to his poem, of a "masculine spirit" who has learned magical arts from her father (the contrast between this fierce and haughty heroine of Scott's and the meek and lowly heroine of *Mansfield Park* makes Austen's allusion to the poem quite comical). On the verge of sending one of her retainers on a dangerous mission that will assist her revenge against those responsible for her husband's death, the Lady pauses to take a look at her infant son.

> The Ladye forgot her purpose high,
>     One moment and no more;
> One moment gaz'd with a mother's eye,
>     As she paused at the arched door.

5 Negus is a beverage combining port or sherry, sugar, hot water, lemon, and nutmeg, named for its early eighteenth-century inventor, Colonel Francis Negus.

# II

1 Literally, she cried *with love*. The phrase *con amore* is a musical direction, indicating a passage to be performed with tenderness.

THE BALL WAS OVER—and the breakfast was soon over too; the last kiss was given, and William was gone. Mr. Crawford had, as he foretold, been very punctual, and short and pleasant had been the meal.

After seeing William to the last moment, Fanny walked back to the breakfast-room with a very saddened heart to grieve over the melancholy change; and there her uncle kindly left her to cry in peace, conceiving perhaps that the deserted chair of each young man might exercise her tender enthusiasm, and that the remaining cold pork bones and mustard in William's plate, might but divide her feelings with the broken egg-shells in Mr. Crawford's. She sat and cried *con amore* as her uncle intended,[1] but it was con amore fraternal and no other. William was gone, and she now felt as if she had wasted half his visit in idle cares and selfish solicitudes unconnected with him.

Fanny's disposition was such that she could never even think of her aunt Norris in the meagreness and cheerlessness of her own small house, without reproaching herself for some little want of attention to her when they had been last together; much less could her feelings acquit her of having done and said and thought every thing by William, that was due to him for a whole fortnight.

It was a heavy, melancholy day.—Soon after the second breakfast, Edmund bad them good bye for a week, and mounted his horse for Peterborough, and then all were gone. Nothing remained of last night but remembrances, which she had nobody to share in. She talked to her aunt Bertram—she must talk to somebody of the ball, but her aunt had seen so little of what passed, and had so little curiosity, that it was heavy work. Lady Bertram was not certain of any body's dress, or any body's place at supper, but her own. "She could not recollect what it was that she had heard about one of the Miss Maddoxes, or what it was that Lady Prescott had noticed in Fanny; she was not sure whether Colonel Harrison had been talking of Mr. Crawford or of William, when he said he was the finest young man in the room; somebody had whispered something to her, she had forgot to ask Sir Thomas what it could be." And these were her longest speeches and clearest communications; the rest was only a languid "Yes—yes—very well—did you?—did he? I did not see *that*—I should not know one from the other." This was very bad. It was only better than Mrs. Norris's sharp answers would have been; but she being gone home with all the supernumerary jellies to nurse a sick maid, there was peace and good humour in their little party, though it could not boast much beside.

The evening was heavy like the day—"I cannot think what is the matter with me!" said Lady Bertram, when the tea-things were removed. "I feel quite stupid. It must be sitting up so late last night. Fanny, you must do something to keep me awake. I cannot work. Fetch the cards—I feel so very stupid."

The cards were brought, and Fanny played at cribbage with her aunt till bed-time; and as Sir Thomas was reading to himself, no sounds were heard in the room for the next two hours beyond the reckonings of the game—"And *that* makes thirty-one;—four in hand and eight in crib.—You are to deal, ma'am; shall I deal for you?"[2] Fanny thought and thought again of the difference which twenty-four hours had made in that room, and all that part of the house. Last night it had been hope and smiles, bustle and motion, noise and brilliancy in the drawing-room, and out of the drawing-room, and every where. Now it was languor, and all but solitude.

A good night's rest improved her spirits. She could think of William the next day more cheerfully, and as the morning afforded her an opportunity of talking over Thursday night with Mrs. Grant and Miss Crawford, in a very handsome style, with all the heightenings of imagination and all the laughs of playfulness which are so essential to the shade of a departed ball, she could afterwards bring her mind

2 Cribbage is a card game for two players. They keep score by moving pegs around on a rectangular board. The card that Fanny has just played, which is also the last card in this hand, brings the total value of the cards played to thirty-one, which in itself earns Fanny two points. She also has another twelve points, "four in the hand and eight in the crib." Lady Bertram apparently requires extra help in coping with the demands of this game much as she did when playing at speculation four chapters earlier.

George Mouton Woodward's 1799 cartoon of two old gentlemen playing cribbage, with their cribbage board visible at the center of the table. The game between Fanny and her aunt was likely a sleepier affair.

without much effort into its everyday state, and easily conform to the tranquillity of the present quiet week.

They were indeed a smaller party than she had ever known there for a whole day together, and *he* was gone on whom the comfort and cheerfulness of every family-meeting and every meal chiefly depended. But this must be learned to be endured. He would soon be always gone; and she was thankful that she could now sit in the same room with her uncle, hear his voice, receive his questions, and even answer them without such wretched feelings as she had formerly known.

"We miss our two young men," was Sir Thomas's observation on both the first and second day, as they formed their very reduced circle after dinner; and in consideration of Fanny's swimming eyes, nothing more was said on the first day than to drink their good health; but on the second it led to something farther. William was kindly commended and his promotion hoped for. "And there is no reason to suppose," added Sir Thomas, "but that his visits to us may now be tolerably frequent. As to Edmund, we must learn to do without him. This will be the last winter of his belonging to us, as he has done."

"Yes," said Lady Bertram, "but I wish he was not going away. They are all going away I think. I wish they would stay at home."

This wish was levelled principally at Julia, who had just applied for permission to go to town with Maria; and as Sir Thomas thought it best for each daughter that the permission should be granted, Lady Bertram, though in her own good nature she would not have prevented it, was lamenting the change it made in the prospect of Julia's return, which would otherwise have taken place about this time. A great deal of good sense followed on Sir Thomas's side, tending to reconcile his wife to the arrangement. Every thing that a considerate parent *ought* to feel was advanced for her use; and every thing that an affectionate mother *must* feel in promoting her children's enjoyment, was attributed to her nature. Lady Bertram agreed to it all with a calm "Yes"—and at the end of a quarter of an hour's silent consideration, spontaneously observed, "Sir Thomas, I have been thinking—

and I am very glad we took Fanny as we did, for now the others are away, we feel the good of it."

Sir Thomas immediately improved this compliment by adding, "Very true. We shew Fanny what a good girl we think her by praising her to her face—she is now a very valuable companion. If we have been kind to *her*, she is now quite as necessary to *us*."

"Yes," said Lady Bertram presently—"and it is a comfort to think that we shall always have *her*."

Sir Thomas paused, half smiled, glanced at his niece, and then gravely replied, "She will never leave us, I hope, till invited to some other home that may reasonably promise her greater happiness than she knows here."

"And *that* is not very likely to be, Sir Thomas. Who should invite her? Maria might be very glad to see her at Sotherton now and then, but she would not think of asking her to live there—and I am sure she is better off here—and besides I cannot do without her."

The week which passed so quietly and peaceably at the great house in Mansfield, had a very different character at the Parsonage. To the young lady at least in each family, it brought very different feelings. What was tranquillity and comfort to Fanny was tediousness and vexation to Mary. Something arose from difference of disposition and habit—one so easily satisfied, the other so unused to endure; but still more might be imputed to difference of circumstances. In some points of interest they were exactly opposed to each other. To Fanny's mind, Edmund's absence was really in its cause and its tendency a relief. To Mary it was every way painful. She felt the want of his society every day, almost every hour; and was too much in want of it to derive any thing but irritation from considering the object for which he went. He could not have devised any thing more likely to raise his consequence than this week's absence, occurring as it did at the very time of her brother's going away, of William Price's going too, and completing the sort of general break-up of a party which had been so animated. She felt it keenly. They were now a miserable trio, confined within doors by a series of rain and snow, with nothing to do and no variety to hope for. Angry as she

was with Edmund for adhering to his own notions and acting on
them in defiance of her, (and she had been so angry that they had
hardly parted friends at the ball,) she could not help thinking of him
continually when absent, dwelling on his merit and affection, and
longing again for the almost daily meetings they lately had. His absence was unnecessarily long. He should not have planned such an
absence—he should not have left home for a week, when her own
departure from Mansfield was so near. Then she began to blame herself. She wished she had not spoken so warmly[3] in their last conversation. She was afraid she had used some strong—some contemptuous
expressions in speaking of the clergy, and *that* should not have been.
It was ill-bred—it was wrong. She wished such words unsaid with all
her heart.

Her vexation did not end with the week. All this was bad, but she
had still more to feel when Friday came round again and brought
no Edmund—when Saturday came and still no Edmund—and when,
through the slight communication with the other family which Sunday produced, she learnt that he had actually written home to defer his return, having promised to remain some days longer with his
friend!

If she had felt impatience and regret before—if she had been sorry
for what she said, and feared its too strong effect on him, she now
felt and feared it all tenfold more. She had, moreover, to contend
with one disagreeable emotion entirely new to her—jealousy. His
friend Mr. Owen had sisters.—He might find them attractive. But
at any rate his staying away at a time, when, according to all preceding plans, she was to remove to London, meant something that she
could not bear. Had Henry returned, as he talked of doing, at the
end of three or four days, she should now have been leaving Mansfield. It became absolutely necessary for her to get to Fanny and try
to learn something more. She could not live any longer in such solitary wretchedness; and she made her way to the Park, through difficulties of walking which she had deemed unconquerable a week before, for the chance of hearing a little in addition, for the sake of at
least hearing his name.

The first half hour was lost, for Fanny and Lady Bertram were together, and unless she had Fanny to herself she could hope for nothing. But at last Lady Bertram left the room—and then almost immediately Miss Crawford thus began, with a voice as well regulated as she could—"And how do *you* like your cousin Edmund's staying away so long?—Being the only young person at home, I consider *you* as the greatest sufferer.—You must miss him. Does his staying longer surprize you?"

"I do not know," said Fanny hesitatingly.—"Yes—I had not particularly expected it."

"Perhaps he will always stay longer than he talks of. It is the general way all young men do."

"He did not, the only time he went to see Mr. Owen before."

"He finds the house more agreeable *now*.—He is a very—a very pleasing young man himself, and I cannot help being rather concerned at not seeing him again before I go to London, as will now undoubtedly be the case.—I am looking for Henry every day, and as soon as he comes there will be nothing to detain me at Mansfield. I should like to have seen him once more, I confess. But you must give my compliments to him. Yes—I think it must be compliments. Is not there a something wanted, Miss Price, in our language—a something between compliments and—and love—to suit the sort of friendly acquaintance we have had together?—So many months acquaintance!—But compliments may be sufficient here.— Was his letter a long one?—Does he give you much account of what he is doing?—Is it Christmas gaieties that he is staying for?"

"I only heard a part of the letter; it was to my uncle—but I believe it was very short; indeed I am sure it was but a few lines. All that I heard was that his friend had pressed him to stay longer, and that he had agreed to do so. A *few* days longer, or *some* days longer, I am not quite sure which."

"Oh! if he wrote to his father—But I thought it might have been to Lady Bertram or you. But if he wrote to his father, no wonder he was concise. Who could write chat to Sir Thomas? If he had written to you, there would have been more particulars. You would have heard of balls and parties.—He would have sent you a description of every thing and every body. How many Miss Owens are there?"

"Three grown up."

"Are they musical?"

"I do not at all know. I never heard."

"That is the first question, you know," said Miss Crawford, trying to appear gay and unconcerned, "which every woman who plays herself is sure to ask about another. But it is very foolish to ask questions about any young ladies—about any three sisters just grown up; for one knows, without being told, exactly what they are—all very accomplished and pleasing, and *one* very pretty. There is a beauty in every family.—It is a regular thing. Two play on the piano-forte, and one on the harp—and all sing—or would sing if they were taught—or sing all the better for not being taught—or something like it."

"I know nothing of the Miss Owens," said Fanny calmly.

"You know nothing and you care less, as people say. Never did tone express indifference plainer. Indeed how can one care for those one has never seen?—Well, when your cousin comes back, he will find Mansfield very quiet;—all the noisy ones gone, your brother and mine and myself. I do not like the idea of leaving Mrs. Grant now the time draws near. She does not like my going."

Fanny felt obliged to speak. "You cannot doubt your being missed by many," said she. "You will be very much missed."

Miss Crawford turned her eye on her, as if wanting to hear or see more, and then laughingly said, "Oh! yes, missed as every noisy evil is missed when it is taken away; that is, there is a great difference felt. But I am not fishing; don't compliment me. If I *am* missed, it will appear. I may be discovered by those who want to see me. I shall not be in any doubtful, or distant, or unapproachable region."

Now Fanny could not bring herself to speak, and Miss Crawford was disappointed; for she had hoped to hear some pleasant assurance of her power, from one who she thought must know; and her spirits were clouded again.

"The Miss Owens," said she soon afterwards—"Suppose you were to have one of the Miss Owens settled at Thornton Lacey; how should you like it? Stranger things have happened. I dare say they are trying for it. And they are quite in the right, for it would be a very pretty establishment for them. I do not at all wonder or blame them.—It is every body's duty to do as well for themselves as they can. Sir Thomas Bertram's son is somebody; and now, he is in their own line. Their father is a clergyman and their brother is a clergyman, and they are all clergymen together. He is their lawful property, he fairly belongs to them. You don't speak, Fanny—Miss Price—you don't speak.—But honestly now, do not you rather expect it than otherwise?"

"No," said Fanny stoutly, "I do not expect it at all."

"Not at all!"—cried Miss Crawford with alacrity. "I wonder at that. But I dare say you know exactly—I always imagine you are perhaps you do not think him likely to marry at all—or not at present."

"No, I do not," said Fanny softly hoping she did not err either in the belief or the acknowledgment of it.

Her companion looked at her keenly; and gathering greater spirit from the blush soon produced from such a look, only said, "He is best off as he is," and turned the subject.

# 12

1 The curved carriage drive leading to the house.

MISS CRAWFORD'S UNEASINESS was much lightened by this conversation, and she walked home again in spirits which might have defied almost another week of the same small party in the same bad weather, had they been put to the proof; but as that very evening brought her brother down from London again in quite, or more than quite, his usual cheerfulness, she had nothing further to try her own. His still refusing to tell her what he had gone for, was but the promotion of gaiety; a day before it might have irritated, but now it was a pleasant joke—suspected only of concealing something planned as a pleasant surprize to herself. And the next day *did* bring a surprize to her. Henry had said he should just go and ask the Bertrams how they did, and be back in ten minutes—but he was gone above an hour; and when his sister, who had been waiting for him to walk with her in the garden, met him at last most impatiently in the sweep,[1] and cried out, "My dear Henry, where can you have been all this time?" he had only to say that he had been sitting with Lady Bertram and Fanny.

"Sitting with them an hour and a half!" exclaimed Mary.

But this was only the beginning of her surprize.

"Yes, Mary," said he, drawing her arm within his, and walking along the sweep as if not knowing where he was, "—I could not get away sooner—Fanny looked so lovely!—I am quite determined, Mary. My mind is entirely made up. Will it astonish you? No—You must be aware that I am quite determined to marry Fanny Price."

The surprize was now complete; for in spite of whatever his consciousness might suggest, a suspicion of his having any such views had never entered his sister's imagination; and she looked so truly the astonishment she felt, that he was obliged to repeat what he had said, and more fully and more solemnly. The conviction of his determination once admitted, it was not unwelcome. There was even pleasure with the surprize. Mary was in a state of mind to rejoice in a connection with the Bertram family, and to be not displeased with her brother's marrying a little beneath him.

"Yes, Mary," was Henry's concluding assurance. "I am fairly caught. You know with what idle designs I began—but this is the end of them. I have (I flatter myself) made no inconsiderable progress in her affections; but my own are entirely fixed."

"Lucky, lucky girl!" cried Mary, as soon as she could speak—"what a match for her! My dearest Henry, this must be my *first* feeling; but my *second,* which you shall have as sincerely, is that I approve your choice from my soul, and foresee your happiness as heartily as I wish and desire it. You will have a sweet little wife; all gratitude and devotion. Exactly what you deserve. What an amazing match for her! Mrs. Norris often talks of her luck; what will she say now? The delight of all the family indeed! And she has some *true* friends in it. How *they* will rejoice! But tell me all about it. Talk to me for ever. When did you begin to think seriously about her?"

Nothing could be more impossible than to answer such a question, though nothing could be more agreeable than to have it asked. "How the pleasing plague had stolen on him" he could not say,[2] and before he had expressed the same sentiment with a little variation of words three times over, his sister eagerly interrupted him with, "Ah! my dear Henry, and this is what took you to London! This was your business! You chose to consult the Admiral, before you made up your mind."

But this he stoutly denied. He knew his uncle too well to consult him on any matrimonial scheme. The Admiral hated marriage, and thought it never pardonable in a young man of independent fortune.

"When Fanny is known to him," continued Henry, "he will doat on her. She is exactly the woman to do away every prejudice of such a man as the Admiral, for she is exactly such a woman as he thinks does not exist in the world. She is the very impossibility he would de-

2 The narrator echoes William Whitehead's "The *Je ne Scai Quoi:* A Song," another poem Austen likely first encountered in Robert Dodsley's 1748 anthology *A Collection of Poems by Several Hands* (rpt. London: J. Dodsley, 1765). Its first quatrain reads:

> Yes, I'm in love, I feel it now,
>   And Cælia has undone me;
> And yet I'll swear I can't tell how
>   The pleasing plague stole on me. (p. 318)

scribe—if indeed he has now delicacy of language enough to embody his own ideas. But till it is absolutely settled—settled beyond all interference, he shall know nothing of the matter. No, Mary, you are quite mistaken. You have not discovered my business yet!"

"Well, well, I am satisfied. I know now to whom it must relate, and am in no hurry for the rest. Fanny Price—Wonderful—quite wonderful!—That Mansfield should have done so much for—that *you* should have found your fate in Mansfield! But you are quite right, you could not have chosen better. There is not a better girl in the world, and you do not want for fortune; and as to her connections, they are more than good. The Bertrams are undoubtedly some of the first people in this country. She is niece to Sir Thomas Bertram; that will be enough for the world. But go on, go on. Tell me more. What are your plans? Does she know her own happiness?"

"No."

"What are you waiting for?"

"For—for very little more than opportunity. Mary, she is not like her cousins; but I think I shall not ask in vain."

"Oh! no, you cannot. Were you even less pleasing—supposing her not to love you already, (of which however I can have little doubt,) you would be safe. The gentleness and gratitude of her disposition would secure her all your own immediately. From my soul I do not think she would marry you *without* love; that is, if there is a girl in the world capable of being uninfluenced by ambition, I can suppose it her; but ask her to love you, and she will never have the heart to refuse."

As soon as her eagerness could rest in silence, he was as happy to tell as she could be to listen, and a conversation followed almost as deeply interesting to her as to himself, though he had in fact nothing to relate but his own sensations, nothing to dwell on but Fanny's charms.—Fanny's beauty of face and figure, Fanny's graces of manner and goodness of heart were the exhaustless theme. The gentleness, modesty, and sweetness of her character were warmly expatiated on, that sweetness which makes so essential a part of every woman's worth in the judgment of man, that though he sometimes loves where it is not, he can never believe it absent. Her temper he had good reason to depend on and to praise. He had often seen it tried. Was there one of the family, excepting Edmund, who had not in some way or other continually exercised her patience and forbearance? Her affections were evidently strong. To see her with her brother! What could more delightfully prove that the warmth of her heart was equal to its gentleness?—What could be more encouraging to a man who had her love in view? Then, her understanding was beyond every suspicion, quick and clear; and her manners were the mirror of her own modest and elegant mind. Nor was this all. Henry Crawford had too much sense not to feel the worth of good principles in a wife, though he was too little accustomed to serious reflection to know them by their proper name; but when he talked of her having such a steadiness and regularity of conduct, such a high notion of honour, and such an observance of decorum as might warrant any man in the fullest dependence on her faith and integrity, he expressed what was inspired by the knowledge of her being well principled and religious.

"I could so wholly and absolutely confide in her," said he; "and *that* is what I want."[3]

Well might his sister, believing as she really did that his opinion of Fanny Price was scarcely beyond her merits, rejoice in her prospects.

"The more I think of it," she cried, "the more am I convinced that you are doing quite right, and though I should never have selected Fanny Price as the girl most likely to attach you, I am now persuaded she is the very one to make you happy. Your wicked project upon her peace turns out a clever thought indeed. You will both find your good in it."

"It was bad, very bad in me against such a creature! but I did not know her then. And she shall have no reason to lament the hour that first put it into my head. I will make her very happy, Mary, happier than she has ever yet been herself, or ever seen any body else. I will not take her from Northamptonshire. I shall let Everingham, and rent a place in this neighbourhood—perhaps Stanwix Lodge.[4] I shall let a seven years' lease of Everingham. I am sure of an excellent tenant at half a word. I could name three people now, who would give me my own terms and thank me."

3 With this statement Henry is probably not suggesting that Fanny would be easy to talk with; instead he is declaring his conviction that he could place his trust in her. As Claudia L. Johnson observes, glossing this piece of Henry's dialogue and the passage of narration preceding it, "Henry's dependence on Fanny's steadiness, honor, decorum, faith, and integrity adds up to the singularly important confidence that she will be above the temptation of adultery. However careless he is about violating the domestic sovereignty of another man, Henry has 'too much sense' to omit forfending against this disgrace in his own home, even though he has been taught to consider the disgrace virtually inevitable" (*Jane Austen: Women, Politics, and the Novel* [Chicago: University of Chicago Press, 1988], p. 109).

4 Stanwick is a village in northeast Northamptonshire.

"Ha!" cried Mary, "settle in Northamptonshire! That is pleasant! Then we shall be all together."

When she had spoken it, she recollected herself, and wished it unsaid; but there was no need of confusion, for her brother saw her only as the supposed inmate of Mansfield Parsonage, and replied but to invite her in the kindest manner to his own house, and to claim the best right in her.

"You must give us more than half your time," said he; "I cannot admit Mrs. Grant to have an equal claim with Fanny and myself, for we shall both have a right in you. Fanny will be so truly your sister!"

Mary had only to be grateful and give general assurances; but she was now very fully purposed to be the guest of neither brother nor sister many months longer.

"You will divide your year between London and Northamptonshire?"

"Yes."

"That's right; and in London, of course, a house of your own; no longer with the Admiral. My dearest Henry, the advantage to you of getting away from the Admiral before your manners are hurt by the contagion of his, before you have contracted any of his foolish opinions, or learnt to sit over your dinner, as if it were the best blessing of life!—*You* are not sensible of the gain, for your regard for him has blinded you; but, in my estimation, your marrying early may be the saving of you. To have seen you grow like the Admiral in word or deed, look or gesture, would have broken my heart."

"Well, well, we do not think quite alike here. The Admiral has his faults, but he is a very good man, and has been more than a father to me. Few fathers would have let me have my own way half so much. You must not prejudice Fanny against him. I must have them love one another."

Mary refrained from saying what she felt, that there could not be two persons in existence, whose characters and manners were less accordant; time would discover it to him; but she could not help *this* reflection on the Admiral. "Henry, I think so highly of Fanny Price, that if I could suppose the next Mrs. Crawford would have half the reason which my poor ill used aunt had to abhor the very name, I would prevent the marriage, if possible; but I know you, I know that a wife you *loved* would be the happiest of women, and that even when you ceased to love, she would yet find in you the liberality and good-breeding of a gentleman."

The impossibilty of not doing every thing in the world to make Fanny Price happy, or of ceasing to love Fanny Price, was of course the groundwork of his eloquent answer.

"Had you seen her this morning, Mary," he continued, "attending with such ineffable sweetness and patience, to all the demands of her aunt's stupidity, working with her, and for her, her colour beautifully heightened as she leant over the work, then returning to her seat to finish a note which she was previously engaged in writing for that stupid woman's service, and all this with such unpretending gentleness, so much as if it were a matter of course that she was not to have a moment at her own command, her hair arranged as neatly as it always is, and one little curl falling forward as she wrote, which she now and then shook back, and in the midst of all this, still speaking at intervals to *me,* or listening, and as if she liked to listen to what I said. Had you seen her so, Mary, you would not have implied the possibility of her power over my heart ever ceasing."

"My dearest Henry," cried Mary, stopping short, and smiling in his face, "how glad I am to see you so much in love! It quite delights me. But what will Mrs. Rushworth and Julia say?"

"I care neither what they say, nor what they feel. They will now see what sort of woman it is that can attach me, that can attach a man of sense. I wish the discovery may do them any good. And they will now see their cousin treated as she ought to be, and I wish they may be heartily ashamed of their own abominable neglect and unkindness. They will be angry," he added, after a moment's silence, and in a cooler tone, "Mrs. Rushworth will be very angry. It will be a bitter pill to her; that is, like other bitter pills, it will have two moments ill-flavour, and then be swallowed and forgotten; for I am not such a coxcomb as to suppose her feelings more lasting than other women's, though *I* was the object of them. Yes, Mary, my Fanny will feel a difference indeed, a daily, hourly difference, in the behaviour of every being who approaches her; and it will be the completion of my happiness to know that I am the doer of it, that I am the person to give the consequence so justly her due. Now she is dependent, helpless, friendless, neglected, forgotten."

"Nay, Henry, not by all, not forgotten by all, not friendless or forgotten. Her cousin Edmund never forgets her."

"Edmund—True, I believe he is (generally speaking) kind to her; and so is Sir Thomas in his way, but it is the way of a rich, superior, longworded, arbitrary uncle. What can Sir Thomas and Edmund together do, what *do* they do for her happiness, comfort, honour, and dignity in the world to what I *shall* do?"

# 13

HENRY CRAWFORD WAS AT Mansfield Park again the next morning, and at an earlier hour than common visiting warrants. The two ladies were together in the breakfast-room, and fortunately for him, Lady Bertram was on the very point of quitting it as he entered. She was almost at the door, and not chusing by any means to take so much trouble in vain, she still went on, after a civil reception, a short sentence about being waited for, and a "Let Sir Thomas know," to the servant.

Henry, overjoyed to have her go, bowed and watched her off, and without losing another moment, turned instantly to Fanny, and, taking out some letters said, with a most animated look, "I must acknowledge myself infinitely obliged to any creature who gives me such an opportunity of seeing you alone: I have been wishing it more than you can have any idea. Knowing as I do what your feelings as a sister are, I could hardly have borne that any one in the house should share with you in the first knowledge of the news I now bring. He is made. Your brother is a Lieutenant. I have the infinite satisfaction of congratulating you on your brother's promotion. Here are the letters which announce it, this moment come to hand. You will, perhaps, like to see them."

Fanny could not speak, but he did not want her to speak. To see the expression of her eyes, the change of her complexion, the progress of her feelings, their doubt, confusion, and felicity, was enough. She took the letters as he gave them. The first was from the Admiral

1 This is a humble commission—a sloop was the smallest navy vessel—but it places William Price on the first rung of the navy's promotion ladder. Austen's extended sentence conveys through its convolutions and formal phrasing the labyrinthine nature of the patronage system that Henry has navigated on Fanny's behalf: William's professional advancement has depended on multiple people exploiting personal contacts and calling in favors. "In all these things, in all these transactions with politicians," says a character in Maria Edgeworth's *Patronage,* "there are wheels within wheels, which we simple people never suspect" (*Patronage,* 4 vols. [London: R. Hunter, 1815], Vol. I, p. 233).

to inform his nephew, in a few words, of his having succeeded in the object he had undertaken, the promotion of young Price, and inclosing two more, one from the Secretary of the First Lord to a friend, whom the Admiral had set to work in the business, the other from that friend to himself, by which it appeared that his Lordship had the very great happiness of attending to the recommendation of Sir Charles, that Sir Charles was much delighted in having such an opportunity of proving his regard for Admiral Crawford, and that the circumstance of Mr. William Price's commission as second Lieutenant of H. M. sloop Thrush, being made out, was spreading general joy through a wide circle of great people.[1]

While her hand was trembling under these letters, her eye running from one to the other, and her heart swelling with emotion, Crawford thus continued, with unfeigned eagerness, to express his interest in the event.

"I will not talk of my own happiness," said he, "great as it is, for I think only of yours. Compared with you, who has a right to be happy? I have almost grudged myself my own prior knowledge of what you ought to have known before all the world. I have not lost a moment, however. The post was late this morning, but there has not been since, a moment's delay. How impatient, how anxious, how wild I have been on the subject, I will not attempt to describe; how severely mortified, how cruelly disappointed, in not having it finished while I was in London! I was kept there from day to day in the hope of it, for nothing less dear to me than such an object would have detained me half the time from Mansfield. But though my uncle entered into my wishes with all the warmth I could desire, and exerted himself immediately, there were difficulties from the absence of one friend, and the engagements of another, which at last I could no longer bear to stay the end of, and knowing in what good hands I left the cause, I came away on Monday, trusting that many posts would not pass before I should be followed by such very letters as these. My uncle, who is the very best man in the world, has exerted himself, as I knew he would after seeing your brother. He was delighted with him. I would not allow myself yesterday to say *how* delighted, or to repeat half that the Admiral said in his praise. I deferred it all, till his praise

Thomas Rowlandson's depiction of the interior of the board room at the Admiralty.
It was included in the publisher Rudolph Ackermann's *The Microcosm of London*
(1808), a three-volume book cataloguing the city's important buildings and centers
of power.

should be proved the praise of a friend, as this day *does* prove it. *Now*
I may say that even *I* could not require William Price to excite a
greater interest, or be followed by warmer wishes and higher commendation, than were most voluntarily bestowed by my uncle, after
the evening they had passed together."

"Has this been all *your* doing then?" cried Fanny. "Good Heaven!
how very, very kind! Have you really—was it by *your* desire—I beg
your pardon, but I am bewildered. Did Admiral Crawford apply?—
how was it?—I am stupefied."

Henry was most happy to make it more intelligible, by beginning
at an earlier stage, and explaining very particularly what he had done.
His last journey to London had been undertaken with no other view
than that of introducing her brother in Hill-street, and prevailing on
the Admiral to exert whatever interest he might have for getting him

on. This had been his business. He had communicated it to no creature; he had not breathed a syllable of it even to Mary; while uncertain of the issue, he could not have borne any participation of his
feelings, but this had been his business; and he spoke with such a
glow of what his solicitude had been, and used such strong expressions, was so abounding in the *deepest interest,* in *twofold motives,* in
*views and wishes more than could be told,* that Fanny could not have remained insensible of his drift, had she been able to attend; but her
heart was so full and her senses still so astonished, that she could listen but imperfectly even to what he told her of William, and saying only when he paused, "How kind! how very kind! Oh! Mr. Crawford, we are infinitely obliged to you. Dearest, dearest William!" She
jumped up and moved in haste towards the door, crying out, "I will
go to my uncle. My uncle ought to know it as soon as possible." But
this could not be suffered. The opportunity was too fair, and his feelings too impatient. He was after her immediately. "She must not go,
she must allow him five minutes longer," and he took her hand and
led her back to her seat, and was in the middle of his further explanation, before she had suspected for what she was detained. When she
did understand it, however, and found herself expected to believe
that *she* had created sensations which his heart had never known before, and that every thing he had done for William, was to be placed
to the account of his excessive and unequalled attachment to her,
she was exceedingly distressed, and for some moments unable to
speak. She considered it all as nonsense, as mere trifling and gallantry, which meant only to deceive for the hour; she could not but
feel that it was treating her improperly and unworthily, and in such a
way as she had not deserved; but it was like himself, and entirely of a
piece with what she had seen before; and she would not allow herself
to shew half the displeasure she felt, because he had been conferring
an obligation, which no want of delicacy on his part could make a
trifle to her. While her heart was still bounding with joy and gratitude on William's behalf, she could not be severely resentful of any
thing that injured only herself; and after having twice drawn back
her hand, and twice attempted in vain to turn away from him, she

got up and said only, with much agitation, "Don't, Mr. Crawford, pray don't. I beg you would not. This is a sort of talking which is very unpleasant to me. I must go away. I cannot bear it." But he was still talking on, describing his affection, soliciting a return, and, finally, in words so plain as to bear but one meaning even to *her*, offering himself, hand, fortune, every thing, to her acceptance. It was so; he had said it. Her astonishment and confusion increased; and though still not knowing how to suppose him serious, she could hardly stand. He pressed for an answer.

"No, no, no," she cried, hiding her face. "This is all nonsense. Do not distress me. I can hear no more of this. Your kindness to William makes me more obliged to you than words can express; but I do not want, I cannot bear, I must not listen to such—No, no, don't think of me. But you are *not* thinking of me. I know it is all nothing."

She had burst away from him, and at that moment Sir Thomas was heard speaking to a servant in his way towards the room they were in. It was no time for further assurances or entreaty, though to part with her at a moment when her modesty alone seemed to his sanguine and pre-assured mind to stand in the way of the happiness he sought, was a cruel necessity.[2]—She rushed out at an opposite door from the one her uncle was approaching, and was walking up and down the east room in the utmost confusion of contrary feelings, before Sir Thomas's politeness or apologies were over, or he had reached the beginning of the joyful intelligence, which his visitor came to communicate.

She was feeling, thinking, trembling, about every thing; agitated, happy, miserable, infinitely obliged, absolutely angry. It was all beyond belief! He was inexcusable, incomprehensible!—But such were his habits, that he could do nothing without a mixture of evil. He had previously made her the happiest of human beings, and now he had insulted—she knew not what to say—how to class or how to regard it. She would not have him be serious, and yet what could excuse the use of such words and offers, if they meant but to trifle?

But William was a Lieutenant.—*That* was a fact beyond a doubt and without an alloy. She would think of it for ever and forget all the

2 Henry Crawford's "pre-assured mind" in this scene links him to a character whom he otherwise resembles very little, Mr. Collins of *Pride and Prejudice*, who is similarly ready to dismiss out of hand Elizabeth Bennet's refusal of his addresses and to ascribe that refusal to her modesty. As Collins puts it to Elizabeth, with exasperating complacency, "perhaps you have even now said as much to encourage my suit as would be consistent with the true delicacy of the female character" (I, 19). Presupposing that the proper young woman is too discreet to express her feelings, or may not yet even know them, neither Collins nor Crawford will take no for an answer.

3 As Mary herself underscores, this is the first time she has addressed Fanny by her first name rather than as Miss Price, risking indecorousness in using the more intimate form of address. Her reference to her stumbles over the title "Miss" are meant to imply that manners have hitherto been an obstacle to a natural affection. From this episode on, John Mullan observes, Mary Crawford's "use of Fanny's name [will be] a constant assault on her defences, often in phrases such as 'dear Fanny' or 'Good, gentle, Fanny.'" Unswayed by these blandishments, Fanny will for her part adhere resolutely to "Miss Crawford" (*What Matters in Jane Austen: Twenty Crucial Puzzles Solved* [London: Bloomsbury, 2012], p. 49).

rest. Mr. Crawford would certainly never address her so again: he must have seen how unwelcome it was to her; and in that case, how gratefully she could esteem him for his friendship to William!

She would not stir farther from the east-room than the head of the great staircase, till she had satisfied herself of Mr. Crawford's having left the house; but when convinced of his being gone, she was eager to go down and be with her uncle, and have all the happiness of his joy as well as her own, and all the benefit of his information or his conjectures as to what would now be William's destination. Sir Thomas was as joyful as she could desire, and very kind and communicative; and she had so comfortable a talk with him about William as to make her feel as if nothing had occurred to vex her, till she found towards the close that Mr. Crawford was engaged to return and dine there that very day. This was a most unwelcome hearing, for though *he* might think nothing of what had passed, it would be quite distressing to her to see him again so soon.

She tried to get the better of it, tried very hard as the dinner hour approached, to feel and appear as usual; but it was quite impossible for her not to look most shy and uncomfortable when their visitor entered the room. She could not have supposed it in the power of any concurrence of circumstances to give her so many painful sensations on the first day of hearing of William's promotion.

Mr. Crawford was not only in the room; he was soon close to her. He had a note to deliver from his sister. Fanny could not look at him, but there was no consciousness of past folly in his voice. She opened her note immediately, glad to have any thing to do, and happy as she read it, to feel that the fidgettings of her aunt Norris, who was also to dine there, screened her a little from view.

> "MY DEAR FANNY,—for so I may now always call you, to the infinite relief of a tongue that has been stumbling at *Miss Price* for at least the last six weeks[3]—I cannot let my brother go without sending you a few lines of general congratulation, and giving my most joyful consent and approval.—Go on, my dear Fanny, and without fear; there can be no difficulties

worth naming. I chuse to suppose that the assurance of *my* consent will be something; so, you may smile upon him with your sweetest smiles this afternoon, and send him back to me even happier than he goes.

Yours affectionately,
M. C."

These were not expressions to do Fanny any good; for though she read in too much haste and confusion to form the clearest judgment of Miss Crawford's meaning, it was evident that she meant to compliment her on her brother's attachment and even to *appear* to believe it serious. She did not know what to do, or what to think. There was wretchedness in the idea of its being serious; there was perplexity and agitation every way. She was distressed whenever Mr. Crawford spoke to her, and he spoke to her much too often; and she was afraid there was a something in his voice and manner in addressing her, very different from what they were when he talked to the others. Her comfort in that day's dinner was quite destroyed; she could hardly eat any thing; and when Sir Thomas good humouredly observed, that joy had taken away her appetite, she was ready to sink with shame, from the dread of Mr. Crawford's interpretation; for though nothing could have tempted her to turn her eyes to the right hand where he sat, she felt that *his* were immediately directed towards her.

She was more silent than ever. She would hardly join even when William was the subject, for his commission came all from the right hand too, and there was pain in the connection.

She thought Lady Bertram sat longer than ever, and began to be in despair of ever getting away; but at last they were in the drawing-room, and she was able to think as she would, while her aunts finished the subject of William's appointment in their own style.

Mrs. Norris seemed as much delighted with the saving it would be to Sir Thomas, as with any part of it. "*Now* William would be able to keep himself, which would make a vast difference to his uncle, for it

4 In his biography of his aunt, Austen's nephew reported that at her nephews' and nieces' request Austen would recount "many little particulars about the subsequent careers of some of her people. In this traditionary way we learned that . . . the 'considerable sum' given by Mrs. Norris to William Price was one pound" (J. E. Austen-Leigh, *A Memoir of Jane Austen,* p. 119).

5 Prized for their warmth, lightness, and intricate patterns, cashmere shawls from India were glamorous status symbols, a status they retained even as less expensive equivalents began to be manufactured in Paisley in Scotland and Norwich in England. Lady Bertram would evidently have no compunction about sending William halfway around the world on a hazardous journey to fetch some.

6 Fanny is struggling to sustain her conviction, formed during the private theatricals chronicled in the novel's first volume, that the Crawfords (who in that episode proved the best actors in the group) are the sort of people who speak lovers' vows only in play and that, paradoxically enough, sincerity would be unnatural in them. Henry's serious words and manner, or seemingly serious words and manner, confront Fanny and Austen's readers with a conundrum. In *The Frame of Art* David Marshall identifies that conundrum as follows: should Henry be considered an example of how, as eighteenth-century theories of acting often maintained, "the ideal actor would forget himself and become the part he was playing" (p. 225 n. 18)?

was unknown how much he had cost his uncle; and indeed it would make some difference in *her* presents too. She was very glad that she had given William what she did at parting, very glad indeed that it had been in her power, without material inconvenience just at that time, to give him something rather considerable; that is, for *her*, with *her* limited means, for now it would all be useful in helping to fit up his cabin. She knew he must be at some expense, that he would have many things to buy, though to be sure his father and mother would be able to put him in the way of getting every thing very cheap—but she was very glad that she had contributed her mite towards it."

"I am glad you gave him something considerable," said Lady Bertram, with most unsuspicious calmness—"for *I* gave him only 10*l.*"[4]

"Indeed!" cried Mrs. Norris, reddening. "Upon my word, he must have gone off with his pockets well lined! and at no expense for his journey to London either!"

"Sir Thomas told me 10*l.* would be enough."

Mrs. Norris, being not at all inclined to question its sufficiency, began to take the matter in another point.

"It is amazing," said she, "how much young people cost their friends, what with bringing them up and putting them out in the world! They little think how much it comes to, or what their parents, or their uncles and aunts pay for them in the course of the year. Now, here are my sister Price's children;—take them all together, I dare say nobody would believe what a sum they cost Sir Thomas every year, to say nothing of what *I* do for them."

"Very true, sister, as you say. But, poor things! they cannot help it; and you know it makes very little difference to Sir Thomas. Fanny, William must not forget my shawl, if he goes to the East Indies; and I shall give him a commission for any thing else that is worth having, I wish he may go to the East Indies, that I may have my shawl. I think I will have two shawls, Fanny."[5]

Fanny, meanwhile, speaking only when she could not help it, was very earnestly trying to understand what Mr. and Miss Crawford were at. There was every thing in the world *against* their being serious, but his words and manner. Every thing natural, probable, reasonable was against it; all their habits and ways of thinking, and all her own demerits.—How could *she* have excited serious attachment in a man, who had seen so many, and been admired by so many, and flirted with so many, infinitely her superiors—who seemed so little open to serious impressions, even where pains had been taken to please him—who thought so slightly, so carelessly, so unfeelingly on all such points—who was every thing to every body, and seemed to find no one essential to him?—And further, how could it be supposed that his sister, with all her high and worldly notions of matrimony, would be forwarding any thing of a serious nature in such a quarter? Nothing could be more unnatural in either. Fanny was ashamed of her own doubts.[6] Every thing might be possible rather than serious attachment or serious approbation of it toward her. She had quite convinced herself of this before Sir Thomas and Mr. Crawford joined them. The difficulty was in maintaining the conviction quite so absolutely after Mr. Crawford was in the room; for once or twice a look seemed forced on her which she did not know how to class among the common meaning; in any other man at least, she would have said that it meant something very earnest, very pointed. But she still tried to believe it no more than what he might often have expressed towards her cousins and fifty other women.

She thought he was wishing to speak to her unheard by the rest. She fancied he was trying for it the whole evening at intervals, whenever Sir Thomas was out of the room, or at all engaged with Mrs. Norris, and she carefully refused him every opportunity.

At last—it seemed an at last to Fanny's nervousness, though not remarkably late,—he began to talk of going away; but the comfort of the sound was impaired by his turning to her the next moment, and saying, "Have you nothing to send to Mary? No answer to her note? She will be disappointed if she receives nothing from you. Pray write to her, if it be only a line."

"Oh! yes, certainly," cried Fanny, rising in haste, the haste of embarrassment and of wanting to get away—"I will write directly."

She went accordingly to the table, where she was in the habit of writing for her aunt, and prepared her materials without knowing

*Evening Shawl Dress*

Engraved for the 1st Number of the New Series of La Belle Assemblee Pub. by J. Bell, May 1, 1810.

A fashion plate from an 1810 issue of the ladies' magazine *La Belle Assemblée*. The sort of shawl that Lady Bertram hopes to obtain should William Price be ordered to the East Indies has here been made up as an evening gown.

what in the world to say! She had read Miss Crawford's note only once; and how to reply to any thing so imperfectly understood was most distressing. Quite unpractised in such sort of note-writing, had there been time for scruples and fears as to style, she would have felt them in abundance; but something must be instantly written, and with only one decided feeling, that of wishing not to appear to think any thing really intended, she wrote thus, in great trembling both of spirits and hand:

> "I AM very much obliged to you, my dear Miss Crawford, for your kind congratulations, as far as they relate to my dearest William. The rest of your note I know means nothing; but I am so unequal to any thing of the sort, that I hope you will excuse my begging you to take no further notice. I have seen too much of Mr. Crawford not to understand his manners; if he understood me as well, he would, I dare say, behave differently. I do not know what I write, but it would be a great favour of you never to mention the subject again. With thanks for the honour of your note,
>
> I remain, dear Miss Crawford, &c&c."

The conclusion was scarcely intelligible from increasing fright, for she found that Mr. Crawford, under pretence of receiving the note, was coming towards her.

"You cannot think I mean to hurry you," said he, in an under voice, perceiving the amazing trepidation with which she made up the note; "you cannot think I have any such object. Do not hurry yourself, I entreat."

"Oh! I thank you, I have quite done, just done—it will be ready in a moment—I am very much obliged to you—if you will be so good as to give *that* to Miss Crawford."

The note was held out and must be taken; and as she instantly and with averted eyes walked towards the fireplace, where sat the others, he had nothing to do but to go in good earnest.

Fanny thought she had never known a day of greater agitation, both of pain and pleasure; but happily the pleasure was not of a sort to die with the day—for every day would restore the knowledge of William's advancement, whereas the pain she hoped would return no more. She had no doubt that her note must appear excessively ill-written, that the language would disgrace a child, for her distress had allowed no arrangement; but at least it would assure them both of her being neither imposed on, nor gratified by Mr. Crawford's attentions.

# VOLUME III

# I

Fanny had by no means forgotten Mr. Crawford, when she awoke the next morning; but she remembered the purport of her note, and was not less sanguine, as to its effect, than she had been the night before. If Mr. Crawford would but go away!—That was what she most earnestly desired;—go and take his sister with him, as he was to do, and as he returned to Mansfield on purpose to do. And why it was not done already, she could not devise, for Miss Crawford certainly wanted no delay.—Fanny had hoped, in the course of his yesterday's visit, to hear the day named; but he had only spoken of their journey as what would take place ere long.

Having so satisfactorily settled the conviction her note would convey, she could not but be astonished to see Mr. Crawford, as she accidentally did, coming up to the house again, and at an hour as early as the day before.—His coming might have nothing to do with her, but she must avoid seeing him if possible; and being then in her way up stairs, she resolved there to remain, during the whole of his visit, unless actually sent for; and as Mrs. Norris was still in the house, there seemed little danger of her being wanted.

She sat some time in a good deal of agitation, listening, trembling, and fearing to be sent for every moment; but as no footsteps approached the east room, she grew gradually composed, could sit down, and be able to employ herself, and able to hope that Mr. Crawford had come, and would go without her being obliged to know any thing of the matter.

Nearly half an hour had passed, and she was growing very comfortable, when suddenly the sound of a step in regular approach was heard—a heavy step, an unusual step in that part of the house; it was her uncle's; she knew it as well as his voice; she had trembled at it as often, and began to tremble again, at the idea of his coming up to speak to her, whatever might be the subject.—It was indeed Sir Thomas, who opened the door, and asked if she were there, and if he might come in. The terror of his former occasional visits to that room seemed all renewed, and she felt as if he were going to examine her again in French and English.

She was all attention, however, in placing a chair for him, and trying to appear honoured; and in her agitation, had quite overlooked the deficiencies of her apartment, till he, stopping short as he entered, said, with much surprise, "Why have you no fire to-day?"

There was snow on the ground, and she was sitting in a shawl. She hesitated.

"I am not cold, Sir—I never sit here long at this time of year."

"But,—you have a fire in general?"

"No, sir."

"How comes this about; here must be some mistake. I understood that you had the use of this room by way of making you perfectly comfortable.—In your bed-chamber I know you *cannot* have a fire. Here is some great misapprehension which must be rectified. It is highly unfit for you to sit—be it only half an hour a day, without a fire. You are not strong. You are chilly. Your aunt cannot be aware of this."

Fanny would rather have been silent, but being obliged to speak, she could not forbear, in justice to the aunt she loved best, from saying something in which the words "my aunt Norris" were distinguishable.

"I understand," cried her uncle recollecting himself, and not wanting to hear more—"I understand. Your aunt Norris has always been an advocate, and very judiciously, for young people's being brought up without unnecessary indulgences; but there should be moderation in every thing.—She is also very hardy herself, which of course will influence her in her opinion of the wants of others. And on another account too, I can perfectly comprehend.—I know what her sentiments have always been. The principle was good in itself, but it may have been, and I believe *has been* carried too far in your case.—I am aware that there has been sometimes, in some points, a misplaced distinction; but I think too well of you, Fanny, to suppose you will ever harbour resentment on that account.—You have an understanding, which will prevent you from receiving things only in part, and judging partially by the event.—You will take in the whole of the past, you will consider times, persons, and probabilities, and you will feel that *they* were not least your friends who were educating and preparing you for that mediocrity of condition which *seemed* to be your lot.—Though their caution may prove eventually unnecessary, it was kindly meant; and of this you may be assured, that every advantage of affluence will be doubled by the little privations and restrictions that may have been imposed. I am sure you will not disappoint my opinion of you, by failing at any time to treat your aunt Norris with the respect and attention that are due to her.—But enough of this. Sit down, my dear. I must speak to you for a few minutes, but I will not detain you long."

Fanny obeyed, with eyes cast down and colour rising.—After a moment's pause, Sir Thomas, trying to suppress a smile, went on.

"You are not aware, perhaps, that I have had a visitor this morning.—I had not been long in my own room, after breakfast, when Mr. Crawford was shewn in.—His errand you may probably conjecture."

Fanny's colour grew deeper and deeper; and her uncle perceiving that she was embarrassed to a degree that made either speaking or looking up quite impossible, turned away his own eyes, and without any farther pause, proceeded in his account of Mr. Crawford's visit.

Mr. Crawford's business had been to declare himself the lover of Fanny, make decided proposals for her, and intreat the sanction of the uncle, who seemed to stand in the place of her parents; and he had done it all so well, so openly, so liberally, so properly, that Sir Thomas, feeling, moreover, his own replies, and his own remarks to have been very much to the purpose—was exceedingly happy to give the particulars of their conversation—and, little aware of what was passing in his niece's mind, conceived that by such details he must be gratifying her far more than himself. He talked therefore for several minutes without Fanny's daring to interrupt him.—She had hardly even attained the wish to do it. Her mind was in too much confusion. She had changed her position, and with her eyes fixed intently on one of the windows, was listening to her uncle, in the utmost perturbation and dismay.—For a moment he ceased, but she had barely become conscious of it, when, rising from his chair, he said, "And now, Fanny, having performed one part of my commission, and shewn you every thing placed on a basis the most assured and satisfactory, I may execute the remainder by prevailing on you to accompany me down stairs, where—though I cannot but presume on having been no unacceptable companion myself, I must submit to your finding one still better worth listening to.—Mr. Crawford, as you have perhaps foreseen, is yet in the house. He is in my room, and hoping to see you there."

There was a look, a start, an exclamation, on hearing this, which astonished Sir Thomas; but what was his increase of astonishment on hearing her exclaim—"Oh! no, Sir, I cannot, indeed I cannot go down to him. Mr. Crawford ought to know—he must know that—I told him enough yesterday to convince him—he spoke to me on this subject yesterday—and I told him without disguise that it was very disagreeable to me, and quite out of my power to return his good opinion."

"I do not catch your meaning," said Sir Thomas, sitting down again.—"Out of your power to return his good opinion! what is all this? I know he spoke to you yesterday, and (as far as I understand) received as much encouragement to proceed as a well-judging young woman could permit herself to give. I was very much pleased with what I collected to have been your behaviour on the occasion; it shewed a discretion highly to be commended. But now, when he has made his overtures so properly, and honourably—what are your scruples *now?*"

"You are mistaken, Sir,"—cried Fanny, forced by the anxiety of the moment even to tell her uncle that he was wrong—"You are quite mistaken. How could Mr. Crawford say such a thing? I gave him no encouragement yesterday—On the contrary, I told him—I cannot recollect my exact words—but I am sure I told him that I would not listen to him, that it was very unpleasant to me in every respect, and that I begged him never to talk to me in that manner again.—I am sure I said as much as that and more; and I should have said still more,—if I had been quite certain of his meaning any thing seriously, but I did not like to be—I could not bear to be—imputing more than might be intended. I thought it might all pass for nothing with *him*."

She could say no more; her breath was almost gone.

"Am I to understand," said Sir Thomas, after a few moments silence, "that you mean to *refuse* Mr. Crawford?"

"Yes, Sir."

"Refuse him?"

"Yes, Sir."

"Refuse Mr. Crawford! Upon what plea? For what reason?"

"I—I cannot like him, Sir, well enough to marry him."

"This is very strange!" said Sir Thomas, in a voice of calm displeasure. "There is something in this which my comprehension does not reach. Here is a young man wishing to pay his addresses to you, with every thing to recommend him; not merely situation in life, fortune, and character, but with more than common agreeableness, with address and conversation pleasing to every body. And he is not an acquaintance of to-day, you have now known him some time. His sister, moreover, is your intimate friend, and he has been doing *that* for your brother, which I should suppose would have been almost sufficient recommendation to you, had there been no other. It is very uncertain when my interest might have got William on. He has done it already."

"Yes," said Fanny, in a faint voice, and looking down with fresh shame; and she did feel almost ashamed of herself, after such a picture as her uncle had drawn, for not liking Mr. Crawford.

"You must have been aware," continued Sir Thomas, presently, "you must have been some time aware of a particularity in Mr. Crawford's manners to you. This cannot have taken you by surprise. You must have observed his attentions; and though you always received

1 As she registers how Fanny's body appears divided against itself to Sir Thomas's inspecting eye, Austen associates her protagonist with a long line of heroines whose blushes seem double signs. Blushing may indicate youthful innocence, but it registers other sorts of inner states as well, including a guilty conscience. In the chapter of Maria Edgeworth's *Belinda* (1801) that is tellingly titled "Rights of Woman," for example, Belinda Portman is forced to listen abashed and tongue-tied as other characters debate whether the glow visible on her face speaks for or against her: is she embarrassed, they wonder, because she doesn't understand their conversation or because she does? (See *Belinda* [London: Everyman, 1993], pp. 216–217). At the start of the eighteenth century, Richard Steele had in *The Spectator* no. 390 (May 28, 1712) sketched a character named Orbicilla, a young woman who *has* reasons to blush, or so he concludes. In that essay Steele calls the blush that "ambiguous Suffusion which is the livery both of guilt and innocence" (*The Spectator*, 5 vols., ed. Donald F. Bond [Oxford: Oxford University Press, 2014], vol. 3 [Oxford Scholarly Editions Online]).

them very properly (I have no accusation to make on that head), I never perceived them to be unpleasant to you. I am half inclined to think, Fanny, that you do not quite know your own feelings."

"Oh! yes, Sir, indeed I do. His attentions were always—what I did not like."

Sir Thomas looked at her with deeper surprise. "This is beyond me," said he. "This requires explanation. Young as you are, and having seen scarcely any one, it is hardly possible that your affections——"

He paused and eyed her fixedly. He saw her lips formed into a *no,* though the sound was inarticulate, but her face was like scarlet. That, however, in so modest a girl might be very compatible with innocence;[1] and chusing at least to appear satisfied, he quickly added, "No, no, I know *that* is quite out of the question—quite impossible. Well, there is nothing more to be said."

And for a few minutes he did say nothing. He was deep in thought. His niece was deep in thought likewise, trying to harden and prepare herself against farther questioning. She would rather die than own the truth, and she hoped by a little reflection to fortify herself beyond betraying it.

"Independently of the interest which Mr. Crawford's *choice* seemed to justify," said Sir Thomas, beginning again, and very composedly, "his wishing to marry at all so early is recommendatory to me. I am an advocate for early marriages, where there are means in proportion, and would have every young man, with a sufficient income, settle as soon after four-and-twenty as he can. This is so much my opinion, that I am sorry to think how little likely my own eldest son, your cousin, Mr. Bertram, is to marry early; but at present, as far as I can judge, matrimony makes no part of his plans or thoughts. I wish he were more likely to fix." Here was a glance at Fanny. "Edmund I consider from his dispositions and habits as much more likely to marry early than his brother. *He,* indeed, I have lately thought has seen the woman he could love, which, I am convinced, my eldest son has not. Am I right? Do you agree with me, my dear?"

"Yes, Sir."

It was gently, but it was calmly said, and Sir Thomas was easy on the score of the cousins. But the removal of his alarm did his niece no service; as her unaccountableness was confirmed, his displeasure increased; and getting up and walking about the room, with a frown, which Fanny could picture to herself, though she dared not lift up her eyes, he shortly afterwards, and in a voice of authority, said, "Have you any reason, child, to think ill of Mr. Crawford's temper?"

"No, Sir."

She longed to add, "but of his principles I have;" but her heart sunk under the appalling prospect of discussion, explanation, and probably non-conviction. Her ill opinion of him was founded chiefly on observations, which, for her cousins' sake,[2] she could scarcely dare mention to their father. Maria and Julia—and especially Maria, were so closely implicated in Mr. Crawford's misconduct, that she could not give his character, such as she believed it, without betraying them. She had hoped that to a man like her uncle, so discerning, so honourable, so good, the simple acknowledgment of settled *dislike* on her side, would have been sufficient. To her infinite grief she found it was not.

Sir Thomas came towards the table where she sat in trembling wretchedness, and with a good deal of cold sternness, said, "It is of no use, I perceive, to talk to you. We had better put an end to this most mortifying conference. Mr. Crawford must not be kept longer waiting. I will, therefore, only add, as thinking it my duty to mark my opinion of your conduct—that you have disappointed every expectation I had formed, and proved yourself of a character the very reverse of what I had supposed. For I *had,* Fanny, as I think my behaviour must have shewn, formed a very favourable opinion of you from the period of my return to England. I had thought you peculiarly free from wilfulness of temper, self-conceit, and every tendency to that independence of spirit, which prevails so much in modern days, even in young women, and which in young women is offensive and disgusting beyond all common offence.[3] But you have now shewn me that you can be wilful and perverse, that you can and will decide for yourself, without any consideration or deference for those who have surely some right to guide you—without even asking their ad-

2 Both the 1814 and 1816 editions have Fanny keeping silent for her "cousin's sake" but that seems to misplace the apostrophe. As the sentence that follows indicates, Fanny's fear is that *neither* of his two daughters has acted in a way Sir Thomas will approve.

3 In identifying insubordination as characteristic of his times, Sir Thomas echoes conservative moralists like Hannah More, who in *Strictures on the Modern System of Female Education* deplored how the French revolution had impacted domestic life and produced, as she said, a "revolutionary spirit in families": "Who can forbear observing and regretting in a variety of instances, that not only sons but daughters have adopted something of that spirit of independence, and disdain of control which characterise the times?" (*Works of Hannah More*, vol. 1, p. 399).

vice. You have shewn yourself very, very different from any thing that I had imagined. The advantage or disadvantage of your family—of your parents—your brothers and sisters—never seems to have had a moment's share in your thoughts on this occasion. How *they* might be benefited, how *they* must rejoice in such an establishment for you—is nothing to *you*. You think only of yourself; and because you do not feel for Mr. Crawford exactly what a young, heated fancy imagines to be necessary for happiness, you resolve to refuse him at once, without wishing even for a little time to consider of it—a little more time for cool consideration, and for really examining your own inclinations—and are, in a wild fit of folly, throwing away from you such an opportunity of being settled in life, eligibly, honourably, nobly settled, as will, probably, never occur to you again. Here is a young man of sense, of character, of temper, of manners, and of fortune, exceedingly attached to you, and seeking your hand in the most handsome and disinterested way; and let me tell you, Fanny, that you may live eighteen years longer in the world, without being addressed by a man of half Mr. Crawford's estate, or a tenth part of his merits. Gladly would I have bestowed either of my own daughters on him. Maria is nobly married—but had Mr. Crawford sought Julia's hand, I should have given it to him with superior and more heartfelt satisfaction than I gave Maria's to Mr. Rushworth." After half a moment's pause—"And I should have been very much surprised had either of my daughters, on receiving a proposal of marriage at any time, which might carry with it only *half* the eligibility of *this,* immediately and peremptorily, and without paying my opinion or my regard the compliment of any consultation, put a decided negative on it. I should have been much surprised, and much hurt, by such a proceeding. I should have thought it a gross violation of duty and respect. *You* are not to be judged by the same rule. You do not owe me the duty of a child. But, Fanny, if your heart can acquit you of *ingratitude*—"

He ceased. Fanny was by this time crying so bitterly, that angry as he was, he would not press that article farther. Her heart was almost broke by such a picture of what she appeared to him; by such accusations, so heavy, so multiplied, so rising in dreadful gradation! Self-willed, obstinate, selfish, and ungrateful. He thought her all this. She had deceived his expectations; she had lost his good opinion. What was to become of her?

"I am very sorry," said she inarticulately through her tears, "I am very sorry indeed."

"Sorry! yes, I hope you are sorry; and you will probably have reason to be long sorry for this day's transactions."

"If it were possible for me to do otherwise," said she with another strong effort, "but I am so perfectly convinced that I could never make him happy, and that I should be miserable myself."

Another burst of tears; but in spite of that burst, and in spite of that great black word *miserable,* which served to introduce it, Sir Thomas began to think a little relenting, a little change of inclination, might have something to do with it; and to augur favourably from the personal intreaty of the young man himself. He knew her to be very timid, and exceedingly nervous; and thought it not improbable that her mind might be in such a state, as a little time, a little pressing, a little patience, and a little impatience, a judicious mixture of all on the lover's side, might work their usual effect on. If the gentleman would but persevere, if he had but love enough to persevere—Sir Thomas began to have hopes; and these reflections having passed across his mind and cheered it, "Well," said he, in a tone of becoming gravity, but of less anger, "well, child, dry up your tears. There is no use in these tears; they can do no good. You must now come down stairs with me. Mr. Crawford has been kept waiting too long already. You must give him your own answer; we cannot expect him to be satisfied with less; and you only can explain to him the grounds of that misconception of your sentiments, which, unfortunately for himself, he certainly has imbibed. I am totally unequal to it."

But Fanny shewed such reluctance, such misery, at the idea of going down to him, that Sir Thomas, after a little consideration, judged it better to indulge her. His hopes from both gentleman and lady suffered a small depression in consequence; but when he looked at his niece, and saw the state of feature and complexion which her crying had brought her into, he thought there might be as much lost as gained by an immediate interview. With a few words,

4 Likely the gravel paths through the shrubbery, where the snow might have been cleared or have melted away.

therefore, of no particular meaning, he walked off by himself, leaving his poor niece to sit and cry over what had passed, with very wretched feelings.

Her mind was all disorder. The past, present, future, every thing was terrible. But her uncle's anger gave her the severest pain of all. Selfish and ungrateful! to have appeared so to him! She was miserable for ever. She had no one to take her part, to counsel, or speak for her. Her only friend was absent. He might have softened his father; but all, perhaps all, would think her selfish and ungrateful. She might have to endure the reproach again and again; she might hear it, or see it, or know it to exist for ever in every connection about her. She could not but feel some resentment against Mr. Crawford; yet, if he really loved her, and were unhappy too!—it was all wretchedness together.

In about a quarter of an hour her uncle returned; she was almost ready to faint at the sight of him. He spoke calmly, however, without austerity, without reproach, and she revived a little. There was comfort too in his words, as well as his manner, for he began with, "Mr. Crawford is gone; he has just left me. I need not repeat what has passed. I do not want to add to any thing you may now be feeling, by an account of what he has felt. Suffice it, that he has behaved in the most gentleman-like and generous manner; and has confirmed me in a most favourable opinion of his understanding, heart, and temper. Upon my representation of what you were suffering, he immediately, and with the greatest delicacy, ceased to urge to see you for the present."

Here Fanny, who had looked up, looked down again. "Of course," continued her uncle, "it cannot be supposed but that he should request to speak with you alone, be it only for five minutes; a request too natural, a claim too just to be denied. But there is no time fixed, perhaps to-morrow, or whenever your spirits are composed enough. For the present you have only to tranquillize yourself. Check these tears; they do but exhaust you. If, as I am willing to suppose, you wish to shew me any observance, you will not give way to these emotions, but endeavour to reason yourself into a stronger frame of mind. I advise you to go out, the air will do you good; go out for an hour on the gravel,[4] you will have the shrubbery to yourself and will be the better for air and exercise. And, Fanny, (turning back again for a moment) I shall make no mention below of what has passed; I shall not even tell your aunt Bertram. There is no occasion for spreading the disappointment; say nothing about it yourself."

This was an order to be most joyfully obeyed; this was an act of kindness which Fanny felt at her heart. To be spared from her aunt Norris's interminable reproaches!—he left her in a glow of gratitude. Any thing might be bearable rather than such reproaches. Even to see Mr. Crawford would be less overpowering.

She walked out directly as her uncle recommended, and followed his advice throughout, as far as she could; did check her tears, did earnestly try to compose her spirits, and strengthen her mind. She wished to prove to him that she did desire his comfort, and sought to regain his favour; and he had given her another strong motive for exertion, in keeping the whole affair from the knowledge of her aunts. Not to excite suspicion by her look or manner was now an object worth attaining; and she felt equal to almost any thing that might save her from her aunt Norris.

She was struck, quite struck, when on returning from her walk, and going into the east room again, the first thing which caught her eye was a fire lighted and burning. A fire! it seemed too much; just at that time to be giving her such an indulgence, was exciting even painful gratitude. She wondered that Sir Thomas could have leisure to think of such a trifle again; but she soon found, from the voluntary information of the housemaid, who came in to attend it, that so it was to be every day. Sir Thomas had given orders for it.

"I must be a brute indeed, if I can be really ungrateful!" said she in soliloquy; "Heaven defend me from being ungrateful!"

She saw nothing more of her uncle, nor of her aunt Norris, till they met at dinner. Her uncle's behaviour to her was then as nearly as possible what it had been before; she was sure he did not mean there should be any change, and that it was only her own conscience that could fancy any; but her aunt was soon quarrelling with her: and when she found how much and how unpleasantly her having only walked out without her aunt's knowledge could be dwelt on, she felt all the reason she had to bless the kindness which saved her from the same spirit of reproach, exerted on a more momentous subject.

"If I had known you were going out, I should have got you just to go as far as my house with some orders for Nanny," said she, "which I have since, to my very great inconvenience, been obliged to go and carry myself. I could very ill spare the time, and you might have saved me the trouble, if you would only have been so good as to let us know you were going out. It would have made no difference to you, I suppose, whether you had walked in the shrubbery, or gone to my house."

"I recommended the shrubbery to Fanny as the dryest place," said Sir Thomas.

"Oh," said Mrs. Norris with a moment's check, "that was very kind of you, Sir Thomas; but you do not know how dry the path is to my house. Fanny would have had quite as good a walk there, I assure you; with the advantage of being of some use, and obliging her aunt: it is all her fault. If she would but have let us know she was going out—but there is a something about Fanny, I have often observed it before,—she likes to go her own way to work; she does not like to be dictated to; she takes her own independent walk whenever she can; she certainly has a little spirit of secrecy, and independence, and nonsense, about her, which I would advise her to get the better of."

As a general reflection on Fanny, Sir Thomas thought nothing could be more unjust, though he had been so lately expressing the same sentiments himself, and he tried to turn the conversation; tried repeatedly before he could succeed; for Mrs. Norris had not discernment enough to perceive, either now, or at any other time, to what degree he thought well of his niece, or how very far he was from wishing to have his own children's merits set off by the depreciation of hers. She was talking *at* Fanny, and resenting this private walk half through the dinner.

It was over, however, at last; and the evening set in with more composure to Fanny, and more cheerfulness of spirits than she could have hoped for after so stormy a morning; but she trusted, in the first place, that she had done right, that her judgment had not misled her; for the purity of her intentions she could answer; and she was willing to hope, secondly, that her uncle's displeasure was abating, and would abate farther as he considered the matter with more impartiality, and felt, as a good man must feel, how wretched, and how unpardonable, how hopeless and how wicked it was, to marry without affection.

When the meeting with which she was threatened for the morrow was past, she could not but flatter herself that the subject would be finally concluded, and Mr. Crawford once gone from Mansfield, that every thing would soon be as if no such subject had existed. She would not, could not believe, that Mr. Crawford's affection for her could distress him long; his mind was not of that sort. London would soon bring its cure. In London he would soon learn to wonder at his infatuation, and be thankful for the right reason in her, which had saved him from its evil consequences.

While Fanny's mind was engaged in these sort of hopes, her uncle was soon after tea called out of the room; an occurrence too common to strike her, and she thought nothing of it till the butler reappeared ten minutes afterwards, and advancing decidedly towards herself, said, "Sir Thomas wishes to speak with you, Ma'am, in his own room." Then it occurred to her what might be going on; a suspicion rushed over her mind which drove the colour from her cheeks; but instantly rising, she was preparing to obey, when Mrs. Norris called out, "Stay, stay, Fanny! what are you about?—where are you going?—don't be in such a hurry. Depend upon it, it is not you that are wanted; depend upon it it is me; (looking at the butler) but you are so very eager to put yourself forward. What should Sir Thomas want you for? It is me, Baddeley, you mean; I am coming this moment. You mean me, Baddeley, I am sure; Sir Thomas wants me, not Miss Price."

But Baddeley was stout. "No, Ma'am, it is Miss Price I am certain of its being Miss Price." And there was a half-smile with the words which meant, "I do not think *you* would answer the purpose at all."

Mrs. Norris, much discontented, was obliged to compose herself to work again; and Fanny, walking off in agitating consciousness, found herself, as she anticipated, in another minute alone with Mr. Crawford.

# 2

THE CONFERENCE WAS NEITHER so short, nor so conclusive, as the lady had designed. The gentleman was not so easily satisfied. He had all the disposition to persevere that Sir Thomas could wish him. He had vanity, which strongly inclined him, in the first place, to think she did love him, though she might not know it herself; and which, secondly, when constrained at last to admit that she did know her own present feelings, convinced him that he should be able in time to make those feelings what he wished.

He was in love, very much in love; and it was a love which, operating on an active, sanguine spirit, of more warmth than delicacy, made her affection appear of greater consequence, because it was withheld, and determined him to have the glory, as well as the felicity, of forcing her to love him.

He would not despair: he would not desist. He had every well grounded reason for solid attachment; he knew her to have all the worth that could justify the warmest hopes of lasting happiness with her; her conduct at this very time, by speaking the disinterestedness and delicacy of her character (qualities which he believed most rare indeed), was of a sort to heighten all his wishes, and confirm all his resolutions. He knew not that he had a pre-engaged heart to attack. Of *that*, he had no suspicion. He considered her rather as one who had never thought on the subject enough to be in danger; who had been guarded by youth, a youth of mind as lovely as of person; whose modesty had prevented her from understanding his attentions, and who was still overpowered by the suddenness of addresses so wholly unexpected, and the novelty of a situation which her fancy had never taken into account.

Must it not follow of course, that, when he was understood, he should succeed?—he believed it fully. Love such as his, in a man like himself, must with perseverance secure a return, and at no great distance; and he had so much delight in the idea of obliging her to love him in a very short time, that her not loving him now was scarcely regretted. A little difficulty to be overcome, was no evil to Henry Crawford. He rather derived spirits from it. He had been apt to gain hearts too easily. His situation was new and animating.

To Fanny, however, who had known too much opposition all her life, to find any charm in it, all this was unintelligible. She found that he did mean to persevere; but how he could, after such language from her as she felt herself obliged to use, was not to be understood. She told him, that she did not love him, could not love him, was sure she never should love him: that such a change was quite impossible, that the subject was most painful to her, that she must intreat him never to mention it again, to allow her to leave him at once, and let it be considered as concluded for ever. And when farther pressed, had added, that in her opinion their dispositions were so totally dissimilar, as to make mutual affection incompatible; and that they were unfitted for each other by nature, education, and habit. All this she had said, and with the earnestness of sincerity; yet this was not enough, for he immediately denied there being anything uncongenial in their characters, or anything unfriendly in their situations; and positively declared, that he would still love, and still hope!

Fanny knew her own meaning, but was no judge of her own manner. Her manner was incurably gentle, and she was not aware how much it concealed the sternness of her purpose. Her diffidence, gratitude, and softness, made every expression of indifference seem almost an effort of self-denial; seem at least, to be giving nearly as much pain to herself as to him. Mr. Crawford was no longer the Mr. Crawford who, as the clandestine, insidious, treacherous admirer of Maria Bertram, had been her abhorrence, whom she had hated to see or to speak to, in whom she could believe no good quality to exist, and whose power, even of being agreeable, she had barely acknowl-

1 The syntax that simulates Fanny's agitated thoughts becomes sufficiently compressed here that many editors of *Mansfield Park* have suspected some corruption of the text, though this wording appears in both the 1814 and the 1816 editions of the novel. Mary Lascelles suggested in 1966, for instance, that "how always" was a misreading for "now as always" and that the passage should be emended to read "And, alas! now as always no known principle to supply as a duty what the heart was deficient in." For Kathryn Sutherland, however, such emendations are symptomatic of modern editors' tendency to underestimate Austen's willingness to experiment with syntax and her interest in rendering the very rhythms of thought in print. To "read the passage aright," Sutherland states, "one must listen to Fanny Price's inner monologue . . . whose irregularly yet insistently repeated structures, *heard* rather than merely seen and read, shape her thoughts and clarify the text" (*Jane Austen's Textual Lives* [Oxford: Oxford University Press, 2005], p. 298).

edged. He was now the Mr. Crawford who was addressing herself with ardent, disinterested, love; whose feelings were apparently become all that was honourable and upright, whose views of happiness were all fixed on a marriage of attachment; who was pouring out his sense of her merits, describing and describing again his affection, proving, as far as words could prove it, and in the language, tone, and spirit of a man of talent too, that he sought her for her gentleness, and her goodness; and to complete the whole, he was now the Mr. Crawford who had procured William's promotion!

Here was a change! and here were claims which could not but operate. She might have disdained him in all the dignity of angry virtue, in the grounds of Sotherton, or the theatre at Mansfield Park; but he approached her now with rights that demanded different treatment. She must be courteous, and she must be compassionate. She must have a sensation of being honoured, and whether thinking of herself or her brother, she must have a strong feeling of gratitude. The effect of the whole was a manner so pitying and agitated, and words intermingled with her refusal so expressive of obligation and concern, that to a temper of vanity and hope like Crawford's, the truth, or at least the strength of her indifference, might well be questionable; and he was not so irrational as Fanny considered him, in the professions of persevering, assiduous, and not desponding attachment which closed the interview.

It was with reluctance that he suffered her to go, but there was no look of despair in parting to bely his words, or give her hopes of his being less unreasonable than he professed himself.

Now she was angry. Some resentment did arise at a perseverance so selfish and ungenerous. Here was again a want of delicacy and regard for others which had formerly so struck and disgusted her. Here was again a something of the same Mr. Crawford whom she had so reprobated before. How evidently was there a gross want of feeling and humanity where his own pleasure was concerned—And, alas! how always known no principle to supply as a duty what the heart was deficient in.[1] Had her own affections been as free—as perhaps they ought to have been—he never could have engaged them.

So thought Fanny in good truth and sober sadness, as she sat musing over that too great indulgence and luxury of a fire upstairs—wondering at the past and present, wondering at what was yet to come, and in a nervous agitation which made nothing clear to her but the persuasion of her being never under any circumstances able to love Mr. Crawford, and the felicity of having a fire to sit over and think of it.

Sir Thomas was obliged or obliged himself to wait till the morrow for a knowledge of what had passed between the young people. He then saw Mr. Crawford, and received his account.—The first feeling was disappointment: he had hoped better things; he had thought that an hour's intreaty from a young man like Crawford could not have worked so little change on a gentle tempered girl like Fanny; but there was speedy comfort in the determined views and sanguine perseverance of the lover; and when seeing such confidence of success in the principal, Sir Thomas was soon able to depend on it himself.

Nothing was omitted, on his side, of civility, compliment, or kindness, that might assist the plan. Mr. Crawford's steadiness was honoured, and Fanny was praised, and the connection was still the most desirable in the world. At Mansfield Park Mr. Crawford would always be welcome; he had only to consult his own judgment and feelings as to the frequency of his visits, at present or in future. In all his niece's family and friends there could be but one opinion, one wish on the subject; the influence of all who loved her must incline one way.

Every thing was said that could encourage, every encouragement received with grateful joy, and the gentlemen parted the best of friends.

Satisfied that the cause was now on a footing the most proper and hopeful, Sir Thomas resolved to abstain from all farther importunity with his niece, and to shew no open interference. Upon her disposition he believed kindness might be the best way of working. Intreaty should be from one quarter only. The forbearance of her family on a point, respecting which she could be in no doubt of their wishes, might be their surest means of forwarding it. Accordingly, on this

2 *Wonderful* as used here is a synonym for astonishing.

principle Sir Thomas took the first opportunity of saying to her, with a mild gravity, intended to be overcoming, "Well, Fanny, I have seen Mr. Crawford again, and learn from him exactly how matters stand between you. He is a most extraordinary young man, and whatever be the event, you must feel that you have created an attachment of no common character; though, young as you are, and little acquainted with the transient, varying, unsteady nature of love, as it generally exists, you cannot be struck as I am with all that is wonderful in a perseverance of this sort,[2] against discouragement. With him, it is entirely a matter of feeling; he claims no merit in it, perhaps is entitled to none. Yet, having chosen so well, his constancy has a respectable stamp. Had his choice been less unexceptionable, I should have condemned his persevering."

"Indeed, Sir," said Fanny, "I am very sorry that Mr. Crawford should continue to— —I know that it is paying me a very great compliment, and I feel most undeservedly honoured, but I am so perfectly convinced, and I have told him so, that it never will be in my power—"

"My dear," interrupted Sir Thomas, "there is no occasion for this. Your feelings are as well known to me, as my wishes and regrets must be to you. There is nothing more to be said or done. From this hour, the subject is never to be revived between us. You will have nothing to fear, or to be agitated about. You cannot suppose me capable of trying to persuade you to marry against your inclinations. Your happiness and advantage are all that I have in view, and nothing is required of you but to bear with Mr. Crawford's endeavours to convince you, that they may not be incompatible with his. He proceeds at his own risk. You are on safe ground. I have engaged for your seeing him whenever he calls, as you might have done, had nothing of this sort occurred. You will see him with the rest of us, in the same manner, and as much as you can, dismissing the recollection of every thing unpleasant. He leaves Northamptonshire so soon, that even this slight sacrifice cannot be often demanded. The future must be very uncertain. And now, my dear Fanny, this subject is closed between us."

The promised departure was all that Fanny could think of with much satisfaction. Her uncle's kind expressions, however, and forbearing manner, were sensibly felt; and when she considered how much of the truth was unknown to him, she believed she had no right to wonder at the line of conduct he pursued. He who had married a daughter to Mr. Rushworth. Romantic delicacy was certainly not to be expected from him. She must do her duty, and trust that time might make her duty easier than it now was.

She could not, though only eighteen, suppose Mr. Crawford's attachment would hold out for ever; she could not but imagine that steady, unceasing discouragement from herself would put an end to it in time. How much time she might, in her own fancy, allot for its dominion, is another concern. It would not be fair to enquire into a young lady's exact estimate of her own perfections.

In spite of his intended silence, Sir Thomas found himself once more obliged to mention the subject to his niece, to prepare her briefly for its being imparted to her aunts; a measure which he would still have avoided, if possible, but which became necessary from the totally opposite feelings of Mr. Crawford, as to any secrecy of proceeding. He had no idea of concealment. It was all known at the parsonage, where he loved to talk over the future with both his sisters; and it would be rather gratifying to him to have enlightened witnesses of the progress of his success. When Sir Thomas understood this, he felt the necessity of making his own wife and sister-in-law acquainted with the business without delay; though on Fanny's account, he almost dreaded the effect of the communication to Mrs. Norris as much as Fanny herself. He deprecated her mistaken, but well-meaning zeal. Sir Thomas, indeed, was, by this time, not very far from classing Mrs. Norris as one of those well-meaning people, who are always doing mistaken and very disagreeable things.

Mrs. Norris, however, relieved him. He pressed for the strictest forbearance and silence towards their niece; she not only promised, but did observe it. She only looked her increased ill-will. Angry she was, bitterly angry; but she was more angry with Fanny for having received such an offer, than for refusing it. It was an injury and af-

3 To humble or demoralize.

4 Compare the rule of conduct that Mary Crawford sets out in a conversation with Mrs. Grant and Henry in the novel's fourth chapter: "every body should marry as soon as they can do it to advantage."

front to Julia, who ought to have been Mr. Crawford's choice; and, independently of that, she disliked Fanny, because she had neglected her; and she would have grudged such an elevation to one whom she had been always trying to depress.[3]

Sir Thomas gave her more credit for discretion on the occasion than she deserved; and Fanny could have blessed her for allowing her only to see her displeasure, and not to hear it.

Lady Bertram took it differently. She had been a beauty, and a prosperous beauty, all her life; and beauty and wealth were all that excited her respect. To know Fanny to be sought in marriage by a man of fortune, raised her, therefore, very much in her opinion. By convincing her that Fanny *was* very pretty, which she had been doubting about before, and that she would be advantageously married, it made her feel a sort of credit in calling her niece.

"Well, Fanny," said she, as soon as they were alone together afterwards,—and she really had known something like impatience, to be alone with her, and her countenance, as she spoke, had extraordinary animation—"Well, Fanny, I have had a very agreeable surprise this morning. I must just speak of it *once,* I told Sir Thomas I must *once,* and then I shall have done. I give you joy, my dear niece."—And looking at her complacently, she added, "Humph—We certainly are a handsome family!"

Fanny coloured, and doubted at first what to say; when hoping to assail her on her vulnerable side, she presently answered—

"My dear aunt, *you* cannot wish me to do differently from what I have done, I am sure. *You* cannot wish me to marry; for you would miss me, should not you?—Yes, I am sure you would miss me too much for that."

"No, my dear, I should not think of missing you, when such an offer as this comes in your way. I could do very well without you, if you were married to a man of such good estate as Mr. Crawford. And you must be aware, Fanny, that it is every young woman's duty to accept such a very unexceptionable offer as this."[4]

This was almost the only rule of conduct, the only piece of advice, which Fanny had ever received from her aunt in the course of eight years and a half.—It silenced her. She felt how unprofitable contention would be. If her aunt's feelings were against her, nothing could be hoped from attacking her understanding. Lady Bertram was quite talkative.

"I will tell you what, Fanny," said she—"I am sure he fell in love with you at the ball, I am sure the mischief was done that evening. You did look remarkably well. Every body said so. Sir Thomas said so. And you know you had Chapman to help you to dress. I am very glad I sent Chapman to you. I shall tell Sir Thomas that I am sure it was done that evening."—And still pursuing the same cheerful thoughts, she soon afterwards added, "And I will tell you what, Fanny—which is more than I did for Maria—the next time pug has a litter you shall have a puppy."[5]

5 In Chap. 7 of Vol. I Lady Bertram's pug was a "he." Perhaps this is a successor, also called Pug?

With slightly comic effects, Thomas Wootton's mid-eighteenth-century oil painting, known by the title *A Pug in a Landscape,* gives its little lapdog subject the sort of artistic treatment that Wootton customarily reserved for thoroughbred stallions.

# 3

EDMUND HAD GREAT THINGS to hear on his return. Many surprises were awaiting him. The first that occurred was not least in interest—the appearance of Henry Crawford and his sister walking together through the village, as he rode into it.—He had concluded,—he had meant them to be far distant. His absence had been extended beyond a fortnight purposely to avoid Miss Crawford. He was returning to Mansfield with spirits ready to feed on melancholy remembrances, and tender associations, when her own fair self was before him, leaning on her brother's arm; and he found himself receiving a welcome, unquestionably friendly, from the woman whom, two moments before, he had been thinking of as seventy miles off, and as farther, much farther, from him in inclination than any distance could express.

Her reception of him was of a sort which he could not have hoped for, had he expected to see her. Coming as he did from such a purport fulfilled as had taken him away,[1] he would have expected any thing rather than a look of satisfaction, and words of simple, pleasant meaning. It was enough to set his heart in a glow, and to bring him home in the properest state for feeling the full value of the other joyful surprises at hand.

William's promotion, with all its particulars, he was soon master of; and with such a secret provision of comfort within his own breast to help the joy, he found in it a source of most gratifying sensation, and unvarying cheerfulness all dinner-time.

1 Since he has just now come back from his ordination, having fulfilled the *purpose* or *purport* of his Christmastime journey from Mansfield in undergoing that ceremony, Edmund does not expect a warm welcome from Miss Crawford.

After dinner, when he and his father were alone, he had Fanny's history; and then all the great events of the last fortnight, and the present situation of matters at Mansfield were known to him.

Fanny suspected what was going on. They sat so much longer than usual in the dining parlour, that she was sure they must be talking of her; and when tea at last brought them away, and she was to be seen by Edmund again, she felt dreadfully guilty. He came to her, sat down by her, took her hand, and pressed it kindly; and at that moment she thought that, but for the occupation and the scene which the tea-things afforded, she must have betrayed her emotion in some unpardonable excess.

He was not intending, however, by such action, to be conveying to her that unqualified approbation and encouragement which her hopes drew from it. It was designed only to express his participation in all that interested her, and to tell her that he had been hearing what quickened every feeling of affection. He was, in fact, entirely on his father's side of the question. His surprise was not so great as his father's, at her refusing Crawford, because, so far from supposing her to consider him with anything like a preference, he had always believed it to be rather the reverse, and could imagine her to be taken perfectly unprepared, but Sir Thomas could not regard the connection as more desirable than he did. It had every recommendation to him, and while honouring her for what she had done under the influence of her present indifference, honouring her in rather stronger terms than Sir Thomas could quite echo, he was most earnest in hoping, and sanguine in believing, that it would be a match at last, and that, united by mutual affection, it would appear that their dispositions were as exactly fitted to make them blessed in each other, as he was now beginning seriously to consider them. Crawford had been too precipitate. He had not given her time to attach herself. He had begun at the wrong end. With such powers as his, however, and such a disposition as hers, Edmund trusted that every thing would work out a happy conclusion. Meanwhile, he saw enough of Fanny's embarrassment to make him scrupulously guard against exciting it a second time, by any word, or look, or movement.

From *The British Theatre,* the multivolume anthology of plays that Elizabeth Inchbald edited in 1808: Charles Heath's frontispiece for *Henry VIII*.

2 The name that Lady Bertram forgets in this paragraph is probably that of Cardinal Wolsey—but (since Lady Bertram's memory is not all it should be) it may be Shakespeare's. The play in question is *Henry VIII,* now thought to have been written jointly by Shakespeare and John Fletcher, a depiction of court intrigue in the period in the sixteenth century in which Henry VIII, with the assistance of his advisor Cardinal Wolsey, divorces his first queen, Katherine of Aragon, in order to wed his second, Anne Boleyn. Dramatizing through this historical episode the origins of England's national church, and doing so with a good deal of pageantry, *Henry VIII* was one of the most popular dramas in the eighteenth-century repertory. Austen's choice of this particular play seems apt on several counts. She would not want readers to miss the resemblance linking Henry Crawford to his namesake, the king whose philandering made history. And Fanny might see herself in Queen Katherine: starting in 1783, Sarah Siddons's performances of that role transformed a drama that had formerly been understood mainly as a story of male ambition and rivalry into one of romantic-period Britain's most influential representations of female virtue in distress.

3 The particular scene of the play whose reading Henry and Edmund have interrupted is likely the one in the third act depicting the fall of Wolsey (a role played for years by Siddons's brother John Philip Kemble). Wolsey has previously been seen engineering the downfall of the pious queen: through Act II, and especially in the scene in which he summons Katherine to a public courtroom, he has pressured her to declare her long marriage to the king an illegal and incestuous sham and warned her darkly of the effects that will follow from any disobedience to the king's will. Katherine has, nonetheless, steadfastly adhered to the truth as she sees it. In Act III, scene 2, Wolsey, knowing that he too has now lost the king's favor, expresses remorse in terms suggesting that he is suddenly able to participate in her patient trust in providence: "I know myself now," says Wolsey to his deputy Thomas Cromwell, "and I feel within me/A peace above all earthly dignities,/A still and quiet conscience" (III, ii, 379–381). Perhaps their encounter with this speech lies be

Crawford called the next day, and on the score of Edmund's return, Sir Thomas felt himself more than licensed to ask him to stay dinner; it was really a necessary compliment. He staid of course, and Edmund had then ample opportunity for observing how he sped with Fanny, and what degree of immediate encouragement for him might be extracted from her manners; and it was so little, so very very little, (every chance, every possibility of it, resting upon her embarrassment only, if there was not hope in her confusion, there was hope in nothing else,) that he was almost ready to wonder at his friend's perseverance.—Fanny was worth it all; he held her to be worth every effort of patience, every exertion of mind—but he did not think he could have gone on himself with any woman breathing, without something more to warm his courage than his eyes could discern in hers. He was very willing to hope that Crawford saw clearer; and this was the most comfortable conclusion for his friend that he could come to from all that he observed to pass before, and at, and after dinner.

In the evening a few circumstances occurred which he thought more promising. When he and Crawford walked into the drawing-room, his mother and Fanny were sitting as intently and silently at work as if there were nothing else to care for. Edmund could not help noticing their apparently deep tranquillity.

"We have not been so silent all the time," replied his mother. "Fanny has been reading to me, and only put the book down upon hearing you coming."—And sure enough there was a book on the table which had the air of being very recently closed, a volume of Shakespeare.—"She often reads to me out of those books; and she was in the middle of a very fine speech of that man's—What's his name, Fanny?—when we heard your footsteps."[2]

Crawford took the volume. "Let me have the pleasure of finishing that speech to your ladyship," said he. "I shall find it immediately." And by carefully giving way to the inclination of the leaves, he did find it, or within a page or two, quite near enough to satisfy Lady Bertram, who assured him, as soon as he mentioned the name of Cardinal Wolsey, that he had got the very speech.[3]—Not a look, or an offer of help had Fanny given; not a syllable for or against. All her attention was for her work. She seemed determined to be interested by nothing else. But taste was too strong in her. She could not abstract her mind five minutes; she was forced to listen; his reading was capital, and her pleasure in good reading extreme. To *good* reading, however, she had been long used; her uncle read well—her cousins all—Edmund very well; but in Mr. Crawford's reading there was a variety of excellence beyond what she had ever met with. The King, the Queen, Buckingham, Wolsey, Cromwell, all were given in turn; for with the happiest knack, the happiest power of jumping and guessing, he could always light, at will, on the best scene, or the best speeches of each; and whether it were dignity or pride, or tenderness or remorse, or whatever were to be expressed, he could do it with equal beauty.—It was truly dramatic.—His acting had first taught Fanny what pleasure a play might give, and his reading brought all his acting before her again; nay, perhaps with greater enjoyment, for it came unexpectedly, and with no such drawback as she had been used to suffer in seeing him on the stage with Miss Bertram.

Edmund watched the progress of her attention, and was amused and gratified by seeing how she gradually slackened in the needlework, which, at the beginning, seemed to occupy her totally; how it fell from her hand while she sat motionless over it—and at last, how the eyes which had appeared so studiously to avoid him throughout the day were turned and fixed on Crawford, fixed on him for minutes, fixed on him in short till the attraction drew Crawford's upon her, and the book was closed, and the charm was broken. Then, she was shrinking again into herself, and blushing and working as hard as ever; but it had been enough to give Edmund encouragement for his friend, and as he cordially thanked him, he hoped to be expressing Fanny's secret feelings too.

"That play must be a favourite with you," said he; "You read as if you knew it well."

"It will be a favourite I believe from this hour," replied Crawford; —"but I do not think I have had a volume of Shakespeare in my hand before, since I was fifteen.—I once saw Henry the 8th acted.—Or I have heard of it from somebody who did—I am not certain which. But Shakespeare one gets acquainted with without knowing how. It

hind the "deep tranquillity" Austen's narrator has just ascribed to Fanny and her aunt. Also notable, though, is the structural resemblance between this chapter of *Mansfield Park* and the earlier scene of *Henry VIII* (III, i) in which Wolsey and his fellow cardinal, Campeius, break in on Katherine and her ladies-in-waiting while they are at their needlework and proceed to give the unwilling Katherine the advice they claim she requires. In this chapter Edmund and Henry may tacitly hold similarly coercive aims when they walk in on an all-female group who sit "intently and silent at work."

Richard Westall's 1795 painting *Wolsey Disgraced,* depicting Act III, scene 2 of *Henry VIII,* was first exhibited in John Boydell's Shakespeare Gallery in London. Scholars have suggested that Austen likely visited this exhibition of paintings representing Shakespearean scenes during the trip to London she took in 1796.

4 Unlike her contemporaries Ann Radcliffe and Walter Scott, Austen avoided using snippets of Shakespeare's works as epigraphs to open her novels' chapters. Nonetheless she might teasingly be challenging her audience to find Shakespeare's celebrated passages—and not only from *Henry VIII*—in the book *we* have just opened. Readers have often discerned echoes of *King Lear,* for example, in *Mansfield Park:* the "nothings" that have in the chapters opening Volume III of the novel punctuated both Fanny's dialogue and the narrator's account of her thoughts might link Fanny to Lear's daughter Cordelia, another young woman accused of ingratitude who cannot feign a feeling she does not feel. "Nothing will come of nothing," Lear warns Cordelia, after she refuses to speak and to enter the competition her father has staged to discover which of his daughters loves him the most (I, i, 88).

The actor John Philip Kemble (1757–1823) in the role of Cardinal Wolsey, whose fall from power *Henry VIII* traces.

is a part of an Englishman's constitution. His thoughts and beauties are so spread abroad that one touches them every where, one is intimate with him by instinct.—No man of any brain can open at a good part of one of his plays, without falling into the flow of his meaning immediately."

"No doubt, one is familiar with Shakespeare in a degree," said Edmund, "from one's earliest years. His celebrated passages are quoted by every body; they are in half the books we open,[4] and we all talk Shakespeare, use his similies, and describe with his descriptions; but this is totally distinct from giving his sense as you gave it. To know him in bits and scraps is common enough; to know him pretty thoroughly, is, perhaps, not uncommon; but to read him well aloud, is no everyday talent."

"Sir, you do me honour;" was Crawford's answer, with a bow of mock gravity.

Both gentlemen had a glance at Fanny, to see if a word of accordant praise could be extorted from her; yet both feeling that it could not be. Her praise had been given in her attention; *that* must content them.

Lady Bertram's admiration was expressed, and strongly too. "It was really like being at a play," said she.—"I wish Sir Thomas had been here."

Crawford was excessively pleased.—If Lady Bertram, with all her incompetency and languor, could feel this, the inference of what her niece, alive and enlightened as she was, must feel, was elevating.

"You have a great turn for acting, I am sure, Mr. Crawford," said her Ladyship soon afterwards—"and I will tell you what, I think you will have a theatre, some time or other, at your house in Norfolk. I mean when you are settled there. I do, indeed. I think you will fit up a theatre at your house in Norfolk."

"Do you, Ma'am?" cried he with quickness. "No, no, that will never be. Your Ladyship is quite mistaken. No theatre at Everingham! Oh! no."—And he looked at Fanny with an expressive smile, which evidently meant, "that lady will never allow a theatre at Everingham."

Edmund saw it all, and saw Fanny so determined *not* to see it, as to make it clear that the voice was enough to convey the full meaning

Late-nineteenth-century engraving of an 1817 painting by George Harlow, *The Trial of Queen Katherine*. Rendering Act II, scene 4 of *Henry VIII* in paint, Harlow also memorializes the performances of the play that took place at Covent Garden between 1806 and 1812 and which featured members of the Kemble family. John Philip Kemble in the part of Wolsey is shown seated on the left, while his sister, Sarah Siddons (1755–1831), dominates center stage.

This portrait print of Sarah Siddons in the role of Queen Katherine is based on George Harlow's 1817 painting. By the early nineteenth century Katherine had come to be seen as an archetype of the virtuous heroine in distress.

of the protestation; and such a quick consciousness of compliment, such a ready comprehension of a hint, he thought, was rather favourable than not.

The subject of reading aloud was farther discussed. The two young men were the only talkers, but they, standing by the fire, talked over the too common neglect of the qualification, the total inattention to it, in the ordinary school-system for boys, the consequently natural, yet in some instances almost unnatural, degree of ignorance and uncouthness of men, of sensible and well-informed men, when suddenly called to the necessity of reading aloud, which had fallen within their notice, giving instances of blunders, and failures with their secondary causes, the want of management of the voice, of proper modulation and emphasis, of foresight and judgment, all proceeding from the first cause, want of early attention and habit; and Fanny was listening again with great entertainment.

"Even in my profession"—said Edmund with a smile—"how lit-

5 With this mention of a "spirit of improvement," Edmund is often thought to be registering the growing influence of evangelicalism within the Church of England, but he might also be referencing the effects of late eighteenth-century Britain's elocution movement: a movement that aimed to regenerate the public speaking of the nation and in particular to improve the speaking that Anglican clergymen did from their pulpits. "The church service," declared Thomas Sheridan, a leader of that movement, "according as it is either well or ill administered, must excite great emotions, or set people to sleep" (*British Education: Or, The Source of the Disorders of Great Britain* [Dublin: George Faulkner, 1756], p. 68). Commentators prior to Sheridan had insistently traced the frequently soporific style of Anglican preachers to the emphasis that the school curriculum in England placed on Latin and Greek; boys trained up in what Edmund has just called the "ordinary school-system" were too prone, it was said, to see themselves as "above English" (or so Richard Steele put it in *Spectator* no. 147 on August 18, 1711: see *The Spectator*, 5 vols., ed. Donald F. Bond [Oxford: Oxford University Press, 2014], vol. 2 [Oxford Scholarly Editions Online]).

6 The liturgy is the order of services that comprise Anglican worship, read out by the minister as he leads the congregation.

Most of these services are reproduced in Thomas Sheridan's *Lectures on the Art of Reading* (2nd ed., London: C. Dilly, J. Dodsley, and T. Evans, 1781), punctuated with the markings Sheridan uses to indicate where a reader's emphasis should fall and where and for how long he should pause. Sheridan aims, in improving clergymen's oral delivery, to improve the worshippers' understanding of the service and heighten their emotional response to it. However, Sheridan also sounds worried that services led by those who have studied his techniques will seem excessively scripted, and as he concludes this section suggests it would be best if clergymen, as soon as "they shall have made themselves masters of the right manner of reading" committed the prayers to memory: "it is impossible whilst the eye is on the book that the heart can be upward" (p. 186). Such questions about rituals' repeti-

tle the art of reading has been studied! how little a clear manner, and good delivery, have been attended to! I speak rather of the past, however, than the present.—There is now a spirit of improvement abroad; but among those who were ordained twenty, thirty, forty years ago, the larger number, to judge by their performance, must have thought reading was reading, and preaching was preaching.[5] It is different now. The subject is more justly considered. It is felt that distinctness and energy may have weight in recommending the most solid truths; and, besides, there is more general observation and taste, a more critical knowledge diffused, than formerly; in every congregation, there is a larger proportion who know a little of the matter, and who can judge and criticize."

Edmund had already gone through the service once since his ordination; and upon this being understood, he had a variety of questions from Crawford as to his feelings and success; questions which being made—though with the vivacity of friendly interest and quick taste—without any touch of that spirit of banter or air of levity which Edmund knew to be most offensive to Fanny, he had true pleasure in satisfying; and when Crawford proceeded to ask his opinion and give his own as to the properest manner in which particular passages in the service should be delivered, shewing it to be a subject on which he had thought before, and thought with judgment, Edmund was still more and more pleased. This would be the way to Fanny's heart. She was not to be won by all that gallantry and wit, and good nature together, could do; or at least, she would not be won by them nearly so soon, without the assistance of sentiment and feeling, and seriousness on serious subjects.

"Our liturgy," observed Crawford, "has beauties, which not even a careless, slovenly style of reading can destroy; but it has also redundancies and repetitions, which require good reading not to be felt.[6] For myself, at least, I must confess being not always so attentive as I ought to be—(here was a glance at Fanny) that nineteen times out of twenty I am thinking how such a prayer ought to be read, and longing to have it to read myself—Did you speak?" stepping eagerly to Fanny, and addressing her in a softened voice; and upon her saying, "No," he added, "Are you sure you did not speak? I saw your lips

move. I fancied you might be going to tell me I *ought* to be more attentive, and not *allow* my thoughts to wander. Are not you going to
tell me so?"

"No, indeed, you know your duty too well for me to—even supposing—"

She stopt, felt herself getting into a puzzle, and could not be prevailed on to add another word, not by dint of several minutes of supplication and waiting. He then returned to his former station, and
went on as if there had been no such tender interruption.

"A sermon, well delivered, is more uncommon even than prayers
well read. A sermon, good in itself, is no rare thing. It is more difficult to speak well than to compose well; that is, the rules and trick of
composition are oftener an object of study. A thoroughly good sermon, thoroughly well delivered, is a capital gratification. I can never
hear such a one without the greatest admiration and respect, and
more than half a mind to take orders and preach myself. There is
something in the eloquence of the pulpit, when it is really eloquence,
which is entitled to the highest praise and honour. The preacher who
can touch and affect such an heterogeneous mass of hearers, on subjects limited, and long worn thread-bare in all common hands; who
can say any thing new or striking, any thing that rouses the attention, without offending the taste, or wearing out the feelings of his
hearers, is a man whom one could not (in his public capacity) honour
enough. I should like to be such a man."

Edmund laughed.

"I should indeed. I never listened to a distinguished preacher in
my life, without a sort of envy.[7] But then, I must have a London audience. I could not preach, but to the educated; to those who were
capable of estimating my composition. And I do not know that I
should be fond of preaching often; now and then, perhaps, once or
twice in the spring, after being anxiously expected for half a dozen
Sundays together; but not for a constancy; it would not do for a constancy."

Here Fanny, who could not but listen, involuntarily shook her
head, and Crawford was instantly by her side again, intreating to
know her meaning; and as Edmund perceived, by his drawing in a

tions and their effect on the sincerity of the Anglican's
devotions were important in Austen's own circle, a sig-
nificance underlined when curators at the Jane Austen
House Museum in Chawton discovered a scrap of paper on which in 1814 Austen appears to have copied out
a sermon by her brother James. The text reads: "Men
may get into a habit of repeating the words of our
Prayers by rote, perhaps without thoroughly understanding—certainly without thoroughly feeling their
full force & meaning."

7 This is the second time we have seen Henry envying
the man who has a profession. William Price's visit to
Mansfield Park had a similar effect on him.

*The Sleeping Congregation,* by William Hogarth, engraved 1736: a humorous depiction of the soporific
effect created when the priest who gives the sermon
has failed to study the art of reading aloud.

8 Early nineteenth-century newspapers were blanketed with advertisements, often, as here, for real estate, educational establishments, and horses. The front page of the issue of the *Times* that on June 22, 1815, announced to Britain the news of Wellington's victory at the Battle of Waterloo displays nothing but advertising, rows upon rows of it, in minuscule print. The victory is announced only on page 2.

Page from Thomas Sheridan's *Lectures on the Art of Reading*. Sheridan has annotated the text of the liturgy so as to indicate the proper places for emphases and pauses when it is read aloud.

chair, and sitting down close by her, that it was to be a very thorough attack, that looks and undertones were to be well tried, he sank as quietly as possible into a corner, turned his back, and took up a newspaper, very sincerely wishing that dear little Fanny might be persuaded into explaining away that shake of the head to the satisfaction of her ardent lover; and as earnestly trying to bury every sound of the business from himself in murmurs of his own, over the various advertisements of "a most desirable estate in South Wales"—"To Parents and Guardians"—and a "Capital season'd Hunter."[8]

Fanny, meanwhile, vexed with herself for not having been as motionless as she was speechless, and grieved to the heart to see Edmund's arrangements, was trying, by every thing in the power of her modest gentle nature, to repulse Mr. Crawford, and avoid both his looks and enquiries; and he unrepulsable was persisting in both.

"What did that shake of the head mean?" said he. "What was it meant to express? Disapprobation, I fear. But of what?—What had I been saying to displease you?—Did you think me speaking improperly?—lightly, irreverently on the subject?—Only tell me if I was. Only tell me if I was wrong. I want to be set right. Nay, nay, I entreat you; for one moment put down your work. What did that shake of the head mean?"

In vain was her "Pray, Sir, don't—pray, Mr. Crawford," repeated twice over; and in vain did she try to move away—In the same low eager voice, and the same close neighbourhood, he went on, re-urging the same questions as before. She grew more agitated and displeased.

"How can you, Sir? You quite astonish me—I wonder how you can"—

"Do I astonish you?"—said he. "Do you wonder? Is there any thing in my present intreaty that you do not understand? I will explain to you instantly all that makes me urge you in this manner, all that gives me an interest in what you look and do, and excites my present curiosity. I will not leave you to wonder long."

In spite of herself, she could not help half a smile, but she said nothing.

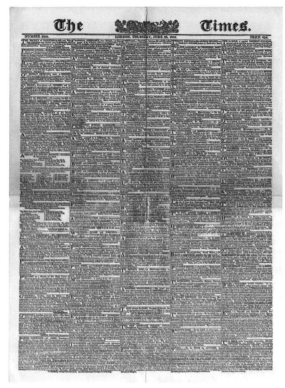

Front page of the June 22, 1815, edition of *The Times* newspaper: the reader is confronted by scores of advertisements, with the news of the day pushed to page 2.

"You shook your head at my acknowledging that I should not like to engage in the duties of a clergyman always for a constancy. Yes, that was the word. Constancy, I am not afraid of the word. I would spell it, read it, write it with any body. I see nothing alarming in the word. Did you think I ought?"

"Perhaps, Sir," said Fanny, wearied at last into speaking—"perhaps, Sir, I thought it was a pity you did not always know yourself as well as you seemed to do at that moment."

Crawford, delighted to get her to speak at any rate, was determined to keep it up; and poor Fanny, who had hoped to silence him by such an extremity of reproof, found herself sadly mistaken, and that it was only a change from one object of curiosity and one set of words to another. He had always something to intreat the explanation of. The opportunity was too fair. None such had occurred since his seeing her in her uncle's room, none such might occur again

9 In using her first name Henry is acting as though Fanny had already accepted his proposal. In *Sense and Sensibility* Elinor Dashwood overhears Willoughby foregoing the title "Miss" and addressing her sister as "Marianne": "From that moment she doubted not of their being engaged to each other" (I, 12).

before his leaving Mansfield. Lady Bertram's being just on the other side of the table was a trifle, for she might always be considered as only half awake, and Edmund's advertisements were still of the first utility.

"Well," said Crawford, after a course of rapid questions and reluctant answers—"I am happier than I was, because I now understand more clearly your opinion of me. You think me unsteady—easily swayed by the whim of the moment—easily tempted—easily put aside. With such an opinion, no wonder that——But we shall see.—It is not by protestations that I shall endeavour to convince you I am wronged, it is not by telling you that my affections are steady. My conduct shall speak for me—absence, distance, time shall speak for me.—*They* shall prove, that as far as you can be deserved by any body, I do deserve you.—You are infinitely my superior in merit; all *that* I know.—You have qualities which I had not before supposed to exist in such a degree in any human creature. You have some touches of the angel in you, beyond what—not merely beyond what one sees, because one never sees any thing like it—but beyond what one fancies might be. But still I am not frightened. It is not by equality of merit that you can be won. That is out of the question. It is he who sees and worships your merit the strongest, who loves you most devotedly, that has the best right to a return. There I build my confidence. By that right I do and will deserve you; and when once convinced that my attachment is what I declare it, I know you too well not to entertain the warmest hopes—Yes, dearest, sweetest Fanny[9]—Nay—(seeing her draw back displeased) forgive me. Perhaps I have as yet no right—but by what other name can I call you? Do you suppose you are ever present to my imagination under any other? No, it is 'Fanny' that I think of all day, and dream of all night.—You have given the name such reality of sweetness, that nothing else can now be descriptive of you."

Fanny could hardly have kept her seat any longer, or have refrained from at least trying to get away in spite of all the too public opposition she foresaw to it, had it not been for the sound of approaching relief, the very sound which she had been long watching for, and long thinking strangely delayed.

The solemn procession, headed by Baddely, of tea-board,[10] urn, and cake-bearers, made its appearance, and delivered her from a grievous imprisonment of body and mind. Mr. Crawford was obliged to move. She was at liberty, she was busy, she was protected.

Edmund was not sorry to be admitted again among the number of those who might speak and hear. But though the conference had seemed full long to him, and though on looking at Fanny he saw rather a flush of vexation, he inclined to hope that so much could not have been said and listened to, without some profit to the speaker.

10 Tea-tray.

# 4

EDMUND HAD DETERMINED that it belonged entirely to Fanny to chuse whether her situation with regard to Crawford should be mentioned between them or not; and that if she did not lead the way, it should never be touched on by him; but after a day or two of mutual reserve, he was induced by his father to change his mind, and try what his influence might do for his friend.

A day, and a very early day, was actually fixed for the Crawfords' departure; and Sir Thomas thought it might be as well to make one more effort for the young man before he left Mansfield, that all his professions and vows of unshaken attachment might have as much hope to sustain them as possible.

Sir Thomas was most cordially anxious for the perfection of Mr. Crawford's character in that point. He wished him to be a model of constancy; and fancied the best means of effecting it would be by not trying him too long.

Edmund was not unwilling to be persuaded to engage in the business; he wanted to know Fanny's feelings. She had been used to consult him in every difficulty, and he loved her too well to bear to be denied her confidence now; he hoped to be of service to her, he thought he must be of service to her, whom else had she to open her heart to? If she did not need counsel, she must need the comfort of communication. Fanny estranged from him, silent and reserved, was an unnatural state of things; a state which he must break through, and which he could easily learn to think she was wanting him to break through.

"I will speak to her, Sir; I will take the first opportunity of speaking to her alone," was the result of such thoughts as these;[1] and upon Sir Thomas's information of her being at that very time walking alone in the shrubbery, he instantly joined her.

"I am come to walk with you, Fanny," said he. "Shall I?"—(drawing her arm within his,) "it is a long while since we have had a comfortable walk together."

She assented to it all rather by look than word. Her spirits were low.

"But, Fanny," he presently added, "in order to have a comfortable walk, something more is necessary than merely pacing this gravel together. You must talk to me. I know you have something on your mind. I know what you are thinking of. You cannot suppose me uninformed. Am I to hear of it from every body but Fanny herself?"

Fanny, at once agitated and dejected, replied, "If you hear of it from every body, cousin, there can be nothing for me to tell."

"Not of facts, perhaps; but of feelings, Fanny. No one but you can tell me them. I do not mean to press you, however. If it is not what you wish yourself, I have done. I had thought it might be a relief."

"I am afraid we think too differently, for me to find any relief in talking of what I feel."

"Do you suppose that we think differently? I have no idea of it. I dare say, that on a comparison of our opinions, they would be found as much alike as they have been used to be: to the point—I consider Crawford's proposals as most advantageous and desirable, if you could return his affection. I consider it as most natural that all your family should wish you could return it; but that as you cannot, you have done exactly as you ought in refusing him. Can there be any disagreement between us here?"

"Oh no! But I thought you blamed me. I thought you were against me. This is such a comfort!"

"This comfort you might have had sooner, Fanny, had you sought it. But how could you possibly suppose me against you? How could you imagine me an advocate for marriage without love? Were I even careless in general on such matters, how could you imagine me so where *your* happiness was at stake?"

1 Commentators often state that Austen, scrupulous in writing only what she knew, deliberately avoided including in her fiction scenes in which only men were present, but *Mansfield Park* represents the exception to this rule. Its readers are positioned so that we more than once listen in on the man-to-man consultations, like this one, that take place between Sir Thomas and his younger son, consultations which have Fanny as their subject but from which she is absent. John Mullan observes that "it is in *Mansfield Park* alone that Austen gives us these accumulated glimpses of men together, as if respecting the Bertrams' aristocratic delusion that all important decisions are made by a father and his sons" (*What Matters in Jane Austen,* p 186)

"My uncle thought me wrong, and I knew he had been talking to you."

"As far as you have gone, Fanny, I think you perfectly right. I may be sorry, I may be surprised—though hardly *that,* for you had not had time to attach yourself; but I think you perfectly right. Can it admit of a question? It is disgraceful to us if it does. You did not love him—nothing could have justified your accepting him."

Fanny had not felt so comfortable for days and days.

"So far your conduct has been faultless, and they were quite mistaken who wished you to do otherwise. But the matter does not end here. Crawford's is no common attachment; he perseveres, with the hope of creating that regard which had not been created before. This, we know, must be a work of time. But (with an affectionate smile), let him succeed at last, Fanny, let him succeed at last. You have proved yourself upright and disinterested, prove yourself grateful and tender-hearted; and then you will be the perfect model of a woman, which I have always believed you born for."

"Oh! never, never, never; he never will succeed with me." And she spoke with a warmth which quite astonished Edmund, and which she blushed at the recollection of herself, when she saw his look, and heard him reply, "Never, Fanny, so very determined and positive! This is not like yourself, your rational self."

"I mean," she cried, sorrowfully, correcting herself, "that I *think,* I never shall, as far as the future can be answered for—I think I never shall return his regard."

"I must hope better things. I am aware, more aware than Crawford can be, that the man who means to make you love him (you having due notice of his intentions), must have very up-hill work, for there are all your early attachments, and habits, in battle array; and before he can get your heart for his own use, he has to unfasten it from all the holds upon things animate and inanimate, which so many years growth have confirmed, and which are considerably tightened for the moment by the very idea of separation. I know that the apprehension of being forced to quit Mansfield will for a time be arming you against him. I wish he had not been obliged to tell you what he was trying for. I wish he had known you as well as I do, Fanny. Between us, I think we should have won you. My theoretical and his practical knowledge together, could not have failed. He should have worked upon my plans. I must hope, however, that time proving him (as I firmly believe it will), to deserve you by his steady affection, will give him his reward. I cannot suppose that you have not the *wish* to love him—the natural wish of gratitude. You must have some feeling of that sort. You must be sorry for your own indifference."

"We are so totally unlike," said Fanny, avoiding a direct answer, "we are so very, very different in all our inclinations and ways, that I consider it as quite impossible we should ever be tolerably happy together, even if I *could* like him. There never were two people more dissimilar. We have not one taste in common. We should be miserable."

"You are mistaken, Fanny. The dissimilarity is not so strong. You are quite enough alike. You *have* tastes in common. You have moral and literary tastes in common. You have both warm hearts and benevolent feelings; and Fanny, who that heard him read, and saw you listen to Shakespeare the other night, will think you unfitted as companions? You forget yourself: there is a decided difference in your tempers, I allow.[2] He is lively, you are serious; but so much the better; his spirits will support yours. It is your disposition to be easily dejected, and to fancy difficulties greater than they are. His cheerfulness will counteract this. He sees difficulties no where; and his pleasantness and gaiety will be a constant support to you. Your being so far unlike, Fanny, does not in the smallest degree make against the probability of your happiness together: do not imagine it. I am myself convinced that it is rather a favourable circumstance. I am perfectly persuaded that the tempers had better be unlike; I mean unlike in the flow of the spirits, in the manners, in the inclination for much or little company, in the propensity to talk or to be silent, to be grave or to be gay. Some opposition here is, I am thoroughly convinced, friendly to matrimonial happiness. I exclude extremes of course; and a very close resemblance in all those points would be the likeliest way to produce an extreme. A counteraction, gentle and continual, is the best safeguard of manners and conduct."

2  "Tempers" here carries the sense of *temperaments*.

Full well could Fanny guess where his thoughts were now. Miss Crawford's power was all returning. He had been speaking of her cheerfully from the hour of his coming home. His avoiding her was quite at an end. He had dined at the parsonage only the preceding day.

After leaving him to his happier thoughts for some minutes, Fanny feeling it due to herself, returned to Mr. Crawford, and said, "It is not merely in *temper* that I consider him as totally unsuited to myself; though in *that* respect, I think the difference between us too great, infinitely too great; his spirits often oppress me—but there is something in him which I object to still more. I must say, cousin, that I cannot approve his character. I have not thought well of him from the time of the play. I then saw him behaving, as it appeared to me, so very improperly and unfeelingly, I may speak of it now because it is all over—so improperly by poor Mr. Rushworth, not seeming to care how he exposed or hurt him, and paying attentions to my cousin Maria, which—in short, at the time of the play, I received an impression which will never be got over."

"My dear Fanny," replied Edmund, scarcely hearing her to the end, "let us not, any of us, be judged by what we appeared at that period of general folly. The time of the play, is a time which I hate to recollect. Maria was wrong, Crawford was wrong, we were all wrong together; but none so wrong as myself. Compared with me, all the rest were blameless. I was playing the fool with my eyes open."

"As a by-stander," said Fanny, "perhaps I saw more than you did; and I do think that Mr. Rushworth was sometimes very jealous."

"Very possibly. No wonder. Nothing could be more improper than the whole business. I am shocked whenever I think that Maria could be capable of it; but if she could undertake the part, we must not be surprised at the rest."

"Before the play, I am much mistaken, if *Julia* did not think he was paying her attentions."

"Julia!—I have heard before from some one of his being in love with Julia, but I could never see any thing of it. And Fanny, though I hope I do justice to my sisters' good qualities, I think it very possible that they might, one or both, be more desirous of being admired by Crawford, and might shew that desire rather more unguardedly than was perfectly prudent. I can remember that they were evidently fond of his society; and with such encouragement, a man like Crawford, lively, and it may be a little unthinking, might be led on to—There could be nothing very striking, because it is clear that he had no pretensions; his heart was reserved for you. And I must say, that its being for you, has raised him inconceivably in my opinion. It does him the highest honour; it shews his proper estimation of the blessing of domestic happiness, and pure attachment. It proves him unspoilt by his uncle. It proves him, in short, every thing that I had been used to wish to believe him, and feared he was not."

"I am persuaded that he does not think as he ought, on serious subjects."[3]

"Say rather, that he has not thought at all upon serious subjects, which I believe to be a good deal the case. How could it be otherwise, with such an education and adviser? Under the disadvantages, indeed, which both have had, is it not wonderful that they should be what they are? Crawford's *feelings,* I am ready to acknowledge, have hitherto been too much his guides. Happily, those feelings have generally been good. You will supply the rest; and a most fortunate man he is to attach himself to such a creature—to a woman, who firm as a rock in her own principles, has a gentleness of character so well adapted to recommend them. He has chosen his partner, indeed, with rare felicity. He will make you happy, Fanny, I know he will make you happy; but you will make him every thing."[4]

"I would not engage in such a charge," cried Fanny in a shrinking accent—"in such an office of high responsibility!"

"As usual, believing yourself unequal to anything!—fancying every thing too much for you! Well, though I may not be able to persuade you into different feelings, you will be persuaded into them I trust. I confess myself sincerely anxious that you may. I have no common interest in Crawford's well doing. Next to your happiness, Fanny, his has the first claim on me. You are aware of my having no common interest in Crawford."

3 Matters of religion.

4 Given that his aim is to "persuade" Fanny into different feelings for Henry, Edmund's emphasis in this sentence on Henry's limitless potential—and the hyperbole of his claim that Fanny could make Henry "every thing"—seem misjudged. An apparent hollowness of identity is what makes Henry a good actor (someone who, as in the previous chapter, can succeed at playing all the roles and simulating all the moods), but it is just what discredits him in Fanny's eyes.

Fanny was too well aware of it, to have anything to say; and they walked on together some fifty yards in mutual silence and abstraction. Edmund first began again:—

"I was very much pleased by her manner of speaking of it yesterday, particularly pleased, because I had not depended upon her seeing every thing in so just a light. I knew she was very fond of you, but yet I was afraid of her not estimating your worth to her brother, quite as it deserved, and of her regretting that he had not rather fixed on some woman of distinction, or fortune. I was afraid of the bias of those worldly maxims, which she has been too much used to hear. But it was very different. She spoke of you, Fanny, just as she ought. She desires the connection as warmly as your uncle or myself. We had a long talk about it. I should not have mentioned the subject, though very anxious to know her sentiments—but I had not been in the room five minutes before she began, introducing it with all that openness of heart, and sweet peculiarity of manner, that spirit and ingenuousness, which are so much a part of herself. Mrs. Grant laughed at her for her rapidity."

"Was Mrs. Grant in the room, then?"

"Yes, when I reached the house I found the two sisters together by themselves; and when once we had begun, we had not done with you, Fanny, till Crawford and Dr. Grant came in."

"It is above a week since I saw Miss Crawford."

"Yes, she laments it; yet owns it may have been best. You will see her, however, before she goes. She is very angry with you, Fanny; you must be prepared for that. She calls herself very angry, but you can imagine her anger. It is the regret and disappointment of a sister, who thinks her brother has a right to every thing he may wish for, at the first moment. She is hurt, as you would be for William; but she loves and esteems you with all her heart."

"I knew she would be very angry with me."

"My dearest Fanny," cried Edmund, pressing her arm closer to him, "do not let the idea of her anger distress you. It is anger to be talked of, rather than felt. Her heart is made for love and kindness, not for resentment. I wish you could have overheard her tribute of praise; I wish you could have seen her countenance, when she said that you *should* be Henry's wife. And I observed, that she always spoke of you as 'Fanny,' which she was never used to do; and it had a sound of most sisterly cordiality."

"And Mrs. Grant, did she say—did she speak—was she there all the time?"

"Yes, she was agreeing exactly with her sister. The surprise of your refusal, Fanny, seems to have been unbounded. That you could refuse such a man as Henry Crawford, seems more than they can understand. I said what I could for you; but in good truth, as they stated the case—you must prove yourself to be in your senses as soon as you can, by a different conduct; nothing else will satisfy them. But this is teazing you. I have done. Do not turn away from me."

"I *should* have thought," said Fanny, after a pause of recollection and exertion, "that every woman must have felt the possibility of a man's not being approved, not being loved by some one of her sex, at least, let him be ever so generally agreeable. Let him have all the perfections in the world, I think it ought not to be set down as certain, that a man must be acceptable to every woman he may happen to like himself. But even supposing it is so, allowing Mr. Crawford to have all the claims which his sisters think he has, how was I to be prepared to meet him with any feeling answerable to his own? He took me wholly by surprise. I had not an idea that his behaviour to me before had any meaning; and surely I was not to be teaching myself to like him only because he was taking, what seemed, very idle notice of me. In my situation, it would have been the extreme of vanity to be forming expectations on Mr. Crawford. I am sure his sisters, rating him as they do, must have thought it so, supposing he had meant nothing. How then was I to be—to be in love with him the moment he said he was with me? How was I to have an attachment at his service, as soon as it was asked for? His sisters should consider me as well as him. The higher his deserts, the more improper for me ever to have thought of him. And, and—we think very differently of the nature of women, if they can imagine a woman so very soon capable of returning an affection as this seems to imply."

"My dear, dear Fanny, now I have the truth. I know this to be the truth; and most worthy of you are such feelings. I had attributed them to you before. I thought I could understand you. You have now given exactly the explanation which I ventured to make for you to your friend and Mrs. Grant, and they were both better satisfied, though your warm-hearted friend was still run away with a little, by the enthusiasm of her fondness for Henry. I told them, that you were of all human creatures the one, over whom habit had most power, and novelty least: and that the very circumstance of the novelty of Crawford's addresses was against him. Their being so new and so recent was all in their disfavour; that you could tolerate nothing that you were not used to; and a great deal more to the same purpose, to give them a knowledge of your character. Miss Crawford made us laugh by her plans of encouragement for her brother. She meant to urge him to persevere in the hope of being loved in time, and of having his addresses most kindly received at the end of about ten years' happy marriage."

Fanny could with difficulty give the smile that was here asked for. Her feelings were all in revolt. She feared she had been doing wrong, saying too much, overacting the caution which she had been fancying necessary, in guarding against one evil, laying herself open to another, and to have Miss Crawford's liveliness repeated to her at such a moment, and on such a subject, was a bitter aggravation.

Edmund saw weariness and distress in her face, and immediately resolved to forbear all farther discussion; and not even to mention the name of Crawford again, except as it might be connected with what *must* be agreeable to her. On this principle, he soon afterwards observed, "They go on Monday. You are sure therefore of seeing your friend either to-morrow or Sunday. They really go on Monday! and I was within a trifle of being persuaded to stay at Lessingby till that very day! I had almost promised it. What a difference it might have made! Those five or six days more at Lessingby might have been felt all my life!"

"You were near staying there?"

"Very. I was most kindly pressed, and had nearly consented. Had I received any letter from Mansfield, to tell me how you were all going on, I believe I should certainly have stayed; but I knew nothing that had happened here for a fortnight, and felt that I had been away long enough."

"You spent your time pleasantly there."

"Yes; that is, it was the fault of my own mind if I did not. They were all very pleasant. I doubt their finding me so. I took uneasiness with me, and there was no getting rid of it till I was in Mansfield again."

"The Miss Owens—you liked them, did not you?"

"Yes, very well. Pleasant, good-humoured, unaffected girls. But I am spoilt, Fanny, for common female society. Good-humoured, unaffected girls, will not do for a man who has been used to sensible women. They are two distinct orders of being. You and Miss Crawford have made me too nice."

Still, however, Fanny was oppressed and wearied; he saw it in her looks, it could not be talked away, and attempting it no more, he led her directly with the kind authority of a privileged guardian into the house.

## 5

EDMUND NOW BELIEVED himself perfectly acquainted with all that
Fanny could tell, or could leave to be conjectured of her sentiments,
and he was satisfied.—It had been, as he before presumed, too hasty
a measure on Crawford's side, and time must be given to make the
idea first familiar, and then agreeable to her. She must be used to the
consideration of his being in love with her, and then a return of affection might not be very distant.

He gave this opinion as the result of the conversation, to his father; and recommended there being nothing more said to her, no farther attempts to influence or persuade; but that every thing should
be left to Crawford's assiduities, and the natural workings of her own
mind.

Sir Thomas promised that it should be so. Edmund's account of
Fanny's disposition he could believe to be just, he supposed she had
all those feelings, but he must consider it as very unfortunate that
she *had;* for, less willing than his son to trust to the future, he could
not help fearing that if such very long allowances of time and habit
were necessary for her, she might not have persuaded herself into receiving his addresses properly, before the young man's inclination for
paying them were over. There was nothing to be done, however, but
to submit quietly, and hope the best.

The promised visit from her "friend," as Edmund called Miss
Crawford, was a formidable threat to Fanny, and she lived in continual terror of it. As a sister, so partial and so angry, and so little scrupulous of what she said; and in another light, so triumphant and

secure, she was in every way an object of painful alarm. Her displeasure, her penetration, and her happiness were all fearful to encounter; and the dependence of having others present when they met, was Fanny's only support in looking forward to it. She absented herself as little as possible from Lady Bertram, kept away from the east room, and took no solitary walk in the shrubbery, in her caution to avoid any sudden attack.

She succeeded. She was safe in the breakfast-room, with her aunt, when Miss Crawford did come; and the first misery over, and Miss Crawford looking and speaking with much less particularity of expression than she had anticipated, Fanny began to hope there would be nothing worse to be endured than an half-hour of moderate agitation. But here she hoped too much, Miss Crawford was not the slave of opportunity. She was determined to see Fanny alone, and therefore said to her tolerably soon, in a low voice, "I must speak to you for a few minutes somewhere;" words that Fanny felt all over her, in all her pulses, and all her nerves. Denial was impossible. Her habits of ready submission, on the contrary, made her almost instantly rise and lead the way out of the room. She did it with wretched feelings, but it was inevitable.

They were no sooner in the hall than all restraint of countenance was over on Miss Crawford's side. She immediately shook her head at Fanny with arch, yet affectionate reproach, and taking her hand, seemed hardly able to help beginning directly. She said nothing, however, but, "Sad, sad girl! I do not know when I shall have done scolding you," and had discretion enough to reserve the rest till they might be secure of having four walls to themselves. Fanny naturally turned up stairs, and took her guest to the apartment which was now always fit for comfortable use; opening the door, however, with a most aching heart, and feeling that she had a more distressing scene before her than ever that spot had yet witnessed. But the evil ready to burst on her, was at least delayed by the sudden change in Miss Crawford's ideas; by the strong effect on her mind which the finding herself in the east room again produced.

"Ha!" she cried, with instant animation, "am I here again? The east room. Once only was I in this room before!"—and after stop-

1 The line Mary cites is one Edmund would have spoken in Act III, scene ii of *Lovers' Vows,* when Anhalt, in dialogue with Amelia, has "two long speeches" that turn respectively on the pleasures and the pains of married life. Tellingly, Mary seems to recall only the first speech.

ping to look about her, and seemingly to retrace all that had then passed, she added, "Once only before. Do you remember it? I came to rehearse. Your cousin came too; and we had a rehearsal. You were our audience and prompter. A delightful rehearsal. I shall never forget it. Here we were, just in this part of the room; here was your cousin, here was I, here were the chairs.—Oh! why will such things ever pass away?"

Happily for her companion, she wanted no answer. Her mind was entirely self-engrossed. She was in a reverie of sweet remembrances.

"The scene we were rehearsing was so very remarkable! The subject of it so very—very—what shall I say? He was to be describing and recommending matrimony to me. I think I see him now, trying to be as demure and composed as Anhalt ought, through the two long speeches. 'When two sympathetic hearts meet in the marriage state, matrimony may be called a happy life.'[1] I suppose no time can ever wear out the impression I have of his looks and voice, as he said those words. It was curious, very curious, that we should have such a scene to play! If I had the power of recalling any one week of my existence, it should be that week, that acting week. Say what you would, Fanny, it should be *that;* for I never knew such exquisite happiness in any other. His sturdy spirit to bend as it did! Oh! it was sweet beyond expression. But alas! that very evening destroyed it all. That very evening brought your most unwelcome uncle. Poor Sir Thomas, who was glad to see you? Yet, Fanny, do not imagine I would now speak disrespectfully of Sir Thomas, though I certainly did hate him for many a week. No, I do him justice now. He is just what the head of such a family should be. Nay, in sober sadness, I believe I now love you all." And having said so, with a degree of tenderness and consciousness which Fanny had never seen in her before, and now thought only too becoming, she turned away for a moment to recover herself. "I have had a little fit since I came into this room, as you may perceive," said she presently, with a playful smile, "but it is over now; so let us sit down and be comfortable; for as to scolding you, Fanny, which I came fully intending to do, I have not the heart for it when it comes to the point." And embracing her very affectionately,—"Good, gentle Fanny! when I think of this being the last time of seeing you; for I do not know how long—I feel it quite impossible to do any thing but love you."

Fanny was affected. She had not foreseen anything of this, and her feelings could seldom withstand the melancholy influence of the word "last." She cried as if she had loved Miss Crawford more than she possibly could; and Miss Crawford, yet farther softened by the sight of such emotion, hung about her with fondness, and said, "I hate to leave you. I shall see no one half so amiable where I am going. Who says we shall not be sisters? I know we shall. I feel that we are born to be connected; and those tears convince me that you feel it too, dear Fanny."

Fanny roused herself, and replying only in part, said, "But you are only going from one set of friends to another. You are going to a very particular friend."

"Yes, very true. Mrs. Fraser has been my intimate friend for years. But I have not the least inclination to go near her. I can think only of the friends I am leaving; my excellent sister, yourself, and the Bertrams in general. You have all so much more *heart* among you, than one finds in the world at large. You all give me a feeling of being able to trust and confide in you; which, in common intercourse, one knows nothing of. I wish I had settled with Mrs. Fraser not to go to her till after Easter, a much better time for the visit—but now I cannot put her off. And when I have done with her, I must go to her sister, Lady Stornaway, because *she* was rather my most particular friend of the two; but I have not cared much for *her* these three years."

After this speech, the two girls sat many minutes silent, each thoughtful: Fanny meditating on the different sorts of friendship in the world, Mary on something of less philosophic tendency. *She* first spoke again.

"How perfectly I remember my resolving to look for you up stairs, and setting off to find my way to the east room, without having an idea whereabouts it was! How well I remember what I was thinking of as I came along; and my looking in and seeing you here, sitting at this table at work; and then your cousin's astonishment when he opened the door at seeing me here! To be sure, your uncle's returning that very evening! There never was anything quite like it."

2 The reference is to the codes of courtly love and amorous service first exhibited in the chivalric romances of the middle ages. In Charlotte Lennox's *The Female Quixote*, Arabella, a bookish heroine whose head has been turned by the seventeenth-century French versions of these romances (Lennox's satiric target), declares it "an unpardonable Presumption" for any man who aims to win her heart "to tell her he loved her, tho' after Ten Years of the most faithful Services" (*The Female Quixote, or, The Adventures of Arabella*, ed. Margaret Dalziel [Oxford: Oxford University Press, 1989], p. 111). Austen read Lennox's 1752 novel at least twice.

3 French for *demanding*.

Another short fit of abstraction followed—when, shaking it off, she thus attacked her companion.

"Why, Fanny, you are absolutely in a reverie! Thinking, I hope, of one who is always thinking of you. Oh! that I could transport you for a short time into our circle in town, that you might understand how your power over Henry is thought of there! Oh! the envyings and heart-burnings of dozens and dozens! the wonder, the incredulity that will be felt at hearing what you have done! For as to secrecy, Henry is quite the hero of an old romance, and glories in his chains.[2] You should come to London, to know how to estimate your conquest. If you were to see how he is courted, and how I am courted for his sake! Now I am well aware, that I shall not be half so welcome to Mrs. Fraser in consequence of his situation with you. When she comes to know the truth, she will very likely wish me in Northamptonshire again; for there is a daughter of Mr. Fraser by a first wife, whom she is wild to get married, and wants Henry to take. Oh! she has been trying for him to such a degree! Innocent and quiet as you sit here, you cannot have an idea of the *sensation* that you will be occasioning, of the curiosity there will be to see you, of the endless questions I shall have to answer! Poor Margaret Fraser will be at me for ever about your eyes and your teeth, and how you do your hair, and who makes your shoes. I wish Margaret were married, for my poor friend's sake, for I look upon the Frasers to be about as unhappy as most other married people. And yet it was a most desirable match for Janet at the time. We were all delighted. She could not do otherwise than accept him, for he was rich, and she had nothing; but he turns out ill-tempered, and *exigeant;*[3] and wants a young woman, a beautiful young woman of five-and-twenty, to be as steady as himself. And my friend does not manage him well; she does not seem to know how to make the best of it. There is a spirit of irritation, which, to say nothing worse, is certainly very ill-bred. In their house I shall call to mind the conjugal manners of Mansfield Parsonage with respect. Even Dr. Grant does shew a thorough confidence in my sister, and a certain consideration for her judgment, which makes one feel there *is* attachment; but of that, I shall see nothing with the Frasers. I shall be at Mansfield for ever, Fanny. My own sister as a wife, Sir Thomas Bertram as a husband, are my standards of perfection. Poor Janet has been sadly taken in;[4] and yet there was nothing improper on her side; she did not run into the match inconsiderately, there was no want of foresight. She took three days to consider of his proposals; and during those three days asked the advice of every body connected with her, whose opinion was worth having; and especially applied to my late dear aunt, whose knowledge of the world made her judgment very generally and deservedly looked up to by all the young people of her acquaintance; and she was decidedly in favour of Mr. Fraser. This seems as if nothing were a security for matrimonial comfort! I have not so much to say for my friend Flora, who jilted a very nice young man in the Blues,[5] for the sake of that horrid Lord Stornaway, who has about as much sense, Fanny, as Mr. Rushworth, but much worse looking, and with a blackguard character. I *had* my doubts at the time about her being right, for he has not even the air of a gentleman, and now, I am sure, she was wrong. By the by, Flora Ross was dying for Henry the first winter she came out. But were I to attempt to tell you of all the women whom I have known to be in love with him, I should never have done. It is you only, you, insensible Fanny, who can think of him with any thing like indifference. But are you so insensible as you profess yourself? No, no, I see you are not."

There was indeed so deep a blush over Fanny's face at that moment, as might warrant strong suspicion in a pre-disposed mind.

"Excellent creature! I will not teaze you. Every thing shall take its course. But dear Fanny, you must allow that you were not so absolutely unprepared to have the question asked as your cousin fancies. It is not possible, but that you must have had some thoughts on the subject, some surmises as to what might be. You must have seen that he was trying to please you, by every attention in his power. Was not he devoted to you at the ball? And then before the ball, the necklace! Oh! you received it just as it was meant. You were as conscious as heart could desire. I remember it perfectly."

"Do you mean then that your brother knew of the necklace beforehand? Oh! Miss Crawford, *that* was not fair."

4 Mary should not be surprised at this outcome. In a conversation with her sister in the novel's first volume she expressed her conviction that "there is not one in a hundred of either sex, who is not taken in when they marry" (I, 5).

5 Nickname for the London-based Royal Regiment of Horse Guards, called the blues because of the color of the officers' uniforms. Membership in this elite regiment was limited to the wealthy and well-connected.

"Knew of it! it was his own doing entirely, his own thought. I am ashamed to say, that it had never entered my head; but I was delighted to act on his proposal, for both your sakes."

"I will not say," replied Fanny, "that I was not half afraid at the time of its being so; for there was something in your look that frightened me—but not at first—I was as unsuspicious of it at first!—indeed, indeed I was. It is as true as that I sit here. And had I had an idea of it, nothing should have induced me to accept the necklace. As to your brother's behaviour, certainly I was sensible of a particularity, I had been sensible of it some little time, perhaps two or three weeks; but then I considered it as meaning nothing, I put it down as simply being his way, and was as far from supposing as from wishing him to have any serious thoughts of me. I had not, Miss Crawford, been an inattentive observer of what was passing between him and some part of this family in the summer and autumn. I was quiet, but I was not blind. I could not but see that Mr. Crawford allowed himself in gallantries which did mean nothing."

"Ah! I cannot deny it. He has now and then been a sad flirt, and cared very little for the havock he might be making in young ladies' affections. I have often scolded him for it, but it is his only fault; and there is this to be said, that very few young ladies have any affections worth caring for. And then, Fanny, the glory of fixing one who has been shot at by so many; of having it in one's power to pay off the debts of one's sex! Oh, I am sure it is not in woman's nature to refuse such a triumph."

Fanny shook her head. "I cannot think well of a man who sports with any woman's feelings; and there may often be a great deal more suffered than a stander-by can judge of."

"I do not defend him. I leave him entirely to your mercy; and when he has got you at Everingham, I do not care how much you lecture him. But this I will say, that his fault, the liking to make girls a little in love with him, is not half so dangerous to a wife's happiness, as a tendency to fall in love himself, which he has never been addicted to. And I do seriously and truly believe that he is attached to you in a way that he never was to any woman before; that he loves you with all his heart, and will love you as nearly for ever as possible.

If any man ever loved a woman for ever, I think Henry will do as much for you."

Fanny could not avoid a faint smile, but had nothing to say.

"I cannot imagine Henry ever to have been happier," continued Mary, presently, "than when he had succeeded in getting your brother's commission."

She had made a sure push at Fanny's feelings here.

"Oh! yes. How very, very kind of him!"

"I know he must have exerted himself very much, for I know the parties he had to move. The Admiral hates trouble, and scorns asking favours; and there are so many young men's claims to be attended to in the same way, that a friendship and energy, not very determined, is easily put by. What a happy creature William must be! I wish we could see him."

Poor Fanny's mind was thrown into the most distressing of all its varieties. The recollection of what had been done for William was always the most powerful disturber of every decision against Mr. Crawford; and she sat thinking deeply of it till Mary, who had been first watching her complacently, and then musing on something else, suddenly called her attention, by saying, "I should like to sit talking with you here all day, but we must not forget the ladies below, and so good bye, my dear, my amiable, my excellent Fanny, for though we shall nominally part in the breakfast parlour, I must take leave of you here. And I do take leave, longing for a happy re-union, and trusting, that when we meet again, it will be under circumstances which may open our hearts to each other without any remnant or shadow of reserve."

A very, very kind embrace, and some agitation of manner, accompanied these words.

"I shall see your cousin in town soon; he talks of being there tolerably soon; and Sir Thomas, I dare say, in the course of the spring; and your eldest cousin and the Rushworths and Julia I am sure of meeting again and again, and all but you. I have two favours to ask, Fanny; one is your correspondence. You must write to me. And the other, that you will often call on Mrs. Grant and make her amends for my being gone."

The first, at least, of these favours Fanny would rather not have been asked; but it was impossible for her to refuse the correspondence; it was impossible for her even not to accede to it more readily than her own judgment authorised. There was no resisting so much apparent affection. Her disposition was peculiarly calculated to value a fond treatment, and from having hitherto known so little of it, she was the more overcome by Miss Crawford's. Besides, there was gratitude towards her, for having made their tête à tête so much less painful than her fears had predicted.

It was over, and she had escaped without reproaches and without detection. Her secret was still her own; and while that was the case, she thought she could resign herself to almost every thing.

In the evening there was another parting. Henry Crawford came and sat some time with them; and her spirits not being previously in the strongest state, her heart was softened for a while towards him —because he really seemed to feel.—Quite unlike his usual self, he scarcely said any thing. He was evidently oppressed, and Fanny must grieve for him, though hoping she might never see him again till he were the husband of some other woman.

When it came to the moment of parting, he would take her hand, he would not be denied it; he said nothing, however, or nothing that she heard, and when he had left the room, she was better pleased that such a token of friendship had passed.

On the morrow the Crawfords were gone.

# 6

MR. CRAWFORD GONE, Sir Thomas's next object was, that he should be missed, and he entertained great hope that his niece would find a blank in the loss of those attentions which at the time she had felt, or fancied an evil. She had tasted of consequence in its most flattering form; and he did hope that the loss of it, the sinking again into nothing, would awaken very wholesome regrets in her mind.—He watched her with this idea—but he could hardly tell with what success. He hardly knew whether there were any difference in her spirits or not. She was always so gentle and retiring, that her emotions were beyond his discrimination. He did not understand her; he felt that he did not; and therefore applied to Edmund to tell him how she stood affected on the present occasion, and whether she were more or less happy than she had been.

Edmund did not discern any symptoms of regret, and thought his father a little unreasonable in supposing the first three or four days could produce any.

What chiefly surprised Edmund was, that Crawford's sister, the friend and companion, who had been so much to her, should not be more visibly regretted. He wondered that Fanny spoke so seldom of *her*, and had so little voluntarily to say of her concern at this separation.

Alas! it was this sister, this friend and companion, who was now the chief bane of Fanny's comfort.—If she could have believed Mary's future fate as unconnected with Mansfield, as she was determined the brother's should be, if she could have hoped her return thither, to be as distant as she was much inclined to think his, she would have been light of heart indeed; but the more she recollected and observed, the more deeply was she convinced that every thing was now in a fairer train for Miss Crawford's marrying Edmund than it had ever been before.—On his side, the inclination was stronger, on hers less equivocal. His objections, the scruples of his integrity, seemed all done away—nobody could tell how; and the doubts and hesitations of her ambition were equally got over—and equally without apparent reason. It could only be imputed to increasing attachment. His good and her bad feelings yielded to love, and such love must unite them. He was to go to town, as soon as some business relative to Thornton Lacey were completed—perhaps, within a fortnight, he talked of going, he loved to talk of it; and when once with her again, Fanny could not doubt the rest.—Her acceptance must be as certain as his offer; and yet, there were bad feelings still remaining which made the prospect of it most sorrowful to her, independently—she believed independently of self.

In their very last conversation, Miss Crawford, in spite of some amiable sensations, and much personal kindness, had still been Miss Crawford, still shewn a mind led astray and bewildered, and without any suspicion of being so; darkened, yet fancying itself light. She might love, but she did not deserve Edmund by any other sentiment. Fanny believed there was scarcely a second feeling in common between them; and she may be forgiven by older sages, for looking on the chance of Miss Crawford's future improvement as nearly desperate, for thinking that if Edmund's influence in this season of love, had already done so little in clearing her judgment, and regulating her notions, his worth would be finally wasted on her even in years of matrimony.

Experience might have hoped more for any young people, so circumstanced, and impartiality would not have denied to Miss Crawford's nature, that participation of the general nature of women, which would lead her to adopt the opinions of the man she loved and respected, as her own.—But as such were Fanny's persuasions, she suffered very much from them, and could never speak of Miss Crawford without pain.

Sir Thomas, meanwhile, went on with his own hopes, and his own observations, still feeling a right, by all his knowledge of human nature, to expect to see the effect of the loss of power and consequence, on his niece's spirits, and the past attentions of the lover producing a craving for their return; and he was soon afterwards able to account for his not yet completely and indubitably seeing all this, by the prospect of another visitor, whose approach he could allow to be quite enough to support the spirits he was watching.—William had obtained a ten days' leave of absence to be given to Northamptonshire, and was coming, the happiest of lieutenants, because the latest made, to shew his happiness and describe his uniform.[1]

He came; and he would have been delighted to shew his uniform there too, had not cruel custom prohibited its appearance except on duty. So the uniform remained at Portsmouth, and Edmund conjectured that before Fanny had any chance of seeing it, all its own freshness, and all the freshness of its wearer's feelings, must be worn away. It would be sunk into a badge of disgrace; for what can be more unbecoming, or more worthless, than the uniform of a lieutenant, who has been a lieutenant a year or two, and sees others made command-

1 William has reason to be delighted, since the full dress and undress uniforms worn by Royal Navy lieutenants were each considerably fancier than those worn by midshipmen. Austen might trade here on her audience's knowledge of improvements recently added to the lieutenants' uniforms under regulations the Royal Navy implemented in 1812. A comic poem of ninety-six lines published in *The Naval Chronicle* for July–December 1812 (vol. 28, pp. 332–333) commemorates the changes, praising the distinctive new navy button and, at some length, the epaulet that the lieutenant was now, for the first time, entitled to wear on his right shoulder:

> No longer will the British fair conceal
> The preference they ever feel
> For Britain's fair defenders;—
> Since these the epaulets display,
> They'll soon "cut out," and keep away,
> All other gay pretenders.
>
> For still the fair, like fish, are caught
> By bait with shining tinsel fraught.
> (As glitters many a beau!)
> Yet not by glare of dress alone
> Are Albion's daughters always won,
> But worth as well as show.

("Lines Addressed to the Lieutenants of the Navy, Upon the Change of Uniform," lines 67–78).

A navy lieutenant who has just been promoted models his showy new uniform for his admiring family.

ers before him? So reasoned Edmund, till his father made him the
confident of a scheme which placed Fanny's chance of seeing the 2d
lieutenant of H. M. S. Thrush, in all his glory in another light.

This scheme was that she should accompany her brother back to
Portsmouth, and spend a little time with her own family. It had occurred to Sir Thomas, in one of his dignified musings, as a right and
desirable measure; but before he absolutely made up his mind, he
consulted his son. Edmund considered it every way, and saw nothing but what was right. The thing was good in itself, and could not
be done at a better time; and he had no doubt of it being highly
agreeable to Fanny. This was enough to determine Sir Thomas; and a
decisive "then so it shall be," closed that stage of the business; Sir
Thomas retiring from it with some feelings of satisfaction, and views
of good over and above what he had communicated to his son, for his
prime motive in sending her away, had very little to do with the propriety of her seeing her parents again, and nothing at all with any
idea of making her happy. He certainly wished her to go willingly, but
he as certainly wished her to be heartily sick of home before her visit
ended; and that a little abstinence from the elegancies and luxuries
of Mansfield Park, would bring her mind into a sober state, and incline her to a juster estimate of the value of that home of greater permanence, and equal comfort, of which she had the offer.

It was a medicinal project upon his niece's understanding, which
he must consider as at present diseased. A residence of eight or nine
years in the abode of wealth and plenty had a little disordered her
powers of comparing and judging. Her Father's house would, in all
probability, teach her the value of a good income; and he trusted that
she would be the wiser and happier woman, all her life, for the experiment he had devised.

Had Fanny been at all addicted to raptures, she must have had a
strong attack of them, when she first understood what was intended,
when her uncle first made her the offer of visiting the parents, and
brothers, and sisters, from whom she had been divided, almost half
her life, of returning for a couple of months to the scenes of her infancy, with William for the protector and companion of her journey;
and the certainty of continuing to see William to the last hour of his
remaining on land. Had she ever given way to bursts of delight, it

must have been then, for she was delighted, but her happiness was of a quiet, deep, heart-swelling sort; and though never a great talker, she was always more inclined to silence when feeling most strongly. At the moment she could only thank and accept. Afterwards, when familiarized with the visions of enjoyment so suddenly opened, she could speak more largely to William and Edmund of what she felt; but still there were emotions of tenderness that could not be clothed in words—The remembrance of all her earliest pleasures, and of what she had suffered in being torn from them, came over her with re-newed strength, and it seemed as if to be at home again, would heal every pain that had since grown out of the separation. To be in the centre of such a circle, loved by so many, and more loved by all than she had ever been before, to feel affection without fear or restraint, to feel herself the equal of those who surrounded her, to be at peace from all mention of the Crawfords, safe from every look which could be fancied a reproach on their account!—This was a prospect to be dwelt on with a fondness that could be but half acknowledged.

Edmund too—to be two months from *him,* (and perhaps, she might be allowed to make her absence three) must do her good. At a distance unassailed by his looks or his kindness, and safe from the perpetual irritation of knowing his heart, and striving to avoid his confidence, she should be able to reason herself into a properer state; she should be able to think of him as in London, and arranging every thing there, without wretchedness.——What might have been hard to bear at Mansfield, was to become a slight evil at Portsmouth.

The only drawback was the doubt of her Aunt Bertram's being comfortable without her. She was of use to no one else; but *there* she might be missed to a degree that she did not like to think of; and that part of the arrangement was, indeed, the hardest for Sir Thomas to accomplish, and what only *he* could have accomplished at all.

But he was master at Mansfield Park. When he had really resolved on any measure, he could always carry it through; and now by dint of long talking on the subject, explaining and dwelling on the duty of Fanny's sometimes seeing her family, he did induce his wife to let her go; obtaining it rather from submission, however, than conviction, for Lady Bertram was convinced of very little more than that Sir Thomas thought Fanny ought to go, and therefore that she must. In the calmness of her own dressing-room, in the impartial flow of her own meditations, unbiassed by his bewildering statements, she could not acknowledge any necessity for Fanny's ever going near a Father and Mother who had done without her so long, while she was so useful to herself.—And as to the not missing her, which under Mrs. Norris's discussion was the point attempted to be proved, she set herself very steadily against admitting any such thing.

Sir Thomas had appealed to her reason, conscience, and dignity. He called it a sacrifice, and demanded it of her goodness and self-command as such. But Mrs. Norris wanted to persuade her that Fanny could be very well spared—(*She* being ready to give up all her own time to her as requested) and in short could not really be wanted or missed.

"That may be, sister,"—was all Lady Bertram's reply—"I dare say you are very right, but I am sure I shall miss her very much."

The next step was to communicate with Portsmouth. Fanny wrote to offer herself; and her mother's answer, though short, was so kind, a few simple lines expressed so natural and motherly a joy in the prospect of seeing her child again, as to confirm all the daughter's views of happiness in being with her—convincing her that she should now find a warm and affectionate friend in the "Mamma" who had certainly shewn no remarkable fondness for her formerly; but this she could easily suppose to have been her own fault, or her own fancy. She had probably alienated Love by the helplessness and fretfulness of a fearful temper, or been unreasonable in wanting a larger share than any one among so many could deserve. Now, when she knew better how to be useful and how to forbear, and when her mother could be no longer occupied by the incessant demands of a house full of little children, there would be leisure and inclination for every comfort, and they should soon be what mother and daughter ought to be to each other.

William was almost as happy in the plan as his sister. It would be the greatest pleasure to him to have her there to the last moment before he sailed, and perhaps find her there still when he came in, from his first cruise! And besides, he wanted her so very much to see the Thrush before she went out of harbour (the Thrush was certainly

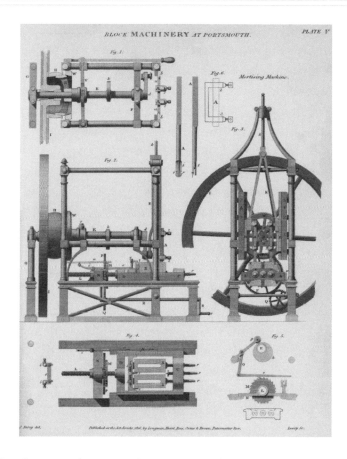

This plate from an early nineteenth-century encyclopedia depicts the Portsmouth dockyard's innovative block-making machinery. This machinery accelerated a process that previously could be done only by hand. Its presence helped make the dockyard a tourist attraction.

2 Under Samuel Bentham, appointed inspector general of naval works in 1796, the dockyard at Portsmouth had been radically enlarged and modernized. Bentham (younger brother of the philosopher Jeremy Bentham) arranged for the newest of the steam engines being designed by Watt and Boulton to be used both for pumping the dry docks in which ships of the line were refitted and, after 1804, for powering the dockyard's wood mills. There the engineer Isambard Brunel installed machinery, the first of its kind, that fully mechanized the manufacture of the wooden pulleys ("blocks") that were required in vast quantities for ships' riggings and guns. Brunel's biographer Richard Beamish wrote admiringly of how by the aid of this machinery ten men could "accomplish with uniformity, celerity, and ease, what formerly required the uncertain labour of one hundred and ten" (*Memoir of the Life of Sir Marc Isambard Brunel*, 2nd ed. [London: Longman, Green, Longman, and Roberts, 1862], p. 98). By the end of the Napoleonic wars these innovations made the Portsmouth dockyard something of a pilgrimage site, and royalty and novelists (Maria Edgeworth and Walter Scott) numbered among its visitors.

the finest sloop in the service). And there were several improvements in the dock-yard, too, which he quite longed to shew her.[2]

He did not scruple to add, that her being at home for a while would be a great advantage to every body.

"I do not know how it is," said he, "but we seem to want some of your nice ways and orderliness at my father's. The house is always in confusion. You will set things going in a better way, I am sure. You will tell my mother how it all ought to be, and you will be so useful to Susan, and you will teach Betsey, and make the boys love and mind you. How right and comfortable it will all be!"

3 Banknotes.

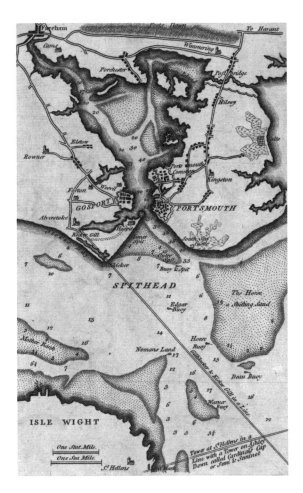

Inset from *A Map of the Western Circuit of England* (published 1784), depicting Portsmouth Harbor and the Spithead Channel.

By the time Mrs. Price's answer arrived, there remained but a very few days more to be spent at Mansfield; and for part of one of those days the young travellers were in a good deal of alarm on the subject of their journey, for when the mode of it came to be talked of, and Mrs. Norris found that all her anxiety to save her Brother-in-law's money was vain, and that in spite of her wishes and hints for a less expensive conveyance of Fanny, they were to travel post, when she saw Sir Thomas actually give William notes for the purpose,[3] she was struck with the idea of there being room for a third in the carriage, and suddenly seized with a strong inclination to go with them—to go and see her poor dear sister Price. She proclaimed her thoughts. She must say that she had more than half a mind to go with the young people; it would be such an indulgence to her; she had not seen her poor dear sister Price for more than twenty years; and it would be a help to the young people in their journey to have her older head to manage for them; and she could not help thinking her poor dear sister Price would feel it very unkind of her not to come by such an opportunity.

William and Fanny were horror-struck at the idea.

All the comfort of their comfortable journey would be destroyed at once. With woeful countenances they looked at each other. Their suspense lasted an hour or two. No one interfered to encourage or dissuade. Mrs. Norris was left to settle the matter by herself; and it ended to the infinite joy of her nephew and niece, in the recollection that she could not possibly be spared from Mansfield Park at present; that she was a great deal too necessary to Sir Thomas and Lady Bertram for her to be able to answer it to herself to leave them even for a week, and therefore must certainly sacrifice every other pleasure to that of being useful to them.

It had, in fact, occurred to her, that, though taken to Portsmouth for nothing, it would be hardly possible for her to avoid paying her own expenses back again. So, her poor dear sister Price was left to all the disappointment of her missing such an opportunity; and another twenty years' absence, perhaps, begun.

Edmund's plans were affected by this Portsmouth journey, this absence of Fanny's. He too had a sacrifice to make to Mansfield Park, as well as his aunt. He had intended, about this time, to be going to

The Swiss painter and traveler Jacques-Laurent Agasse's 1815 painting *The Last Stage on the Portsmouth Road*. For all its beauty, Agasse's painting vividly evokes the discomforts and the delays that travelers on early nineteenth-century post roads had to endure.

London, but he could not leave his father and mother just when everybody else of most importance to their comfort, was leaving them; and with an effort, felt but not boasted of, he delayed for a week or two longer a journey which he was looking forward to, with the hope of its fixing his happiness for ever.

He told Fanny of it. She knew so much already, that she must know every thing. It made the substance of one other confidential discourse about Miss Crawford; and Fanny was the more affected from feeling it to be the last time in which Miss Crawford's name would ever be mentioned between them with any remains of liberty. Once afterwards, she was alluded to by him. Lady Bertram had been telling her niece in the evening to write to her soon and often, and promising to be a good correspondent herself; and Edmund, at a convenient moment, then added, in a whisper, "And *I* shall write to you, Fanny, when I have any thing worth writing about; any thing to say, that I think you will like to hear, and that you will not hear so soon from any other quarter." Had she doubted his meaning while she listened, the glow in his face, when she looked up at him, would have been decisive.

For this letter she must try to arm herself. That a letter from Edmund should be a subject of terror! She began to feel that she had not yet gone through all the changes of opinion and sentiment, which the progress of time and variation of circumstances occasion in this world of changes. The vicissitudes of the human mind had not yet been exhausted by her.

Poor Fanny! though going, as she did, willingly and eagerly, the last evening at Mansfield Park must still be wretchedness. Her heart was completely sad at parting. She had tears for every room in the house, much more for every beloved inhabitant. She clung to her aunt, because she would miss her; she kissed the hand of her uncle with struggling sobs, because she had displeased him; and as for Edmund, she could neither speak, nor look, nor think, when the last moment came with *him,* and it was not till it was over that she knew he was giving her the affectionate farewell of a brother.

All this passed over night, for the journey was to begin very early in the morning; and when the small, diminished party met at breakfast, William and Fanny were talked of as already advanced one stage.

# 7

THE NOVELTY OF TRAVELLING, and the happiness of being with William, soon produced their natural effect on Fanny's spirits, when Mansfield Park was fairly left behind, and by the time their first stage was ended, and they were to quit Sir Thomas's carriage, she was able to take leave of the old coachman, and send back proper messages, with cheerful looks.

Of pleasant talk between the brother and sister, there was no end. Every thing supplied an amusement to the high glee of William's mind, and he was full of frolic and joke, in the intervals of their higher-toned subjects, all of which ended, if they did not begin, in praise of the Thrush, conjectures how she would be employed, schemes for an action with some superior force, which (supposing the first lieutenant out of the way—and William was not very merciful to the first lieutenant) was to give himself the next step as soon as possible, or speculations upon prize money, which was to be generously distributed at home, with only the reservation of enough to make the little cottage comfortable, in which he and Fanny were to pass all their middle and latter life together.[1]

Fanny's immediate concerns, as far as they involved Mr. Crawford, made no part of their conversation. William knew what had passed, and from his heart lamented that his sister's feelings should be so cold towards a man whom he must consider as the first of human characters; but he was of an age to be all for love, and therefore unable to blame; and knowing her wish on the subject, he would not distress her by the slightest allusion.

1 The fantasizing in which William indulges involves the *Thrush's* victory against the odds in some sea battle ("an action against some superior force"), a battle that ideally would take place soon and in circumstances that would lead automatically to William's promotion to the next rank and his receipt of much "prize money." "Prize money" was the bonus the Crown awarded navy crews when they had sunk or, better still, captured an enemy ship or a trading vessel flying an enemy flag, with the overall size of the award being calculated according to the value the Crown placed on the ship and its cargo. Controversially, shares in this money were far from even, with the captain receiving a share amounting to three-eighths of the whole (after an 1808 reform, a quarter), and the remainder distributed among all the crew members according to a graduated scale. In *Persuasion,* the "five-and-twenty thousand pounds" the narrator ascribes to Captain Wentworth in the novel's final chapter—the reason that even Sir Walter Elliot no longer dares dismiss him as a "nobody"—would most certainly derive from prize money rather than from Wentworth's navy salary (II, 12). In his edition of *Persuasion* Robert Morrison points out that even during this period there were critics who found the whole system of prize money a kind of "legalized piracy," a system that encouraged (as a character in Edgeworth's *Manoeuvring* puts it) "honest tars" to become "calculating pirates": see *Persuasion: An Annotated Edition* (Cambridge, Mass.: Belknap Press of Harvard University Press, 2011), p. 52.

Early nineteenth-century caricature by Thomas Tegg, who comments on the navy's controversial policies involving prize money. As a ship prepares for an enemy attack, the officer standing on the left concludes too hastily that the kneeling crew member's prayers betray his cowardice. Instead those prayers are for justice: "I was only praying that the enemies shot may be distributed in the same proportion as the prize money, the greatest part among the Officers."

She had reason to suppose herself not yet forgotten by Mr. Crawford.—She had heard repeatedly from his sister within the three weeks which had passed since their leaving Mansfield, and in each letter there had been a few lines from himself, warm and determined like his speeches. It was a correspondence which Fanny found quite as unpleasant as she had feared. Miss Crawford's style of writing, lively and affectionate, was itself an evil, independent of what she was thus forced into reading from the brother's pen, for Edmund would never rest till she had read the chief of the letter to him, and then she had to listen to his admiration of her language, and the warmth of her attachments.—There had, in fact, been so much of message, of allusion, of recollection, so much of Mansfield in every letter, that Fanny could not but suppose it meant for him to hear; and to find herself forced into a purpose of that kind, compelled into a correspondence which was bringing her the addresses of the man she did not love, and obliging her to administer to the adverse passion of the man she did, was cruelly mortifying. Here, too, her present removal promised advantage. When no longer under the same roof with Edmund, she trusted that Miss Crawford would have no motive for writing, strong enough to overcome the trouble, and that at Portsmouth their correspondence would dwindle into nothing.

With such thoughts as these among ten hundred others, Fanny proceeded in her journey, safely and cheerfully, and as expeditiously as could rationally be hoped in the dirty month of February. They entered Oxford, but she could take only a hasty glimpse of Edmund's College as they passed along, and made no stop any where, till they reached Newbury, where a comfortable meal, uniting dinner and supper, wound up the enjoyments and fatigues of the day.[2]

The next morning saw them off again at an early hour; and with no events and no delays they regularly advanced, and were in the environs of Portsmouth while there was yet daylight for Fanny to look around her, and wonder at the new buildings.—They passed the Drawbridge, and entered the town;[3] and the light was only beginning to fail, as, guided by William's powerful voice, they were rattled into a narrow street, leading from the high street, and drawn up before the door of a small house now inhabited by Mr. Price.

Fanny was all agitation and flutter—all hope and apprehension. The moment they stopt, a trollopy-looking maid-servant, seemingly in waiting for them at the door, stept forward, and more intent on telling the news, than giving them any help, immediately began with "the Thrush is gone out of harbour, please Sir, and one of the officers has been here to"— — She was interrupted by a fine tall boy of eleven years old, who rushing out of the house, pushed the maid aside, and while William was opening the chaise door himself, called out, "you are just in time. We have been looking for you this half hour. The Thrush went out of harbour this morning. I saw her. It was a beautiful sight. And they think she will have her orders in a day or two.[4] And Mr. Campbell was here at four o'clock, to ask for you; he has got one of the Thrush's boats, and is going off to her at six, and hoped you would be here in time to go with him."

2 Fanny and William have broken their journey into two stages. Newbury in Berkshire, where they spend the night, is about sixty miles north of Portsmouth. The mud of the coach roads on which they travel—in an era prior to the introduction of macadamized roads—makes February a "dirty month."

3 Portsmouth was then a fortified town, protected by ramparts and a moat. The drawbridge over the moat, known as Landport Gate, led from the north end of the old town onto the High Street.

4 The *Thrush* has sailed out of Portsmouth harbor and anchored at Spithead. There she awaits the orders that will determine the direction of her voyage.

A stare or two at Fanny, as William helped her out of the carriage, was all the voluntary notice which this brother bestowed;—but he made no objection to her kissing him, though still entirely engaged in detailing farther particulars of the Thrush's going out of harbour, in which he had a strong right of interest, being to commence his career of seamanship in her at this very time.

Another moment, and Fanny was in the narrow entrance-passage of the house, and in her mother's arms, who met her there with looks of true kindness, and with features which Fanny loved the more, because they brought her aunt Bertram's before her; and there were her two sisters, Susan, a well-grown fine girl of fourteen, and Betsey, the youngest of the family, about five—both glad to see her in their way, though with no advantage of manner in receiving her. But manner Fanny did not want. Would they but love her, she should be satisfied.

She was then taken into a parlour, so small that her first conviction was of its being only a passage-room to something better, and she stood for a moment expecting to be invited on; but when she saw there was no other door, and that there were signs of habitation before her, she called back her thoughts, reproved herself, and grieved lest they should have been suspected. Her mother, however, could not stay long enough to suspect any thing. She was gone again to the street door, to welcome William. "Oh! my dear William, how glad I am to see you. But have you heard about the Thrush? She is gone out of harbour already, three days before we had any thought of it; and I do not know what I am to do about Sam's things, they will never be ready in time; for she may have her orders to-morrow, perhaps. It takes me quite unawares. And now you must be off for Spithead too. Campbell has been here, quite in a worry about you; and now, what shall we do? I thought to have had such a comfortable evening with you, and here every thing comes upon me at once."

Her son answered cheerfully, telling her that every thing was always for the best; and making light of his own inconvenience, in being obliged to hurry away so soon.

"To be sure, I had much rather she had stayed in harbour, that I might have sat a few hours with you in comfort; but as there is a boat ashore, I had better go off at once, and there is no help for it. Where-

Miniature portrait of Austen's brother Francis in his naval uniform. Austen playfully arranges for the fictional *Thrush,* the sloop on which William will serve as second lieutenant, to lie alongside the real *H. M. S. Canopus,* Captain Francis Austen's command during 1805–1806.

*Portsmouth Harbour,* early nineteenth-century color lithograph, originally painted by Thomas Rowlandson.

abouts does the Thrush lay at Spithead? Near the Canopus?[5] But no matter—here's Fanny in the parlour, and why should we stay in the passage?—Come, mother, you have hardly looked at your own dear Fanny yet."

In they both came, and Mrs. Price having kindly kissed her daughter again, and commented a little on her growth, began with very natural solicitude to feel for their fatigues and wants as travellers.

"Poor dears! how tired you must both be!—and now what will you have? I began to think you would never come. Betsey and I have been watching for you this half hour. And when did you get anything to eat? And what would you like to have now? I could not tell whether you would be for some meat, or only a dish of tea after your journey, or else I would have got something ready. And now I am afraid

5 Throughout this chapter, Austen borrows the names of actual navy vessels on which her two brothers who were officers had served: first the *Canopus,* which her elder brother Frank captained in 1805–1806; and further on in the chapter the *Elephant,* Frank's next command; the *Endymion,* on which her younger brother Charles served two tours of duty between 1797 and 1804, first as a midshipman and then as First Lieutenant; and the *Cleopatra,* whose command Charles assumed in 1810. On July 3, 1813, around the time she was finishing work on *Mansfield Park,* Austen wrote to Frank, then serving on the *Elephant* in the Baltic, and, after mentioning the new novel she had in hand, asked: "shall you object to my mentioning the Elephant in it, & two or three other of your old Ships?—I *have* done it, but it shall not stay, to make you angry" (*Letters,* p. 226).

6 Half-dead with cold. "Starved with cold" is a homely, colloquial expression, likely not one ever heard in the drawing room at Mansfield. Norman Page writes of Mrs. Price's frequent lapses into such expressions (see also her reference to their "sad fire") as "the linguistic correlate of the process whereby her whole style of living has been insidiously corrupted over a long period by poverty and fecklessness": *The Language of Jane Austen* (1972; rept. New York: Routledge, 2011), p. 160.

7 Bandboxes, used to transport ladies' bonnets, were made from either cardboard or very thin wood and were generally of slight construction. Mr. Price has likely done damage already.

8 The 1814 edition reads "Alert is the word." When she prepared the new edition of *Mansfield Park* for John Murray, this paragraph in which Fanny's father describes the *Thrush*'s progress from Portsmouth's inner harbor to Spithead was the passage that Austen revised most extensively, commencing with this sentence. It is generally thought that Austen consulted with her brothers Frank and Charles before implementing these alterations, which in the main seem intended to make the nautical jargon in which Mr. Price speaks more realistic. ("Alert," for example, might retroactively have been seen as too strong a word, one reserved in shipboard life for a situation in which an attack is in the offing.) While working on his *Life of Nelson* Robert Southey likewise had to draw on a seafaring brother for advice, admitting, "I walk among sea terms as a cat goes in a china pantry, in bodily fear of doing mischeif, & betraying myself" (quoted in Southam, *Jane Austen and the Navy,* p. 210). It is worth noting that Fanny is likely to find her father's speech—so different from the conversation heard at Mansfield—as opaque as many modern readers do.

9 "Mess" is the nautical term for provisions, the private store of food and tableware that William as an officer would be expected to carry aboard with him: in the 1816 *Mansfield Park* "mess" replaces the vaguer "things," which Austen had Mr. Price use in the 1814 edition. Turner's was an actual business in the Portsmouth High Street. Two of Austen's letters (from April 8–11, 1805, and January 10–11, 1809) mention using the

Campbell will be here, before there is time to dress a steak, and we have no butcher at hand. It is very inconvenient to have no butcher in the street. We were better off in our last house. Perhaps you would like some tea, as soon as it can be got."

They both declared they should prefer it to anything. "Then, Betsey, my dear, run into the kitchen, and see if Rebecca has put the water on; and tell her to bring in the tea-things as soon as she can. I wish we could get the bell mended—but Betsey is a very handy little messenger."

Betsey went with alacrity; proud to shew her abilities before her fine new sister.

"Dear me!" continued the anxious mother, "what a sad fire we have got, and I dare say you are both starved with cold.[6] Draw your chair nearer, my dear. I cannot think what Rebecca has been about. I am sure I told her to bring some coals half an hour ago. Susan, *you* should have taken care of the fire."

"I was up stairs, mamma, moving my things;" said Susan, in a fearless, self-defending tone, which startled Fanny. "You know you had but just settled that my sister Fanny and I should have the other room; and I could not get Rebecca to give me any help."

Farther discussion was prevented by various bustles; first, the driver came to be paid—then there was a squabble between Sam and Rebecca, about the manner of carrying up his sister's trunk, which he would manage all his own way; and lastly in walked Mr. Price himself, his own loud voice preceding him, as with something of the oath kind he kicked away his son's portmanteau, and his daughter's bandbox in the passage,[7] and called out for a candle; no candle was brought, however, and he walked into the room.

Fanny, with doubting feelings, had risen to meet him, but sank down again on finding herself undistinguished in the dusk, and unthought of. With a friendly shake of his son's hand, and an eager voice, he instantly began—"Ha! welcome back, my boy. Glad to see you. Have you heard the news? The Thrush went out of harbour this morning. Sharp is the word, you see.[8] By G—, you are just in time. The doctor has been here enquiring for you; he has got one of the boats, and is to be off for Spithead by six, so you had better go with him. I have been to Turner's about your mess;[9] it is all in a way to be done. I should not wonder if you had your orders to-morrow; but you cannot sail with this wind, if you are to cruize to the westward; and Captain Walsh thinks you will certainly have a cruize to the westward, with the Elephant. By G—, I wish you may. But old Scholey was saying just now, that he thought you would be sent first to the Texel.[10] Well, well, we are ready, whatever happens. But by G—, you lost a fine sight by not being here in the morning to see the Thrush go out of harbour. I would not have been out of the way for a thousand pounds. Old Scholey ran in at breakfast time, to say she had slipped her moorings and was coming out. I jumped up, and made but two steps to the platform.[11] If ever there was a perfect beauty afloat, she is one; and there she lays at Spithead, and anybody in England would take her for an eight-and-twenty.[12] I was upon the platform two hours this afternoon, looking at her. She lays close to the Endymion, between her and the Cleopatra, just to the eastward of the sheer hulk."[13]

"Ha!" cried William, "*that's* just where I should have put her myself. It's the best birth at Spithead. But here is my sister, Sir, here is Fanny;" turning and leading her forward;—"it is so dark you do not see her."[14]

With an acknowledgment that he had quite forgot her, Mr. Price now received his daughter; and, having given her a cordial hug, and observed that she was grown into a woman, and he supposed would be wanting a husband soon, seemed very much inclined to forget her again. Fanny shrunk back to her seat, with feelings sadly pained by his language and his smell of spirits; and he talked on only to his son, and only of the Thrush, though William, warmly interested, as he was, in that subject, more than once tried to make his father think of Fanny, and her long absence and long journey.

After sitting some time longer, a candle was obtained; but as there was still no appearance of tea, nor, from Betsey's reports from the kitchen, much hope of any under a considerable period, William determined to go and change his dress, and make the necessary preparations for his removal on board directly, that he might have his tea in comfort afterwards.

9 services of a "Mr. Turner" when the Austen family needs help in conveying a letter or parcel to Frank and Charles aboard their ships (*Letters*, pp. 106, 171).

10 The Texel is the channel dividing the Dutch mainland from the Friesian islands off the coast. If the *Thrush*'s orders take her east to the Texel, she will be joining the part of the fleet that has been trusted with the Royal Navy's blockade of Napoleonic Europe (ships leaving the naval base at Amsterdam would have to traverse the channel to access the North Sea). A cruise westward into the Atlantic would present more opportunities for capturing a prize.

11 To get a good view Mr. Price hurried to a spot called the Saluting Platform, located at the south end of the High Street. It formed part of the harbor fortifications that dated back to the Tudor era.

12 To Mr. Price, the *Thrush*, though only a sloop, a small vessel, looks as good as though it were a frigate, a vessel large enough to carry twenty-eight guns.

13 A hulk is a vessel that is no longer seaworthy. Some of the hulks in Portsmouth harbor in the early nineteenth century functioned as floating prisons (their portholes on the landward side were boarded up to deter escapes), but Southam suggests in *Jane Austen and the Navy* that the sheer hulk would have been a vessel dedicated to the maintenance of other ships and equipped with sheers for the removal and fitting of their masts and spars (p. 210). William's response in the next sentence to his father's narrative, an addition Austen made for the 1816 edition, indicates his local knowledge.

14 The sharp eyes Mr. Price evidently had for that "perfect beauty," the *Thrush*, momentarily fail him where Fanny is concerned.

15 A merchant vessel belonging to the East India
Company and engaged in trade with India.

This rather crudely designed early nineteenth-century painting shows the Saluting
Platform that makes up a portion of Portsmouth's ramparts. The port's semaphore
tower is visible in the image's center.

As he left the room, two rosy-faced boys, ragged and dirty, about
eight and nine years old, rushed into it just released from school, and
coming eagerly to see their sister, and tell that the Thrush was gone
out of harbour; Tom and Charles: Charles had been born since Fanny's going away, but Tom she had often helped to nurse, and now felt
a particular pleasure in seeing again. Both were kissed very tenderly,
but Tom she wanted to keep by her, to try to trace the features of the
baby she had loved, and talked to, of his infant preference of herself.
Tom, however, had no mind for such treatment: he came home, not
to stand and be talked to, but to run about and make a noise; and
both boys had soon burst from her, and slammed the parlour door
till her temples ached.

She had now seen all that were at home; there remained only two
brothers between herself and Susan, one of whom was a clerk in a
public office in London, and the other midshipman on board an In-
diaman.[15] But though she had *seen* all the members of the family, she
had not yet *heard* all the noise they could make. Another quarter of

an hour brought her a great deal more. William was soon calling out from the landing-place of the second story, for his mother and for Rebecca. He was in distress for something that he had left there, and did not find again. A key was mislaid, Betsey accused of having got at his new hat, and some slight, but essential alteration of his uniform waistcoat, which he had been promised to have done for him, entirely neglected.

Mrs. Price, Rebecca, and Betsey all went up to defend themselves, all talking together, but Rebecca loudest, and the job was to be done as well as it could, in a great hurry; William trying in vain to send Betsey down again, or keep her from being troublesome where she was; the whole of which, as almost every door in the house was open, could be plainly distinguished in the parlour, except when drowned at intervals by the superior noise of Sam, Tom, and Charles chasing each other up and down stairs, and tumbling about and hallooing.

Fanny was almost stunned. The smallness of the house, and thinness of the walls, brought every thing so close to her, that, added to the fatigue of her journey, and all her recent agitation, she hardly knew how to bear it. *Within* the room all was tranquil enough, for Susan having disappeared with the others, there were soon only her father and herself remaining; and he taking out a newspaper—the accustomary loan of a neighbour,[16] applied himself to studying it, without seeming to recollect her existence. The solitary candle was held between himself and the paper, without any reference to her possible convenience; but she had nothing to do, and was glad to have the light screened from her aching head, as she sat in bewildered, broken, sorrowful contemplation.

She was at home. But, alas! it was not such a home, she had not such a welcome, as——she checked herself; she was unreasonable. What right had she to be of importance to her family? She could have none, so long lost sight of! William's concerns must be dearest—they always had been—and he had every right. Yet to have so little said or asked about herself—to have scarcely an enquiry made after Mansfield! It did pain her to have Mansfield forgotten; the friends who had done so much—the dear, dear friends! But here, one subject swallowed up all the rest. Perhaps it must be so. The destina-

16 With taxes on newspapers kept high by a government made anxious by the freedom of the press, they were expensive to buy and were often shared. In *Waverley; Or, 'Tis Sixty Years Since* Walter Scott describes how a newspaper is passed from Waverley-Honour, having regaled the master of the house, his sister, and his butler, to the nearby rectory, and thence "to Squire Stubbs's at the Grange, from the squire to the baronet's steward . . . from the steward to the bailiff, and from him through a huge circle of honest dames and gaffers" (*Waverley,* ed. Claire Lamont [Oxford: Oxford University Press, 1986], p. 7). Scott's novel from 1814 is set in the 1740s: a modern road system and post office and communications technologies like the telegraph disseminated the news more quickly seventy years later, but the taxes on knowledge, as they were called, remained.

17 The boatswain was the officer responsible for the crew's work on the ship's sails, rigging, and cables. An overseer of sorts, he called the crew to their labors using a special whistle (hence the pun in Mr. Price's reference to Sam's "confounded pipe").

18 Tired out.

tion of the Thrush must be now pre-eminently interesting. A day or two might shew the difference. *She* only was to blame. Yet she thought it would not have been so at Mansfield. No, in her uncle's house there would have been a consideration of times and seasons, a regulation of subject, a propriety, an attention towards every body which there was not here.

The only interruption which thoughts like these received for nearly half an hour, was from a sudden burst of her father's, not at all calculated to compose them. At a more than ordinary pitch of thumping and hallooing in the passage, he exclaimed, "Devil take those young dogs! How they are singing out! Ay, Sam's voice louder than all the rest! That boy is fit for a boatswain. Holla—you there—Sam—stop your confounded pipe, or I shall be after you."[17]

This threat was so palpably disregarded, that though within five minutes afterwards the three boys all burst into the room together and sat down, Fanny could not consider it as a proof of any thing more than their being for the time thoroughly fagged,[18] which their hot faces and panting breaths seemed to prove—especially as they were still kicking each other's shins, and hallooing out at sudden starts immediately under their father's eye.

The next opening of the door brought something more welcome; it was for the tea-things, which she had begun almost to despair of seeing that evening. Susan and an attendant girl, whose inferior appearance informed Fanny, to her great surprise, that she had previously seen the upper servant brought in every thing necessary for the meal; Susan looking as she put the kettle on the fire and glanced at her sister, as if divided between the agreeable triumph of shewing her activity and usefulness, and the dread of being thought to demean herself by such an office. "She had been into the kitchen," she said, "to hurry Sally and help make the toast, and spread the bread and butter—or she did not know when they should have got tea—and she was sure her sister must want something after her journey."

Fanny was very thankful. She could not but own that she should be very glad of a little tea, and Susan immediately set about making it, as if pleased to have the employment all to herself; and with only a little unnecessary bustle, and some few injudicious attempts at keeping her brothers in better order than she could, acquitted herself very well. Fanny's spirit was as much refreshed as her body; her head and heart were soon the better for such well-timed kindness. Susan had an open, sensible countenance; she was like William—and Fanny hoped to find her like him in disposition and good will towards herself.

In this more placid state of things William re-entered, followed not far behind by his mother and Betsey. He, complete in his Lieutenant's uniform, looking and moving all the taller, firmer, and more graceful for it, and with the happiest smile over his face, walked up directly to Fanny—who, rising from her seat, looked at him for a moment in speechless admiration, and then threw her arms round his neck to sob out her various emotions of pain and pleasure.

Anxious not to appear unhappy, she soon recovered herself: and wiping away her tears, was able to notice and admire all the striking parts of his dress—listening with reviving spirits to his cheerful hopes of being on shore some part of every day before they sailed, and even of getting her to Spithead to see the sloop.

The next bustle brought in Mr. Campbell, the Surgeon of the Thrush, a very well behaved young man, who came to call for his friend, and for whom there was with some contrivance found a chair, and with some hasty washing of the young tea-maker's, a cup and saucer; and after another quarter of an hour of earnest talk between the gentlemen, noise rising upon noise, and bustle upon bustle, men and boys at last all in motion together, the moment came for setting off; every thing was ready, William took leave, and all of them were gone—for the three boys, in spite of their mother's intreaty, determined to see their brother and Mr. Campbell to the sally-port;[19] and Mr. Price walked off at the same time to carry back his neighbour's newspaper.

Something like tranquillity might now be hoped for, and accordingly, when Rebecca had been prevailed on to carry away the tea-things, and Mrs. Price had walked about the room some time looking for a shirt-sleeve, which Betsey at last hunted out from a drawer in the kitchen, the small party of females were pretty well composed, and the mother having lamented again over the impossibility of get-

19 The landing-place from which the *Thrush*'s boat will leave to take William and any other men on shore back to the sloop.

20 Domestic servants were usually hired by the year. As Rebecca and her mistress would each have been aware, there was a chronic shortage of women willing to fill the lowly position of maid-of-all-work in less affluent households like the Prices'.

ting Sam ready in time, was at leisure to think of her eldest daughter and the friends she had come from.

A few enquiries began; but one of the earliest—"How did sister Bertram manage about her servants? Was she as much plagued as herself to get tolerable servants?"—soon led her mind away from Northamptonshire, and fixed it on her own domestic grievances; and the shocking character of all the Portsmouth servants, of whom she believed her own two were the very worst, engrossed her completely. The Bertrams were all forgotten in detailing the faults of Rebecca, against whom Susan had also much to depose, and little Betsey a great deal more, and who did seem so thoroughly without a single recommendation, that Fanny could not help modestly presuming that her mother meant to part with her when her year was up.

"Her year!" cried Mrs. Price; "I am sure I hope I shall be rid of her before she has staid a year, for that will not be up till November. Servants are come to such a pass, my dear, in Portsmouth, that it is quite a miracle if one keeps them more than half-a-year.[20] I have no hope of ever being settled; and if I was to part with Rebecca, I should only get something worse. And yet I do not think I am a very difficult mistress to please—and I am sure the place is easy enough, for there is always a girl under her, and I often do half the work myself."

Fanny was silent; but not from being convinced that there might not be a remedy found for some of these evils. As she now sat looking at Betsey, she could not but think particularly of another sister, a very pretty little girl, whom she had left there not much younger when she went into Northamptonshire, who had died a few years afterwards. There had been something remarkably amiable about her. Fanny, in those early days, had preferred her to Susan; and when the news of her death had at last reached Mansfield, had for a short time been quite afflicted.—The sight of Betsey brought the image of little Mary back again, but she would not have pained her mother by alluding to her, for the world.—While considering her with these ideas, Betsey, at a small distance, was holding out something to catch her eyes, meaning to screen it at the same time from Susan's.

"What have you got there, my love?" said Fanny, "come and shew it to me."

It was a silver knife. Up jumped Susan, claiming it as her own, and trying to get it away; but the child ran to her mother's protection, and Susan could only reproach, which she did very warmly, and evidently hoping to interest Fanny on her side. "It was very hard that she was not to have her *own* knife; it was her own knife; little sister Mary had left it to her upon her death-bed, and she ought to have had it to keep herself long ago. But mamma kept it from her, and was always letting Betsey get hold of it; and the end of it would be that Betsey would spoil it, and get it for her own, though mamma had *promised* her that Betsey should not have it in her own hands."

Fanny was quite shocked. Every feeling of duty, honour, and tenderness was wounded by her sister's speech and her mother's reply.

"Now, Susan," cried Mrs. Price in a complaining voice, "now, how can you be so cross? You are always quarrelling about that knife. I wish you would not be so quarrelsome. Poor little Betsey; how cross Susan is to you! But you should not have taken it out, my dear, when I sent you to the drawer. You know I told you not to touch it, because Susan is so cross about it. I must hide it another time, Betsey. Poor Mary little thought it would be such a bone of contention when she gave it me to keep, only two hours before she died. Poor little soul! she could but just speak to be heard, and she said so prettily, 'Let sister Susan have my knife, mamma, when I am dead and buried.'— Poor little dear! she was so fond of it, Fanny, that she would have it lay by her in bed, all through her illness. It was the gift of her good godmother, old Mrs. Admiral Maxwell, only six weeks before she was taken for death. Poor little sweet creature! Well, she was taken away from evil to come. My own Betsey, (fondling her), *you* have not the luck of such a good godmother. Aunt Norris lives too far off, to think of such little people as you."

Fanny had indeed nothing to convey from aunt Norris, but a message to say she hoped that her god-daughter was a good girl, and learnt her book.[21] There had been at one moment a slight murmur in the drawing-room at Mansfield Park, about sending her a Prayer-

21  Worked hard at learning to read.

William Marshall Craig's 1804 watercolor depicting a
street vendor selling bonnet boxes. Fanny would have
transported bonnets to Portsmouth in a box resembling his wares.

book; but no second sound had been heard of such a purpose. Mrs.
Norris, however, had gone home and taken down two old Prayer-
books of her husband, with that idea, but upon examination, the ardour of generosity went off. One was found to have too small a print
for a child's eyes, and the other to be too cumbersome for her to
carry about.

Fanny fatigued and fatigued again, was thankful to accept the first
invitation of going to bed; and before Betsey had finished her cry at
being allowed to sit up only one hour extraordinary in honour of sister, she was off, leaving all below in confusion and noise again, the
boys begging for toasted cheese, her father calling out for his rum
and water, and Rebecca never where she ought to be.

There was nothing to raise her spirits in the confined and scantily-
furnished chamber that she was to share with Susan. The smallness
of the rooms above and below indeed, and the narrowness of the
passage and staircase, struck her beyond her imagination. She soon
learnt to think with respect of her own little attic at Mansfield Park,
in *that* house reckoned too small for anybody's comfort.

# 8

COULD SIR THOMAS have seen all his niece's feelings, when she wrote her first letter to her aunt, he would not have despaired; for though a good night's rest, a pleasant morning, the hope of soon seeing William again, and the comparatively quiet state of the house, from Tom and Charles being gone to school, Sam on some project of his own, and her father on his usual lounges,[1] enabled her to express herself cheerfully on the subject of home, there were still to her own perfect consciousness, many drawbacks suppressed. Could he have seen only half that she felt before the end of a week, he would have thought Mr. Crawford sure of her, and been delighted with his own sagacity.

Before the week ended, it was all disappointment. In the first place, William was gone. The Thrush had had her orders, the wind had changed, and he was sailed within four days from their reaching Portsmouth; and during those days, she had seen him only twice, in a short and hurried way, when he had come ashore on duty. There had been no free conversation, no walk on the ramparts, no visit to the dock-yard, no acquaintance with the Thrush—nothing of all that they had planned and depended on. Every thing in that quarter failed her, except William's affection. His last thought on leaving home was for her. He stepped back again to the door to say, "Take care of Fanny, mother. She is tender, and not used to rough it like the rest of us. I charge you, take care of Fanny."

William was gone;—and the home he had left her in was—Fanny could not conceal it from herself—in almost every respect, the very

1 Strolls.

2 The most popular of these lists was *Steel's Original and Correct List of the Royal Navy,* a periodical updated monthly and sold for sixpence. Though it contained other information, its main attraction was its alphabetical list of navy officers, sorted according to rank. For regular readers *Steel's* provided a kind of Facebook of the Royal Navy, complete with status updates. Navy lists figure in *Persuasion* as well. In Vol. I, Chap. 5, the narrator identifies them, along with newspapers, as sources for Anne Elliot's knowledge of the professional success that Captain Wentworth met with in the years that followed their estrangement. In Vol. I, Chap. 8, Henrietta and Louisa Musgrove, smitten with Wentworth, hasten to obtain "their own" copy of the navy list, "the first that had ever been at Uppercross," the better to follow the handsome captain's stories of his life at sea.

3 Another anchorage near Portsmouth harbor, located to the west of Spithead.

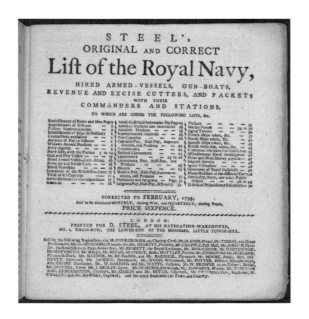

Steel's Navy List, reading matter to which Fanny's father probably resorts both to keep tabs on his former shipmates and to wile away his many hours of leisure.

reverse of what she could have wished. It was the abode of noise, disorder, and impropriety. Nobody was in their right place, nothing was done as it ought to be. She could not respect her parents, as she had hoped. On her father, her confidence had not been sanguine, but he was more negligent of his family, his habits were worse, and his manners coarser, than she had been prepared for. He did not want abilities; but he had no curiosity, and no information beyond his profession; he read only the newspaper and the navy-list;[2] he talked only of the dockyard, the harbour, Spithead, and the Motherbank;[3] he swore and he drank, he was dirty and gross. She had never been able to recal anything approaching to tenderness in his former treatment of herself. There had remained only a general impression of roughness and loudness; and now he scarcely ever noticed her, but to make her the object of a coarse joke.

Her disappointment in her mother was greater; *there* she had hoped much, and found almost nothing. Every flattering scheme of being of consequence to her soon fell to the ground. Mrs. Price was not unkind—but, instead of gaining on her affection and confidence,[4] and becoming more and more dear, her daughter never met with greater kindness from her, than on the first day of her arrival. The instinct of nature was soon satisfied, and Mrs. Price's attachment had no other source. Her heart and her time were already quite full; she had neither leisure nor affection to bestow on Fanny. Her daughters never had been much to her. She was fond of her sons, especially of William, but Betsey was the first of her girls whom she had ever much regarded. To her she was most injudiciously indulgent. William was her pride; Betsey, her darling; and John, Richard, Sam, Tom, and Charles, occupied all the rest of her maternal solicitude, alternately her worries and her comforts. These shared her heart; her time was given chiefly to her house and her servants. Her days were spent in a kind of slow bustle; all was busy without getting on, always behindhand and lamenting it, without altering her ways; wishing to be an economist, without contrivance or regularity; dissatisfied with her servants, without skill to make them better, and whether helping, or reprimanding, or indulging them, without any power of engaging their respect.

Of her two sisters, Mrs. Price very much more resembled Lady Bertram than Mrs. Norris. She was a manager by necessity, without any of Mrs. Norris's inclination for it, or any of her activity. Her disposition was naturally easy and indolent, like Lady Bertram's; and a situation of similar affluence and do-nothing-ness would have been much more suited to her capacity, than the exertions and self-denials of the one, which her imprudent marriage had placed her in. She might have made just as good a woman of consequence as Lady Bertram, but Mrs. Norris would have been a more respectable mother of nine children, on a small income.

Much of all this, Fanny could not but be sensible of. She might scruple to make use of the words, but she must and did feel that her mother was a partial, ill-judging parent, a dawdle, a slattern, who neither taught nor restrained her children, whose house was the scene of mismanagement and discomfort from beginning to end, and who had no talent, no conversation, no affection towards herself; no curiosity to know her better, no desire of her friendship, and no inclination for her company that could lessen her sense of such feelings.

Fanny was very anxious to be useful, and not to appear above her home, or in any way disqualified or disinclined, by her foreign education, from contributing her help to its comforts, and therefore set about working for Sam immediately,[5] and by working early and late, with perseverance and great dispatch, did so much, that the boy was shipped off at last, with more than half his linen ready. She had great pleasure in feeling her usefulness, but could not conceive how they would have managed without her.

Sam, loud and overbearing as he was, she rather regretted when he went, for he was clever and intelligent, and glad to be employed in any errand in the town; and though spurning the remonstrances of Susan, given as they were—though very reasonable in themselves, with ill-timed and powerless warmth, was beginning to be influenced by Fanny's services, and gentle persuasions; and she found that the best of the three younger ones was gone in him; Tom and Charles being at least as many years as they were his juniors distant from that age of feeling and reason, which might suggest the expediency of making friends, and of endeavouring to be less disagreeable. Their

4  Instead of becoming her confidante.

5  Laboring for Sam by sewing some of the clothing the boy will take to sea.

Early nineteenth-century comic print showing a young midshipman's sea chest being packed in preparation for his voyage. Intent on practicing his swordsmanship, the boy seems, perhaps like young Sam Price, to have delegated all the actual packing to the female members of his family.

sister soon despaired of making the smallest impression on *them;* they were quite untameable by any means of address which she had spirits or time to attempt. Every afternoon brought a return of their riotous games all over the house; and she very early learnt to sigh at the approach of Saturday's constant half holiday.

Betsey too, a spoilt child, trained up to think the alphabet her greatest enemy, left to be with the servants at her pleasure, and then encouraged to report any evil of them, she was almost as ready to despair of being able to love or assist; and of Susan's temper, she had many doubts. Her continual disagreements with her mother, her rash squabbles with Tom and Charles, and petulance with Betsey, were at least so distressing to Fanny, that though admitting they were by no means without provocation, she feared the disposition that could push them to such length must be far from amiable, and from affording any repose to herself.

Such was the home which was to put Mansfield out of her head, and teach her to think of her cousin Edmund with moderated feelings. On the contrary, she could think of nothing but Mansfield, its beloved inmates, its happy ways. Every thing where she now was was in full contrast to it. The elegance, propriety, regularity, harmony—and perhaps, above all, the peace and tranquillity of Mansfield, were brought to her remembrance every hour of the day, by the prevalence of every thing opposite to them *here*.

The living in incessant noise was to a frame and temper, delicate and nervous like Fanny's, an evil which no superadded elegance or harmony could have entirely atoned for. It was the greatest misery of all. At Mansfield, no sounds of contention, no raised voice, no abrupt bursts, no tread of violence was ever heard; all proceeded in a regular course of cheerful orderliness; every body had their due importance; every body's feelings were consulted. If tenderness could be ever supposed wanting, good sense and good breeding supplied its place; and as to the little irritations, sometimes introduced by aunt Norris, they were short, they were trifling, they were as a drop of water to the ocean, compared with the ceaseless tumult of her present abode. Here, every body was noisy, every voice was loud, (excepting, perhaps, her mother's, which resembled the soft monotony of Lady Bertram's, only worn into fretfulness.)—Whatever was wanted, was halloo'd for, and the servants halloo'd out their excuses from the kitchen. The doors were in constant banging, the stairs were never at rest, nothing was done without a clatter, nobody sat still, and nobody could command attention when they spoke.

In a review of the two houses, as they appeared to her before the end of a week, Fanny was tempted to apply to them Dr. Johnson's celebrated judgment as to matrimony and celibacy, and say, that though Mansfield Park might have some pains, Portsmouth could have no pleasures.[6]

6 The reference is to the "oriental tale" *Rasselas* (1759), in which Samuel Johnson recounts the investigations that Rasselas and his companions undertake into the nature of the good life. In chapter 26, Rasselas's philosophizing sister Princess Pekuah turns the group's attention to the discords that frequently make family life a scene of discontent; nonetheless, she declares that "Marriage has many pains, but celibacy has no pleasures" (*The History of Rasselas, Prince of Abissinia,* ed. Thomas Keymer [Oxford: Oxford University Press, 2009], p. 59). Despite this decision, Johnson eschews for his fiction the marriage plot that was increasingly central to the new novels of his day, and when *Rasselas* concludes Pekuah remains single, as do the book's other characters.

*Dr. Samuel Johnson,* portrait after Sir Joshua Reynolds, circa 1772. When in his Biographical Notice of his sister Henry Austen lists Jane Austen's favorite authors, Johnson (1709–1784) figures alongside Cowper and Crabbe.

9

FANNY WAS RIGHT ENOUGH in not expecting to hear from Miss Crawford now, at the rapid rate in which their correspondence had begun; Mary's next letter was after a decidedly longer interval than the last, but she was not right in supposing that such an interval would be felt a great relief to herself.—Here was another strange revolution of mind!—She was really glad to receive the letter when it did come. In her present exile from good society, and distance from every thing that had been wont to interest her, a letter from one belonging to the set where her heart lived, written with affection, and some degree of elegance, was thoroughly acceptable.—The usual plea of increasing engagements was made in excuse for not having written to her earlier, "and now that I have begun," she continued, my letter will not be worth your reading, for there will be no little offering of love at the end, no three or four lines passionnées[1] from the most devoted H. C. in the world, for Henry is in Norfolk; business called him to Everingham ten days ago, or perhaps he only pretended to call, for the sake of being travelling at the same time that you were. But there he is, and, by the by, his absence may sufficiently account for any remissness of his sister's in writing, for there has been no 'well, Mary, when do you write to Fanny?—is not it time for you to write to Fanny?' to spur me on. At last, after various attempts at meeting, I have seen your cousins, 'dear Julia and dearest Mrs. Rushworth;' they found me at home yesterday, and we were glad to see each other again. We *seemed very* glad to see each other, and I do really think we were a little.—We had a vast deal to say.—Shall I tell you how Mrs. Rushworth looked when your name was mentioned? I did not use to think her wanting in self-possession, but she had not quite enough for the demands of yesterday. Upon the whole Julia was in the best looks of the two, at least after you were spoken of. There was no recovering the complexion from the moment that I spoke of 'Fanny,' and spoke of her as a sister should.—But Mrs. Rushworth's day of good looks will come; we have cards for her first party on the 28th.—Then she will be in beauty, for she will open one of the best houses in Wimpole Street.[2] I was in it two years ago, when it was Lady Lascelles's, and prefer it to almost any I know in London, and certainly she will then feel—to use a vulgar phrase—that she has got her pennyworth for her penny. Henry could not have afforded her such a house. I hope she will recollect it, and be satisfied, as well as she may, with moving the queen of a palace, though the king may appear best in the back ground; and as I have no desire to tease her, I shall never *force* your name upon her again. She will grow sober by degrees.—From all that I hear and guess, Baron Wildenhaim's attentions to Julia continue, but I do not know that he has any serious en-

2 The Rushworths have taken up residence in Marylebone, an expensive district in London first developed in the mid-eighteenth century and soon associated in the public mind with the West Indian sugar magnates who flocked there from the Caribbean and brought their often phenomenal wealth with them. Edward Long, owner of the misleadingly named Lucky Valley plantation in Clarendon, Jamaica, and, as author of a *History of Jamaica* and a tract deploring the Mansfield Judgment, a leading proslavery publicist, lived on Wimpole Street. Later, so did the poet Elizabeth Barrett Browning, whose father and grandfather owed their wealth to Jamaican plantations.

Devonshire Place and Wimpole Street, as viewed in an engraving from 1793. The Rushworths have taken up residence on this fashionable street.

3 An efficient but snide way to refer to Mr. Yates, whose income does not match his aristocratic title.

Thomas Rowlandson, *Portsmouth Point,* 1811: an especially seedy district in the early nineteenth century. The bustle, noise, and carousing evoked in Rowlandson's water-color sketch suggest why Fanny might be predisposed to find the inhabitants of Portsmouth uncongenial company.

couragement. She ought to do better. A poor honourable is no catch,[3] and I cannot imagine any liking in the case, for, take away his rants, and the poor Baron has nothing. What a difference a vowel makes!— if his rents were but equal to his rants!—Your cousin Edmund moves slowly; detained, perchance, by parish duties. There may be some old woman at Thornton Lacey to be converted. I am unwilling to fancy myself neglected for a *young* one. Adieu, my dear sweet Fanny, this is a long letter from London; write me a pretty one in reply to gladden Henry's eyes, when he comes back—and send me an account of all the dashing young captains whom you disdain for his sake."

There was great food for meditation in this letter, and chiefly for unpleasant meditation; and yet, with all the uneasiness it supplied, it connected her with the absent, it told her of people and things about whom she had never felt so much curiosity as now, and she would have been glad to have been sure of such a letter every week.

Her correspondence with her aunt Bertram was her only concern of higher interest.

As for any society in Portsmouth, that could at all make amends for deficiencies at home, there were none within the circle of her father's and mother's acquaintance to afford her the smallest satisfaction; she saw nobody in whose favour she could wish to overcome her own shyness and reserve. The men appeared to her all coarse, the women all pert, every body under-bred; and she gave as little contentment as she received from introductions either to old or new acquaintance. The young ladies who approached her at first with some respect, in consideration of her coming from a Baronet's family, were soon offended by what they termed "airs"—for as she neither played on the pianoforte nor wore fine pelisses,[4] they could, on farther observation, admit no right of superiority.

The first solid consolation which Fanny received for the evils of home, the first which her judgment could entirely approve, and which gave any promise of durability, was in a better knowledge of Susan, and a hope of being of service to her. Susan had always behaved pleasantly to herself, but the determined character of her general manners had astonished and alarmed her, and it was at least a fortnight before she began to understand a disposition so totally different from her own. Susan saw that much was wrong at home, and wanted to set it right. That a girl of fourteen, acting only on her own unassisted reason, should err in the method of reform was not wonderful;[5] and Fanny soon became more disposed to admire the natural light of the mind which could so early distinguish justly, than to censure severely the faults of conduct to which it led. Susan was only acting on the same truths, and pursuing the same system, which her own judgment acknowledged, but which her more supine and yielding temper would have shrunk from asserting. Susan tried to be useful, where *she* could only have gone away and cried; and that Susan was useful she could perceive; that things, bad as they were, would have been worse but for such interposition, and that both her mother and Betsey were restrained from some excesses of very offensive indulgence and vulgarity.

4 The pelisse was a fitted, ankle-length coat worn over a dress.

5 That Susan has made mistakes is *not surprising*.

In every argument with her mother, Susan had in point of reason the advantage, and never was there any maternal tenderness to buy her off. The blind fondness which was for ever producing evil around her, *she* had never known. There was no gratitude for affection past or present, to make her better bear with its excesses to the others.

All this became gradually evident, and gradually placed Susan before her sister as an object of mingled compassion and respect. That her manner was wrong, however, at times very wrong—her measures often ill-chosen and ill-timed, and her looks and language very often indefensible, Fanny could not cease to feel; but she began to hope they might be rectified. Susan, she found, looked up to her and wished for her good opinion; and new as any thing like an office of authority was to Fanny, new as it was to imagine herself capable of guiding or informing any one, she did resolve to give occasional hints to Susan, and endeavour to exercise for her advantage the juster notions of what was due to every body, and what would be wisest for herself, which her own more favoured education had fixed in her.

Her influence, or at least the consciousness and use of it, originated in an act of kindness by Susan, which after many hesitations of delicacy, she at last worked herself up to. It had very early occurred to her, that a small sum of money might, perhaps, restore peace for ever on the sore subject of the silver knife, canvassed as it now was continually, and the riches which she was in possession of herself, her uncle having given her 10*l.* at parting, made her as able as she was willing to be generous. But she was so wholly unused to confer favours, except on the very poor, so unpractised in removing evils, or bestowing kindnesses among her equals, and so fearful of appearing to elevate herself as a great lady at home, that it took some time to determine that it would not be unbecoming in her to make such a present. It was made, however, at last; a silver knife was bought for Betsey, and accepted with great delight, its newness giving it every advantage over the other that could be desired; Susan was established in the full possession of her own, Betsey handsomely declaring that now she had got one so much prettier herself, she should never want *that* again—and no reproach seemed conveyed to the equally satisfied mother, which Fanny had almost feared to be impossible.

The deed thoroughly answered; a source of domestic altercation was entirely done away, and it was the means of opening Susan's heart to her, and giving her something more to love and be interested in. Susan shewed that she had delicacy; pleased as she was to be mistress of property which she had been struggling for at least two years, she yet feared that her sister's judgment had been against her, and that a reproof was designed her for having so struggled as to make the purchase necessary for the tranquillity of the house.

Her temper was open. She acknowledged her fears, blamed herself for having contended so warmly, and from that hour Fanny understanding the worth of her disposition, and perceiving how fully she was inclined to seek her good opinion and refer to her judgment, began to feel again the blessing of affection, and to entertain the hope of being useful to a mind so much in need of help, and so much deserving it. She gave advice; advice too sound to be resisted by a good understanding, and given so mildly and considerately as not to irritate an imperfect temper; and she had the happiness of observing its good effects not unfrequently; more was not expected by one, who, while seeing all the obligation and expediency of submission and forbearance, saw also with sympathetic acuteness of feeling, all that must be hourly grating to a girl like Susan. Her greatest wonder on the subject soon became—not that Susan should have been provoked into disrespect and impatience against her better knowledge—but that so much better knowledge, so many good notions, should have been hers at all; and that, brought up in the midst of negligence and error, she should have formed such proper opinions of what ought to be—she, who had had no cousin Edmund to direct her thoughts or fix her principles.

The intimacy thus begun between them was a material advantage to each. By sitting together up stairs, they avoided a great deal of the disturbance of the house; Fanny had peace, and Susan learnt to think it no misfortune to be quietly employed. They sat without a fire; but *that* was a privation familiar even to Fanny, and she suffered the less because reminded by it of the east-room. It was the only point of resemblance. In space, light, furniture, and prospect, there was nothing alike in the two apartments; and she often heaved a sigh at the

6 Circulating libraries were commercial establishments that lent out books to their subscribers. The rates for subscriptions varied, but from an anonymously authored pamphlet published in London in 1797 entitled *The Use of Circulating Libraries Considered* it appears that at the end of the eighteenth century subscribers could count on paying as little as eighteen pence or two shillings for a month's worth of borrowing privileges (p. 10). (The "yearly subscriber," this author continues enthusiastically, could "read as many books for one guinea, which, to purchase, would cost ONE HUNDRED" [p. 10].) The spread of these libraries throughout Britain at the end of the eighteenth century transformed reading into a pastime that was accessible even to those, like Fanny, with limited incomes. For some commentators, however, made anxious by the many novels found on circulating library shelves, these establishments were to be deplored for purveying a kind of "mischievous trash" that would create in young women an "aversion" to serious literature—or so declares the Reverend Thomas Gisborne in his *Enquiry into the Duties of the Female Sex* (p. 353)—or, worse still, that would give their minds the "romantic turn" that would occasion "fatal mistakes in their conduct"—as Sarah Pennington puts it in another moralizing book, *An Unfortunate Mother's Advice to her Absent Daughters* (3rd ed. [London: W. Bristow, 1761], p. 40). Fanny's choice of reading matter—biography and poetry, and also history, as we will see later, but *not* novels—might reassure those holding such views.

Isaac Cruikshank, *The Circulating Library,* circa 1800–1811. As the state of the shelves behind the counter indicates, Cruikshank represents the female clientele of this commercial lending library as very keen to borrow novels, romances, and tales and very reluctant to borrow books of sermons.

remembrance of all her books and boxes, and various comforts there. By degrees the girls came to spend the chief of the morning up stairs, at first only in working and talking; but after a few days, the remembrance of the said books grew so potent and stimulative, that Fanny found it impossible not to try for books again. There were none in her father's house; but wealth is luxurious and daring—and some of hers found its way to a circulating library.[6] She became a subscriber—amazed at being any thing in *propria persona,* amazed at her own doings in every way; to be a renter, a chuser of books! And to be having any one's improvement in view in her choice! But so it was. Susan had read nothing, and Fanny longed to give her a share in her own first pleasures, and inspire a taste for the biography and poetry which she delighted in herself.

In this occupation she hoped, moreover, to bury some of the recollections of Mansfield which were too apt to seize her mind if her
fingers only were busy; and especially at this time, hoped it might
be useful in diverting her thoughts from pursuing Edmund to London, whither, on the authority of her aunt's last letter, she knew he
was gone. She had no doubt of what would ensue. The promised no-
tification was hanging over her head. The postman's knock within
the neighbourhood was beginning to bring its daily terrors[7]—and if
reading could banish the idea for even half an hour, it was something gained.

7 Fanny can hear the postman knocking at the doors
of the other houses in the neighborhood, something
he would do so as to rouse the people within and collect the postage for the letters he had brought them.

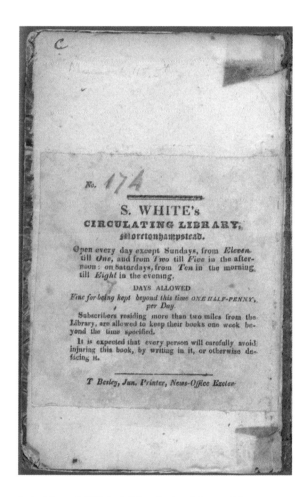

Label from S. White's Circulating Library, Moretonhampstead. This label is pasted to the inside cover of
all three volumes of the copy of the 1816 *Mansfield
Park* that is now preserved at Houghton Library, Harvard University. Though the label prohibits any writing in the library's property, pencil marks and scrib-
bled notes can be found throughout the book.

# 10

A WEEK WAS GONE since Edmund might be supposed in town, and Fanny had heard nothing of him. There were three different conclusions to be drawn from his silence, between which her mind was in fluctuation; each of them at times being held the most probable. Either his going had been again delayed, or he had yet procured no opportunity of seeing Miss Crawford alone—or, he was too happy for letter writing!

One morning about this time, Fanny having now been nearly four weeks from Mansfield—a point which she never failed to think over and calculate every day—as she and Susan were preparing to remove as usual up stairs, they were stopt by the knock of a visitor, whom they felt they could not avoid, from Rebecca's alertness in going to the door, a duty which always interested her beyond any other.

It was a gentleman's voice; it was a voice that Fanny was just turning pale about, when Mr. Crawford walked into the room.

Good sense, like hers, will always act when really called upon; and she found that she had been able to name him to her mother, and recal her remembrance of the name, as that of "William's friend," though she could not previously have believed herself capable of uttering a syllable at such a moment. The consciousness of his being known there only as William's friend, was some support. Having introduced him, however, and being all re-seated, the terrors that occurred of what this visit might lead to were overpowering, and she fancied herself on the point of fainting away.

While trying to keep herself alive, their visitor, who had at first approached her with as animated a countenance as ever, was wisely and kindly keeping his eyes away, and giving her time to recover, while he devoted himself entirely to her mother, addressing her, and attending to her with the utmost politeness and propriety, at the same time with a degree of friendliness—of interest at least—which was making his manner perfect.

Mrs. Price's manners were also at their best. Warmed by the sight of such a friend to her son, and regulated by the wish of appearing to advantage before him, she was overflowing with gratitude, artless, maternal gratitude, which could not be unpleasing. Mr. Price was out, which she regretted very much. Fanny was just recovered enough to feel that *she* could not regret it; for to her many other sources of uneasiness was added the severe one of shame for the home in which he found her. She might scold herself for the weakness, but there was no scolding it away. She was ashamed, and she would have been yet more ashamed of her father, than of all the rest.

They talked of William, a subject on which Mrs. Price could never tire; and Mr. Crawford was as warm in his commendation, as even her heart could wish. She felt that she had never seen so agreeable a man in her life; and was only astonished to find, that so great and so agreeable as he was, he should be come down to Portsmouth neither on a visit to the port-admiral, nor the commissioner,[1] nor yet with the intention of going over to the island,[2] nor of seeing the Dockyard. Nothing of all that she had been used to think of as the proof of importance, or the employment of wealth, had brought him to Portsmouth. He had reached it late the night before, was come for a day or two, was staying at the Crown, had accidentally met with a navy officer or two of his acquaintance, since his arrival, but had no object of that kind in coming.

By the time he had given all this information, it was not unreasonable to suppose, that Fanny might be looked at and spoken to; and she was tolerably able to bear his eye, and hear that he had spent half an hour with his sister, the evening before his leaving London; that she had sent her best and kindest love, but had had no time for writ-

1 Each Royal Navy base had a port-admiral appointed to it, who during the absence onshore of those vessels' usual commanders would be in charge of commissioned ships in the harbor and at anchorage nearby. The commissioner, a member of the Navy Board, ran the dockyard.

2 The Isle of Wight.

3 Mrs. Price likely uses *sad* as a synonym for *bad*. Portsmouth suffered from the usual problems of an early nineteenth-century port city—including those created by a transient, rowdy population of sailors and marines either on shore leave or awaiting ships, and the sex workers who dealt with these men and were often forced to resort to robbing their clients in order to make up their income. Genteel young women like Fanny and Susan would be reluctant to walk unescorted in Portsmouth's streets.

George Mouton Woodward and Thomas Rowlandson's caricature print *Accommodation, or Lodgings to Let at Portsmouth* trades on the port town's reputation for sexual immorality.

ing; that he thought himself lucky in seeing Mary for even half an hour, having spent scarcely twenty-four hours in London after his return from Norfolk, before he set off again; that her cousin Edmund was in town, had been in town, he understood, a few days; that he had not seen him, himself, but that he was well, had left them all well at Mansfield, and was to dine, as yesterday, with the Frasers.

Fanny listened collectedly even to the last-mentioned circumstance; nay, it seemed a relief to her worn mind to be at any certainty; and the words, "then by this time it is all settled," passed internally, without more evidence of emotion than a faint blush.

After talking a little more about Mansfield, a subject in which her interest was most apparent, Crawford began to hint at the expediency of an early walk;—"It was a lovely morning, and at that season of the year a fine morning so often turned off, that it was wisest for everybody not to delay their exercise;" and such hints producing nothing, he soon proceeded to a positive recommendation to Mrs. Price and her daughters, to take their walk without loss of time. Now they came to an understanding. Mrs. Price, it appeared, scarcely ever stirred out of doors, except of a Sunday; she owned she could seldom, with her large family, find time for a walk.—"Would she not then persuade her daughters to take advantage of such weather, and allow him the pleasure of attending them?"—Mrs. Price was greatly obliged, and very complying. "Her daughters were very much confined—Portsmouth was a sad place—they did not often get out[3]—and she knew they had some errands in the town, which they would be very glad to do."—And the consequence was, that Fanny, strange as it was—strange, awkward, and distressing—found herself and Susan, within ten minutes, walking towards the High Street, with Mr. Crawford.

It was soon pain upon pain, confusion upon confusion; for they were hardly in the High Street, before they met her father, whose appearance was not the better from its being Saturday. He stopt; and, ungentlemanlike as he looked, Fanny was obliged to introduce him to Mr. Crawford. She could not have a doubt of the manner in which Mr. Crawford must be struck. He must be ashamed and disgusted altogether. He must soon give her up, and cease to have the smallest inclination for the match; and yet, though she had been so much wanting his affection to be cured, this was a sort of cure that would be almost as bad as the complaint; and I believe, there is scarcely a young lady in the united kingdoms, who would not rather put up with the misfortune of being sought by a clever, agreeable man, than have him driven away by the vulgarity of her nearest relations.

Mr. Crawford probably could not regard his future father-in-law with any idea of taking him for a model in dress; but (as Fanny instantly, and to her great relief discerned), her father was a very different man, a very different Mr. Price in his behaviour to this most highly-respected stranger, from what he was in his own family at home. His manners now, though not polished, were more than passable; they were grateful, animated, manly; his expressions were those of an attached father, and a sensible man;—his loud tones did very well in the open air, and there was not a single oath to be heard. Such was his instinctive compliment to the good manners of Mr. Crawford; and be the consequence what it might, Fanny's immediate feelings were infinitely soothed.

The conclusion of the two gentlemen's civilities was an offer of Mr. Price's to take Mr. Crawford into the dock-yard, which Mr. Crawford, desirous of accepting as a favour, what was intended as such, though he had seen the dock-yard again and again; and hoping to be so much the longer with Fanny, was very gratefully disposed to avail himself of, if the Miss Prices were not afraid of the fatigue; and as it was somehow or other ascertained, or inferred, or at least acted upon, that they were not at all afraid, to the dock-yard they were all to go; and, but for Mr. Crawford, Mr. Price would have turned thither directly, without the smallest consideration for his daughters' errands in the High Street. He took care, however, that they should be allowed to go to the shops they came out expressly to visit; and it did not delay them long, for Fanny could so little bear to excite impatience, or be waited for, that before the gentlemen, as they stood at the door, could do more than begin upon the last naval regulations, or settle the number of three deckers now in commission,[4] their companions were ready to proceed.

They were then to set forward for the dock-yard at once, and the walk would have been conducted (according to Mr. Crawford's opinion) in a singular manner, had Mr. Price been allowed the entire regu-

*Fanny was obliged to introduce him to Mr. Crawford.*

Hugh Thomson's illustration depicts the meeting in the Portsmouth street between the visiting Henry Crawford and Fanny's father. Thomson's Mr. Price, befuddled by surprise or perhaps by drink, is slow to conform to the usual etiquette of such an occasion and doff his hat to the younger man.

5  A ship under construction.

6  Early March is not the usual time for a gentleman like Henry to go down into the country; London's winter season of parties and dinners continues in full swing.

7  Henry's estate at Everingham, another property in the novel owned by a mainly absentee landlord, is managed by a steward, likely an attorney, who oversees its finances and takes charge of finding tenants to farm the land.

lation of it, as the two girls, he found, would have been left to follow, and keep up with them, or not, as they could, while they walked on together at their own hasty pace. He was able to introduce some improvement occasionally, though by no means to the extent he wished; he absolutely would not walk away from them; and, at any crossing, or any crowd, when Mr. Price was only calling out, "Come, girls—come, Fan—come, Sue—take care of yourselves—keep a sharp look-out," he would give them his particular attendance.

Once fairly in the dock-yard, he began to reckon upon some happy intercourse with Fanny, as they were very soon joined by a brother lounger of Mr. Price's, who was come to take his daily survey of how things went on, and who must prove a far more worthy companion than himself; and after a time the two officers seemed very well satisfied in going about together and discussing matters of equal and never-failing interest, while the young people sat down upon some timbers in the yard, or found a seat on board a vessel in the stocks which they all went to look at.[5] Fanny was most conveniently in want of rest. Crawford could not have wished her more fatigued or more ready to sit down; but he could have wished her sister away. A quick looking girl of Susan's age was the very worst third in the world—totally different from Lady Bertram—all eyes and ears; and there was no introducing the main point before her. He must content himself with being only generally agreeable, and letting Susan have her share of entertainment, with the indulgence, now and then, of a look or hint for the better informed and conscious Fanny. Norfolk was what he had mostly to talk of; there he had been some time, and every thing there was rising in importance from his present schemes. Such a man could come from no place, no society, without importing something to amuse; his journeys and his acquaintance were all of use, and Susan was entertained in a way quite new to her. For Fanny, somewhat more was related than the accidental agreeableness of the parties he had been in. For her approbation, the particular reason of his going into Norfolk at all, at this unusual time of year,[6] was given. It had been real business, relative to the renewal of a lease in which the welfare of a large and (he believed) industrious family was at stake. He had suspected his agent of some underhand dealing[7]—of meaning to bias him against the deserving—and he had determined to go himself, and thoroughly investigate the merits of the case. He had gone, had done even more good than he had foreseen, had been useful to more than his first plan had comprehended, and was now able to congratulate himself upon it, and to feel, that in performing a duty, he had secured agreeable recollections for his own mind. He had introduced himself to some tenants, whom he had never seen before; he had begun making acquaintance with cottages whose very existence, though on his own estate, had been hitherto unknown to him. This was aimed, and well aimed, at Fanny. It was pleasing to hear him speak so properly; here, he had been acting as he ought to do. To be the friend of the poor and oppressed! Nothing could be more grateful to her,[8] and she was on the point of giving him an approving look when it was all frightened off, by his adding a something too pointed of his hoping soon to have an assistant, a friend, a guide in every plan of utility or charity for Everingham, a somebody that would make Everingham and all about it, a dearer object than it had ever been yet.

She turned away, and wished he would not say such things. She was willing to allow he might have more good qualities than she had been wont to suppose. She began to feel the possibility of his turning out well at last; but he was and must ever be completely unsuited to her, and ought not to think of her.

He perceived that enough had been said of Everingham, and that it would be as well to talk of something else, and turned to Mansfield. He could not have chosen better; that was a topic to bring back her attention and her looks almost instantly. It was a real indulgence to her to hear or to speak of Mansfield. Now so long divided from every body who knew the place, she felt it quite the voice of a friend when he mentioned it, and led the way to her fond exclamations in praise of its beauties and comforts, and by his honourable tribute to its inhabitants allowed her to gratify her own heart in the warmest eulogium, in speaking of her uncle as all that was clever and good, and her aunt as having the sweetest of all sweet tempers.

He had a great attachment to Mansfield himself; he said so; he looked forward with the hope of spending much, very much of his

8 *Grateful* in the older sense meaning *agreeable* or *pleasant*.

9 A small house to be occupied during the hunting
season.

time there—always there, or in the neighbourhood. He particularly
built upon a very happy summer and autumn there this year; he felt
that it would be so; he depended upon it; a summer and autumn infinitely superior to the last. As animated, as diversified, as social—but
with circumstances of superiority undescribable.

"Mansfield, Sotherton, Thornton Lacey," he continued, "what a
society will be comprised in those houses! And at Michaelmas, perhaps, a fourth may be added, some small hunting-box in the vicinity
of every thing so dear⁹—for as to any partnership in Thornton Lacey,
as Edmund Bertram once good-humouredly proposed, I hope I foresee two objections, two fair, excellent, irresistible objections to that
plan."

Fanny was doubly silenced here; though when the moment was
passed, could regret that she had not forced herself into the acknowledged comprehension of one half of his meaning, and encouraged him to say something more of his sister and Edmund. It was
a subject which she must learn to speak of, and the weakness that
shrunk from it would soon be quite unpardonable.

When Mr. Price and his friend had seen all that they wished, or
had time for, the others were ready to return; and in the course of
their walk back, Mr. Crawford contrived a minute's privacy for telling Fanny that his only business in Portsmouth was to see her, that
he was come down for a couple of days on her account and hers only,
and because he could not endure a longer total separation. She was
sorry, really sorry; and yet, in spite of this and the two or three other
things which she wished he had not said, she thought him altogether
improved since she had seen him; he was much more gentle, obliging, and attentive to other people's feelings than he had ever been at
Mansfield; she had never seen him so agreeable—so *near* being agreeable; his behaviour to her father could not offend, and there was
something particularly kind and proper in the notice he took of Susan. He was decidedly improved. She wished the next day over, she
wished he had come only for one day—but it was not so very bad as
she would have expected; the pleasure of talking of Mansfield was so
very great!

Before they parted, she had to thank him for another pleasure, and one of no trivial kind. Her father asked him to do them the honour of taking his mutton with them, and Fanny had time for only one thrill of horror, before he declared himself prevented by a prior engagement. He was engaged to dinner already both for that day and the next; he had met with some acquaintance at the Crown who would not be denied; he should have the honour, however, of waiting on them again on the morrow, &c. and so they parted—Fanny in a state of actual felicity from escaping so horrible an evil!

To have had him join their family dinner-party and see all their deficiencies would have been dreadful! Rebecca's cookery and Rebecca's waiting, and Betsey's eating at table without restraint, and pulling every thing about as she chose, were what Fanny herself was not yet enough inured to, for her often to make a tolerable meal. *She* was nice only from natural delicacy, but *he* had been brought up in a school of luxury and epicurism.[10]

10 Fine dining, of the kind sought out by an epicure with cultivated tastes.

# II

1 The chapel, formerly part of a medieval hospice for pilgrims on their way to and from the shrines in Canterbury and Winchester, had by this date been rebuilt and assigned to the use of the men and officers of the Portsmouth Garrison and their families.

2 Why is the group "obliged to divide" after they arrive at the chapel? It is uncertain what Austen is indicating with that statement. Traditionally men and women had been seated in separate sections of church buildings during services (segregation by marital status and by rank was sometimes conventional as well). However, by the nineteenth century, as family pews became more common, most Anglican churches had evolved a combination of mixed and single-sex pews. It might simply be the case that there is insufficient seating for the many members of the Price family, and that the male and female members are accustomed to going their separate ways at the church door.

3 In his 1817 *History of Portsmouth* Lake Allen boasts patriotically about the ramparts, "about a mile and a quarter in circumference" and "edged with elm trees, whose spreading foliage affords one of the most delightful promenades that can possibly be conceived" (p. 149).

THE PRICES WERE JUST setting off for church the next day when Mr. Crawford appeared again. He came—not to stop—but to join them; he was asked to go with them to the Garrison chapel,[1] which was exactly what he had intended, and they all walked thither together.

The family were now seen to advantage. Nature had given them no inconsiderable share of beauty, and every Sunday dressed them in their cleanest skins and best attire. Sunday always brought this comfort to Fanny, and on this Sunday she felt it more than ever. Her poor mother now did not look so very unworthy of being Lady Bertram's sister as she was but too apt to look. It often grieved her to the heart—to think of the contrast between them—to think that where nature had made so little difference, circumstances should have made so much, and that her mother, as handsome as Lady Bertram, and some years her junior, should have an appearance so much more worn and faded, so comfortless, so slatternly, so shabby. But Sunday made her a very creditable and tolerably cheerful-looking Mrs. Price, coming abroad with a fine family of children, feeling a little respite of her weekly cares, and only discomposed if she saw her boys run into danger, or Rebecca pass by with a flower in her hat.

In chapel they were obliged to divide, but Mr. Crawford took care not to be divided from the female branch;[2] and after chapel he still continued with them, and made one in the family party on the ramparts.[3]

Mrs. Price took her weekly walk on the ramparts every fine Sunday throughout the year, always going directly after morning service and staying till dinner-time. It was her public place; there she met her acquaintance, heard a little news, talked over the badness of the Portsmouth servants, and wound up her spirits for the six days ensuing.

Thither they now went; Mr. Crawford most happy to consider the Miss Prices as his peculiar charge; and before they had been there long—somehow or other—there was no saying how—Fanny could not have believed it—but he was walking between them with an arm of each under his, and she did not know how to prevent or put an end to it. It made her uncomfortable for a time—but yet there were enjoyments in the day and in the view which would be felt.

The day was uncommonly lovely. It was really March; but it was April in its mild air, brisk soft wind, and bright sun, occasionally clouded for a minute; and every thing looked so beautiful under the influence of such a sky, the effects of the shadows pursuing each other, on the ships at Spithead and the island beyond, with the ever-varying hues of the sea now at high water, dancing in its glee and dashing against the ramparts with so fine a sound, produced altogether such a combination of charms for Fanny, as made her gradually almost careless of the circumstances under which she felt them. Nay, had she been without his arm, she would soon have known that she needed it, for she wanted strength for a two hours' saunter of this kind, coming as it generally did upon a week's previous inactivity. Fanny was beginning to feel the effect of being debarred from her usual, regular exercise; she had lost ground as to health since her being in Portsmouth, and but for Mr. Crawford and the beauty of the weather, would soon have been knocked up now.

The loveliness of the day, and of the view, he felt like herself. They often stopt with the same sentiment and taste, leaning against the wall, some minutes, to look and admire; and considering he was not Edmund, Fanny could not but allow that he was sufficiently open to the charms of nature, and very well able to express his admiration. She had a few tender reveries now and then, which he could some-

*Only discomposed if she saw Rebecca pass by with a flower in her hat.*

Hugh Thomson's 1897 depiction of the ungovernable Rebecca, the Prices' maid-of-all-work, glimpsed by her mistress who is en route to Sunday services.

times take advantage of, to look in her face without detection; and the result of these looks was, that though as bewitching as ever, her face was less blooming than it ought to be. — She *said* she was very well, and did not like to be supposed otherwise; but take it all in all, he was convinced that her present residence could not be comfortable, and, therefore, could not be salutary for her, and he was growing anxious for her being again at Mansfield, where her own happiness, and his in seeing her, must be so much greater.

"You have been here a month, I think?" said he.

"No. Not quite a month. — It is only four weeks to-morrow since I left Mansfield."

"You are a most accurate and honest reckoner. I should call that a month."

"I did not arrive here till Tuesday evening."

"And it is to be a two months' visit, is not it?"

"Yes. — My uncle talked of two months. I suppose it will not be less."

"And how are you to be conveyed back again? Who comes for you?"

"I do not know. I have heard nothing about it yet from my aunt. Perhaps I may be to stay longer. It may not be convenient for me to be fetched exactly at the two months' end."

After a moment's reflection, Mr. Crawford replied, "I know Mansfield, I know its way, I know its faults towards *you.* I know the danger of your being so far forgotten, as to have your comforts give way to the imaginary convenience of any single being in the family. I am aware that you may be left here week after week, if Sir Thomas cannot settle every thing for coming himself, or sending your aunt's maid for you, without involving the slightest alteration of the arrangements which he may have laid down for the next quarter of a year. This will not do. Two months is an ample allowance, I should think six weeks quite enough. — I am considering your sister's health," said he, addressing himself to Susan, "which I think the confinement of Portsmouth unfavourable to. She requires constant air and exercise. When you know her as well as I do, I am sure you will

View of Portsmouth Harbor and Portsea Island, looking south from the top of
Portsdown Hill: aquatint by the author included in William Gilpin's travelogue *Observations on the Coasts of Hampshire, Sussex, and Kent; Relative Chiefly to Picturesque
Beauty* (1804). Gilpin writes that from this spot "we had a view grander in its kind
than perhaps any part of the globe can exhibit."

agree that she does, and that she ought never to be long banished
from the free air, and liberty of the country.—If, therefore, (turning
again to Fanny) you find yourself growing unwell, and any difficulties
arise about your returning to Mansfield—without waiting for the
two months to be ended—*that* must not be regarded as of any consequence, if you feel yourself at all less strong, or comfortable than
usual, and will only let my sister know it, give her only the slightest
hint, she and I will immediately come down, and take you back to
Mansfield. You know the ease, and the pleasure with which this
would be done. You know all that would be felt on the occasion."

Fanny thanked him, but tried to laugh it off.

"I am perfectly serious,"—he replied,—"as you perfectly know.—
And I hope you will not be cruelly concealing any tendency to indisposition.—Indeed, you shall *not,* it shall not be in your power, for so

long only as you positively say, in every letter to Mary, 'I am well.'—and I know you cannot speak or write a falsehood,—so long only shall you be considered as well."

Fanny thanked him again, but was affected and distressed to a degree that made it impossible for her to say much, or even to be certain of what she ought to say.—This was towards the close of their walk. He attended them to the last, and left them only at the door of their own house, when he knew them to be going to dinner, and therefore pretended to be waited for elsewhere.

"I wish you were not so tired,"—said he, still detaining Fanny after all the others were in the house; "I wish I left you in stronger health.—Is there any thing I can do for you in town? I have half an idea of going into Norfolk again soon. I am not satisfied about Maddison.—I am sure he still means to impose on me if possible, and get a cousin of his own into a certain mill, which I design for somebody else.—I must come to an understanding with him. I must make him know that I will not be tricked on the south side of Everingham, any more than on the north, that I will be master of my own property. I was not explicit enough with him before.—The mischief such a man does on an estate, both as to the credit of his employer, and the welfare of the poor, is inconceivable. I have a great mind to go back into Norfolk directly, and put every thing at once on such a footing as cannot be afterwards swerved from.—Maddison is a clever fellow; I do not wish to displace him—provided he does not try to displace *me;*—but it would be simple to be duped by a man who has no right of creditor to dupe me—and worse than simple to let him give me a hard-hearted, griping fellow for a tenant, instead of an honest man, to whom I have given half a promise already.—Would it not be worse than simple? Shall I go?—Do you advise it?"

"I advise!—you know very well what is right."

"Yes. When you give me your opinion, I always know what is right. Your judgment is my rule of right."

"Oh, no!—do not say so. We have all a better guide in ourselves, if we would attend to it, than any other person can be. Good bye; I wish you a pleasant journey to-morrow."

"Is there nothing I can do for you in town?"

"Nothing, I am much obliged to you."

"Have you no message for anybody?"

"My love to your sister, if you please; and when you see my cousin —my cousin Edmund, I wish you would be so good as to say that—I suppose I shall soon hear from him."

"Certainly; and if he is lazy or negligent, I will write his excuses myself—"

He could say no more, for Fanny would be no longer detained. He pressed her hand, looked at her, and was gone. *He* went to while away the next three hours as he could, with his other acquaintance, till the best dinner that a capital inn afforded, was ready for their enjoyment, and *she* turned in to her more simple one immediately.

Their general fare bore a very different character; and could he have suspected how many privations, besides that of exercise, she endured in her father's house, he would have wondered that her looks were not much more affected than he found them. She was so little equal to Rebecca's puddings, and Rebecca's hashes, brought to table as they all were, with such accompaniments of half-cleaned plates, and not half-cleaned knives and forks, that she was very often constrained to defer her heartiest meal, till she could send her brothers in the evening for biscuits and buns. After being nursed up at Mansfield, it was too late in the day to be hardened at Portsmouth; and though Sir Thomas, had he known all, might have thought his niece in the most promising way of being starved, both mind and body, into a much juster value for Mr. Crawford's good company and good fortune, he would probably have feared to push his experiment farther, lest she might die under the cure.[4]

Fanny was out of spirits all the rest of the day. Though tolerably secure of not seeing Mr. Crawford again, she could not help being low. It was parting with somebody of the nature of a friend; and though in one light glad to have him gone, it seemed as if she was now deserted by everybody; it was a sort of renewed separation from Mansfield; and she could not think of his returning to town, and being frequently with Mary and Edmund, without feelings so near akin to envy, as made her hate herself for having them.

Her dejection had no abatement from anything passing around her; a friend or two of her father's, as always happened if he was not with them, spent the long, long evening there; and from six o'clock

4 Sir Thomas's "medicinal project" upon his niece's "diseased" understanding appears in a new guise in this sentence: Fanny now looks to be enduring the period of fasting and penitence that is appropriate to the Lenten season, the interval in the Christian calendar between Ash Wednesday and Easter.

till half past nine, there was little intermission of noise or grog. She was very low. The wonderful improvement which she still fancied in Mr. Crawford, was the nearest to administering comfort of anything within the current of her thoughts. Not considering in how different a circle she had been just seeing him, nor how much might be owing to contrast, she was quite persuaded of his being astonishingly more gentle, and regardful of others, than formerly. And if in little things, must it not be so in great? So anxious for her health and comfort, so very feeling as he now expressed himself, and really seemed, might not it be fairly supposed, that he would not much longer persevere in a suit so distressing to her?

# 12

It was presumed that Mr. Crawford was travelling back to London, on the morrow, for nothing more was seen of him at Mr. Price's; and two days afterwards, it was a fact ascertained to Fanny by the following letter from his sister, opened and read by her, on another account, with the most anxious curiosity:—

"I have to inform you, my dearest Fanny, that Henry has been down to Portsmouth to see you; that he had a delightful walk with you to the Dock-yard last Saturday, and one still more to be dwelt on the next day, on the ramparts; when the balmy air, the sparkling sea, and your sweet looks and conversation were altogether in the most delicious harmony, and afforded sensations which are to raise ecstasy even in retrospect. This, as well as I understand, is to be the substance of my information. He makes me write, but I do not know what else is to be communicated, except this said visit to Portsmouth, and these two said walks, and his introduction to your family, especially to a fair sister of your's, a fine girl of fifteen, who was of the party on the ramparts, taking her first lesson, I presume, in love. I have not time for writing much, but it would be out of place if I had, for this is to be a mere letter of business, penned for the purpose of conveying necessary information, which could not be delayed without risk of evil. My dear, dear Fanny, if I had you here, how I would talk to you!— You should listen to me till you were tired, and advise me till you were still tired more; but it is impossible to put a hundredth part of my great mind on paper, so I will abstain altogether, and leave you to guess what you like. I have no news for you. You have politics of course; and it would be too bad to plague you with the names of people and parties, that fill up my time. I ought to have sent you an account of your cousin's first party, but I was lazy, and now it is too long ago; suffice it, that every thing was just as it ought to be, in a style that any of her connections must have been gratified to witness, and that her own dress and manners did her the greatest credit. My friend Mrs. Fraser is mad for such a house, and it would not make *me* miserable. I go to Lady Stornaway after Easter. She seems in high spirits, and very happy. I fancy Lord S. is very good-humoured and pleasant in his own family, and I do not think him so very ill-looking as I did, at least one sees many worse. He will not do by the side of your cousin Edmund. Of the last-mentioned hero, what shall I say? If I avoided his name entirely, it would look suspicious. I will say, then, that we have seen him two or three times, and that my friends here are very much struck with his gentleman-like appearance. Mrs. Fraser (no bad judge), declares she knows but three men in town who have so good a person, height, and air; and I must confess, when he dined here the other day, there were none to compare with him, and we were a party of sixteen. Luckily there is no distinction of dress now-a-days to tell tales,[1] but—but—but.

Your's, affectionately."

"I had almost forgot (it was Edmund's fault, he gets into my head more than does me good), one very material thing I had to say from Henry and myself, I mean about our taking you back into Northamptonshire. My dear little creature, do not stay at Portsmouth to lose your pretty looks. Those vile sea-breezes are the ruin of beauty and health. My poor aunt always felt affected, if within ten miles of the sea, which the Admiral of course never believed, but I know it was so. I am at your service and Henry's, at an hour's notice. I should like

*St. George's, Hanover Square, London,* engraving by T. Malton. This church was known as a locale for fashionable weddings.

2 A church in the modern and fashionable Mayfair district of London: the lively Lady G.——in Samuel Richardson's *History of Sir Charles Grandison* is married there. As John Wiltshire explains in his annotations to this passage (p. 728 n. 4), this eighteenth-century church's undistinguished interior makes it unlikely that it is being mentioned as a London tourist attraction. Instead, Mary has teasingly recommended to Fanny a travel route that is intended to take her to the altar; and if Edmund were nearby at that moment, Mary fears, she might be tempted to make it a double wedding.

the scheme, and we would make a little circuit, and shew you Everingham in our way, and perhaps you would not mind passing through London, and seeing the inside of St. George's, Hanover-Square. Only keep your cousin Edmund from me at such a time, I should not like to be tempted.[2] What a long letter!—one word more. Henry I find has some idea of going into Norfolk again upon some business that *you* approve, but this cannot possibly be permitted before the middle of next week, that is, he cannot any how be spared till after the 14th, for *we* have a party that evening. The value of a man like Henry on such an occasion, is what you can have no conception of; so you must take it upon my word, to be inestimable. He will see the Rushworths, which I own I am not sorry for—having a little curiosity—and so I think has he, though he will not acknowledge it."

This was a letter to be run through eagerly, to be read deliberately, to supply matter for much reflection, and to leave every thing in greater suspense than ever. The only certainty to be drawn from it was, that nothing decisive had yet taken place. Edmund had not yet spoken. How Miss Crawford really felt—how she meant to act, or might act without or against her meaning—whether his importance to her were quite what it had been before the last separation—whether if lessened it were likely to lessen more, or to recover itself, were subjects for endless conjecture, and to be thought of on that day and many days to come, without producing any conclusion. The idea that returned the oftenest, was that Miss Crawford, after proving herself cooled and staggered by a return to London habits, would yet prove herself in the end too much attached to him, to give him up. She would try to be more ambitious than her heart would allow. She would hesitate, she would teaze, she would condition, she would require a great deal, but she would finally accept. This was Fanny's most frequent expectation. A house in town!—*that* she thought must be impossible. Yet there was no saying what Miss Crawford might not ask. The prospect for her cousin grew worse and worse. The woman who could speak of him, and speak only of his appearance!—What an unworthy attachment!—To be deriving support from the commendations of Mrs. Fraser! *She* who had known him intimately half a year! Fanny was ashamed of her. Those parts of the letter which related only to Mr. Crawford and herself, touched her in comparison, slightly. Whether Mr. Crawford went into Norfolk before or after the 14th, was certainly no concern of her's, though, every thing considered, she thought he *would* go without delay. That Miss Crawford should endeavour to secure a meeting between him and Mrs. Rushworth, was all in her worst line of conduct, and grossly unkind and ill-judged; but she hoped *he* would not be actuated by any such degrading curiosity. He acknowledged no such inducement, and his sister ought to have given him credit for better feelings than her own.

She was yet more impatient for another letter from town after receiving this, than she had been before; and for a few days, was so unsettled by it altogether, by what had come, and what might come, that her usual readings and conversation with Susan were much suspended. She could not command her attention as she wished. If Mr. Crawford remembered her message to her cousin, she thought it very likely, *most* likely, that he would write to her at all events; it would be most consistent with his usual kindness, and till she got rid of this idea, till it gradually wore off, by no letters appearing in the course of three or four days more, she was in a most restless, anxious state.

At length, a something like composure succeeded. Suspense must be submitted to, and must not be allowed to wear her out, and make her useless. Time did something, her own exertions something more, and she resumed her attentions to Susan, and again awakened the same interest in them.

Susan was growing very fond of her, and though without any of the early delight in books, which had been so strong in Fanny, with a disposition much less inclined to sedentary pursuits, or to information for information's sake,[3] she had so strong a desire of not *appearing* ignorant, as with a good clear understanding, made her a most attentive, profitable, thankful pupil. Fanny was her oracle. Fanny's explanations and remarks were a most important addition to every essay, or every chapter of history. What Fanny told her of former times, dwelt more on her mind than the pages of Goldsmith;[4] and she paid her sister the compliment of preferring her style to that of any printed author. The early habit of reading was wanting.

Their conversations, however, were not always on subjects so high as history or morals. Others had their hour; and of lesser matters, none returned so often, or remained so long between them, as Mansfield Park, a description of the people, the manners, the amusements, the ways of Mansfield Park. Susan, who had an innate taste for the genteel and well-appointed, was eager to hear, and Fanny could not but indulge herself in dwelling on so beloved a theme. She hoped it was not wrong; though after a time, Susan's very great admiration of every thing said or done in her uncle's house, and earnest longing to go into Northamptonshire, seemed almost to blame her for exciting feelings which could not be gratified.

Poor Susan was very little better fitted for home than her elder sister; and as Fanny grew thoroughly to understand this, she began to feel that when her own release from Portsmouth came, her happiness would have a material drawback in leaving Susan behind. That a girl so capable of being made, every thing good, should be left in such

3 Here again the meaning of *information* is tricky. Rachel Brownstein suggests that Susan's lack of interest in "information for information's sake" ought to be understood as a lack of interest in "disinterested reading"—in reading that is intellectually enriching precisely because it is not easily converted to utilitarian ends (*Why Jane Austen?*, p. 234).

4 Probably Oliver Goldsmith's frequently reprinted and frequently abridged *The History of England from the Earliest Times to the Death of George II* (4 vols., 1771). The margins of the Austen family's copy of Goldsmith's *History* contain multiple, occasionally combative annotations in Jane Austen's hand, which Peter Sabor, in his Cambridge University Press edition of the *Juvenilia*, dates to 1791, when Austen was fifteen.

hands, distressed her more and more. Were *she* likely to have a home to invite her to, what a blessing it would be!—And had it been possible for her to return Mr. Crawford's regard, the probability of his being very far from objecting to such a measure, would have been the greatest increase of all her own comforts. She thought he was really good-tempered, and could fancy his entering into a plan of that sort, most pleasantly.

# 13

SEVEN WEEKS OF THE TWO MONTHS were very nearly gone, when the one letter, the letter from Edmund so long expected, was put into Fanny's hands. As she opened and saw its length she prepared herself for a minute detail of happiness and a profusion of love and praise towards the fortunate creature, who was now mistress of his fate. These were the contents.

"*Mansfield Park*.

"My dear Fanny,

"Excuse me that I have not written before, Crawford told me that you were wishing to hear from me, but I found it impossible to write from London, and persuaded myself that you would understand my silence.—Could I have sent a few happy lines, they should not have been wanting, but nothing of that nature was ever in my power.—I am returned to Mansfield in a less assured state than when I left it. My hopes are much weaker.—You are probably aware of this already.—So very fond of you as Miss Crawford is, it is most natural that she should tell you enough of her own feelings, to furnish a tolerable guess at mine.—I will not be prevented, however, from making my own communication. Our confidences in you need not clash.—I ask no questions.—There is something soothing in the idea, that we have the same friend, and that whatever unhappy differences of opinion may exist between us, we are united in our love of you. — It will be a comfort to me to tell you how things now are, and what are my present plans, if plans I can be said to have. — I have been returned since Saturday. I was three weeks in London, and saw her (for London) very often. I had every attention from the Frasers that could be reasonably expected. I dare say I was *not* reasonable in carrying with me hopes of an intercourse at all like that of Mansfield. It was her manner, however, rather than any unfrequency of meeting. Had she not been different when I did see her, I should have made no complaint, but from the very first she was altered; my first reception was so unlike what I had hoped, that I had almost resolved on leaving London again directly. — I need not particularize. You know the weak side of her character, and may imagine the sentiments and expressions which were torturing me. She was in high spirits, and surrounded by those who were giving all the support of their own bad sense to her too lively mind. I do not like Mrs. Fraser. She is a cold-hearted, vain woman, who has married entirely from convenience, and though evidently unhappy in her marriage, places her disappointment, not to faults of judgement or temper, or disproportion of age, but to her being after all, less affluent than many of her acquaintance, especially than her sister, Lady Stornaway, and is the determined supporter of every thing mercenary and ambitious, provided it be only mercenary and ambitious enough. I look upon her intimacy with those two sisters, as the greatest misfortune of her life and mine. They have been leading her astray for years. Could she be detached from them! — and sometimes I do not despair of it, for the affection appears to me principally on their side. They are very fond of her; but I am sure she does not love them as she loves you. When I think of her great attachment to you, indeed, and the whole of her judicious, upright conduct as a sister, she appears a very different creature, capable of every thing noble, and I am ready to blame myself for a too harsh construction of a playful manner. I cannot give her up, Fanny.

She is the only woman in the world whom I could ever think of as a wife. If I did not believe that she had some regard for me, of course I should not say this, but I do believe it. I am convinced, that she is not without a decided preference. I have no jealousy of any individual. It is the influence of the fashionable world altogether that I am jealous of. It is the habits of wealth that I fear. Her ideas are not higher than her own fortune may warrant, but they are beyond what our incomes united could authorise. There is comfort, however, even here. I could better bear to lose her, because not rich enough, than because of my profession. That would only prove her affection not equal to sacrifices, which, in fact, I am scarcely justified in asking; and if I am refused, *that,* I think, will be the honest motive. Her prejudices, I trust, are not so strong as they were. You have my thoughts exactly as they arise, my dear Fanny; perhaps they are some times contradictory, but it will not be a less faithful picture of my mind. Having once begun, it is a pleasure to me to tell you all I feel. I cannot give her up. Connected, as we already are, and, I hope, are to be, to give up Mary Crawford, would be to give up the society of some of those most dear to me, to banish myself from the very houses and friends whom, under any other distress, I should turn to for consolation. The loss of Mary I must consider as comprehending the loss of Crawford and of Fanny. Were it a decided thing, an actual refusal, I hope I should know how to bear it, and how to endeavour to weaken her hold on my heart—and in the course of a few years—but I am writing nonsense—were I refused, I must bear it; and till I am, I can never cease to try for her. This is the truth. The only question is *how?* What may be the likeliest means? I have sometimes thought of going to London again after Easter, and sometimes resolved on doing nothing till she returns to Mansfield. Even now, she speaks with pleasure of being in Mansfield in June; but June is at a great distance, and I believe I shall write to her. I have nearly determined on explaining myself by letter. To be at an early

certainty is a material object. My present state is miserably
irksome. Considering every thing, I think a letter will be decidedly the best method of explanation. I shall be able to
write much that I could not say, and shall be giving her time
for reflection before she resolves on her answer, and I am less
afraid of the result of reflection than of an immediate hasty
impulse; I think I am. My greatest danger would lie in her
consulting Mrs. Fraser, and I at a distance, unable to help my
own cause. A letter exposes to all the evil of consultation, and
where the mind is any thing short of perfect decision, an adviser may, in an unlucky moment, lead it to do what it may
afterwards regret. I must think this matter over a little. This
long letter, full of my own concerns alone, will be enough to
tire even the friendship of a Fanny. The last time I saw Crawford was at Mrs. Fraser's party. I am more and more satisfied
with all that I see and hear of him. There is not a shadow of
wavering. He thoroughly knows his own mind, and acts up to
his resolutions—an inestimable quality. I could not see him,
and my eldest sister in the same room, without recollecting what you once told me, and I acknowledge that they did
not meet as friends. There was marked coolness on her side.
They scarcely spoke. I saw him draw back surprised, and I
was sorry that Mrs. Rushworth should resent any former
supposed slight to Miss Bertram. You will wish to hear my
opinion of Maria's degree of comfort as a wife. There is no
appearance of unhappiness. I hope they get on pretty well
together. I dined twice in Wimpole Street, and might have
been there oftener, but it is mortifying to be with Rushworth
as a brother. Julia seems to enjoy London exceedingly. I had
little enjoyment there—but have less here. We are not a
lively party. You are very much wanted. I miss you more than
I can express. My mother desires her best love, and hopes to
hear from you soon. She talks of you almost every hour, and I
am sorry to find how many weeks more she is likely to be
without you. My Father means to fetch you himself, but it
will not be till after Easter, when he has business in town.

You are happy at Portsmouth, I hope, but this must not be a yearly visit. I want you at home, that I may have your opinion about Thornton Lacey. I have little heart for extensive improvements till I know that it will ever have a mistress. I think I shall certainly write. It is quite settled that the Grants go to Bath; they leave Mansfield on Monday. I am glad of it. I am not comfortable enough to be fit for any body; but your aunt seems to feel out of luck that such an article of Mansfield news should fall to my pen instead of her's. Your's ever, my dearest Fanny."

"I never will—no, I certainly never will wish for a letter again," was Fanny's secret declaration, as she finished this. "What do they bring but disappointment and sorrow?—Not till after Easter!—How shall I bear it? And my poor aunt talking of me every hour!"

Fanny checked the tendency of these thoughts as well as she could, but she was within half a minute of starting the idea, that Sir Thomas was quite unkind, both to her aunt and to herself.—As for the main subject of the letter—there was nothing in that to soothe irritation. She was almost vexed into displeasure, and anger, against Edmund. "There is no good in this delay," said she. "Why is not it settled?—He is blinded, and nothing will open his eyes, nothing can, after having had truths before him so long in vain.—He will marry her, and be poor and miserable. God grant that her influence do not make him cease to be respectable!"—She looked over the letter again. "'So very fond of me!' 'tis nonsense all. She loves nobody but herself and her brother. 'Her friends leading her astray for years!' She is quite as likely to have led *them* astray. They have all, perhaps, been corrupting one another; but if they are so much fonder of her than she is of them, she is the less likely to have been hurt, except by their flattery. 'The only woman in the world, whom he could ever think of as a wife.' I firmly believe it. It is an attachment to govern his whole life. Accepted or refused, his heart is wedded to her for ever. 'The loss of Mary, I must consider as comprehending the loss of Crawford and Fanny.' Edmund, you do not know *me*. The families would never be connected, if you did not connect them! Oh! write, write. Finish it

1 In "*A Simple Story:* From Inchbald to Austen" (*Romanticism* 5 [1999]: 161–171), the critic Paula Byrne proposes that with the Mary-Edmund plot of *Mansfield Park* Austen rewrites the first part of Inchbald's *Simple Story.* Where Inchbald's Miss Milner delights in demonstrating her sexual power over Dorriforth, a man who is supposed to be her guardian and who at the novel's opening is also a Catholic priest, Austen's Mary exults in the prospect of drawing Edmund from his religious vocation. Byrne connects the confessional letter that Fanny receives from Edmund in this chapter to the episode in Inchbald's novel in which Dorriforth wavers between keeping his engagement to Miss Milner and breaking with her forever. Feeling as though he were doing battle with this young woman for Dorriforth's soul, Dorriforth's confessor Father Sandford responds angrily to the sight of his friend's psychological tumult in terms that anticipate Fanny's response to Edmund: "And yet, notwithstanding all this provocation, he has not come to the determination to think no more of her—he lingers and hesitates—I never saw him so weak upon any occasion before" (p. 169).

*Gimcrack on Newmarket Heath,* by George Stubbs. In this 1765 oil painting, one of several he painted to document the Newmarket Races, Stubbs depicts the famous racehorse Gimcrack twice. The horse can be seen on the right winning a race, and on the left, outside the stables with a trainer, a stable boy, and a jockey.

at once. Let there be an end of this suspense. Fix, commit, condemn yourself."[1]

Such sensations, however, were too near a kin to resentment to be long guiding Fanny's soliloquies. She was soon more softened and sorrowful.—His warm regard, his kind expressions, his confidential treatment touched her strongly. He was only too good to every body.—It was a letter, in short, which she would not but have had for the world, and which could never be valued enough. This was the end of it.

Every body at all addicted to letter writing, without having much to say, which will include a large proportion of the female world at least, must feel with Lady Bertram, that she was out of luck in having such a capital piece of Mansfield news, as the certainty of the Grants going to Bath, occur at a time when she could make no advantage of it, and will admit that it must have been very mortifying to her to see it fall to the share of her thankless son, and treated as concisely as possible at the end of a long letter, instead of having it to spread over the largest part of a page of her own.—For though Lady Bertram rather shone in the epistolary line, having early in her marriage, from the want of other employment, and the circumstance of Sir Thomas's being in Parliament, got into the way of making and keeping correspondents, and formed for herself a very creditable, commonplace, amplifying style, so that a very little matter was enough for her; she could not do entirely without any; she must have something to write about, even to her niece, and being so soon to lose all the benefit of Dr. Grant's gouty symptoms and Mrs. Grant's morning calls, it was very hard upon her to be deprived of one of the last epistolary uses she could put them to.

There was a rich amends, however, preparing for her. Lady Bertram's hour of good luck came. Within a few days from the receipt of Edmund's letter, Fanny had one from her aunt, beginning thus:—

"My Dear Fanny,

"I take up my pen to communicate some very alarming intelligence, which I make no doubt will give you much concern."

This was a great deal better than to have to take up the pen to acquaint her with all the particulars of the Grants' intended journey, for the present intelligence was of a nature to promise occupation for the pen for many days to come, being no less than the dangerous illness of her eldest son, of which they had received notice by express,[2] a few hours before.

Tom had gone from London with a party of young men to Newmarket,[3] where a neglected fall, and a good deal of drinking, had brought on a fever; and when the party broke up, being unable to move, had been left by himself at the house of one of these young men, to the comforts of sickness and solitude, and the attendance only of servants. Instead of being soon well enough to follow his friends, as he had then hoped, his disorder increased considerably, and it was not long before he thought so ill of himself, as to be as ready as his physician to have a letter dispatched to Mansfield.

"This distressing intelligence, as you may suppose," observed her Ladyship, after giving the substance of it, "has agitated us exceed-

2 The news would have been brought by a specially dispatched messenger riding on horseback.

3 The famous horse-racing course near Cambridge.

ingly, and we cannot prevent ourselves from being greatly alarmed,
and apprehensive for the poor invalid, whose state Sir Thomas fears
may be very critical; and Edmund kindly proposes attending his
brother immediately, but I am happy to add, that Sir Thomas will
not leave me on this distressing occasion, as it would be too trying
for me. We shall greatly miss Edmund in our small circle, but I trust
and hope he will find the poor invalid in a less alarming state than
might be apprehended, and that he will be able to bring him to Mansfield shortly, which Sir Thomas proposes should be done, and thinks
best on every account, and I flatter myself, the poor sufferer will
soon be able to bear the removal without material inconvenience or
injury. As I have little doubt of your feeling for us, my dear Fanny,
under these distressing circumstances, I will write again very soon."

Fanny's feelings on the occasion were indeed considerably more
warm and genuine than her aunt's style of writing. She felt truly for
them all. Tom dangerously ill, Edmund gone to attend him, and the
sadly small party remaining at Mansfield, were cares to shut out every other care, or almost every other. She could just find selfishness enough to wonder whether Edmund *had* written to Miss Crawford before this summons came, but no sentiment dwelt long with
her, that was not purely affectionate and disinterestedly anxious.
Her aunt did not neglect her; she wrote again and again; they were
receiving frequent accounts from Edmund, and these accounts were
as regularly transmitted to Fanny, in the same diffuse style, and the
same medley of trusts, hopes, and fears, all following and producing
each other at hap-hazard. It was a sort of playing at being frightened.
The sufferings which Lady Bertram did not see, had little power over
her fancy; and she wrote very comfortably about agitation and anxiety, and poor invalids, till Tom was actually conveyed to Mansfield,
and her own eyes had beheld his altered appearance. Then, a letter
which she had been previously preparing for Fanny, was finished in a
different style, in the language of real feeling and alarm; then, she
wrote as she might have spoken. "He is just come, my dear Fanny,
and is taken upstairs; and I am so shocked to see him, that I do not
know what to do. I am sure he has been very ill. Poor Tom, I am quite
grieved for him, and very much frightened, and so is Sir Thomas; and

how glad I should be, if you were here to comfort me. But Sir Thomas hopes he will be better to-morrow, and says we must consider his journey."

The real solicitude now awakened in the maternal bosom was not soon over. Tom's extreme impatience to be removed to Mansfield, and experience those comforts of home and family which had been little thought of in uninterrupted health, had probably induced his being conveyed thither too early, as a return of fever came on, and for a week he was in a more alarming state than ever. They were all very seriously frightened. Lady Bertram wrote her daily terrors to her niece, who might now be said to live upon letters, and pass all her time between suffering from that of to-day, and looking forward to to-morrow's. Without any particular affection for her eldest cousin, her tenderness of heart made her feel that she could not spare him; and the purity of her principles added yet a keener solicitude, when she considered how little useful, how little self-denying his life had (apparently) been.

Susan was her only companion and listener on this, as on more common occasions. Susan was always ready to hear and to sympathize. Nobody else could be interested in so remote an evil as illness, in a family above an hundred miles off—not even Mrs. Price, beyond a brief question or two if she saw her daughter with a letter in her hand, and now and then the quiet observation of "My poor sister Bertram must be in a great deal of trouble."

So long divided, and so differently situated, the ties of blood were little more than nothing. An attachment, originally as tranquil as their tempers, was now become a mere name. Mrs. Price did quite as much for Lady Bertram, as Lady Bertram would have done for Mrs. Price. Three or four Prices might have been swept away, any or all, except Fanny and William, and Lady Bertram would have thought little about it; or perhaps might have caught from Mrs. Norris's lips the cant of its being a very happy thing,[4] and a great blessing to their poor dear sister Price to have them so well provided for.

4 Samuel Johnson's definition of *cant* in his *Dictionary* illuminates what is being said here about Mrs. Norris's pious resignation: *cant* is a "whining pretension to goodness, in formal and affected terms."

## 14

1 Symptoms that include weakness, wasting, and vomiting. Bartholomew Parr's *The London Medical Dictionary* (Philadelphia: Mitchell, Ames, and White, 1819) states that "intemperate drinkers, and those who indulge in excess of any kind" are often subject to hectic disorders (p. 735).

AT ABOUT THE WEEK'S END from his return to Mansfield, Tom's immediate danger was over, and he was so far pronounced safe, as to make his mother perfectly easy; for being now used to the sight of him in his suffering, helpless state, and hearing only the best, and never thinking beyond what she heard, with no disposition for alarm, and no aptitude at a hint, Lady Bertram was the happiest subject in the world for a little medical imposition. The fever was subdued; the fever had been his complaint, of course he would soon be well again; Lady Bertram could think nothing less, and Fanny shared her aunt's security, till she received a few lines from Edmund, written purposely to give her a clearer idea of his brother's situation, and acquaint her with the apprehensions which he and his father had imbibed from the physician, with respect to some strong hectic symptoms,[1] which seemed to seize the frame on the departure of the fever. They judged it best that Lady Bertram should not be harassed by alarms which, it was to be hoped, would prove unfounded; but there was no reason why Fanny should not know the truth. They were apprehensive for his lungs.

A very few lines from Edmund shewed her the patient and the sick room in a juster and stronger light than all Lady Bertram's sheets of paper could do. There was hardly any one in the house who might not have described, from personal observation, better than herself; not one who was not more useful at times to her son. She could do nothing but glide in quietly and look at him; but, when able to talk or be talked to, or read to, Edmund was the companion he preferred.

His aunt worried him by her cares, and Sir Thomas knew not how to bring down his conversation or his voice to the level of irritation and feebleness. Edmund was all in all. Fanny would certainly believe him so at least, and must find that her estimation of him was higher than ever when he appeared as the attendant, supporter, cheerer of a suffering brother. There was not only the debility of recent illness to assist; there was also, as she now learnt, nerves much affected, spirits much depressed to calm and raise; and her own imagination added that there must be a mind to be properly guided.

The family were not consumptive,[2] and she was more inclined to hope than fear for her cousin—except when she thought of Miss Crawford—but Miss Crawford gave her the idea of being the child of good luck, and to her selfishness and vanity it would be good luck to have Edmund the only son.

Even in the sick chamber, the fortunate Mary was not forgotten. Edmund's letter had this postscript. "On the subject of my last, I had actually begun a letter when called away by Tom's illness, but I have now changed my mind, and fear to trust the influence of friends. When Tom is better, I shall go."

Such was the state of Mansfield, and so it continued, with scarcely any change till Easter. A line occasionally added by Edmund to his mother's letter was enough for Fanny's information. Tom's amendment was alarmingly slow.

Easter came—particularly late this year, as Fanny had most sorrowfully considered, on first learning that she had no chance of leaving Portsmouth till after it. It came, and she had yet heard nothing of her return—nothing even of the going to London, which was to precede her return. Her aunt often expressed a wish for her, but there was no notice, no message from the uncle on whom all depended. She supposed he could not yet leave his son, but it was a cruel, a terrible delay to her. The end of April was coming on; it would soon be almost three months instead of two that she had been absent from them all, and that her days had been passing in a state of penance, which she loved them too well to hope they would thoroughly understand;—and who could yet say when there might be leisure to think of, or fetch her?

2 Consumption, tuberculosis of the lungs, was then believed, wrongly, to be a hereditary disease.

3 Fanny draws once more on her favorite author, quoting Cowper's "Tirocinium, or, A Review of Schools," first published alongside *The Task* in 1785. The poem condemns the grand boarding schools of the era and recommends that the sons of gentlemen be educated at home by their fathers. Changing the pronouns in Cowper's lines, Fanny re-genders Cowper's schoolboy, who, in the poem, is imagined counting off the days until he can return home from school for the holidays: "Th'indented stick that loses day by day / Notch after notch, 'till all are smooth'd away, / Bears witness, long 'ere his dismission come, / With what intense desire he wants his home" ("Tirocinium," in *The Task: A Poem* [London: J. Johnson, 1785], p. 322, lines 559–562).

Her eagerness, her impatience, her longings to be with them, were such as to bring a line or two of Cowper's Tirocinium for ever before her.—"With what intense desire she wants her home," was continually on her tongue, as the truest description of a yearning which she could not suppose any school-boy's bosom to feel more keenly.[3]

When she had been coming to Portsmouth, she had loved to call it her home, had been fond of saying that she was going home; the word had been very dear to her; and so it still was, but it must be applied to Mansfield. *That* was now the home. Portsmouth was Portsmouth; Mansfield was home. They had been long so arranged in the indulgence of her secret meditations; and nothing was more consolatory to her than to find her aunt using the same language.—"I cannot but say, I much regret your being from home at this distressing time, so very trying to my spirits.—I trust and hope, and sincerely wish you may never be absent from home so long again"—were most delightful sentences to her. Still, however, it was her private regale.—Delicacy to her parents made her careful not to betray such a preference of her uncle's house: it was always, "when I go back into Northamptonshire, or when I return to Mansfield, I shall do so and so."—For a great while it was so; but at last the longing grew stronger, it overthrew caution, and she found herself talking of what she should do when she went home, before she was aware.—She reproached herself, coloured and looked fearfully towards her Father and Mother. She need not have been uneasy. There was no sign of displeasure, or even of hearing her. They were perfectly free from any jealousy of Mansfield. She was as welcome to wish herself there, as to be there.

It was sad to Fanny to lose all the pleasures of spring. She had not known before what pleasures she *had* to lose in passing March and April in a town. She had not known before, how much the beginnings and progress of vegetation had delighted her.—What animation both of body and mind, she had derived from watching the advance of that season which cannot, in spite of its capriciousness, be unlovely, and seeing its increasing beauties, from the earliest flowers, in the warmest divisions of her aunt's garden, to the opening of

leaves of her uncle's plantations, and the glory of his woods.—To be
losing such pleasures was no trifle; to be losing them, because she
was in the midst of closeness and noise, to have confinement, bad
air, bad smells, substituted for liberty, freshness, fragrance, and verdure, was infinitely worse;—but even these incitements to regret,
were feeble, compared with what arose from the conviction of being
missed, by her best friends, and the longing to be useful to those who
were wanting her!

Could she have been at home, she might have been of service to
every creature in the house. She felt that she must have been of use
to all. To all, she must have saved some trouble of head or hand; and
were it only in supporting the spirits of her aunt Bertram, keeping
her from the evil of solitude, or the still greater evil of a restless, officious companion, too apt to be heightening danger in order to enhance her own importance, her being there would have been a general good. She loved to fancy how she could have read to her aunt,
how she could have talked to her, and tried at once to make her feel
the blessing of what was, and prepare her mind for what might be;
and how many walks up and down stairs she might have saved her,
and how many messages she might have carried.

It astonished her that Tom's sisters could be satisfied with remaining in London at such a time—through an illness, which had now,
under different degrees of danger, lasted several weeks. *They* might
return to Mansfield when they chose; travelling could be no difficulty to *them,* and she could not comprehend how both could still
keep away. If Mrs. Rushworth could imagine any interfering obliga-
tions, Julia was certainly able to quit London whenever she chose.—
It appeared from one of her aunt's letters, that Julia had offered to
return if wanted—but this was all.—It was evident that she would
rather remain where she was.

Fanny was disposed to think the influence of London very much
at war with all respectable attachments. She saw the proof of it in
Miss Crawford, as well as in her cousins; *her* attachment to Edmund
had been respectable, the most respectable part of her character,
her friendship for herself, had at least been blameless. Where was
either sentiment now? It was so long since Fanny had had any letter

from her, that she had some reason to think lightly of the friendship
which had been so dwelt on.—It was weeks since she had heard any
thing of Miss Crawford or of her other connections in town, except
through Mansfield, and she was beginning to suppose that she might
never know whether Mr. Crawford had gone into Norfolk again or
not, till they met, and might never hear from his sister any more this
spring, when the following letter was received to revive old, and create some new sensations.

"Forgive me, my dear Fanny, as soon as you can, for my
long silence, and behave as if you could forgive me directly.
This is my modest request and expectation, for you are so
good, that I depend upon being treated better than I deserve—and I write now to beg an immediate answer. I want
to know the state of things at Mansfield Park, and you, no
doubt, are perfectly able to give it. One should be a brute not
to feel for the distress they are in—and from what I hear,
poor Mr. Bertram has a bad chance of ultimate recovery. I
thought little of his illness at first. I looked upon him as the
sort of person to be made a fuss with, and to make a fuss himself in any trifling disorder, and was chiefly concerned for
those who had to nurse him; but now it is confidently asserted that he is really in a decline, that the symptoms are
most alarming, and that part of the family, at least, are aware
of it. If it be so, I am sure you must be included in that part,
that discerning part, and therefore intreat you to let me
know how far I have been rightly informed. I need not say
how rejoiced I shall be to hear there has been any mistake,
but the report is so prevalent, that I confess I cannot help
trembling. To have such a fine young man cut off in the
flower of his days, is most melancholy. Poor Sir Thomas will
feel it dreadfully. I really am quite agitated on the subject.
Fanny, Fanny, I see you smile, and look cunning, but upon my
honour, I never bribed a physician in my life. Poor young
man!—If he is to die, there will be *two* poor young men less
in the world; and with a fearless face and bold voice would I

say to any one, that wealth and consequence could fall into no hands more deserving of them. It was a foolish precipitation last Christmas, but the evil of a few days may be blotted out in part. Varnish and gilding hide many stains. It will be but the loss of the Esquire after his name.[4] With real affection, Fanny, like mine, more might be overlooked. Write to me by return of post, judge of my anxiety, and do not trifle with it. Tell me the real truth, as you have it from the fountain head. And now, do not trouble yourself to be ashamed of either my feelings or your own. Believe me, they are not only natural, they are philanthropic and virtuous. I put it to your conscience, whether 'Sir Edmund' would not do more good with all the Bertram property, than any other possible 'Sir.' Had the Grants been at home, I would not have troubled you, but you are now the only one I can apply to for the truth, his sisters not being within my reach. Mrs. R. has been spending the Easter with the Aylmers at Twickenham (as to be sure you know), and is not yet returned; and Julia is with the cousins, who live near Bedford Square;[5] but I forgot their name and street. Could I immediately apply to either, however, I should still prefer you, because it strikes me, that they have all along been so unwilling to have their own amusements cut up, as to shut their eyes to the truth. I suppose, Mrs. R.'s Easter holidays will not last much longer; no doubt they are thorough holidays to her. The Aylmers are pleasant people; and her husband away, she can have nothing but enjoyment. I give her credit for promoting his going dutifully down to Bath, to fetch his mother; but how will she and the dowager agree in one house? Henry is not at hand, so I have nothing to say from him. Do not you think Edmund would have been in town again long ago, but for this illness?—Yours ever, Mary."

"I had actually began folding my letter, when Henry walked in; but he brings no intelligence to prevent my sending it. Mrs. R. knows a decline is apprehended; he saw her this morning, she returns to Wimpole Street to-day, the old

4 Edmund's ordination, the "foolish precipitation at Christmas" Mary has in mind, will, she thinks, be of little consequence once he becomes the only son and heir to Mansfield Park. The courtesy title *Esquire* was not used for gentlemen in clerical orders.

5 A less fashionable area of London than Wimpole Street in Marylebone, Bedford Square, about a mile to the east, is still a prestigious address. The Lord Chancellor of England, Lord Eldon, lived at no. 6 Bedford Square in 1814.

6  A village southeast of London, Richmond is immediately across the river Thames from Twickenham,
where Maria Rushworth has been paying a visit.

lady is come. Now do not make yourself uneasy with any
queer fancies, because he has been spending a few days at
Richmond.[6] He does it every spring. Be assured, he cares for
nobody but you. At this very moment, he is wild to see you,
and occupied only in contriving the means for doing so, and
for making his pleasure conduce to yours. In proof, he re-
peats, and more eagerly, what he said at Portsmouth, about
our conveying you home, and I join him in it with all my soul.
Dear Fanny, write directly, and tell us to come. It will do us all
good. He and I can go to the Parsonage, you know, and be no
trouble to our friends at Mansfield Park. It would really be
gratifying to see them all again, and a little addition of society might be of infinite use to them; and, as to yourself, you
must feel yourself to be so wanted there, that you cannot in
conscience (conscientious as you are,) keep away, when you
have the means of returning. I have not time or patience to
give half Henry's messages; be satisfied, that the spirit of
each and every one is unalterable affection."

Fanny's disgust at the greater part of this letter, with her extreme
reluctance to bring the writer of it and her cousin Edmund together,
would have made her (as she felt), incapable of judging impartially
whether the concluding offer might be accepted or not. To herself,
individually, it was most tempting. To be finding herself, perhaps,
within three days, transported to Mansfield, was an image of the
greatest felicity—but it would have been a material drawback, to
be owing such felicity to persons in whose feelings and conduct,
at the present moment, she saw so much to condemn; the sister's
feelings—the brother's conduct—*her* cold-hearted ambition—*his*
thoughtless vanity. To have him still the acquaintance, the flirt, perhaps, of Mrs. Rushworth!—She was mortified. She had thought better of him. Happily, however, she was not left to weigh and decide
between opposite inclinations and doubtful notions of right; there
was no occasion to determine, whether she ought to keep Edmund
and Mary asunder or not. She had a rule to apply to, which settled
every thing. Her awe of her uncle, and her dread of taking a liberty

with him, made it instantly plain to her, what she had to do. She must absolutely decline the proposal. If he wanted, he would send for her; and even to offer an early return, was a presumption which hardly any thing would have seemed to justify. She thanked Miss Crawford, but gave a decided negative.—"Her uncle, she understood, meant to fetch her; and as her cousin's illness had continued so many weeks without her being thought at all necessary, she must suppose her return would be unwelcome at present, and that she should be felt an incumbrance."

Her representation of her cousin's state at this time, was exactly according to her own belief of it, and such as she supposed would convey to the sanguine mind of her correspondent, the hope of every thing she was wishing for. Edmund would be forgiven for being a clergyman, it seemed, under certain conditions of wealth; and this, she suspected, was all the conquest of prejudice, which he was so ready to congratulate himself upon. She had only learnt to think nothing of consequence but money.

## 15

1 French for a thoughtless slip, a piece of imprudence.

As FANNY COULD NOT DOUBT that her answer was conveying a real disappointment, she was rather in expectation, from her knowledge of Miss Crawford's temper, of being urged again; and though no second letter arrived for the space of a week, she had still the same feeling when it did come.

On receiving it, she could instantly decide on its containing little writing, and was persuaded of its having the air of a letter of haste and business. Its object was unquestionable; and two moments were enough to start the probability of its being merely to give her notice that they should be in Portsmouth that very day, and to throw her into all the agitation of doubting what she ought to do in such a case. If two moments, however, can surround with difficulties, a third can disperse them; and before she had opened the letter, the possibility of Mr. and Miss Crawford's having applied to her uncle and obtained his permission, was giving her ease. This was the letter.

"A most scandalous, ill-natured rumour has just reached me, and I write, dear Fanny, to warn you against giving the least credit to it, should it spread into the country. Depend upon it there is some mistake, and that a day or two will clear it up—at any rate, that Henry is blameless, and in spite of a moment's *etourderie* thinks of nobody but you.[1] Say not a word of it—hear nothing, surmise nothing, whisper nothing, till I write again. I am sure it will be all hushed up, and noth-

ing proved but Rushworth's folly. If they are gone, I would lay
my life they are only gone to Mansfield Park, and Julia with
them. But why would not you let us come for you? I wish you
may not repent it.

Yours, &c."

Fanny stood aghast. As no scandalous, ill-natured rumour had
reached her, it was impossible for her to understand much of this
strange letter. She could only perceive that it must relate to Wimpole
Street and Mr. Crawford, and only conjecture that something very
imprudent had just occurred in that quarter to draw the notice of
the world, and to excite her jealousy, in Miss Crawford's apprehension, if she heard it. Miss Crawford need not be alarmed for her. She
was only sorry for the parties concerned and for Mansfield, if the report should spread so far; but she hoped it might not. If the Rushworths were gone themselves to Mansfield, as was to be inferred
from what Miss Crawford said, it was not likely that any thing unpleasant should have preceded them, or at least should make any impression.

As to Mr. Crawford, she hoped it might give him a knowledge of
his own disposition, convince him that he was not capable of being
steadily attached to any one woman in the world, and shame him
from persisting any longer in addressing herself.

It was very strange! She had begun to think he really loved her, and
to fancy his affection for her something more than common—and
his sister still said that he cared for nobody else. Yet there must have
been some marked display of attentions to her cousin, there must
have been some strong indiscretion, since her correspondent was
not of a sort to regard a slight one.

Very uncomfortable she was and must continue till she heard
from Miss Crawford again. It was impossible to banish the letter
from her thoughts, and she could not relieve herself by speaking of it
to any human being. Miss Crawford need not have urged secrecy
with so much warmth, she might have trusted to her sense of what
was due to her cousin.

The next day came and brought no second letter. Fanny was disappointed. She could still think of little else all the morning; but when her father came back in the afternoon with the daily newspaper as usual, she was so far from expecting any elucidation through such a channel, that the subject was for a moment out of her head.

She was deep in other musing. The remembrance of her first evening in that room, of her father and his newspaper came across her. No candle was *now* wanted. The sun was yet an hour and half above the horizon. She felt that she had, indeed, been three months there; and the sun's rays falling strongly into the parlour, instead of cheering, made her still more melancholy; for sun shine appeared to her a totally different thing in a town and in the country. Here, its power was only a glare, a stifling, sickly glare, serving but to bring forward stains and dirt that might otherwise have slept. There was neither health nor gaiety in sun-shine in a town. She sat in a blaze of oppressive heat, in a cloud of moving dust; and her eyes could only wander from the walls marked by her father's head, to the table cut and knotched by her brothers, where stood the tea-board never thoroughly cleaned, the cups and saucers wiped in streaks, the milk a mixture of motes floating in thin blue, and the bread and butter growing every minute more greasy than even Rebecca's hands had first produced it. Her father read his newspaper, and her mother lamented over the ragged carpet as usual, while the tea was in preparation—and wished Rebecca would mend it; and Fanny was first roused by his calling out to her, after humphing and considering over a particular paragraph—"What's the name of your great cousins in town, Fan?"

A moment's recollection enabled her to say, "Rushworth, Sir."

"And don't they live in Wimpole Street?"

"Yes, Sir."

"Then, there's the devil to pay among them, that's all. There, (holding out the paper to her)—much good may such fine relations do you. I don't know what Sir Thomas may think of such matters; he may be too much of the courtier and fine gentleman to like his daughter the less. But by G—if she belonged to *me,* I'd give her the

*The Point of Honor,* caricature print by George Cruikshank, 1825. The print shows a sailor tied to a grate and about to undergo the flogging that was a standard part of the arsenal of punishments administered onboard navy vessels. As an officer in the marines, entrusted with the task of enforcing the authority of the navy officers, Mr. Price would have witnessed many scenes like this one.

rope's end as long as I could stand over her. A little flogging for man and woman too, would be the best way of preventing such things."[2]

Fanny read to herself that "it was with infinite concern the newspaper had to announce to the world, a matrimonial *fracas* in the family of Mr. R. of Wimpole Street; the beautiful Mrs. R. whose name had not long been enrolled in the lists of hymen,[3] and who had promised to become so brilliant a leader in the fashionable world, having quitted her husband's roof in company with the well known and captivating Mr. C. the intimate friend and associate of Mr. R. and it was not known, even to the editor of the newspaper, whither they were gone."[4]

"It is a mistake, Sir," said Fanny instantly; "it must be a mistake—it cannot be true—it must mean some other people."

2 The rope's end—a short length of rope that had been bound at the end with thread—was used for "smacking" (as it was called), a painful punishment sailors endured on an everyday basis aboard ship. It was administered on the spot for minor infractions of discipline or simply because to someone in charge the offender seemed to require some hurrying up. Floggings were more consequential disciplinary measures, recorded in the ship's log, and staged in front of the entire crew.

3 In Greek mythology Hymen is the god of marriage. In a roundabout and arch way, the newspaper is identifying this "Mrs. R." as a newlywed.

4 Gossip columns recounting with heavy innuendo the sex scandals among celebrities and members of the social elite were standard features of period newspapers like the *Morning Post* and the *Morning Chronicle.* One reason Austen is able to mimic so plausibly the style of such reports is that, as her letters attest, she read such papers herself. A letter to Cassandra from June 20–22, 1808, mentions, for instance, how in yesterday's *Courier* Austen has spotted a hint, "with Initials," of a "sad story" involving a certain Mrs. Powlett. R. W. Chapman found that *Courier* was in this letter Austen's mistake for *Morning Post.* He transcribed the bulletin that he discovered in the latter newspaper, which reads (as reproduced in Deirdre Le Faye's edition of the *Letters*): "Another elopement has taken place in high life. A Noble Viscount, Lord S., has gone off with a Mrs. P., the wife of a relative of a Noble Marquis" (*Letters,* p. 401 n. 13).

5 Fanny's response to the news of Maria's adultery is at
once emotional and physical, as John Wiltshire notes
in *Jane Austen and the Body: "The Picture of Health"* (Cambridge: Cambridge University Press, 1992), so that in
this narrative passage she all but replicates the symptoms of Tom Bertram's fever (p. 105).

She spoke from the instinctive wish of delaying shame, she spoke
with a resolution which sprung from despair, for she spoke what she
did not, could not believe herself. It had been the shock of conviction as she read. The truth rushed on her; and how she could have
spoken at all, how she could even have breathed—was afterwards
matter of wonder to herself.

Mr. Price cared too little about the report, to make her much answer. "It might be all a lie, he acknowledged; but so many fine ladies
were going to the devil now-a-days that way, that there was no answering for anybody."

"Indeed, I hope it is not true," said Mrs. Price plaintively, "it
would be so very shocking!—If I have spoken once to Rebecca about
that carpet, I am sure I have spoke at least a dozen times; have not I,
Betsey?—And it would not be ten minutes work."

The horror of a mind like Fanny's, as it received the conviction of
such guilt, and began to take in some part of the misery that must
ensue, can hardly be described. At first, it was a sort of stupefaction;
but every moment was quickening her perception of the horrible
evil. She could not doubt; she dared not indulge a hope of the paragraph being false. Miss Crawford's letter, which she had read so often as to make every line her own, was in frightful conformity with
it. Her eager defence of her brother, her hope of its being *hushed up,*
her evident agitation, were all of a piece with something very bad;
and if there was a woman of character in existence, who could treat
as a trifle this sin of the first magnitude, who would try to gloss it
over, and desire to have it unpunished, she could believe Miss Crawford to be the woman! Now she could see her own mistake as to *who*
were gone—or *said* to be gone. It was not Mr. and Mrs. Rushworth, it
was Mrs. Rushworth and Mr. Crawford.

Fanny seemed to herself never to have been shocked before.
There was no possibility of rest. The evening passed, without a pause
of misery, the night was totally sleepless. She passed only from feelings of sickness to shudderings of horror; and from hot fits of fever
to cold.[5] The event was so shocking, that there were moments even
when her heart revolted from it as impossible—when she thought it
could not be. A woman married only six months ago, a man profess-

ing himself devoted, even *engaged,* to another—that other her near relation—the whole family, both families connected as they were by tie upon tie, all friends, all intimate together!—it was too horrible a confusion of guilt, too gross a complication of evil, for human nature, not in a state of utter barbarism, to be capable of!—yet her judgment told her it was so.[6] *His* unsettled affections, wavering with his vanity, *Maria's* decided attachment, and no sufficient principle on either side, gave it possibility—Miss Crawford's letter stampt it a fact.

What would be the consequence? Whom would it not injure? Whose views might it not effect?[7] Whose peace would it not cut up for ever? Miss Crawford herself—Edmund; but it was dangerous, perhaps, to tread such ground. She confined herself, or tried to confine herself, to the simple, indubitable family-misery which must envelope all, if it were indeed a matter of certified guilt and public exposure. The mother's sufferings, the father's—there, she paused. Julia's, Tom's, Edmund's—there, a yet longer pause. They were the two on whom it would fall most horribly. Sir Thomas's parental solicitude, and high sense of honour and decorum, Edmund's upright principles, unsuspicious temper, and genuine strength of feeling, made her think it scarcely possible for them to support life and reason under such disgrace; and it appeared to her, that as far as this world alone was concerned, the greatest blessing to every one of kindred with Mrs. Rushworth would be instant annihilation.

Nothing happened the next day, or the next, to weaken her terrors. Two posts came in, and brought no refutation, public or private. There was no second letter to explain away the first, from Miss Crawford; there was no intelligence from Mansfield, though it was now full time for her to hear again from her aunt. This was an evil omen. She had, indeed, scarcely the shadow of a hope to soothe her mind, and was reduced to so low and wan and trembling a condition as no mother—not unkind, except Mrs. Price, could have overlooked, when the third day did bring the sickening knock, and a letter was again put into her hands. It bore the London postmark, and came from Edmund.

6 The diction here and the complex syntax, with its double negative, together betray Fanny's efforts, even in thought, to deny her own emotional implication in the family scandal. Not only does she herself figure in this sentence only in the third person, as "another" and as "that other," but she lets herself dally with the idea that such moral transgressions—possible, she illogically insists, only in a "state of utter barbarism"—may be kept at a safe geographical and temporal distance from modern, civilized Britain. Fanny is trying here to do what at a crucial moment in *Northanger Abbey* Henry Tilney (arguably with equal bad faith) advises Catherine Morland to do—"Remember the country and the age in which we live" (II, 9)—but in this case that effort is ineffectual.

7 Editors of *Mansfield Park* have tended to substitute *affect* for *effect* in this sentence, but in the text as it stands in both the 1814 and the 1816 editions, Fanny can be understood to be musing about whose plans or prospects ("views") will not be brought to pass or be realized, that is, "effected," in the wake of the scandal—and maybe also, more tacitly, musing about whose will. Of course, Fanny's own views, plans for her happiness she has never consciously avowed, are now closer to being effected than they have ever been. But to think that is, as Fanny tells herself only two sentences later, to stray into "dangerous" territory.

8 The laws that after 1753 regulated marriages in England did not extend to Scotland: couples there were
exempt from the requirement that they either be resident in a parish for a three-week period prior to their
wedding ceremony or agree to purchase an expensive
special license from the bishop. The result was that,
after 1770, which was when the "turnpike road network reached Scotland," "a steady stream of matrimonial traffic" regularly journeyed across the border from
England to Scotland (Lisa O' Connell, "Gretna Green
Novels," *The Oxford Encyclopedia of British Literature,*
ed. David Scott Kastan [New York: Oxford University
Press, 2005], p. 477). In eloping to Scotland, Julia Bertram and Mr. Yates have taken a route very familiar to
novel-readers. In Frances Burney's *Camilla* the heroine's sister is abducted by a fortune-hunting villain who
plans to marry her against her will at Gretna Green,
the tiny border village that by the late eighteenth century had become the center of the trade in instant
marriages. In *Pride and Prejudice,* the first reports about
the whereabouts of Lydia Bennet and Mr. Wickham
have this eloping couple heading in Gretna Green's direction as well (III, 4).

9 Edmund will travel from London to Portsmouth by
the overnight mail coach.

10 A restorative drink.

"Dear Fanny,

You know our present wretchedness. May God support
you under *your* share. We have been here two days, but there
is nothing to be done. They cannot be traced. You may not
have heard of the last blow—Julia's elopement; she is gone
to Scotland with Yates.[8] She left London a few hours before
we entered it. At any other time, this would have been felt
dreadfully. Now it seems nothing, yet it is an heavy aggravation. My father is not overpowered. More cannot be hoped.
He is still able to think and act; and I write, by his desire, to
propose your returning home. He is anxious to get you there
for my mother's sake. I shall be at Portsmouth the morning
after you receive this, and hope to find you ready to set off
for Mansfield. My Father wishes you to invite Susan to go
with you, for a few months. Settle it as you like; say what is
proper; I am sure you will feel such an instance of his kindness at such a moment! Do justice to his meaning, however I
may confuse it. You may imagine something of my present
state. There is no end of the evil let loose upon us. You will
see me early, by the mail.[9] Your's, &c."

Never had Fanny more wanted a cordial.[10] Never had she felt such
a one as this letter contained. To-morrow! to leave Portsmouth to-
morrow! She was, she felt she was, in the greatest danger of being
exquisitely happy, while so many were miserable. The evil which
brought such good to her! She dreaded lest she should learn to be insensible of it. To be going so soon, sent for so kindly, sent for as a
comfort, and with leave to take Susan, was altogether such a combination of blessings as set her heart in a glow, and for a time, seemed
to distance every pain, and make her incapable of suitably sharing
the distress even of those whose distress she thought of most. Julia's
elopement could affect her comparatively but little; she was amazed
and shocked; but it could not occupy her, could not dwell on her
mind. She was obliged to call herself to think of it, and acknowledge
it to be terrible and grievous, or it was escaping her, in the midst of

all the agitating, pressing, joyful cares attending this summons to herself.

There is nothing like employment, active, indispensable employment, for relieving sorrow. Employment, even melancholy, may dispel melancholy, and her occupations were hopeful. She had so much to do, that not even the horrible story of Mrs. Rushworth (now fixed to the last point of certainty), could affect her as it had done before. She had not time to be miserable. Within twenty-four hours she was hoping to be gone; her father and mother must be spoken to, Susan prepared, every thing got ready. Business followed business; the day was hardly long enough. The happiness she was imparting too, happiness very little alloyed by the black communication which must briefly precede it—the joyful consent of her father and mother to Susan's going with her—the general satisfaction with which the going of both seemed regarded—and the ecstacy of Susan herself, was all serving to support her spirits.

The affliction of the Bertrams was little felt in the family. Mrs. Price talked of her poor sister for a few minutes—but how to find any thing to hold Susan's clothes, because Rebecca took away all the boxes and spoilt them, was much more in her thoughts, and as for Susan, now unexpectedly gratified in the first wish of her heart, and knowing nothing personally of those who had sinned, or of those who were sorrowing—if she could help rejoicing from beginning to end, it was as much as ought to be expected from human virtue at fourteen.

As nothing was really left for the decision of Mrs. Price, or the good offices of Rebecca, every thing was rationally and duly accomplished, and the girls were ready for the morrow. The advantage of much sleep to prepare them for their journey, was impossible. The cousin who was travelling towards them, could hardly have less than visited their agitated spirits, one all happiness, the other all varying and indescribable perturbation.

By eight in the morning, Edmund was in the house. The girls heard his entrance from above, and Fanny went down. The idea of immediately seeing him, with the knowledge of what he must be suffering, brought back all her own first feelings. He so near her, and in

*Gretna Green, or The Red Hot Marriage,* mezzotint from 1795. Many of the runaway marriages contracted in the Scottish village of Gretna Green took place in the village blacksmith's shop, with the blacksmith, the so-called anvil priest, acting as the minister conducting the ceremony.

misery. She was ready to sink, as she entered the parlour. He was alone, and met her instantly; and she found herself pressed to his heart with only these words, just articulate, "My Fanny—my only sister—my only comfort now." She could say nothing; nor for some minutes could he say more.

He turned away to recover himself, and when he spoke again, though his voice still faltered, his manner showed the wish of self-command, and the resolution of avoiding any farther allusion. "Have you breakfasted?—When shall you be ready?—Does Susan go?"— were questions following each other rapidly. His great object was to be off as soon as possible. When Mansfield was considered, time was precious; and the state of his own mind made him find relief only in motion. It was settled that he should order the carriage to the door in half an hour; Fanny answered for their having breakfasted, and being quite ready in half an hour. He had already ate, and declined staying for their meal. He would walk round the ramparts, and join them with the carriage. He was gone again, glad to get away even from Fanny.

He looked very ill; evidently suffering under violent emotions, which he was determined to suppress. She knew it must be so, but it was terrible to her.

The carriage came; and he entered the house again at the same moment, just in time to spend a few minutes with the family, and be a witness—but that he saw nothing—of the tranquil manner in which the daughters were parted with, and just in time to prevent their sitting down to the breakfast table, which by dint of much unusual activity, was quite and completely ready as the carriage drove from the door. Fanny's last meal in her father's house was in character with her first; she was dismissed from it as hospitably as she had been welcomed.

How her heart swelled with joy and gratitude, as she passed the barriers of Portsmouth, and how Susan's face wore its broadest smiles, may be easily conceived. Sitting forwards, however, and screened by her bonnet, those smiles were unseen.

The journey was likely to be a silent one. Edmund's deep sighs often reached Fanny. Had he been alone with her, his heart must have opened in spite of every resolution; but Susan's presence drove him quite into himself, and his attempts to talk on indifferent subjects could never be long supported.

Fanny watched him with never-failing solicitude, and sometimes catching his eye, revived an affectionate smile, which comforted her; but the first day's journey passed without her hearing a word from him on the subjects that were weighing him down. The next morning produced a little more. Just before their setting out from Oxford, while Susan was stationed at a window, in eager observation of the departure of a large family from the inn, the other two were standing by the fire; and Edmund, particularly struck by the alteration in Fanny's looks, and from his ignorance of the daily evils of her father's house, attributing an undue share of the change, attributing *all* to the recent event, took her hand, and said in a low, but very expressive tone, "No wonder—you must feel it—you must suffer. How a man who had once loved, could desert you! But *your's*—your regard was new compared with——Fanny, think of *me!*"

The first division of their journey occupied a long day, and brought them almost knocked up, to Oxford; but the second was over at a much earlier hour. They were in the environs of Mansfield long before the usual dinner-time, and as they approached the beloved place, the hearts of both sisters sank a little. Fanny began to dread the meeting with her aunts and Tom, under so dreadful a humiliation; and Susan to feel with some anxiety, that all her best manners, all her lately acquired knowledge of what was practised here, was on the point of being called into action. Visions of good and ill breeding, of old vulgarisms and new gentilities were before her; and she was meditating much upon silver forks, napkins, and finger glasses.[11] Fanny had been every where awake to the difference of the country since February; but, when they entered the Park, her perceptions and her pleasures were of the keenest sort. It was three months, full three months, since her quitting it; and the change was from winter to summer. Her eye fell every where on lawns and plantations of the freshest green; and the trees, though not fully clothed, were in that delightful state, when farther beauty is known to be at hand, and when, while much is actually given to the sight, more yet remains for

12  As John Wiltshire notes, Austen works into this account of Fanny's homecoming a faint recollection of the New Testament story of the prodigal son. When the errant child of Christ's parable was returning home, his forgiving father spotted him while he was yet "a great way off . . . and had compassion, and ran, and fell on his neck, and kissed him" (Luke, chapter 15, verse 20). See Wiltshire, *The Hidden Jane Austen* (Cambridge: Cambridge University Press, 2014), p. 118.

the imagination. Her enjoyment, however, was for herself alone. Edmund could not share it. She looked at him, but he was leaning back, sunk in a deeper gloom than ever, and with eyes closed as if the view of cheerfulness oppressed him, and the lovely scenes of home must be shut out.

It made her melancholy again; and the knowledge of what must be enduring there, invested even the house, modern, airy, and well situated as it was, with a melancholy aspect.

By one of the suffering party within, they were expected with such impatience as she had never known before. Fanny had scarcely passed the solemn-looking servants, when Lady Bertram came from the drawing room to meet her; came with no indolent step; and, falling on her neck,[12] said, "Dear Fanny! now I shall be comfortable."

# 16

IT HAD BEEN A MISERABLE PARTY, each of the three believing themselves most miserable. Mrs. Norris, however, as most attached to Maria, was really the greatest sufferer. Maria was her first favourite, the dearest of all; the match had been her own contriving, as she had been wont with such pride of heart to feel and say, and this conclusion of it almost overpowered her.

She was an altered creature, quieted, stupefied, indifferent to every thing that passed. The being left with her sister and nephew, and all the house under her care, had been an advantage entirely thrown away; she had been unable to direct or dictate, or even fancy herself useful. When really touched by affliction, her active powers had been all benumbed; and neither Lady Bertram nor Tom had received from her the smallest support or attempt at support. She had done no more for them, than they had done for each other. They had been all solitary, helpless, and forlorn alike; and now the arrival of the others only established her superiority in wretchedness. Her companions were relieved, but there was no good for *her*. Edmund was almost as welcome to his brother, as Fanny to her aunt; but Mrs. Norris, instead of having comfort from either, was but the more irritated by the sight of the person whom, in the blindness of her anger, she could have charged as the dæmon of the piece. Had Fanny accepted Mr. Crawford, this could not have happened.

Susan, too, was a grievance. She had not spirits to notice her in more than a few repulsive looks, but she felt her as a spy, and an intruder, and an indigent niece, and every thing most odious. By her other aunt, Susan was received with quiet kindness. Lady Bertram could not give her much time, or many words, but she felt her, as Fanny's sister, to have a claim at Mansfield, and was ready to kiss and like her; and Susan was more than satisfied, for she came perfectly aware, that nothing but ill humour was to be expected from Aunt Norris; and was so provided with happiness, so strong in that best of blessings, an escape from many certain evils, that she could have stood against a great deal more indifference than she met with from the others.

She was now left a good deal to herself, to get acquainted with the house and grounds as she could, and spent her days very happily in so doing, while those who might otherwise have attended to her, were shut up, or wholly occupied each with the person quite dependant on them, at this time, for every thing like comfort; Edmund trying to bury his own feelings in exertions for the relief of his brother's, and Fanny devoted to her aunt Bertram, returning to every former office, with more than former zeal, and thinking she could never do enough for one who seemed so much to want her.

To talk over the dreadful business with Fanny, talk and lament, was all Lady Bertram's consolation. To be listened to and borne with, and hear the voice of kindness and sympathy in return, was every thing that could be done for her. To be otherwise comforted was out of the question. The case admitted of no comfort. Lady Bertram did not think deeply, but, guided by Sir Thomas, she thought justly on all important points; and she saw, therefore, in all its enormity, what had happened, and neither endeavoured herself, nor required Fanny to advise her, to think little of guilt and infamy.

Her affections were not acute, nor was her mind tenacious. After a time, Fanny found it not impossible to direct her thoughts to other subjects, and revive some interest in the usual occupations; but whenever Lady Bertram *was* fixed on the event, she could see it only in one light, as comprehending the loss of a daughter, and a disgrace never to be wiped off.

Fanny learnt from her, all the particulars which had yet transpired. Her aunt was no very methodical narrator; but with the help of some letters to and from Sir Thomas, and what she already knew herself, and could reasonably combine, she was soon able to understand quite as much as she wished of the circumstances attending the story.

Mrs. Rushworth had gone, for the Easter holidays, to Twickenham, with a family whom she had just grown intimate with—a family of lively, agreeable manners, and probably of morals and discretion to suit—for to *their* house Mr. Crawford had constant access at all times. His having been in the same neighbourhood, Fanny already knew. Mr. Rushworth had been gone, at this time, to Bath, to pass a few days with his mother, and bring her back to town, and Maria was with these friends without any restraint, without even Julia; for Julia had removed from Wimpole Street two or three weeks before, on a visit to some relations of Sir Thomas; a removal which her father and mother were now disposed to attribute to some view of convenience on Mr. Yates's account. Very soon after the Rushworths' return to Wimpole Street, Sir Thomas had received a letter from an old and most particular friend in London, who hearing and witnessing a good deal to alarm him in that quarter, wrote to recommend Sir Thomas's coming to London himself, and using his influence with his daughter, to put an end to the intimacy which was already exposing her to unpleasant remarks, and evidently making Mr. Rushworth uneasy.

Sir Thomas was preparing to act upon this letter, without communicating its contents to any creature at Mansfield, when it was followed by another, sent express from the same friend, to break to him the almost desperate situation in which affairs then stood with the young people. Mrs. Rushworth had left her husband's house; Mr. Rushworth had been in great anger and distress to *him* (Mr. Harding), for his advice; Mr. Harding feared there had been *at least,* very flagrant indiscretion. The maid-servant of Mrs. Rushworth, senior, threatened alarmingly. He was doing all in his power to quiet every thing, with the hope of Mrs. Rushworth's return, but was so much counteracted in Wimpole Street by the influence of Mr. Rushworth's mother, that the worst consequences might be apprehended.

This dreadful communication could not be kept from the rest of the family. Sir Thomas set off; Edmund would go with him; and the others had been left in a state of wretchedness, inferior only to what followed the receipt of the next letters from London. Every thing

1 As Roger Sales notes, this maid-servant who knows too much is at once "serving her mistress" and "shifting the balance of power between them" by setting aside the code of deference that is supposed to regulate the interactions between servants and their employers ("In the Face of All the Servants: Spectators and Spies in Austen," in *Janeites: Austen's Disciples and Devotees,* ed. Deidre Lynch [Princeton: Princeton University Press, 2000], p. 200). Eighteenth-century writers could be quite explicit about the anxiety that servants' opportunities for inside knowledge created among their masters and mistresses. Samuel Johnson observed in his *Rambler* essay of November 10, 1750, for example, that "no condition is more hateful or despicable, than his who has put himself in the power of his servant" (*Yale Edition of the Works of Samuel Johnson,* vol. 3, ed. W. J. Bate and Albrecht B. Strauss [New Haven: Yale University Press, 1969], p. 362). In his 1794 novel *Things as They Are, or, The Adventures of Caleb Williams,* William Godwin took up the storyline that Johnson's observation implies but narrated it from the servant's point of view.

2 Reputation.

was by that time public beyond a hope. The servant of Mrs. Rushworth, the mother, had exposure in her power, and, supported by her mistress, was not to be silenced.[1] The two ladies, even in the short time they had been together, had disagreed; and the bitterness of the elder against her daughter-in-law might perhaps, arise almost as much from the personal disrespect with which she had herself been treated, as from sensibility for her son.

However that might be, she was unmanageable. But had she been less obstinate, or of less weight with her son, who was always guided by the last speaker, by the person who could get hold of and shut him up, the case would still have been hopeless, for Mrs. Rushworth did not appear again, and there was every reason to conclude her to be concealed somewhere with Mr. Crawford, who had quitted his uncle's house, as for a journey, on the very day of her absenting herself.

Sir Thomas, however, remained yet a little longer in town, in the hope of discovering, and snatching her from farther vice, though all was lost on the side of character.[2]

*His* present state, Fanny could hardly bear to think of. There was but one of his children who was not at this time a source of misery to him. Tom's complaints had been greatly heightened by the shock of his sister's conduct, and his recovery so much thrown back by it, that even Lady Bertram had been struck by the difference, and all her alarms were regularly sent off to her husband; and Julia's elopement, the additional blow which had met him on his arrival in London, though its force had been deadened at the moment, must, she knew, be sorely felt. She saw that it was. His letters expressed how much he deplored it. Under any circumstances it would have been an unwelcome alliance, but to have it so clandestinely formed, and such a period chosen for its completion, placed Julia's feelings in a most unfavourable light, and severely aggravated the folly of her choice. He called it a bad thing, done in the worst manner, and at the worst time; and though Julia was yet as more pardonable than Maria as folly than vice, he could not but regard the step she had taken, as opening the worst probabilities of a conclusion hereafter, like her sister's. Such was his opinion of the set into which she had thrown herself.

Fanny felt for him most acutely. He could have no comfort but in Edmund. Every other child must be racking his heart. His displeasure against herself she trusted, reasoning differently from Mrs. Norris, would now be done away. *She* should be justified. Mr. Crawford would have fully acquitted her conduct in refusing him, but this, though most material to herself, would be poor consolation to Sir Thomas. Her uncle's displeasure was terrible to her; but what could her justification, or her gratitude and attachment do for him? His stay must be on Edmund alone.

She was mistaken, however, in supposing that Edmund gave his father no present pain. It was of a much less poignant nature than what the others excited; but Sir Thomas was considering his happiness as very deeply involved in the offence of his sister and friend, cut off by it as he must be from the woman, whom he had been pursuing with undoubted attachment, and strong probability of success; and who in every thing but this despicable brother, would have been so eligible a connection. He was aware of what Edmund must be suffering on his own behalf in addition to all the rest, when they were in town; he had seen or conjectured his feelings, and having reason to think that *one* interview with Miss Crawford had taken place, from which Edmund derived only increased distress, had been as anxious on that account as on others, to get him out of town, and had engaged him in taking Fanny home to her aunt, with a view to his relief and benefit, no less than theirs. Fanny was not in the secret of her uncle's feelings, Sir Thomas not in the secret of Miss Crawford's character. Had he been privy to her conversation with his son, he would not have wished her to belong to him, though her twenty thousand pounds had been forty.

That Edmund must be for ever divided from Miss Crawford, did not admit of a doubt with Fanny; and yet, till she knew that he felt the same, her own conviction was insufficient. She thought he did, but she wanted to be assured of it. If he would now speak to her with the unreserve which had sometimes been too much for her before, it would be most consoling; but *that* she found was not to be. She seldom saw him—never alone—he probably avoided being alone with her. What was to be inferred? That his judgment submitted to all his own peculiar and bitter share of this family affliction, but that it was too keenly felt to be a subject of the slightest communication. This must be his state. He yielded, but it was with agonies, which did not admit of speech. Long, long would it be ere Miss Crawford's name passed his lips again, or she could hope for a renewal of such confidential intercourse as had been.

It *was* long. They reached Mansfield on Thursday, and it was not till Sunday evening that Edmund began to talk to her on the subject. Sitting with her on Sunday evening—a wet Sunday evening—the very time of all others when if a friend is at hand the heart must be opened, and every thing told—no one else in the room, except his mother, who, after hearing an affecting sermon, had cried herself to sleep—it was impossible not to speak; and so, with the usual beginnings, hardly to be traced as to what came first, and the usual declaration that if she would listen to him for a few minutes, he should be very brief, and certainly never tax her kindness in the same way again—she need not fear a repetition—it would be a subject prohibited entirely—he entered upon the luxury of relating circumstances and sensations of the first interest to himself, to one of whose affectionate sympathy he was quite convinced.

How Fanny listened, with what curiosity and concern, what pain and what delight, how the agitation of his voice was watched, and how carefully her own eyes were fixed on any object but himself, may be imagined. The opening was alarming. He had seen Miss Crawford. He had been invited to see her. He had received a note from Lady Stornaway to beg him to call; and regarding it as what was meant to be the last, last interview of friendship, and investing her with all the feelings of shame and wretchedness which Crawford's sister ought to have known, he had gone to her in such a state of mind, so softened, so devoted, as made it for a few moments impossible to Fanny's fears, that it should be the last. But as he proceeded in his story, these fears were over. She had met him, he said, with a serious—certainly a serious—even an agitated air; but before he had been able to speak one intelligible sentence, she had introduced the subject in a manner which he owned had shocked him. "I heard you were in town," said she—"I wanted to see you. Let us talk over this sad business. What can equal the folly of our two relations?"—"I could not answer, but I believe my looks spoke. She felt reproved. Sometimes how quick to feel! With a graver look and voice she then added—'I do not mean to defend Henry at your sister's expence.' So she began—but how she went on, Fanny, is not fit—is hardly fit to be repeated to you. I cannot recall all her words. I would not dwell upon them if I could.[3] Their substance was great anger at the *folly* of each. She reprobated her brother's folly in being drawn on by a woman whom he had never cared for, to do what must lose him the woman he adored; but still more the folly of—poor Maria, in sacrificing such a situation, plunging into such difficulties, under the idea of being really loved by a man who had long ago made his indifference clear. Guess what I must have felt. To hear the woman whom—no harsher name than folly given!—So voluntarily, so freely, so coolly to canvass it!—No reluctance, no horror, no feminine—shall I say? no modest loathings!—This is what the world does. For where, Fanny, shall we find a woman whom nature had so richly endowed?—Spoilt, spoilt!—"

After a little reflection, he went on with a sort of desperate calmness—"I will tell you every thing, and then have done for ever. She saw it only as folly, and that folly stamped only by exposure. The want of common discretion, of caution—his going down to Richmond for the whole time of her being at Twickenham—her putting herself in the power of a servant;—it was the detection, in short— Oh! Fanny, it was the detection, not the offence which she reprobated. It was the imprudence which had brought things to extremity, and obliged her brother to give up every dearer plan, in order to fly with her."

He stopt.—"And what," said Fanny, (believing herself required to speak), "what could you say?"

"Nothing, nothing to be understood. I was like a man stunned. She went on, began to talk of you;—yes, then she began to talk of you, regretting, as well she might, the loss of such a— —. There she spoke very rationally. But she has always done justice to you. 'He has thrown away,' said she, 'such a woman as he will never see again. She

3  As D. A. Miller notes in *Narrative and Its Discontents* (Princeton: Princeton University Press, 1981), Austen goes to pains in this chapter not simply to sacrifice Mary to the demands of narrative closure but also to call attention to the fact that she is doing so. In the novel's last hundred pages or so Mary disappears from direct view: Austen has arranged the novel so that readers' access to this character is mediated, first, by her letters as they are read by Fanny and, finally, in this scene, by Edmund's report on his last meeting with her. In reading this scene we cannot help realizing that in being confined to Edmund's vantage point and being subjected to Edmund's understanding of what is and isn't "fit to be repeated" to Fanny, we are not getting the full story. Is Mary so definitively removed from the foreground of the novel, Miller asks, in order that knowledge of her "real character," a phrase the narrator will use later in the chapter, may be "more easily secured—behind her back, as it were?" (p. 87).

4 Edmund's language takes on biblical cadences with an unconscious echo of Psalm 32, verse 2: "Blessed is the man unto whom the Lord imputeth not iniquity, and in whose spirit there is no guile."

would have fixed him, she would have made him happy for ever.'—My dearest Fanny, I am giving you I hope more pleasure than pain by this retrospect of what might have been—but what never can be now. You do not wish me to be silent?—if you do, give me but a look, a word, and I have done."

No look or word was given.

"Thank God!" said he. "We were all disposed to wonder—but it seems to have been the merciful appointment of Providence that the heart which knew no guile, should not suffer.[4] She spoke of you with high praise and warm affection; yet, even here, there was alloy, a dash of evil—for in the midst of it she could exclaim 'Why would not she have him? It is all her fault. Simple girl!—I shall never forgive her. Had she accepted him as she ought, they might now have been on the point of marriage, and Henry would have been too happy and too busy to want any other object. He would have taken no pains to be on terms with Mrs. Rushworth again. It would have all ended in a regular standing flirtation, in yearly meetings at Sotherton and Everingham.' Could you have believed it possible?—But the charm is broken. My eyes are opened."

"Cruel!" said Fanny—"quite cruel! At such a moment to give way to gaiety and to speak with lightness, and to you!—Absolute cruelty."

"Cruelty, do you call it?—We differ there. No, her's is not a cruel nature. I do not consider her as meaning to wound my feelings. The evil lies yet deeper; in her total ignorance, unsuspiciousness of there being such feelings, in a perversion of mind which made it natural to her to treat the subject as she did. She was speaking only, as she had been used to hear others speak, as she imagined every body else would speak. Her's are not faults of temper. She would not voluntarily give unnecessary pain to any one, and though I may deceive myself, I cannot but think that for me, for my feelings, she would—Her's are faults of principle, Fanny, of blunted delicacy and a corrupted, vitiated mind. Perhaps it is best for me—since it leaves me so little to regret.—Not so, however. Gladly would I submit to all the increased pain of losing her, rather than have to think of her as I do. I told her so."

"Did you?"

"Yes, when I left her I told her so."

"How long were you together?"

"Five and twenty minutes. Well, she went on to say, that what remained now to be done, was to bring about a marriage between them. She spoke of it, Fanny, with a steadier voice than I can." He was obliged to pause more than once as he continued. "'We must persuade Henry to marry her,' said she, 'and what with honour, and the certainty of having shut himself out for ever from Fanny, I do not despair of it. Fanny he must give up. I do not think that even *he* could now hope to succeed with one of her stamp, and therefore I hope we may find no insuperable difficulty. My influence, which is not small, shall all go that way; and, when once married, and properly supported by her own family, people of respectability as they are, she may recover her footing in society to a certain degree. In some circles, we know, she would never be admitted, but with good dinners, and large parties, there will always be those who will be glad of her acquaintance; and there is, undoubtedly, more liberality and candour on those points than formerly.[5] What I advise is, that your father be quiet. Do not let him injure his own cause by interference. Persuade him to let things take their course. If by any officious exertions of his, she is induced to leave Henry's protection, there will be much less chance of his marrying her, than if she remain with him. I know how he is likely to be influenced. Let Sir Thomas trust to his honour and compassion, and it may all end well; but if he get his daughter away, it will be destroying the chief hold.'"

After repeating this, Edmund was so much affected, that Fanny, watching him with silent, but most tender concern, was almost sorry that the subject had been entered on at all. It was long before he could speak again. At last, "Now, Fanny," said he, "I shall soon have done. I have told you the substance of all that she said. As soon as I could speak, I replied that I had not supposed it possible, coming in such a state of mind into that house, as I had done, that any thing could occur to make me suffer more, but that she had been inflicting deeper wounds in almost every sentence. That, though I had, in the course of our acquaintance, been often sensible of some difference in our opinions, on points too, of some moment, it had not entered my imagination to conceive the difference could be such as she had now proved it. That the manner in which she treated the dreadful

5 Mary is using *candour* in an older sense of the word and suggesting that fashionable society is more open-minded than it once was.

6 Mary's rejoinder to Edmund's reproaches implies that there is something plebeian and vulgar about his piety and moral rigor. As she is aware, the Society of Methodists, which had by the end of the eighteenth century broken away altogether from the Church of England, had been derided through the century for its powerful appeals to the illiterate and the poor. Her comment derives additional sting from the fact that few missionaries at the start of the nineteenth century were beneficed clergymen—that is, gentlemen—as Edmund is. Andrew F. Walls reports that of the thirty missionaries who in 1796 set out for the Pacific as representatives of the London Missionary Society, only four were ordained, and most of the remainder were artisans or laborers ("The Missionary Movement: A Lay Fiefdom?" in *The Rise of the Laity in Evangelical Protestantism,* ed. Deryck W. Lovegrove [London: Routledge, 2003], p. 176).

crime committed by her brother and my sister—(with whom lay the greater seduction I pretended not to say)—but the manner in which she spoke of the crime itself, giving it every reproach but the right, considering its ill consequences only as they were to be braved or overborne by a defiance of decency and impudence in wrong; and, last of all, and above all, recommending to us a compliance, a compromise, an acquiescence in the continuance of the sin, on the chance of a marriage which, thinking as I now thought of her brother, should rather be prevented than sought—all this together most grievously convinced me that I had never understood her before, and that, as far as related to mind, it had been the creature of my own imagination, not Miss Crawford, that I had been too apt to dwell on for many months past. That, perhaps it was best for me; I had less to regret in sacrificing a friendship—feelings—hopes which must, at any rate, have been torn from me now. And yet, that I must and would confess, that, could I have restored her to what she had appeared to me before, I would infinitely prefer any increase of the pain of parting, for the sake of carrying with me the right of tenderness and esteem. This is what I said—the purport of it—but, as you may imagine, not spoken so collectedly or methodically as I have repeated it to you. She was astonished, exceedingly astonished—more than astonished. I saw her change countenance. She turned extremely red. I imagined I saw a mixture of many feelings—a great, though short struggle—half a wish of yielding to truths, half a sense of shame—but habit, habit carried it. She would have laughed if she could. It was a sort of laugh, as she answered, 'A pretty good lecture upon my word. Was it part of your last sermon? At this rate, you will soon reform every body at Mansfield and Thornton Lacey; and when I hear of you next, it may be as a celebrated preacher in some great society of Methodists, or as a missionary into foreign parts.'[6] She tried to speak carelessly; but she was not so careless as she wanted to appear. I only said in reply, that from my heart I wished her well, and earnestly hoped that she might soon learn to think more justly, and not owe the most valuable knowledge we could any of us acquire—the knowledge of ourselves and of our duty to the lessons of affliction—and immediately left the room. I had gone a few steps, Fanny, when I heard the door open behind me. 'Mr. Bertram,' said she.

I looked back. 'Mr. Bertram,' said she, with a smile—but it was a smile ill-suited to the conversation that had passed, a saucy playful smile, seeming to invite, in order to subdue me; at least, it appeared so to me. I resisted; it was the impulse of the moment to resist, and still walked on. I have since—sometimes—for a moment—regretted that I did not go back; but I know I was right; and such has been the end of our acquaintance! And what an acquaintance has it been! How have I been deceived! Equally in brother and sister deceived! I thank you for your patience, Fanny. This has been the greatest relief, and now we will have done."

And such was Fanny's dependance on his words, that for five minutes she thought they *had* done. Then, however, it all came on again, or something very like it, and nothing less than Lady Bertram's rousing thoroughly up, could really close such a conversation. Till that happened, they continued to talk of Miss Crawford alone, and how she had attached him, and how delightful nature had made her, and how excellent she would have been, had she fallen into good hands earlier. Fanny, now at liberty to speak openly, felt more than justified in adding to his knowledge of her real character, by some hint of what share his brother's state of health might be supposed to have in her wish for a complete reconciliation. This was not an agreeable intimation. Nature resisted it for a while. It would have been a vast deal pleasanter to have had her more disinterested in her attachment; but his vanity was not of a strength to fight long against reason. He submitted to believe, that Tom's illness had influenced her; only reserving for himself this consoling thought, that considering the many counteractions of opposing habits, she had certainly been *more* attached to him than could have been expected, and for his sake been more near doing right. Fanny thought exactly the same; and they were also quite agreed in their opinion of the lasting effect, the indelible impression, which such a disappointment must make on his mind. Time would undoubtedly abate somewhat of his sufferings, but still it was a sort of thing which he never could get entirely the better of; and as to his ever meeting with any other woman who could—it was too impossible to be named but with indignation. Fanny's friendship was all that he had to cling to.

# 17

1 In this sentence the narrator is almost comically direct, even testy, but her language even so recalls a line from the Anglican Morning Prayer, "Restore thou them that are penitent."

LET OTHER PENS DWELL on guilt and misery. I quit such odious subjects as soon as I can, impatient to restore every body, not greatly in fault themselves, to tolerable comfort, and to have done with all the rest.[1]

My Fanny indeed at this very time, I have the satisfaction of knowing, must have been happy in spite of every thing. She must have been a happy creature in spite of all that she felt or thought she felt, for the distress of those around her. She had sources of delight that must force their way. She was returned to Mansfield Park, she was useful, she was beloved; she was safe from Mr. Crawford, and when Sir Thomas came back she had every proof that could be given in his then melancholy state of spirits, of his perfect approbation and increased regard; and happy as all this must make her, she would still have been happy without any of it, for Edmund was no longer the dupe of Miss Crawford.

It is true, that Edmund was very far from happy himself. He was suffering from disappointment and regret, grieving over what was, and wishing for what could never be. She knew it was so, and was sorry; but it was with a sorrow so founded on satisfaction, so tending to ease, and so much in harmony with every dearest sensation, that there are few who might not have been glad to exchange their greatest gaiety for it.

Sir Thomas, poor Sir Thomas, a parent, and conscious of errors in his own conduct as a parent, was the longest to suffer. He felt that he ought not to have allowed the marriage, that his daughter's senti-

Film still showing one of the series of stagy tableaux that the director Patricia Rozema sets up to conclude her film adaptation of Austen's novel. Through this closing sequence, in which the film's characters are reassembled on the lawn of the Bertrams' country house, Rozema creates a cinematic equivalent to the intrusive narrator whom readers encounter in this final chapter of *Mansfield Park*.

ments had been sufficiently known to him to render him culpable in authorising it, that in so doing he had sacrificed the right to the expedient, and been governed by motives of selfishness and worldly wisdom. These were reflections that required some time to soften; but time will do almost every thing, and though little comfort arose on Mrs. Rushworth's side for the misery she had occasioned, comfort was to be found greater than he had supposed, in his other children. Julia's match became a less desperate business than he had considered it at first. She was humble and wishing to be forgiven, and Mr. Yates, desirous of being really received into the family, was disposed to look up to him and be guided. He was not very solid; but there was a hope of his becoming less trifling—of his being at least tolerably domestic and quiet; and, at any rate, there was comfort in finding his estate rather more, and his debts much less, than he had feared, and in being consulted and treated as the friend best worth attending to. There was comfort also in Tom, who gradually regained his health, without regaining the thoughtlessness and selfishness of his previous habits. He was the better for ever for his illness. He had suffered, and he had learnt to think, two advantages that he had never known before; and the self-reproach arising from the deplorable event in Wimpole Street, to which he felt himself accessory by all the dangerous intimacy of his unjustifiable theatre, made an impression on his mind which, at the age of six-and-twenty, with no want of sense, or good companions, was durable in its happy effects. He became what he ought to be, useful to his father, steady and quiet, and not living merely for himself.

Here was comfort indeed! and quite as soon as Sir Thomas could place dependence on such sources of good, Edmund was contributing to his father's ease by improvement in the only point in which *he* had given him pain before—improvement in his spirits. After wandering about and sitting under trees with Fanny all the summer evenings, he had so well talked his mind into submission, as to be very tolerably cheerful again.

These were the circumstances and the hopes which gradually brought their alleviation to Sir Thomas, deadening his sense of what was lost, and in part reconciling him to himself; though the anguish arising from the conviction of his own errors in the education of his daughters, was never to be entirely done away.

Too late he became aware how unfavourable to the character of any young people, must be the totally opposite treatment which Maria and Julia had been always experiencing at home, where the excessive indulgence and flattery of their aunt had been continually contrasted with his own severity. He saw how ill he had judged, in expecting to counteract what was wrong in Mrs. Norris, by its reverse in himself, clearly saw that he had but increased the evil, by teaching them to repress their spirits in his presence, as to make their real disposition unknown to him, and sending them for all their indulgences to a person who had been able to attach them only by the blindness of her affection, and the excess of her praise.

Here had been grievous mismanagement; but, bad as it was, he gradually grew to feel that it had not been the most direful mistake in his plan of education. Something must have been wanting *within,* or time would have worn away much of its ill effect. He feared that principle, active principle, had been wanting, that they had never been properly taught to govern their inclinations and tempers, by that sense of duty which can alone suffice. They had been instructed theoretically in their religion, but never required to bring it into daily practice. To be distinguished for elegance and accomplishments—the authorised object of their youth—could have had no useful influence that way, no moral effect on the mind. He had meant them to be good, but his cares had been directed to the understanding and manners, not the disposition; and of the necessity of self-denial and humility, he feared they had never heard from any lips that could profit them.

Bitterly did he deplore a deficiency which now he could scarcely comprehend to have been possible. Wretchedly did he feel, that with all the cost and care of an anxious and expensive education, he had brought up his daughters, without their understanding their first duties, or his being acquainted with their character and temper.

The high spirit and strong passions of Mrs. Rushworth especially, were made known to him only in their sad result. She was not to be prevailed on to leave Mr. Crawford. She hoped to marry him, and they continued together till she was obliged to be convinced that such hope was vain, and till the disappointment and wretchedness arising from the conviction, rendered her temper so bad, and her feelings for him so like hatred, as to make them for a while each other's punishment, and then induce a voluntary separation.

She had lived with him to be reproached as the ruin of all his happiness in Fanny, and carried away no better consolation in leaving him, than that she *had* divided them. What can exceed the misery of such a mind in such a situation?

Mr. Rushworth had no difficulty in procuring a divorce;[2] and so ended a marriage contracted under such circumstances as to make any better end, the effect of good luck, not to be reckoned on. She had despised him, and loved another—and he had been very much aware that it was so. The indignities of stupidity, and the disappointments of selfish passion, can excite little pity. His punishment followed his conduct, as did a deeper punishment, the deeper guilt of

2 Until new laws were made in 1857, divorces could be obtained only through private acts of Parliament, a slow and expensive process that involved hearings in the civil and ecclesiastical courts as well as a "criminal conversation" trial, as it was called, in which the wronged husband would sue his wife's seducer for damages. Conservative estimates place the cost of a divorce at this moment at 1,000*l*, suggesting that only the Mr. Rushworths of this world could extricate themselves from failed marriages in this manner. Adultery on the part of a husband was scarcely recognized as a legitimate ground for divorce: before 1857 only four women in England succeeded in petitioning Parliament to dissolve their marriages.

3 A house and servants are found for them in another part of England; *country* here means county.

his wife. *He* was released from the engagement to be mortified and unhappy, till some other pretty girl could attract him into matrimony again, and he might set forward on a second, and it is to be hoped, more prosperous trial of the state—if duped, to be duped at least with good humour and good luck; while *she* must withdraw with infinitely stronger feelings to a retirement and reproach, which could allow no second spring of hope or character.

Where she could be placed, became a subject of most melancholy and momentous consultation. Mrs. Norris, whose attachment seemed to augment with the demerits of her niece, would have had her received at home, and countenanced by them all. Sir Thomas would not hear of it, and Mrs. Norris's anger against Fanny was so much the greater, from considering *her* residence there as the motive. She persisted in placing his scruples to *her* account, though Sir Thomas very solemnly assured her, that had there been no young woman in question, had there been no young person of either sex belonging to him, to be endangered by the society, or hurt by the character of Mrs. Rushworth, he would never have offered so great an insult to the neighbourhood, as to expect it to notice her. As a daughter—he hoped a penitent one—she should be protected by him, and secured in every comfort, and supported by every encouragement to do right, which their relative situations admitted; but farther than *that,* he would not go. Maria had destroyed her own character, and he would not, by a vain attempt to restore what never could be restored, be affording his sanction to vice, or in seeking to lessen its disgrace, be anywise accessory to introducing such misery in another man's family, as he had known himself.

It ended in Mrs. Norris's resolving to quit Mansfield, and devote herself to her unfortunate Maria, and in an establishment being formed for them in another country[3]—remote and private, where, shut up together with little society, on one side no affection, on the other, no judgment, it may be reasonably supposed that their tempers became their mutual punishment.

Mrs. Norris's removal from Mansfield was the great supplementary comfort of Sir Thomas's life. His opinion of her had been sinking from the day of his return from Antigua; in every transaction together from that period, in their daily intercourse, in business, or in chat, she had been regularly losing ground in his esteem, and convincing him that either time had done her much disservice, or that he had considerably over-rated her sense, and wonderfully borne with her manners before. He had felt her as an hourly evil, which was so much the worse, as there seemed no chance of its ceasing but with life; she seemed a part of himself, that must be borne for ever. To be relieved from her, therefore, was so great a felicity, that had she not left bitter remembrances behind her, there might have been danger of his learning almost to approve the evil which produced such a good.

She was regretted by no one at Mansfield. She had never been able to attach even those she loved best, and since Mrs. Rushworth's elopement, her temper had been in a state of such irritation, as to make her every where tormenting. Not even Fanny had tears for aunt Norris — not even when she was gone for ever.

That Julia escaped better than Maria was owing, in some measure, to a favourable difference of disposition and circumstance, but in a greater to her having been less the darling of that very aunt, less flattered, and less spoilt. Her beauty and acquirements had held but a second place. She had been always used to think herself a little inferior to Maria. Her temper was naturally the easiest of the two; her feelings, though quick, were more controulable; and education had not given her so very hurtful a degree of self-consequence.

She had submitted the best to the disappointment in Henry Crawford. After the first bitterness of the conviction of being slighted was over, she had been tolerably soon in a fair way of not thinking of him again; and when the acquaintance was renewed in town, and Mr. Rushworth's house became Crawford's object, she had had the merit of withdrawing herself from it, and of chusing that time to pay a visit to her other friends, in order to secure herself from being again too much attracted. This had been her motive in going to her cousins. Mr. Yates's convenience had had nothing to do with it. She had been allowing his attentions some time, but with very little idea of ever accepting him; and, had not her sister's conduct burst forth as it did, and her increased dread of her father and of home, on that event — imagining its certain consequence to herself would be greater severity and restraint — made her hastily resolve on avoiding such immediate horrors at all risks, it is probable that Mr. Yates would never have succeeded. She had not eloped with any worse feelings than those of selfish alarm. It had appeared to her the only thing to be done. Maria's guilt had induced Julia's folly.

Henry Crawford, ruined by early independence and bad domestic example, indulged in the freaks of a cold-blooded vanity a little too long. Once it had, by an opening undesigned and unmerited, led him into the way of happiness. Could he have been satisfied with the conquest of one amiable woman's affections, could he have found sufficient exultation in overcoming the reluctance, in working himself into the esteem and tenderness of Fanny Price, there would have been every probability of success and felicity for him. His affection had already done something. Her influence over him had already given him some influence over her. Would he have deserved more, there can be no doubt that more would have been obtained; especially when that marriage had taken place, which would have given him the assistance of her conscience in subduing her first inclination, and brought them very often together. Would he have persevered, and uprightly, Fanny must have been his reward—and a reward very voluntarily bestowed—within a reasonable period from Edmund's marrying Mary.

Had he done as he intended, and as he knew he ought, by going down to Everingham after his return from Portsmouth, he might have been deciding his own happy destiny. But he was pressed to stay for Mrs. Fraser's party; his staying was made of flattering consequence, and he was to meet Mrs. Rushworth there. Curiosity and vanity were both engaged, and the temptation of immediate pleasure was too strong for a mind unused to make any sacrifice to right; he resolved to defer his Norfolk journey, resolved that writing should answer the purpose of it, or that its purpose was unimportant—and staid. He saw Mrs. Rushworth, was received by her with a coldness which ought to have been repulsive, and have established apparent indifference between them for ever; but he was mortified, he could not bear to be thrown off by the woman whose smiles had been so wholly at his command; he must exert himself to subdue so proud a display of resentment; it was anger on Fanny's account; he must get the better of it, and make Mrs. Rushworth Maria Bertram again in her treatment of himself.

In this spirit he began the attack; and by animated persever-ance had soon re-established the sort of familiar intercourse—of gal-lantry—of flirtation which bounded his views, but in triumphing over the discretion, which, though beginning in anger, might have saved them both, he had put himself in the power of feelings on her side, more strong than he had supposed.—She loved him; there was no withdrawing attentions, avowedly dear to her. He was entangled by his own vanity, with as little excuse of love as possible, and with-out the smallest inconstancy of mind towards her cousin.—To keep Fanny and the Bertrams from a knowledge of what was passing be-came his first object. Secrecy could not have been more desirable for Mrs. Rushworth's credit than he felt it for his own.—When he re-turned from Richmond, he would have been glad to see Mrs. Rush-worth no more.—All that followed was the result of her imprudence; and he went off with her at last, because he could not help it, regret-ting Fanny, even at the moment, but regretting her infinitely more, when all the bustle of the intrigue was over, and a very few months had taught him, by the force of contrast, to place a yet higher value on the sweetness of her temper, the purity of her mind, and the ex-cellence of her principles.

That punishment, the public punishment of disgrace, should in a just measure attend *his* share of the offence, is, we know, not one of the barriers, which society gives to virtue.[4] In this world, the penalty is less equal than could be wished; but without presuming to look forward to a juster appointment hereafter, we may fairly consider a man of sense like Henry Crawford, to be providing for himself no small portion of vexation and regret—vexation that must rise some-times to self-reproach, and regret to wretchedness—in having so re-quited hospitality, so injured family peace, so forfeited his best, most estimable and endeared acquaintance, and so lost the woman whom he had rationally, as well as passionately loved.

After what had passed to wound and alienate the two families, the continuance of the Bertrams and Grants in such close neighbour-hood would have been most distressing; but the absence of the latter,

4  Barrier in the sense of *bulwark* or *defense*. This is one of Austen's most explicit statements on the sexual dou-ble standard.

5  Promoted to the office of canon at Westminster Abbey.

6  In *The Common Reader* Virginia Woolf took notice of this sentence in particular and wrote of how in Austen's fiction "a divine justice is meted out; Dr. Grant, who begins by liking his goose tender, ends by 'bringing on apoplexy and death, by three great institutionary dinners in one week.' Sometimes it seems as if her creatures were born merely to give Jane Austen the supreme delight of slicing their heads off" (*The Common Reader,* p. 176).

for some months purposely lengthened, ended very fortunately in the necessity, or at least the practicability of a permanent removal. Dr. Grant, through an interest on which he had almost ceased to form hopes, succeeded to a stall in Westminster,[5] which, as affording an occasion for leaving Mansfield, an excuse for residence in London, and an increase of income to answer the expenses of the change, was highly acceptable to those who went, and those who staid.

Mrs. Grant, with a temper to love and be loved, must have gone with some regret, from the scenes and people she had been used to; but the same happiness of disposition must in any place and any society, secure her a great deal to enjoy, and she had again a home to offer Mary; and Mary had had enough of her own friends, enough of vanity, ambition, love, and disappointment in the course of the last half year, to be in need of the true kindness of her sister's heart, and the rational tranquillity of her ways. —They lived together; and when Dr. Grant had brought on apoplexy and death, by three great institutionary dinners in one week, they still lived together;[6] for Mary, though perfectly resolved against ever attaching herself to a younger brother again, was long in finding among the dashing representatives, or idle heir apparents, who were at the command of her beauty, and her 20,000*l.* any one who could satisfy the better taste she had acquired at Mansfield, whose character and manners could authorise a hope of the domestic happiness she had there learnt to estimate, or put Edmund Bertram sufficiently out of her head.

Edmund had greatly the advantage of her in this respect. He had not to wait and wish with vacant affections for an object worthy to succeed her in them. Scarcely had he done regretting Mary Crawford, and observing to Fanny how impossible it was that he should ever meet with such another woman, before it began to strike him whether a very different kind of woman might not do just as well— or a great deal better; whether Fanny herself were not growing as dear, as important to him in all her smiles, and all her ways, as Mary Crawford had ever been; and whether it might not be a possible, an hopeful undertaking to persuade her that her warm and sisterly regard for him would be foundation enough for wedded love.

I purposely abstain from dates on this occasion, that every one may be at liberty to fix their own, aware that the cure of unconquerable passions, and the transfer of unchanging attachments, must vary much as to time in different people. — I only intreat every body to believe that exactly at the time when it was quite natural that it should be so, and not a week earlier, Edmund did cease to care about Miss Crawford, and became as anxious to marry Fanny, as Fanny herself could desire.

With such a regard for her, indeed, as his had long been, a regard founded on the most endearing claims of innocence and helplessness, and completed by every recommendation of growing worth, what could be more natural than the change? Loving, guiding, protecting her, as he had been doing ever since her being ten years old, her mind in so great a degree formed by his care, and her comfort depending on his kindness, an object to him of such close and peculiar interest, dearer by all his own importance with her than any one else at Mansfield, what was there now to add, but that he should learn to prefer soft light eyes to sparkling dark ones. — And being always with her, and always talking confidentially, and his feelings exactly in that favourable state which a recent disappointment gives, those soft light eyes could not be very long in obtaining the preeminence.

Having once set out, and felt that he had done so, on this road to happiness, there was nothing on the side of prudence to stop him or make his progress slow; no doubts of her deserving, no fears of opposition of taste, no need of drawing new hopes of happiness from dissimilarity of temper. Her mind, disposition, opinions, and habits wanted no half concealment, no self deception on the present, no reliance on future improvement. Even in the midst of his late infatuation, he had acknowledged Fanny's mental superiority. What must be his sense of it now, therefore? She was of course only too good for him; but as nobody minds having what is too good for them, he was very steadily earnest in the pursuit of the blessing, and it was not possible that encouragement from her should be long wanting. Timid, anxious, doubting as she was, it was still impossible that such tenderness as hers should not, at times, hold out the strongest hope of success, though it remained for a later period to tell him the whole delightful and astonishing truth. His happiness in knowing himself to have been so long the beloved of such a heart, must have been great enough to warrant any strength of language in which he could clothe it to her or to himself; it must have been a delightful happiness! But there was happiness elsewhere which no description can reach. Let no one presume to give the feelings of a young woman on receiving the assurance of that affection of which she has scarcely allowed herself to entertain a hope.

Their own inclinations ascertained, there were no difficulties behind, no drawback of poverty or parent. It was a match which Sir Thomas's wishes had even forestalled. Sick of ambitious and mercenary connections, prizing more and more the sterling good of principle and temper, and chiefly anxious to bind by the strongest securities all that remained to him of domestic felicity, he had pondered with genuine satisfaction on the more than possibility of the two young friends finding their mutual consolation in each other for all that had occurred of disappointment to either; and the joyful consent which met Edmund's application, the high sense of having realised a great acquisition in the promise of Fanny for a daughter, formed just such a contrast with his early opinion on the subject when the poor little girl's coming had been first agitated, as time is for ever producing between the plans and decisions of mortals, for their own instruction, and their neighbor's entertainment.

Fanny was indeed the daughter that he wanted. His charitable kindness had been rearing a prime comfort for himself. His liberality had a rich repayment, and the general goodness of his intentions by her, deserved it. He might have made her childhood happier; but it had been an error of judgment only which had given him the appearance of harshness, and deprived him of her early love; and now, on really knowing each other, their mutual attachment became very strong. After settling her at Thornton Lacey with every kind attention to her comfort, the object of almost every day was to see her there, or to get her away from it.

Selfishly dear as she had long been to Lady Bertram, she could not be parted with willingly by *her.* No happiness of son or niece could make her wish the marriage. But it was possible to part with her, because Susan remained to supply her place.—Susan became the stationary niece—delighted to be so!—and equally well adapted for it by a readiness of mind, and an inclination for usefulness, as Fanny had been by sweetness of temper, and strong feelings of gratitude. Susan could never be spared. First as a comfort to Fanny, then as an auxiliary, and last as her substitute, she was established at Mansfield, with every appearance of equal permanency. Her more fearless disposition and happier nerves made every thing easy to her there.—With quickness in understanding the tempers of those she had to deal with, and no natural timidity to restrain any consequent wishes, she was soon welcome, and useful to all; and after Fanny's removal, succeeded so naturally to her influence over the hourly comfort of her aunt, as gradually to become, perhaps, the most beloved of the two.—In *her* usefulness, in Fanny's excellence, in William's continued good conduct, and rising fame,[7] and in the general well-doing

7 Tim Fulford reads this sentence as sketching a revitalization of the landed interest Sir Thomas represents: the gentry, he says, "has been renewed by the careers its less wealthy sons have taken up," "revitalized by opportunities that empire gives for character-building employment" ("Romanticizing the Empire: The Naval Heroes of Southey, Coleridge, Austen, and Marryat," *Modern Language Quarterly* 69, 2 [1999]: 190). Austen will put this storyline front and center in her final novel, *Persuasion;* its heroine, Anne Elliot, will renounce a life in the English country house to opt for a life as wife to a Royal Navy captain, "that profession which is [the narrator says] if possible more distinguished in its domestic virtues than in its national importance" (II, 12).

*A Married Sailor's Adieu,* by Julius Caesar Ibbetson, circa 1800. Like Austen's fiction, Ibbetson's painting associates the men of the Royal Navy with domestic virtues.

Cassandra Austen's watercolor, signed "C. E. A.,
1804," is generally thought to be the sketch that her
niece Anna Austen remembered years later, which,
said Anna, pictured Jane outdoors on a hot summer's
day, with her bonnet strings untied. There is perhaps
something apt about the view from the back. By
withholding the face of its sitter, the portrait evokes
all the more powerfully the teasing aspect of Austen's
fictions, how they often force us to draw our own
conclusions about their moral implications.

and success of the other members of the family, all assisting to advance each other, and doing credit to his countenance and aid, Sir
Thomas saw repeated, and for ever repeated reason to rejoice in
what he had done for them all, and acknowledge the advantages of
early hardship and discipline, and the consciousness of being born to
struggle and endure.

With so much true merit and true love, and no want of fortune
and friends, the happiness of the married cousins must appear as secure as earthly happiness can be.—Equally formed for domestic life,
and attached to country pleasures, their home was the home of affection and comfort; and to complete the picture of good, the acquisition of Mansfield living by the death of Dr. Grant, occurred just after they had been married long enough to begin to want an increase
of income, and feel their distance from the paternal abode an inconvenience.

On that event they removed to Mansfield, and the parsonage
there, which under each of its two former owners, Fanny had never
been able to approach but with some painful sensation of restraint
or alarm, soon grew as dear to her heart, and as thoroughly perfect
in her eyes, as every thing else, within the view and patronage of
Mansfield Park, had long been.

APPENDIX

LIST OF EMENDATIONS

FURTHER READING

ILLUSTRATION CREDITS

ACKNOWLEDGMENTS

# Appendix

## "Opinions of *Mansfield Park*"

Not long after the publication of the first edition of *Mansfield Park,* Jane Austen set to gathering—from, it seems, letters, conversations, and comments relayed to her secondhand—the reactions her first readers had to the book. She transcribed these "Opinions" into a handmade booklet of eight pages, to which she gave the title "Opinions of *Mansfield Park*." Many of the comments are from family members, whose identities are given below in square brackets. Many of the others are from neighbors living near Chawton or near Godmersham, the country house that Austen's brother Edward Knight owned in Kent.

"We certainly do not think it as a <u>whole</u> equal to P. & P.–but it has many & great beauties. Fanny is a delightful Character! And Aunt Norris is a great favourite of mine. The Characters are natural & well supported, & many of the Dialogues excellent. You need not fear the publication being considered as discreditable to the talents of its author."—F. W. A. [Austen's brother Francis William Austen, of the Royal Navy]

Not so clever as P. & P.–but pleased with it altogether. Liked the character of Fanny. Admired the Portsmouth scene.—Mr. K. [Austen's brother Edward, who took the surname Knight in 1812]

Edward & George. [Edward Knight's sons]–Not liked it near so well as P. & P.–Edward admired Fanny–George disliked her.–George interested by nobody but Mary Crawford. Edward, pleased with Henry C.–Edmund objected to, as cold & formal.–Henry C.s going off with Mrs. R. at such a time when so much in love with Fanny thought unnatural by Edward.–

Fanny Knight. [Edward Knight's daughter]–Liked it; in many parts, very much in-deed; delighted with Fanny;–but not satisfied with the end–wanting more Love be-tween her & Edmund–& could not think it natural that Edmd shd be so much at-tached to a woman without Principle like Mary C.–or promote Fanny's marrying Henry.–

Anna [Anna Lefroy, the eldest daughter of Austen's eldest brother, James, who mar-ried Benjamin Lefroy in 1814] liked it better than P.&P.– but not so well as S.&S.– could not bear Fanny.–Delighted with Mrs. Norris, the scene at Portsmouth, & all the humorous parts.–

Mrs. James Austen, very much pleased. Enjoyed Mrs. Norris particularly, & the scene at Portsmouth. Thought Henry Crawford's going off with Mrs. Rushworth, very natural.

Miss Clewes' [the governess at Godmersham] objections much the same as Fan-ny's.–

Miss Lloyd preferred it altogether to either of the others.–Delighted with Fanny–Hated Mrs. Norris.–

My Mother–not liked it so well as P. & P.–Thought Fanny insipid.–Enjoyed Mrs. Norris.–

Cassandra–thought it quite as clever, tho' not so brilliant as P. & P.–Fond of Fanny–Delighted much in Mr. Rushworth's stupidity.–

My Eldest Brother [James Austen]–a warm admirer of it in general.–Delighted with the Portsmouth Scene.

Edward [James Austen's son, later Jane Austen's biographer]–Much like his Father.–Objected to Mrs. Rushworth's Elopement as unnatural.

Mr. B. L. [Benjamin Lefroy, husband to Austen's niece Anna]–Highly pleased with Fanny Price–& a warm admirer of the Portsmouth Scene.–Angry with Edmund for not being in love with her, & hating Mrs. Norris for teazing her.–

Miss Burdett–Did not like it so well as P. & P.

Mrs. James Tilson–Liked it better than P. & P.

Fanny Cage–did not much like it–not to be compared to P. & P. –nothing interesting in the characters–Language poor.–Characters natural & well supported–Improved as it went on.–

Mr. & Mrs. Cooke–very much pleased with it–particularly with the manner in which the Clergy were treated–Mr. Cooke called it "the most sensible novel he had ever read."–Mrs. Cooke wished for a good Matronly Character.–

Mary Cooke–quite as much pleased with it, as her Father & Mother; seemed to enter into Lady B.'s character & enjoyed Mr. Rushworth's folly. Admired Fanny in general, but thought she ought to have been more determined on overcoming her own feelings, when she saw Edmund's attachment to Miss Crawford.–

Miss Burrel–admired it very much–particularly Mrs. Norris & Dr. Grant.–

Mrs. Bramstone–much pleased with it, particularly with the character of Fanny, as being so very natural. Thought Lady Bertram like herself.–Preferred it to either of the others.–but imagined <u>that</u> might be her want of Taste.–as she does not understand Wit.–

Mrs. Augusta Bramstone–owned that she thought S. & S.–and P. & P. downright nonsense, but expected to like MP. better, & having finished the 1st vol–flattered herself that she has got through the worst.

The families at Dean– all pleased with it–Mrs. Anna Harwood delighted with Mrs. Norris & the green Curtain.

The Kintbury Family–very much pleased with it; preferred it to either of the others.–

Mr. Egerton the Publisher–praised it for it's morality, & for being so equal a composition.–no weak parts

Lady Rob: Kerr wrote–"You may be assured I read every line with the greatest interest & am more delighted with it than my humble pen can express. The excellent delineation of Character, sound Sense, elegant language, & the pure morality with which it abounds, makes it a most desirable as well as useful work, & reflects the highest honour &c. &c–Universally admired in Edinburgh, by all the <u>wise ones</u>–indeed I have not heard a single fault given to it."–

Miss Sharpe–"I think it excellent–& of its good sense & moral Tendency there can be no doubt. Your characters are drawn to the Life–so <u>very, very</u> natural & fresh–but as you beg me to be perfectly honest, I must confess I prefer P.& P."–

Mrs. Carrick–"All who think deeply & feel much will give the Preference to Mansfield Park."

Mr. J. Plumptre.–"I never read a novel which interested me so very much throughout, the characters are all so remarkably well kept up & so well drawn, & the plot is so well constructed that I had not an idea til the end which of the two wd. marry Fanny, H. C. or Edmund. Mrs. Norris amused me particularly, & Sir Thos. is very clever, & his conduct proves admirably the defects of the modern system of Education."–Mr. J. P. made <u>two</u> objections, but only one of them was remembered, the want of some character more striking & interesting to the generality of Readers, than Fanny was likely to be:–

Sir James Langham & Mr. H. Sanford, having been told that it was much inferior to P.&P.–began it expecting to dislike it, but were very soon extremely pleased with it–& I <u>beleive</u> did not think it at all inferior.

Alethea Bigg–"I have read MP & heard it very much talked of, very much praised, I like it myself & think it very good indeed, but as I never say what I do not think, I will add that although it is superior in a great many points in my opinion to the other two works, I think it has not the spirit of P. & P., except perhaps the <u>Price</u> family at Portsmouth, and they are delightful in their way."–

Charles [Charles Austen, Austen's younger brother, another Royal Navy captain]– did not like it near so well as P. & P.–thought it wanted Incident.–

Mrs. Maling– (Lady Mulgrave's mother)–delighted with it; read it through in a day & a half–

Mrs. Dickson. "I have bought M. P. – but it is not equal to P. & P.–"

Mrs. Lefroy–liked it, but thought it a mere Novel.–

Mrs. Portal–admired it very much–objected cheifly to Edmund's not being brought more forward.–

Lady Gordon wrote "In most novels you are amused for the time with a set of Ideal People whom you never think of afterwards or whom you the least expect to meet in common life, whereas in Miss A–s works, & especially in MP. you actually live with them, you fancy yourself one of the family; & the scenes are so exactly descriptive, so perfectly natural, that there is scarcely an Incident a conversation or a person that you are not inclined to imagine you have at one time or other in your Life been a witness to, born a part in, & been acquainted with."

Mrs. Pole wrote, "There is a particular satisfaction in reading all Miss A's works– they are so evidently written by a Gentlewoman–most novelists fail & betray themselves in attempting to describe familiar scenes in high life, some little vulgarism escapes & shews that they are not experimentally acquainted with what they describe, but here it is quite different Everything is natural, & the situations & incidents are told in a manner which clearly evinces the writer to <u>belong</u> to the society whose manners she so ably delineates." Mrs. Pole also said that no Books had ever occasioned so much canvassing & doubt, & that everybody was desirous to attribute them to some of their own friends, or to some person of whom they thought highly.–

# List of Emendations

Volume II

|  |  | *The 1816 text* | *Emended to* |
|---|---|---|---|
| Chapter 1 | page 215, lines 28–29 | Why do not I see my little Fanny?"<br>And on perceiving her, | Why do not I see my little Fanny?",<br>and on perceiving her, |
| Chapter 6 | page 265, line 8 | most be grown two inches, | must be grown two inches, |
| Chapter 7 | page 276, lines 20–21 | two persons cards | two persons' cards |
|  | page 280, lines 17–18 | be yours, turning to her again— | be yours (turning to her again)— |
| Chapter 8 | page 291, lines 10–11 | two cousins enjoyment | two cousins' enjoyment |
| Chapter 9 | page 295, lines 8–9 | I come to look for you, | I came to look for you, |
| Chapter 10 | pages 310–311, lines 37–1 | general prevailing desire | generally prevailing desire |
| Chapter 11 | page 320, line 25 | had sisters—He might | had sisters.—He might |
| Chapter 12 | page 324, line 20 | where he was "—I | where he was, "—I |
| Chapter 13 | page 335, lines 22–23 | confusion of contrary feeling, | confusion of contrary feelings, |
|  | page 338, line 12 | must unsuspicious calmness— | most unsuspicious calmness— |

Volume III

|  |  | *The 1816 text* | *Emended to* |
|---|---|---|---|
| Chapter 1 | page 350, line 1 | on that head,) | on that head), |
|  | page 351, line 12 | cousin's sake, | cousins' sake, |
|  | page 352, lines 7–8 | a young, heated fancy imagine | a young, heated fancy imagines |
|  | page 357, line 23 | depend upon it is me; | depend upon it it is me; |
| Chapter 3 | page 366, line 10 | unquestionably friendly | unquestionably friendly, |
|  | page 371, lines 7–8 | natural—yet in some instances almost<br>unnatural degree | natural, yet in some instances almost<br>unnatural, degree |
| Chapter 9 | page 430, line 33 | possession of her own. | possession of her own, |
| Chapter 10 | page 437, lines 27–28 | daughters errands | daughters' errands |
| Chapter 13 | page 456, lines 9–10 | Had she been different | Had she not been different |
|  | page 459, line 26 | "Her friends leading her astray" | 'Her friends leading her astray' |
|  | page 462, line 22 | did not neglet her; | did not neglect her; |
| Chapter 14 | page 471, lines 14–15 | and this she suspected, | and this, she suspected, |
| Chapter 15 | page 473, line 5 | "Yours, | Yours, |
|  | page 478, line 20 | Your's &c. | Your's &c." |

| | VOLUME III | *The 1816 text* | *Emended to* |
|---|---|---|---|
| Chapter 16 | page 485, line 14 | Rushworths return | Rushworths' return |
| | page 489, line 5 | added —I do not mean | added —'I do not mean |
| | page 490, lines 11–12 | Why, would not she have him? | Why would not she have him? |
| | page 491, line 5 | "We must | "'We must |
| | page 491, line 24 | hold." | hold.'" |
| Chapter 17 | page 496, line 5 | he felt himself accessary | he felt himself accessory |
| | page 497, line 29 | such a mind in such a situation" | a mind in such a situation? |
| | page 498, line 26 | accessary to introducing | accessory to introducing |
| | page 503, lines 28–29 | no reliance future improvement. | no reliance on future improvement. |

# Further Reading

Generally, I have limited myself in this list to full-length books; additional references to articles and chapters in books may be found in the notes to the novel.

Auerbach, Nina. *Romantic Imprisonment: Women and Other Glorified Outcasts.* New York: Columbia University Press, 1985.

Butler, Marilyn. *Jane Austen and the War of Ideas.* Oxford: Clarendon Press, 1975; 2nd ed., 1987.

Byrne, Paula. *The Real Jane Austen: A Life in Small Things.* London: HarperPress, 2013.

Copeland, Edward, and Juliet McMaster, eds. *The Cambridge Companion to Jane Austen.* Cambridge: Cambridge University Press, 1997; 2nd ed., 2011.

Deresiewicz, William. *Jane Austen and the Romantic Poets.* New York: Columbia University Press, 2004.

Duckworth, Alistair M. *The Improvement of the Estate.* Baltimore: Johns Hopkins University Press, 1971; 2nd ed., 1994.

Ferguson, Moira. *Colonialism and Gender Relations from Mary Wollstonecraft to Jamaica Kincaid.* New York: Columbia University Press, 1993.

François, Anne-Lise. *Open Secrets: The Literature of Uncounted Experience.* Stanford: Stanford University Press, 2008.

Galperin, William H. *The Historical Austen.* Philadelphia: University of Pennsylvania Press, 2003.

Gay, Penny. *Jane Austen and the Theatre.* Cambridge: Cambridge University Press, 2002.

Halsey, Katie. *Jane Austen and Her Readers, 1786–1945.* London: Anthem Press, 2012.

Heydt-Stevenson, Jillian. *Austen's Unbecoming Conjunctions: Subversive Laughter, Embodied History.* New York: Palgrave Macmillan, 2005.

Johnson, Claudia L. *Jane Austen: Women, Politics, and the Novel.* Chicago: University of Chicago Press, 1988.

——. *Jane Austen's Cults and Cultures.* Chicago: University of Chicago Press, 2012.

——, and Clara Tuite, eds. *A Companion to Jane Austen.* Malden: Wiley-Blackwell, 2009.

Kirkham, Margaret. *Jane Austen: Feminism and Fiction.* Brighton: Harvester, 1983.

Knox-Shaw, Peter. *Jane Austen and the Enlightenment.* Cambridge: Cambridge University Press, 2004.

Lynch, Deidre, ed. *Janeites: Austen's Disciples and Devotees.* Princeton: Princeton University Press, 2000.

Mandal, Anthony. *Jane Austen and the Popular Novel: The Determined Author.* Basingstoke: Palgrave Macmillan, 2007.

Miller, D. A. *Jane Austen, or The Secret of Style.* Princeton: Princeton University Press, 2003.

Moore, Roger E. *Jane Austen and the Reformation: Remembering the Sacred Landscape.* Farnham: Ashgate, 2016.

Morgan, Susan. *In the Meantime: Character and Perception in Jane Austen's Novels.* Chicago: University of Chicago Press, 1980.

Park, You-Me, and Rajeswari Sunder Rajan, eds. *The Postcolonial Jane Austen.* New York: Routledge, 2000.

Said, Edward. *Culture and Imperialism.* New York: Knopf, 1993.

Simons, Judy, ed. *Manfield Park* and *Persuasion: Contemporary Critical Essays.* Basingstoke: Palgrave Macmillan, 1997.

Southam, Brian. *Jane Austen and the Navy.* London and New York: Hambledon, 2000.

Stewart, Maaja. *Domestic Realities and Imperial Fictions: Jane Austen's Novels in Eighteenth-Century Contexts.* Athens: University of Georgia Press, 1993.

Sutherland, Kathryn. *Jane Austen's Textual Lives: From Aeschylus to Bollywood.* Oxford: Oxford University Press, 2005.

Tandon, Bharat. *Jane Austen and the Morality of Conversation.* London: Anthem, 2003.

Tanner, Tony. *Jane Austen.* Cambridge: Harvard University Press, 1986.

Thompson, James. *Between Self and World: The Novels of Jane Austen.* University Park: Pennsylvania State University Press, 1988.

Todd, Janet, ed. *Jane Austen in Context.* Cambridge: Cambridge University Press, 2003.

Trumpener, Katie. *Bardic Nationalism: The Romantic Novel and the British Empire.* Princeton: Princeton University Press, 1997.

Tuite, Clara. *Romantic Austen: Sexual Politics and the Literary Canon.* Cambridge: Cambridge University Press, 2002.

Waldron, Mary. *Jane Austen and the Fiction of Her Time.* Cambridge: Cambridge University Press, 1999.

White, Laura Mooneyham. *Jane Austen's Anglicanism.* Farnham: Ashgate, 2011.

Williams, Raymond. *The Country and the City.* London and New York: Oxford University Press, 1973.

Wiltshire, John. *The Hidden Jane Austen.* Cambridge: Cambridge University Press, 2014.

———. *Jane Austen and the Body: "The Picture of Health."* Cambridge: Cambridge University Press, 1992.

# Illustration Credits

*Stoke Park,* color lithograph, after John Gendall, published in *Ackermann's Repository of Arts,* c. 1826. Private collection/The Stapleton Collection/Bridgeman Images.  *frontispiece, 86*

Map of the world of *Mansfield Park* by Isabelle Lewis.  *vi*

*Castle Ashby, Northamptonshire,* colored engraving, 19th century, by Frederick William Hulme. Private collection/© Look and Learn/Bridgeman Images.  *2*

Title page, Jane Austen, *Mansfield Park: A Novel* (London: Thomas Egerton, 1814). Houghton Library, Harvard University.  *7*

Title page, Jane Austen, *Mansfield Park: A Novel,* 2nd ed. (London: J. Murray, 1816). Houghton Library, Harvard University.  *7*

Frontispiece and title page, *The History of Little Goody Two-Shoes* (London: T. Carnan and F. Newbery, 1777). Houghton Library, Harvard University.  *9*

*Portrait of William Murray, 1st Earl of Mansfield,* oil in canvas, 18th century, by John Singleton Copley. National Portrait Gallery, London/Bridgeman Images.  *14*

Title page, Maria Edgeworth, *Patronage,* vol. 1 (London, 1814). Houghton Library, Harvard University.  *16*

First page of "Opinions of *Mansfield Park*" ms. British Library (CC by 4.9)  *20*

"In vain did Lady Bertram smile and make her sit on the sofa with herself and pug," from Jane Austen, *Mansfield Park,* illustrated by Hugh Thomson (New York: The Macmillan Company, 1902).  *41*

*Silhouette Representation of the Adoption of Edward Austen by Thomas and Catherine Knight,* 1783, by William Wellings. Chawton House Library.  *49*

*Lady Charlotte Finch, Governess to the Children of King George III,* oil on canvas, 1787, by William Hopkins. GAC3810, Government Art Collection, UK.  *51*

Facsimile of an Austen family letter. Jane Austen's House Museum, Jane Austen Memorial Trust. *55*

Photograph of pen-knives at Chawton Cottage. Jane Austen's House Museum, Jane Austen Memorial Trust. *57*

Puzzle map, 18th century, from Puzzles, Box Game, and Playing Cards, 1785–190-. Houghton Library, Harvard University. *58*

*Portrait of Miss Margaret Casson at the Piano,* oil on canvas, 1781, by George Romney. Private collection/photo © Philip Mould Ltd., London/Bridgeman Images. *59*

Map of the island of Antego, by Herman Moll, geographer, early eighteenth century. Harvard Map Collection, Pusey Library, Harvard College Libraries. *62*

*Andrews's New Map of the West Indies and Part of the Coast of South America,* 1783. Harvard Map Collection, Pusey Library, Harvard College Libraries. *65*

Kirby Hall, near Corby, Northamptonshire, UK, exterior seen from the grounds, photo. Photo © Mark Fiennes/Bridgeman Images. *72*

The Bertram family reacts to Mary and Henry Crawford in director Patricia Rozema's 1999 film adaptation of *Mansfield Park* (Miramax Films). *83*

*The Moor Park Apricot,* from William Hooker, *Pomona Londinensis: Containing Colored Engravings of the Most Esteemed Fruits Cultivated in British Gardens,* vol. 1 (London: W. Hooker, 1818), plate IX. Houghton Library, Harvard University. *90*

*Humphry Repton Surveying with a Theodolite,* color lithograph, 18th century, after Humphry Repton. Private collection/The Stapleton Collection/Bridgeman Images. *92*

"The Alcove from the Avenue," from James Sargent Storer and John Greig, *Cowper Illustrated in a Series of Views* (London: Vernor and Hood, 1803). opp. p. 12. Houghton Library, Harvard University. *94*

*William Cowper,* engraving, English School, 19th century. Private collection/Ken Walsh/Bridgeman Images. *96*

*A Barouche with Ackermann's Patent Moveable Axles,* colored engraving, English School, 19th century. Private collection/© Look and Learn/Peter Jackson Collection/Bridgeman Images. *99*

*A View of the Royal Navy of Great Britain,* colored engraving, 1804, by Nicolaus von Heideloff. © Royal Naval Museum, Portsmouth, Hampshire, UK/Bridgeman Images. *100*

"Artificial Scenery" and "Natural Scenery," from Humphry Repton, *Observations on the Theory and Practice of Landscape Gardening* (London: J. Taylor, 1805), opp. p. 48. Houghton Library, Harvard University. *102*

*Riding Dress,* color lithograph, c. 1806, English School. Fashion Museum, Bath and North East Somerset Council/Bridgeman Images. *106*

*A Quiet Moment,* pen and ink on paper, 19th century, by John Harden. Abbot Hall Art Gallery, Kendal, Cumbria, UK/Bridgeman Images. *111*

*Portrait of Jane Austen,* watercolor on paper, English School, 18th century. Private collection/Bridgeman Images. *114*

*Stoneleigh Abbey,* color photograph, English photographer, c. 1905. Private collections/© Look and Learn/Bridgeman Images. *122*

John Cordrey, "A Gentleman with his Pair of Bays Harnessed to a Curricle," 1806. Yale Center for British Art. *123*

*Sir Walter Scott,* engraving by Charles Turner, 1810, after Henry Raeburn. Yale Center for British Art, Paul Mellon Collection/Bridgeman Images. *126*

*Melrose Abbey: An Illustration to Sir Walter Scott's "The Lay of the Last Minstrel,"* pencil and watercolor, 1831, by J. M. W. Turner. Private collection/photo © Christie's Images/Bridgeman Images. *127*

"A plain appears on a hill, or a hill a plain, according to the point of view from whence each is seen," engraving, by Humphry Repton. Private collection/The Stapleton Collection/Bridgeman Images. *133*

Page from Laurence Sterne, *Sentimental Journey through France and Italy* (London: W. Holland, 1795). Houghton Library, Harvard University. *136*

*Laurence Sterne,* engraving by Edward Fisher, 18th century, after Joshua Reynolds. Private collection, Bridgeman Images. *139*

"He walked to the gate and stood there without seeming to know what to do," illustration by Charles Edmund Brock, from Jane Austen, *Mansfield Park* (London: Dent, 1922). University of Toronto Libraries. *140*

*Portrait of John Murray,* engraving by E. Finden, published 1838, after Henry William Pickersgill. Private collection/© Look and Learn/Elgar Collection/Bridgeman Images. *142*

Frontispiece to Hester Chapone, *Letters on the Improvement of the Mind* (London: J. Sharpe, 1829). The University of California, Berkeley, Library. *151*

*Dilettanti Theatricals, or A Peep in the Green Room,* hand-colored etching, by James Gillray, published by Hannah Humphrey in 1803. Courtesy of the Warden and Scholars of New College, University of Oxford/Bridgeman Images.  *157*

*Mr Suett as Dicky Gossip in "My Grandmother,"* oil on canvas, 1797, by Samuel DeWilde. WA1924.1, © Ashmolean Museum, University of Oxford.  *160*

*David Garrick between the Muses of Tragedy and Comedy,* oil on canvas, 1760–1761, after Joshua Reynolds. Somerset Maugham Theatre Collection, London/Bridgeman Images.  *161*

*Playbill Advertising a Performance of Lovers' Vows at the Theatre Royal Edinburgh,* 1820. Reproduced by permission of the National Library of Scotland.  *163*

*The Billiard Table,* aquatint, by Thomas Rowlandson, from William Combe, *The Tour of Dr Syntax,* 1812–1821. Private collection/The Stapleton Collection/Bridgeman Images.  *164*

Mary Ann Yates in the Character of Medea, mezzotint by William Dickinson, 1771, after Robert Edge Pine. National Portrait Gallery London.  *169*

*"I'll Tell You What! That Such Things Are We Must Allow, But Such Things Never Were Till Now,"* color engraving, c. 1790, by Henry Wigstead. Private collection/photo © Liszt Collection/Bridgeman Images.  *186*

*Outside of a Castle,* transparency etching, 1798, by Edward Orme. (GC138) GA 2009.00439. Optical Devices and Views Collection, Graphic Arts Collection, Department of Rare Books and Special Collections, Princeton University Library.  *189*

Charlotte Brontë's workbox, photo. © Brontë Parsonage Museum, Haworth, Yorkshire UK/Bridgeman Images.  *191*

*George Crabbe,* oil on canvas, c. 1819, by Henry William Pickersgill. National Portrait Gallery, London/Pictures from History/Bridgeman Images.  *192*

*Reception of the Diplomatique and His Suite at the Court of Pekin,* color etching, c. 1793, by James Gillray. Victoria and Albert Museum, London/Bridgeman Images.  *194*

*Dr Syntax at Covent Garden Theatre, London,* colored engraving, 19th century, by Thomas Rowlandson. Private collection/© Look and Learn/Peter Jackson Collection/Bridgeman Images.  *203*

"My father is come!" from Jane Austen, *Mansfield Park,* illustrated by Hugh Thomson (New York: The Macmillan Company, 1902), first edition with Hugh Thomson's Illustrations 1897. Mt. Holyoke College Archives and Special Collections.  *209*

"Put round her shoulders by Mr. Crawford's quicker hands," from Jane Austen, *Mansfield Park,* illustrated by Hugh Thomson (New York: The Macmillan Company,

1902), first edition with Hugh Thomson's Illustrations 1897. Mt. Holyoke College Archives and Special Collections. *211, 286*

Frontispiece to *Lovers' Vows,* by Charles Heath, in Mrs. Inchbald, *The British Theatre,* vol. 23 (London: Longman, Hurst, Rees, and Orme, 1808). Houghton Library, Harvard University. *221*

"Mr. Yates felt it accutely," illustration by Charles Edmund Brock, from Jane Austen, *Mansfield Park* (London: Dent, 1922). University of Toronto Libraries. *227*

*A New and Accurate Map of the Island of Antigua or Antego,* 1780, by Emanuel Bowen. Royal Geographical Society (with the Institute of British Geographers). *233*

*Reverend Thomas Clarkson, M.A.,* engraving by John Young, 1789, after Carl Frederik van Breda. © Guildhall Art Gallery, City of London/Bridgeman Images. *234*

*Slaves Planting Cane Cuttings,* colored engraving, by William Clark, from *Ten Views in the Island of Antigua* (1823). British Library, London/© British Library Board. All rights reserved/Bridgeman Images. *235*

"Am I Not a Woman and a Sister," abolitionist seal depicting a chained slave kneeling, clear glass, c. 1830. Private collection/© Michael Graham-Stewart/Bridgeman Images. *237*

*Progress of Female Dissipation,* etching and aquatint heightened with white and brown gouache, by Antoine Cardon, 1800, after Maria Hadfield Cosway. Yale University Art Gallery, gift of Joseph Lanman Richards. *244*

Evening dress, cotton muslin and glass beads, 1800, English School. Fashion Museum, Bath and North East Somerset Council/Gift of Barbara Jones/Bridgeman Images. *258*

Embeth Davidtz as Mary Crawford and Alessandro Nivola as Henry Crawford in director Patricia Rozema's 1999 film adaptation of *Mansfield Park* (Miramax Films). *267*

*Lady Orde with Her Daughter Anne,* oil on canvas, 1810–1812, by Thomas Lawrence. bpk, Berlin/Neue Pinakothek, Bayerische Staatsgemaeldesammlungen, Munich/ Art Resource, NY. *271*

Capture of *La Tribune,* from *The Naval Achievements of Great Britain, From the Year 1793 to 1817,* by J. Jenkins, 1817. The Unicorn Preservation Society, HM Frigate Unicorn, Dundee, Scotland, www.frigateunicorn.org. *273*

*The Whist Party,* color lithograph, English School, 19th century. Private collection/ The Stapleton Collection/Bridgeman Images. *275*

Thirteen various carved mother-of-pearl game counters in the form of fish, Denham's, The Sussex Auctioneers. *280*

*Horatio Nelson as a Midshipman,* watercolor on paper, 1774, by E. Fane. The Samuel Courtauld Trust, The Courtauld Gallery, London. *282*

*The School for Love, or Beauty and Music,* mezzotint, c. 1780s, anonymous artist British School. © The Trustees of the British Museum. *285*

Topaz crosses. Jane Austen's House Museum, Jane Austen Memorial Trust. *288*

Charles Austen, by an unknown artist. Jane Austen's House Museum, Jane Austen Memorial Trust. *288*

Frontispiece, Jane Austen, *Mansfield Park: A Novel* (London: Richard Bentley, 1833). Houghton Library, Harvard University. *292*

*Portrait of Jane Austen,* watercolor on paper, c. 1810, by Cassandra Austen. National Portrait Gallery, London/De Agostini Picture Library/Bridgeman Images. *298*

*Shooting Pieces,* chromolithograph, 19th century, after George Morland. Private collection/© Look and Learn/Illustrated Papers Collection/Bridgeman Images. *300–301*

George Cruikshank, *La Belle Assemblée, or Sketches of Characteristic Dancing,* cartoon, 1817. Courtesy of the Lewis Walpole Library, Yale University. *306–307*

Title page, Thomas Wilson, *An Analysis of Country Dancing* (London: W. Calvert, 1808). Houghton Library, Harvard University. *308*

Instructions for steps, from Thomas Wilson, *An Analysis of Country Dancing* (London: W. Calvert, 1808), pp. 10–11. Houghton Library, Harvard University. *311*

"She Thought Some Spirit of the Sky," engraving by Charles Heath, drawn by Richard Westall, from Walter Scott, *The Lay of the Last Minstrel* (London: John Sharpe, 1809). Edinburgh University Library. *314*

*Twopenny Cribbage,* hand-colored etching by Thomas Rowlandson, drawn by George Mouton Woodward, published by R. Akerman, 1799. Courtesy of the Lewis Walpole Library, Yale University. *317*

*Board Room of The Admiralty, 1808,* color engraving, 1808, after T. Rowlandson and A. C. Pugin. Private collection/Bridgeman Images. *333*

*Evening Shawl Dress,* engraving, from *La Belle Assemblée,* n.s. (May 1810). University of Washington Libraries, Special Collections, COS031. *339*

"Fanny was obliged to introduce him to Mr. Crawford," from Jane Austen, *Mansfield Park,* illustrated by Hugh Thomson (New York: The Macmillan Company, 1902), first edition with Hugh Thomson's Illustrations 1897. Mt. Holyoke College Archives and Special Collections. *343, 437*

*A Pug in a Landscape,* oil on canvas, 18th century, by John Wootton. Private collection/© Arthur Ackermann Ltd., London/Bridgeman Images. *365*

Frontispiece to Shakespeare's *Henry VIII,* by Charles Heath, in Mrs. Inchbald, *The British Theatre,* vol. 3 (London: Longman, Hurst, Rees, and Orme, 1808). Houghton Library, Harvard University. *367*

*Wolsey Disgraced,* oil on canvas, 1795, by Richard Westall. Folger Shakespeare Library. *369*

King Henry VIII, *Kemble as Cardinal Wolsey,* crayon drawing, 18th or 19th century, by George Henry Harlow. Folger Shakespeare Library. *370*

*The Trial of Catherine of Aragon, 1529,* engraving, c. 1880, after George Henry Harlow. Private collection/© Look and Learn/Bridgeman Images. *371* (left)

*Mrs. Siddons as Queen Katherine* [*in Shakespeare's*] *Henry the Eighth,* engraving by W. T. Fry, 1822, after George Henry Harlow. Folger Shakespeare Library. *371* (right)

*The Sleeping Congregation,* engraving, 1736, William Hogarth. Private collection/ Bridgeman Images. *373*

Page from Thomas Sheridan, *Lectures on the Art of Reading: First Part Containing the Art of Reading Prose* (London: J. Dodsley, J. Wilkie, C. Dilly, and T. Davies, 1775), p. 156. Houghton Library, Harvard University. *374*

Front page of the *Times,* Thursday, June 1815. Detail at left. *375*

*A newly promoted lieutenant (post-1812) shows off his epaulette.* From Brian Lavery, *Nelson's Navy: The Ships, Men and Organisation, 1793–1815* (London: Conway Maritime Press, 1989), p. 92. Houghton Library, Harvard University. *399*

*Block Machinery at Portsmouth,* from Abraham Rees, *The Cyclopedia,* vol. 2, plate 5. © Science Museum/Science & Society Picture Library, all rights reserved. *403*

*A Map of the Western Circuit of England,* inset of the Spithead Channel with Portsmouth Harbor, by Benjamin Donne and Son, 1784. Harvard Map Collection, Pusey Library, Harvard College Libraries. *404*

*Last Stage on the Portsmouth Road,* oil on canvas, 1815, by Jacques-Laurent Agasse. Oskar Reinhart Foundation, Winterthur, Switzerland. *405*

*Equity or a Sailor's Prayer before Battle. Anecdote of the Battle of Trafalgar* (caricature), hand-colored etching, c. 1805, by Thomas Tegg. National Maritime Museum, Greenwich, London. *408*

Francis Austen, by an unknown artist. Jane Austen's House Museum, Jane Austen Memorial Trust. *410*

*Portsmouth Harbour,* color lithograph, 19th century, by Thomas Rowlandson. Private collection/Bridgeman Images. *411*

*Platform, Portsmouth, with a Distant View of the Isle of Wight.* Royal Museums Greenwich Picture Library. 414

*Buy a Bonnet Box,* watercolor, pen and ink on paper, 1804, by William Marshall Craig. © Victoria and Albert Museum, London. *420*

*Steel's Original and Correct List of the Royal Navy,* corrected to February 1799. Harry Ransom Center, The University of Texas at Austin. *422*

From Brian Lavery, *Nelson's Navy: The Ships, Men and Organisation, 1793–1815* (London: Conway Maritime Press, 1989), p. 89. Houghton Library, Harvard University. *424*

*Portrait of Dr. Samuel Johnson,* oil on canvas, 18th century, after Joshua Reynolds. Private collection/Bridgeman Images. *425*

*Devonshire Place and Wimpole Street from the New Road, St. Marylebone,* engraving, English School, published 1793. Private collection/© Look and Learn/Peter Jackson Collection/Bridgeman Images. 427

*Portsmouth Point,* 1811, by Thomas Rowlandson. Portsmouth City Art Gallery, Hampshire, UK/Bridgeman Images. *428*

*The Circulating Library,* pen and ink and watercolor and wash on wove paper, by Isaac Cruikshank. Yale Center for British Art, Paul Mellon Collection/Bridgeman Images. *432*

Label from S. White's Circulating Library, Moretonhampstead. Houghton Library, Harvard University. *433*

*Lodgings for Single Men and Their Wives,* by Thomas Rowlandson. Bibliothèque Nationale, Paris, France/Archives Charmet/Bridgeman Images. 436

"Only discomposed if she saw Rebecca pass by with a flower in her hat," from Jane Austen, *Mansfield Park,* illustrated by Hugh Thomson (New York: The Macmillan Company, 1902), first edition with Hugh Thomson's Illustrations 1897. Mt. Holyoke College Archives and Special Collections. *443*

View of Portsmouth Harbor and Portsea Island, from William Gilpin, *Observations on the Coasts of Hampshire, Sussex, and Kent; Relative Chiefly to Picturesque Beauty* (London: Printed for T. Cadell and W. Davies, 1804), following p. 14. Harvard College Library. *445*

*St. George's, Hanover Square, London,* engraving, by Thomas Malton. British Library, London/© The British Library Board. 451

*Gimcrack on Newmarket Heath with a Trainer, a Jockey and a Stable Lad,* oil on canvas, 18th century, by George Stubbs. Private collection/photo © Christie's Images/ Bridgeman Images. *460*

*The Point of Honor,* caricature print by George Cruikshank, 1825. © National Maritime Museum, Greenwich, London. *475*

*Gretna Green, Or the Red-Hot Marriage,* colored engraving, English School, published by Aurrie & Whittle, 1794. Private collection/The Stapleton Collection/Bridgeman Images. *479*

Closing sequence in director Patricia Rozema's 1999 film adaptation of *Mansfield Park* (Miramax Films). *495*

*A Married Sailor's Adieu,* oil on panel, c. 1800, by Julius Caesar Ibbetson. Yale Center for British Art, Paul Mellon Collection/Bridgeman Images. *505*

Watercolor of Jane Austen painted by her sister, Cassandra, around 1802. National Portrait Gallery, London. *506*

# Acknowledgments

My greatest debt is to the undergraduates who have studied Austen's works with me at the University of Toronto and Harvard College. Their passionate engagement with the subtleties of *Mansfield Park* has energized my writing on the novel for years. Beyond the reading lessons I have received from those students, I have also learned an immense amount from other Austenian critics and editors, fellow editors of this series of Austen's novels most of all: that debt should be everywhere apparent in these pages.

I am also grateful to Gillian Dow, Executive Director of the Chawton House Library, for organizing in March 2014 a stimulating day-long conference commemorating the bicentennial of the publication of *Mansfield Park*. Her invitation enabled me to exchange a central Canadian winter for sunshine and daffodils in the Chawton woods. More important, the conversations I had that day with Gillian, with the audience she drew to Chawton, and with my fellow speakers, Antony Mandal, Katie Halsey, and Mary Ann O'Farrell, have shaped my thinking about the novel ever since. Later that year, the Eighteenth-Century Studies seminar, which meets under the auspices of Harvard's Mahindra Humanities Center, organized another bicentennial commemoration, from which I also benefited: my thanks go to my fellow panelists and to the seminar's co-directors, Sue Lanser, Yoon Sun Lee, and Ruth Perry especially.

My editor at Harvard University Press, John Kulka, has been patient, supportive, and wise. His wisdom extended to finding the perfect readers for the edition: the sharp-eyed, generous, and thorough commentaries I received from Patricia Meyer Spacks, Katie Trumpener, and Susan Wolfson guided me tremendously in the last stage of my work on the Introduction and notes. Thanks to John, I also received expert assistance with illustration research from Joy Deng and Hope Stockton, and benefited from Christine Thorsteinsson's skills as a copy editor.

It is my pleasure, as well, to register my gratitude to Julia Grandison, Elissa Gurman, Melissa Patterson, Mario Menendez, and David Weimar for various forms of research assistance, large and small, over the last five years; to Robert Clark for sharing his work on the background to *Mansfield Park*; to Evelyne Ender, Tom Keirstead, and Paul Stevens for smart, supportive eleventh-hour readings; and to Tom, again, because so consistently in our daily lives he knows just how to restore me to more than tolerable comfort. He, of course, is much too good for me--but, as *Mansfield Park*'s narrator observes shrewdly, nobody minds having what is too good for them.